"In this captivating world there are three types of magic, each of which has its own rules, limits and variables. Kellen sets down a road he never expected to take, on a journey of dire importance. The narrative speeds to the end, leaving the reader satisfied and wanting to know more." —*Publishers Weekly*

"Once Kellen realizes there is a world full of wonders, diversity, and people who think and live differently, he cannot return to the oppressive sameness of City life. The Wild Magic has an agenda for him, involving an acerbic unicorn and a woman to learn the Wild (but not sex) Magic from. Delightful." —*Booklist*

* * *

Kellen Tavadon, son of the Arch-Mage Lycaelon, thought he knew the way the world worked. His father, leading the wise and benevolent Council of Mages, protected and guided the citizens of the Golden City of the Bells.

Then Kellen found the forbidden books of Wild Magic—or did *they* find *him*? Their magic felt like a living thing, guided by the hearts and minds of those who practiced it and benefited from it.

Questioning everything he has known, Kellen discovers too many of the City's dark secrets. Banished, with the Outlaw Hunt on his heels, Kellen invokes Wild Magic—and finds himself running for his life with a unicorn at his side.

Rescued by a unicorn, healed by a female Wildmage who knows more about Kellen than anyone outside the City should, meeting Elven royalty and warriors in a world full of magical beings—Kellen both revels in and fears his new freedom. All the Mages of the City agreed that practicing Wild Magic corrupted a Mage. Turned him into a Demon. Would that be Kellen's fate?

Deep in Obsidian Mountain, the Demons are waiting. Since their defeat in the last great War, they've been biding their time, sowing seeds of distrust between their human and Elven enemies. When the Demons rise to make war, there will be no alliance between High and Wild Magic to stand against them. And then all the world will belong to the

THE OBSIDIAN TRILOGY
BY MERCEDES LACKEY AND JAMES MALLORY

The Outstretched Shadow
To Light a Candle
When Darkness Falls

TOR BOOKS BY MERCEDES LACKEY

THE HALFBLOOD CHRONICLES
(with Andre Norton)
The Elvenbane
Elvenblood
Elvenborn

DIANA TREGARDE NOVELS
Burning Water
Children of the Night
Jinx High

Firebird
Sacred Ground

ALSO BY JAMES MALLORY

Merlin: The Old Magic
Merlin: The King's Wizard
Merlin: End of Magic

The Outstretched Shadow

THE OBSIDIAN TRILOGY:
BOOK ONE

Mercedes Lackey
and James Mallory

TOR®
fantasy

A TOM DOHERTY ASSOCIATES BOOK
NEW YORK

This is a work of fiction. All the characters and events portrayed in this book are fictitious or are used fictitiously.

THE OUTSTRETCHED SHADOW: THE OBSIDIAN TRILOGY:
BOOK ONE

Copyright © 2003 by Mercedes Lackey and James Mallory

A Tor Book
Published by Tom Doherty Associates, LLC
175 Fifth Avenue
New York, NY 10010

www.tor.com

Tor® is a registered trademark of Tom Doherty Associates, LLC.

ISBN-13: 978-0-765-34141-9
ISBN-10: 0-765-34141-7

First Edition: October 2003
First Mass Market Edition: September 2004

Printed in the United States of America

0 9 8 7 6 5

BC # 33307

105 ٧. Mat٤ LIBEd/Tech '06

Contents

ONE   In the City of Golden Bells   1

TWO   Dark Lightning   33

THREE   The Books of the Wild Magic   53

FOUR   Music in Chains   77

FIVE   The Courts of Nightmare   105

SIX   A College of Magicks   118

SEVEN   Magic Unmasked   145

EIGHT   By the Light of the Moon   179

NINE   Facing the Outlaw Hunt   207

TEN   Hunters of the Dark   223

ELEVEN   Reborn to Magic   249

TWELVE   Apples and Apparitions   273

THIRTEEN   The World Without Sun   300

FOURTEEN   Storms and Bright Water   316

FIFTEEN   Darkness and Lies   347

SIXTEEN   Revelry and Ashes   376

SEVENTEEN   Into Elven Lands   412

EIGHTEEN   The City Never Sleeps   447

NINETEEN   The Fruit of the Tree of Night   497

TWENTY   A Circle of Silver Fire   521

TWENTY-ONE   Beyond the Elven Lands   571

TWENTY-TWO   Visions of the Past   619

TWENTY-THREE   Allies and Enemies   626

TWENTY-FOUR   A Pause Before the Storm   655

TWENTY-FIVE   Battle at the Cairn   675

TWENTY-SIX   Storm Wind and Silver Feather   690

The Outstretched Shadow

Chapter One

In the City of Golden Bells

The garden market positively *thronged* with people, clustered around the wagons just in from the countryside. *What a fuss over strawberries—you'd think they were made of solid ruby.*

Perhaps—to some—they were. Certainly the number of superior kitchen servants that filled the streets of the Garden Market, their household livery enveloped in spotless aprons, pristine market baskets slung over their arms, suggested that the gourmets of the City treasured them as much as if they were, indeed, precious gems.

Kellen Tavadon supposed it was all a matter of taste. The strawberries were said to be particularly good this year, and there must have been a hundred people waiting impatiently for the three ox-carts in from the country to unload the second picking of the day, great crates full of the tender fruit, layered in fresh straw to keep from bruising the delicate flesh. The air was full of the scent of them, a perfume that made even Kellen's mouth water.

"Out of the way, young layabout!"

A rude shove in Kellen's back sent him staggering across the cobbles into the arms of a marketplace stall-holder, who caught him with a garlic-redolent oath just in time to keep him from landing face first in the cart full of the man's neatly heaped-up vegetables. Behind Kellen, the burly armsman dressed in purple-and-maroon livery and bearing nothing more lethal than an ornamental halberd dripping purple-and-maroon ribbons shoved another man whose only crime was in being a little too tardy at clearing the path. This victim, a shabby farmer, went stumbling in the opposite direction, and looked far more cowed than Kellen had. A third, a boy picked up by the collar and tossed aside, saved himself from taking down another stall's awning by going into the stone wall behind it instead.

All this rudeness was for no greater purpose than so the armsman's master need not be jostled by the proximity of mere common working-folk who had been occupying the space that their superior wished to cross.

Kellen felt his lip curling in an angry sneer as he mumbled a hurried apology to the fellow who'd caught him. *Damn the idiot that has to make a display of himself here! He picked a fine time to come parading through, whoever he is! The Garden Market couldn't be more crowded if you stood on a barrel and yelled, "Free beer!"*

Then again—maybe that was the point. Some people couldn't see an opportunity to flaunt their importance without grabbing it and wringing every last bit of juice out of it.

Father, for instance . . .

Kellen turned just in time to see that the Terribly Important Person in question this time was High Mage Corellius, resplendent in his velvet robes and the distinctive hat that marked him as a High Mage and thus a creature of wealth, rank, and power. Quite a hat it was, and Corellius held his scrawny neck very upright and stiff supporting it—a construction with a square brim as wide as his arm was long that curled up on the right and the left. It had three gold cords that knotted around the crown and trailed down his back, cords ending in bright golden tassels as long as Kellen's hand. Corellius's colors were purple and maroon, and they suited him vilely. Not only did the shades clash, they made him look as if he had a permanent case of yellow jaundice, which condition was not at all improved by the wattles of his throat and the mottled jowls hanging down from his narrow vulpine jaw. His beady little eyes fastened on Kellen just long enough for Kellen to be certain the smirk on the thin lips was meant for him, then moved on, recognizing Kellen and dismissing him as a thing of no importance.

Kellen flushed involuntarily. *Which I am, of course. Fa-*

ther's position and glory hardly reflect on his so-disappointing son. And if I were as properly ambitious as I'm supposed to be, I wouldn't be wandering about in the market in the first place. I'd be at my studies.

The official ranks of Magecraft progressed from the Student at the very beginning of the discipline, through Apprentice, to Journeyman, to Mage, to High Mage. Kellen, as a student, was beneath Corellius's notice under the usual circumstances. But Kellen was no ordinary Student. Not with the Arch-Mage Lycaelon—head of the High Council, and therefore Lord of all the Mages in the City—as his father.

Kellen glowered at the High Mage's back. There was no doubt in his mind Corellius had recognized him, even dressed as he was. How could he not, considering who Kellen's father was?

"That'd be a High Mage, then?" asked the stall-holder, conversationally. "Don't suppose ye know which one?"

Kellen shrugged, not at all inclined to identify himself as someone who would know High Mages on sight. He'd worn his oldest clothes into the City for just this reason.

"Maroon and purple, that's all I know," he replied untruthfully. "Don't know why a High Mage would be barging through the Garden Market, though."

"Wondered that myself." The stall-holder shrugged, then lost interest in Corellius and Kellen, as a housewife squeezed out of the press, positioned herself under the man's red-striped awning, and began to pick over the carrots.

Kellen moved on, taking a path at right angles to Corellius's progress. He didn't want to encounter the High Mage again, but he also didn't want to fight his way through the wake of disturbance Corellius had left behind him. The Garden Market, with its permanent awnings that were fastened into the stone of the warehouse buildings behind them and unfurled every morning, was full every day, but other markets were open only once every Sennday, once a moonturn, or once a season. The Brewers' and Vintners' Market was open today, though, over in Barrel Street, for instance. The brewers were in with Spring Beer today, which, along with the new crop of strawberries, probably accounted for the heavy traffic here in the Market Quarter.

Probably accounts for Corellius, too. Kellen knew the High Mage's tastes, thanks to overheard conversations among Lycaelon and his friends. Corellius might *pretend* to favor wine, a much more sophisticated beverage than beer, but his pretense was as bogus as—as his apparent height! Just as he wore platform soles to his shoes, neatly hidden under the skirt of his robe, to hide his true stature, his carefully cultivated reputation as a gourmet concealed coarser preferences. His drink of choice was the same beer his carpenter father had consumed, and the stronger, the better. He might have a reputation for keeping an elegant cellar among his peers and inferiors, but his superiors knew his every secret "vice."

They had to: only a convocation of High Mages could invest a Mage into their exalted ranks, and it behooved them to know everything about a potential candidate. Little did Corellius know that a frog would fly before he was invested with the rank he so coveted. The High Mages would have understood and accepted a man who clung to his culinary roots openly—but a Mage who dissembled and created a false image of himself might find it easy to move on to more dangerous falsehoods. So Lycaelon said—loudly, and often.

So Kellen steered clear of the Brewers' and Vintners' Market. Corellius would be in there for bells, tasting, comparing, pretending he was buying for the table of his servants, while brewers fell over themselves trying to impress him and gain his patronage. And as long as the Mage dallied in the market, no one else would be served, which would make for a backlog of a great many impatient and disgruntled would-be customers.

But they would just have to wait. This was the Mage-City of Armethalieh and only another Mage, senior in age or higher in rank, could displace Corellius from his position of importance. Mages had built it, Mages ruled it, and Mages were the only people of any real consequence in it, though it had nobility and rich men in plenty.

It didn't matter if Armethalieh traded with the entire world and held rich merchants within her walls, or that she could boast nobles whose bloodlines went back centuries, some with more wealth than any ten merchants combined. When it came to power and the wielding of it—well—Mages were the only men who had it, and they guarded their privileges jealously.

Not that they didn't earn those privileges. Magick infused and informed this City, often called "Armethalieh of the Singing Towers" for all of the bell spires piercing the sky. Magick ensured that the weather was so controlled that—for instance—rain only fell between midnight and dawn, so that the inhabitants need not be inconvenienced. Magick kept the harbor clear and unsilted, guided ships past the dangerous Sea-Hag's Teeth at the mouth of it, and cleansed the ships that entered it of vermin. There was magick to reinforce any construction, so that (in the wealthiest parts, at least) the City looked like a fantastic confection, a sugar-cake fit for a high festival. The City stretched toward the sun with stonework as delicate as lace and hard as diamonds, be-towered and be-domed, gilded and silvered, jeweled with mosaics, frosted with fretwork. Things were less fanciful in less exalted quarters, but still ornamented with gargoyle downspouts and carved and glazed friezes of ceramic tiles. Magick reinforced these, too, and nearly every block boasted its own bell tower, with still more magick ensuring that all of the songs of the towers harmonized, rather than clashed, with each other.

Magick set the scales in the marketplace and ensured their honesty. Magick at the Mint guaranteed that the square coins of the City, the Golden Suns of Armethalieh, were the truest in the world, and the most trusted. Magick kept the City's water supply sweet and uncontaminated, her markets filled with fresh wholesome food at every season, her buildings unthreatened by fire. There were entire cadres of Mages on the City payroll, dedicated to magick for the public good. If they were well paid and well respected, they had earned both the pay and the respect. Even Kellen, no friend of Mages, had to admit to that. Life in the City was sweet and easy.

As for the private sector, where the *real* wealth was to be made, there were far more opportunities for a Mage to enrich himself. There was virtually no aspect of life that could not be enhanced by magick. Domestic magick, for instance. If you had the money, you could hire a Mage to thief-proof your house or shop, to keep vermin out of it, to keep disease from your family, and to heal their injuries. If you had the money, you could even hire a Mage to create a winter-box where you could put perishables to keep them from spoiling. And there were even greater magicks to be had—magicks that melded brick-and-mortar into a whole more solid than stone and harder than adamant. Magicks that kept a ship's sails full of favoring wind no matter what the real conditions were. Money bought magick, and magick made money, and no matter how lowly born a Mage was—and the Magegift could appear in any family, regardless of degree of birth (Corellius, for example)—he could count on becoming rich before he was middle-aged. He might become *very* rich. He might aspire to far more than mere wealth, if he was powerful enough: a seat on the High Council, and a voice in ruling the City itself.

Most important of all of the folk of the City were the Mages, and the most important of all the Mages were those High Mages who formed the elite ruling body of the City, the High Council. They were considered to be the wisest of the wise; they were certainly the most powerful of the powerful. If there was a decision to be made about anything inside the walls of the City, it was the High Council that made it.

And that was what stuck in Kellen's throat and made him wild with pent-up frustration.

If there is a way to fetter a person's life a little further, it is the High Council that puts the pen to the parchment, Kellen thought sourly as he made his way past the Tailors' Mart and the stalls of those who sold fabric and trimmings. His goal was the little by-water of booksellers, but he would have to make his way through most of the markets to get there, since Corellius was blocking the short route.

Kellen was seventeen, and had been a Student for three years now, and although that was probably the acme of ambition for most young men in this City, he would rather have forgone the "honor" entirely. It would have been a great deal easier, all things considered, if he had never been born among the Gifted. On the whole, he would much rather have been completely and utterly ordinary. His father would have been disgusted.

And I could have gotten out of this place. I could have gone to be a sailor . . . It would have gotten him as far as the Out Islands, at least. And from there, who knew?

Mages weren't *always* born to Mage fathers, and certainly not *only* to Mages, but in Kellen's case, if he *hadn't* been among the Gifted, Lycaelon would probably have had apoplexy—or gone looking for his wife's extramarital interest. Or both. The blood in Kellen's veins contained—as he was reminded only too often—the distillation of a hundred Arch-Mages past, half of whom had held the seat of a Lord of the High Council at some point during their lifetimes.

That was difficult enough to live up to, but he was also the son of the Arch-Mage Lycaelon Tavadon, ruler of the City and the current Arch-Mage of the High Council.

That made his life so unbearably stultifying that Kellen would gladly have traded places with an apprentice pig-keeper, if there were such a thing to be found within the walls of Armethalieh.

Wherever Kellen went in his father's world, there were critical eyes on him, weighing his lightest deed, his least word. Only here, in the "common" quarters of the artisans, the shopkeepers, and the folk for whom magick was a rare and expensive commodity, here where no one knew who he was, did Kellen feel as if he could be himself.

And yet, even here, the heavy hand of Arch-Magisterial regulation intruded.

For these were the markets of Armethalieh, and Armethalieh was the greatest city in the world, after all. This should have been a place where wonders and novelties abounded. The harbor welcomed ships from every place, race, and culture, and caravans arrived at the Delfier Gate daily laden with goods from every conceivable place. There should be a hundred, a thousand new things in the market whenever it opened. And yet—

And yet the High Council intruded, even here.

They, and not the merchants, determined what could be sold in the marketplace. And only products that had been approved by the High Council could make an appearance here. Inspectors roamed the streets, casting their critical eyes over the stalls and stores, and *anything* that looked new or different was challenged.

In fact, there was one such Inspector in his black-and-yellow doublet and parti-colored hose just ahead of Kellen now. The Inspector was turning to look at the contents of a ribbon-seller's stall with a frown.

"What's this?" he growled, poking with his striped baton of office at something Kellen couldn't see.

The stall-holder didn't even bother to answer or argue; he just slapped his permit down atop the offending object. Evidently, this Inspector was a fellow well known to the merchant.

"Council's allowed it, Greeley, so take your baton off my property afore you spoil it," the man growled back. From his look of offended belligerence, Kellen guessed that the merchant had been targeted by this particular Inspector in the past.

The Inspector removed his baton, but also picked up the permit and examined it minutely—and managed to block all traffic down this narrow street as he did so. Kellen wasn't the only one to wait impatiently while the surly, mustachioed official took his time in assuring himself that the permit was entirely in order. Granted, some merchants had tried—and probably would continue to try—to use an old permit for a new offering, bypassing the inspection process, but that didn't mean the old goat had call to block the street!

"It's in order," Greeley grunted at last, and finally moved away from the stall so that people could get by again.

"Interfering bastard," the merchant muttered just as Kellen went past. "Even if it wasn't, what difference would a new pattern of woven ribbons make, for the Eternal Light's sake?"

Kellen glanced down curiously to see the disputed objects that had so raised the Inspector's ire. The merchant was smoothing out his wares, and Kellen could easily see why the Inspector's interest had been aroused. The ribbons in question were of the usual pastel colors that custom decreed for female garb, but the patterns woven into them were angular, geometric, and intricate, like the mosaics made from square ceramic tiles by the Shanthin farmers of the north. There wasn't a hint of the flowers and leaves usually woven into such ribbons, and although he wasn't exactly the most expert in matters of lady's dresses, Kellen didn't think he'd ever seen ribbons like this before. Well! Something new!

And the merchant was right—what difference *could* this make to anyone?

Despite the Council's eternal restrictions, the Market Quarter was still a lush, rich place to wander through, from the heady scents of the Spice Market to the feast for the eyes of the fabrics in the Clothworkers' and Trimmers' Market.

But though there was a great deal of *abundance,* and it was all wonderfully extravagant (at least, in the markets that Kellen's class frequented), creating an impression of wealth and plenty, it was all the same as it ever had been, or ever would be, except in the minutest of details. It was the same way throughout the entire City—throughout Kellen's entire *life*— tiny meaningless changes that made no difference. A pattern here, a dance step there, a scarf added or subtracted from one's attire—someone who had lived in Armethalieh five hundred years ago could come back and be perfectly at home and comfortable now.

And if the High Council continued to govern as it had, someone who would live here five hundred years *hence* could return and find nothing of note changed.

Is that any way to live?

Somehow, that chance encounter with the Inspector had given form to Kellen's vague discontent. *That* was what was wrong with this place! That was why he felt as if he was being smothered all the time, why he was so restless and yearned to be anywhere but here!

Abruptly, Kellen changed his mind. He was *not* going to the Booksellers' Market. Instead, he would go to the Low Market. Maybe among the discards of generations past he *might* find something he hadn't seen a thousand times. He hadn't *ever* been to the Low Market, where (it was said) all the discards of the City eventually ended up. It was in a quarter inhabited by the poorest workers, the street-sweepers, the scullery-help, the collectors of rubbish, the sewer-tenders—people who had a vested interest in allowing those merchants of detritus to camp on their doorsteps twice a sennight.

Yes, he would go *there* and hope to find something different. And even if he didn't, well, at least being in the Low Market would be something akin to novelty, with the added fillip of knowing that if Lycaelon found out about where his son had gone, he would be utterly horrified.

THERE were no "stalls" as such in the Low Market, and no awnings sheltering goods and merchants, only a series of spaces laid out in chalk on the cobbles of Bending Square. The "square" itself was a lopsided space surrounded by apartment buildings of four and five stories, centered by a public pump. Within each space each would-be merchant was free to display what he or she had for sale in whatever manner he or she chose. No Inspectors ever bothered to come *here*, and in fact, it wasn't even "officially" a market.

Some of the sellers laid out a pitiful assortment of trash directly on the stones; some had dirty, tattered blankets upon which to display their findings; some presided over a series of wooden boxes through which the customers rummaged. The most prosperous had actual tables, usually with more boxes piled beneath. Kellen stopped before one of these, inspecting the seller's wares curiously.

He fingered an odd piece of sculpture made of brass with just enough silver in the crevices to tell him it had once been plated. The table was heaped with odd metal bric-a-brac, doorknobs, hinges and latches, old keys, tiny dented dishes meant for salt, pewter spoons.

"That there's a knife-rest, sor," said the ugliest cheerful man—or the cheerfullest ugly man—Kellen had ever seen. He picked up the object that Kellen had been examining with puzzlement, a sort of two-headed horse no longer than his finger. "Gentry used to have 'em at dinner, so's not to soil the cloth when they put their knives down." He set the object in the middle of a minuscule clear spot, and demonstrated, setting a knife with the blade on the horse's back and the handle on the table.

Well—something I never heard of! Kellen thought, pleased.

"Fell out of fashion, oh, in my great-great-granddam's time," the man continued, looking at the object with fondness, and Kellen conceived an irrational desire for the thing. It was absurd, a foolish bit of useless paraphernalia to clutter up an already cluttered dinner table, and he wanted it.

"How much?" he asked, and the haggling began.

Irrational desire or not, Kellen wasn't going to be taken for a gull, if only for the reason that if he paid the asking price, every creature in the market with something to sell would be on him in a heartbeat, determined not to let him go until every coin in his pocket was spent.

It was only when the knife-rest was his that Kellen gave it a good look, and discovered it wasn't a two-headed horse at all—but a two-headed unicorn, the horns worn down by much handling to mere nubs. For some reason, the discovery made him feel immensely cheered, and he tucked it in his pocket, determined to have it re-silvered and start using it at dinner.

And his father wouldn't be able to say a word. There were no edicts against reviving an *old* fashion, after all, even a foolish one, only against starting something new. The little sculpture rested heavily, but comfortably, in the bottom of his pocket; it felt like a luck-piece.

Maybe I won't use it. Maybe I'll just have it plated and keep it as a charm against boredom.

At the farther end of the square, Kellen spotted a bookseller—one of the prosperous individuals who had tables *and* boxes of books beneath. The errand that had originally sent Kellen to the Booksellers' Market had been to find a cheap edition of one of the Student Histories—Volume Four, *Of Armethalieh and Weather,* to be precise. Lycaelon's personal library had one, of course—how could it not?—but Kellen wanted one of his own that he could mark up with his own notes in the margins. This was a practice that infuriated his tutor, Anigrel, and frustrated his father, but as long as he did it in his *own* books, rather than in the pristine volumes in Lycaelon's library, there was nothing either of them could really say about it. He was, after all, studying.

I might as well see if there's one here. It'll be cheaper, and besides, if it's full of someone else's notes from lectures, I might not need to take any of my own.

Besides, it might be amusing to read what some other Student had thought of the Histories.

He didn't go straight to the bookstall, however, for that would be advertising his interest. Instead, he worked his way down the aisle between the chalk lines, examining a bit of broken clockwork here, a set of mismatched napkins there. It had the same sort of ghoulish fascination as watching the funeral of a stranger, this pawing over the wreckage, the flotsam and jetsam of other people's lives. Who had torn the sleeves out of this sheepskin jacket, and why? How had the hand got bitten off this carved wooden doll? What on earth use was a miniature funeral carriage? If it was a play-toy, it was certainly a ghoulish one. If those rusty stains on this shirt were blood—then was *that* slash a knife wound?

People came and went from the apartment buildings surrounding the vendors; tired and dirty and coming home from their work, or clean and ready for it. One thing living here *did* guarantee—that you had a job, a roof over your head, and enough money to feed you. If the roof was a single room and you crammed yourself, your spouse, and half a dozen children into it, well, that was your business and your problem. At least the building was going to be kept in good repair by your City taxes, your spouse and your children could find work to bring in enough to feed all the mouths in the family, and just perhaps one of your kids would turn out to be Gifted and become a Mage—and support the whole family.

Eventually he got to his goal, and feigning complete disinterest, began digging through the books. The bookseller himself looked genuinely disinterested in the possibility of a sale; from his expression, Kellen guessed that he was suffering either from a headache or a hangover, and would really rather have been in bed.

Luck was with him, or perhaps his new little mascot had brought it—Kellen found not only the Volume Four he was looking for—in a satisfyingly battered and annotated condition—but Volumes Five, Six, and Seven, completing the set. They had stiff, pasteboard bindings of the cheapest sort, with the edges of the covers bent and going soft with use and abuse. They looked as if they'd been used for everything *but* study, which made them all the more valuable in Kellen's eyes, for the worse they looked, the less objection Anigrel could have to his marking them up further. And the more Lycaelon would wince when he saw his son with them.

I can hear him now—"We're one of the First Families of the City, not some clan of rubbish-collectors! If you must have your own copies to scribble in, for the One's sake, why couldn't you at least have bought a proper set in proper leather bindings!" And I'll just look at him and say, "Are the words inside any different?" And of course he'll throw up his hands and look disgusted.

Baiting his father was one of Kellen's few pleasures, although it had to be done carefully. Pushed too far, Lycaelon could restrict him to the house and grounds, allowing him to leave only to go to his lessons. And an Arch-Mage found enforcing his will a trivial matter—and one unpleasant for his victim.

He was about to get the bookseller's attention, when a faint hint of gilding caught his eye. It was at the bottom of a pile he'd dismissed as holding nothing but old ledgers. There were three books there, in dark bindings, and yes, a bit of gilding. Rather out-of-keeping with the rest of these shabby wares.

Huh. I wonder what that is—

Whatever it was, the very slender volumes bound in some fine-grained, dark leather, with just a touch of gilt on the spine, seemed worth the effort of investigating. At the worst, they'd turn out to be some silly girl's private journals of decades past, and he might find some amusement in the gossip of a previous generation.

If he'd been in a regular bookseller's stall, Kellen might not have bothered. But . . .

It might be something interesting. And it's bound to be cheap.

If it wasn't a set of journals, the books might even do as a present for his father if the books were in halfway decent shape. An obsessive bibliophile, Lycaelon was always looking for things for his library. Literally anything would do so long as it wasn't a book he already had, and his Naming Day Anniversary would be in two moonturns.

It would be a bit better than the usual pair of gloves I've gotten him for the past three years.

It took Kellen some work to get down to the three volumes on the bottom of the pile, but when he did, he found himself turning them over in his hands with some puzzlement. There was nothing on the spine of each but a single image—a sun, a crescent moon, and a star. Nothing on the cover, not even a bit of tooling, and the covers themselves were in pristine condition—

Odd. Definitely out of keeping with the rest of the wares here.

He opened the front covers to the title pages.

Handwritten, not printed, title pages . . .

The Book of Sun. That was the first, and the other two were *The Book of Moon* and *The Book of Stars.* Journals after all? He leafed through the pages, trying to puzzle out the tiny writing. The contents were handwritten as well, and so far from being journal entries, seemingly dealt with magick.

They shouldn't be here at all! Kellen thought with a sudden surge of glee. They looked like workbooks of some sort, but books on magick were very closely kept, with Students returning their workbooks to their tutors as they outgrew them, and no book on magick that wasn't a part of a Mage's personal library was supposed to leave the grounds of the Mage College at all.

Perhaps some Student had made his own copies for his own use, and they'd gotten lost, to end up here?

But they weren't any of the recognized Student books, or anything like them, as far as Kellen could tell. The handwriting was neat but so small that the letters danced in front of his eyes, and the way that the letters were formed was unfamiliar to him, slightly slanted with curved finials. But it seemed to him that he recognized those three titles from *somewhere*.

Father be hanged. I want these. Without bothering to look through them any further, he put them on the top of his pile and caught the stall-holder's eye. The poor fellow, sweating furiously, heaved himself up out of his chair, and got a little more lively when Kellen made only a token gesture at bargaining. Profit, evidently, was the sovereign remedy for what ailed him.

He got out a bit of old, scraped paper and even began writing up a bill of sale with the merest stub of a graphite-rod, noting down titles and prices in a surprisingly neat hand.

"Ah, got younger sibs at home, do you?" the man asked when he got to the last three special volumes.

"No—" Kellen said, startled by the non sequitur. "Why do you ask?"

"Well, children's stories—" The man gestured at Kellen's three prizes. "I just thought—" Then he shrugged, wrote down three titles and prices, and handed the receipt to Kellen, who looked down at it in confusion.

There were his Student's Histories, Volumes Four, Five, Six, and Seven—but what was this? *Tales of the Weald, Fables of Farm and Field,* and *Hearth-side Stories?*

There was nothing like that, nothing like that *at all*, inside the covers of those three books.

He thought quickly. Perhaps he had better go along with this . . .

"Cousins," he said briefly, with a grimace, as if he was plagued with a horde of small relatives who needed to be amused.

"Ah," the man said, his curiosity turning to satisfaction, and stuffed the purchases in the carry-bag that Kellen handed to him without a second look.

There was something very odd about those books . . . and Kellen wanted to get home *now,* before his father returned from the Council House to plague him, and give them a very close examination. An examination that could be made without any danger of interference. Armethalieh held many magical oddities, but where had he ever heard of a book that could disguise itself? *How* was a very interesting question— but more pressing than that was—

Why?

⌒

THE house of Lycaelon Tavadon was not set apart from the street by a wall. It didn't need to be. The two great stone mastiffs on either side of the walkway to the front door were not mere ornaments, but guardians. Anyone not invited, or not belonging to the household, would be . . . discouraged from entering. And as one long-ago thief had discovered, a knife has very little effect on a stone dog. Lycaelon's guardians were very, very good.

The front garden, a geometric arrangement of walkway, sculptural shrubbery, and guardians, was not particularly large. The back garden was larger, but no more inviting. The former served to isolate the house from the common thoroughfare and as an ornament against the white stone walls of the mansion. The latter—well, Kellen would have thought that a back garden should be a private place to relax; a spot insulated and surrounded by greenery, to enjoy a bit of sun away from the prying eyes and the noise of the City. Lycaelon's back garden, home to tall, dark, somber cypresses planted along the wall, kept it too shaded for that, and far too cold except in the heat of summer when the sun was

overhead. No grass grew there; only careful, somber evergreen plantings in raised beds, separated by gravel, and more
statuary, though at least the statuary in the back garden wasn't
animated. There was nothing to sit on, in any event, except
the edges of the beds or the gravel. There was a single water-
spike of a fountain that stabbed up at the sky. Not even birds
could find anything to like in this place—though it was possible that, to spare his statues, Lycaelon had worked a little
spell to chase the birds away.

Kellen carried his burden up the walkway between the
stone mastiffs. As he passed them, there was, as ever, the
faintest suggestion of movement; the barest tilt of neck in his
direction, the tiniest twitching of stone noses as the household
guardians tested him, the hint of the glitter of life in those
deeply carved and polished granite eyes.

As always, the back of his neck crawled when he passed
them. But he refused to go around by the back entrance just
because the damned things intimidated him. He hated the
sight of them, though—they were too like the worst aspects
of their master, hard and cold, unchangeable and unyielding.

The ebony door, inlaid with silver runes, swung open at
his touch, and closed behind him without any effort on his
part. More magick, of course; you could hardly do without
ostentatious use of magick at every possible opportunity in
the home of a High Mage. And when that High Mage was
the head of the Council, well, it was actually more surprising
that Lycaelon had human servants at all.

He could have done without them, had he chosen to—but
it would have meant a great deal of work on his part. Nothing
came for free, after all; magick servants in the form of sim-
ulacra or homunculi were difficult to create and required an
endless supply of magick to keep them working. The alternative, literally making dust vanish, food appear, clothes to
clean themselves, was even more time and effort-consuming.
Lycaelon *would* dispense with servers if he had an important
gathering of his fellow Mages here, animating a single sim-
ulacra that he kept on view, serving double-duty the rest of
the time as a chaste statue of a shepherd-boy, but with no

one here to impress but his son, human servants were cheaper, easily replaced if they gave offense, and took very little thought on his part—only orders.

On *their* part—well, the servants knew who they had to please. Lycaelon was generous with his money, but not with forgiveness if anything went wrong. Kellen, however, mattered not at all—except as Lycaelon ordered.

As soon as Kellen set foot in the entryway—black and white marble floor, the pattern being square-in-square rather than checks, white walls, a few tasteful black plinths with tasteful black urns standing against the walls at aesthetic intervals—one of the servants materialized, dressed in the household livery of black and white. An oh-so-refined and elegant livery; hose with one black leg and one white, black half-boots, black, long-sleeved tunic coming to the knee, crisp, white shirt beneath it. The careful, rigid correctness of the man's expression relaxed a trifle when he saw who it was.

"Good afternoon, Kellen," the servant said. He did not offer to take Kellen's book-bag from him. There was nothing about Kellen to command fear or respect from the servants, and no real consequences if they didn't offer him deference. Politeness, yes, they would be polite to him. If they were cheeky, it was possible that Lycaelon would come to hear about it, and then they'd find themselves on the street without references. But they regarded him, Kellen suspected, as a damned nuisance, and did their best to encourage him to stay out of their way as much as possible.

Politely, of course.

The servant turned and vanished before Kellen could return his greeting. Kellen shrugged, and followed in the man's footsteps, into the vast and echoing reception room at the end of the entryway. Here the decor was varied a trifle from the stark black and white of the entryway by the addition of two shades of blue. The ceiling was dark blue, with little Mage-stars glittering above, mimicking the movement of the stars in the night sky. And the three long, low couches and the discreet scattering of chairs were upholstered in satin a slightly paler shade of the same color. All the tables, ornaments, and other accoutrements (including a fireplace big enough to stand or lie down in) were white or black—alabaster and ebony. Even the famous simulacrum, standing on (what else?) another black marble plinth, looked like the finest white alabaster.

There wasn't anything alive in this room; sometimes the rare female visitor would look about, smile knowingly, and say something about the place needing a "woman's touch." Such ladies were never invited back a second time. It was quite true, though, that Kellen couldn't remember flowers ever being in the vases, and the air in here never seemed to warm, no matter how the fire in the fireplace roared.

There were no apparent doors, no openings into this room, other than the one by which he had just entered. Not even windows; the light came from glowing panels set high on the walls, which was how anyone who could afford Magelights would generally illuminate a windowless room.

The servant was nowhere to be seen, which was no great surprise; having ascertained that the master was not the one who had just entered the front door, he considered his duty discharged. Kellen took a few echoing steps into the reception chamber, then turned right and went straight toward a panel of white marble set in the wall between two blue-and-ebony chairs. At a touch, it dissolved before him and he stepped through and onto a fine, handsome staircase.

The panel was keyed to him and other members of the immediate household, of course; a stranger would still be facing a blank slab of marble. He was now in his own portion of the house; House Tavadon was a vast mausoleum, and there were probably sections he had never been in and never would have access to until Lycaelon died and the magic doors all opened. He had never been in his father's wing, for instance, and wasn't even quite sure where it was. He could come and go as he liked within his own rooms—bedroom, separate small library and study, magical workroom, bathroom—and within the set of public rooms comprising the main library, dining chamber, reception room, his father's "public" study—and he could make free use of the guest quarters, which were in this wing below his rooms, reached by a separate entrance from the reception chamber below. Kellen also knew from experimentation that he could also get into the servants' quarters and the kitchen, cellars, and storerooms, but he was usually ushered summarily back to the "proper" parts of the Tavadon manse if he was found in any of those areas.

And the Chapel, oh, the Light forfend I should forget the Chapel! The Chapel had a wing all to itself, and differed from the rest of the house in that it was *not* done in black and white, but in honey alabaster and gold, as befitted the Eternal Light. Such a tasteful Chapel that it was, so pure and refined in style, with the Everburning Flame on a simple altar, and all the niches for the ancestral ashes set into the walls so that no one could *ever* forget just how many generations of important men had borne the familial name . . .

Oh, no, never.

Kellen hardly knew for certain how deeply his father believed in the Eternal Light—but he certainly believed in the name of Tavadon.

He climbed the stairs to the third floor, where his own rooms were. Here things were no longer in stark black and white—in his own suite, he had a certain say in the way things were decorated. The walls were still white, the floors black and white marble again, but there were colorful tapestries on the walls, and fruit in a dish on a plinth beside the top of the stairs, perfuming the air with the scent of apples. He took an apple as he passed it, and got as far as the door to his room, when another servant materialized behind him.

"You'll be having a bath, Kellen?" said the man—Kellen didn't know his name; he wasn't encouraged to learn the servants' names. All women except Cook were "my girl" and all men were "my man." Lycaelon didn't approve of familiarity with the servants.

Kellen had never even known the names of the succession of nursemaids he'd had as a small child; they had only been "Nursie," an endless series of interchangeable middle-aged women with gentle hands and soft voices, the last of which had left when he turned five. Then he'd been on his own in his rooms, his nights filled with loneliness, his days turned over to a succession of tutors who had schooled him according to his father's expectations until he had started attending the Mage College at fourteen.

Servants tended only to impinge on him when *they* had orders concerning Kellen. Like the bath.

Kellen would have been perfectly happy to do without that bath, but it had not been phrased as a question. This was one of his father's rules, and there was to be no argument about it—when one went out into the streets, among the common folk, one had a bath immediately on return. Lycaelon's abode must not be soiled with the common dust of Armethalieh; the air must be as pure as a breeze passing over an alpine glacier, with no hint of the City outside brought within the walls.

"Of course," he replied with resignation, and left the book-bag just inside the door to his room. At least the fellow wouldn't touch it if he wasn't specifically ordered to—the servants served Lycaelon out of fear and awe rather than loyalty, and seldom did things voluntarily. Lycaelon's standards were exacting enough to make plenty of work, with no need to look for more of it, Kellen supposed.

The bathroom was something he had never figured out how to decorate; as a result, it was entirely white, entirely marble, and as chill and uninviting as being in the center of a cube of snow. The square marble tub sunk into the floor was already full. The water was, as he had expected, cold. It was always cold. Even in the dead of winter, it was cold. He scarcely remembered what a hot bath felt like—he hadn't had one since the last incarnation of "Nursie" had gone, never to return, no matter how much he wept at night for her.

Kellen knew he never got hot water for his bath on purpose, and it wasn't only because the servants were disinclined to stir themselves on his behalf. His father felt that this was an incentive to Kellen's mastering his lessons so that he could heat his own bathwater with magick—as Lycaelon probably did. And Kellen was just stubborn enough that even if he *had* mastered magick enough to heat the water, he might not have done it, just out of spite.

Well, at least after a long walk followed by the three-story climb, a cold bath wasn't as much of an ordeal as usual. But it certainly didn't make one inclined to linger . . .

RECLOTHED—in the fresh and considerably more ornate garments the servant had left for him—Kellen was still shivering when he closed the door of his room and unpacked his book-bag. His father wouldn't be home for bells, Kellen knew from long experience. Lycaelon's long bells at the Mage Court kept him away from home most of the time. He usually left after a leisurely breakfast, but often didn't return until well into Night Bells.

And now that the tub had been drained, Kellen wouldn't see a servant in his suite unless he called for one. He was more or less used to being alone most of the time when he wasn't studying, but now and again, it felt eerily as if everyone in the world had forgotten his existence. Sometimes Kellen fantasized that he himself was like a mouse wandering through a giant machine, which would run just the same whether he was there or not. It seemed to him that nothing he ever did made any real mark on the place—that House Tavadon existed for empty display and heartless show, and was less a home than an extension of one of Armethalieh's great public buildings, or Temples of the Light.

Or just a bigger version of Lycaelon's simulacrum-servant.

Although other rooms in this suite had only been opened up for him as he grew older and needed them, this room had been his for as long as he could remember. It had begun as his nursery, with his Nursie sleeping in the same room, or the one adjoining. His cradle had been here, and the box-bed that prevented his falling out as a toddler. The tapestries on the wall covered whitewashed plaster that had been laid over the painted animals of his childhood. The floor was wood, not marble, and brown, not black. The wardrobe, the bed, the chests and bookcases, all were the same pieces he'd had since he was a boy, all were fine pieces, but plain—expensive, but an honest golden brown, not black, not white, and just a little battered by hard use at the hands of an active child. Thick, brightly patterned rugs were on the floor, multicolored cushions were piled in a corner, and there was a single window that looked out on the street. He could see *out,* but due to the same magic that hid the passages from the reception room into the other parts of the house, no one could see *in.* His fireplace was of reasonable size, and when it was not in use, it held scented candles that he had selected for himself in the Perfumers' Market. This was the only room in the house that he ever felt warm in.

He never felt entirely undisturbed here, not since the day that he'd found one of the servants clearly rummaging through his wardrobe, but at least he could relax to a certain extent here. Lycaelon might send servants in here to spy, but he never troubled to come himself.

For a moment Kellen paused in his unpacking. He'd forgotten about the servants, and the way they periodically went through his belongings and reported the results to his father. How was he going to hide those books—

Then he laughed. *Stupid! They're going to hide themselves, of course.* These books clearly didn't show their true nature to just anyone. Probably only a Mage would see them for what they were—and there were only three Mages that ever entered this part of the house, and of the three, two, Lycaelon and Anigrel, never entered this room.

So he put his new acquisitions in with the old, battered storybooks from his nursery days. If they'd disguised themselves as children's stories before, they probably would again. No one would ever notice that there were three more books on that shelf than there had been before.

What he *wanted* to do was to open the books then and there and try to read them—but there were rules in the house of Arch-Mage Lycaelon, and one of those rules was that of routine and schedule.

He heard the sound of Noontide Bells begin to ring—the

high clear note of the crystal bell of the Temple of the Light struck first, followed by the bells of the other towers in the City, and last of all the great bronze bell atop the Council House added its deep note to the chorus.

A blind man could tell time—and even the season of the year—in Armethalieh, for the intricate pattern of her bells told the hour of the day, the season, and more.

The only towers that rang all the bells were the Temple of the Light and the Council House. You could actually tell which bell of the day it was by the sound of the ring: at Midnight Bells, only those two rang together, making a beautiful and eerie sound. At Evensong, Noontide, and Morning Bells (a few bells later than actual dawn, fortunately for light sleepers), all the towers in the City rang out. And at every bell and season, the pattern changed: it was one of the duties of the Mage Council to set the towers by magic.

From Evensong until Midnight Bells, fewer and fewer towers would ring each bell, until the Temple and the Council House rang alone. Then, slowly, a few privileged towers would add their voices to each bell through the rest of the night—first the Mage College, then the Great Library, then the Merchants' Guild—until all the towers throughout the City rang out Morning Bells, as they would ring each bell throughout the day, until Evensong, when once again, they began to fall silent.

By the sound of the bells—the pattern of the ring would have told him it was the Noontide Bells, even if he hadn't been able to see the sun—and, by the emptiness of his stomach, Kellen knew it was time for dinner. Even though the Arch-Mage himself might not be home for it, dinner *would* be served. And if Kellen wanted anything to eat before supper, he'd better be there when the plates went on the table.

Just as he left his room, the soft gong that announced that very fact sounded through the corridors.

Down the stairs and out into the reception chamber he went, and from there to another blank panel that let him into the main part of the house. When Lycaelon entertained, this panel was left open, and the suite of enormous "public" rooms beyond it, a music room, the library, the dining room, and a garden room were all lit and furnished with anything that a guest could conceivably want. Now they were all left in shadowy half-darkness, with curtains drawn, except for the dining room at the very end of the corridor.

The same color scheme of black, white, and blue held here. The enormous ebony table, stretching the length of the room, could easily seat thirty or forty guests; there were two place settings laid as usual. One at the very head of the table was meant for Lycaelon—he appeared only rarely, but woe betide the servants if they weren't prepared for that eventuality!— the other, roughly halfway down the table, for Kellen. A series of covered dishes waited on the sideboard; a single liveried servant stood there, waiting to serve them.

In silence, Kellen took his seat, and the meal began.

One by one the dishes were presented to Kellen, and he either shook his head or nodded acceptance. Hot food stayed hot, and cold nicely chilled, thanks to more small magicks on the depressions in which the dishes rested. Kellen's bath might be cold, but his father didn't have to share that particular discomfort, whereas he did share Kellen's meals. Lycaelon spared no effort or expense when it came to the pleasures of the table.

Kellen ate with a good appetite, and was not particularly surprised to find that the meal ended with a dish of strawberries, beaten cream, and white cake. He helped himself, thinking wryly that if he'd looked closely at the mob in the Garden Market this morning he might well have seen his father's black-and-white livery on one of the servants there.

The entire meal took place in total silence, except for the faint clink of cutlery and the sounds of plates being picked up and set down. Kellen was used to it; even when his father was here, there was no conversation during a meal. Lycaelon did not believe in conversation at mealtime. He had to put up with it when he entertained, but when he and Kellen were alone, silence prevailed. And certainly in Lycaelon's absence, Lycaelon's servants would not presume to begin any conversation with his son.

When he was finished, Kellen pushed his chair away from the table and left the footman to clear up. *The library—I should go look through the books in the library,* he thought. *I'll bet that's where I found those references to my books. If I go check now, I should have plenty of time to look in the likeliest places long before Father gets home.*

Books that hid their nature . . .

Lycaelon apparently had never even noticed that Kellen used his library on a regular basis. *I think I'd like to keep things that way, too,* he thought as he walked in through the library door and headed straight for the curtains, to pull them wide and let pale sunshine stream in through the windows. In fact, he had been reading the books on magick for a very long time now—and he was at least familiar with a *great* deal more than his father or Anigrel suspected, even if he couldn't yet manage to put his knowledge into practice.

And I know things that neither of them want anyone under the rank of High Mage to know about, he thought, pulling one of the ladders over to the bookcase that housed some very esoteric volumes on the top shelves—volumes that, had Lycaelon or anyone else known *he* was poking around in the place, would surely have been removed or locked up. There were a lot of things on those shelves that were not meant for a Student's eyes.

It didn't take long at all for Kellen to find what he was looking for, because the more he thought about his finds, the more convinced he became that they were books that were hiding their nature for a very good reason.

Sure enough, he found the reference precisely where he'd begun to suspect it was, in the *Ars Perfidorum,* the *Book of Forbidden Acts.*

Kellen wasn't even supposed to be aware that the *Ars Perfidorum* existed, much less have leafed through it. For that matter, he didn't even think his *tutor* was supposed to know about it; knowledge of this particular book was, if he recalled correctly, restricted to members of the Council and specific senior Mages. And the reason *Kellen* knew that was because Lycaelon had once allowed one of his fellow Council members to use the library, and the fellow had carelessly left the *Ars Perfidorum* and two other similarly restricted books out in the music room where he had been reading them. The resulting explosion when Lycaelon found them there had been memorable.

Lycaelon had not been aware that Kellen was anywhere about, and the entertainment value of hearing his father swear and curse the stupidity of another adult—a High Mage at that!—had been so great that Kellen took his chances on being caught in order to eavesdrop. He made very sure to get back to his own rooms as soon as the coast was clear—but after that he'd been afire to find those books and see them for himself.

He vividly recalled his disappointment at finding them to be deadly dull. It had seemed to him that a book with such an exciting title should have been *full* of horrors—bloodcurdling *examples* of Forbidden Acts, in excruciating detail, so that Mages down the centuries would know *exactly* how to recognize a Forbidden Act when they saw it. In fact, *Ars Perfidorum* was a mealymouthed prude of a book, more intent on outlining the punishments to be meted out for each perfidious deed than describing the deeds themselves. It was—it was a *clerkly* sort of book, and sent him off into a near-doze when he tried to read it.

Maybe I thought that book was dull then, he thought, swiftly leafing through the text, *but that was before anybody shoved the* History of the City in Seven Volumes *under my nose—hah!*

There they were—just as he remembered. His three books—titles and all.

He leafed back a page.

"The Foule and Invidious Practices of Wilde Magick." *Now what in the name of the Light is* that *supposed to mean?* Kellen wondered, frowning.

The chapter in question didn't exactly answer any of his questions, although *Ye Boke of Sunne, Ye Boke of Moone,* and *Ye Boke of Starres* were named as the "prime texts of the heinous practitioners of those who seek anarchy and chaos." In fact, except for that single item of hard fact, the chapter was singularly unhelpful. It railed at great length against the "Wilde Mages," suggested any number of unpleasant means to deal with them, and attributed all manner of evils to them (always prefacing the accusation with the words "it is said") but it didn't say anything about what this "Wilde Magick" *was,* or why it should be so bad.

In fact, the worst accusations that the author seemed to be able to come up with were that it was unpredictable, that it could not be controlled, and that some of the so-called lesser races such as Centaurs and fauns were known to practice it. "And well we knowe that these creatures are closer to the Beaste in nature than to Noble Manne—"

Huh. "And in particular, Wilde Magick is the greatest seducer of Womyn, who are weak in Mind and Spirit and inclined to Corruption." Now what did *that* mean? That women could and did use it—or that it could be used to seduce women?

Hmm . . . Now there was a possibility that had all manner of pleasant ramifications . . .

Well, at least he knew *now* what the books were, and why they were passing themselves off as children's tales. He put the *Ars Perfidorum* back in its proper place, taking care that it fit exactly into the place where he'd pulled it down from, then moved the ladder back to where he'd found it. It looked as if the only place he was going to find any answers about the books was within their covers.

He grinned to himself. And what good luck that he had the entire rest of the day free! *I got* just *what I wished for,* Kellen thought with glee, *something new—something new— at last!*

———

NIGHT had fallen over the City while Kellen puzzled his way through the Books' peculiar crabbed handwriting in the safety of his room, although it was never really dark here. Lamps, magickal and otherwise, kept the darkness at bay all night long, in every season. Lamps illuminated the streets and decorated the gardens; lamps even lit alleyways to discourage the presence of thieves. Not that anyone would be foolish enough to attempt to rob the household of a Mage of any sort. Not twice, anyway.

He'd skimmed through all three of the Books once quickly, finding little that made sense to him. *The Book of Sun* was composed partly of philosophy, partly of spells, but the spells were not of a kind that he recognized, and Kellen was doubtful that they could actually work. They seemed to verge on wondertale superstition. Burn this leaf. Say those rhymes. He could imagine nothing further from the abstruse disciplines of the High Magick.

But at least *The Book of Sun* did contain things Kellen recognized as magick. *The Book of Moon* didn't even seem to contain any actual spells, just hints at spells—as far as he could tell from a quick skim, it was something halfway between an etiquette book and a philosophy text—and *The Book of Stars* made no sense to him at all. He had the odd feeling, though, that there was *something* there, if he could only figure it out.

The house was utterly silent, with all of the household in bed, from which comfort no one would stir until they had to. That Lycaelon was a stern master was no secret; he did not approve of his servants "prowling," as he put it, during the bells of proper sleep. This included Kellen, of course, and after having been caught by Lycaelon once or twice, he kept to his own part of the mansion when restlessness kept him awake.

Tonight was one of those nights.

He had his shutters open on the small balcony that overlooked the gardens, and across the gardens he could see the lights of the other homes of the Mage elite. Soft globes of pastel colors lit their gardens—you could tell where one garden took over from the next by the color of the lamps. Only a few lights were burning in the homes themselves, and those were probably night-lights, not an indication that anyone was wakeful or working. In the distance he could see the Council

House, facing the Delfier Gate that opened onto the forest road.

The Council House stood symbolic guard over the gate and access into the City. Or was it more than merely symbolic?

There were a few farming villages in that direction—the City claimed extensive lands outside itself. Certainly soldiers were sent out there, and tax collectors, the latter to feed the City's prosperity, and the former—perhaps to ensure the City's prosperity?

But Kellen had never been there, and emigration between village and City was strongly discouraged, or so he'd been told, though never *why*.

He could understand why the Council wouldn't want too many people trying to move *into* the City; conditions were crowded enough without adding more people. But why keep citizens from leaving if they wanted to?

It was a puzzle for which he had no answer. Unless it was simply that City-dwellers had few, if any, skills that would be of use in a rural or agrarian society. Perhaps the idea was merely to save them from inevitable failure . . .

Still, shouldn't people be allowed to learn this for themselves?

If would-be City-folk-turned-rustics came trailing back with their tails between their legs after failing some bucolic experiment to the ridicule of their former neighbors, surely that would be more effective than any reprimand from the Council.

The Council House itself was ablaze with light, for Mages worked there all night, every night, weaving spells for the good of the City. It was the only place in the City that never slept. Of course, all those lights so nearby meant that the stars were hard to see from the gardens of those living nearby.

Someday Kellen would spend his nights there too, if his father's plans for his future went according to Lycaelon's oft-expressed wishes.

A night owl by nature, that hadn't seemed so bad in the past, for he would be well out of Lycaelon's purview most of the time once he went to night duties—but for some reason now, the thought seemed stifling. As stifling as the High Magick itself had seemed of late, for it required a finicking obsession with detail that, applied to anything else, would be considered unhealthy. Kellen had come to realize of late that High Magick was *boring*, that—once certain tools of memory and power manipulation were mastered—it was entirely composed of written spells that were descriptions of the change in reality that the Mage would like to produce. Very exact descriptions, very *minute* descriptions, down to the smallest detail, written in a kind of mystical shorthand and forced into the face of reality-as-it-was by magickal power.

Frankly, if the simple spells were enough to induce yawns, the advanced spells that he'd managed to glimpse looked to Kellen a very great deal like abstruse mathematical problems expressed in words and symbols of the sort that drove schoolboys mad—"If *A* leaves his house on the corner of Bodhran Street and approaches Taman Square at the same time *B*—"

Learning how to read, write, and thoroughly comprehend this sigil-language and apply it to the world in the form of memorized spells was what the Mage-in-training first learned. Only then was he allowed to *do* anything with his knowledge.

It was bloodless and terribly boring, when it came right down to it. There was so much preparation and memorization and detail required to do even the simplest thing that by the time you actually accomplished what you'd set out to do, you were probably so bored with the process that the accomplishment came as an anticlimax. And in any case, the tiny things Kellen was allowed to do now—and so far, all he'd managed to do successfully was light a candle once or twice—were so simple and so insignificant that he hardly knew why anyone had ever bothered to write down the spells for them.

He looked out at the City, looked at what little he could see beyond the City walls from his third-floor balcony, and it gradually came over him that not only was he not happy, but for most of his life, save only a few stolen moments, he had *never* been happy. Other people were happy—why wasn't he? Why wasn't any Mage, really?

He *knew* they weren't.

His father wasn't, and his father was Arch-Mage, the highest and most powerful rank any Mage could attain. But Lycaelon was perpetually dissatisfied. When was the last time he'd ever seen his father *enjoy* anything? Other than finding an excuse to browbeat his son, that is . . .

And none of Lycaelon's colleagues seemed any more content with their lives, even though they had wealth and power and the envy of everyone in the City who wasn't them. When was the last time he'd seen *any* of the Mages take pleasure in anything, other than humiliating one another?

Being a Mage doesn't make you happy, Kellen realized with something very much like fear.

He'd never thought about it before.

He hated the lessons, was bored by the memorization, and didn't like his fellow Mage Students very much. But he'd always, well, sort of assumed that he'd get through all of it somehow, become a Mage, and things would get better.

What if they didn't?

Suddenly, staring out at the brightly-lit Council House, Kellen confronted his own life, and the prospects for the future, and he didn't like what he saw. And the more he pondered it, the less he liked it, and he began to come to some uncomfortable conclusions.

One of which was that his studies were going to drive him mad before too long, all this obsession with pointless detail. He brooded on the view without seeing it, wondering why *anyone* would choose to be a Mage when a Mage had so little room in his life *for* life. If he did as Lycaelon wanted, Kellen would only trade the stultifying life of a Student for the tedious life of an Apprentice, and then for an even more restrictive and obsessive life of a Journeyman, and then what? Spend his entire life like his father, with a fantastic home he never saw, a garden he never went into, possessions he never used, and colleagues—not friends—he couldn't stand? Was he to live a life so measured, so controlled, that all the juice was sucked out of it?

He shuddered, appalled by the prospect of becoming like one of them—with a dry little mummified excuse for a soul, spending his days contriving ways to control other people's lives for them, his evenings spent building baroque and convoluted spells, or equally baroque and convoluted schemes for the downfall of his political rivals. Where was the joy, the life, the *pleasure* in that?

There *had* to be some other alternative . . .

His mind turned naturally to the Books of the Wild Magic, which seemed, from the little he'd managed to understand so far, to be all that the High Magick was not.

And if they were—if they were, in fact, the very opposite of High Magick—it would be very surprising indeed to find that Lycaelon looked upon them with favor . . . Furthermore, there might, there just *might* be something in them that would lead him to freedom.

And that alone decided him. He got them from his hiding place, lit a single, well-shielded candle, and began to read *The Book of Sun* in earnest.

Chapter Two

Dark Lightning

The Arch-Mage Lycaelon Tavadon was a very busy man. Arch-Mage of the High Council of Mages that, in turn, governed all the lesser Mages who kept the Golden City running smoothly, his days were filled, not with spells and magicks as the commonfolk might think, but rather with the tedium of endless paperwork. A pile of unread reports sat now at his left elbow, teetering dangerously. A far smaller pile—read and annotated in his crabbed scholar's hand—waited for his secretary to come and bear them away. And at that, a day devoted to such tedium was a welcome change from the endless rounds of judgments and formal hearings that his rank demanded his attendance upon. Arch-Mage! The least of his Journeymen, it seemed, spent more of his time in practice of the Art than did Lycaelon these days.

But we all serve the City, each doing his part in service to Armethalieh the Golden, the Arch-Mage reminded himself.

He took a moment to indulge in a bit of pardonable pride in himself; not for *him* the plaints of lesser men, who bleated about the fettering of their great gifts to the rock of bureaucracy, the loss of their personal time, the sacrifice of their relationships and families on the altar of Duty. *He* had never once complained, and did not begrudge such sacrifice, though his late wife had shown her displeasure in no uncertain terms. But then even the best of women were lesser creatures, and could hardly be expected to understand when sacrifice for the greater good of all was required of a man. Which was only one more reason why they could never understand, nor be permitted to practice, High Magick, for they could never be depended upon to act selflessly when sacrifice was called for. Lycaelon often wondered why the Light had created them at all except as a vehicle for the perpetuation of a man's line.

If only a man didn't need them for that purpose! How much easier, how much more serene and well tempered a man's life would be without the tears, the hysterics, the white, clinging arms that held him *back* even as they held him *close* . . .

Not that females didn't have their uses, and their bodies certainly gave pleasure, but a well-made and finely crafted simulacrum would do as well, and could be left on a plinth or in a closet when not needed. Unlike a wife.

He toyed with the notion for just a moment of finding a spell that would allow a Mage to reproduce himself without the intercession of a woman—say, perhaps from his own essence, making an exact duplicate of himself in infant form.

But—no. That was forbidden magick. Only the Light could create life, and any attempt for a mortal to do so would invite in the Darkness. He gave up the idea with regret, and turned his attention back to the reports of the Mages of the Water-Works.

He scribbled his recommendations on the last page, then

paused for a moment to stand and stretch the kinks out of his back, looking down the length of his imposing work chamber.

The Arch-Mage's private offices were in a wing of the Council House itself, so that he could be summoned at any moment to join the Council in its deliberations. No Magery had been spared in its construction; his desk, of a rare blood-red wood, was situated atop a dais elevated above the rest of the floor so that to reach it required ascending three steps of black marble. Few received such an invitation, least of all such supplicants who found their way to this office, but it was good to have that extra level of intimidation here in case it was required.

The walls were of white alabaster, intricately carved in elaborate geometric patterns at the bidding of some long-dead Arch-Mage, giving the whole room the look of a chamber deep inside some enormous machine. The floor carried out the pattern begun upon the walls, only here the pattern was repeated in colored marbles, giving the illusion of texture and depth. Non-Mages had been known to trip upon that disorienting floor, to Lycaelon's private amusement. Fools of un-Gifted, not to be able to accurately see what their eyes presented them—it was fortunate for all concerned that they had the High Council to rule them!

At the end of the chamber, the pattern repeated again upon the far wall, only this time in an enormous window of colored glass wrought of hues so piquant and intense that Magery must have played a hand in their crafting, for each pane was flawless and brilliant, a rainbow of colors framing the large disk of pure clear glass at its center, through which Lycaelon could see the Delfier Gate set into the City wall across the square from the Council House, and the Western Road beyond it. As always, the gate stood closed and barred: the only time it opened was to allow the entrance of City buyers bringing the fruits of trade caravans or the produce from the outlying villages that served the Golden City to the City warehouses.

Once they had allowed farmers and traders to enter the City itself, but that course of action had proven . . . unwise. Now

City buyers went out and brought the produce into the City, where it was kept fresh and vermin-free under spells of containment until the Merchants and Provenders Council was ready to release it to the City markets. Under their guidance—advised by the Mage Council, of course—all ran smoothly, with neither glut nor famine to disturb the steady workings of the City. Only a few choice items were permitted to enter the markets directly from the fields, to create an illusion of scarcity and a kind of aura of festival—the first crop of early-summer strawberries for instance, and Spring Beer. Such occasions were necessary to give the populace something to look forward to. Gorging on strawberries once a year was hardly harmful, and allowed the masses a chance to feel that they were indulging themselves. Indulgence bred content, and a content population was a quiet one.

As for the traders . . .

They traded now in Nerendale, the closest of the farming villages, less than a day's ride from the City gates, offering goods to a Journeyman-Undermage who acted as broker. Those that were on the Approved List—or which Armethal-ieh's broker thought *might* be approved—were sent on into the City.

It was much tidier.

Lycaelon settled himself in his chair again and reached for his jade teacup, then drew back his hand when he realized the cup had grown stone cold. It would be the work of an instant to summon enough Magefire to warm it, but reheated tea was an abomination. Better to send servants to the kitchens for fresh.

He was reaching for the bell-pull when the door to his office opened, and his confidential secretary, Chired Anigrel, entered. Anigrel was as fair as Lycaelon was dark, and many decades younger than his master, but both men bore the unmistakable stamp of Mage breeding: the narrow saturnine features, high forehead, and slender, long-boned build that set them apart from ordinary men. Anigrel wore the dark grey robes of a Journeyman-Undermage; in a few years, he would be a Master Undermage, released from mundane tasks such as this and on his way to the years of study that would lead to full Magehood. But for now he served and learned.

But given his somewhat elevated position as Lycaelon's assistant and tutor to Kellen, Anigrel was permitted something other than *plain* grey robes. Although he was not allowed any variation in color, his robes were made of somewhat finer materials than most, and were tastefully ornamented with cursive grey embroidery. It did not suit Lycaelon to have his personal aide taken for an ordinary Journeyman; not when Anigrel carried his master's word and prestige. It had only taken a single instance of Anigrel wasting half the day cooling his heels in some officious little noble's hall instead of discharging his errand and returning to his duties before Lycaelon had ordered the change in wardrobe.

"Master," Anigrel said, folding his hands and bowing his head submissively.

"There is a problem?" Lycaelon asked, attempting to mask his irritation. Anigrel knew better than to interrupt him with trifles.

"A . . . small problem. But one that can be handled by no one else, Arch-Mage."

Lycaelon sat back in his chair, sighing. He trusted Anigrel's judgment—or else the man would not have long survived in his current post—but he loathed being interrupted.

"You may continue," he said grudgingly.

"A merchant family has lodged a complaint—of sorcery within their home," Anigrel said reluctantly.

Lycaelon leaned forward. "Sorcery? Uncontrolled Magery? Piffle! More likely their cook has been using the wrong sort of mushrooms in the stew—and if it is sorcery, any trained Undermage could deal with it. *You* could deal with it!" He glared at the secretary.

Anigrel cleared his throat nervously. "Forgive me, my lord Arch-Mage, for not making myself entirely clear. The family involved is the Tasoaire family. Apparently this . . . sorcery

. . . has been going on for some days. They are quite distracted, if I may say so."

He hummed under his breath for a moment, then added, reluctantly, "Actually, things are at a bad pass with them, by the report they have given us. It is my opinion that it should be . . . dealt with, immediately. They are not of exalted status by birth, but they are . . . influential."

And very, very rich. Lycaelon added what Anigrel was too tactful to mention aloud. The Tasoaires were one of the wealthy trading families who controlled much of Armethalieh's material wealth, and paid a great deal in taxes for the privilege. Whatever the true nature of their problem, they were important enough to need their feelings soothed by having no less a personage than the Arch-Mage himself deal with their problem, whatever it was.

He focused his attention on Anigrel again. "Very well. You were quite right to come to me with this. I will go to see them. And now you may stop quaking in your slippers and tell me what else you know about this problem, the part you are certain I will very much dislike."

Anigrel swallowed hard. "Naturally we did a preliminary investigation of the complaint—without bringing it to the attention of the family, of course. There does seem to be some actual cause for alarm. And the focus of the disturbance seems to be the, ah, *daughter* of the house . . ."

⌐

A scant quarter-chime later, Lycaelon Tavadon strode down the main thoroughfare of Armethalieh, his heavily embroidered black-on-silver Arch-Mage robes belling behind him with the force of his passage, and the wide-brimmed, pointed hat that matched them held on to his head by a clever cantrip. The afternoon sunlight flashed off the bright ornament at the tip of his Staff of Office, its gold-and-crystal finial meant to depict the Unbounded Light in all its glory. He could certainly have taken his carriage, or a sedan chair, or even a horse, but he knew he needed the walk to clear his head and calm his feelings, or else he'd risk blasting the entire family to ashes where they stood, and wouldn't *that* set the merchant families fluttering like chickens with the fox among them! Not so easy to deal with at the next Trade Council meeting, half of which seemed to be spent soothing ruffled feathers and smoothing over imagined slights at the best of times.

The crowd parted before him, giving him a wide berth even without the need for his retainers to clear the way. In fact, people pressed back against the walls as he passed, their faces blank, transfixed with awe and a little fear. They might not know one Mage from another, usually, but *everyone* knew what his staff of office looked like, and knew by extension who the bearer must be. Their deference soothed him, but only a little. Anigrel was right, he could not delegate this particular task, much as he would like to: Arch-Magisterial oil was needed to calm these waters.

But . . .

A girl! A puling insignificant maggot of a female, Tradeborn to boot, working magick, or trying to. Of *course* it had gone wrong! And now he must come in and deal with it, and calm their superstitious fears—for as Anigrel had reminded him several times, the Tasoaires were the wealthiest of the merchant families, terrified beyond reason by this firebird in a hen's nest, and fear could quickly turn to anger . . .

Anger was the bane of every Mage, from the lowliest Student to the Arch-Mage himself. No one, not even a streetsweeper, much less a wealthy merchant, should ever look upon the works of a Mage with anything other than the deepest and most profound gratitude, a gratitude all-important and all-encompassing. The City could not survive without that gratitude, though the citizens knew it not.

These idiot Tradeborn fools—they would never, ever guess what the Arch-Mage had saved them from, *besides* their folly, that is, when he finished with this mess. For there was a worse thing that the girl could become if she continued down the path she was on; something so dreadful he *dared* not even hint at it to anyone outside the most trusted of the Mageborn.

There were times when he wished devoutly to sink every

female in the world to the bottom of the Selken Sea. Only a female could create such havoc with so little effort!

So. He took a deep breath, and another, willing himself to be calm in the face of this mortal insult to his Art. No one would see his inner feelings. He went to pacify, not to frighten. *We all serve the City, each doing his part in service to Armethalieh the Golden.*

Although sometimes only the Light can see how!

⌒

HE would easily have found the Tasoaire home even without the uniformed servant who was waiting at the nearest cross-street to lead him to it. The man was wearing a livery more suited to a captaincy in one of Armethalieh's little-used cavalry regiments than to a footman of a proper merchant family, but the Tasoaires had done more than well for themselves, and were not averse to letting the world know it. Wealth had long since outstripped good taste, and though the Tasoaires were not so blind to all good sense and common decency to think of moving out of the Merchants' Quarter, they had certainly let their good fortune seduce them into making such extensive changes to what had once been a modest and sensible home that Lycaelon could almost have imagined for a moment that it was one of the mansions of the Mage aristocracy, grotesquely distorted and crammed into a space far too small for it.

As Lycaelon followed the man to his destination, he kept his face from showing the disdain he felt. The house stood out from its fellows in a way that was almost—Lycaelon's lip curled—*foreign.* Honest timber and stone had been replaced with golden marble that would not have been out of place in Lycaelon's own courtyard (and so was *very* much out of place here), and instead of the neat stone walls and colorful glazed pots filled with seasonal flowers that graced the forecourts of other merchant houses, the Tasoaire home was enclosed by a fanciful iron gate with gilded accents behind which a fountain—small, but still far too large for the

space it occupied, and covered with vulgar imported colored
tiles besides—sprayed jets of water into the sky. Anyone approaching their door, tradesman or guest, was sure to receive
a soaking, regardless of the weather.

But "anyone" was not the Arch-Mage Lycaelon Tavadon.
He paused for a moment before the gates, and concentrated
on a simple Binding Spell, drawing on the stored power in
the Talisman around his neck and one of the many simple
cantrips he had memorized years before. There was a stut-
tering sound from deep beneath the earth, and the arcing jets
of water drooped and died.

The servant stared up at him, wide-eyed and anxious. Lycaelon allowed himself a thin smile. Let them all wonder—
or, if they thought about it at all, perhaps they would blame
the fountain's sudden failure on the madness they were har-
boring within their own walls. The madness he had come to
end, and the sooner, the better.

Straightening his robes, Lycaelon tapped the butt of his
staff meaningfully on the paving. The servant stopped staring
and scurried to open the gate. The Arch-Mage's escort peeled
off to stand at strict attention on either side of the gate, while
the Arch-Mage entered.

Before Lycaelon had taken three steps up the walk, the
door of the house was swinging open at the hand of an even
more ornately uniformed personage than the footman who
had guided him to the house. Correctly identifying this apparition as the Tasoaires' butler, Lycaelon surrendered his
cloak, hat, gauntlets, and staff. He imagined the servant
looked embarrassed to be seen in such an outfit—as well he
ought, in such a hideously indecent household! Wealth, like
power, belonged only in those hands suited to wield it properly.

It occurred to Lycaelon that perhaps something could be
done about the Tasoaires' improper good fortune. Some grad-
ual readjustment of their affairs—for the good of the City,
of course. He would look into it once he got back to the
Council House. But at the moment, he had a more immediate
problem to solve . . .

"I am expected," he announced austerely.

"Of course, Lord Arch-Mage. If you will accompany me?"

Lycaelon followed the butler into the house, amusing himself by attempting to discern the bones of the original building beneath the veneer of its clownish makeover. It was like walking through a jackdaw's nest—there was no regard for taste and balance, only for vulgarity and expensive display. And he was certain that at least a few of these items had made it off the Selken ships without the Council's imprimatur.

He was also interested to note that there seemed to be gaps—prominent, but irregular—in the overabundance of tawdry ornament, as if broken items had been hastily removed and the survivors had not yet been rearranged to hide the absence. Apparently the girl had indeed broken most of what was breakable in the Tasoaire household, for which he held himself much in her debt.

But to Lycaelon's faint disappointment, the room to which he was led seemed to have suffered the least from the Tasoaires' new wealth. The heart-room of the house still displayed its timber and plaster walls unchanged, and the large tiled fireplaces at each end of the room were lovely and tasteful examples of merchant-class craftsmanship. Small-paned windows, open to the unusually warm spring day, showed glimpses of a small back garden that was very much as it ought to be. Carved oak settles, their wood honey-dark with years of beeswax polishing, flanked each hearth, and there was a small writing desk under one window, angled to catch the natural light. There was a sideboard on the wall facing the windows, and Lycaelon was interested to see that where he would have expected to see fiery cut-crystal, he saw instead a pewter jug and a collection of mismatched pewter cups, badly dented but polished to a satiny gleam.

But the seemly and modest effect was spoiled by an enormous gilded chair with a scarlet velvet cushion that squatted in the middle of the room, obviously carried in for his benefit, with a painted and gilded table beside it that was undoubtedly more suitable to a whorehouse than a merchant's townhouse.

The two people awaiting him arose from their seats on one of the settles as the door opened, and moved hesitantly forward to greet him.

Lycaelon recognized Ioan Tasoaire from his many appearances before the Council, and the painfully overdressed woman beside him must be his wife, though Lycaelon didn't trouble himself to recall her name. Both were upholstered in so much satin, multicolored brocade, gold lace, and velvet piping that they looked like a pair of overstuffed chairs designed by a madman. Both of them looked worn and frightened. Lycaelon smiled, radiating charm—a simple enough cantrip, really, among the many every High Mage always kept in readiness for situations such as this.

"Come, Ioan, you know me," Lycaelon said, injecting good humor and warmth into his voice. "I'm here to help. And who is this lovely young thing? Surely this isn't your daughter?"

Ioan Tasoaire smiled, and Lycaelon could see that it cost him some effort. "Nay, Lord Arch-Mage, this is my wife, Yanalia."

"You can help her, can't you, Lord Arch-Mage? Help our Darcy?" the woman burst out. "You do know what it is with her, don't you? Don't you?"

"Hush now, Yana," Ioan said, pulling his wife back before she could approach Lycaelon. "I'm sure the Arch-Mage will do all he can."

"Of course I will," Lycaelon said, settling himself in the garish throne-chair, inasmuch as seemed to be expected of him. "I came as soon as I heard there was trouble—in fact, I'm a little hurt, Ioan, that you didn't come to me sooner. What are friends for, if not to help one another?"

Yanalia began to weep in harsh strangled sobs, clinging to her husband. Lycaelon forced himself to keep his face smooth, his expression benign. Puling and weeping with hysteria already, and he hadn't been in the house more than a few moments! How like a woman!

"We were afraid," Ioan said slowly.

Lycaelon composed his features into an expression of hurt

regret and bowed his head. "If that is the case . . . if that is
truly the case . . . then I have failed you, failed all the people
of Armethalieh. How can I help you, if you won't come to
me for help? Look at me, Ioan." He spread his hands, a sad
smile on his face. "I'm a Mage. That's all I am. That's all I
do. I don't plant crops, or spin cloth—or make gold out of
thin air like *you* do, Ioan!" He allowed himself a rueful smile
at the small joke, and was pleased to see Ioan smile in return.
"All I do is help people. That's all any Mage does. That's all
the Art Magickal is *for*. But when people won't come to me
for help, then, well . . . I'm useless. I can't help you if I don't
know that you need help, and my Gifts go to waste."

He lowered his head again, as if meeting their eyes was
too much for him. Had he overplayed his hand, laid it on too
thick? But no. They were distracted, afraid, and from the
looks of things hadn't been sleeping well at all. If he could
get them feeling guilty as well, they should be supremely easy
to manipulate.

"It weren't—it wasn't that." Ioan had made his way up
from the laboring classes and married a minor merchant's
daughter, taking her name, as was customary when marrying
into a higher-ranked family. When he was upset, his low-
class origins showed in his speech.

"We thought it would go away. It didn't, but then we
thought she'd get better!" Yanalia burst out, her voice still
thick with tears. "But it's only gotten worse, Arch-Mage. The
fires, and the breaking things, well, at first we thought it
might be a spirit or something, not *her*—we had a Light-
Priest in to bless the house, and it stopped for a while, but
then it started up again. Then I began thinking about old tales
and when we realized it was her, not a spirit, we thought it
would get better . . ." Her voice faltered, and for a moment
Lycaelon thought she was finished speaking, but she composed herself with an effort and went on. "After all, don't all
Apprentices have trouble when they start learning magick?"

Only years of self-discipline and iron self-control kept Lycaelon's features composed in a benign mask. He even managed to smile at the witless creature. "Perhaps you had better

begin at the beginning," he said smoothly. "Tell me everything. Leave nothing out."

It was an old and not unfamiliar story, a mainstay of the
romances so beloved of the lower classes. A child of humble
parents—a merchant, a tavern-keeper, or perhaps even a
farmer—begins to find bizarre things happening around him
at the same time his body begins changing from child to
adult. Things vanish, only to reappear in strange places.
Stones rain down on his house. Plates, cups, and other small
objects fly through the air around him as if thrown, though
no one seems to have touched them. Mysterious voices are
heard, music, odd sounds. Sometimes spontaneous fires start,
or the boy sleepwalks, going into trances and speaking of
things he has no way of knowing. And then, to provide the
story with a happy ending, just as things seem darkest, a
Mage comes, and recognizes the child's power, and takes him
away for training in the Art Magickal, elevating him into a
world of privilege, duty, and entitlement.

These people had heard such stories a hundred times, and
when the same things started happening in their home, and
they eliminated the possibility that it was some spirit of mischief, doubtless had visions of the glory that having a Mage
in the household would bring them.

But it is always a boy of whom the storytellers write and
sing. Because there never has been, and never would be, a
female Mage in the Golden City of Armethalieh.

"And you say there have been fires?" Lycaelon asked
smoothly, when it became clear that the story Ioan and Yanalia had to tell was degenerating into a recital of a long series
of boring incidents, and they had no more real details to give.
Fires . . . well, that put the cap on it. If there were fires starting, it wouldn't be long before what was happening *inside*
these walls would migrate outside, endangering far more than
a few trinkets, no matter how strong the Protection Spells on
the surrounding buildings were.

"They started a day or two ago," Ioan said, sighing heavily.
"And now Deglas says the fountain has stopped running as
well, and where will we get the water to put out the next

one? Lord Arch-Mage, what can we do? Protective amulets just shatter. Beating the girl does no good—it only makes matters worse!"

"Broke all my best dishes after that," Yanalia said, dabbing at her eyes. "Oh, not *her*—but they flew around the kitchen like bats for half a bell, all smashed to flinders, and the cook left and both the scullery-maids; I haven't been able to keep a girl since! You *must* help us! Please! You must take her now!"

"Take her now." The Light preserve us. The daft woman really does think we'll take the wretched creature and make a Mage of her!

"Rest assured, Goodlady Tasoaire; your problems are at an end. You and your husband have done the right thing by coming to me." He kept his voice soothing, although his own emotions could best be described as "seething" rather than "soothing." "I will deal with this myself, here and now. Your Darcilla will never again be troubled by these strange and unwelcome visitations. I will see to it that her energies are redirected into some other activity that is more suited to her sex," Lycaelon told her, though in truth, he wanted to grab the idiot creature by the brocaded shoulders and shake her until her teeth rattled for being such a fool. "Obviously, since it is a girl-child involved, and not a boy, we will have to take action before she harms herself with this—unnatural power. Quite impossible for any girl to use such a thing, of course. Quite, quite impossible. Now, if you will send for the girl . . ."

"But why aren't you going to take her and make her into a Mage?" Yanalia asked, taken aback. "I thought—the stories all say—she has such power . . ."

Lycaelon stared at her, too stunned for a moment to retain his mask of avuncular calm. Was it actually possible that despite what he had just told her, this cretinous female was going to insist that her *daughter* be taken in and trained by the Mages?

Clearly, she was not listening. And he was going to have to take a stronger stand. Much. In fact, he was going to have to be disagreeable with her. He got to his feet, frowning sternly. "My good woman, try not to be any more feather-brained than absolutely required by your female nature. Do *think*, will you? Have you *ever* seen a female Mage in this City?"

Yanalia cowered back, aware that she had somehow offended the Arch-Mage but not quite sure what she'd done.

"Well . . . no," she admitted. "But I don't see . . ."

"Precisely. You don't see. Because, my good woman, you are not a Mage. But surely you have eyes." He waved his hand around. "Look at the shambles she's made of your house, and imagine what a disaster she could make of the City were she turned loose upon it. It's the simple truth that women lack the emotional detachment necessary to master the High Magick; a truth that has been proven time and time again, and sometimes with tragic results. Their gifts lie elsewhere—in the arts, in business, in the home. She is as unhappy now as you would be, madame, should I ask you to strap on sword and armor and patrol the City walls. Bring her to me and I shall heal her of this inconvenient fever, and you will all be more comfortable for it."

"She'll be all right?" Ioan asked uncertainly.

Lycaelon smiled at Ioan, man-to-man, allowing a faint undercurrent of magic to speak to him, silently. *Your wife, as you have always thought, is a fool. You and I know better than any mere female. You must be the master in your house. Put your foot down with her, put her in her place, and your world will become infinitely more comfortable and harmonious.* "It will be as if this last moonturn never happened. She'll be your own happy grateful child once more. Peace beneath your own roof, Ioan, what more could any man ask for, eh?"

Ioan smiled, letting out a long sigh of relief. "Ah, that's that, then. Go and fetch the girl, Yana."

Yanalia Tasoaire still looked doubtful, but not quite uncertain enough to be willing to argue with her husband in front of the Arch-Mage of Armethalieh. She bobbed a hasty curtsy and left the room.

"She'll be a while," Iaon said, with the air of one who has had long experience with wives and daughters. Whatever he was like normally with his wife, he had drunk deeply of the spine-strengthener supplied by Lycaelon, and was acting accordingly. He stepped to the sideboard. "Care for a stiffener while you wait?"

"Ah . . . no. My Art prevents, you will understand."

While it was partly true—no Adept of the Art Magickal partook of senses-clouding substances lightly, least of all when about to perform magic—it would have been a simple matter for Lycaelon to change the contents of the cup until it was no more potent than spring water. Refusing to drink with his host was all part of a certain mystique the Mages wove about themselves, a dance of etiquette designed to set them apart from the average citizens whom they governed. The people of the Golden City must never be allowed to forget that their servant-Masters were woven of finer cloth than they themselves were.

"But do go ahead," Lycaelon said generously. "I imagine this has all been quite a strain for you and your good lady."

Ioan laughed raggedly. "Like a wondertale come to life— and not one of Perulan's, where you know all will end well!" He poured himself a full cup and drank, and Lycaelon smelled the rich scent of good brandy.

"I must admit, I was never convinced that Darcy was ever going to control this—"

"Inconvenient fever," Lycaelon supplied smoothly.

"Cursed inconvenient. It just kept getting worse, not better. But my wife—" He coughed. "You know how women are. They get harebrained notions and nothing will shake them loose of it."

Lycaelon judged it time to change the subject. "Tell me, Ioan, this Darcilla of yours, what are her interests? Will she be following you into the business?"

"Nay, not she—that's for her older sister; Mora's been mad for the counting-house ever since she could hold a string of tally-beads. No, for Darcilla it's always been the music." The man looked bemused. "Even before she could walk or talk, it was the music."

Ah. Lycaelon felt a small spark of satisfaction. So the girl had some small spark of talent for music, did she? All to the good. It would make what he was about to do that much easier; music required some of the same abilities and talents as the Art Magickal, so redirecting the girl's interests wouldn't be as painful or difficult as it could have been.

"Conservatory isn't cheap," Ioan went on, "but what's money for if not to spend, says I?"

"Indeed," Lycaelon agreed smoothly. *And you will have every opportunity to spend a great deal of your money on this daughter of yours. I shall see to that.*

The door opened again and Yanalia entered with her daughter. Though barely out of childhood, Darcilla Tasoaire was already taller than her mother, with something of her father's dark good looks. She was clean, though slatternly dressed; a worn pink house-tunic, several sizes too big for her, dragged, unbelted, on the floor, and her long dark hair hung lank and uncombed down her back. Darcilla's cheeks were flushed, and her eyes flashed dangerously; she and her mother had obviously been fighting over how she should appear before this important guest, and the lightnings of uncontrolled Mage-potential crackled around her like the warnings of a storm to Lycaelon's finely attuned senses.

For a moment he felt a flash of pity for the young victim. Who knew what would happen if things were allowed to go on as they were? Powers such as the girl now possessed didn't simply go away, and no mere female could possibly learn to control such subtle and powerful energies. She could only be led down the paths of madness and chaos, dragging the Light knew how many innocents in her wake. Curse her parents for letting this go on as long as they had out of foolish pride and misplaced pity! It only proved once again how unfit ordinary folk were to involve themselves in any dealings with High Magick.

And females. Most especially females.

"Now I must ask you to leave us alone together for a short time," Lycaelon said, rising to his feet.

He saw Yanalia brace herself to argue, but Ioan was already moving toward her, detaching his wife from his daughter and moving her briskly through the open door. The door shut behind them, and the Arch-Mage was alone with Darcilla Tasoaire.

"You would do well to heed me," Lycaelon said in a slow, deep resonant voice quite unlike the one he had used with her parents. The words themselves were unimportant; he actually had no interest in speaking with the girl. Speaking was only a way of catching her attention, to key the prepared cantrip that would place her into a trance so that he could do the work that must be done.

He saw the girl's lashes flutter as she fell quickly into trance—those with the Gift were far more susceptible to it than those with no talent whatsoever, oddly enough—and he moved to catch her before she fell. Under his guidance, she walked over to the enormous gilded chair and seated herself docilely in it.

He took a moment to prepare himself, just as a surgeon does before making the first incision. Like a master surgeon, this was an operation the High Mage had performed hundreds of times, for not all of those born with the ability to learn the High Art, despite what the talespinners said, were suited to practice it, either for reasons of temperament or birth—or sex. For the good of the City, it was often the unpleasant duty of a Mage to protect both the Art and the people by removing the Gift from an ill-suited practitioner, as well as to perform other delicate operations on the mind. Armethalieh had no prisons. There was no need of them, in a city ruled by the Mages who wielded this most delicate and subtle of all the High Art's Gifts.

With quick deftness Lycaelon entered the girl's mind. To his Magesight, the parts of her brain that sensed and handled Mage-energy glowed brightly, as brightly as a diseased organ beneath a surgical spell. He drew upon his Talisman, focusing its stored Mage-energy upon each of those centers in turn, burning and destroying them until they were cold and dark.

It would not affect her normal functioning. No one but Mages used those parts of their brain, after all. With Mage-sight he watched carefully as their glow faded like the embers of a dying fire, vanishing away into darkness. And when all the glow was gone, there was nothing left but a perfectly ordinary girl, like hundreds of others throughout the City.

Now that part of his task was done, Darcilla could no longer sense, evoke, or work with any of the energies called magick.

But her memories of doing so remained, and to leave them in place would be to leave his task half-finished. The desires that had turned her toward magick in the first place were still there, and if they weren't attached to some new interest, they would fester and lead to anger and discontent. She would be angry with her parents for turning her over to the Arch-Mage and "robbing" her of what she undoubtedly considered her "rightful" powers. She would be even angrier with the Arch-Mage, and it was truly said that there was no creature more dangerous than a woman bent on avenging a personal grudge; she was young, and she would have a long, long time to plan her revenge. He could not leave such a dangerous creature loose and unfettered—what if she decided that the way to repay the "wrong" was to ruin Anigrel or subvert Kellen?

He was here in the first place because her father was a powerful man, with a seat on the Trade Council. He could not allow an embittered child to jeopardize that delicate po-litical balance, either. Let Ioan be grateful for this day's work, and the City would run that much more smoothly . . . best for everyone if the girl was subtly molded into a shape more pleasing for all concerned.

Slowly, carefully, like riffling through the pages of a book, Lycaelon sought through Darcilla's memories. Each time he found one attached to magick—even one so seemingly in-nocuous as listening to a song, attending a play, reading a book—he reached in and changed it, erasing some parts, changing others, connecting all of them with music. Slowly he rebuilt her personality, making only tiny individual changes, but attaching all her interests, her drive, her will, to music. She would, without a shadow of a doubt, become as great a musician as he had promised her father—she now had the dedication and the drive, as well as the talent. He'd made sure of that. And if she seemed a little obsessed with it for the next few moonturns, well, that would pass as the spell settled into place, and what silly young girl wasn't obsessed with something or other at this age? Her parents should thank him for ensuring that she wouldn't be climbing out of her window every night to keep a rendezvous with some pimply young laborer intent upon marrying into wealth, just as her father had! No indeed, if—no, *when*, for Lycaelon would see to it that an invitation to audition came from the Conservatory by the next Sennday—she entered the Conservatory as a student, that single-minded obsession alone would guarantee her success. In the practice of music, like the practice of magick, success went to the single-minded, those who devoted the most time to practice.

He had done her the greatest favor possible. She might have become just one more featherwitted girl of wealth, unfocused, bored, and restless, with no other prospects than marriage. Now she would become a rising star in the Conservatory, and eventually a great artist. Eventually, she would be as great, in her own sphere, as any Mage. She would certainly have more *public* acclaim.

His task complete, Lycaelon withdrew from her mind, and sent her from a trance into a deep sleep. She'd awaken in a day or so unable to remember her part in any of what had happened, feeling that she was just as she had always been, her memories an unbroken line from her earliest days till now. The Tasoaires would engage a new flock of servants who had not been around during the recent unpleasantness, and all would be well.

The Arch-Mage stepped back, gazing down at the sleeping girl with a certain satisfaction. Everything had been set right. Things were now as they were meant to be. Trouble had been avoided for the good of the City, what was wrong had been set right, and in fact, the world would be a better place for his actions. Thanks to him, the City would now nurture a budding artist of exceptional ability, who would one day bring pleasure to thousands.

Straightening his robes, he went to give final instructions to her parents.

Chapter Three

The Books of the Wild Magic

"**K**ellen, you're not attending."

Three mornings a week, Kellen went off to private lessons with his tutor in one of the heavily warded private workrooms at the Mage College of Armethalieh.

The Mage College was a complex of buildings set among beautifully landscaped grounds in the heart of the Mage Quarter. It was surrounded by the homes of the Mages, and no one who was not himself a Mage or a Mage-to-be had ever set foot upon its grounds. Many of the wondertales circulating about the City dealt at great length with a young Apprentice's first sight of the College. All were completely inaccurate, as none of the fabulists had ever actually seen it.

Kellen regarded the fables with a mixture of disgust and amusement. The reality was nothing like they imagined: no talking fountains, no trees bearing every kind of fruit out of season, no herds of animated statuary in every conceivable shape and color wandering over the lawns, no beds of jeweled flowers wafting jets of strange perfumes into the air, no kindly elderly Mages wandering the grounds, trailing clouds of rainbows and Magelights . . .

No kindly elderly Mages at all. Crotchety, arrogant Mages in plenty, though.

. . . and no circles of eager Apprentices standing about

chattering among themselves as they worked on great spells . . .

Lots of Apprentices scurrying from class to class, but that's about it.

And certainly no strange collections of Other Races, kept here out of sight of the common run of Armethaliehans.

Everything was just ordinary. And *boring*.

The only statues that might possibly be animated were the two lions that flanked the main gate, and Kellen had never actually seen them move, though rumor had it that if a non-Mageborn ever tried to pass between them, they would leap down and rend him to bits. It was unlikely that a non-Mageborn would ever get that far, though. Not only would custom and common sense—and the Constabulary—keep ordinary citizens away, there were simple wards all around the grounds, to turn back the drunk, the sick, and the mad.

Unfortunately, no matter how hard he'd tried, Kellen had never been sick enough to be turned back.

He stared blankly at his tutor, Undermage Anigrel. He stared *blankly* because he knew better than to stare with challenge in his gaze. Anigrel looked like a younger—and blond—version of Kellen's father; tall, lean, and saturnine, with just a hint of pointed beard and a pencil line of moustache. All the Mageborn were slender and fine-boned, their bodies shaped by no physical labor more arduous than lifting a wand or a pen. Their coloration was vivid; black, blond, or red hair running strongly in particular Mage families. They were elegant.

Kellen . . . wasn't.

His classmates called him "farmer" and "laborer" behind his back, and in truth, he *did* tower over most of them, especially since his last growth-spurt. Muscles meant for use, and honed by climbing walls and trees, and simply walking for miles through the City, bulked the fabric of his tunic and the loose-fitting trousers he preferred to the fashionable hose worn by some of his more daring classmates. He bet Anigrel wore hose—not that he'd ever seen his tutor without his grey

Journeyman robes, or was likely to. Or wanted to, come to that.

Chired Anigrel wasn't from a prominent enough family to have family colors, and as a Journeyman-Undermage he wasn't yet entitled to colors of his own, so he wore the universal uniform of the Mages of the City, the long grey robes and sleeveless, floor-length vest that would someday—if he was fortunate and worked hard—bear the colors of a full-fledged High Mage. Anigrel *was* in high favor with Lycaelon, however, which meant that his personal fortune stretched to a finer style of clothing than most—soft grey linen in this weather, with a discreet trimming of darker grey and equally discreet silver-grey geometric motifs in fine embroidery on the front and back panels of the vest.

It occurred to Kellen at that moment that he hadn't ever really *noticed* the way that the differences between those who were in favor with someone of high position and those who were not were subtly displayed despite the plain grey "uniform" that was supposed to be identical for every Mage, regardless of class or social background. Once again—as usual—fine words fell short of reality where the Mages were concerned.

"Begin again, Kellen," Anigrel said crossly, and Kellen sighed and raised his Student wand. Anigrel began to chant the names of the sigils that Kellen was supposed to have memorized.

"Eleph. Vath. Kushon. Deeril. Ashan . . ."

As Anigrel spoke the name of the sigil, Kellen was supposed to trace it in the air. In this order they were meaningless, and not even the magick stored in the wand did more than permit them to glow in the air for a few moments before fading. But assembled together in set orders, they would make the key components of the first-level spells that every Student Mage had to master before moving on to the next level. Kellen was only a Student-Apprentice; not even a full Apprentice. He was unable to cast even the simplest spell of the High Magick—or at least, he was *supposed* to be unable to.

Kellen was very well aware that he should be long past memorizing sigil-lists by now. He should, in fact, be mastering the first-level spells and well into the groundwork for second-level spells, which involved more complicated structures of sigils and words of Power. And in fact he actually had mastered one or two second-level spells, even though he didn't really know the groundwork—though *that* was something he kept to himself.

The trouble was, of course, that all this business with tracing sigils in the air without much result was boring. When he'd been a lot younger, there had been a certain excitement in seeing the sigils glowing with magick as they hung in the air before him; there was even a kind of aesthetic pleasure in creating them, for like ornamental writing, they were pretty in an austere, yet baroque fashion. But that had been a long time ago. These days, Anigrel kept finding all manner of little defects to correct in the sigils he'd mastered, and lists of new sigils to learn. He was tired of it; tired of rote memorization and repetition without any results.

His mind kept drifting off to the very different sort of magick that he had found in *The Book of Sun.* There was substance there, a kind of magick you could get your teeth into. And it was a magick anyone could understand. There didn't seem to be any nonsense with memorizing books full of sigils and words of power.

The Book of Sun was the easiest of the three Books to understand, a primer on personal energy and how magick actually worked. It was the first time he'd ever *seen* anything about how magick worked. The High Mages didn't want to explain anything—at least to a lowly Student like Kellen— his studies consisted of endless drill, and he was supposed to take it on faith that someday the endless round of memorization would make sense.

Not like the Books of the Wild Magic. They actually *told* you things; how things worked, why they worked, why they *didn't* work. Even better, they had actual *spells.*

He'd discovered that the back half of *The Book of Sun* was mostly full of little cantrips and minor spells to make things

happen—everything from lighting a candle to sending a one-
or two-word message to scrying what was happening at a
distance.

If these Books were intended to serve the same purpose
for young Wildmages as his textbooks on High Magick, they
were certainly a lot more straightforward—and you actually
got to *do* something besides memorize!

"Kellen!" Anigrel said sharply. "Your line is drifting to the
right—I've told you over and over: you *must* keep your sigil
centered directly in front of you! Now, again—retrace that
Methra—"

Kellen sighed; *he* didn't think he was off-center. He began
retracing the sigil.

Well, while it was true that you could start doing the Wild
Magic immediately, there also seemed to be—ramifications.
The spells in the three Books didn't seem all that different
from the basic High Magick spells he'd been learning (if not
actually using), but now that he'd finished the first Book he
was starting to get an idea of why the Books were anathema
to the High Mages. Wild Magic seemed to be utterly unpredictable.

And oh, how the High Mages *hated* the unpredictable! Absolutely *hated* it! As far as they were concerned, everything
ought to be regulated, measured, moderated, and controlled,
and Wild Magic just . . . wasn't. You could cast your spell,
set the process in motion, and as far as Kellen could figure
out, there was no telling just how your end would be accomplished, or even if it would be attained at all. That point was
made over and over again in *The Book of Moon*. Spontaneity,
variety, unpredictability, all linked into that most powerful of
things, *magick*—the High Mages couldn't possibly do anything other than hate the Wild Magic, now, could they?

And despite the fact that you might not get what you
wanted, that was part of what Kellen found so attractive about
Wild Magic, just when he was the most unhappy with his
life and the future his father had all planned out for him.

It was very strange, finding the Books in the Low Market
like that, though perhaps it would be better to say that *they*

found *him*. Perhaps that was just one more demonstration of how unpredictable Wild Magic was.

Perhaps he had *been* practicing Wild Magic even before he'd found the Books, even without knowing it, and because of that he had sensed the Books and been drawn to them just when he had been longing for the new and different, for excitement and change. Maybe his longing had *become* the instrument of Wild Magic . . .

Or Wild Magic had used him . . .

And that sudden thought made him just a bit uncomfortable.

"Xota. Jald. Eron. Batun," Anigrel chanted, as Kellen traced sigil after sigil, each one more complicated than the last. The first set had only glowed with a single color; now that he was into the more advanced of the sigils, the lines that he drew in the air boasted three different—though always harmonious—colors, or three shades of the same color. And now the sigils themselves pointed out where he went wrong, for the colors would not be *quite* right if his tracing was off even a little. And if they were wrong altogether, well, he'd often get vile shades that set his teeth on edge.

I wonder what would happen to a color-blind Mage? Kellen thought suddenly. That would hardly be a problem for a Wildmage, now, would it?

Of course, there were other difficulties with Wild Magic. . . .

His mind wandered again; there was something else that had occurred to him that made him more than a little uneasy about his three Books.

The Books, if they had not actively sought him out, had surely *picked* him—or something connected with them had. Probably they had sat in that merchant's stock for years, and before that, perhaps in some other merchant's stock or some forgotten library. So. What was it about *him* that had made them pick him? Whoever had copied out the three Books had set a spell on them to enable them to stay together as a set, and must have set a second to ensure that only someone who was "right" for them would find them. The question in Kellen's mind was—just what was it about *him* that was "right"?

Obviously the Books knew they had to go to someone who wouldn't automatically turn them over to the High Mages, which probably ought to bother him more than it did. And they had to go to someone who had the personal energy to be a Wildmage. But what else was involved? Was it only that the person had to be willing, even eager, to accept something that was different, someone who was tired of the endless sameness enforced by the Council? Or was there something more to it than that?

Was it a weakness in him? Something, as the *Ars Perfidorum* suggested, corruptible?

And of course, he had another worry altogether. Whether or not the *Ars Perfidorum* was correct about the Wild Magic being bad, there was still the law. The three Books were anathema; there was no arguing with that. At the very least, if they were discovered in his possession, they'd be taken from him and burned. At worst . . . well, he wasn't sure what the worst would be. He had to hope that the Books would continue to hide themselves—but what if he *was* found out?

He tried to picture his father coming across them. Asking where he'd gotten them. Asking if he'd read them. Just how much trouble would he be in?

He wanted to think that it couldn't be *that* bad; after all, they were only Books. It wasn't as if he'd done anything, even if he had read them. Right?

Nevertheless, he had the horrible feeling that it would be a lot worse than anything he had ever gotten into before.

⟳

UNDERMAGE Anigrel felt a headache coming on.

Being appointed as the tutor to the only son of Arch-Mage Lycaelon was a great honor, one he had fought tooth-and-nail for.

Life had not been easy for him, although it also had not been particularly difficult, either. He'd been just wealthy enough to see *true* wealth and long for it; just exalted enough in status to know what real status was and crave it. Perhaps, in a way, that had been worse than being born impoverished and ignorant.

Chired Anigrel was the grandson of a tradesman. His father had shown Magegift and been taken away by the Mages to be trained. Anigrel knew nothing of his father's family, and little more of his Mageborn mother's, who had cut her off completely when she had married the son of a tradesman, even though he was a promising young Mage. She had died bringing Anigrel into the world, despite all that High Magick could do, and after that, Torbet Anigrel's fate had been sealed. He had been a wealthy man by the standards of the City, but in comparison to the fees the High Mages *could* command for their work, he'd been a pauper, and his dead wife's family had made it crystal clear that Torbet Anigrel would never rise above the ranks of the plain, common Mages who labored at the thankless jobs of the City.

If Anigrel had learned one lesson from his father's life, it was not to let family stand in his way. His father had died untimely early, while his son was still at his own magickal studies, and once his father was dead, Anigrel had sold the house and everything in it and set about erasing every link that bound him to the tradesman's son, the upstart Mage who had killed a Mageborn daughter. Everyone would still know, but they would admire the effort he used to try to make them forget.

The money after the estate was settled hadn't gone far, but it had bought him a new set of friends, ones with more important fathers, important enough to counteract everything that his mother's family could muster to pull him down. At length, Anigrel was on his way up in the world—the only world that counted, the one ruled by Mages, and if his mother's family was no help to him, they did not go out of their way to hinder him, either. With time, the path of friendships and carefully tended connections had led to the House of Tavadon, to the Arch-Mage himself. The Arch-Mage had a young son, and young sons grew, and needed tutors . . .

Anigrel knew Kellen's bloodline, knew his potential, and

had cherished daydreams of great reward from his father when he turned over to him a polished and accomplished young Apprentice to follow in the Arch-Mage's footsteps.

The trouble was, Kellen wasn't cooperating. Light knew he'd done his best to make things easy for the boy—he gained nothing from producing a failure, after all!

But no matter what he did, Kellen would not apply himself to his studies. Would not memorize the basic groundwork, the framework upon which the architecture of High Magick must be built. And without that, Anigrel could do nothing. In fact, as the years passed, Kellen actually seemed to manage to *unlearn* some of his lessons, if that was possible!

As time passed, he felt the unspoken pressure from Lycaelon and the increasing resistance from Kellen and felt very much as if he was being squeezed between the two.

Well, of the two, Kellen was the one he could break the easiest. Much depended on it.

"Kellen," he said, tinging his voice with heavy disappointment layered with an artful coloring of scorn, "I am not certain what your difficulty is today—if I didn't know how intelligent you are *supposed* to be, I'd consign you to the ranks of the useless dullards. And I fear that your father would not be at all surprised."

The boy flushed, and his mouth took on that pouting downturn that made him look even more sullen than usual. Anigrel scowled. Kellen was a singularly unpromising specimen, all things considered. He had nothing of the look of the Mageborn—there was some scandal there, something to do with the Arch-Mage's late and unknown wife, but Anigrel was far too clever a social-climber to ever touch on such a sensitive issue. In his private hours, however, Anigrel sometimes wondered what the nameless female might have had to recommend her to the Arch-Mage's attention.

Undoubtedly she had been a beauty, but surely a Mage would seek for more than that in a marriage alliance that would produce sons? The features that commended themselves to masculine attention upon a female face could be unfortunate when passed on to male offspring, after all. That girlish face and pouting mouth might be quite beguiling on a young maiden, but Kellen was far too heavy-featured to make them into assets. In fact, Kellen seemed to take no pains with his appearance at all. Above heavy eyebrows was a thatch of curling brown hair that always looked a little too long no matter how often or expertly it was cut, and never looked neat. Kellen loomed above his peers, with hands and feet too big for the rest of him, and even the most expertly tailored robes and tunics never seemed to quite fit. He was nothing like his elegant father—no ambition, no drive—and Anigrel was more than tired of Kellen's constant sulking.

Well, it was time to pass some of that irritation back to the appropriate recipient.

"Sit down, and take out your notes," Anigrel continued. "You *can* take notes, can't you? Your mind hasn't gone so dull that you can't write your letters?"

The boy flushed again, and this time there was a flash of anger in the dark eyes. Good. He'd finally struck a nerve.

Anigrel waited while the boy took his seat at the small table just under the single window in the workroom, and took out the book of blank pages in which he was supposed to take notes while Anigrel lectured. Anigrel regularly inspected this book to be certain that the boy understood the lectures delivered to him—or at least understood enough to note down the salient points of each lecture. And to be certain the boy wasn't just doodling or writing nonsense.

"Power," he began, pacing slowly back and forth while he spoke, "and by that I mean magickal power, does not arise out of nothing. As you know, every Mage has his own personal reserves of power, and this is all very well for small matters, but for greater Workings, power must be pooled. This is part of every Mage's training, how to cooperate and meld the power each one holds into a greater whole. But even this is not enough to supply the needs of our City and its people. Therefore, in the distant past, the Arch-Mages discovered and learned to harvest a still greater source of this power."

He paused in his pacing to glance aside at his pupil, whose

head was bent over his book, his pen scratching diligently on the pages.

Well, regardless of how absentminded the boy was today, the information that Anigrel was about to give him should certainly wake him up.

"You know that every Mage has his own personal reserve of power," Anigrel continued. "But you may not have realized it is not only Mages who have stores of this power. All people have it, although of course they can never use it themselves."

The boy looked up sharply at that. Anigrel smiled slightly. It was about time that the boy began to understand how the world really worked! Perhaps some inside knowledge would give him the motivation to succeed! "Yes, you may well stare! Now, do you know *why* a Mage needs to learn how to share his power with others?"

Kellen shook his head mutely.

"Because, boy, only one born to the power of a Mage can *resist* someone trying to take his power from him, and he instinctively does so when he feels his power being drained from him. It takes training and will to overcome that instinct. The ordinary person, one who has no notion that he has this power, does not resist when it is harvested. And that is what we do, we Mages in the service of the City. Fully half of us spend all our waking time harvesting the power of our citizens to serve the City itself.

"Not, as you may have thought, in using our own little stores of power in long and involved spells that make the maximum use of tiny amounts of it, in order to do the work that we must. No, we constantly harvest the power of the people of the entire City, storing it, so that we need not deplete ourselves in order to do the work of the City."

Rather elegant, he'd always thought; like an invisible tax. Take *from* the citizens to do the work that they insisted in having done: purifying water, destroying vermin, creating the Golden Suns that Armethalieh spent so lavishly in trade with the outside world. And if the Mages siphoned off a bit here and there to make their own lives easier, well, that was only fair. Nothing in life was free.

The boy gaped at him, as if he didn't quite understand what he had heard. "You mean, you *take* it from them? Without asking? Without them even knowing?" he asked incredulously.

"And what would be the point of telling them?" Anigrel demanded sharply. "Half of them wouldn't believe it, and the other half would want to be paid for it, somehow—as if living in the City weren't payment enough. Ridiculous—they don't *use* it, they *can't* use it, they don't miss it, and if it weren't harvested, it would just drain away, accomplishing nothing. All things have their price, and the good of the City is paid for by the power of its citizens. Why should *we* deplete ourselves for them, when they can supply the power instead?"

"But—we should tell them, at least," Kellen persisted, then shut his mouth as Anigrel frowned at him furiously. Had the boy no higher instincts at all?

"Stupid sentimentality!" Anigrel snapped. "They are beneath us; uneducated, without the wisdom that knowledge gives to *us;* they are not fit to make decisions in this regard. Yet they are pleased to accept all the benefits that living within the walls of Armethalieh brings. They must pay for it somehow—just as they pay other taxes, *this* is a tax that they must pay to the Mages and the Council. That they do not know they pay it is irrelevant. Everything has a price. Everything. And that is the way that the real world works."

KELLEN bent his head back down over his book and scribbled Anigrel's words down verbatim, hiding his unease as best he could. So *this* was how all the magick of the City was fueled! He was very certain now that none of the Mages ever used his innate personal power for anything except his own personal needs. Why should they, even though the Mages benefited as much as anyone else from all of the municipal magicks, when they could save their own power for themselves and use the power of the citizens instead?

The problem was, *The Book of Moon* seemed to say that whenever you were the one who benefited from magick, you were the one who had to pay the price. Maybe that was only true in Wild Magic, but Kellen had to wonder. Wasn't all magick essentially the same, all governed by the same underlying rules?

He guessed that was why High Mages and Wildmages— if there still were any—couldn't agree about anything, if they couldn't agree about that. From his lessons with Undermage Anigrel, Kellen already knew that the larger the effect of the spell you cast, the higher the price in terms of raw power you had to pay for it, and where High Magick was utterly indifferent to the possibility of a *personal* price, Wild Magic seemed to say that not only was there always one, but that it *had* to be paid, and by the person casting the spell.

He bet the High Mages hadn't liked hearing that, if anyone had ever told them.

It had taken him a good part of last night to get his mind wrapped around that concept, but once he'd managed it, it seemed both logical and inevitable, if not precisely something that made him comfortable.

The personal price wasn't directly related to what was being done—that was what had been so hard to understand. So in Wild Magic, the more powerful the spell, the more likely it was that you'd have to *do* something besides supply your own personal power—like copy out and bespell those three Books, for instance, in exchange for, perhaps, creating a well or healing an injury.

The thing was—yet another concept he'd had trouble with—there was just no way of telling in advance *what* the price of any given spell would be. And if paying the "price" for a spell involved casting more spells, you could spend all your time in an endless cycle of "Magedebt" to the Wild Magic that way, always trying to "pay off" obligations for magick you'd used to pay off previous obligations! *My head hurts,* Kellen thought. It all seemed so complicated!

The Book of Moon said that the reason the price was never

the same was that the caster of the spell wasn't the same person he was the last time he cast it, which seemed, well, kind of an odd thing to claim. How could you be a different person today from the one who'd cast, oh, say, a Finding Spell yesterday? People didn't change overnight!

Kellen knew that people changed, of course. He wasn't the same person at seventeen that he'd been at seven. But that was *normal*. Everyone changed while they were growing up.

But then they stopped. His father had been the same person for as long as Kellen had known him, and if Lycaelon lived another fifty years, Kellen was sure that he wouldn't change a single habit or opinion.

Kellen tried to imagine people continuing to change all their lives—and for that matter, changing *quickly*. It would be like, like . . .

Like waking up one morning and finding you were living in a strange and unfamiliar house.

He felt a faint thrill of excitement at the thought. Could the Wild Magic make that happen? What if the prices you had to pay somehow changed you? What if the price *was* to change?

That would be another thing the High Mages wouldn't like. As far as *he* could tell, the whole point of High Magick was to keep anything from changing. Ever.

Anigrel blatted on about how the citizens of the City owed their energies to the Mages, his face set in an expression of self-satisfied arrogance that just made Kellen sick. He didn't want to listen to it. Didn't the Mages get rewarded enough, being paid for the work they did, and handsomely, too? There wasn't such a thing as a *poor* Mage in the entire City—once you were a full Mage, you had as good a house, servants, food, and clothing as any well-off merchant in the City, and for a lot less work, too! A nice life . . . no wonder everyone wanted it.

Everyone but Kellen, maybe.

"Kellen!"

The sharp tone of Anigrel's voice brought Kellen's attention back to his tutor, and the annoyance in Anigrel's face made it very clear that while he'd been thinking, his pen hadn't been moving . . .

"I do not know what could possibly have gotten into you, boy," Anigrel said with smoldering irritation, "but you clearly are not prepared to pay attention—and *I* am not prepared to waste my valuable time on a pupil who doesn't wish to learn."

Oh, grand. Father is certainly going to hear about this, Kellen thought with a sinking feeling. And what could he say? That he didn't like the way the City was run? But he *had* liked it, mostly, up until now.

He guessed . . .

Anigrel made a shooing motion with his hands, frowning exasperatedly. "Get out of here, boy. Go play, since that is obviously the only thing you're fit for today. I shall attempt to salvage something out of this morning while you idle your way about the City, child that you are. Be grateful I don't call for a nurse to take you to your room to play with toys."

Release, but with a sting in it.

Kellen picked up his notes and strode out of the room before Anigrel changed his mind.

Release—but at the cost of being treated like a child, like an *infant*, at being insulted and abused by a fatuous prig who thought he was *owed* everything he got!

Kellen set his chin stubbornly and left the workroom.

He stopped on the way out of the College and deposited his books in his locker, hoping he wouldn't run into any of his year-mates at the Mage College who would wonder why he wasn't still at his morning's lessons with his tutor—or worse, that he wouldn't run into his father, who sometimes visited the College between Council sessions to check up on some of the more promising senior pupils.

He thought of going home, but the thought of going back to Tavadon House, to the chilly corridors and grudging servants, nearly made him ill. He had to get out, somewhere far from here, from there, from Mages and magick. He needed free air and—if there was such a thing in this City—free talk.

There was only one place to go for both of those things.

Kellen opened his locker again and pulled off his robe, wadding it up and stuffing it in atop his books and tools. Where he was going, it would be a disadvantage to be recognized as a Student of the Mage College of Armethalieh.

A definite disadvantage.

⟜

WHEN the foreign ships from the Out Islands and the lands beyond the bounds of those claimed by the City were in, there was one place in Armethalieh where there was little or no chance that anyone would recognize him for who and what he was. The docks were the one place where Mages didn't go if they could help it.

Sailors distrusted them, captains did not like having to depend on the magicks that they bought at such high prices from them—the Talismans that brought fair following winds, the Amulets that directed storms to move out of the path of a ship, the Runestones that dispelled fog, the Wands that warned the man at the tiller of shoals and dangerous rocks. Yet those who failed to purchase such aids often came to grief—far oftener, said the whispers, than mere bad luck could account for . . .

And as for the merchants, well—it was the Mages who dictated what could and could not be sold. It was hardly to be expected that *they* would welcome the sight of those who restricted their ability to profit.

Foreign sailors were confined to the area of the docks; only the merchant-captain of a ship—or better still, his City-born representative—was allowed into the City proper to present samples of the cargo for inspection or deliver promised goods. The dock even had its own market, plenty of taverns and inns, and in any case the sailors were kept busy enough even in port that they didn't have much time to spend wandering the streets of Armethalieh.

The citizens were not encouraged to wander the docks, either, and generally everyone had heard tales of drunken sailors quarreling with peaceful citizens, starting fights, and generally behaving in an uncivilized manner. That was enough to keep most folk away. But Kellen had learned—by going there himself—that very few of those stories were true, and of the rest, well, people got drunk and got into fights, robbed and were robbed across the breadth of the City every day. Sailors and foreigners were as apt to be victims as victimizers.

But the area of dockside *was* a rough neighborhood, and a Mage who wandered in there, if he kept his nose in the air as most did, was apt to be greeted with jeers and rudeness. If the sailors and travelers weren't welcome in the City proper, well, they returned the favor in their own territory. So when Kellen went to the docks, he was careful to do so wearing inconspicuous clothing. He watched what he said and who he said it to. Mostly, he just looked and listened, and tried to stay out of the way.

The boundary dividing the dockside from the rest of the City was nothing more than a very wide boulevard, but it was patrolled by regular City Guards, who questioned anyone who crossed that particular street quite closely, and turned back anyone going in either direction if he didn't seem to have appropriate business where he was going. And "I'm just going to look around" was *not* considered to be appropriate business.

However, there were other places the guards didn't bother to check; one of them was a section of large warehouses that, rebuilt after a great fire a hundred years ago, had spread across the boulevard into the City. There was always so much coming and going there, wains being loaded and unloaded, men and boys heaving bales and barrels of goods about, that the guards couldn't have questioned everyone, and didn't bother trying. Kellen slipped across the border there, along with a gang of men and an empty wain; once on the dockside, he separated from the group and headed for the wharves.

He knew by now how to move out of the way of the stevedores and *stay* out of the way, and before too very long, he was perched on a piling in a disused slip, with the salt breeze blowing his hair away from his face, looking out at the harbor and the sea beyond.

If he squinted into the sunlight, it was possible to see a sort of shimmer across the mouth of the harbor—if he had used the spell that allowed him to see magick in action, he'd have seen what that shimmer really was. A curtain of power hung across the mouth of the harbor, the result of a spell that protected the harbor from the waves and winds and storms—but could also be "tightened" to keep everything, including ships, out . . . or in.

It could have been made completely invisible, of course, but the Mages of the City didn't want that. They *wanted* the foreign captains and their sailors to see that faint shimmer, to feel a little tingle as they crossed it, and know that while it protected them, it could also exclude them if they became too troublesome. The City was a huge, voracious creature. It devoured entire cargoes, disgorging in return other goods and minted gold coins so pure and so exact in weight that they were the standard against which all other currencies everywhere in the world were measured. The square Golden Suns of Armethalieh were accepted everywhere, for thanks to the special magicks worked at the City Mint, they could not be melted down, debased, shaved, or otherwise adulterated—unless another Mage broke the spell, at which point they lost their stampings and ceased to be Golden Suns, becoming only blank shapes of gold.

The foreign ships were in, and Kellen watched the pre-approved cargoes being unloaded. The wharf was full, every mooring place taken, and the masts of all the ships formed a kind of leafless forest, stripped of the sails that had carried them all this way. In their holds were things that would never be allowed to leave the confines of the ships; perhaps perfectly ordinary things, perhaps wonderful things. Kellen would never know, for he would never be permitted to see them. No one except the Mages of the Council would ever be permitted to see them. He could only wonder what *might* be there.

Still, even to be *close* to so much freedom made him feel

better. He took a seat on a piling, out of the way, and watched the sailors of the ship nearest him unloading their cargo. *Are there things in that hold that Wild Magic made?* he wondered. *Or things that Wild Magic has touched?* He wouldn't be able to tell, not from here, not with the aura of High Magick everywhere, overwhelming anything subtle. And Wild Magic was nothing if not subtle. Did anyone outside of the City know about Wild Magic? Surely they must.

High Magick—the Mages were more disciplined than the soldiers of the Council's Army, and they imposed *their* will upon the cosmos to the exclusion of any other possibility with the iron of that discipline. There was no room for error, for creativity, even for much experimentation in High Magick. A Mage could work for years, decades, just to develop a single variant in an existing spell, and even when he had spent his life upon it, it *still* might not be approved by the Council.

Kellen was supposed to feel comforted by this; the fact that nothing changed, nothing *would* change, was supposed to make people feel secure. But he wasn't—

The slip next to the one that Kellen sat beside held a slim little trading vessel of the sort that specialized in speed rather than bulk to make a profit. It rode high in the water, and was in the process of being loaded with small casks—probably distilled spirits—and wooden boxes—which would be spices, incense, and medicines, particular specialties of Armethalieh. The ship's master himself was at hand, helping to load the cargo; a vessel like this, Kellen had learned, seldom had a crew larger than ten, with perhaps a passenger, and since it dealt in cargoes of small valuable objects easy to steal, the crew never allowed anyone to load or unload but themselves.

The Dock Patrol—a detachment of the City Guard that regularly worked the dock area—came down the pier, eyed the ship and her crew, then cast a glance over at Kellen. But Kellen was prepared for them. He had a stick and a string he'd picked up from the rubbish waiting for the trash collectors, and the moment he'd taken his seat on the piling, he'd tossed the string into the water. It looked enough like a fishing-rod at a distance to fool the guards, and anyone could come down to the docks to augment his dinner with a little fish, if he chose.

It was odd, considering how much trouble the regular City Guard went to to keep citizens away from the docks, that the Dock Patrols so rarely chased people away from the wharves, but Kellen had found, to his surprise, that it was true. But perhaps it wasn't so odd after all. Only the poorest of Armethalieh's citizens would risk the social stigma of coming here—no one with any money at all would stoop to gleaning "trash" fish from the harbor for their suppers—and there was always the possibility of being "contaminated" by alien ways that would keep any Armethaliehan with a pretense of respectability far from the foreigners. Perhaps the Dock Patrol thought it was easier to keep an eye on the usual visitors to the docks than to simply try to keep them all out. Perhaps they relied on the fact that the regular City Guard, or the Constables of the Watch (who generally patrolled only the residential districts of Armethalieh), would turn back any really suspicious characters before they reached their patrol area. For whatever reason, the Dock Patrol favored Kellen with no more than a single glance before turning away to resume their patrol of the wharf.

He was just as glad that he'd worn his oldest clothes beneath his Student robes today. He'd found out a long time ago that nobody at the College cared what you wore *beneath* the stiff, bulky, light blue Student robes that covered the Students—from neck to ankle, and Kellen took great advantage of that freedom. Once he'd pulled off his robe and stuffed it into his locker, his clothing didn't mark him out—at least not too much—from anyone else in the City. Anyone who wasn't a Mage, at least.

It was only when the Dock Patrol was well out of sight that a newcomer slipped out of the cover of an alley, and hastened over to the captain of the trader. Kellen was careful not to turn, careful not to draw attention to himself. Another "respectable" citizen of the City—here! One who was neither an Inspector nor a merchant, nor—from his dress—a member of the lowest classes. What could he be doing here?

The newcomer was a young man, perhaps a year or two older than Kellen. His clothing was of good quality; he carried a bag and wore a harried expression.

He did not seem particularly well-to-do, although he was perhaps a cut or two above a common laborer—perhaps a tradesman. He was a little older than Kellen, but the look of stifled, sullen dissatisfaction on his face was—oh, that was very familiar. It was the one Kellen saw in his own mirror nearly every day.

The ship's captain spotted the young man on the dock as he stood looking up at the ship with mingled hope and doubt. Mutual recognition appeared on both their faces, and relief as well on the young man's as the captain hurried down the gangplank to meet him.

Kellen remained very still, willing them to ignore him.

It seemed to work.

The captain reached out his hand, and clasped the one the newcomer extended to him. "I'm pleased that you haven't changed your mind," he said. "I was afraid that you might. Many do. When the time comes to leave the City forever, they find it isn't worth the sacrifice."

"Not me," the young man said, his chin thrust forward stubbornly. "I *can't* go back in any event. I've been thrown out by my father, disowned by my mother—"

"Ah," the captain said. "Your mother—that's different, then. Mothers forgive nearly everything, but when your mother disowns you, there's no going back."

"Hmph." The young man shook his head. "They don't forgive it when you've besmirched their social standing by insulting the most important person they've ever managed to lure to the dinner table, I can tell you that."

Since Kellen had wanted to do just that, and more than once, his admiration for the young man soared. But the captain was most concerned with the reactions of the man's parents, it seemed.

"So what did they *say* exactly?" the captain persisted.

"That I was to leave and never return, never use their name, never intimate that I even know them, much less am related to them. It was more than just *saying* it," he continued bitterly. "They made quite a production of it, gathered all the servants and my brother and sister, and threw me out with what I'm carrying."

All this only made the captain more cheerful. "Ah, good!" he exclaimed. "Then there won't be any problem!"

"Problem?" The young man seemed confused.

So was Kellen. The captain, apparently, was in a mood to explain.

"Here, take a seat." The captain took his own invitation, and perched himself on a nearby piling. "It's like this—the way things are, here in this City of yours, your Council wants everybody happy with the way things are, so that everything runs smooth as fine sailing. So they go out of their way to *keep* everybody happy. Now, a lot of times, young fellows like you get itchy feet, get the idea of traveling outside the City walls, maybe even have a bit of a to-do with their parents and decide they'd be better off somewhere else. Well, that may be so, but their parents aren't any too pleased if they find 'em gone, and it could be they've got skills or they're doing a job that needs doing here. So"—the captain shrugged—"when someone like me takes 'em aboard, sometimes there's trouble. Sometimes there's a search before we leave the dock, sometimes before we leave the harbor, and sometimes, if the lad's got an important enough family, those magick barriers that keep the storms *out* keep us *in* until we've handed the lad over."

I knew it! I knew it! Kellen thought. *I knew the Mages were keeping people from leaving, somehow—*

But there went any hope *he* had of escaping. Not with Lycaelon as a father. If he went missing, well—Lycaelon would probably keep anything larger than an ant from getting out of the City until Kellen was found and brought back.

"But for you," the captain continued, looking positively gleeful, "well, your parents have done it, haven't they? And the Council knows that tryin' to keep their paws on a restless lad like you, cast out of his own family and liable to cause trouble, even if he doesn't mean it, well, that's not going to make for a peaceful City. Bet you've been doin' a bit of tavern brawling, hmm? Been in trouble with the Watch, just a bit?"

The young man flushed. "And if I have?" he demanded.

"Now, don't come all over toplofty on me!" the captain remonstrated. "Really, it's all to your good! Council *knows* they're better off lettin' you go! And you aren't the only one, not by a stretch! There's a steady leak of young fellows like you, and a few older ones too, all heading for the Out Isles like you, or the Selken Holds, or maybe through the gates for the farms, I don't know. Not a lot of you, maybe, but it lets the steam out, so to speak. Council knows they've *got* to do that, or face trouble, later."

The young man took a deep breath, then let it out, his anger going with it. "All right for me, then, I suppose. I shouldn't take it amiss. And I won't." His expression cleared. "No, I won't! It's a gift, and I'll take it." He stood up, and slung his bag over his shoulder. "Mind if I come aboard, then?"

"Be my guest," the captain replied genially. "We sail in an hour—that's half a bell to you—our cargo has already gotten its inspection, and there won't be anyone by to look at it before we leave," the captain said. "We'll be under way as soon as we get this lot loaded."

The two of them went up the gangplank, still oblivious to Kellen. He might not have even been there.

Or had it been the Wild Magic helping him? It could have been, easily enough, even though he hadn't actually *done* anything with it. *The Book of Sun* said that it might act on its own, through him or on him, when it wanted something done. It might have wanted him to know that escape was possible. It might also have wanted him to know that *he* would not be able to get out as easily as the young man he'd just seen.

Suddenly Kellen lost his taste for the docks, and for gazing out at a freedom he could not have.

There was money in his pocket, and a tavern nearby. Not

that he was going to get drunk . . . No, but if he bought a round of drinks, he'd soon find someone willing to tell him tales of their travels in return for more drinks. Perhaps he could steer the conversation in the direction of magick, if he was very careful. He might even learn something more about the Wild Magic that way.

He tossed string and stick into the water, and left his perch, weaving his way carefully among the dock laborers until he came to the door of what passed for a respectable drinking establishment out here. It was dark, reeked of fish, and the furnishings were crude benches and tables. The only food available was battered, fried, and highly salted to encourage thirst. As he entered, the half-dozen sailors perched at the tables eyed him with suspicion. Kellen ordered a fish-roll, and after a careful look around at the clientele, a round of beer for the house.

His generosity was greeted with an upwelling of warmth, and Kellen took a seat across from a fellow who looked as if he was a bit more intelligent and observant than the rest, and might have a tale or two to tell.

"Workingmen got to stick together, eh?" he said as he sat down and clinked mugs with the weather-beaten sailor. "Came down here to get a bit of sun and fresh air on my day off, and what do you think happens?"

The sailor spat off to the side. "Guard gives you trouble?" he asked, though they both knew it wasn't a question.

Kellen grimaced. "Too true, mate. Dunno what they thought I was gonna get up to—I told 'em I had a fancy for fried fish, and was there a law against that now?"

The sailor guffawed. "Good answer. What's your trade?"

"Scribe-in-training. Got a letter you need written? Don't mind doing a favor for a tale or two," Kellen said quickly, knowing he would never pass for an ordinary laborer. But a scribe was a workingman, no higher in rank than the laborers he served, since no one of any means at all needed them. "I'd leave if I could—but my mother—" He shrugged helplessly. "If I can't leave, I'd as lief hear a tale."

"Aye, that's a fair trade," the sailor said cheerfully, and

called for pen and paper, which the bartender brought, and
which the sailor paid for himself. He dictated his letter, a
common enough epistle. Kellen read it back, and the sailor
took possession of it with great satisfaction. "I'll hand it off
to someone on the *Sea Sprite*," the man said, looking pleased.
"They're on the inbound leg, and my Evike will be right glad
to get a word of me so soon. Now, young friend, you were
after a tale. Well, I mind me of something that happened two
voyages back, on a dark night with no moon, when we were
near dead in the water . . ."

Kellen settled back to listen with an intensity that his tutor
Anigrel would have been surprised to see.

Chapter Four

Music in Chains

The chamber in which the High Council of Armethalieh
met was a vast space devoted by day to meetings of the
Council. By night, it was used as a secure chamber for the
workings of the High Magick that guaranteed the smooth
functioning of the City of a Thousand Bells. The enormous
circular chamber occupied most of the center wing of the
Council House, and was easily the largest single enclosed
space in the entire City. Save for a star-shaped ring of windows at the apex of its vast domed golden ceiling, it was
windowless, its enormous interior space lit by the sourceless
blue-white glow of shadowless, unchanging Magelight. The
soft directionless light made day and night as one: the only
hint of time's passage was the movement of the sunlight or
moonlight that spilled through the windows at the apex of
the dome, and the muffled chiming of the City bells.

Few of Armethalieh's ordinary citizens ever saw this place,
for a hearing before the assembled High Council was reserved

for those occasions when every other means of resolving a situation in accordance with the City's ancient Laws had been exhausted—for that, and for the few necessary dealings of Armethalieh with foreigners. And for these reasons, and others not known to most of the inhabitants of the Golden City, the chamber's designers, in the long-ago time of the City's first founding, had taken great care to make the High Council chamber as stark and intimidating as possible.

The walls of the Council chamber were of featureless white marble, polished so perfectly that their smooth curve gleamed like a dull mirror, broken only by two golden doors set into their surface at opposite sides of the circular chamber. Each door was wrought with the symbol of the Eternal Light in gleaming high relief, so that the planes and angles of their exquisite surfaces glittered, even in this diffuse light, as if they were aflame. The floor was inlaid in a complex pattern of polished black and white marble—to the uninitiated eye, no more than a slightly disorienting decorative pattern, but in fact a series of keys that allowed Adepts to keep their proper places during the nighttime Workings. It was a singularly cold room, designed to chill the spirit and numb the ability to think. It took some time for even a Mage to become accustomed to these surroundings and work unaffected by them.

At one end of the windowless room, its curve echoing that of the curving wall behind it, there stood a judicial bench of black marble twice the height of a tall man, behind which the thirteen members of the High Council sat to make their solemn deliberations. The Arch-Mage of Armethalieh, chief of the High Council, Lycaelon Tavadon, sat at the center of them, the back of his unadorned thronelike chair of black marble rising high above the other seats, a stark silhouette against the white wall behind him. Six unbreathing stone golems, seven-foot statues given life and motion by the High Magick, stood guard in the room to protect the Mages from their supplicants, their mirror-polished grey granite skin reflecting the softer stone of their surroundings. The elaborate and distinctive embroidery on the thirteen Mages' formal grey robes of Judgment—from which those who were versed in such things could discern not only rank and family, but much of that Mage's personal history and record of achievement and awards as well—was the only spot of color in the entire room—and of course, since Lycaelon's "colors" were black and white, he looked of a piece with the room, and scarcely more human than the golems.

Yesterday the Selken trading fleet had docked, and as was traditional, Undermages from the Customs House had gone aboard to inspect the cargoes, releasing those items that had been approved on previous voyages to the traders' warehouses for inspection and sale. But the traders were always bringing new wares to offer to the City of a Thousand Bells, and so today, as had been set down in custom from time immemorial, each trading captain must bring samples of his new merchandise to the Council House to see if it might also be approved for sale in Armethalieh.

As the merchant-captains stood in an apprehensive gaggle several yards away in the center of the room, Lycaelon and his fellows conferred over the sample wares. No matter how many times some of them might have stood there, Lycaelon was pleased to see the foreigners never lost their proper awe of the High Mages of Armethalieh. A Spell of Judgment, carefully cast over the chamber before the captains had been allowed to enter, allowed each member of the council to share the feelings at the surface of the others' minds, projecting them so that each member of the Council could be aware of the opinion of all the others, whether favorable or otherwise.

The High Council had spent the morning on cloth, ribbons, beads, and dyes—simple enough matters all, but each was new to the City, and each must be carefully weighed and judged for its possible impact on the well-being of the populace before being released into the marketplace. Changes in fashion should be subtle things; it was difficult for most men to imagine what difference something like a change of sleeve or ornament might make—frankly, most men wouldn't even *notice*—but women were profoundly influenced by such things. If one woman snatched up a new ornament to set a radical new fashion, it wouldn't be long before the desire to replicate or better her effort would spread through the City like a fever, begetting an orgy of spending, a frenzy of stitching and cutting, and then—well, then the rot would set in, the wish for change, just for the sake of change, which would spread at last from the women to their men. All from a new bead, a new color, a new ribbon, something that the ordinary man would think was insignificant.

So the Council was careful, very careful, even with something as tiny as a bead or a button. Beginning with dyes, they had moved on to perfumes and spices. Most of the perfumes had been rejected out of hand for being simply too *foreign,* and of all of the senses, the most subtle and most open to unconscious seduction was that of smell—but the spices were a more difficult matter.

Lycaelon touched his finger to his tongue, and took up a small amount of the brownish powder on the twist of paper before him. He held it beneath his nose for a moment, then touched it to his tongue. It had a sweet, nutlike flavor, elusively familiar, tasting of anise and cinnamon. It was enough like both that its introduction into City marketplaces would cause no disturbances in the even tenor of City life; earlier this morning, before it had even reached the Council, an Undermage had inspected it by magick for narcotic properties and other dangerous side effects, and found none. Had Lycaelon not known this, he might have suspected some tranquilizing property in the stuff, for his reaction to it was to find the taste curiously comforting. Well, a feeling of *comfort* was something to be cultivated among the populace. Comfort bred contentment, and a disinclination to change.

"Interesting. What do they call this?" he asked, leaning toward his nearest colleague.

"*Rendis,*" Mage Volpiril said. The Magister-Regnant very much wished to succeed Lycaelon as Arch-Mage of Armethalieh, and regarded his superior with an interest that Lycaelon found simple to interpret, even without High Magick's aid: Should Volpiril express approval? Disapproval? Which would best further his own interests?

"I call the vote," Lycaelon said formally, ending the period of inquiry by raising his right hand, palm out, to signal approval of the new spice. Palm down would indicate disapproval.

Unsurprisingly, Volpiril raised his own hand in the same fashion, and the rest of the Council unanimously followed suit. A public vote was a matter of show for their trader-audience, really; if a matter really required a discussion to reach a consensus, it would hardly be dealt with in front of foreigners.

But, as with so many things the Mage Council did, it was good to preserve an illusion of open discussion before the foreigners. If any of the Council had serious reservations about something brought before them, something that could not be projected into the Judgment Spell, he would use his Art for a moment of Silent Speech with Lycaelon, who would simply defer the "vote" if the matter truly seemed to warrant it. Before foreigners, the Council would always present a united front. That was the path of Power.

An Undermage came to clear away the small packets of spices and to serve the Council small cups of strong *kaffeyah* to clear away the lingering scents. The next class of items was usually a difficult one—whole manufactured items of foreign origin—so to keep the Council from becoming over-tired in its deliberations, it was interspersed with something quite simple: book approvals, both new works by current City authors, and reprintings of old tales. While naturally books by foreign authors, containing as they did foreign and dangerous notions, could never be allowed into the City, often the trade ships brought foreign editions of books by approved City authors, frequently authors who had been so long out of print in the City that their works were a novelty again. These exotics sold very well, but it was the Council's job to be certain that there had been no disturbing additions made to them in their foreign manufacture.

But before the books, some difficult decisions needed to be made. "What is the first item?" the Arch-Mage asked his page, who was standing just behind his chair of state with the long list of items that needed to be approved in today's Council session.

"A . . . *'cittern,'* Lord Arch-Mage," Auronwy said, stumbling over the foreign word. "It is a stringed instrument for making music, I have been told. The captain has asked to be allowed to demonstrate the item to you."

Lycaelon suppressed a faint spark of irritation. Really, the presumption of these Selkens was truly amazing. No matter how much liberty the Council granted them, they always demanded more. Still, a show of mercy and fair-dealing was one of the City's greatest strengths, and each time the Selkens overstepped the bounds of civility and good taste, they only harmed themselves and strengthened Lycaelon's own position.

"Very well. Have him approach." And watching barbarians caper should do a little something to relieve the tedium, at least.

Auronwy descended the steps behind the judicial bench and approached the waiting captains. He spoke briefly with one of them, who came forward and retrieved a peculiar instrument from the pile of trade goods that waited beneath the watchful eyes of the motionless guard golems.

The *cittern* appeared to Lycaelon's eyes like some sort of giant, misshapen lute—flat on both sides, its sound box pulled into a sort of peculiar sand-glass shape. The neck was grotesquely elongated, and it seemed to have only half the proper number of strings. No fretwork covered the hole in the soundbox, either; if you stood close enough, you could probably see all the way down into the body of the instrument. How crude it looked, and how unfinished! Lycaelon steeled himself; surely this instrument's sound would be as unpolished as its appearance.

The captain slung the *cittern*'s strap over his shoulder, plinked a few strings hesitantly, and began to play.

Lycaelon resisted, though with difficulty, the impulse to cover his ears, and felt the wave of disgust from his fellow Mages through the Judgment Spell. It was like nothing any of them had ever heard—not like the lute, nor the harp, nor the viol, nor any other stringed instrument known in the City. It was loud. It *jangled*. It was infernally cheerful. Very raucous, barbaric, and not in the least bit calming. If the drinking songs caterwauled in taverns could have been turned into an instrument upon which they might be played, this was it.

As the captain himself seemed about to break into song (which only confirmed the Arch-Mage's impression of the instrument), Lycaelon raised his hand.

"That will be quite sufficient," he said firmly. He shook his head very slightly, not needing to look to the rest of the Council to feel their agreement and relief. This decision, at least, would be an easy one, with no dissension and no need for a discussion. "The Council regrets, we cannot permit you to sell this . . . *'cittern'* here."

"But why?" The captain looked honestly surprised—and hurt, as if he'd offered them a rare treat and been spurned. Lycaelon sighed inwardly. The Light blast all overemotional thin-skinned barbarians back to the First Cause and beyond! If there were some way for the City to do without the trade ships, he, personally, would weave such a spell as would seal Armethalieh's harbors off from the outside world for a thousand years . . .

"Please understand," Lycaelon said, projecting a warmth and regret he did not feel into his words. Beneath them, he let an undercurrent of magick flow outward toward the captain: *If it were my choice alone, I would welcome this innovation. But we are both of us at the mercy of forces greater than ourselves, and cannot always act as we choose. You and I, we must both make hard choices for the good of those we serve.* "I am certain that this *'cittern'* is a lovely instrument, cherished in your homeland. But we of the City have never heard anything like it. It would require new compositions to be written for it, new musicians to be trained in its use. Our City simply isn't ready to accept so great an innovation, we regret."

He saw the captain step back, glancing toward the rest of the Council, confusion, acceptance—and regret—plain on his features. He would return to his ship, convinced that the High

Council—and especially Lycaelon—acted out of hard necessity, but were themselves good men.

As it should be. As it must be—for the good of the City.

"Perhaps next time you might have a new lute to demonstrate instead."

The captain still looked as if he might be about to protest, but one of his fellows caught his eye, shook his head slightly. The first fellow clamped his jaw shut with a visible effort, bowed, and withdrew, taking his abominable instrument with him.

Lycaelon let him go without comment. "What is the next item on the agenda?" he asked briskly.

"A new illustrated edition of *Pastoral Poems of Golden Days* by a Gentleman of Leisure, printed and illustrated in Bariona," Auronwy announced smoothly, setting the book before Lycaelon with a practiced gesture.

TWO more books—both passed—then a music box that was found acceptable both in form and content, then two more books, one of which was found to have entirely unsuitable illustrations. Why the publisher had chosen to dress the characters in the costumes of the Lothien Archipelago when the book was intended for the City baffled Lycaelon; he must have known they would never allow depictions of barbarian dress within their walls! It was most peculiar.

The Council was preparing to consider an item that its importer assured them was a new timepiece of heretofore impossible accuracy, when a Senior Undermage from the Printers Council appeared in the doorway.

Without being told, Auronwy hurried over to him, and was back in a moment with his message, which he whispered into Lycaelon's ear.

"Lord Arch-Mage. A few days ago Citizen Perulan brought his latest book to the Council to receive his license to publish—"

Though everywhere else in the City the degrees of class

and birth were closely noted and observed in forms of observance and address, here within the Council chamber there were only two classes: Mages and citizens. And Perulan, no matter to what class he had been born, now belonged unequivocally to the latter.

Perulan was a fabulist whose popular pastoral fantasies of a magickal idealized life in the farming communities west of the City had gained him fame and following over the last several years. His latest book had been eagerly awaited.

"Challenged on first reading by Banarus, wasn't it? Unpublishable. *Nothing* like his usual work. Pity," Lycaelon said softly, leaning back in his chair. The acoustics of the Council chamber were such that nothing said behind the judicial bench would carry to those standing in the center of the floor, though the rest of the Council would be able to hear him if he wished them to.

"He demands a hearing before the High Council, Lord Arch-Mage," Auronwy said, equally softly. "He is . . . not in agreement with Undermage Banarus's decision."

While it was every citizen's right to take any grievance, no matter how minor, to the High Council itself, it was a right rarely invoked. Ninety-nine times out of a hundred, it was a waste of the Council's time and annoyed them to boot. But artists had no sense of proportion or reality; they saw things only in terms of their own "vision," regardless of what was good for the City.

"Is he here?" Lycaelon asked, hoping that the answer was "no." This was likely to become a very unpleasant scene, one he was certainly *not* going to begin in front of the foreigners.

"Outside, my lord. With his manuscript," Auronwy confirmed.

Lycaelon felt his jaw tense. Why was it that these artists always *had* to have an audience, even for their tantrums? "He can wait until our *proper* business is completed. See that he remains."

Auronwy bowed and withdrew.

Lycaelon returned his attention to the approvals.

IT was nearly Evensong Bells by the time the Council chamber was cleared of the day's legitimate business. Banarus and Perulan entered, Perulan clutching a leather-wrapped bundle.

Perulan was tall and slender, his pale hair going to grey. He had been born into a Mage family, a younger son, and while it had been something of a scandal for him to turn his back upon the High Art and follow his passion to become a teller of tales, it was only a small scandal, and his success had done nothing to bring real disgrace upon his family. Perulan lived suitably and modestly in the Artists Quarter of Armethalieh upon a small allowance his family made him and the revenues from his writings, and had made no trouble . . . until now.

If the man had followed proper procedure, he was now holding the only copy of his manuscript, having destroyed all notes and drafts once he had made the fair copy. They would see.

"Who comes before the Council?" Lycaelon asked.

"Perulan, son of Nadar, of House Arbathil," Banarus answered formally.

"What justice does Perulan Arbathil seek?" Lycaelon responded, equally formally.

"Lord Arch-Mage," Banarus said, bowing. "Citizen Perulan seeks a license to publish for his latest work. The Printers Council has reviewed it and found it . . . unacceptable. Citizen Perulan challenges this decision, as is his right."

"Let the manuscript be brought before the High Council for fair, final, just, and merciful irrevocable judgment, as is the right of every citizen of Armethalieh," Lycaelon said.

Banarus took the manuscript from Perulan's arms and brought it to the end of the bench. Auronwy accepted the hefty bundle and brought it to Lycaelon, setting it on the polished marble before him.

Faintly curious now, Lycaelon untied the leather covering and exposed the first page. The title was written large, in Perulan's flowing clear scribe-hand: *Golden Chains: A Tale of the City.*

Not an auspicious title—why should an author of pastoral fantasies now choose to write about the City? And the Arch-Mage did not in the least care for the sound of "Golden Chains" either. Unless, perhaps, it was a romantic tale, of the sort that foolish women devoured, and the chains were those of love? Lycaelon frowned, and marshaled a small cantrip, one foolishly relied upon far too often by Student-Apprentices: *Knowing That Which Is Written.* While *Knowing* would not allow one to master the intricacies of a thick technical volume of Magecraft, no matter how many times it was cast, it was certainly sufficient to put a Master Mage in possession of the contents of a simple work of fiction, no matter how long.

In moments, the contents of the book rushed into Lycaelon's mind. And he was appalled.

It was a saga of love indeed, among other things, and unhappily unlike any other Perulan had ever written. People died unhappily and for no reason at all, true loves proved false, Priests of the Light were corrupt, servants betrayed and were betrayed by their masters for personal gain, masters repaid the loyalty of lifelong servants with indifference, discarding them to poverty when they were no longer useful . . .

In short, it was "reality," and not fantasy, unvarnished, unmasked, and horribly uncomfortable. It was *not* the escape that the readers of Perulan's previous tales would expect, and in a lesser author, disgust would lead a disappointed reader to fling the book across the room. But Perulan was skilled, highly skilled, brilliant even. No, the reader would persist, drawn into the story against his will, and when he was finished—

Discontent. Unhappiness. Restlessness and a sense of injustice that *would* seek an outlet.

This cannot possibly be published! Lycaelon thought in stormy shock, and felt the assent of the Mages around him as his knowledge of the manuscript spilled into the Judgment Spell. This was nothing less than an attack upon the City itself!

"Is this your only copy? You cannot re-create this book? Answer truly," Lycaelon said.

Out of Perulan's line of sight, Banarus's fingers went up to touch the Talisman around his neck as the Undermage cast a Truthspell upon the writer, cued by Lycaelon's demand for the truth. Perulan's next words would be the whole and complete truth, whether he wished to tell it or not.

"Lord Arch-Mage, this is truly my only copy of the book. I burned all my notes and drafts. I spent years writing it—it comes from my heart—I can never re-create it. It is my finest work—a work of truth—the truth that no one wishes to see."

The truth-aura around him burned blue and steady to Lycaelon's Magesight. Perulan was telling the truth. In all things. The foolish man really believed it was a masterpiece, the crowning achievement of his career.

Idiot. He was Mageborn; he should have known better. Of all things, the Mages could not tolerate discontent. Just as there could be no new and strange goods in the markets to startle people and make them think that other places might be better, there could be no new thoughts in books, no new ways of painting a picture, no innovations in music, because all of those things would wake up the imagination. There must be nothing within the walls of the Golden City that might make her citizens think, wonder—and start to look outside the walls.

For only within these walls could there be safety. Without lay chaos, madness, and anarchy, the years of Blood and Darkness awaiting the spark that would kindle their rebirth. To open Armethalieh to change was to court her destruction.

"It cannot be published," Lycaelon said flatly. He held out his hand over the manuscript and spoke a simple spell: *Magefire*. There was a bright flash, and the manuscript and its leather wrapping were gone, burned away to a few wisps of ash.

Perulan cried out, once. It was a heartrending sound, not loud, but so full of pain that it gave even Lycaelon pause for a moment. Half protest and disbelief, half wail of despair, like a mother who sees her child murdered before her eyes.

Perulan's face went grey, and he swayed unsteadily on his feet.

"How *could* you?" he whispered in a shaking voice. "It was my *life*! All my skill—all I knew . . ."

"It was not suitable," Lycaelon told him sternly. "Why, when it is unsafe to go outside the City walls, should you write some poisonous fable to make the people of Armethalieh doubt that their rulers know what is best for them? Why should you seek to make them believe that their betters rule only for the sake of gain, and not to make them safe and happy? Why, above all things, should you write something that was calculated to stir rebellion in their hearts and discontent in their souls? They might begin to believe that other places are better than here; they *might* begin to believe that they would make better rulers than those who are wiser than they. And, in their profound ignorance, they might seek to put themselves in our places, and that would be—not to be thought of. Go, and write something more pleasing next time—or don't write at all."

Perulan only stared at him, eyes wide with shock, as if he had not heard—or did not understand—Lycaelon's words. The Arch-Mage gestured impatiently, and Banarus half led, half carried the writer from the Council chamber. Perulan accompanied him like a man in a trance, moving as unsteadily as one who has received a mortal wound.

What a fuss to make over a few scraps of paper and a silly story! Just as well Nadar excised the Magegift from his mind; the man was far too emotional to ever have been trusted with the disciplines of the High Art . . .

Lycaelon dismissed the matter from his mind. Banarus would see to the man, and do all that was necessary to conclude the matter properly.

"Well, that was unpleasant enough," Lord-Mage Perizel said sourly when the door had shut behind the pair.

Lord-Mage Meron, sitting beside him, nodded his head. "Won't be the end of it. You mark my words, my lord Mages. Talespinners! Always scribbling something, and all of it nonsense."

There was a general murmur of agreement, and Volpiril leaned close to Lycaelon. "If you will permit, my lord Arch-Mage, perhaps someone should be placed in Perulan's household? He might bear further watching—just to make sure he doesn't do something foolish, of course."

There was no expression on his bland face, but Lycaelon, who was about to order the same thing, wondered why Volpiril felt it necessary to suggest such a move before Lycaelon could do so.

"Of course," Lycaelon said, keeping his own countenance as bland as Volpiril's. "Are we all in agreement on that? I will leave you to see to it, Mage Volpiril."

And I will remember that you will bear further watching, as well, my lord Volpiril . . .

He glanced down with sudden distaste at the mass of ashes and crisped leather on the table, and added, with just a touch of venom, "And someone clean up this mess!"

AS the shadows lengthened and the cool spring air filled with the music of Evensong, Kellen realized, with resignation and great reluctance, that it was time to be returning home. It wouldn't do for him to be anywhere but his rooms when his father arrived—Lycaelon had made it clear on several memorable occasions what he thought of a scion of House Tavadon wandering the streets of Armethalieh like one of the common folk.

But with any luck, his father would still be busy at the Council House, and Undermage Anigrel would have found something else dull and boring to do as well—something that would keep him away from both Tavadon House and Lycaelon. No one needed to ever know that Kellen hadn't gone straight home after his unfortunate early dismissal from his lessons. With further luck, Anigrel might even forget to tell Lycaelon about the whole incident, though that was probably too much to hope for.

Kellen approached Tavadon House through the mazelike

network of back and side alleyways that ran between the great houses of the Mage Quarter. It was easy to get lost here—there were no signs, and nothing to distinguish one seamless Magecrafted stone wall from another, but Kellen had no difficulty in finding his way. He knew the back alleys of the Mage Quarter as well as any refuse hauler or rag-and-bone dealer did; the narrow streets were much used by those vendors and tradesmen whose business was not quite appropriate for the front doors—or even the main service entrance—of the imposing houses of Armethalieh's Mageborn aristocracy.

The Mageborn preferred that the messier aspects of life be tended to invisibly, and the noble and wealthy aped their habits. Kellen doubted that any of them had ever seen a refuse hauler in their lives.

But in his seventeen years of life Kellen had discovered, as many had before him, that there was no privacy to be had in a house full of servants, and if he did not want to alert everyone in House Tavadon to all of his comings and goings—most of which weren't supposed to be taking place in the first place—the best thing to do was to find a more private way in and out of the house. Though he could not use it too often without drawing attention to it, the small side door at the bottom of the kitchen garden, where the garbage from the kitchen was left every morning in neat bins, filled his needs nicely: he could let himself in and out whenever he wanted without alerting the servants, and if anyone missed him and wanted to make a fuss, who was to say he hadn't simply been somewhere in the formal garden—or the house—the whole time he'd been supposedly "missing"?

Though of course the door was warded against intruders, as a son of the house, Kellen could pass through those wards without triggering them. And although it was kept locked from the inside, Kellen simply took the key with him when he went and left the door unlocked behind him. The servants rarely had business in the garden, and the gardener never bothered about anything that close to the house itself. So far his tampering had gone undiscovered, and Kellen had been able to come and go as he pleased.

He reached his destination—a nondescript (though, of course, costly and well-made) wooden door set into the tall, plaster-covered brick wall—and confidently gave it a shove, expecting it to swing inward, revealing the sere Tavadon garden.

The door didn't move.

Kellen tried again, pushing more slowly and with greater force. Still nothing. The door was locked. Sometime in the last several bells, some overzealous servant must have come down into the garden and locked it.

Well, that was all of a piece with the way his day had been going until now. Kellen sighed, reaching into his belt-pouch for his key, only to discover that his bad luck was still in full flower, and likely to get worse.

His key wasn't there.

Oh, no—

Now what was he to do? Never mind that Anigrel had virtually ordered him to go hare off on his own. Anigrel would be certain to deny it, and say he'd meant Kellen to go home and study, and certainly that was what an obedient son of House Tavadon would have done. If anyone found out he'd actually been *wandering around the City* until Evensong, he'd really be in for it!

Not yet in a panic, but not far from that state, Kellen spun around, gazing around the empty alley wildly, as though by some miracle the key to the garden door might suddenly materialize.

Think, you cloudwit!

He was sure—he was almost sure—he'd had it with him when he'd left for his lesson with Anigrel this morning. Could he have dropped it somewhere? It was a big heavy brass key; he was certain he would have noticed the sudden absence of its weight from his pouch, or heard the noise it would have made when it fell to the street.

Unsurprisingly, the key was nowhere to be seen; after all, he hadn't *left* by this door. And retracing his steps—well, that was an exercise in futility; a key that big would have been found and picked up, for the value of the scrap metal if nothing else . . .

Kellen sighed gustily, running his hand through his disorderly mop of long brown curls distractedly. Where was the Light-forgotten thing?

All right. No need to get in a state. Nothing's going to happen just yet. If the garden door was locked, there was still the front door . . . but that meant going in past the mastiffs, and that would rouse the servants—there'd be no chance of sneaking in. And if his father or Anigrel had left instructions that he hadn't been here to receive . . . well, it would mean an unpleasant scene at the least. If his father found out he hadn't gone straight home from his morning's lesson, Lycaelon would want to know where he'd been, and if he couldn't think of something innocuous and impossible to disprove, he'd be in deeper trouble yet.

Why is it that everything I do ends up with me in trouble?

No. He'd find another way.

He looked up at the wall, gauging his chances of simply scaling the wall. But the wall had been plastered smooth to discourage just such a possibility, and the errant coil of bramble-rose vine that trailed down just above his head was far too slender—and prickly—to serve as a climbing rope. He couldn't use a cantrip to unlock the door from outside, either, even if he knew the right spell, because the locks were counterspelled against just that.

But there was another way. He had his new magick. And if he couldn't use it to unlock a door (and so far there didn't seem to be an Unlocking Spell anywhere in the three Books, or at least not one that he'd discovered), he could use it in some other way to get in. And the simplest was—to find that blasted key.

With the Wild Magic, he could cast a Finding Spell, get his key back, open the door, and slip inside. He'd be safe in his rooms before Lycaelon arrived, and no one would be the wiser about just how long it had taken Kellen to come home from lessons. And a Finding Spell was such a small magick—harmless. All it involved was getting back what was his in the first place. What could that hurt? No one would see, and no one would know. And he had everything he needed to cast it right here: his desire—and a drop of his own blood was easily come by, with the bramble-roses to help.

Pleased at his own cleverness at finding so simple a solution to a potentially embarrassing problem, Kellen reached up and pulled the bramble-vine down toward him. He selected a particularly large and sharp-looking thorn and drove it into the ball of his thumb, wincing at the sudden pain, and as the bright drop of blood welled out, he focused all his will on the key to the garden gate and his *need* to have it in his hands.

There was a faint tingle, as if someone had thrown a handful of snowflakes at him, and he held his breath in anticipation. What would happen? Would the key just *appear*? Would someone bring it, looking for the owner?

But—nothing. The tingle faded, and nothing whatsoever happened. Nothing changed, not even the faint stink of produce past its prime that came up from the sunbaked stone of the alley. Obscurely disappointed, Kellen let go of the vine—it snapped back into place with a dry shaking of leaves—and sucked at his injured thumb, walking absently up the alleyway.

I might as well give up, and use the front door, and take my chances . . .

Wait. Where am I going?

As he'd started walking he'd told himself he'd given up and was going around to his front door, but then he found himself turning *away* from the house, in a direction he'd never gone before, unable to stop or turn back. The more he tried to fight against this compulsion, the faster he went, until he found himself running, losing track of the turns he made, until he was entirely lost in the warren of Mage Quarter back alleys.

And still he ran on, as if there was something pulling him—or chasing him. The Wild Magic had him, he had no doubt whatsoever of *that,* and it wasn't going to let go!

He was finally allowed to stop in front of another wall elsewhere in the Mage Quarter, but whatever force had taken possession of him when he cast his Wild Magic spell of Finding wasn't through with him yet. The walls here were green with ivy, providing easy access to the garden beyond to anyone who cared to climb the wall, and to his horror and amazement, Kellen found his arms and legs acting as if they belonged to another person, sending him up the ladder of vines as if he were a squirrel.

Over the top he went on his belly. He slid down through the thick mass of ivy on the interior side and froze, holding his breath. If anyone caught him here, if he couldn't talk his way out of this . . . they'd turn him over to the City Constables, or at the very least, they'd summon his father out of his Council meeting, and what could Kellen possibly say to explain what he was doing trespassing in some other Mage's garden? He didn't even know whose garden this was! And if it belonged to one of his father's many political enemies . . . Oh, Light defend him! What could Kellen possibly say to explain? He was trapped by his own decisions to cast a Wild Magic spell. What had he done to himself?

As he stood frozen, trying to figure out what had just happened to him, Kellen became aware that somewhere nearby someone was crying—the choked, grief-stricken sounds of someone terrified and in complete despair, but equally afraid of being overheard.

A very *young* someone; from the high voice, it must be a child.

And at that moment, Kellen stopped worrying about himself; his own predicament could wait. Whoever was making that sort of weeping sound was in more trouble than he could ever possibly get into. He knew the difference between the way a child sounded when it was crying angrily over a hurt, real or imagined, when it was crying out of self-pity, and when it was crying because it was truly, deeply, in despair. And this was the latter.

As silently as he could, Kellen moved away from the wall and toward the source of the crying.

Coming out from behind a screen of bushes, Kellen saw a little girl—no more than seven or eight—wearing the simple clothing of an under house servant. She wasn't old enough to have much responsibility; she was probably a kitchen maid—children usually apprenticed in the kitchens of a Great House, where there were fewer things to break, and much fetching and carrying to be done—which meant she certainly had no right to be in the master's garden at all.

Her shoulders drooped with fatigue, and her little body trembled with each suppressed whimper. She was kneeling at the base of an enormous magnolia tree that was the focal point of the garden, looking up into its branches. He stepped on a bit of gravel that crunched under his boot, and she swiveled around, her round, tear-streaked face white with fear. The moment she saw him, she got to her feet with a strangled sob. In a moment she would run, and he knew, without knowing how or why, that *she* was the reason he was here.

"Don't be afraid," Kellen said quickly. "I'm not supposed to be here either. I climbed over the wall. In fact, if anybody sees me, they'll probably run for the nearest Constable. I heard you crying—will you tell me what's the matter?" He bestowed his most winning smile on her, the one that had usually gotten him out of trouble with every one of his "Nursies."

The girl hesitated, then stood where she was, shifting her weight from foot to foot, regarding him doubtfully. She had certainly been told to be wary of housebreakers and thieves, but even dressed in his oldest clothes, Kellen figured he didn't look very much like either one.

"I live nearby," he said coaxingly. "Won't you tell me why you're so unhappy?"

That seemed to decide her, and her face regained a little color. "Can—can you help me, goodsir?" she asked hopefully. She gestured up at the branches over her head with a slim little hand. "Milady is in the tree—she got out of the kitchen and climbed up, and if Mistress finds us here, she'll have me whipped—and she'll drown Milady!" Fresh tears began to roll down the girl's face.

"I *know* she will, I *know* she will, and Milady—"

—Is probably the only friend this little one has, Kellen

supplied for himself, feeling a surge of anger at a woman he didn't even know, who would be so heartless as to snuff out the life of a child's pet because it did what any cat would do. When she'd first started to speak, he'd wondered if Milady might be a child of the house that the girl was supposed to be watching, but if the girl was afraid that Mistress would drown her . . .

It had to be a cat—though the Light help him if it turned out to be a white squirrel, or a monkey, or a ferret, or some other form of outlandish pet. A cat he could probably coax down; with an exotic, he'd probably wind up with a handful of sharp teeth.

"Hush now, don't cry." Kellen rummaged inside his tunic for a clean handkerchief—reasonably clean, anyway—and handed it to the girl. "Blow your nose and dry your eyes. I'm sure we can do something about your problem."

He approached her; she wasn't going to run now. "Can you show me where she is?"

The girl stood beside him and pointed up into the tree. Kellen looked in the direction she indicated, squinting against the last rays of the setting sun. High in the tree, perched on one of the topmost branches, he could barely make out a small grey fuzzy kitten, its fur nearly the same color as the slippery bark of the tree. It edged back and forth on its branch, which shifted dangerously with every move it made.

Kellen sighed, just a little. Still, he couldn't leave the little thing up there to get all three of them in trouble. And he couldn't just leave the poor little girl here to try to coax it down. Kittens had the bad habit of climbing into inaccessible places, then being too frightened to get down by themselves.

He glanced over his shoulder. A high hedge of ornamental shrubbery screened the bottom of the garden from the view of the house, and at this chime, the inhabitants would be dressing for dinner and the staff would be preparing it. For a little while, at least, it wasn't likely that they'd be found here. He thought hard, coming up with a plan.

He patted her clumsily; she didn't seem to mind. "Now look here, I'll see if I can't help you out. I'll climb up and get your kitten down. If anyone comes while I'm up there, you must scream as loud as you can, and point up at me. Don't say anything, just scream. Do you understand?" Kellen asked.

The little girl looked puzzled. "But why?"

Kellen smiled ruefully. "Well as to that, sweeting, I think you're far too pretty to be whipped for wanting to save your kitten. If you make a lot of noise, they'll all think you came out in the garden chasing me, and you'll be a great heroine."

"But what about you?" she asked. She might not be very old, but she was evidently wise enough in the ways of her household to know that if *she* acted as if he were an interloper rather than someone who'd come to help her, *he* would be in serious trouble.

Then again, anyone who had spoken so casually of being whipped knew plenty about punishment.

"Oh, I'll think of something," he said airily. And thought: *I just hope I don't have to.*

And keeping that thought in mind, Kellen turned away from her, put foot and hand to the trunk of the tree, and began to climb.

The lower branches were easy, though the fine-grained bark was as slick as polished wood. The flowers had an overpowering sweet and slightly unpleasant scent as if they were *just* on the wrong side of decay, even in the cool of the evening, and he dared not get any of their fleshy, greasy petals between his hands and the bark. Once he was higher in the tree he could hear the kitten mewing—hoarsely, as if it had been doing it for some time—but with the leaves in his face Kellen could no longer see it. He did know it was still somewhere above him.

"Here, kitty-kitty-kitty," Kellen muttered, mostly to himself, for he doubted that the cat could hear him over its own plaintive cries. As a matter of fact, at the moment he felt like making a few plaintive cries of his own . . .

The tree was very tall. He looked out once, and found himself on a level with the third-floor windows of whatever Mage-house's gardens he was trespassing in, and fought down his vertigo with an effort. After that, he kept his eyes firmly focused on the trunk of the tree and the branches in front of his face.

Then, at last, the cries were near at hand. He moved aside a branch while clinging desperately with his other hand, and there it was.

And it was not at all happy to see him. Rather than regard him as a rescuer, it apparently thought he was there to eat it. He reached toward it—and it backed away, then scrambled off down a side branch, forcing him to leave the trunk and follow.

Then began a pursuit that would have been comical if Kellen hadn't been so petrified of falling. Several times he was almost within reach of the kitten. Each time it regarded Kellen's outstretched hand in pop-eyed horror and retreated out of reach, either around the trunk or out along a limb. Several times it fell, slipping to a lower branch to glare at him in affronted indignation before bouncing off—*just* out of reach— to resume its piteous cries for rescue.

You stupid lint-brained furball! Can't you see I'm trying *to rescue you?* Kellen thought with something more than irritation.

Finally, he'd gone as high as he could go without falling himself. The tree trunk itself swayed slowly with his weight, a slow sickening motion that would surely give away his presence here if anyone bothered to look. The kitten was just above him, on an even narrower branch.

And for one brief moment, all its featherbrained feline attention was devoted to keeping its balance. Kellen lunged, grabbed it around its middle, tore it loose from its perch, and stuffed it down into his tunic as deep as he could, wrapping one arm around himself to keep it from struggling free.

Kittens, Kellen discovered at that very moment, might be small and helpless-looking, but they had a very large number of very sharp claws. The claws weren't big, but they made up for their lack of size in degree of sharpness. He was being lacerated by needles. He clamped his mouth shut on a yell, which would only have attracted unwanted attention.

Gritting his teeth and trying to concentrate, he turned toward the trunk, feeling with his foot for the branch below.

And slipped.

His descent from the tree was much faster and far less comfortable than his ascent. Kellen grabbed one-handed at everything he could to slow his fall, but his weight and the speed of his fall tore the branches from his fingers almost as soon as he grasped them.

At last he stopped.

Abruptly. On his back.

He struggled to breathe for a moment, and his vision greyed out, then returned as he managed to gasp in a breath.

Kellen lay on the ground, panting, taking in huge gulps of air, looking up at the tree. He was dimly aware of something struggling free of his tunic and worming its way out through the neck-hole.

I've broken my back. Father will have a fit.

A healing-Mage could mend a broken back of course, and it wasn't as if Lycaelon couldn't afford the best there was—but oh, what he'd have to say about it!

He twitched feet and hands experimentally, then moved arms and legs. They all worked, and no movements produced any stabbing pains . . .

Oh, good. I haven't *broken my back. Or anything else, I guess.*

Groggily he sat up, shaking his head. Leaves, flower petals, and bits of twig rained down on him from his hair and from the hole he'd left through the branches as he fell.

He looked up at the little kitchen maid. She was clutching the kitten beneath her chin and beaming at him, her tears forgotten. The kitten was purring loudly and looking smug. Wretched little monster. For a brief moment Kellen could see why someone would be tempted to drown it.

Maybe I should have left it up there . . .

But—no. The tear streaks remaining on the child's face reminded Kellen of why he really didn't mean that last thought.

"Are you all right?" the girl asked anxiously.

"I think so," Kellen said, though he really didn't think anything of the sort. He shifted, and heard something crackle beneath him as he moved. For a moment, he was afraid it was his spine after all.

But if his spine had made a noise like that, he wouldn't have been able to move. Kellen got to his knees, pulling the object out from beneath him.

A bird's nest. A big one, the size of a soup plate, woven of sticks, and full of . . . junk?

"A jackdaw's nest," Kellen said aloud, identifying the item. "I must have knocked it free when I fell."

Jackdaws were notorious thieves, attracted to anything that was colorful or shiny. Curious, he began to pick through the jackdaw's trove.

Bits of tinsel and glass. Faded hair ribbons. Pieces of painted tin, relics of the last Festival day. Among the junk, a real treasure—a gold and emerald chain.

"That belongs to Mistress!" the little girl gasped, staring at it. "She was looking everywhere for it!"

"Here," Kellen said, tucking it into a pocket in the girl's smock. "Tell her you found it somewhere. Um—tell her that you saw the jackdaw carrying it off and you threw stones at the nest until it came down. That will explain this mess, and it should save you and Milady from a few whippings in the future."

There was one more thing at the bottom of the nest: a key. Kellen's key.

When he held it in his hand, all his unease at the Wild Magic and the *geas* its spell had cast upon him came rushing back. *"All magic has a price,"* it had said in *The Book of Sun.* Kellen had thought his blood was the price of the magick, but he'd been wrong. That was only the price of the *spell.* Rescuing the kitten had been the price for finding the key, because if he hadn't rescued the kitten, he'd never have found the key.

But I chose to rescue the kitten, didn't I? Kellen wondered uneasily. *Magick didn't make me do it.*

He'd thought the Wild Magic was just like the High Magick, just with fewer rules: you did the spell and you got the result. But it wasn't. The spell had only brought him here. If he hadn't cared about the girl and her kitten, he'd never have found the key. It was what was in him, what he was, that made the magick work the way it did—as if, when he looked into the Books of the Wild Magic, somehow the Wild Magic was also looking into him, and judging him.

I don't like this, Kellen thought apprehensively. *What if I weren't* me? *How would the magick work then?*

He got to his feet, putting the key into his pocket.

"I've got to go now," he said, feeling uncomfortable. "Could you show me where the garden door is?"

He hated to involve the girl in any more trouble, but the way he was feeling right now, another climb over the wall was the last thing he could manage.

"It's right over here. No one will see you. And . . . thank you, goodsir."

"Thank *you*, gentle miss. I learned a lot here today," Kellen said honestly. *More than I wanted to learn, if the truth be told.*

She led him across the garden—Kellen limping along behind her—and when the door had closed behind him, he wasn't really surprised to see he was in an alley he recognized, only a few turnings from home.

⌐

IT was full dark—first Night Bells had rung—by the time Kellen reached his own garden door once more, for he had been moving rather slowly as he'd left that garden gate. He was lucky not to have any broken bones or bad sprains from his fall, but by tomorrow morning he'd have a rainbow of bruises, and he felt stiff all over. He was thinking longingly of sneaking down to the laundry for a long soak in one of the spell-heated washtubs as he crossed the garden—there'd be nobody there at this time of night, and the water in the washing vats was always hot—and he wished he could soak out the memory of the Wild Magic as easily as he could soak out the stiffness of his bruises.

Why did it work the way it did? How *could* it work the way it did? If it worked like this for a simple Finding Spell, what would happen if he dared to cast one of the greater spells described in the Books? What sort of price might the Wild Magic ask then?

Kellen was so engrossed in his own thoughts on his way to his room to pick up fresh clothes for after his bath that he failed to see his father on the stairs leading to his suite. And unfortunately, Lycaelon saw him. Apparently Lycaelon had gotten home early for once—and had been looking for him.

"Kellen!"

Kellen froze where he was, stunned. It had never occurred to him that he'd run into his father *now*—Lycaelon was rarely home before midnight, and sometimes not before dawn, if he was participating in a Greater Working, not just a Council session. Kellen wished suddenly that he was a Mage out of the wondertales—one who could stop time, turn himself invisible, or simply teleport himself away with no more than a thought. But Mages like that only existed in stories, not real life.

Lycaelon reached the top of the stairs, a ball of blue Magelight hovering behind his left shoulder. As its cerulean radiance reached Kellen, the boy saw his father's expression change from one of irritation to actual anger.

"I see. What have you to say for yourself?" Lycaelon said.

He always starts arguments in the middle and expects me to play catch-up! Kellen thought, becoming angry in turn. *He sees* what, *exactly?* He felt his mouth settle into a sullen line, and said nothing. What was there to say, when he didn't even know what he was being accused of. *Except it's always the same thing, isn't it—not being him, not being the kind of son that would be happy to be a mindless little copy of him? A model of exemplary behavior to be held up to every other Mage who has a son?*

"Undermage Anigrel told me you'd shirked your lessons

today to go off and wander around the City again like an out-of-work laborer—and from the look of you, you've spent that day rolling around under hedges. Mend your ways, or you will be dead weight, Kellen, dead weight—and the City has no place for dead weight!" Lycaelon thundered.

Thundered? Maybe he *thought* he sounded impressive, but to Kellen's ears, Lycaelon's voice was pompous, not awe-inspiring. He sounded more like the outraged patriarch in a bad play, the one that the lovers were going to outwit, no matter what he did.

"It isn't—" Kellen tried to interrupt. *I didn't SHIRK them! He sent me away! But I don't suppose he bothered to tell you that part, did he? Oh, no, whatever happens, it's always MY fault, isn't it? Light blast it, I can say the truth, that I was rescuing a little girl's kitten, without giving away what happened! He's always telling me to be more responsible, and isn't that the sort of thing he means?*

It wasn't though, and Kellen knew it. Now, if he'd rescued the kitten of a wealthy, noble, or Mageborn child, oh, that would be entirely different . . .

Lycaelon raised a hand. "No! I have coddled you long enough. I spend my days in long and thankless labor to keep the City running smoothly, and you spend yours attempting to destroy everything I'm trying to build for your future! You cannot just step into a position such as mine by simple right of birth—it takes a lifetime of preparation and study—preparation which you do not seem willing to make! A person in our position in society has duties as well as privileges—he must behave suitably as an example to those below him, for the good of the City, and this is a responsibility you have so far ignored. How are you ever going to take your proper place in society if you keep shirking your obligations this way?"

Duties—obligations—suitable behavior—meaning suitably arrogant, suitably deceptive, suitably oh-so-superior to any poor fool who doesn't happen to be Mageborn! Kellen thought mutinously. And somehow he just couldn't hold his feelings in any longer.

"You're always bleating at me as if I *want* people bowing and scraping to me all day and looking for new ways to humiliate themselves! Well, maybe I don't! Maybe I don't want a place in your precious society, if to get it I have to stick my nose in the air, act like a prig, and turn into a slavish copy of *you*!" Kellen burst out. He turned away and stormed into his room, slamming the door behind him.

Chapter Five

❦

The Courts of Nightmare

The world without Sun was a wonderful place, just as vast and far more beautiful than the Bright World. For centuries Queen Savilla had ruled over its lightless halls and shadow caverns, its vast subterranean seas and darkling plains.

But like all rulers, she loved her palace best, for here all the good things in her world were distilled to their ultimate perfection. Here, in the Heart of Darkness, she tended the strands of her web of knowledge and power, patiently awaiting the day when the Tree of Night would bear that fruit whose harvest would prove so bitter to the Brightworlders.

Once—twice—the Endarkened had not been so patient, and He Who Is, their master, had chosen to teach them patience, allowing them to be defeated in their battles for mastery in the World Above. In the last battle—called in the Bright World the Great War—their defeat had been so profound and all-encompassing that they had been swept from their every stronghold in the World Above, forced back into their most secret strongholds, there to lie hidden, recovering their strength—and their numbers—for centuries.

But they had not been defeated. No. Let the haughty Elves, the foolish Centaurs, the arrogant humans think that. Let them revel in their false victory and turn in their false peacetime upon each other, dissolving their ancient Alliance and retreating each to his own place. That suited Savilla's plans very well. From the very moment of the Endarkened's last retreat, while the wings of dragons still blackened the sky and the music of the victory horns still sounded among the armies in the World Above, Savilla had begun to plan for the day that now, at last, seemed so near. Centuries had passed before she had first dared to send forth her agents into the Bright World once more, but she had waited patiently, and now her plans began their final, ever-accelerating plunge to fruition at last.

Did not the humans isolate themselves in their Golden City, certain that they were the masters of the world and that all lesser races must bow before them?

Did not the Elves retreat to their Forest of Flowers, too content with their own ways to look outside themselves and see how the world had changed?

Had not the dragons vanished altogether, seen never by humans, seldom by others, and only at a distance?

Were not the other races so fragmented and harassed by the humans of the Golden City that it was far more likely that they would abandon the City to any enemy that should appear than to ever ally themselves with it?

So it was.

And ancient allies became present enemies—with the help of the Endarkened and their agents—insulated, isolated, each in his own petty world, each nursing exasperations and minor grievances to the exclusion of intelligence and common sense, each combating problems he was certain were his and his alone and were the most important and terrible difficulties in the universe.

Each with misfortunes that could be solved by the other, did he only know it. And that was the beauty, the artistry of her plan—that salvation should be within the grasp of each, and that they would turn a blind eye to it, choked by their own baseness and pride, until they died of it.

Savilla smiled, exposing long gleaming white fangs, as she reclined on her royal couch, prodding the quivering mass at her feet with one taloned foot, still preoccupied with her thoughts of the Endarkened victory to come.

It was wonderful to contemplate the suffering of her enemies, and still more delightful to know that none of them even suspected that the Endarkened were the architects of their quiet misery and diminution, moving against them even now. Nor would they suspect it, until it was far too late. This was the way to win a war. Not on the battlefield, with banners, bright swords, and brave words, but by weakening a foe until he destroyed himself. That was where the former ruler of the Endarkened, her predecessor, King Virulan, had made his fundamental errors; he had counted on brute force to ensure his conquest.

That was why he was the *former* ruler.

Perhaps she would even set her ancient enemies to warring with one another. It would not matter who won that war . . . the victor would be weak, exhausted by his battles, easy prey for her Endarkened legions and their subject-allies. Whoever triumphed would fall to her, and after the great city-states had gone down into defeat and shadows, then would fall their shattered exiles and former enemies. She would pick them off, one by one.

And then the world—both worlds—the World Without Sun and the Bright World—would belong to the Endarkened and to He Who Is.

Savilla regarded her surroundings with complacent approval before turning her attention to the treat before her. Work was done for now, and it was time for pleasure. To the Endarkened—those whom the Brightworlders in their bigoted ignorance called Demons—torture was the highest art, one requiring the most luxurious setting. Where a mortal or even an Elven ruler would have ornamented his throne room, libraries, or law courts with fine paintings and sculptures, the Endarkened lavished all such skills and embellishments on their torture chambers. The devices that could cause hideous pain and damage were crafted of precious metals, rare woods, and ivories, inlaid with a jeweler's skill, and the walls of such chambers were lined with comfortable couches and divans, so that favored friends and confederates could come to spend a pleasant afternoon listening to screams of pain and whimpers for mercy and release as masters plied their most refined arts upon their victims.

Every Endarkened noble had a private torture chamber, but Queen Savilla's was the most beautiful of all, its painted and jeweled walls covered with detailed and elaborate depictions of agony, its vaulted dome crafted of black crystal mirror, and its lovely mosaic floor an intricate inlay of gold and polished skull-ivory, so that Savilla could walk upon the bones of vanished victims and cherish the memory of their deaths.

She reclined upon her satin couch—black, to enhance the deep warm scarlet of her skin—and stroked the arm lovingly. It was inlaid with a pure spiral of unicorn horn, harmless to her now with the death of its owner. How well she remembered the wonderful months she had spent torturing the magnificent creature slowly to death, for the Endarkened did not rush their pleasures, and even the death of a magicless mortal could take a very long time. The Endarkened were master magicians, and all magic must be paid for. They gained their power through the pain and suffering of others, and there were so very many sorts of pain that could be inflicted, even before the first welt had been raised upon the skin.

Savilla looked around herself, regarding her courtiers complacently. Only a favored few had been invited to witness this very special day—those who stood high in her esteem . . . or those who needed a very special lesson in what it meant to lose her favor.

In the Courts of the Endarkened, it was often difficult to tell ally from enemy. Savilla knew. She made it her business to know. But those who had eagerly accepted the invitation to this particular treat could not, themselves, be certain *why* they had been invited, and that undercurrent of uncertainty only added to her pleasure. Mental cruelty, emotional suffering—there was a saying among the Endarkened: *Each tear shed is Power gained.*

Tanilak was far beyond tears.

Savilla looked down at the body lying on the velvet cushion at her feet, taking a deep breath of pure delight. She had taken the Endarkened noble as her lover over a year ago, knowing when she first welcomed him to her bed that the affair would end in the scene now playing out here. She had raised him high in her favor, plied him with honors, and then sent him into the Bright World to accomplish a small—but very difficult—task for her.

It would have been lovely had he been able to accomplish it to her satisfaction, and in fact he had done far better than Savilla had expected, for Tanilak had honestly wanted to please her. That was the beauty of it. The anguish of his failure, the terror of his punishment, the horror of going as her prey and victim to that place where he had gone so many times as a spectator, all were heady wine to her Endarkened senses. He might have hoped for mercy, for allies to engineer his rescue. But Tanilak had no friends at Court. She'd made sure of that as she'd engineered his downfall. By raising him high and encouraging arrogance, she had invoked jealousy and resentment in even those who once had allied with him. He'd left no grieving hearts behind to make trouble later.

When she'd had him seized, he'd done everything he could think of to save himself. For weeks she'd fed his hope, letting him think it was possible. She'd even engineered—and foiled—an escape attempt, tactics that would not have worked a few weeks before, but Tanilak was maddened with fear and hope, credulous as a child. When she'd come to him in his cell, he'd clung to her skirts and wept, clutching her barbed tail, kissing it and begging to be allowed to do something, anything, to prove himself, in the name of the love they'd shared.

Savilla smiled reminiscently at the memory, flexing her clawed toes in remembered ecstasy. How wonderful that moment had been, to see his yellow eyes well up with tears, their slitted pupils wide in the dimness, to see the moment when all hope died. She shivered with remembered delight, rubbing her hands over her bare gold-dusted arms.

But then, at last, it had been time to move on, to show him the engines that he knew so well, to explain what she would use on him, and how, and when, to savor his utter despair and feel his desperate search for a way to kill himself before she began. That, too, she frustrated.

And then, when he thought himself unable to feel anything more, Savilla proved him wrong again. Once more they were united in bonds of flesh and blood, until he yielded to her more completely than any lover possibly could.

And now, the last and sweetest consummation.

It was something impossible save with one of their own flesh, for in the case of another Endarkened, when at last the victim had been reduced to a quivering mass of agonized protoplasm, the final outcome was to be absorbed completely by their torturer—to yield up everything—life, soul, spirit, memory—knowing at every moment what was happening, feeling the slow and inexorable death of the "self" as it was taken away to feed the life and power of the one it had come to hate and fear and worship.

Her skirts swishing about her slender ankles, Savilla rose gracefully to her feet and knelt beside the body before her, furling her delicate membranous wings tightly against her back.

Only its scarlet skin revealed that this had once been a noble of the Court. Horns, tail, ears, nose, teeth, eyes, fingers, and toes had all long since been removed, and all the rest reduced to a jellylike consistency, held together only by the skin. The shapeless mass was far smaller than Tanilak had been in the days of his glory, but deep inside, what had once been Tanilak was still aware, was still himself. And now she was going to devour him.

Savilla leaned forward and placed her lips against his skin, biting down just enough to pierce the surface with her fangs. She began to suck gently. The taste of his essence filled her mouth, as warm and delightful as the taste of a fine brandy.

She sat back, sighing with pleasure. It had been too long since she had partaken of this particular delicacy. Her enjoyment was heightened by the sight of her Court favorites seated upon divans about her, watching her with greedy envy. It was rare that any of the Pure Blood transgressed so thoroughly as to render themselves prey for the rapacious appetites of their peers.

As she bent to sip again, her attention was caught by movement on the far side of the room, and she heard excited whispering among the Endarkened gathered here to watch her finish Tanilak.

Prince Zyperis had entered the Heart of Darkness, but he was not here to observe his mother's pleasure—or not entirely. Zyperis had brought a companion with him—a human.

The Prince towered over the human, and his scarlet skin made the human look as pale as a glistening grub. Zyperis was a truly beautiful creature, with waist-length hair as black as Savilla's own, curving golden horns, an elegant barbed tail, and large, graceful ribbed wings—a mark of his noble blood. He was dressed all in white and gold, from his elegant sandals to his flowing silk trousers, gilded codpiece, and diaphanous jeweled sleeves. A large pearl drop glowed in one ear, and his hair was held back from his face with a set of matching pearl combs.

His companion, Savilla was pleased to see, was clean and well fed and dressed in the most opulent of human finery. Zyperis had a fine touch with the Art, and would ensure that his own offering to the Art lasted a very long time. For now, the human's every physical need was being fully met, while Prince Zyperis played upon his mind and nerves. Bringing him here today was only the first step in the campaign that the Prince would wage upon those citadels, Savilla thought proudly. Zyperis would extract every ounce of torment possible from the human's fear and uncertainty before moving on to the first taste of physical pain.

She bent forward and let Tanilak's essence fill her mouth again, drinking in his memories, his long-buried desires.

⟶

PRINCE Zyperis regarded the human beside him with pleasure and interest. Henamor Lear had been of little use in the fashion he had sworn he could be, but the man would yet have his opportunity to repair that insult—and provide Zyperis great entertainment into the bargain.

"If you will only give me another chance, Exalted One," Henamor whimpered desperately. He was barely able to keep his attention upon the Prince, for Henamor Lear had never seen so many of the Demonkind in one place together, and certainly he had never before been so deep within their realm. He only hoped he could still escape alive—for if he did, this was the end of his dealing with Demons!

Zyperis smiled, knowing full well the direction and content of his captive's thoughts. Yes, let the man still hope for a reprieve . . . for a time . . . even though his fate was irrevocably sealed. There were so many humans, after all, each willing to exchange freedom and safety for the powers of Darkness. With so many eager to take Henamor's place, the human was entirely disposable.

"But why should I do that, when you failed so dreadfully on your last attempt? You assured me it would be so simple, so possible, to find a dragon and bond with it through your spells, O Great Magician," Zyperis said playfully.

"But it is—it will be!" The human whispered, shrinking in upon himself, as one of the nearest Endarkened turned her gaze away from the Queen and rested it upon the human. "Only let me draw near to it, and it will fall prey to my spells—then you will have all its power—and mine—for your own, to use as you choose!"

"But I already have you, and all your power, Henamor," Zyperis pointed out with mock-obliviousness. "How could I possibly be greedy enough to wish for anything more?"

"Only let me try again," Henamor begged. "It must have detected me somehow, hidden itself before I could discover its den. I have done all that you asked, Exalted One—for years I have been your eyes and ears in the Bright World, doing all that you asked of me, growing in your power, working your Dark Arts. I have given you many slaves, even my own wife and children—"

"But you promised me a dragon," Zyperis said in jesting singsong tones. "And you didn't give me a dragon. Now why should I give you a second chance to fail at what you didn't manage to accomplish once? I really don't think another failure would be at all good for you, my Henamor. Now come. You have always been curious about our secrets. Let me show you the heart of our power."

He put an arm around the human's shoulders, and drew him close to his side, savoring the shudders of fear that Henamor tried hard to suppress, drawing ever-so-delicately upon that anguish. Zyperis directed his agent's attention to the wall paintings, as if to praise their beauty, knowing the man would only see their subject, the endless and exquisite ways that the Endarkened had devised for their victims to die, and think of his own fate. He summoned a servant—one of the Lesser Endarkened, its hoofed and scaled form such that the Brightworlders found especially hideous—and pressed wine upon his guest, before directing his attention to a pair of golden boots. They stood upon a long wooden rack beside several other sets of oddly shaped footwear, all metal.

"Are they not lovely? Rather bulky, I'm afraid, but that is because there are hollows built into the outer shell that can be filled with boiling oil. And the wonder of it is that even filled, they are light enough to dance in. Imagine!" Zyperis smiled proudly at his guest. The Court ladies in attendance upon the Queen giggled approvingly, flirting their jeweled fans as they tried to catch the young Prince's eye. "Have you ever seen such craftsmanship, such cunning?"

"A-amazing," Henamor whispered. He gazed pleadingly at the Prince, begging silently for mercy. Zyperis pretended not to see.

"It is a wonderful thing to have a creature entirely at your mercy—but I need hardly tell you that, my friend," Zyperis said. "You, too, have accomplished great things in your time."

"And I will do more, if you will permit me, Master," Henamor gasped, seizing the opening. "I know I have failed you—"

"Now, now—what are two old friends such as we to talk of failure?" Zyperis said chidingly. "Still, I should so very

much have liked to have had a dragon . . . But perhaps another time. Please allow me to show you the flaying knives.
They are so wonderfully sharp and thin that it is quite possible to remove a man's skin in one piece, you know, though
it can take weeks—sennights as you call them—to properly
loosen the skin of the face. I understand that the best method
is to make a small incision and then to inject brine beneath
the skin—did you not tell me you had done that once?" Zyperis allowed his brow to furrow, as if in thought. "Oh, yes,
now I remember. You said the man died of the pain, but I
assure you, that won't happen here," the Prince added, in
soothing tones.

Like all the so-called Masters of the Dark Arts with whom
Zyperis had dealt in his lifetime, Henamor was brave enough
when inflicting pain on others, but the mere thought of receiving such treatment himself made him weep like a child.
Zyperis reveled in this delicious foretaste of the banquet to
come—and the beauty of it was, the human had no notion
his Demonic host was already siphoning off his pain and
despair, while leaving its wellspring intact. Patience; that was
the essence of success. Queen Savilla was right; patience won
all, with patience, one could create a feast of fear and pain
that would satisfy the most finicky of appetites.

Henamor was weeping now, quite frantic with terror, and
Zyperis judged that it was time to offer some small modicum
of relief, lest matters progress too swiftly.

"But I am sure that you will want to tell me more of what
you know about the dragons, leaving nothing back," Zyperis
said, drawing the human away from his horrified contemplation of the crystal cases filled with slender glittering knives.

When Henamor had come here, the man had intended to
withhold some of his information, to use it to bargain for his
freedom, or at the very least, to persuade the Prince of his
continued usefulness. Now he found himself telling everything he knew, or guessed, or suspected about the caverns
where the dragons might be found—how to seek them out,
the spells that might be used to compel them, how to force
a bond upon one of them.

Zyperis listened intently, sipping the fear that radiated from the human just as he absorbed the information—though this was hardly the last time he would have this information from Henamor's lips before the Mage-man died. If only he could use it himself—but unfortunately, his race was unable to make an alliance with the dragons. Only a Mage could bond with a dragon, and only a human could become a Mage. But once bonded, a dragon was psychically and emotionally vulnerable to anything that its rider was vulnerable to, and humans were so very, very vulnerable . . .

As he listened, he watched Queen Savilla at her feast, savoring Tanilak's destruction nearly as much as she did. Though she had not taken him into her confidence, he had guessed her plans from the moment she had first begun to show favor to Tanilak, and had secretly been delighted when he was proven right. Zyperis had never tired of watching the two of them here together in the Heart of Darkness, glorying in the anticipation of the moment he knew was to come.

Henamor's words faltered to a stop, his eyes following the direction of Zyperis's gaze. "What . . . *is* that?" he whispered.

"That is my mother the Queen," Zyperis said, pretending to take offense. "The most beautiful and accomplished of all of the host of Endarkened—"

"No!" Henamor protested frantically, terrified of causing new trouble for himself. "I meant no disrespect! I meant . . . *with* the Queen."

"Ah." Zyperis smiled, and allowed himself to be pleased. Henamor had recovered his equilibrium, and was ready to be frightened once more. "That was once a noble of this Court, who failed to give satisfaction in a far more trivial matter than you have, my dear friend. The Queen's abilities in the Art far exceed my own, and as you see, she has quite destroyed poor Tanilak. Now she consumes him utterly."

Already the scarlet pulsing mass had much decreased in size, while Queen Savilla glowed with increased power and life. Zyperis felt the intimate tug of her beauty.

"She's . . . *eating* him," Henamor moaned.

"So she is," Prince Zyperis said, as if he'd only just discovered that fact. "And do you know, as she does, she is consuming every one of his memories, and his soul as well. There will be no rebirth for Tanilak upon the branches of the Tree of Night."

The frisson of despair that jolted Henamor played deliciously on all of Zyperis's senses, and he luxuriated in it. Not quite so delicious a vintage as the essence of Tanilak, but savory in its own small way. Let Henamor believe for as long as possible that this could be his own ultimate fate. Humans were so short-lived that they set great store by their souls' fates.

And even though it was not possible for Zyperis to do to Henamor precisely what Queen Savilla was doing to Tanilak, the Prince had plans for the human Mage's immortal spark. Plans that he would reveal to his victim at the appropriate time in their relationship . . .

"But come," Zyperis said. "I know that our afternoon together has tired you, and you will wish to spend some time alone meditating upon your numerous failings and considering how you can best please me. Although of course," he added, almost as an afterthought, "I can think of no way that you can save yourself from your fate."

He turned away, knowing that in Henamor's wearied and distracted condition it would take several seconds for the meaning of his words to sink in, and raised his hand. One of the Lesser Endarkened hurried over, its hooves clicking against the glittering mosaic floor. It bowed low before the Prince, casting a greedy glance toward the human.

"Return my guest to his rooms and see that he has food and drink, for I anticipate many long hours of pleasure spent in his company in the future."

The Prince turned back to Henamor, who was only now beginning to realize what Prince Zyperis had said. He would still deny it to himself, and hope he had heard wrong— Zyperis meant to fan the flames of hope and uncertainty for many days yet, before dashing those hopes forever.

"Please—Prince Zyperis—Your Highness—"

"Your company grows tedious, my friend. Do not make it

entirely offensive," Zyperis said gently. He watched as Henamor reluctantly allowed himself to be led away by the Lesser Endarkened, and heard the sibilant sound as it whispered to the human, telling him horrors—on Prince Zyperis's orders, of course—that would cause Henamor Lear a long and sleepless night.

The Prince smiled, and returned his attention to the enchanting tableau before him. Tanilak was so diminished by now that the Queen could cradle what was left of him in her cupped palms like a malign scarlet fruit, and as Zyperis watched, she sucked him in with one last deep swallow.

A murmur of appreciation passed through the watching Endarkened, and a ripple of gentle applause.

Zyperis approached, bowing low.

SAVILLA regarded her son with approval. He had handled the ugly little human splendidly, feeding from him so subtly that the human Mage probably wasn't even aware that the vampirism had taken place. Now he knelt before her, flushed with power—and quite the most attractive member of her Court, at least since the day, so many years ago, when his father went the way that Tanilak had just gone. Dear Urallesse—in so many ways he had been her equal, save in guile, and there was no one in all the Court these days to match him.

Save Prince Zyperis. Strong and handsome, ambitious and utterly merciless . . . he was her peer, almost her equal.

She rose gracefully to her feet, regarding him through lowered lashes. He stared back at her with a hot-eyed gaze of frank admiration, as drawn by her increase in power as she was captivated by his youthful charms.

She held out her hand. He took it, first kneeling gracefully in homage, then rising to his feet and bringing her hand to his mouth, kissing first the palm, then the wrist where the pulse of stolen life beat strongly. Their eyes met, and there was no doubt between them where this unspoken conversation would lead.

"I shall be in my chambers for the rest of the afternoon," Savilla announced, leading Zyperis toward the door that led to her rooms. "My . . . private chambers."

Chapter Six

A College of Magicks

Kellen was sure there would be further repercussions from the quarrel in the morning. He'd rarely dared to contest his father's will openly in the past—certainly he'd never before gone so far as to *raise his voice* to his father—and the punishment for not falling immediately into line with whatever Lycaelon had planned for him had always been swift, unpleasant, and crushing.

But to his faint surprise and great relief, Lycaelon seemed disinclined to pursue the matter this time. Maybe having his offspring talk back to him had taken him by surprise. Or maybe he just hadn't yet managed to think of a punishment commensurate with the "crime."

Whatever the reason, Lycaelon was already gone by the time Kellen came downstairs in the morning. Second Morning Bells were ringing throughout the City, and the breakfast table was cleared. The servants didn't seem to have any "special orders" regarding Kellen, so he resorted to his usual morning habit of sneaking into the kitchen and filching leftovers from the sideboard, then hurried off to class.

Fortunately this wasn't one of the mornings that he had to face his tutor. Having seen Anigrel yesterday, he wouldn't see him again until tomorrow. All he had to suffer through was the regular round of classes and lectures that were the lot of every Student in Magecraft.

PASSING through the main gate of the College, Kellen entered the Quadrangle. At this time of day it was filled with bodies—Students in their plain blue robes, Entered Apprentices in grey robe and soft cap, Journeymen in grey robe and tabard, Mages in their colors, all hurrying (in the case of Student, Apprentice, and Journeyman) or going leisurely (in the case of Mages) about their business.

The principal buildings of the Mage College were grouped around the Quadrangle. Just as the wondertales told, there was a fountain in the center of the Quad, but it was of the most mundane sort, a statue of a triton with water spewing from the tips of his trident. The Library and the Chapel of the Light were on the left, the imposing building that held the classrooms and lecture halls on his right. Straight ahead was the building that held the offices of the College, and the tutors' workrooms that had been Kellen's destination yesterday. Beyond that—and most carefully and thoroughly warded—was a building containing another series of workrooms, where senior Apprentices and Journeyman Mages practiced and tested their work in spellcraft. They certainly didn't do so in public on the lawn—another thing the wondertales always got wrong. Though Kellen supposed it would make a very pretty picture—if the Mages had actually been the sort of people the wondertales presented them as being . . .

Elsewhere on the grounds—though not near the Quadrangle, which tended to be noisy—were the residence halls of those Mages who, for whatever reason, did not wish to either live with their families or put themselves to the trouble and expense of keeping a house. For the few children from non-Mage families who were discovered to be worth training, other arrangements were made.

As Kellen crossed the Quadrangle, the bells in the carillon of the Temple of the Light began to chime Third Morning Bells. The sound was picked up by towers throughout the City—though of course the Temple of the Light began every ring, as was only proper—and Kellen realized that if he did not hurry, he'd be late for his first class. And that was the last thing he wanted to be today. He hurried, and was in his appointed seat before the last echoes of Third Bells had sounded.

THE course was "History of the City," and here at the College, that meant it was the history of the High Mages as well, for as Mage Hendassar, the Master Undermage who taught them, had told them over and over, the Mages were the City, and the City was the Mages. Kellen generally found the lectures not only pointless, but painful, for Mage Hendassar delighted in humiliating those of his Students whom he could catch unprepared, and Kellen was usually among them.

But today, it seemed, Mage Hendassar had chosen another victim.

"Come now, young Master Cilarnen. Surely you can recite for me the names of the Arch-Mages who have led the High Council since the founding of the City. Or perhaps thoughts of *romance* have distracted you from your studies . . . ?"

Kellen glanced up, and saw Cilarnen slide down in his seat as far as he dared, looking uncomfortable. He wondered what was going on. Cilarnen was the son of a high-ranking Mage family—his father was the High Mage Lord Setarion Volpiril—and until now he'd been one of Hendassar's pets.

Hendassar turned away from Cilarnen and strode to the front of the room.

"Gentlemen," he said. "Behold before you a young man of flawless birth and impeccable breeding—and heretofore undeniable gifts—who believes that there is something more important than serving the City! Now, can any of you imagine what that is?"

Kellen shrank down in his own seat in sympathy. Whatever Cilarnen had done, it must be awful.

All twenty students regarded Mage Hendassar with silent fascination.

"Women—!" Mage Hendassar said in hushed disgusted tones.

Several of the bolder members of the class burst into stifled snickers.

"Now, of course, women are important. Most of you will—eventually—marry, in order to breed strong Mage-sons to serve the City. And of course, your wives will produce daughters as well, since Mages must marry Mageborn daughters in order to keep the bloodline pure. However, we must never forget that women are essentially unimportant to the life of a Mage, unable to participate in or even understand the actual concerns of his life: the practice and study of the Art Magickal."

Hendassar broke off to glare at Cilarnen again.

"There is a time and a place for everything. And certainly when one should be devoting all of one's energies to the mastery of those concerns which will occupy one's entire future, one should *not* be occupying one's energy in writing love poetry to Lady Amintia. Such as this example."

Mage Hendassar reached into his sleeve and withdrew a slender scroll.

Oh, no. Kellen groaned inwardly. He didn't like Cilarnen particularly—he didn't even know him. Lord Volpiril was one of Lycaelon's rivals on the Council just to begin with, and Lycaelon had disliked his son fraternizing with lesser beings—and in Lycaelon's mind, even his fellow Mages were lesser beings—but Kellen didn't like to see anyone publicly humiliated.

Mage Hendassar began to read out the poem, playing it for laughs—which he got. Kellen didn't know a lot about poetry; he guessed it was pretty bad, but still, nobody deserved to be treated this way. If Lord Volpiril didn't want Cilarnen to see Amintia, why hadn't he just told him so, rather than doing something like this to him?

At least Kellen's father had never made *him* into a public spectacle. He supposed he ought to be grateful for that much. But he knew it wasn't because Lycaelon cared about him in any way. It was because Lycaelon couldn't bear the thought of seeming less than perfect: the perfect Arch-Mage with the perfect—and perfectly obedient—son.

By the time Mage Hendassar had finished reading out the poem, the rest of the class was roaring with laughter, and Kellen was filled with an odd cold anger.

Why were Mages supposed to be so different from ordinary folk? Kellen had spent a lot of time—much more than either Lycaelon or Anigrel suspected—in the poorer quarters of Armethalieh. He'd had to learn to be handy with his fists, to earn his place among the children there, but once he'd won a few street-fights—his size and strength had served him well, there—they'd accepted him as more than a nasty interloping Mageborn brat, and he'd learned a lot about how the "other folk" lived.

For instance, he knew that at among tradesmen and laborers—and even among a lot of the non-Mage nobles—people were courting and marrying. Yet the Mageborn weren't even supposed to *think* about such a thing until they had reached Journeyman Undermage rank at least, if not Master Undermage—and that could take another decade of studying.

And where did they *find* the women they were supposed to marry? If Kellen had stayed where he was supposed to stay and only gone where he was told to go, he knew, he doubted he'd ever even *see* a woman. As a child, he'd played with children in the parks and made friends with them when he'd been under the care of his "Nursies," but all that had changed as soon as he was deemed old enough and Gifted enough to someday become a Student. Then, Lycaelon had done his best to cut Kellen off from all human contact. If Kellen had not continued to sneak out onto the streets—and carefully concealed the fact—and managed to make friends of his own, however fleeting, he'd have grown up completely alone, for he had no friends among what his father would have called "his own kind."

As he'd grown older, Kellen's own attitude to the hypocrisy he saw in the Mages that were his father's cronies, as much as the growing rivalry for future place among their sons, had done much to keep him isolated by his own wish, even from those who would have sought to curry favor with the Arch-Mage by cultivating a friendship with his son.

Kellen did not want friendship on those terms, even if Lycaelon would have permitted it. But it did make him wonder where Lycaelon thought his future daughter-in-law was going to come from. He knew that some of his fellow Students had sisters—they must have, from what Mage Hendassar had said, but . . .

There was no point in thinking about it. It wasn't, after all, a subject that actually interested Kellen very much. And he didn't need another thing to get himself into trouble about.

Eventually Mage Hendassar relented, and restored the class to order, assigning Cilarnen a long punishment essay—due at the beginning of the next class—on the History of the Great Arch-Mages. With a few more blighting remarks on the irrelevancy of females to a Mage's life, he returned to his scheduled lecture.

After that, it was hard for Kellen to keep his mind on the assigned subject, but he was safe at the back of the room, and Mage Hendassar didn't seem to be looking for any more victims today. Kellen let his mind drift back to more familiar questions.

The map of the City, ancient and yellowed, hanging on the wall behind Mage Hendassar, caught his eye. Though he'd seen it a thousand times before, today an errant beam of light fell on the legend "Delfier Gate."

What was beyond the Delfier Gate? What lands did the Selken Traders sail to? Where *were* the Out Islands, exactly? Somewhere beyond the mouth of the harbor, but *where*?

Like every other inhabitant of the City, Kellen knew—vaguely—about the Home Farms, the villages that grew the food the City consumed. He knew the Mountain Traders brought things down from the High Hills that made their way into the City in the trading caravans—furs and spices and medicinals—but the High Hills were no more than a name to him. He knew there must be lands beyond the sea that produced the goods that came in the Traders' ships and appeared in the City markets. But those places weren't even names.

Why not?

He'd never thought about it before.

He'd been carefully encouraged not to, Kellen realized, just as he'd been encouraged not to think about marriage and family and Mageborn girls—about anything outside of his studies, in fact. The only histories he'd learned were the history of the City and its inhabitants and the history of the High Magick. As for geography . . . he could draw a map of the better quarters of the City from memory, but set him one foot outside its walls, and he'd be lost.

That wasn't right.

Was it?

Surely the information existed somewhere, even if it wasn't being taught.

After History came Geography—another boring useless class—and then Natural Philosophy. And then the day's lessons were done. Kellen headed for his locker to put away his books and then headed quickly out through the gates, his robe bundled beneath his arm, intent on finding the answers to at least some of his questions.

Though the information he sought might very well be archived within the walls of the Library of the Mage College, there was no possibility of Kellen's getting at it there. No one below the rank of Entered Apprentice was allowed beyond the small first-floor Student Reference Library, and Entered Apprentice was a rank Kellen had yet to reach—he was still a lowly Student, not yet allowed to exchange his humble blue robe for one of magickal grey.

But there was more than one library in the Golden City . . .

Without anyone noticing, he made his way to the Great Library that stood at the center of the City, across from the Main Temple of the Light. The two buildings had been designed to complement each other: Wisdom and Knowledge marching hand in hand.

Uneasily, Kellen touched the Talisman he wore around his

neck on a heavy gold chain, the golden symbol of his citizenship. Though they might wear it on a leather cord or a cotton string or a silver chain or one of gold and jewels, every citizen of Armethalieh wore the same gold rectangle, marking them as a citizen of Armethalieh. Each month you brought it to the Temple of the Light and exchanged it for a new one. You came to the Temple of the Light for your new Talisman on the moonday on which you had been born, so that everyone didn't end up coming on the same day. Kellen had been born on the eighth day of the moon, and so, ever since his Naming, when he had received his first Talisman, he had been brought—or later, came alone—to the appropriate Temple of the Light (the main one in the City Square, of course; Lycaelon's social consequence would admit of no less) to receive a fresh Talisman.

The ceremony was simple: the old Talisman went into one bowl, the new Talisman came out of another, was blessed by the Arch-Priest, and placed into the worshiper's hand. As the bowls filled (or emptied) they were taken away by Deacons of the Light, and new bowls were brought.

Then you stepped aside, and someone else took your place. There were always a dozen young Deacons of the Light standing around to help make sure you could get your Talisman back onto its keeper-chain again without trouble, and to be sure you were wearing it when you left.

It had always seemed like a great deal of unnecessary fuss, when keeping the same identification Talisman until it wore out, was damaged, or was lost would surely have served the City's purposes (so he'd once thought) just as well. He'd never questioned why—like so many things in the City, it was just the way things were, and custom was custom, not to be questioned.

But now, after what Anigrel had told him, Kellen wondered if he could ever do it again, could ever face the Light-Priest and hand over his Talisman with the same calm acceptance, knowing that when he did so he was giving up a part of himself? How could he, knowing that the Mages fed upon him, upon all the citizens of Armethalieh, as if they were no more than a herd of milk-cattle?

It was disgusting. No, worse than that. It was *sick*.

And worst of all, Kellen didn't see a single thing he could do about it.

Gritting his teeth, Kellen turned away from the Temple of the Light and strode up the steps into the Great Library.

It was City Law that one copy of every book that came into the City had to be kept available here. Most people who used the Library had to go to one of the Reading Rooms, fill out a request, and wait for the books they wanted to be brought to them, but there were some advantages to being the Arch-Mage's son. Kellen was greeted personally by the Chief Librarian, and after a few vague comments about needing to do some research—Kellen didn't say for what, and if the Chief Librarian assumed it was for his magickal studies, well, he didn't say anything to correct the man's mistake—the Chief Librarian presented him with an "All Access" pass to the stacks.

Kellen hung the square silver tag around his neck so that it would be plainly visible, thanked the man politely and profusely, assured him he would remember him to his father the Arch-Mage, and made his escape into the stacks.

⌒

THIS was not the first time he'd been here—Anigrel had brought him once or twice before—but it was the first time Kellen had been here unescorted. Panels of Magelight illuminated the long shelves of books in the windowless corridors, and the faint hum of Preservation Spells, endlessly renewed, made the air sleepy and thick. Fortunately, the Great Library used the same cataloguing system as the smaller Student Reference Library at the Mage College did, so Kellen knew where to look for what he wanted.

He began with travelogues. Surely there would be some information there about the lands beyond the City.

But though he made a promising beginning—all the books

in that section were marked "Do Not Circulate," which meant they must contain something interesting—Kellen discovered to his disgust that every single one of them was fiction. Tales of travel to the moon, beneath the sea, to ridiculous wonder-tale kingdoms at the center of the earth. None of them had anything to do with the real world.

By the time he finished his investigations, the closing bell had rung—joined, he could hear faintly, by the echoing bells of Evensong sounding throughout the City. Kellen tucked his pass inside his tunic—he had no intention of giving it up just yet—and hurried out of the Library. He was far from finished.

BUT his experiences the following day mirrored those of the first. As soon as his lesson with Anigrel was finished, Kellen returned to the Great Library—making sure the key to the garden was safe in his pocket, this time. Now he turned his searches to books of geography, to anything with maps, and was similarly disappointed. Either the books were missing entirely from the Library's shelves—although you really couldn't say they were missing, when it was obvious they'd never been there in the first place—or they were obviously fantasies. And even the fantasies were marked "Do Not Circulate," as if someone didn't want the citizens of Armethal-ieh—or at least, the ones who couldn't afford to buy books of their own—to even *think* about the possibility of a world beyond the City walls.

Growing more frustrated—and just a little frightened, something he wasn't quite prepared to admit to himself—Kellen began delving into any book that might contain even a passing reference to the world outside the City walls. Each day, once his lessons were done, he returned to the Great Library—it was a safe enough destination, should Lycaelon ever discover he hadn't actually been at home. A little odd, perhaps, but scholarship was a respectable thing for one of the Mageborn to be engaged in, and there were a lot of per-fectly reasonable things Kellen *could* have been looking up.

As the days passed, he continued to return to the Library. Kellen consulted histories of the City, plays, popular fiction, looking for anything that even mentioned the fact that there was a whole world that didn't stop at the Delfier Gate and the harbor mouth.

And he found nothing.

At last, after a whole sennight of fruitless searching, he set the book he'd been looking at back in its place on the shelf with a disgusted sigh. There was no point in going on. He'd spent a sennight here, and if he spent a dozen sennights, if he read every book in the Great Library cover to cover, he knew he wouldn't find anything different.

It was as if the world stopped at the City walls, and nobody cared. At least, nobody cared so long as the strawberries and beer came in through the gates in their seasons, and they had hot water and vermin-free kitchens.

Nobody but Kellen Tavadon. Or those few people who were lucky enough to be parentless, or to have their parents disinherit them, so that they could get passage on a Selken ship out of the City.

Well, if the Library couldn't help him, he had other resources.

He had the Wild Magic.

Kellen had done a lot more reading in his three Books while he'd been working his way through the contents of the Great Library—not only *The Book of Sun*, but also *The Book of Moon*, which explained a lot more about what he'd gone through with that first Finding Spell. He realized that he'd actually gotten off pretty easily, all things considered, and now that he'd actually *done* a Wild Magic spell, he understood a lot more about it than he had when he'd just been daydreaming about it during Undermage Anigrel's lecture.

While High Magick and Wild Magic were alike in requiring a "payment" for their working, with the Wild Magic, the payment was not just the personal or group energy involved in setting the spell, but a further personal cost that could not be determined in advance. For the Wildmage, the more powerful the spell, the more likely that the price of actually getting what he wanted would require the Wildmage to act as a human agent of the Wild Magic's "desires."

And whatever the personal price might be, there was a good chance it wouldn't be the same thing twice. He'd actually read that part before, but he'd been, well, careless. He'd thought that a Finding Spell was small enough to be exempt from that personal cost, but he'd obviously been wrong about that.

That led to all kinds of questions, and Kellen had no one he could possibly ask. Was the Wild Magic alive? Did it "want" things—and if so, *why* did it "want" things—and even more importantly, what did it want them *for*? How could getting a servant-girl's kitten out of a tree be a part of anything, well, *bigger*? The *Ars Perfidorum* in his father's library talked about how dangerous and terrible the Wild Magic was, and Kellen hadn't really liked having his will taken away like that, but once he'd gone over the garden wall, he hadn't felt the compulsion any longer. He'd just acted naturally, and in the end he'd gotten what he'd asked for, and been able to help someone else, too, almost by accident.

Except that this was *magick,* and in magick there were no accidents. So the Wild Magic had *meant* him to help the girl, while helping himself at the same time.

Kellen shrugged, staring at the shelves of books that hadn't answered any of his questions, and shook his head. He didn't understand it, but nobody had gotten hurt, and so he was willing to risk trying it again. The Library had told him nothing—but somewhere in the City someone *had* to have the answers he needed! All he had to do was find them.

With the Wild Magic. Finding answers was a Finding Spell, after all. How much could it cost him?

He left the Library, stopping to turn in his pass at the Chief Librarian's office and thank the man for all his help. There'd been no classes—and no tutorial—today, so Kellen had gotten an early start at the Library. He still had most of the day before him. Plenty of time to cast a spell and see where it took him.

He spent a short time searching for a secluded place where

he wouldn't be disturbed; easy enough to find here in the center of the City on the Light's Day. As before, the Finding Spell took him only a little time to cast. This time he wasn't as specific: he wasn't asking it to find a specific object, only information—about life outside the City, or, failing that, why the information couldn't be found. The Books said that the less specific you made your goal, the lower the price that would be asked of you, and the more likely you would be to gain what you sought.

This time, when the compulsion took him, Kellen didn't fight it, simply following where the pull led him.

He was surprised to find himself drawn down into the Artists' Quarter, where the painters, poets, musicians, and writers of Armethalieh tended to gather. It was one of the oldest parts of the City—the streets here were narrow, with taverns, boardinghouses, printing shops, and *kaffeyah*-parlors all crammed in together. Music floated through the air as musicians practiced their craft or gave lessons in upper rooms, and the sharp smells of drying paint and turpentine were strong in the cool air.

I could live here, Kellen thought hopefully. He didn't know what he could do to earn a place for himself here—he had no particular talent for the arts—and he wasn't sure he'd fit in, but at least these people didn't look as if they were spending their lives practicing for their own funerals and hoping to attend the funerals of their rivals first.

Distracted from the spell-*geas* by the color and gaiety, he slowed down to peer into a shop filled with colorful pottery, but the pull of the spell drew him onward, and Kellen reluctantly obeyed, promising himself to return another time.

Urged onward, he turned a corner, then another, and found himself on a quiet back street with fewer shops and more houses. This street wasn't as well kept up as the others he'd gone down, and large grey creatures scurried out of his way as he approached.

Ugh. Rats.

At last he felt the compulsion to move on lift as he reached the end of a dead-end street. He looked around. He was on a narrow street of shabby two-story brick houses that had seen better days. The City services that kept the better quarters of the City clean and orderly were less in evidence here—such services cost money beyond the house tax that paid for the City Watch and for the spells that kept house fires from spreading out of control, and those who lived in places like these rarely had the ready coin to pay for them.

A scent of brackish water and rotting garbage assailed his nostrils, and he traced it to an old cistern in an empty corner lot beside one of the houses. Once it might have been used to catch rainwater, or even have been used as a communal well, but now it was choked with garbage and trash, and was obviously a clubhouse for the local rats.

Kellen felt a sensation inside himself as if a key had turned in a lock, and realized exactly what he had to do. He didn't understand how cleaning the cistern out and filling it in with clean dirt would lead him to the information he sought, but he had no doubt that this was the price the Wild Magic wanted him to pay.

And me in my good clothes, he thought with a sigh.

He stripped off his tunic and undertunic, folding them carefully and setting them to one side, and got to work. He couldn't finish this task in a day, and he'd be sure to bring tools and wear more suitable clothes when he returned tomorrow. But the Wild Magic had brought him here, so he'd better start now.

Hesitantly, Kellen approached the cistern.

⟳

"YOU! Boy! What are you doing there!"

Kellen had become so involved in his task—he'd started by dragging away the heavy boards that were balanced precariously at the top of the trash heap that covered the cistern, and when he'd pulled the first of them loose, several rats had bolted out of the cistern, squeaking angrily as they ran—that the shout took him entirely by surprise. He dropped the board he was holding (narrowly missing his own foot) and turned in the direction of the voice.

A man in a yellow tunic—he had the look, but hardly the manner, of one of the Mageborn—was leaning out the side window of the house, staring at him in surprise. Kellen stared back for a long moment before realizing he really needed to come up with an explanation. A *good* explanation. One that didn't involve the Wild Magic.

"I'm, uh, cleaning out your cistern, goodsir. It's full of garbage, you see, and, well, there are rats . . ."

"I know there are rats! Their squeaking keeps me up half the night—but will the Council do anything about it? No! They say it isn't on public property, so it isn't their responsibility! *You're* not from the Council, are you?"

"Me? No, I'm just . . . me," Kellen said. "But I really want to clean it out," he added hastily.

The man in the window stared at him for a long moment, as if attempting to judge just exactly how crazy Kellen was. "You ought to have work gloves," he said after a moment. "Wait there."

He withdrew from the window, leaving Kellen staring after him, wondering what he ought to do. After less than a tenth-chime, the man returned with a pair of heavy leather work gloves in his hand.

"I knew I still had these somewhere. Mind you put them back on the front step when you're finished for the day."

He tossed them out the window. They landed at Kellen's feet.

"Yes, goodsir," Kellen said meekly. "Ah, goodsir? I'm going to have to come back tomorrow. And maybe for a few days. To finish."

"Well, see that you don't come too early," the man said, and closed the window firmly.

Well, he's an odd one, Kellen thought to himself, going to pick up the gloves. They were a little small, but he was able to force his hands into them. They made the work go a lot easier, and he was careful to leave them just where the man had said when he'd done all he could for the day.

I wonder who he is? Kellen thought as he left.

———

THE next day Kellen came back just after Second Morning Bells wearing his oldest clothes, with a pick and shovel and some burlap bags he'd taken from the gardener's hut at the bottom of his garden. Even a garden that was home to nothing but gravel required constant tending, Kellen had discovered, and the tools were going to come in handy.

The gloves were where he'd left them the night before, and he put them on and set to work.

As Kellen dug, he sorted his "finds" as best he could— rotting garbage (which went into the bags), clean garbage (broken pottery, small bits of wood or bone), which he could use when he filled in the cistern again, and large unidentifiable *things,* which would have to be hauled away somehow, unless he could manage to break them up into small pieces with the pick or shovel. It was hot, dirty work that kept him stooped over, and he didn't dare step down into the cistern to work from there. Not yet, anyway. He had no idea how deep it went, and even though he was now wearing heavy work boots, he had no desire to slice his foot open on a piece of rusty metal or glass that had been steeped in rotting garbage.

It certainly explained why the cistern hadn't been cleaned out before now. If the Council wouldn't pay to have it done because it lay on private land, the land's owner would have to pay someone privately to do it, and Kellen could hardly begin to imagine how much someone would charge to do this work. A lot, probably. More than someone down here had, almost certainly.

At least most of the big stuff seemed to be near the top, where he could hook it with the pick and drag it up.

"You! Boy!"

Kellen heaved his latest "find"—a tangled mass of bailing wire—to the edge of the cistern, and looked toward the house. The man who had given him the gloves the day before was looking out the window at him again. This time the tunic was red, its sleeves spotted with old ink stains.

"Yes, goodsir?" Kellen said politely. He assumed the man was a "goodsir," and not a "gentlesir," for all his aristocratic looks. It was not unknown for Mageblood to appear elsewhere in the City—that was where lowborn Mages came from, according to Mage Hendassar. Perhaps this man's sire or grandsire had been a Mage on the wrong side of the blanket. It did happen, though hardly as often as the wondertales claimed.

"I suppose you're going to dig all day?" the man said.

"Yes, goodsir, I think I am," Kellen said, glancing down at the cistern. With the largest of the objects removed, he could now see that the cistern—a stone circle about six feet across—was full of an inky black sludge starting about three feet below its lip. Kellen had no idea how far down it went.

"And I suppose you didn't bring any lunch with you?" the man asked waspishly.

"No, goodsir," Kellen admitted sheepishly. He'd forgotten about that until just now.

"Well, come around to the back of the house, then." The man withdrew and the window was shut once more.

Kellen gazed at the closed window for a moment, then meekly did as the man said, picking up his discarded tunic—one of his most disreputable—on the way. The man was waiting at the door with a tin bucket and a towel.

"Rinse yourself off and come in. You've done a good day's work so far; I won't have you fainting dead away from hunger before you finish."

Kellen took the bucket and stepped back to pour its contents over his head and shoulders. The icy shock made him gasp, and he shook his head, toweling his head and chest quickly dry before slipping into his tunic. He followed the man inside, setting the bucket and the damp towel down just inside the door.

"Come—come!" his host urged, more cordially now, and Kellen passed through the kitchen into the room beyond.

It was a parlor, dominated by a large table covered with a white cloth upon which had been set a sizable plain luncheon. His host was seated at the head of the table, and gestured for Kellen to sit beside him.

"My boots—" Kellen began, stopping at the edge of the rug.

"It's only a little mud," his host said graciously, "and my girl hasn't enough to do just looking after me. My name is Perulan. And yours?"

"Kellen," Kellen said, sitting as he'd been bid. Perulan poured him a large beaker of cider, and Kellen drained it thirstily, then, at Perulan's urging, poured himself another, of water this time. He'd gotten very thirsty digging outdoors all morning.

The servant-girl Perulan had mentioned a moment before entered, carrying a large china tureen, and for a while there was silence while Kellen satisfied the hunger honed by several bells of hard labor. There was hot thick vegetable soup, hefty slices of cold mutton, large chunks of golden cheese, and thick slices of warm bread with fresh butter. Perulan watched him eat, a faint approving smile on his face, but restricted himself to no more than his soup and a little cider.

"So, Master Kellen," he said when Kellen had slowed down a little, "what do you do when you aren't cleaning out cisterns for . . . former . . . writers?"

"You're *that* Perulan?" Kellen asked without thinking. He suddenly wished he'd curbed his tongue, for the older man winced, as if Kellen had spoken of something very painful. "I mean, I'm a Student, Gentlesir Perulan," he said hastily, trying to remember if it should be "gentlesir," "noblesir," or "lord." "I study."

"Just 'Perulan' if you please, Master Kellen. My family has disowned me long since, and I have no patience with empty honorifics, nor do they have any place between friends. As for study . . . it can be a broadening thing, if a bit dangerous," Perulan said. "You must be careful in your studies, Master Kellen. You might learn things you didn't wish to discover."

"I know," Kellen said, sighing. "Look, I was wondering if you could tell me . . . do you know how deep that cistern is?"

Perulan had obviously been expecting him to ask something else: his face first showed surprise, then relief. "I believe it goes down about ten feet. Certainly not much deeper."

"And . . . do you know if it feeds into a spring? Or is it solid at the bottom?"

Perulan smiled. "Quite solid, young Kellen. When I was a young man, and first bought this house, that cistern was still empty. I recall making plans to turn it into a fish pond, or something of the like, but those plans, like so many others I made as a young man, came to naught. But I think it best if you fill it in now, or people will simply come and throw more garbage into it."

"That's what I plan to do," Kellen said, relieved to have Perulan fall in so easily with his own plans. "It needs doing."

AFTER lunch, he worked for a few bells more, marking time by the distant echo of the carillons that sounded faintly over the roofs of the City, for the nearest bell tower was several streets away, and had not paid its bell tax in some time. He would have continued working far longer, but Perulan called him back into the house and insisted on giving him tea before sending him home for the day. It occurred to Kellen that the old man must be lonely, and he wondered if Perulan might be the source of information the Wild Magic had sent him to.

He wondered about that all the next day as well, while shoveling smelly black muck out of the cistern. From somewhere, Perulan had provided a bucket and wheelbarrow for his use: Kellen would fill the bucket, use it to fill the barrow, wheel the barrow to the back of the lot, and dump the contents into an ever-growing, stinking pile. Maybe the sun would dry the sludge out into something he could use. Maybe he could dig it into the ground and bury it when he dug up fresh earth to fill in the cistern.

As he worked, he wondered if it would be just too cold-blooded to *ask* Perulan what he wanted to know about the City and the lands beyond. He liked Perulan, and he didn't want to make trouble for him, and Kellen had already come to realize that there were some questions meant never to be asked—or answered.

But even without asking outright, Kellen found out some things that, just as Perulan had warned, he would have been happier not knowing.

⇁

"SO you're from a Mage family, young Kellen?" Perulan asked. "I would not have thought it. You haven't the look, as you are no doubt long tired of hearing."

Kellen choked on his lunchtime cider, managing (with an effort) to swallow decorously. "But how did you know?" he asked when he was able.

"Come come, young sir. A writer must be observant, and I was born into a Mage-family myself, as you are certainly aware. While you have a talent for hard labor, you're no laborer, and a member of a Trade family would be hard at his apprenticeship at your age. What does that leave?"

"Mages," Kellen said bitterly.

Perulan raised his eyebrows and smiled faintly.

"Ah, speak softly of our beloved rulers—or else they'll find what you love best and cherish most, and turn it to ash before your very eyes."

Kellen stared at him.

"I'm Perulan the Writer, as you know—only Perulan the Writer's last and greatest work was denied a publication license, and so it was destroyed by the High Council before his very eyes. For the good of the City, of course. It is always for the good of the City." The smile faded, and Perulan stared bleakly off into space, contemplating something Kellen couldn't see.

"Do you think it really is?" Kellen asked before he could stop himself. "How can they *know*? Aren't they just trying to—well—make all of us quiet and fat and not think, just so we'll want to keep things as they are, like them? So we won't want to even think about leaving the City? But the City isn't the only place in the world!"

"No," Perulan agreed. "There are other places—across the sea, across the forest—and they do things very differently there. To be different is not to be wrong, or even inferior. Only . . . different."

"Can you—" Kellen said, and stopped himself.

"Can I tell you about them?" Perulan asked. "Yes, and perhaps I will, if you are certain that is what you wish. But not now. Think about whether you really want to know, Kellen-of-a-Mage family, and ask me again. Perhaps you will come to dinner, and we will talk, once you have finished with my cistern."

﹏

IT was the backbreaking work of several more days, but at last Kellen had dug down to bare stone, and then filled in the cistern again. From somewhere a load of old brick appeared to greet him one morning, and on another day, an iron-bound cistern cover cut to size—Perulan's doing, Kellen supposed. Kellen tumbled the bricks into the hole, layering them in with fresh-dug clean dirt from the lot and stamping on each layer to pack it tight as he put it in. He buried the muck and trash he'd dug out of the cistern in the hole he'd dug to get the fill dirt, and stacked the bigger pieces of trash to be hauled away.

Last of all, he used the back of the shovel to bang the heavy wooden stakes that would hold the cover in place into the dirt around the edges of the cistern, then stepped back to admire his work.

No more rats, no more garbage, no more stink.

He was done.

"Excellent work, young Kellen," Perulan said. The older man came to stand beside him, gazing down at the cistern cover. It was the first time Kellen had seen Perulan leave his house. "I suppose now that your task is done, our fair neighborhood will no longer be graced with your presence?"

"I . . ." In truth, Kellen hadn't thought much past getting the cistern filled in.

"No matter," Perulan said graciously. "I think I shall not be here much longer myself. And now, the time grows late. Would you care to join me in my evening meal?"

Looking around, only now did Kellen realize that he had grown so engrossed in his task that he had not even heard the sound of Evensong Bells. In fact, he had stayed later at Perulan's house than ever before. The sun was westering, and it was already almost too dark to see. But his father wouldn't be home yet—and even if he was, what would it matter? Whether Kellen tried to do what Lycaelon wanted or not, the end result was the same: these days, it seemed, they always ended up arguing.

"Sure. I mean, I'd like that, gentlesir."

Dinner was a more elaborate meal than the lunches Kellen had enjoyed at Perulan's house, with a large hot meat pie brought from the local cookshop, roast fowl and potatoes prepared by Perulan's all-but-invisible maidservant, baked apples roasted on the hearth, and candied fruits and wine to follow.

The parlor was mellow in the golden light cast by the fat white candles in the fixture hanging over the table, and warmth radiated from the tiled hearth tucked into one corner.

"You asked me once what I knew of the world outside the City," Perulan said when the servant had cleared away the dishes and retired to the kitchen. "Would it surprise you to know that when I was a young man, I had a correspondence with, well, let us call them Folk From Away?"

Kellen stared at him, a piece of candied ginger halfway to his lips. "But how? That's not possible!" he stammered.

"Not quite impossible, merely difficult, my young Student. The Selken-folk smuggled my letters out, and smuggled my correspondents' replies back in. It can be done, with trust, and for a price—the Selken-folk have no love for the Mage

Council, and are happy to trick them if they can. And I was young and adventurous—just as you are now—and wanted to know everything about the world and all it contains.

"But—alas!—then I grew famous, and well regarded, and had more to lose than when I was a hungry young struggling writer. I thought of that and became cowardly. I stopped writing to my friends across the sea because I feared the risk of discovery."

Perulan stopped, and took a long drink from his wine cup, staring down into it broodingly. "But now . . . I no longer have anything to lose. Now, I think, I will pay my Selken friends to smuggle *me* away. It will hurt to leave Armethalieh, but if I cannot write the books I want to write, I might as well be dead, and in the face of death, exile holds no terrors."

"But—But—Why can't you just go live in the country if you don't like the City anymore?" Kellen asked, floundering to accept this torrent of new ideas. It was one thing to see someone leave, to dream of leaving himself, but to actually *talk* to someone about leaving . . .

Perulan smiled sadly, shaking his head.

"My dear young Kellen, have you *ever* heard of anyone who did? The villages exist to serve the City with their crops and their taxes and their labor, as much our beasts of burden as the horses who pull our carts. Citizens and villagers don't mix and never have, despite the foolish fables I have written. If I were to go out into the villages, the villagers would know me for a Citizen and hate me for it—and for the hope of reward, cheerfully turn me over to the Council's soldiery to be returned to the City. No. If I am to leave, I must leave Armethalieh entirely: leave the City and all its lands."

"But couldn't you just go openly?" Kellen asked. It was true that he'd never heard of anyone doing that, but surely *some* people . . .

He realized that, deep down inside, even though he had imagined leaving, buried in that daydream had been the surety of coming back someday. As much as he hated the restrictions Armethalieh placed upon its citizens, hated the thought of living the life his father had planned out for him, the City was the only home he had ever known.

Perulan laughed bitterly and patted his hand. "Dear boy! I forget how young you are! I assure you: the Council would *never* let someone go forth to bear tales to 'unknown enemies.' No, Armethalieh the Golden hoards her treasures—and her people—for always. But I hope, if the Light is kind, that there may be a way for one of her Golden Children to escape her . . ."

Kellen turned his head, distracted by a flicker of movement at the kitchen door. But when he looked, there was no one there.

"But how?" he asked, turning back and forgetting the momentary distraction. "If the Council won't *let* you go—?"

"It is best that I tell you nothing more. What you do not know, you cannot reveal, even under Truthspell, and more lives than mine are at risk upon this venture. But though we may see one another again, I think it best if we say our true good-byes now. I have enjoyed our friendship, Kellen, and allow me to offer you one last piece of advice: if you ever think to leave Armethalieh the Golden, go quickly, go far, and trust none of her citizens with your intentions."

"I won't," Kellen said, getting to his feet. "Good-bye, sir. May the Light go with you."

"And with you," Perulan said gravely.

⌒

IT was nearly midnight when Kellen reached home, for he had gone slowly, his thoughts full of his conversation with Perulan. To leave the City! It was one thing to stow away on a ship as a young man of Kellen's age, like the fellow he'd seen down at the docks. But for someone as important, as well connected, as Perulan to be contemplating it . . .

Where did they go, the ones who successfully escaped Armethalieh's golden chains of privilege? What other lands did the Selken ships trade with? What was beyond the Delfier Forest, beyond the City lands whose farms fed the City?

The Council didn't want anyone to know.

Why not? What was so bad about them? And if the places over the Sea and Beyond the Forest were so bad, why did Armethalieh *trade* with those places? Yet they did: by ship and trading caravan both.

It didn't make sense.

Nothing made sense.

The house was dark when he eased open the unlocked garden gate, carefully locking it again behind him in case someone should check in the morning. This was no time to rouse the servants. He'd remembered to bring the pick and shovel with him, and groped his way down to the gardener's cottage to put them away. He didn't think they'd been missed in the last sennight, and as long as they were back now, there shouldn't be any trouble about them having been gone in the first place.

Mission accomplished, Kellen headed up to the house. He'd better find some way to get rid of the clothes he'd been wearing all this time as well—even if he washed them, he didn't think they'd pass muster as something suitable for a son of the House of Tavadon.

HE knew something was wrong the moment he came through the servants' quarters into the main part of the house—knew without having any way to forestall whatever disaster was to come. All he could do was just walk right into it, and hope the consequences weren't too terrible.

"Don't you know that people talk?"

His father came out of his first-floor study—just like an adder out of its hole, Kellen thought unkindly—just as Kellen entered the reception chamber. Kellen froze, his hand on the panel of white marble that led to his staircase, then turned back to face his father. Lycaelon was standing in the doorway of the study, backlit by the yellow glow of candles.

"Why is it, do you suppose, that you have plenty of time to spend digging ditches and wallowing in muck but not one moment to attend to your studies?" Lycaelon asked him, in

the same voice Kellen's professors used when they asked him
a question they didn't really want an answer to.

Kellen stared at his father in dawning horror. He'd been
so focused—obsessed, really—with getting the cistern
cleared, with paying the price the Wild Magic asked, that it
hadn't occurred to him until this moment that he'd simply
disappeared for a sennight—cut his regular lessons at the
Mage College, missed his private sessions with Undermage
Anigrel, everything! What could he possibly say?

"I was busy," he muttered. "I'll do better, I promise." He
winced inwardly at the sound of his own words, knowing
they were a feeble and inadequate defense.

"You'll forgive me, Kellen, if I don't think your promises
are worth very much. Promises, excuses—all they are is evasions—evasions of your duties and responsibilities! All you
care about is yourself and your own pleasures," Lycaelon
answered scornfully.

"That's not true! You think cleaning out a clogged cistern
is a *pleasure*? It wasn't—but at least it helped someone, and
it was more constructive than sitting around repeating sigils
that I've done a hundred times already and listening to useless
lectures! You don't know me—you don't know who I am or
what I think about!" Kellen burst out angrily.

" 'Think'?"

He should have known better than to try to justify what
he'd done. Lycaelon obviously wasn't listening. He'd probably been planning his little lecture for bells now, and he was
going to deliver it intact no matter what Kellen said to him.

" 'Think'? I don't believe you *think* at all. You certainly
don't act as if you do. Don't you know that people see you—
and talk? Don't you know that everything you do reflects on
my position? Don't you know that you have a tradition to
live up to?"

Every time he tried to talk to his father, it always came
back to this: duties, responsibilities, behave like a good little
Tavadon-golem to make everything easy for the great and
powerful Arch-Mage! It was all about Lycaelon Tavadon, and
nothing about Kellen!

"Don't you *think*," Kellen shot back, angrily mimicking his father's tone, "that if you care so much about things like that you'd be better off not having a son at all? Or why don't you just *make* a son with magick, so you can get one that's exactly what you want?" He turned away, opened the panel, and ran up the stairs, ignoring his father's angry shouts to return.

Kellen slammed the door to his room behind him and leaned against it, half afraid—and half hopeful—that his father would come after him. Why couldn't they ever just *talk*? He knew his father only wanted the best for him, just as Lycaelon wanted the best for the City, but for the past few years, ever since Kellen had started studying the High Magick when he turned fourteen, it seemed they couldn't even say "good morning" without arguing about Kellen's behavior.

Not that Kellen had many opportunities to say "good morning" to his father. For as long as he could remember, Lycaelon Tavadon had been Arch-Mage of Armethalieh, spending more bells at the Council House than he did in his own home. Kellen had been raised by a succession of servants, each staying for a few years before moving on. He saw more of Undermage Anigrel than he did of his own father!

When it became clear that once again Lycaelon was not going to pursue the matter, Kellen sighed and moved away from the door. He stripped off his dirty, sweaty clothing, and gave himself an unsatisfactory sponge bath from the bowl and pitcher that stood on his night table. At least he'd gotten a good dinner at Perulan's.

It was while he was pulling his nightshirt on over his head that it occurred to him Lycaelon must have known more or less where he'd been all week—that crack about "digging ditches" had been pretty close to the mark, after all.

He frowned for a moment, and then his brow cleared. Well, Perulan had known he was from a Mage family, and had probably just been too polite to admit he knew which one. Gossip was gossip, after all, and gossip was the one thing that could run through the streets of the City of a Thousand Bells faster than a Mage-spell. Probably someone had mentioned to someone else that he was down there, and it had gotten back to his father somehow.

Mystery solved to his satisfaction, Kellen flung himself down on his bed and slept.

Chapter Seven

Magic Unmasked

The early morning sunlight woke him only a few bells later, and the music of First Morning Bells echoing through the City told him just how early it was. For a moment Kellen contemplated just pulling the covers over his head and going back to sleep, but with a deep sigh, he changed his mind. He was going to prove to his father that he wasn't the self-seeking irresponsible wilding Lycaelon seemed to think he was. He'd get up and go off to the precinct for his morning lesson with Undermage Anigrel—and get there early for once! He'd even let the Undermage bore him silly with all the dustiest cantrips in all the High Magick repertoire without a single yawn of complaint. He'd apply himself to his studies, he'd pay attention . . .

And maybe—just once—his father would admit he was proud of him.

For once, Kellen paid attention to his clothes, dressing with particular care in his best green velvet day-tunic and cream linen undertunic, a new pair of low kidskin City boots, and a pair of fawn trousers so form-fitting they were *almost* hose. He added his usual belt, and after a moment's thought, added two items he'd never worn before, an elaborately ornamented pencase and matching coinpouch—Naming Day gifts from his father, never worn until now. He transferred some personal items from his old pouch and case to the new one— his pens and knife, some small money, the unicorn knife-rest that he carried as a luck-piece—ran a comb through his unruly hair, glanced at the result in the mirror, and sighed. Time for another haircut, he supposed. Well, Father would have nothing to complain of in his clothes, at least.

Kellen's hopeful mood lasted until he reached the kitchens. Though breakfast would have been laid out in the sunny morning parlor for his father, Kellen was usually up too late for it, and made a habit of picking over the remains of the dishes after they'd been returned to the kitchen. The servants turned a blind eye to this particular intrusion into their domain, as it made less work for them than setting out a second breakfast service would, something Kellen would be well within his rights to demand. And as such a demand would reflect directly upon Lycaelon's own consequence as master of Tavadon House, it would have been enforced, unlike so many of Kellen's other wishes.

Seeing the butler's sideboard empty, Kellen realized that for once he was too early for leftovers and was about to retreat when he heard the servants talking around the corner.

"—such a shame about that poor man! And him a writer! Criminal, it was."

He wasn't sure who was speaking; thanks to Lycaelon's efforts, Kellen had only the vaguest notions of the size and composition of the household staff. He heard the clink of cups and plates, and knew that the upper servants must be having their breakfast during this lull in the day's activities; he knew that the servants ate before their masters. Kellen pulled back farther into the shadows, out of sight—but not out of earshot—of the gossiping servants.

"Drowned at midnight. It's like something out of a play," a woman said, sounding pleased.

"Well, what I want to know is, what was Lord Perulan *doing* down at the docks at midnight? Nothing decent—you may take that from me." Kellen recognized the voice of the house's butler.

Perulan—*dead?* The servants were unlikely to be misinformed—house-servant gossip was generally a fast and reliable source of information about everything that went on in the City.

And he knew, he *knew*, that this was no coincidence.

It's my fault.

Every time he used those three Books of the Wild Magic, every time he cast a spell, something happened that just seemed to make Kellen's life darker and more uncertain. If he'd never met Perulan, never talked to Perulan, maybe the writer would have gotten over his loss. Maybe he would have decided it was worth writing again, and gone back to his wondertales. He would have stayed safe in his little house, and not gone down to the docks for a reason Kellen could well guess. And he'd still be alive.

That does it. That's it. I'm never, ever casting another Wild Magic spell!

He turned to leave the kitchen, but the thought of running into his father somewhere in the house stopped him. If he saw Lycaelon now, Kellen knew, he'd only say something unforgiveable. His father would never understand what it was about Perulan's death that upset him so.

You burned his book—and he killed himself!

No. He *couldn't* say that to his father. His father had only been doing his job.

I have to get out of here. I have to calm down. I have to think.

Almost running, Kellen hurried through the kitchen, past the startled servants, out through the garden, and out through the garden gate into the street.

⌐

IN the sunny breakfast parlor, Arch-Mage Lycaelon Tavadon sat over his morning tea, wondering, without any real expectation that it would come to pass, if his errant son would come to join him at the morning meal.

He should have dealt with the boy firmly last night, but there had been no time. He had been needed at the Council House to oversee the Working, and once it was over, had spent the rest of a long sleepless night brooding over the current problem before the Council. And now Kellen was lying abed as usual. Just as well, Lycaelon supposed, for he had much to occupy his mind this day.

At dawn, a messenger had come to let him know that the Working in the matter of the writer Perulan had run its course. Just as Volpiril had suggested, a spy had been set in Perulan's house the very day Perulan had come before the Council. A serving-girl; men of Perulan's sort never took any notice of what their servants did, and the girl had been able to listen and hear much in the days that followed. She had been able to inform the Council that Perulan meant to flee the City; to escape by ship through the help of contacts cultivated in former years. The Council had been given no choice but to act.

To give water form and then life was a difficult business, requiring both great skill and great power, but the High Council of Armethalieh possessed both in abundance. They had sent a water golem to follow Perulan once he reached the docks, to make sure he never spoke with any of the Selken captains . . . or indeed with anyone else, ever again.

Once it had completed that grisly task, it had left Perulan's body where it was sure to be found, for if Perulan were simply to vanish, there were sure to be others infected with his sickness who would believe he had managed to successfully escape. And that could not be allowed.

No one escaped from Armethalieh. Even those few fools who managed to bribe the Selken-folk to smuggle them out—and Lycaelon knew that there were a few such reckless and determined folk, every year—would mysteriously sicken and die within a few moonturns, at the very most, after they had passed beyond the magickal barrier at the edge of the harbor. The spell was a simple one, renewed each moonturn at the same time their power was harvested through the exchange of the City Talisman each citizen wore about his or her neck.

And should anyone be rash enough to try to flee overland—a far more difficult proposition to keep secret—there was no need for a similar spell upon the Western Gates. The farmers in the surrounding villages well knew the terrible price of doing aught but holding such a fugitive prisoner to face the City's swift justice. Escape by land was even less possible than escape by sea.

No, Armethalieh's greatest treasure—her citizens—were hers and hers alone. Hers to keep. Forever.

But with all his heart, Lycaelon wished there had been some other way than the unpleasant course of action he had been forced to permit. Why couldn't Perulan have taken the opportunities the Council had given him to live out his days in peace and happiness here among folk who loved and understood him? Armethalieh was the best place in the world, his home, filled with people who cared for him. Even at the last, his family would have willingly taken him back. The loss of a single book was no great matter—he should have looked upon the experience for what it was, a necessary correction to his thinking, a lesson in responsibility! Then he could have returned to penning the bucolic tales that were the proper exercise of his talent!

But instead of seeking healing, Perulan had hugged the sickness of his despair to himself like an addiction and let it destroy him. He'd turned away from everything good, becoming a danger to himself and to others—like a mad dog. And like a mad dog, finally Perulan had to be put down for the good of the City.

And Kellen had been with Perulan in the last sennight of his life. Only Lycaelon's influence had kept Kellen from being brought immediately before the Council to be questioned about his knowledge of Perulan's intentions, and that only because Lycaelon promised to handle the matter himself. But influence—even the influence of the Arch-Mage of Armethalieh—could only extend so far. It would be a grave transgression of the oaths he had sworn in defense of the City for Lycaelon to blind himself to evil beneath his own roof out of misplaced familial loyalty.

That, as much as anything else, had kept him from acting last night, dearly though he had wished to strike the boy down for his unthinking insolence. He owed House Tavadon better than that. He must be strong. He must be clear-sighted and calm. It was his duty—both as a father, and as Arch-Mage—to consider the matter carefully before he acted.

Was Kellen going down the same dark road of anarchy and chaos that Perulan had? The boy was young yet, but it was also true that Kellen's behavior had become increasingly erratic and disrespectful of late—not only to his father, but to his tutor, and to others, highly placed and deserving of his respect and deference, as well.

I have given him every advantage—every warning—and it has done no good! Lycaelon thought; his sense of anguish tempered by his sense that justice *needed* to be dispensed, regardless of whom it fell upon.

In fact, rather than seeing the error of his ways and moderating his wild, improper behavior, Kellen only grew worse—actively seeking out Perulan only a few days after the writer had been censured by the Council, constantly wandering the streets of Low Town (to meet with who-knew-what other disreputable elements of society?), neglecting his studies in a fashion that showed his utter contempt for the Armethaliehan way of life. The boy seemed intent on rejecting everything about his upbringing—for surely, if Kellen felt he could not confide in his father or his magickal tutor, he would at least seek counseling from a Priest of the Light?

But Lycaelon had made inquiries among the Priesthood, and none of them reported speaking with his son.

There must be a reason!

All of Lycaelon's life was built on a foundation of reason, and truth, and Law. If Kellen was behaving in this heretical fashion, there must be a reason for it. Lycaelon would make one last attempt to discover what it was before resorting to stronger measures.

Kellen would certainly still be in his bed at this bell. He would go, rouse the boy out of bed, and get to the bottom of this once and for all, for both their sakes.

And for the good of the City.

⏤

BUT when Lycaelon reached Kellen's room, Kellen was already gone. Lycaelon stood for a moment in the middle of the teenaged disorder—Kellen having forbidden the servants access to his rooms a year and more before—and stared at the empty bed, pondering what to do.

Surely, if there was a clue to the soul-sickness that had befallen his son, it would be here.

Hesitantly, and then with increasing fervor, Lycaelon searched his son's room. Though he was thorough, opening every drawer, shuffling through every paper and book, he found nothing inappropriate, and after a tenth-chime of searching Lycaelon realized that this was only a sign that things were worse than he thought. No rude, high-spirited young man slowly turning bad—like Kellen Tavadon—left no signs of the cause of his dissipation! Where was the stash of brandy bottles; the hidden box of dream-smoke herb so beloved of the laboring classes; the stash of gambling winnings or record of debts; the bundle of perfumed love letters from some cozening lowborn female looking to snare a Mageborn son? *Something* was at the root of Kellen's increasingly antisocial behavior, and if the boy was taking such pains to hide it, that something must be very bad indeed—worse than anything Lycaelon had thought of so far. Kellen's room had been his own as a boy, and Lycaelon was familiar with its "secret hiding places," but so far, every hiding place he'd found was empty, or obviously hadn't been used for years, containing such outgrown boyish treasures as dried frogs and old birds' nests crumbling away to dust.

At last Lycaelon did as he knew he ought to have done from the first. He called upon the power stored in his Arch-Mage's Talisman and cast the strongest Illusion-Dispelling Spell he knew, one that would counter every form of magic designed to conceal or misdirect, one that would bring all hidden things to light.

He spoke the Word that held the whole of the spell in concentrated form, and for a moment Time itself seemed to slow, as the ripples of the spell spread outward from Lycaelon, washing over every object within its radius, making the outlines of every object appear momentarily sharper and more real. When the spell settled, Lycaelon looked around.

The old bookshelf, filled with ancient tattered picture books from Kellen's nursery days, drew his attention strongly. With a sinking heart, he went to it and riffled through the volumes there one more time. Tucked casually in among the outworn relics of childhood were three small books.

Filled with dread—knowing already what he would find—Lycaelon reached out and picked them up. He knew them by reputation, knew of their unclean glamouries that kept all but their intended victim from seeing their true nature, and kept even that victim from seeing his danger until far too late.

The Book of Moon.

The Book of Sun.

The Book of Stars.

Lycaelon felt his heart swell with grief and fury. This was far beyond anything a father, no matter how indulgent, could overlook or ignore. He must bring these Books before the Council at once, and tell his brother Mages all.

For the good of the City.

⌒

THIS was, bar none, the most soothing and engrossing class of Kellen's studies. *Maths* . . . he thought with a feeling of comfort as he settled into his seat.

He was on time; the rest were late, and took their places with an air of resignation. Most of Kellen's fellow Students hated Maths. At one point, Kellen had, too. It had seemed only one more set of things to learn by rote for no reason. But that was before the lessons progressed beyond simple Maths to the elegance of geometry.

Here, as nowhere else, he found something that made absolute sense, followed clear rules, where A plus B always equaled C and the equation could be applied to the ordinary world; a science that described the visible world and could be used to *do* things. Useful things.

It was the one class he seldom skipped. And, as was all too often the case in his life, it was the one class that was held only once a fortnight. The instructor was the least-regarded Mage in the entire Mage College; an old, old man, an Undermage all of his life, an Undermage still, who would die an Undermage. His robes were plain and uncared for, and though clean, were threadbare about the hem; his eyes were distant and a little sad beneath his heavy white brows. There was a dispirited air about him, a sense that he had given up long ago, and was merely marking time here, teaching the one thing he knew well to Students and Apprentices who did not value it, until the Council would permit him to retire to a little set of rooms somewhere.

And die.

Not that anyone would ever notice. Possibly the old Mage himself might not notice.

But he was very good at teaching Maths. It probably was the only thing he *was* good at. And even if Lycaelon wasn't impressed by Kellen's high marks in the subject, the old man seemed to revive just a little whenever his eyes fell on his prize pupil.

Kellen had thrown himself into work on the hardest problem they'd ever been set the moment he had arrived in class—because while he was working on the pure *rightness* of the puzzle, he didn't have to think about anything that had been happening to him. He could forget his father, forget the Wild Magic and the three Books, forget what had happened to poor Perulan. Everything between the covers of his workbook was a matter of figures, line, and angle, and there was only ever one right answer.

But his concentration was interrupted when he was only halfway through the complex calculation by a heavy hand falling on his shoulder.

Startled, he looked up, for the old Mage had never gripped his shoulder like *that* before.

It wasn't his instructor.

The burly, sallow-faced fellow in the uniform tabard of a servant of the Council looked down at him with an unreadable face.

Kellen clamped down on his jolt of fear.

It wasn't just the lack of expression in the man's face that made him unreadable, it was the feeling that this man had only a trifle more life and thought in him than one of the Council's stone golems . . .

"Kellen Tavadon?" the man asked, completely without inflection except for the slight rise at the end of the two words that made it a question instead of a statement.

Kellen wondered what the man would do if he denied being himself; considered doing just that for one fleeting moment, then nodded, reluctantly.

"You are summoned to attend the High Council at the third bell of afternoon."

By now the rest of his class was staring at him—and at the stony-faced apparition that had delivered the Council's message. It was the most attention he'd gotten from his fellow Students in moonturns. Some of them were whispering to each other. The poor old Mage just looked confused.

"The third bell," the man repeated.

"I—understand," Kellen managed to say.

A cold hand closed around his heart, and a cold finger traced its way down his spine. The Council! This could only be Lycaelon's work. So he was to be punished for last night's rebellion after all.

"The third bell." With a *thud,* the messenger let fall something on Kellen's workbook. Kellen picked it up; it was a heavy brass plate engraved with the Council sigil, the sign that he had been called before them. Having said his piece and delivered his burden, the Council's retainer turned on his heel and left. Kellen picked up the little brass plate and shoved it into his pocket, then tried to go back to his Maths problem, but he had completely lost the ability to concentrate.

What do they want? Surely my having an argument with Father is no matter for the Council?

Unless Father makes it one . . .

The rest of the members of the class murmured to each other as he bent his head over his paper.

The sound of the voices, though—there was nothing in their tone to warn him that *they* had any notion why he was being summoned.

But he did. Oh, yes, *he* did. He just didn't want to even consider it.

But he had to; even if you were the Arch-Mage of Armethalieh, you didn't hail your son in front of the High Council just to deliver a lecture on filial duty. Besides, for Lycaelon that would be tantamount to admitting that he was a failure at bringing his offspring to heel, and Lycaelon could not bear admit he was a failure at *anything*.

No, there was only one thing that Kellen could think of that would cause the High Council to haul him in for a confrontation.

Wild Magic.

The Books.

Father found the Books.

After all, Lycaelon had known he'd been talking to Perulan, and that meant the Arch-Mage was keeping a watch on Kellen somehow. If he'd learned that, he surely would have learned other things.

Or he decided to search my room.

He *knew* he shouldn't have left early this morning! If he'd *been* there, surely Lycaelon wouldn't even have thought of searching the room—or if he had, he'd have left it to the servants, who would, as usual, have found nothing.

And though the three Books could disguise their nature from ordinary servants, they probably couldn't hold up their glamourie against the magic of the Arch-Mage of Armethalieh.

So Lycaelon knew about the Books, and if *he* knew, the whole High Council knew. Lycaelon would never keep something so illegal, so potentially scandalous, secret.

But if anyone here at the Mage College had any idea why Kellen was being called up before the High Council, they wouldn't be whispering, they'd be getting out of their seats and trying to get out of the room before the dangerous criminal noticed them.

So no one here knows, and the High Council has decided not to say anything yet, Kellen thought with a faint pang of relief. Rumors usually spread through the Mage College like wildfire, so there wasn't a rumor. Yet.

Which doesn't mean a thing. The High Council was perfectly capable of being closemouthed when it suited them.

Kellen gave up on trying to concentrate, or even pretend to, shoved away from his desk, and stood up to leave. The whispering stopped, and every eye in the room was riveted on him. Even though the appointed time was bells away— probably calculated that way by Lycaelon, to allow his son to stew and fret until the appointed time—everyone knew that a summons before the High Council had to be answered immediately. In fact, they were probably wondering why he hadn't gone already.

Kellen stalked out of the classroom, keeping his back rigid and his head held high with a bravado that was entirely feigned.

THE other Students and his teacher would probably assume that he would go straight to the Council House to cool his heels in one of the waiting rooms and reflect upon his sins. That, however, was not what Kellen had in mind.

He stopped at his locker—probably for the last time—to deposit his books and his robes. He spared a moment of thanks that today he was dressed in his best clothes beneath the all-concealing Student Blues: to think that only this morning he'd been planning to start afresh, to impress his father and Anigrel with his devotion to the ways of the Mage life, to study and conform and be a good son of House Tavadon!

He'd been so stupid.

For the first time ever, he went openly to the harbor, glaring defiance at the Watch as he crossed the street into the harbor district.

The Constables didn't try to stop him, but perhaps because he was dressed as ostentatiously as any City noble, they thought he was there on some legitimate business. The more fools they.

He stalked across the street and plunged in among the offices of the various shipping companies and merchants, giving the Constables about as much attention as he would a piece of statuary. His pencase and coinpouch bounced against his thigh as he strode angrily along—oh, he looked a proper son of House Tavadon today. All he lacked was a cloak and sword, and a pair of ornamental gloves thrust through his belt to be the image of a proper petty lordling. And who cared?

He did. If there was something Kellen knew he didn't want to be, it was that.

When he reached the wharves themselves, Kellen took a moment to simply breathe in the fresh salt air and get his bearings. He wanted to remember this day clearly—every sight, every sound, every smell. After all, this might well be the last time he would be able to come here.

Might? That's a virtual certainty. If I'm lucky, I'll only be confined to my room for the rest of the year. If I'm not, it'll be the rest of my life . . .

There were several ships in today, and more waiting outside the harbor to come in; their sails tacking back and forth just over the horizon. It was a busy day, one that usually meant a lot of work for the High Council . . . which meant that the High Council considered *his* situation to be a serious one, worth interrupting their day over.

Not good.

Kellen picked a spot out of the way of anyone working around the ships, and watched a new vessel sail in and tie up. He was full of restless energy, discontent, and a sick undercurrent of fear that he tried hard to ignore. Never had he felt so much raw envy for the Selken-folk, or for the few nameless Armethaliehans who managed to escape on their ships. He watched the half-naked sailors bringing a ship skillfully in to its mooring, scrambling up into the rigging and furling the sails, heaving ropes over the side and tying up to the piers. Wood creaked; the wood of the dock, and of the ship. Men called to each other, up in the rigging, and a group of them, hauling on a rope wrapped around a capstan, chanted in unison. Their captain shouted orders at them, punctuated by strange, wild oaths, and waves splashed against the pilings and the sides of the ship. The air smelled of fish, tar, sun-baked wood, and salt, with an undercurrent of strange scents too faint to be identified.

On another ship, a little farther down the dock, another crew was unloading their ship's cargo. They traded insults with the crew of the new arrival while Kellen watched and listened, and tried not to think too hard about how much he wished he could just saunter aboard and sail away with them when they left.

I don't suppose there's a chance that Father would disinherit me and let me go with them... Kellen thought wistfully.

No. Not Lycaelon. The Arch-Mage's motto should have been, "What I have, I hold." No matter what Kellen did, Lycaelon would never let him go.

The anger and discontent swelled in him until he thought he would burst from it. Probably the only thing that *did* keep him from bursting was the fear he felt inside . . . for he knew now that there was no place for him in the City unless he conformed to every one of his father's wishes. He could never escape what Lycaelon wanted, not even if he tried to renounce his own Mageborn talents and turn common laborer. No matter what he did, Lycaelon would have him followed and brought back, and once again, there would be the edict: *Obey.* If he didn't do so of his own free will, he'd be forced into it.

Conform—or—

Well, he'd butted heads with the "or" many times in his seventeen years, but this time the "or" had more than just his father behind it. This time he was going to face the entire High Council. And although he had no doubt that whatever they decided to do with him would be what Lycaelon had already decided, *their* edict would be enforced by Constables, Council retainers, and if necessary, other means. And the High Council had a great many options under that last category.

One of the farther ships pulled away from the dock even as he watched, and began its slow, graceful tack toward the harbor mouth. Its sails filled with a Mage-conjured breeze, belling out like great white wings, carrying its crew away from Armethalieh and out to freedom.

Freedom that *he* was never going to taste.

The ship passed through the shimmering curtain of magick, its own outline shivering a little as if seen through a heat haze. And at that moment, Noontide Bells rang out. Kellen felt a surge of guilty nausea. He just had time to get to the Council House before the appointed hour.

Glumly, he trudged out to meet his fate.

⌒

THE Council House was at the opposite side of the City from the docks, facing the Delfier Gate in the west, and Kellen realized, as he trudged up the almost-empty avenue that led to the Council House and the gate beyond, that he had never actually seen the Delfier Gate open. Citizens were not encouraged to linger near the gates when the farm carts and trade caravans were moving in and out—not that citizens were encouraged to linger in the Mage Quarter in the first place.

Not for the first time, Kellen wondered what it would be like to go through those gates and take the road that led into the forest and what lay beyond.

Perulan had said that no citizen had, that none *could*. But Perulan had been referring to trying to take shelter with the villagers out there. What if someone decided to live out in the forest itself? Could anyone be found who really wanted to hide out there?

Don't be an idiot, he scolded himself. *You aren't exactly a woods-wise forester out of a wondertale. How, exactly, would you live out there? What would you eat? Roots and berries? Have you ever even seen a berry that wasn't already picked and in a basket?*

Crumbs, he hadn't even ever *cooked* for himself. Just how did he think he was going to survive in a forest?

But, oh, the idea was so tempting . . .

Anywhere but here, Kellen thought to himself. *Anywhere has GOT to be better than here!*

━━▶

THE Council House was a tall, round white marble building with a domed and gilded roof, and it was *much* bigger on the inside than it appeared on the outside. Magick, of course. A little glamourie to let it look important and imposing, but not *too* important or imposing, of course. Kellen's teachers had explained that this was to ensure that every Citizen felt free to come before the Council, whether of his own will or if summoned. Now Kellen wondered if there was another reason for the spells entirely.

To keep the ordinary citizen from knowing just how little freedom he truly has? Or to keep him from realizing just how much power over him the Mages have?

Both, probably.

It was as if—now, when it was too late to do him any good—fear suddenly made Kellen able to think of the questions he'd never been able to even think of before.

The gleaming bronze doors, ornamented with the portraits of the greatest Arch-Mages of the past, were guarded by two stone golems, seven feet tall and looking just like the animated polished black granite statues that they were.

The Mages of the High Council preferred golems as guardians. Any jumped-up merchant could hire a small army of human guards and spear-carriers, but no one but a Mage could have a golem to guard his door. And besides, nothing short of being shattered into a hundred thousand bits would stop a golem in the course of its duty. If that duty was to rend interlopers into component parts, well, too bad for the interlopers if they hadn't hired a Mage who'd come prepared with counterspells (assuming anyone could find a Mage who would work against his fellow Mages) or brought a big contingent of followers with stone-breaking hammers.

The golems allowed Kellen to pass unmolested when he held up the Council sigil he was sent with his summons. If passing between the stone mastiffs at Tavadon House made his flesh creep, walking between the two utterly silent human-shaped statues, their eyes glittering malevolently at him as he entered the gilded door, made every hair on his body stand up.

Once inside, the door swung shut behind him with a thunderous *boom*. It had been dark and shadowy when the door opened, but now the place was flooded with light, and he blinked in surprise.

He was standing inside the Council chamber.

How had he gotten into the Council chamber from the main door? When he'd been here before, at the age of twelve, when he was first made a full citizen, he'd come with a gaggle of his Mageborn year-mates. Then they'd passed by the door of the Council chamber, and the Council chamber had been at the end of a long corridor, *not* right inside the main door. This time, magick had brought him straight to this room, without passing through any of the intervening spaces. Why? Did his father not want anyone to see him but the High Council? Then why go to the trouble of tracking him down at his lesson and presenting the summons in public in front of all his classmates?

To overawe me, Kellen thought sourly, unimpressed. *To make sure I know what they're capable of—as if I didn't know that already.*

He looked around. White marble walls, a black and white marble floor; facing him at the far end of the room was the High Council sitting at a high horseshoe-shaped black marble table, their aides standing behind their chairs.

High up so they can look down upon their victims, he

thought. And he shuddered, frightened in spite of all of his attempts at bravado. Was this what poor Perulan had faced, in defense of his book? *He was braver than I thought. . . .*

Arch-Mage Lycaelon, tall, saturnine, and imposing in his robes of state, stared down at his son, his face as expressionless as those of the stone golems outside, but his eyes glittering just as dangerously.

"Kellen Tavadon!" he said, his voice echoing hollowly in the vast chamber. "You have been summoned here by the High Council on a matter of gravest concern to all good citizens of the City. Step forward!"

Much as he would have liked to disobey, Kellen knew better than to try. Reluctantly, he walked across that vast expanse of black and white marble until he stood just below the dais.

Lycaelon glared down at his son for a moment, looking as if he'd never seen him before, then pointed a monitory finger at him. "Kellen Tavadon! Three forbidden Books were found in your quarters. Do you deny that they are your possessions?"

Lycaelon's voice boomed and echoed in a most imposing fashion; even though Kellen knew it was all a trick of acoustics and clever architecture, it still made him want to grovel.

But he was too overcome with the nightmare feeling that his worst fears were about to be realized to even make the attempt.

For the offending Books were brought forth by another golem, a smaller one this time. It was scarcely six feet tall—about his own height—but it was no less intimidating for all that; its feet clattered like steel-shod hooves against the marble floor, and he could see the chessboard reflection of the floor against its highly polished grey skin. In its hands were three small shabby books. Kellen felt himself grow sick with dread; he had no difficulty in recognizing the Books that the golem carried. *The Book of Sun, The Book of Moon,* and *The Book of Stars,* his three finds, that had hidden their nature from all eyes but his.

Or at least, they had until now.

Father searched my room. And he used magick to do it.
Just as Kellen had feared.

"I see by the guilt and shame on your face that these are yours," Lycaelon said with disgust and utter contempt. "Where did you get them?"

Kellen clamped his mouth shut. There wasn't much he could do right now, but at least he wasn't going to get that poor old fellow in the Low Market in trouble—not when he knew very well that Lycaelon would make some sort of scapegoat out of him.

Instead, he just stared at the marble at his feet. He would have *liked* to have stared defiantly into his father's eyes, but he knew that if he did that, his father would know just how to get every bit of information he wanted out of him.

"Speak!" Lycaelon roared, his voice echoing in the chill room. "Be aware, we will find the criminal that supplied them to you! Was it Perulan?"

Kellen stared at his own boots. *That* was a thought that hadn't occurred to him. And they couldn't hurt Perulan any more than they already had. *He was Mageborn too. That'll stick in their throats.* He recognized most of the faces behind the dais from his father's infrequent entertainments: Volpiril, Lycaelon's particular enemy; Isas and Harith, who his father considered spineless allies; and the other nine, any of whom would be glad to step into the Arch-Mage's seat and probably saw today as a stepping-stone to that end.

"What if it was?" he replied sullenly, still staring at the floor. "What are you going to do? Dig him up and use nec- romancy on him?"

A gasp from his left told him that he'd struck a nerve. Necromancy was as forbidden as Wild Magic, if not more so. He wondered if they would have tried it, maybe one or two of them, in secret . . . if *he* hadn't said something about it. Now they wouldn't dare. Not with the other ears in the room, their aides, and servants, and the ears that were prob- ably outside, pressed to the door.

"If you hurry," he added nastily, "he probably won't smell *too* much or lose *too* many body parts while you question him. Of course, in this heat, you never know—"

"Enough!" Lycaelon roared, going red and white by turns. "Wretched boy! Do not presume on our patience, and confine your speech to answering our questions! Have you been practicing this foul perversion called Wild Magic?"

He *could* claim that he hadn't, and unless they had someone using a Truthspell on him, they'd never know any differently. He *could* claim that Perulan had given him the Books at their last meeting, and that he hadn't had time to look at them yet.

But if he did that, they'd just take the Books and destroy them, punish him *anyway,* and aside from being punished, nothing else about his life would change. *Aside* from being punished? What was he thinking? From this moment on, he'd probably have a watcher with him every moment, waking and sleeping! But if he didn't—

You wanted something that would make your father disinherit you, didn't you? Well, this is probably it. Your one chance to get on a ship and escape.

And besides, they probably had someone casting a Truthspell on him anyway.

Better to remain silent about it, though—not confess, but not deny it either.

He raised his eyes to his father's face and summoned as much defiance as he could. "What do *you* think?" he asked, keeping his voice even with a great effort.

Lycaelon began to turn a striking shade of cerise.

"Boy," interrupted Lord-Mage Vilmos, "Wild Magic is anathema for a good reason. It is totally unpredictable. It offers you your desires, but grants them in its own twisted fashion—affecting not only you, not only those you know, but innocent parties who have never met you and *certainly* do not deserve to be caught up in your spells and have their lives ruined by your foul meddling."

Perulan, Kellen thought, and suppressed a wince. Was it his fault that Perulan was dead?

"It is a perverted form of *true* magick," Vilmos continued, managing to sound both angry and pompous at the same time.

"It requires no study, no discipline, no thought at all, thus appealing to inferior persons of inferior intellect and no sense of proper responsibility."

That stung. And Kellen, goaded, replied just as angrily. "Inferior by *your* standards, maybe! Just because they don't want to waste their lives learning to lick your boots for a taste of what *you've* got! I don't think so! And I don't think that the mere fact that Wild Magic isn't predictable was *ever* a good reason to outlaw it then, or to ban it now! This place could do with a little less *predictability!* Maybe it would stop being a stagnant suck-hole that chokes the life out of anything that's new and good!"

The startled and offended glares he got from every live creature in the room would have been funny if the situation hadn't been so serious. This was not what the Mages in general and his father in particular wanted to hear from him— they had expected him to be terrified and penitent.

Well, I'm not! And they can damn well deal with it! He felt energized and alive in a way he hadn't been for longer than he could remember. He felt ready to take them *all* on, singly or together! Stupid, hidebound old fools, it was *their* fault Perulan was dead, not his, and how many other people did they kill or ruin every day, refusing to change, refusing to see what was right in front of them? A fire built in his gut, and he matched them glare for glare, prepared to say and do anything to wipe those looks of smug superiority off their faces.

"Maybe I haven't done much of any kind of magick," he snarled, "but I've read all three Wild Magic Books from cover to cover. Have any of you? Do you really know what it is that you've outlawed, or are you just flapping and squawking like a lot of mocker-birds, repeating the decisions of a bunch of people afraid of their own shadows, people dead so long that you don't even remember their names?" He snorted derisively. "Mocker-birds! You aren't even that! You're a bunch of old hens, cackling and shrieking about nothing because every other old hen is cackling 'Danger! Danger!' at the top of her lungs!"

Mage Isas was sitting there with such a stunned look on his face that Kellen wondered if he was about to fall out of his chair. Harith worked his mouth, but no sound came out.

The rest were various shades of interesting colors, from white to purple, his own father included.

"And just what is wrong with being unpredictable, with change, with innovation?" he flung at them. "Just why is it that everybody has to be *protected* all the time? Last time I looked, the rest of the world didn't need all of that protection, and they were getting along just fine!"

Finally Mage Breulin managed to get to his feet, his stiff silver beard waggling with the force of his indignation. "*You* don't see any reason, do you, you mutinous young puppy? And of course, you are so very learned, you who cannot even produce an adequate understanding of the history of the City, much less that of the world!"

How am I supposed to have an understanding of the history of the world when you don't let me see it? Kellen thought angrily. "You—" he began.

"I *have* an answer for you, insolent brat—Wild Magic is the magick of chaos and anarchy; using it brings down the darkness of confusion, and there is no room for anarchy and confusion in a civilized world!" Mage Breulin had the wind in his sails now, and was prepared to run down anything in his path. "Where there is chaos, evil finds a way in, as it did before. No one who dares to practice Wild Magic can remain untainted by evil!"

And you've got every incentive to lie to me, and none to tell me the truth. "You don't know that!" Kellen shouted back. "There's a whole world outside the City, and I bet *some* of them know Wild Magic! And most of them don't give a toss about *High* Magick—look at the Selken-folk! They do without you just fine, and they can't all be evil, or you'd never even allow the little trickle of trade with them that you've got! You're just afraid that if you let people see there's a different way possible, they'll decide they can do very nicely without you, and you'll all be left to have to make an honest living for a change!"

"*Enough!*" Lycaelon bellowed, the acoustics of the place giving *his* voice far more strength than Kellen's. "We aren't here to listen to the ignorant nonsense of children. Kellen! You will either make a public apology, personally burn the books, and renounce your wayward behavior, or—you *will* face Banishment! Not mere disinheritance, you miserable, ignorant brat—though, by the Light, I swear I *should* disinherit you no matter how sincere your apology—but *Outlawry*, you puling whelp! To be cast out through the Delfier Gate into the forest with nothing but the clothes on your back and provisions for a single day!"

Lycaelon's face was so suffused with anger it had become a mask indistinguishable from the golems' carved faces. "Light save me, would that I had never had a child at all, would that you had died with your mother, would that *she* had died in infancy, rather than spawn *you!*"

Kellen could hardly recognize his own father in this rigid, unyielding, intolerant demagogue, thundering down judgment as if he thought he was a god—

Right, then, Kellen thought furiously. *You wish I'd never been born, well so do I! I'd rather starve to death in the forest than eat another bite of food at your table!*

"Kiss my foot," Kellen sneered, in a voice he hardly recognized as his own. "You don't want me? Well, I don't want *you,* old man. I'd rather have a wolf for a father." He thrust out his chin, and crossed his arms over his chest. "Go ahead. Banish me."

Lycaelon barked a single word in the tongue of the High Magick, and before Kellen could wonder what it meant, his arms were seized from behind. And in the next moment, he was pulled off his feet and dragged out of the Council chamber by two of the stone golems.

And behind him, as the doors closed, he could hear the chamber erupt into a tumult of noise as all the members of the Council began to shout at once.

⟶

KELLEN staggered forward, thrown off-balance as the golems thrust him through the open doorway. He'd thought the room beyond would be larger, for some reason, and as he fumbled against the far wall of the cell, too stunned to quite understand where he was, he heard the door of the cell close behind him with an awful finality, cutting off most of the light.

There was no point in crying out in protest. The golems lacked the power to answer him.

In fury and outrage—the only things keeping his growing despair at bay—Kellen whirled and stared at the six-inch square opening in the door. Its grill admitted the unwavering pale blue Magelight of the corridor, providing the only light in his cell.

He stood as rigidly still as if he were made of stone himself, listening to the clatter of the golem's footsteps as they walked away, slowly rubbing his arms where they had gripped him. Hard enough to bruise, not hard enough to break bone. Not quite. But it had hurt, and the pain had shocked him in a way that nothing else had, not even hearing about Perulan's death. No one had ever manhandled him before; not even his father. Punishment had always meant being confined to his room on a diet of nourishing gruel and water. The implied violence in the golems' treatment of him caught him right in the gut.

The footsteps faded away, and slowly Kellen became aware that the only sound was his own shallow frightened breathing. He forced himself to move, to take a step, to breathe deeply, and to see what he could of his surroundings.

The cell was even smaller than he'd thought. Smooth grey stone, a cubicle a bit less than eight feet square, a stone bench at one end, all with the perfect seamlessness of Magecrafting. When Kellen looked up, the ceiling was lost in darkness, too far away to see. A cell—and not a Mage's meditation cell, either!

This was a prison cell. So there were cells beneath the Council House to house people the Council deemed inconvenient. Another thing to mar the pretty picture the High Council painted for the people of Armethalieh of how things worked. How many people before him had stood in this very spot? Kellen wondered. What had been *their* crimes—and what had happened to them?

Reflexively, his hand sought his golden City Talisman for comfort, but when he touched it, he recoiled as if he'd been burned. No. Not after what Anigrel had told him about the Talismans and their *real* purpose.

He forced himself to take a step, to turn his back on the door. The Council—his *father*—wanted him to recant, to humiliate himself in public, to help them destroy the first breath of fresh air the City had seen in a thousand years, to say he'd been wrong to study the three Books of the Wild Magic. To go back to them and be a good little Kellen-golem and do whatever he was told, and believe whatever they told him to believe.

But he hadn't been wrong in what he'd done. Kellen knew he hadn't. And he wouldn't say he had. *Lycaelon searched my room. He used a spell to find those Books—he had to have! If anyone's done something wrong, it's him!* Wasn't he, wasn't everyone entitled to privacy? Wasn't he old enough to make up his own mind about the world? *Everyone says that Armethalieh is a city of Law—but where's the Law in the things that the Council's done lately? The Mages live off the citizens like leeches, they destroyed Perulan, and even if they didn't kill him they put him into a state where he went where he would get into trouble and they probably knew he would! How many other people have they destroyed? They do what they want to because they can, that's all. That's the way it's always been.*

Let them Banish me if that's what they want now. I won't play their games anymore.

It was an easy vow to make, and a harder one to keep in the forefront of his mind as the time stretched on, seamlessly, and with no way to mark its passing, down here in the dark. Did the Council mean just to leave him down here and forget about him? He couldn't even hear the City bells, and he hadn't thought there was *anywhere* in the City where you couldn't hear the bells of Armethalieh.

He paced until he got tired, then he sat down in a corner with his back against the wall. How long had he been here? Did the Council mean just to leave him down here and forget about him so that he could just vanish quietly? Somehow that frightened him more than the idea of Banishment. The cell was just chilly enough to be uncomfortable, and Kellen could stand and think, or sit and think, but either way he was as much a prisoner of his own thoughts as of the stone around him.

If he had wanted a demonstration of the absolute power the Council could wield when it chose, he was receiving it now. Everyone at the College had seen him receive the summons. No one would be surprised if he simply disappeared, not really.

And nobody would talk about it, either, at least not openly. That wasn't the way the citizens of the City did things. After all, the Council knew best, didn't they? They only acted for the good of all citizens. If there was no announcement that he had been Banished—and Kellen suddenly realized just how embarrassing such an announcement would be for his father—well, everyone knew how rebellious he was, and what a poor student he was. There might be some idle speculation, but most of it would be around the suggestion that Lycaelon had sent him away to someplace where he'd "learn proper discipline." And in time, people would forget about him.

He was so wrapped up in his own thoughts and fears—with very little sense of how much time had passed since the golems had shoved him roughly into this dark, chilly stone box—that at first the renewed sound of footsteps didn't penetrate Kellen's gloom and self-absorption. But he was quickly summoned to full awareness by the sound as it came nearer: not the heavy impact of stone-on-stone, but the softer sound of leather City-boots on stone floors.

Someone—a person—was coming.

Despite his best intentions of standing up to his captors and showing a defiant face, Kellen backed away from the door as far as he could, his heart beating faster.

The door swung open, filling the cell with light from the corridor, and a robed Mage, accompanied by a hovering ball of Magelight, stepped into the cell.

"Kellen," Arch-Mage Lycaelon said, inclining his head. He made a small gesture, and the blue ball of Magelight soared up to hover several feet above their heads, bathing the whole cell in its even unchanging brightness. Somehow that made the cell seem both larger and smaller, all at the same time. The height of it made Kellen feel insignificant; the length and width so small as to give him a feeling of claustrophobia.

"Father," Kellen answered evenly. Too many emotions to sort out filled him all at once. Relief that someone had come—anger, at the Mages and at Lycaelon personally—a sense of betrayal so intense that it made his whole body tremble.

"I trust you're as well as possible under the circumstances? The golems were not intended to injure you. But they are, when all is said and done . . . stone," Lycaelon said.

Kellen recognized his father's "public" voice, smooth and confident. Why was Lycaelon here? Surely his father had said everything to his wilding son he intended to say back in the Council chamber? Why this display of parental devotion now, when nobody was here to witness it?

Or maybe what had gone before had been the public act . . . and this was to be the private truth?

"I'm fine," Kellen said crossly. He rubbed his arms, wincing again as he touched the developing bruises. He saw Lycaelon sigh, watching the gesture.

"In a way, Kellen, it is . . . unfortunate that you were halted in your studies when you were."

Kellen stared at his father. He'd expected more threats, more denunciations. Not this. Despite everything, he felt a tiny spark of hope.

Lycaelon smiled thinly. "You accused us of never having

read the Books of the Wild Magic, Kellen—and it is true that no Mage of this generation has done so, but do you think that no student of the High Art ever has fallen afoul of them, in all the years since the founding of the Golden City? Why in the name of the Light would Wildmagery then be so grave an offense? No, Kellen. The Council isn't as arbitrary as it seems to you. Our ancient brothers in the High Art studied the Books of the Wild Magic in full, to their peril and their cost, and discovered what I believe you would have discovered yourself with only a little more time."

"Then why can't I have that time?" Kellen burst out. "If—"

Lycaelon raised a hand. "Please, my son. Hear me out. The risk is too great—not only to you alone, but to all those you might endanger through studies that seem innocent now. Think hard, and answer honestly: In all the time you have studied and worked with those Books, have you never felt even a little uneasy about what you do?"

Kellen blushed angrily, hanging his head. He thought of every time he'd vowed to set *The Book of Moon, The Book of Sun,* and *The Book of Stars* aside forever. Hadn't both the spells he'd done spiraled out of control, involving him in things he never would have gotten into if he hadn't cast them?

"You need not speak aloud," Lycaelon said soothingly. "Nor are you to blame. It is the very nature of the Books of the Wild Magic to seem—at first—nothing more than an innocent and powerful tool, capable of being used for good. But the Wild Magic is as seductive as the Elvenkind, using the Wildmage for its own secret purposes, luring him slowly away from his own path, and into convoluted schemes of its own, plans of darkest Evil. There are Mages who recognized them for what they were and rejected their lure in time to save themselves . . . from what you do not say, I pride myself that you would have soon realized that what they purport to teach are not lessons, but tainted fantasies, foul sorcery that is the enemy of the Light, and rejected their false teachings before it was too late. But now, I must burden you with knowledge normally given only to those far above your rank."

Really. How . . . privileged I feel, Kellen thought sardonically.

Lycaelon, of course, read a willingness to listen into his silence.

"For centuries we of the City attempted to tame the power of the Wild Magic . . . and failed. In time, the High Mages realized Wildmagery could not be practiced safely, even by Master Mages—not even by the Arch-Mage himself. If you had gotten further in your legitimate studies, you would have been taught to recognize the Books, and taught why they must be destroyed wherever they are found."

So just how is it, then, that they keep popping up? Kellen wondered silently.

"You see, Kellen, every single Mage who worked with the Wild Magic without rejecting it not only went to the bad, but lost his mind into the bargain, ultimately destroying not only his own life but the lives of those around him. You have already seen that the Wild Magic seems to have an ultimate purpose of its own, one that it hides from you. In ancient days, we discovered to our sorrow what that purpose is. Practice of the Wild Magic leads to conversation with Demons, monstrous creatures who are the enemy of all Light and Life, and any Mage who deals with Demonfolk is inevitably corrupted and seduced by the Darkness, in the end betraying his own kind to the Demons' embrace. The High Magick is an alliance with the Light, and the Wild Magic is its opposite, an exaltation of Darkness. And so, in the end, the Wildmage becomes the tool of Darkness."

Demons? Kellen fought to keep his face expressionless. He had thought his father might bring any number of arguments to bear on him, but he never would have dreamed that Lycaelon would use the terror of the nursery as a serious ploy.

"Nursie" had terrified Kellen with tales of Demons as a child . . . to scare him into behaving. They were supposed to belong to the Darkness that was the opposite of the Light, but the Priests of the Eternal Light actually tended to discourage belief in them, saying that Demons were only a children's tale, that the Light, which was all-powerful, would certainly not permit something as dark and twisted as Demons to exist, and in fact, they weren't even discussed in his magickal studies or his Natural Philosophy courses. Kellen had read far deeper in the Art Magickal than either Lycaelon or Anigrel suspected—and there was nothing there about Demons, either!

But Lycaelon continued speaking, oblivious to Kellen's expression—if he'd even noticed it.

"And so the Council was formed, to cast out the Wildmages forever, to banish the Demon-taint from Armethalieh, and to let the Light shine free and unfettered over the Golden City and all her people. And the greatest gift of all the gifts we have given them is freedom from the memory of those terrible ancient days. Only we of the High Council retain any access to the histories of so long ago, and because of that we know that the Black Days when Demons walked the land were so terrible that any risk, no matter how slight, of the Demons' return is too great. Wildmagery opens a door to that return, and for that reason, the Council cannot tolerate the taint of Wild Magic, the barest possibility that Demons could get a toehold in this City again. No mercy can be shown, not even when the Mage in question is my own son." Lycaelon bowed his head for a moment, and drew a deep breath.

"I know this is terribly hard for you to believe now, when the Wild Magic is helping you find lost objects and light candles, and other seemingly innocent pastimes, but even the most treacherous mountain has soft and pleasant foothills. You do not know what your future holds if you do not renounce your present course, Kellen. I beg you, my son. Turn back. There is still time. If you will not do it for your own sake, then, please—do it for the sake of the City, for your honor here as a Tavadon, for the glory of our ancient name—"

KELLEN grimaced in self-disgust, shaking off the spell of his father's words. For a moment he'd almost *believed* Ly-

caelon, and he hated himself for it, and for hoping, even for
a moment, that his father had come down here to talk because
his father cared for him. But no. It was more of the same
practiced tricks that Lycaelon used on everyone to get what
he wanted—and at the end, the Arch-Mage hadn't been able
to resist throwing in that last turn of the knife, about doing
it for House Tavadon, and that proved all the rest was a lie,
didn't it? Lycaelon would do anything rather than suffer the
humiliation of having a Wildmage for a son, including coming down here to try to feed Kellen a pack of lies as if he
were seven instead of seventeen!

Demons—why hadn't his father just said "bogeymen" and
had done with it? Kellen should have recognized the plot line
of this particular story a little sooner—it was right out of the
Ars Perfidorum, after all—with the addition of "Demons" to
make it more interesting.

So. His father hadn't even bothered trying to talk to him
as an adult. He'd come down here with this wondertale to
try to scare Kellen into doing what he wanted, and it wasn't
going to work. *If there were such things as Demons, wouldn't
there be at least some sign of defenses against them? I
wouldn't imagine that mere walls would keep them out. You'd
think that someone, somewhere, in all the books in Father's
library would have let something slip about how to protect
yourself from them!*

But no. And that was because nobody created a counterspell against something that didn't exist. His father had come
down here with this nonsense to try to scare Kellen into doing
what he wanted, just so Lycaelon could look good for the
Council. The mighty Arch-Mage, so persuasive he even managed to turn a budding Wildmage back to the paths of order
and obedience and Law! Well, Kellen was tired of performing
that particular function in his father's life, thank you very
much. The Wild Magic had never *really* hurt anybody, which
was more than Kellen could say for the Council and its tricks.
In fact, everything it had made him do had *helped* other people! Even Perulan: it wasn't Kellen's fault that Perulan had
decided to flee the City—from what Perulan himself had said,

the writer might very well have decided to try to escape the
City long before Kellen ever came on the scene.

He stood silent, head down, no longer meeting his father's
gaze. Kellen thought he'd been angry in the Council chamber;
now he knew he'd only been disgusted. He was furious now,
and more. Emotions he did not want to name boiled up within
him, and with all his strength, Kellen fought to keep from
letting any of them show on his face. All his concentration
was focused on one thing—to keep from lashing out at his
father with words and fists, to keep from giving back one iota
of the pain his father had given him with his contempt.

Contempt. Yes. That was the word. Long, long ago, Kellen
had learned never to expect love or even kindness from his
father. But the realization of the utter contempt in which Lycaelon held him was a sharp new blow, more painful than
any bone-bruise given by unliving stone golems ever could
be. Only a man who truly despised his fellows would attempt
to manipulate them the way Lycaelon was trying to manipulate his son.

*I've never been anything more than an object to him; a
trophy, something to show off to the other Mages. The proof
that his bloodline breeds true.*

The realization carried with it a sense of loss so intense it
shocked him, for Kellen had thought he had nothing left to
lose, and the realization that he did took him by surprise. But
it was true. Lycaelon did not even treat his servants as badly
as he treated his only son. He only ignored his servants, and
sent them away if they displeased them. He'd showed his son
no such mercy. For Kellen there had been no escape from
that constant torture in all the years of his life.

Until now.

Now Kellen saw an escape. And he was going to take it.

"HAVE you nothing to say?" Lycaelon said, his voice growing harsh and impatient. "I see," he said after a pause that
Kellen did nothing to fill. "You persist in your ignorant de-

fiance. No doubt you have some childish romantic notion of Banishment, of making a life for yourself outside the City. Allow me to disabuse you of one more infantile delusion. I shall explain to you precisely the terms of your Banishment, and you shall have one last chance to recant."

You'd like that, wouldn't you? After all, if I don't recant—you lose. You lose the game, you lose face, and you lose me. Surprise, Father. You lost me a long time ago.

"At sunset, you will be stripped of your Talisman, don the Felon's Cloak, and be set outside the walls of the City. The terms of Banishment are these: that you have until sunrise to be outside the boundaries of the City lands, or face the Outlaw Hunt. At dawn, the City gates will open again and the Outlaw Hunt will fare forth to hunt you down and tear you to pieces if you are still within our bounds. But I will tell you one thing more: the Outlaw Hunt will certainly reach you."

Lycaelon took a step nearer. Another. And his voice descended to a sinister growl.

"Do not delude yourself about that. No power under the heavens could carry you to the edge of the City lands in a night—not the fastest horse ever foaled, were you permitted to claim a horse from the City stables, could bear you beyond the boundaries of the City lands. Banishment is a death sentence. No one has ever escaped an Outlaw Hunt. *No one!*"

Kellen glanced up then, shocked at the triumph in his father's voice, and caught Lycaelon's smile of victory. The Arch-Mage was certain he'd won, certain that now Kellen would give in, give up, submit tamely to punishment and public humiliation.

But he hadn't counted on the depth of Kellen's anger.

"I'll die then! I'd rather die—it's better than living on your terms, as your lackey, as your *nothing,* as less than a dog that eats your scraps!" Kellen shouted. He took a step forward, unable to control himself any longer, fists clenched until they ached.

In the cool azure Magelight, he could see the dark blood

fill his father's face until Lycaelon's complexion was nearly purple. The Arch-Mage took a step backward, raising his hand.

"By the Light, I should have known you'd live down to your bad blood!" Lycaelon roared, his voice thick with fury. The Arch-Mage whirled, flinging the cell door open with a gesture, then cast a killing look over his shoulder at Kellen. "There's bad blood in you from your mother's folk—you're just like your sister, and you'll come to the same end!"

Lycaelon stepped out into the hallway. The door of Kellen's cell slammed between them so hard the wood groaned and protested, the sound deafeningly loud in such a small space. The echoes of its crash blotted out any sound Lycaelon might have made in his departure.

Kellen stood where he was for a long moment, his heart hammering in his chest until he thought it might burst. At last he drew a deep breath and moved shakily over to the stone bench, sitting down carefully. He'd won—he thought he'd won—but it didn't feel like it. The unleashed anger of Arch-Mage was more than a temper tantrum. It could have serious consequences for everyone in his presence. Kellen felt ill with more than the aftermath of his own fury. He leaned his head against the cold stone of the wall and tried to slow his racing heart.

After a few moments he felt better. Lycaelon hadn't been trying to hurt him at the last. Why should he? According to him, by morning, the Outlaw Hunt was going to rip the Arch-Mage's inconvenient son to pieces.

Just like it had his sister.

Sister?

Puzzled, Kellen forced himself to concentrate on Lycaelon's parting words, setting aside his other painful thoughts. *"You're just like your sister,"* Lycaelon had shouted . . . but Kellen didn't remember having a sister, and it wasn't the sort of thing you just forgot.

Although she'd probably died before he'd been born. Died, another victim of the Outlaw Hunt, probably spending some of her last bells in this very cell.

He wondered what she'd done. He hoped, whatever it was, that it had been something really, truly excessive. Not something like theft or murder—but something bold and brave, a strike against Lycaelon and for freedom.

Something worth dying for.

He looked up. The Magelight was still there, hovering near the ceiling. Lycaelon had been so furious when he left that he'd forgotten to summon it to follow him. Well, it would have to stay there until Lycaelon or some other Mage came back to retrieve it.

Kellen grinned irrepressibly, his spirits recovering a little. Maybe it would stay there forever. Lycaelon had been so furious when he left that he'd probably forgotten about it completely, and nobody was likely to remind him.

He guessed whatever his lost sister had done to merit Banishment, it had been pretty annoying after all.

Chapter Eight

By the Light of the Moon

A short time later, two Constables in the deep scarlet uniform of the City Watch opened the door to Kellen's cell once again. Both carried the long halberds that—along with the truncheons slung at their belts—were the only weapons of the Watch. Kellen supposed he ought to be grateful the Council hadn't sent the Guard and a couple of detachments of the Militia as well. Then again, there wouldn't be enough room for them down here.

"Time for you to go, boy," the older one said, not unkindly. Despite the gentleness of his tone, Kellen noticed the man did not look directly toward him. Neither of them did. It was as if Kellen had already begun to cease to exist.

The Constable tossed a leather day-pack to the floor of the

cell. It skidded across the smooth stone floor until it bumped gently against Kellen's feet.

"Best you check that all's accounted for there. I'll have no one saying that prisoners are ill done by on my watch."

Because it seemed to be expected of him, Kellen leaned over from his seat on the stone bench and picked up the pack. It was cheap leather, held shut with crude horn toggles. He opened it. Inside was a flat loaf of penance-bread—of the sort that minor criminals condemned to bread-and-water punishments were forced to subsist on—and a waterskin. He hefted it experimentally. It sloshed, full.

Kellen replaced both items in the pack and closed it, and put it back down on the floor, his throat suddenly tight. He looked up and nodded, not trusting himself to speak.

This was no game. They were really going to do it. This was supposed to be food and water for the journey, to preserve the fiction that there would be a journey of Banishment, one that didn't end with sunrise and the release of the Outlaw Hunt.

He wondered if either of the Constables knew that every Banishment ended in death. He wondered if either of them would believe him if he told them. Or care. After all, he was a lawbreaker, or he wouldn't be getting Banished right now, so how much consideration did a lawbreaker deserve?

"And this." The Senior Constable tossed a bundle of bright yellow cloth toward Kellen. It landed in the middle of the floor. Kellen got slowly to his feet and picked it up. His legs were still a bit shaky, and he took a deep breath, refusing to show these two strangers any hint of what he was feeling now.

It was a thin hooded cloak of coarse weaving, its fabric of the cheapest possible material. The black symbol of Felony had been painted on its back with thin tar, making the fabric there stiff. It tied at the throat with a drawstring.

"You'll be wanting to put that on before we go. But first, we'll be needing your Talisman. You don't belong to the City anymore," the Senior Constable said, a little less patient now.

Slowly Kellen worked the golden rectangle up from beneath his clothes and slipped the long golden chain off over his neck. He tossed the Talisman, chain and all, to the floor. It struck the stone with a high sweet ringing sound, and even though he knew what the Talisman *really* represented, being without it made Kellen feel oddly naked.

The Junior Constable reached out with his halberd and scooped the Talisman across the floor to where he could pick it up, transferring it to a pouch that hung at his belt. His face was set in firm lines of disapproval. The Senior Constable just looked tired and old.

Kellen felt paralyzed with inertia. As if, as long as he just stood here, it wasn't real, and nothing would happen.

"Well, go on, boy. Sun's westering, and you've got to be out of the City by dusk," the Senior Constable said. He stared, not at Kellen, but at some place on the wall just behind Kellen's shoulder.

Setting his jaw, Kellen bent down and picked up the pack, slipping it on over his shoulders. He picked up the cloak next—shoddy workmanship, the coarse cloth barely suitable for sacking vegetables, for all its lurid color, but at least it was clean, having obviously never been used before—and flung it over his shoulders. He resisted the momentary urge to pull the hood up over his face. He had nothing to hide. It was the *Council* that should be hiding their faces in shame, not him! He'd done nothing he was ashamed of, while they—they'd lied, cheated, stolen . . . and the worst of it was, most of their victims didn't even know it.

He straightened and faced the two Constables once more. Both of them held their halberds in front of them, as if they were afraid he might be tempted to attack them. The Junior Constable was unable to keep from flicking suspicious glances upward at the ball of hovering Magelight, as if he suspected Kellen of having something to do with it.

Not me. Blame that one on the Arch-Mage.

Silently they stepped back, indicating he should go before them through the open door of the cell.

In silence, Kellen preceded the two Constables down the hallway along which he'd been dragged by the stone golems such a short time earlier. He felt numb, still unable to completely believe this was happening to him, even with the harsh dye-smell of the Felon's Cloak tickling his nostrils, and the lying weight of the day-pack tugging at his shoulders, filled with rations for a journey he would not live to complete. He, Kellen Tavadon, was being Banished from the Golden City!

Only it wasn't really Banishment, was it? It was execution, a death sentence carried out in such a way that the High Council could pretend to be merciful, so that their victims could cherish hope until the very last moment, so that the citizens of Armethalieh would never know that they were being governed by a pack of murderers.

At the foot of the stairs that led to the surface he stopped, wanting to say something, to tell them the truth, only to receive the sharp prod of a halberd point in the small of the back.

"None of that," the Senior Constable said quietly. "Don't say nothin', lad. You're not to talk to us."

In mutinous silence, Kellen climbed the stairs. He wasn't surprised to find that this time they led directly to the outside world. He was in the courtyard directly outside the Council House, a short walk from the Delfier Gate. The lesser gates of gilded bronze, set into the Great Gate that hadn't been opened in all of Kellen's lifetime, stood open, glowing gold in the last rays of the setting sun, and as he took a step toward them, the bells of the City began to ring the Evensong.

First one bell—the great crystal bell in the Main Temple of the Light—began to toll, in long ringing notes that hung in the air, and then, at its signal, every bell in the City joined in, each with its own special tone and cadence, until the air was filled with sound. Last of all, the deep-throated golden bell of the Council House itself joined in, so close that Kellen's bones vibrated with every stroke.

If he turned and looked, he could see Tavadon House from

where he stood, but another jab in the back discouraged that impulse before it was fully formed. Herded forward like a pig to market, Kellen approached the Delfier Gate, feeling more alone than he'd ever felt in his life.

Beneath his feet were the usual eight-sided granite cobble-stones that covered most of the better City streets. At the gate, they stopped abruptly, as if to underscore the fact that here Civilization ended. Beyond was a wide well-used dirt road, hammered smooth by generations of trade caravans and farm carts. Conscious of the two Constables at his back—and the round dozen uniformed City Guards waiting to close and bar the gates—Kellen walked out of the City.

For the first and last time.

⌒

THE lesser gates—together only large enough to admit a single cart at a time—clanked shut behind him, and through, the chiming of the City bells, Kellen heard the booming of the bolts being thrown home, cutting him off from the City forever.

He looked back.

On the inside, the walls and gates of Armethalieh were lavishly ornamented. The gates were gilded bronze, covered with bas-relief sculpture depicting the joys of living in the City. The walls themselves were glazed and colored tile. Even in the poorest quarters of the City, the City wall itself was a work of art, beautifully painted if nothing else.

Outside was a different matter, so it seemed.

Here the gates were plain unadorned bronze, the wall itself plain dark stone, its true color difficult to tell in the twilight. Automatically, he pulled the thin yellow cloth of his Felon's Cloak tighter around him and shivered, although he wasn't really cold. Not yet.

This was the face that the City showed to outsiders. And Kellen was an outsider now. Cast out by the City, cut off from the only life he'd ever known. He'd never felt so completely alone in his life.

As he stared at the blank forbidding walls, out of the corner of his eye he caught a flicker of movement high above him. He glanced farther up, and saw one of the City Guards staring down at him, grinning nastily.

Kellen quickly turned his back to the City, blotting out the sight of the guard's gloating expression. The sunset was a thin line of gold through the trees toward the west. In less than a tenth-chime more, the sun would set completely.

He was cast out. *Banished*—from the City and all its lands. And in the morning, when the first rays of the sun rose to gild the dome of the Council House, the Outlaw Hunt that the Mages would have spent all night enchanting would be sent forth through the very gate he had just walked through to rip him to shreds if he was still within reach.

Without conscious thought, Kellen began to move, heading down the Western Road at a fast trot.

This was the road the farmers from the villages used to bring their produce to the City. Though it was only used during harvest season, it should be smooth and even enough for him to make good time on, even in the dark. And the moon was full tonight—that was another stroke of luck. It would be rising in a bell or two, and a full moon would surely give him enough light to travel by.

Kellen winced, listening to the direction of his own thoughts. He slowed to a walk, and then stopped, realizing it had become too dark to see, at least for running. He risked a glance back over his shoulder. The Evensong Bells were silent now, and he could no longer make out the City behind him, though he knew it would probably be visible in daylight. The walls blocked off all sight of the buildings—and their warm and comforting lights—from outside.

All at once the enormity of his situation seemed to settle over him like a far heavier version of the Felon's Cloak. Who was he trying to kid? Even if he could manage to run full-out all night long there was no way he could reach the edge of City lands by dawn. He didn't even know how far they extended—or where this road led. He could use the moon to

keep himself heading due west, though there was no guarantee that the road would oblige him by going the same way.

For once his father had been telling the simple truth, just
as Perulan had. *"My dear young Kellen, have you ever heard
of anyone who simply LEFT the City?"*

No, Perulan. Not even you, Kellen thought mournfully.

Banishment wasn't banishment—it was murder. Banishment was just a convenient and innocuous way for the Council to explain how they got rid of troublemakers. A bloodless
death sentence that the Council could claim—assuming anyone ever dared to ask—represented a fair chance for the victim. And until his father had told him the truth down there
in the cell, Kellen would have believed them, just like everyone else in the City believed in the myth that the Banished
just went elsewhere to live. Of course they did. The High
Council was wise and kind; the Mages wouldn't condone
anything that wasn't in the best interests of everyone involved. As for the Outlaw Hunt, well, that was just to make
certain that the Banished didn't sneak back inside the City
with the farmers to make more trouble, of course.

But Lycaelon had given him the reality behind the pretty
myth. And no matter how much Kellen was inclined to doubt
everything his father had to say, there was something about
standing all alone in the middle of a dark forest on a road
that led to nowhere that made Lycaelon's words ring with
truth. *"Banishment is a death sentence. No one has ever escaped an Outlaw Hunt. No one!"*

Banishment was murder.

How could *anyone* find the edge of the City lands when
no one knew where they were? In all his fruitless days of
searching the City Library for information about the lands
outside the City, Kellen had never even encountered one
scrap of information about the extent of the City lands beyond
the City walls—nor had anyone volunteered to provide that
vital piece of survival information to a Banished Outlaw.

So that much of what Lycaelon had told him must be true.

Kellen began walking again, more slowly now, as furious

with himself for believing the High Mages' lies so easily as
he was with the Council for having lied to him—to all of
them—for all these years. Why couldn't they just be honest
enough to admit they were executing people? Why did they
have to play at being merciful?

*Because if they didn't people would object to the killings.
And there would have to be more executions. And then people
would see them for what they are,* a small voice inside Kellen
said reasonably.

It was all part of a pattern of life in the Golden City. The
Council saw to it that there was nothing new that might make
people think. Nothing to excite people, or upset them. Nothing that would make people question the way things were, or
question the fact that the High Council acted for the good of
all, *always.* Nothing that would make people question the
way things were. In the City, anything unpleasant or distress-
ing simply . . . disappeared.

Just the way Kellen was going to disappear now.

*"Oh, Kellen? I remember him. Lycaelon's son. He wasn't
happy here, so the Council Banished him, for the good of the
City."* And everyone would nod their heads, thinking of how
wise, how just, how kind, how *merciful* the High Council
was. And life would go on, following the rules the Council
laid down for it.

*But at least I have until morning before they release the
Hunt. They'll have to work all night to enchant the stone
Hounds, and even if they're ready early, the Council will
abide by the letter of its decree and not release them until
morning.* If there was anything left for Kellen to be certain
of among all the lies and betrayal, it was that. Why should
they put themselves to the trouble of breaking one of their
endless petty rules when the Outlaw Hunt could find him
wherever he went, and they *knew* there was no way for Kellen
to escape them?

But they were wrong. Lycaelon had been wrong. Kellen
did have a way. He just wasn't sure he was going to use it
yet. He needed to think very carefully about it first, and he

wasn't yet certain, *really, truly* certain, deep in his gut, that he'd come to the point where he had no other options.

He walked on until it was too dark to see at all, stumbling several times on the wagon-rutted road before he tripped over some unseen obstacle and landed heavily on his hands and knees. That was the point that almost broke him; tears of fear, frustration, and anger welled up in his eyes and despair enveloped his heart as the Felon's Cloak enveloped his body, and at last he was finally willing to admit that he'd reached that point. Groping carefully around himself, Kellen sat down in the middle of the road, facing back the way he'd come.

There was nothing to see. If he'd hoped for a glimpse of the lights of Armethalieh on the horizon, he was disappointed. There was nothing there to see—not even the lights of the highest towers, for some reason. Nothing but more darkness, and more shadows.

It was spring, but it was still early enough in the season that the temperature dropped sharply at night this close to the coast. Kellen shivered now in earnest, pulling his inadequate cloak tighter around himself. If he'd known when he got up this morning that he was going to be arrested and Banished, he'd have dressed more warmly and worn stout walking boots at the very least.

At least there was nothing there he'd really miss. Everything he'd owned had been bought as part of Lycaelon's idea of what Lycaelon's perfect son should have. The few things he'd bought on his own, from the allowance that was also a part of what Lycaelon's perfect son should have somehow never managed to stay around very long if they were deemed too unsuitable. Kellen had learned very early not to get too attached to possessions.

Still, he had a good pair of heavy boots there, and a warm sturdy cloak that would come in handy right now. If the Council had really wanted to even *pretend* to be fair, they would have let him get proper clothes from home. But the Council only wanted to make a good show for its citizens, not for its victims, and right now Kellen had other concerns. Right now he had to think—hard—about what to do next.

He didn't have his Books of the Wild Magic with him. The Council had those. And they probably thought that without them he was defenseless, but he actually didn't need them. He'd been right when he accused the Council of not having any idea of how the Wild Magic worked, and despite all Lycaelon's fine words about how they'd studied it a long time ago (he bet they hadn't) they were assuming it was just like the High Magick they were familiar with.

But unlike High Magick, which needed so much calculation, preparation, tools, and endless memorization of stock formulas, Wild Magic, as Kellen had already learned, was driven far more by the intent of the caster than by calculation. He didn't need pages of written-out spellcasting—a grimoire, a temple full of tools and furniture, and rigid observance of planetary hours—to be able to use it. He could cast an effective spell with what he already knew and what was around him.

But what kind of a spell?

What did he want?

To stay alive was the easy and obvious answer, but maybe it was a little *too* easy. There was always a price, and for a need this *big,* the price would be high. That much Kellen knew already. What price would the Wild Magic ask for the gift of his life? How would it answer such a request?

Was it a price he was willing to pay?

He hadn't, after all, been willing to pay *Lycaelon's* price for remaining in the City, so Kellen already knew that some prices were too high.

Better not ask for just staying alive, then, Kellen decided warily. He thought carefully about all he'd read. The three Books were less about spells than about the principles behind them—the physics, not the ethics. Ethics, apparently, was something the Wildmage had to work out for him or herself.

But as he recalled from *The Book of Moon,* the less you specified in Wild Magic, the better your response was likely to be. Getting specific meant getting selfish—thinking too much, and at the same time, not thinking enough.

I guess . . . maybe . . . if when you ask for something from

*the Wild Magic you're always promising to give something
in return . . . the easier you make it for Something to give to
you . . . maybe the easier it becomes for you to repay in return?*

*Or maybe I'm completely wrong! I have no idea what I'm
doing here!* he thought in frustration.

Kellen sighed. What was the smallest, simplest, least thing
that he needed? The less he asked for, the less he'd have to
give, after all. Or so it seemed to him right now.

*To be out of City lands by sunrise. I need help to be out
of City lands by sunrise. I don't care how, or where I end
up, but that's what I need—REALLY need. And I don't care
what I have to pay for it—no, that's not true, I won't murder
to pay for it, and there are probably other pretty horrible
things I wouldn't do, but something personal probably
wouldn't be a problem. And that's what I need—REALLY
need.*

He felt a great sense of relief, as if he'd managed to solve
a riddle correctly. That was what he needed, and that was
what he'd ask for. And how badly awry could the spell possibly go? According to *The Book of Stars,* if he didn't specify
a payment limit, he would be granted the chance to turn down
what he was offered—with no hard feelings, as it were. For
instance, if he was asked to murder someone . . .

Because some things, as Kellen was already discovering,
came at too high a price. And if, just *if,* as Lycaelon claimed,
there were Demons involved, Kellen knew there might be a
price worse than that of giving up his own life.

With the matter settled to his own satisfaction, Kellen
waited some more, this time with a purpose. At last the moon
rose through the trees, shedding its dappled light through
trees rustling with the new leaves of early spring. Finally, he
could see where he was, and what he needed to get.

The Calling Spell he intended to try was a bit more elaborate than the simple Finding Spell he had cast twice before,
and required more ingredients. Fortunately the trees were already in leaf, and those simple ingredients were easy enough
to find. Two chimes' search allowed him to collect leaves

from each of three trees: an oak, an ash, and a thorn tree, and to amass a good handful of tinder and dry sticks from the forest floor to build the fire to burn them.

Returning to the center of the cart track, he piled his kindling and tinder carefully in a heap, then took the strongest of the sticks he had gathered and carefully drew a circle around himself, digging the line as deeply as he could into the rutted bare-earth surface of the road. He broke up the stick and added it to the pile, and then with a flick of his fingers, set the small pile of sticks and tinder alight.

It was such an easy spell—the first one in *The Book of Moon,* the first one that the Student of High Magick studied—that for a moment Kellen wasn't sure which method he'd used to summon the flames. He felt disoriented, caught between two paths: the rigid discipline of the High Magick, the fluid inspiration of the Wild Magic.

There's still time to back out.

But there wasn't. Not really. There was going forward, or there was giving up and staying where he was out of fear. Those were his only real choices just now. The City would not take him back. When morning came, the Outlaw Hunt would kill him.

He bent down and picked up the three leaves that he'd set aside. There was one last thing he needed to cast the spell. Still holding the fresh green leaves between the fingers of his left hand, he opened his pencase and pulled out his little penknife. Holding it carefully in his right hand, he cut a shallow scratch along his left palm. They'd taken none of his possessions from him except his Talisman—he even still had the key to the back garden. He wondered if Lycaelon would miss it and change all the locks.

The blood welled up, pooling in the palm of his hand. He wiped the penknife dry on his pant leg and replaced it in the pencase, and took each leaf in turn, dabbing it in the blood until each had been marked. Probably there wasn't any need to make quite so much of a mess, but he wanted to be sure he was doing everything right.

Then he dropped the leaves—and his blood—carefully into

the fire, willing his spell, his call, as they burned and sizzled, sending up a thin plume of peculiar-smelling smoke. Help to leave the City lands by daybreak. Nothing more. Help unspecified, for a price unspecified.

Kellen had expected—or at least hoped—for fireworks and drama, but there were no bright lights, no mystic bells. The fire was small, and a few minutes later it had burned away to embers and ash. Kellen rubbed it out with the sole of his boot. His left hand itched, and he licked it clean, then rubbed it gingerly against his velvet tunic, wary of starting it bleeding again.

Still nothing happened. Kellen stalked back and forth, stopping automatically at the edges of his circle. The moon was above the trees now, and he could see his shadow on the ground pacing him as he turned, but though he strained all his senses, he heard nothing more than the cry of a night-hunting bird, the faint rustle of its prey, and the rhythm of the wind through the trees, and he saw nothing at all.

How long do I wait?

Emotionally battered by the events of the day, Kellen couldn't stop himself from wondering: What if there had been truth in more of his father's words than he wanted to believe? What if the Wild Magic was . . . unreliable? What if it was going to betray him now, just as everything else in his life had?

No.

Kellen wasn't sure where that conviction came from, but it was deep and sure. The response to his attempts at spell-casting might not be exactly what he'd like—it might be downright scary in fact, confusing, unexpected, utterly puzzling, but the Wild Magic was not a cheat and a lie.

Finally he stopped fidgeting and looked up at the moon. It was still rising. Kellen wasn't sure how long it had been since he'd cast the spell—at least half a bell. No matter what, he knew he couldn't simply stand here all night, waiting for help that might never come. Maybe the spell *hadn't* worked—that wouldn't be the Wild Magic's fault, after all. He wasn't exactly a full-fledged Wildmage, was he? Maybe he already had all the "help to get out of City lands by daybreak" he actually needed. Maybe he *could* reach the edge of City lands on his own two feet, unlikely though that seemed. Lycaelon might have lied about that, hoping to make him give up without trying.

He sighed. *Might as well start walking, anyway. If help is coming, it can find me wherever I am. No harm in that.*

He was about to step out of his circle when he saw a flicker of something white and glowing heading toward him from the west. It looked as bright as the moon itself, but it was clearly coming through the trees toward him. The hair on the back of his neck rose. Was *this* the answer to his call? Was it a ghost, or some other noncorporeal creature?

Kellen took a deep breath and resolved to stand his ground.

It approached cautiously, as if, whatever it was, it was as wary of him as he was of it. As it came closer he could see that it had four legs—a deer? No, a horse.

Then it stepped through the trees and out onto the road, and Kellen saw that it was neither.

It was a unicorn.

The unicorn was about the size of a small pony, but there the resemblance to anything equine ended. It had long slender legs and a long, lithe, slender—almost feline—body, covered with short plush silvery-white fur, fluffed out against the nocturnal chill. It had a lionlike tufted tail—which it carried, catlike, curled up and away from its body—and narrow pale cloven hooves, like a deer's or a goat's. It had a long slender neck, with a short roached mane that stopped just short of its horn. Its head wasn't really shaped like either a deer's, a goat's, or a horse's, though a little like each.

But its *horn . . . !*

The unicorn's horn was the most beautiful thing Kellen had ever seen—like polished diamond, or perhaps silver, if silver were somehow transparent. The horn was set in the middle of the unicorn's wide forehead, between its large dark eyes, and seemed to drink in the moonlight from the air around it and glow with a blue light that came from within. It was spiral-shaped, like the narwhal-teeth the Selken-folk sometimes brought to the City for sale, but where they were blunt, the unicorn's horn tapered to an elegant point sharper than any needle . . .

"If you're *quite* through staring," the unicorn said acerbically, "I believe we need to get on with this."

Kellen blinked, then stumbled back in alarm. While he'd been gawking in awestruck wonder, the unicorn had walked right up to him and stopped, close enough to reach out and touch. Its eyes were on a level with his own—deep fathomless pools of spring green, fringed with long thick silver lashes. Its small elegant ears flicked back and forth as it spoke, signaling amusement—or was it annoyance?

"Well," the unicorn said. "You know why I'm here, Wildmage."

Finally it seemed as if Kellen was able to think again, and not just stare. Not only a unicorn—but a *talking* unicorn. It was too much to comprehend all at once. "You're—going to get me out?" Kellen suggested feebly. "Of the City lands?" he added, stammering.

"Yes, but—you know why *I* am here," the unicorn said implacably.

Kellen suddenly remembered something he'd read about unicorns and felt himself blushing hotly. Unicorns only came to virgins. A virgin could tame a unicorn; non-virgins got skewered if they approached too closely or threatened one.

"There is a price for my help, and it is this: that you will remain chaste and celibate—you *do* know the difference?" the unicorn asked, interrupting itself.

There was a pause. Kellen realized that the unicorn was waiting for him to answer. Fortunately his lessons with Undermage Anigrel had been of some use, and he *did* know the difference. Celibate meant simply that he wouldn't marry. Chaste meant that he also wouldn't have sex, or engage in sexual or erotic practices of any sort. He nodded, swallowing hard to cover his embarrassment at the topic of the conversation.

"—for a year and a day from now," the unicorn finished. "If you break this promise . . ." It lowered its head and brandished its horn meaningfully. The tip—just as sharp as it had looked—whispered against the front of Kellen's tunic, barely touching it, below the belt line.

Up this close, now that he wasn't just dazzled by its eldritch beauty, Kellen could see that the unicorn was male. Its implication was clear: break his promise, and *he* wouldn't be any longer. Well, he hadn't had any trouble staying a virgin until now, and it didn't seem like a price that would be particularly difficult to pay—or one that would hurt other people if he paid it.

You can still back out, a small voice inside him said.

"I . . . yes. Okay. I agree," Kellen said quickly.

"Then by the blood you have sacrificed, Wildmage, you are bound by your vow," the unicorn said formally. "Now get on my back—quickly. We have a long way to go before sunrise." It turned sideways, lashing its tufted tail just like an impatient cat.

Awkwardly, Kellen stepped forward. He was worried about hurting it—it was so small, so graceful, and thinking about getting on its back was like thinking of riding a deer, or a foal—but refusing to do as the unicorn asked was impossible now, and Kellen had to suppose it knew what it was doing. With only a little difficulty, he managed to scramble onto its narrow back. The thick fur was just as soft as a cat's fur—and just as slippery. Feeling the flex of its muscles between his thighs, Kellen realized the unicorn was much stronger than it looked.

It was also much harder to stay aboard than any horse Kellen had ever ridden, bareback or otherwise. Kellen began sliding sideways on the oil-slick fur just as the unicorn went from a dead stop to a full-out running plunge into the forest. He grabbed at its mane, but found no handholds in the short coarse bristles, and barely managed to fling himself forward and wrap his arms around the unicorn's slender neck in time to keep from falling off altogether as the creature broke into a clearing.

Its fur smelled like cinnamon.

If he'd thought about riding a unicorn at all—and he hadn't—Kellen would have imagined that it would gallop like a horse.

It didn't.

Once it reached its top speed, the unicorn bounded like a deer in full flight—not that Kellen, child of the City, had ever *seen* a deer except in carefully tended City parks—launching itself directly into the deepest part of the forest. It bounded over fallen logs and through thickets, occasionally running flat-out for a minute or two before gathering itself to spring into the air once more. Every time it sprang forward, Kellen thought he'd slide right off the back, and when it landed, he nearly broke his nose on the unicorn's neck.

Speed seemed to be its only concern. It paid no attention to the branches that whipped and tore at Kellen's flesh and clothing, lacerating him as if he were running a gantlet of riding-crops wielded by sadistic riders. He buried his face in the unicorn's neck, low against its shoulder, to protect his eyes, and was very glad he had—brambles plucked at his arms and legs, ripped his clothing, tore at his hair, and once, for one terrifying moment, the hood of his cloak caught on something, threatening to strangle him or drag him from the unicorn's back. He clung to its neck with all his strength as the unicorn strained, until at last the cheap cloth of the Felon's Cloak gave, tearing free to be left behind.

And still it ran, tireless, faster than the fastest horse Kellen could imagine. He knew from the burning along every exposed part of him, the outsides of arms and legs, and to a lesser extent his shoulders and back, that he was bleeding from a thousand scrapes and scratches all along his arms and legs—if he had not shed enough blood to seal the pact between them before, he was certainly shedding it now.

His chest was bruised, he was battered from neck to toes by collisions with branches, and he was having trouble breathing as his arms and chest muscles began to ache from the sheer effort of holding on. Battered and breathless with sheer speed, Kellen wondered if he'd specified anything in his spell about reaching the boundaries of City lands *alive*—

this almost seemed worse than anything the Outlaw Hunt could do to him.

When the unicorn seemed to have settled into a straightforward bounding motion—and Kellen hadn't been hit by anything for a while—he decided to risk a glimpse at his surroundings. Raising his head cautiously, he looked around.

They were out in the open, and up ahead, Kellen could see the flicker of moonlight on water. There was a stream ahead, its flat surface glistening in the moonlight, a stretch of water perhaps a hundred yards wide. He loosened his stranglehold on the unicorn's neck, assuming he was going to dismount and wade across.

"Don't do that," the unicorn said briefly.

It didn't slow down.

Kellen watched in horror as the unicorn approached the river at top speed and launched itself from the bank with an enormous leap. It hit the water with a splash that drenched both of them, but the river was only a few feet deep and it forged quickly across through the chest-high water while Kellen clung on for dear life. It lunged up the other bank and was running again before Kellen had even managed to catch his breath from the icy shock of his dousing.

Fortunately, that was the widest of the streams they had to cross that night, because, as Kellen quickly discovered, the unicorn did not mean to stop for anything. It jumped ditches and logs and rivulets; what it could not jump it climbed. What it could neither jump nor climb it went through, leaving Kellen to cling to its back like a tick, and fend for himself as best he could. He was chilled to the bone, with every scratch tracing a separate line of fire along his skin, and every bruise aching with every jolt.

They soon found themselves back among trees again. Kellen had long since buried his face against the unicorn's neck once more, risking only occasional quick glimpses of his surroundings. Even so, he got the impression that the ground was rising, and that their path was becoming even more difficult. Once or twice the unicorn actually had to slow down, as if it had to pick its way carefully, and a couple of times it came to a complete stop before launching itself vigorously into space. At those times, Kellen was just as glad he couldn't see where they were going. He certainly wasn't eager to look down at any point.

He could tell that it was getting colder, though, even if his stream-soaked clothes had long since been air-dried to no more than a faint clamminess by the speed of their flight and the heat of the unicorn's body. There was a sharp *different* smell in the air; the scent of pine trees.

Nothing had hit him for the past chime or so, so he raised his head cautiously again and looked around. It seemed they had been fleeing forever.

Once again, as his arms complained that he had been holding on for far too long, he noted that they seemed to be moving through a more open area, one where it might be safe to risk a look around. Cautiously—*very* cautiously—he raised his head again.

By now Kellen had lost all real sense of time, but he knew they'd been going for a long time—bells, and not just a few chimes. Every muscle he possessed cried out with cold and stiffness as it flexed; he was utterly spent, but if he was exhausted from nothing more than clinging to the unicorn's back all night, how much more weary must the magical creature itself be? It had never slowed its hectic pace for more than a tenth-chime; even now it moved forward as fast as a galloping horse, its footfalls eerily muffled by the bed of fallen pine needles. The trees on either side were little more than a dark blur as they passed.

The forest through which they now rode was mostly evergreen, with little in the way of treacherous underbrush to attack Kellen. He sat up as far as he could while still holding tightly on to the unicorn's neck and realized that when he looked back through a gap in the trees he could see down into the valley behind. He could see for leagues.

Surely they'd reached the edge of the City lands by now?

He looked up, into the sky overhead, and could no longer see the moon, only the bright unfamiliar stars of the darkest part of the night. He looked ahead, and when he could not see the moon through the trees, Kellen realized it must be low in the western sky. It was setting. The night must be nearly over. In a bell—less—dawn would come.

And with dawn, the Outlaw Hunt would be released.

The horror of the thought made him flinch. He would certainly have lost his grip on the unicorn's neck then except for the fact that by now his clenched hands seemed frozen in place.

A low-hanging branch brushed his cheek, and Kellen quickly ducked his head again.

⇌

AFTER that, if possible, the terrain over which they rode got even rougher. They seemed to spend as much time going down as up, over territory that would have made a mountain goat think twice. Half the time, Kellen was hanging over the unicorn's shoulder, the other half, trying to keep from sliding off the unicorn's rump. He'd have offered to walk, but there was no way he, a City-bred boy whose only experience in climbing was in climbing stairs and the occasional wall or tree, could have kept up with the unicorn. Their path led them down into deep ravines, into which the unicorn slid as much as galloped, and up the other side, with Kellen dangling from its neck, his whole weight hanging from his aching arms. He tried to wrap his legs around the unicorn's narrow torso, but the slick fur didn't give him much to grip on to.

The unicorn pushed its way through thickets that reopened the crusted scratches on his arms and legs and gouged new ones, and once, leaping some obstacle Kellen couldn't see in the dark, it landed badly, slipping and falling and rolling over and over down a slope covered with the rotting remains of last year's leaves, Kellen tangled up with it and desperately trying to avoid its razor-sharp horn and thrashing hooves.

He thought he'd been in pain before; he realized in that moment that he'd had no idea of how much pain a single person could be in. It felt as if every bone in his body was being systematically broken; he yelped with every impact until the moment when a boulder hit him square in the stomach. He finally rolled free and landed against a rock—*hard*— gasping in protest as the breath was knocked out of him.

He sat up, blinking and shaking his head, trying to see where they were. He was liberally smeared with mud and last year's rotting leaves; they had a sour smell, like the dregs of cold tea left too long. This was much worse than falling out of the tree back in the garden.

"Come on. Get up," the unicorn said remorselessly. It was standing a few feet away. Kellen could see it, faintly glowing in the darkness exactly as if it were the ghost of a unicorn, but he could see nothing else. If it had been injured at all in the fall, it certainly didn't sound like it.

Kellen shook his head. Stars danced in his vision, and pain lanced through his head and ribs when he moved. In that moment he hated the unicorn, hated magic, hated everyone and everything that had brought him to this place—bruised, aching, and essentially alone in the freezing dark. He didn't know where he was, or what he was doing here, he didn't know how any of this would end—he was cut off from both the future and the past, and he had no way to predict what might happen next.

"Don't tell me you can't," the unicorn said nastily. "If you're still alive, you *can*."

With a snarl, Kellen used the rock to push himself to his feet. He staggered through the slippery stinking mush of last autumn's leaves toward the unicorn, certain that when he reached it he would use the last of his strength to throttle the life out of the maddening creature. But when he reached it, he was too tired—

So there was nothing to do but drag himself onto its back once more, gasping hollowly with the dull, bone-deep ache of hot new bruises that screamed in agony when he moved and throbbed with pain when he didn't. His muscles shook as he forced his arms around the unicorn's neck once more.

And they were off again.

At that point, in the midst of the pain and the dark and cold, Kellen felt tears prickle at the back of his eyes—not because of the fall, or the pain, but because he knew that somehow he was going to get through all this. Thanks to the unicorn, he was going to live to see the border and beyond. And then he'd be out of City lands, in a whole new world, and—

And then what?

He had no idea. Where would he go? What would he do?

This was all just too much. He couldn't do this, whatever it was. He didn't know what he'd meant to do when he'd faced down his father and the High Council, but it hadn't been this.

The unicorn, paying about as much attention to Kellen's internal turmoil as Lycaelon ever had, kept running.

Kellen's world narrowed to one of utter physical misery, and his mind centered on one thought only: *Don't fall off*.

Don't fall off, because he knew he couldn't find the strength to mount the unicorn one more time.

Don't fall off, because falling off the unicorn again would hurt more than he could bear.

Don't fall off, because the Outlaw Hunt was somewhere back behind him, and if he fell off, he'd never get to the border.

Everything hurt. And he very much feared that what didn't hurt, didn't work anymore. He closed his eyes and clung on, grinding his teeth with every jolt and leap. Then, finally, there were no jolts and leaps . . .

After a very long time, Kellen opened his eyes, feeling dull and stupid with pain, and realized two things.

The unicorn had stopped moving.

And the sky was light.

He sat up with a startled gasp, struggling as if he were trying to wake up from a long nightmare, and instantly fell off the unicorn's back.

"Don't get comfortable," the unicorn said tauntingly, looking down at him. "This is just a very brief stop to rest, nothing more. We've still got a long way to go to get out of the lands claimed by your City."

"It isn't my City anymore," Kellen muttered under his

breath, getting stiffly to his knees. He blinked and looked around, rubbing his eyes.

It was just dawn. They were at the edge of a stream, and the sound of running water made Kellen's throat convulse with thirst. He knelt over the flow on hands and knees and scooped up palmfuls of the icy water, drinking thirstily before remembering he had a water-bottle with him. Moving a little less stiffly now, he shrugged the backpack off his back—somehow it had managed to survive the night's ride—and pulled out its contents, the leather water-bottle and a loaf of bread. He'd fallen on the bread several times that night, but it was still in pretty good shape, considering. He emptied the water-bottle into the stream—for the water was stale and musty by now, and there was no reason to drink it when there was fresh at hand—and then refilled the bottle and used it to drink from. The water still tasted a bit of boiled leather, but it was faster than using his hands. Downstream, the unicorn was quenching its thirst as well.

He drank and drank until he couldn't hold any more water, then sat back on his heels to look around.

There was no sign of the sun; from the treetops upward, the sky was a uniform shade of pale grey and mist shrouded the tops of the trees and sent little wisps down into the gaps between them. The air was damp and chill, with fog scent in it, and this little stream ran down a long, rocky slope from some point above them. The trees were a great deal taller than the ones in the gardens of the City, they seemed to be mostly conifers, and they had a wilder, gnarled look to them, as if they often had to contend with storm winds.

They were up in the hills—to Kellen, an unimaginable distance from Armethalieh. Everything around them was mist-shrouded, and the nearby pine boughs were thick with heavy dew, turning them green and silver. The boulders of the stream bed were scoured bare, but ones on the banks were heavily covered in moss, with tiny ferns growing between them. All around was the sound of dripping water, interrupted by the occasional clear birdcall.

Kellen stretched and yawned, getting to his feet, working more of the kinks out, and wincing as he discovered new bruises. Now that he wasn't acquiring new lacerations with every passing moment, and now that his arms weren't being jerked from their sockets, he realized that he wasn't—quite— as badly hurt as he'd thought. Though he certainly *hurt.* And with every movement, he wanted nothing more than to crawl first into a hot bath, and then into a bed. His good clothes and thin leather boots—just fine for a morning of school in Armethalieh—were ruined beyond repair. The skin beneath the tattered clothing was covered with scratches and bruises, and the low soft boots were torn completely through in a couple of places. He pulled off his overtunic—there wasn't much left of it after the night's ride and the roll down the hillside—and after soaking it in the stream, used the make-shift washcloth to clean away some of the caked dirt and blood from his arms and legs. As he did, he caught sight of the deep livid hand-shaped bruises on his arms where the stone golems had gripped him, and felt a faint weary spark of anger. It seemed a lifetime ago, but the bruises were black and fresh. Rinsing the tattered cloth clean one last time, he washed his face, wincing when he encountered a deep gouge over one eye. He hadn't known *that* was there! He ran his hands through his hair, dislodging a small shower of leaves and twigs, and felt his ribs experimentally. Nothing grated, and he only aroused the dull pain of bruises, not the sharp one of a broken bone. Things could be worse. They could, most certainly, be *better,* but they could also be worse.

His stomach rumbled, reminding him he'd missed the last several meals, and he returned to the day-pack. He was a little surprised to find that the bread, though coarse and a little stale by now, was perfectly edible, but then he realized there was actually no reason for it to be otherwise. Most of those involved in his Banishing must have really believed they were preparing him to spend his life as a hunted Outlaw. The Council would certainly have done everything in its power to maintain the fiction of Kellen's possible survival, after all, just as it pretended that every Banishing was merely that—and not murder in disguise.

Though Kellen could cheerfully have eaten twice as much as was there, he carefully divided the loaf in half. For the first time, he thought—really thought—about the unicorn. It had gone through just as much as *he* had tonight, and more: *it* had been the one doing the running, and with him on its back, as well.

And it hadn't had to do it, any of it. The unicorn hadn't been Banished from Armethalieh, after all. It had come to save Kellen's life of its own free will, and what had it gotten so far for its trouble? A litany of complaint.

Despite his fear and weariness, Kellen felt his ears burn with shame. He'd thought he was so much *better* than everyone in Armethalieh, and the moment things got rough, what did he turn into? A spoiled City brat!

Only you aren't a citizen of Armethalieh now, spoiled or otherwise.

"There's food," he said, holding out half the loaf to the unicorn. "And, look, I . . ."

His voice died in his throat as he turned and took a *really* good look at his companion for the first time.

If possible, the magical creature looked even more improbable in the daylight than it had by the light of the moon—at one and the same time, ethereal as the mist and as solid and present as the trees. He stared at it in fascination, both self-pity and good resolutions momentarily forgotten, for in all of Armethalieh, known for its magick, he had never seen anything quite so—well—*magickal.*

Its downy coat was fluffed out against the morning chill, and dew sparkled on its silver-white fur, making it shimmer like the most expensive silk velvet. Its head was as long, proportionately, as a horse's, and the ears were much the same shape as a horse's, but there was more space for intelligence behind the wide speaking eyes, the muzzle smaller and more delicate in comparison. And there all resemblance to a horse ended.

A unicorn. I'm looking at a REAL UNICORN.

It wasn't that Kellen had ever been told that unicorns didn't exist, or anything like that, because they certainly existed in wondertales and were discussed in the history of the City and in his magickal texts. As a Student at the Mage College, he'd studied them, just as he'd studied other creatures of magick and the inferior Other Races that the Light had seen fit to create in his Natural History courses.

But he now suspected that the Natural Histories he'd studied had been written by people who'd never seen one, since they compared unicorns to horses, deer, lions, and even goats! Now that he'd actually seen one, Kellen didn't think you could really compare a unicorn to anything besides another unicorn.

And he suspected that no one in the City had seen one for a very long time.

"No," the unicorn said in answer to his offer, nostrils flaring. "But I thank you for the thought. You should eat it all. You'll need your strength."

Kellen did not need to be told twice. He sat by the stream and wolfed down the rest of the coarse loaf quickly, along with a great deal of stream water, then filled and stoppered the water-bottle for later use, putting it carefully into the knapsack. He'd once heard someone say that hunger made everything taste good, but to tell the truth, he was so busy cramming the bread into his stomach that he didn't taste it at all.

He decided to use the damp remains of his overtunic to make a sort of handhold or collar, so he wouldn't need to cling so tightly to the unicorn's throat. Provided, of course, that the unicorn didn't object . . .

"Now what, unicorn?" Kellen asked, getting to his feet again and stretching.

"Now, Kellen, we go on," the unicorn answered, picking its way carefully among the moss-covered boulders, so that Kellen could mount once more. "And—since we are bound together in this, you might as well call me by my name. That would be—Shalkan."

NOW that there was light, Kellen could at least see when to duck, and Shalkan was not going nearly as fast as he had been while it was dark. Kellen's makeshift handhold worked fairly well; with the rags of his overtunic looped around the unicorn's neck, he could hold on to the knotted ends and sit almost upright, instead of lying along Shalkan's back.

"Are you sure we're still in City lands?" Kellen asked tentatively. All he could see in any direction was trees: climbing up the rocky slopes, trailing down them, their tops vanishing into the dawn mist—trees so enormous they'd stifled most of the undergrowth beneath their canopy.

"I'm sure," Shalkan said. "And next you're going to ask me how the Outlaw Hunt can possibly find us all this long way from the City."

"No I'm not," Kellen protested, stung—although that had been the question on the tip of his tongue. "It's enchanted. It has magick. Like bloodhounds, I suppose; the Mages would give it some kind of scent and turn it loose."

"But you have no idea of what it actually is. Have you ever *seen* an Outlaw Hunt?" Shalkan asked.

"I . . . no," Kellen admitted sheepishly. He wasn't sure anyone had. He doubted anyone had been Banished from the City in his lifetime. Or—at least, not that he'd *heard*. There was the matter of the sister he didn't remember . . . "Have you?" he said boldly.

"Let us say I have a certain experience with the Hunt, just as you are about to, unless we are very lucky." Shalkan shook his head, and the sharp tip of his horn seemed to give off a little more light. "So, allow me to enlighten you. The Hunt is composed of Hounds—stone statues in the shape of hounds, animated by the Mages just as they animate statues of humans to do their bidding."

"Stone golems," Kellen said aloud. He thought of the stone guardians in front of House Tavadon, and shivered.

"Exactly so." Shalkan continued, his voice sounding dispassionate and pitiless. "The Hounds are tireless, relentless, and voiceless. Give them the scent, and they pursue until they catch their prey—or until they reach the borders of the lands claimed by the City. And when—*if*—they catch you, they will tear you to ribbons." Shalkan cocked his head to look back over his shoulder at his rider. "And me, of course," he added, matter-of-factly. "I'm helping you, after all. They'll kill anything that stands between them and their prey. Your City Mages have gone to a great deal of trouble to ensure that not only do those who have been Banished not survive the experience, but to discourage anyone outside of the City from even considering helping them."

"But of course, it's all out of sight of the Mages who sent them, so their hands and consciences are clean," Kellen added bitterly. He thought about a pack of the same Hounds that guarded the front of House Tavadon running silently along his trail, and winced inwardly. Somehow, knowing exactly what was after him made it worse. He wondered if somehow he'd always known he was going to end up this way, and that was why he'd particularly hated the mastiffs, then dismissed the thought with a shrug. It couldn't matter now.

But he couldn't help wondering why, if Shalkan *knew* what was coming, the unicorn was trying to get him to safety . . . Did *Shalkan* owe a debt to the Wild Magic? Or was this just another instance of some poor innocent bystander being dragged into *his* problems?

Like Perulan . . .

Shalkan flicked an ear back in his direction again and suddenly seemed to quiver all over. "The Hounds have been released," he said abruptly. "They're behind us somewhere, running free. I can feel them. The question is, which of us will reach the border first?"

A few moments later, the unicorn had resumed his headlong bounding gait to the west.

Chapter Nine

Facing the Outlaw Hunt

Kellen was almost used to the way that Shalkan bounded through the forest by now; he was beginning to get the rhythm of it and move with it. They'd left the deep forest behind a few hours before and were now in an area that was—well—mountainous, if the descriptions in the proscribed wondertales he'd seen in the Great Library were anything to go by, with jutting granite outcroppings, sheer drop-offs, and pocket canyons. The mist had either lifted, or they had passed out of the region where it lingered, and the sun shone down on them with a cheer that was all out-of-keeping with the grimness of their situation. Here the trees grew in thickets, easy to avoid, and they rode through bright cloudless daylight. In full sunlight Shalkan was even more dazzling than he had been by moonlight and morning mist: his thick white fur had the same crystalline dazzle as the winter's first fall of snow, and his spiral horn had the prismatic fire of polished crystal. Yet Shalkan was undeniably as much a palpable living creature as Kellen was: real and earthly (though obviously magical), and not an illusion that might vanish at any moment. And not much like that little silver-plated mascot Kellen still carried, except as to general shape. The heat of the day intensified the spicy scent of the unicorn's fur, making Kellen's stomach rumble and causing him to think longingly of bakeshops and plates of fried sweet cakes.

More bells—as the City he had left reckoned time—passed as they fled, and as they continued to climb, Kellen was able to look back and see the hills spread out behind them;

thousands of acres of land that seemed to be completely un-
inhabited—at least by humans.

Yet Shalkan said it was all City lands, and undoubtedly
the unicorn was right.

Why did the City claim so much territory? The two of them
must have covered hundreds of leagues in their escape, or at
least it seemed that way. They were heading almost directly
west, and they still weren't out of reach of the Outlaw Hunt.

"Why?" Kellen said aloud.

"Why what?" Shalkan responded, dropping back to a trot.
The unicorn was looking from side to side, as it had been
since midmorning, as if it were searching for something specific. A landmark?

"Why does the City claim so much land?" Kellen asked,
repeating his thoughts aloud. "The farmlands, okay, I can see
that—we need the farmlands for the crops, but this isn't farmland—"

"Because they're greedy idiots," the unicorn said bluntly.

Kellen flinched. He knew he shouldn't care. The City had
condemned him to death, after all. He was an Outlaw. But at
this time yesterday he'd been heading down to the docks,
with no real idea any of this was going to happen. And somehow he could not help but feel obscurely guilty that *his* former home was so cordially disliked as to evoke *that* sort of
response from the unicorn. Fine, it wasn't *Kellen's* fault, but
he still felt guilty, tainted by association.

Shalkan sighed. "Kellen, I'm sorry. You deserve a better
answer, and I don't have one. Ask me something else."

"How long until we reach the border?" Kellen asked.

There was a long silence, and from it, Kellen could already
read the answer that Shalkan didn't want to give.

"The Hounds will reach us first, won't they?" he said quietly.

Shalkan stopped and looked back at him. "They're about
an hour—four chimes—behind us. The border is . . . farther
than that. We need to find a place to make a stand. That's
what I've been looking for. I'm sorry, Kellen, but it's going
to come to a fight after all."

Shalkan turned back to the trail and put on a burst of speed then that surprised even Kellen, who dropped his makeshift rein and went back to clinging tightly to the unicorn's neck with both arms in order to hold on.

At last the unicorn stopped again, so suddenly that Kellen's whole body was flung forward against his neck.

"Here."

Kellen raised his head and looked around, blinking at the brightness that confronted him.

He was facing a sheer wall of white granite. It reflected the midday sun with a bright eye-hurting intensity. A gentle slope of gravel and granite chips led up to a shallow opening in the rock, as if two blocks of granite had been eased a few feet apart by some master hand. The trail they'd been following led on around the edge of the cliff, and the path Shalkan stood on was only a few feet wide. The ground dropped off into a steep, brush-filled gully on the far side of the path, and beyond, the ground sloped sharply away in a tangle of granite outcroppings and barren sloping hills, all bathed in harsh, cloudless spring sunlight.

"We're running out of time, and this is the best we've got. They can't get behind us there, and we'll have room to fight. But you'll need a weapon." The unicorn raised his head and sniffed the air, and added, "Quickly. We probably won't hear them coming until it's too late."

Kellen slid from Shalkan's back, his hand automatically going to his belt. But his penknife was a tiny thing, suitable for sharpening quills and cutting paper, not to doing battle with monstrous stone dogs.

He cast a frantic look around. At the end of the path was a conifer tree, its trunk gnarled and twisted by years of exposure to the elements in this hostile place. The branches should have been covered with green needles, but instead, they were bare and stark. Dead. Maybe dry enough to break off a piece, but not so brittle the piece would be useless. Kellen ran toward it.

When he reached it, he saw that it had been struck by lightning, shearing away most of the trunk and burning the core to charcoal. One thick smooth branch, solid and heavy as iron, the bark long polished away by the wind, came away easily in his hands. He returned, panting, with his makeshift club.

"Good," Shalkan said brusquely. The unicorn turned and lunged up the slope. Kellen scrambled after him, slipping and sliding on the loose rock that covered the ground. The uncertain footing would be another advantage for them when the Hounds came for them.

Once Kellen had armed himself, the two of them climbed to the cleft in the granite wall. It was shallow and narrow—only four feet deep, narrowing to a point at the back, and a bit over a yard wide at the opening. No room for a Hound to get around them and come at them from behind. Though the mountain air had a cool bite to it, the pale walls of the pocket canyon radiated heat, as warm as living flesh to the touch.

Kellen clutched at his wooden club tightly, aware in the sudden stillness that he could hear a scrabbling sound, like rats in a rockfall, disturbing pebbles as they ran, only much louder.

It was the sound of rock on rock. The Hounds.

The next thing he saw was the bright flash of sun as it struck a polished surface, and then Kellen saw his first Hound, surging up over the edge of the gully.

It charged up the gravel slope at a dead run, as unnervingly silent as Shalkan had warned. It looked *exactly* like the ones outside his front door, aside from being carved from a different color of granite, and that somehow added an element of horror to the whole situation, as if this were a strange waking nightmare. It made him feel as if he and Shalkan were being attacked by the City itself.

The Hound was the shape and size of a regular mastiff, carved all out of mirror-polished red granite, lovingly detailed by its maker-Mage down to the studded collar about its neck. Its red, blank eyes, like featureless marbles, glared unseeing in their direction; its red tongue lolled between its red teeth; its red lips were drawn back in a red snarl; and it lunged up the treacherous slope with those polished granite eyes fixed unblinkingly on Kellen's face.

Behind it came more—a dozen, twenty, too many to count. All identical to the first save for the color of the granite from which they'd been carved: red, white, black, grey. All silent, save for the thud of their stone feet against the ground, the clatter of stone paws on more stone, the clicking of dislodged gravel rolling downslope, or the smack of their granite flanks against each other as they jostled for position. How many *were* there? Two dozen? More?

Kellen had a moment for one pang of terror—when Shalkan had first described the Hunt, he'd thought there'd be only a few Hounds, six, perhaps, or eight—before the first one reached him. Then there was no more time for thought at all, as the Hounds surged up the graveled slope, the red one in the lead, fangs bared for his throat.

He swung his club, aiming low at the first Hound's brittle and vulnerable legs. Once, when he was a child, he'd seen a stone golem slip and break. He knew that even though they were enchanted, the Hound golems were still as fragile as the carved stone they really were, and for all its bulk, a Hound's legs were comparatively slender in proportion to its size.

His club connected with a dull impact of wood against stone. With a pang of savage delight, Kellen saw the Hound's foreleg break off with a crack, and the three-legged Hound lost its balance and rolled backward down the slope, bowling over several of the Hounds behind it with dull tombstone thuds. They milled and snapped at each other just as if they were dogs of flesh, making a sound like boulders tumbling together.

But a moment later, they seemed to recall their task, and surged in a body up the hill—and they just kept coming.

Out of the corner of his eye he saw a flicker of magic. One of the Hounds had reached Shalkan. The unicorn had reached out and touched it with his horn, and the Hound had stiffened, becoming a nonmagical stone statue once more. It tumbled down, just like any other boulder, away from the canyon opening. Bits of it cracked off and went flying in all directions as it fell.

A flash of memory told Kellen what had happened. A unicorn's horn could purify anything it touched, and break all magick, Kellen remembered from his studies, and felt a sudden flash of hope. Because of that, at least they had a chance.

But as fast as Shalkan was, the Hounds were faster. If one of them got its jaws around Shalkan's throat, the unicorn would be dead.

Shalkan's hooves were all-but-useless here; only his horn was going to be at all effective.

Another Hound leaped at Kellen. This time Kellen was too slow. He missed when he swung at it, and Shalkan had too many problems of his own to come to Kellen's rescue. Kellen found himself with his arms full of writhing, silently snarling stone Hound, heavy as granite yet horribly alive.

Its jaws snapped inches from his throat as its clawed paws scrabbled at his arms and stomach. He dropped his club. A second Hound had darted in beneath it; he felt its jaws closing on his leg. One good snap—and his leg would be useless, broken, and it would all be over.

With a shout of fear and pain, Kellen kicked at the stone face of the second Hound, keeping it from getting a good bite in, and shoved the first Hound away from his face. Somehow, he grabbed it by its hind legs; it tried to escape him, but this was a smaller Hound, about the size of a greyhound, and a lot lighter than its fellows. He used the Hound itself as a club, swinging it at the head of the second Hound golem until its jaws shattered and the legs in his hands snapped off. He flung and kicked them both away, screaming wordlessly. He snatched up his club and hammered at the next one as it rushed him, sweeping low with his club, then turned to protect Shalkan.

Out of his line of sight, Kellen heard the dull impact of stone on stone as the Hounds now tried to rush them in a pack, and those that missed slammed against the granite walls to either side of the canyon opening. Some slid back to the bottom of the slope. Others tried to rush in from the side.

Their jaws clattered as they snapped at Kellen and missed, and when he looked, he could *see* them barking, or at least their jaws working as if they were barking, but there was no sound other than the impact of stone on stone, and wood on stone, and the faint sizzle as Shalkan managed to disenchant another of the Hound golems.

If the Outlaw Hunt had been smarter than the mastiffs they resembled, Kellen and Shalkan would have been dead in the first few instants of the attack. But the stone Hounds were only stronger, and faster, and tireless, and nearly invulnerable.

Nearly, that was the key thing. Mastiffs weren't the brightest dogs in the world, and these stone versions seemed even dimmer. They didn't even try to protect themselves, and they didn't learn from the mistakes of the ones that were eliminated. That was what gave him and Shalkan a chance. A slim chance, but a real one, and a far, far better one than any of the Mages would have believed, back in the City. Quickly their strategy evolved—Kellen stood in front, beating the Hounds back, breaking their legs off when he could, protecting Shalkan so that the unicorn could dart out and destroy each one permanently. Even if Kellen managed to break off two legs, or a lower jaw, the maimed-but-still-enchanted Hound would just keep on coming, crawling up the slope as long as it could still move in order to get at its prey.

He could not kill the creatures, but he could cripple them— Shalkan couldn't hurt them, but he could destroy them. The Hunt climbed over its weaker members, trying to get at him and Shalkan indiscriminately, not realizing that of the two of them, Shalkan was the most dangerous. The two of them took advantage of that.

And slowly, slowly, Kellen and Shalkan winnowed the pack, until the Hounds coming against them were few enough to count, and all of them were chipped and battered by previous attacks.

As their numbers diminished, the Hounds seemed to sense the fact—their leaps grew more frantic, their assaults more desperate. Once Kellen was bitten: the Hound's jaws closed over his forearm, its teeth just about to break the skin before Shalkan turned the Hound into lifeless stone. But even so, Kellen had to batter the stone body against the wall of the pocket canyon to loosen its unliving grip from his flesh.

And in that moment of distraction, two more attacked.

"Kellen!"

One was missing one of its forelegs. The other had lost its lower jaw and half its head. Kellen managed to knock the three-legged one sideways, away from Shalkan, before the other leaped into the air and bore Kellen down.

His head hit the ground with an impact that jarred his teeth, and then the Hound, shaking its head like a terrier with a rat, hit him across the side of the head with the ragged remains of its muzzle.

It could not bite. But it did not have to bite to kill him. All it had to do was batter him to death with blows from its flailing stone head—or hold him, helpless, while others of its pack arrived to finish him.

"Hold it still!" Shalkan shouted, and Kellen, grimly, struggled to obey.

There was a jarring impact, and the Hound flew off his chest as the unicorn pivoted and kicked. Kellen heard the sound of breaking stone.

"Up!" Shalkan cried desperately.

Kellen dragged himself to his feet, scrabbling for his club. He staggered, dazed and unable to see as dark spots filled his vision. His nose was bleeding, and he snorted, spraying blood. He swung wildly, and felt the blow connect, felt the jarring hardness of wood against stone as he knocked one of the golems flying.

They fought on. If there was a Hell, this was surely it . . .

Finally—silence.

No thudding of stone-on-stone, no dark bodies rushing at him, no more Hounds were coming up the slope. Exhausted and drenched in sweat, his clothing in rags, Kellen looked around. The ground was littered with broken stone statues that had once been the Hounds of the Outlaw Hunt. Not one of them was whole.

Horribly, there were lots of bits that were still moving, still writhing, still trying to get *at* their quarry. But nothing that could do him or Shalkan any harm.

"We did it—" Kellen said in dull and weary disbelief. He wanted to feel relief, but—well, perhaps there was a spark of it. He hadn't the strength to sustain more than that little spark, though. Every muscle hurt. He would have given up long since except for the need to protect Shalkan. "We—"

"No," Shalkan said bleakly, interrupting him. "Listen."

There was the sound of scrabbling stone feet over rock.

"No . . ." Kellen said in angry disbelief. *More Hounds.* "No. *That's not fair!*"

A second pack of Hounds swarmed into view, a pack even larger than the first.

Kellen stared, watching them come, frozen in shock.

The City had sent a second Outlaw Hunt. Against all Law and Custom, they'd sent a second pack of Hounds, a second Hunt, to kill him—to kill *them*. They'd hated him enough to do that—his *father* hated him enough to do that—and not only was he, Kellen, going to die here because of that, *Shalkan* was going to die, too, because of the spell Kellen had cast and the vow Shalkan had sworn, to take Kellen over the border of City lands. Shalkan would not leave him, and the Hounds would kill Shalkan too.

His fault. Because the Council cheated. His fault. Because the Council lied. His fault. Because Lycaelon Tavadon had cheated and lied. His *father,* the noble, the honorable, the *respected* Arch-Mage of Armethalieh. The *trusted* leader of the High Council.

Someplace in the back of his mind, Kellen had still believed in Lycaelon, believed at least that the Arch-Mage would keep his word. Perhaps even believed that, no matter what had passed between them, there was still *something* binding them together, and that his father would, in all decency, allot him some sort of fair chance, no matter how tiny. But Lycaelon could not bear to be contradicted, could not bear to be defeated, and clearly would do anything to revenge himself on the person who had done both.

A vast fury filled Kellen—if there'd still been love there between the two of them, father and son, that love had been betrayed and defiled so utterly and completely that it left a terrible vacuum; and this rage rushed in to take its place. It swept away Kellen's pain and exhaustion. In his rage, he felt nothing but the need to destroy this terrible thing, this thing that should not be. He stepped forward and struck at the first of the Hounds, tears of grief and fury streaming unnoticed down his face. In his blind, berserker *anger,* he felt nothing but the need to destroy.

There was not even room in his mind for *thoughts,* only a focused and diamond-hard rage, white-hot, searing away everything else. He stepped forward and struck at the first of the Hounds with a strength he didn't even recognize as his own. His eyes blurred and cleared; there was wetness on his cheeks. His tears were irrelevant. All that mattered was the enemy before him and the weapon in his hand.

He'd ridden all night and fought off one pack of Hounds already. Kellen didn't care. He was beyond thinking. It didn't matter. None of it mattered. Rage filled him but did not overmaster him. He was beyond thinking, but that only freed him to *act.* As if he, too, were made of stone, he fought, drawing on reserves he did not know he had and did not question the source of. He could not lose this fight—whatever the cost, whatever the price he must pay later, he could not lose. His whole world narrowed to the few feet of space just before the mouth of the canyon. Whatever entered that space he hit.

Afterward Kellen retained only a blurred and confused body-memory of disjointed moments of the fight, as though once the picture of what had happened had been whole, then someone had smashed it and left Kellen with nothing more than a handful of jagged pieces.

He remembered doing things that were impossible, and doing them because he had to.

He remembered batting a Hound out of the air, feeling as if he had all the time in the world to strike the blow because the creature just seemed to hang there, as if Time itself had stopped.

He remembered the feel of stone jaws closing on his flesh. No pain, just a crushing coldness, as if the cold of the stone had somehow transferred itself to his body.

He remembered forcing his fingers once again around the shaft of the club, seeing that one of them wouldn't move, seeing that it was broken, closing his other hand over it and forcing the broken finger into place. He did not feel the pain.

He remembered how quietly the Hounds' legs sheared away, how the place where the stone broke glittered like fresh-spilled salt in the afternoon sun. He remembered how the light flashed off their polished skins, making the moving pack flicker like the surface of the harbor on a bright day when the wind was blowing over the water, and in the back of his mind, Kellen could almost hear the faint scream of gulls. He did not remember his own screams, how as the battle wore on, his voice cracked and broke, and became only a whisper of unyielding fury.

And still the Hounds came. And still Kellen fought.

—

"KELLEN. *Kellen.*"

Someone was calling his name.

"Kellen. KELLEN!"

Dazedly, Kellen tried to raise his club once more, and realized that at last he had no strength left. His muscles shook; a slow constant tremor as if he were wracked by fever-chill, but he felt almost as if he were floating, somehow distant from his body, as if everything he had done, he had done almost in his sleep.

He was staring at the ground. He couldn't raise the club, because he wasn't holding the club. The world around him was silent, without the clack and rattle of living stone moving to attack. Somehow there was a wrongness to that, and Kellen felt a faint pang of alarm. Where was his club? Where were the Hounds?

He raised his head, slowly. The effort made him nauseous and light-headed. He blinked. It took a conscious effort, and his eyes felt gritty and dry. He knew, obscurely, that he should be in pain, but he wasn't yet. Just—numb. Exhausted, and numb.

Shalkan was standing beside him, gazing at him with a worried expression. The unicorn looked rumpled, his head hanging with exhaustion, but there was no blood on his silver fur.

Kellen raised his hand to touch that fur, and gasped as shooting pain lanced through his body, shocking him back to himself. He looked down. Swollen and bloody against his forearm was the deep print of mastiff jaws.

"We have to go now," Shalkan said gently, raising his head with an effort. The unicorn's voice was hoarse, and Kellen felt a dim flare of alarm for his companion.

"But the Hounds," Kellen said. His voice sounded clumsy and strained, as if he'd forgotten how to speak. He looked around, blinking at the brightness of sun on stone.

"They're all dead," Shalkan said flatly. "Or if they aren't, they're no danger to us."

The ground around the pocket canyon was littered with the lifeless broken statues and scattered limbs that had been the Outlaw Hunt—and worst of all, here and there, the limbless bodies of still-animate Hounds, helpless but still attempting to reach their prey, squirming like hideous caterpillars of stone.

"Get on," Shalkan said again, taking another step closer to him. "They'll have figured out by now that we've managed to get rid of the first packs. They'll be creating more. Fortunately, it will take them some time, and the new packs won't get here until morning. But we're only safe over the Border. Get on. You have to get on; we have to get out of here."

"I can't do that again," Kellen said in a ragged whisper. "I can't."

"Kellen," Shalkan said harshly. "Are you listening to me? Get on. We have to go now. We have to get over the Border before they send another pack."

Kellen finally turned toward Shalkan, but when he moved,

his knees buckled and he fell. The unicorn moved forward quickly, so that Kellen fell half across his back, stomach down.

Shalkan stood steadily beneath his weight. Kellen sprawled there for a long moment, his body suddenly aware of how much it hurt, and wondered how he would ever find the strength to lift his leg across the unicorn's haunches.

But he had to. Because if they stayed here, another Hunt would come. And this time, they'd both die.

He couldn't let that happen to Shalkan.

Gritting his teeth, Kellen swung his right leg across Shalkan's back.

The bolt of sudden unexpected agony shocked him back to full consciousness. He realized that there was a deep welling bite high on the outside of his right thigh, and that his left ankle had been bruised between a Hound's jaws sometime during the fight. It twisted beneath him as he put his full weight on it to mount, and he grabbed Shalkan's shoulders, gasping for breath. As he did, his broken finger momentarily hurt worse than all the other injuries put together, and he gasped and coughed, choking on the pain. Shalkan half crouched, and suddenly Kellen was on his back, sprawled astride. There was no way he could hold on—but at least he was in place. More or less. For now.

"Comfy?" the unicorn asked sardonically, shifting his weight to settle Kellen more securely on his back. And somehow, that single word—or perhaps the tone, laden with heavy irony—brought a little more life back into Kellen, though he could not have said why. Maybe because, if Shalkan was feeling strong enough to be sarcastic, there was still hope.

Kellen laughed raggedly, feeling blood from his thigh starting to trickle down his leg and into what remained of his boot. "Oh, yeah." His voice was hoarse and cracked, and his throat hurt.

"Don't fall off," Shalkan advised.

"Right."

Shalkan picked his way carefully down the slope, avoiding the still-moving bodies of the crippled Hounds, and continued along the trail, still at a slow walk. All the grace and vitality of the unicorn's gait was gone now. Forget bounding across the forest, Shalkan moved as ploddingly as if each step was an effort. Kellen empathized with his friend—for at some point during the fight, Shalkan had become just that—but at the same time a small selfish part of himself was grateful, because he could not possibly have managed to stay on Shalkan's back if the unicorn had set any faster pace. As it was, each footfall jarred him all the way through, making everything hurt afresh with each step Shalkan took, and Kellen bit his lip to keep from crying out as they moved slowly down the trail. He realized as he did so that he'd bitten it before—or something had. His face was a mask of blood. His nose felt swollen and hot; he started to touch it, and thought better of doing so. Maybe it was broken. It was a lot easier to breathe through his mouth.

As the combination of adrenaline and stupor wore off, Kellen gradually became aware of just how extensively he'd been hurt. The bite on his thigh was only the bloodiest of his injuries; Kellen had been bitten in half a dozen places during the battle; crushing or tearing wounds that burned and throbbed, the bruising almost more agonizing than the pain. The hand with the broken finger was swelling and starting to turn dark, making his right hand stiff and almost impossible to use. His muscles ached with strain; his head hurt as if it had been hit—*hard*—several times . . . in fact, he didn't think there was any part of him that *didn't* hurt just now.

"Do you suppose they're poisoned?" Kellen asked, to distract himself. "The Hound's teeth, I mean?" Talking still hurt, but he found he really wanted to know.

"The strangest things entertain you," Shalkan said, but Kellen could hear a note of relief in the unicorn's voice that he was asking the question—or any question at all. "No, I don't think so. But cheer up—there's always the chance of infection. Or gangrene. Or maggots. Now why don't you see if your water-bottle survived intact and have a nice drink?"

Kellen had forgotten about his backpack—though he'd fallen on it a couple of times during the fight—and completely forgotten about the water-bottle he'd filled at the stream at dawn today. Balancing himself carefully on Shalkan's back, he managed to get the backpack off and open it with his good hand.

The water in the small waterskin was warm and tasted of leather, but Kellen had never in his life tasted anything so delicious. He drained it in a few thirsty swallows before replacing the bottle and shrugging the backpack carefully into position once more. It hurt, but it was worth it.

It was the last halfway pleasant experience of the afternoon.

Kellen's sense of victory at having defeated and escaped the Outlaw Hunt swiftly disappeared in the presence of the grinding pain of his injuries. His entire body slowly became one throbbing, feverish ache, interrupted by unexpected lances of fiery agony. As the pain increased, the afternoon sun seemed fiendishly bright, the cool air of the high hills alternately freezing in the shade, or a choking furnace heat in the sun.

"I have to get down and walk," Kellen said at one point, barely aware of what he was saying. He knew that Shalkan was as exhausted as he was, though he didn't think the unicorn had actually been injured in the fight. He had a vague notion that it would hurt both of them less if he walked; he'd managed to forget that he was too badly hurt to take even a few steps.

"No you don't. Just hold on," Shalkan said soothingly.

Kellen leaned forward, resting his whole weight against the unicorn's neck and awkwardly embracing it. It was easy enough to do; the unicorn's head hung low now, his neck parallel to the ground. Shalkan's bristly mane dug into Kellen's neck and chest, pressing now against bare skin, because his undertunic had been reduced to rags by the Hounds' attacks, but Kellen barely noticed that small discomfort. Dimly, he remembered that there were things he ought to be doing, things he should be worrying about, but the pain was like a vast thick liquid that was slowly submerging him, taking away his ability to reason, to think.

They crossed the ridge and went down into forest again. Kellen's head ached fiercely, the pounding pain throbbing in time with his heartbeat. He groaned aloud, unable to understand why they were back among the trees—were they going back to the City? Why?—but glad to be away from the bright sunlight. Sometimes he heard Shalkan speaking to him, repeating the same words over and over with weary patience, but he was unable to rouse himself enough to make sense of what the unicorn was saying. Sometimes he tried to answer, not sure if his answers made any sense, but finally he was unable to make even that much effort, and sometime after that, Shalkan stopped talking to him.

An eternity seemed to pass as they walked—slowly—toward the setting sun. Kellen never lost consciousness, not completely. A tiny part of his mind was always aware that he had to hold on, though at times he wasn't sure where he was or even, near the end, what he was holding on to. When he felt himself drifting too far into unconsciousness he fought to bring himself back by forcing his broken hand into a fist, or slapping it against Shalkan's shoulder—making the unicorn stagger—and that worked for a while.

But at last he lost the strength for even that.

"WE'RE across."

The pain ebbed, a little. Just a little. Just enough for Kellen to understand that the unicorn had stopped moving. "We're across," Shalkan repeated. The unicorn staggered to a stop and stood splay-legged, swaying.

Kellen opened his eyes. Either it was dusk, or his vision was failing. He closed them again, and tried not to move.

Something was pulling at him, dragging him from the unicorn's back. In his mind, Kellen struggled wildly, but his body had no more left to give. He tried to see his attacker, but it was too dark, or his vision was gone at last. He felt himself being pulled upright, away from Shalkan. His feet brushed the ground and he cried out, a hoarse cawing sound, as pain lanced upward from his ankle to the crown of his head, making the world flare lightning-bright for a brief moment. Then the oblivion he had been fighting against all day swept over him in a sudden wave.

And then nothing.

He roused again at the touch of cool patient hands. He was lying down somewhere dark and shadowy, but he could tell nothing beyond than that. He blinked, trying to force his eyes open, but he couldn't make them focus. All he saw was a vague shape, dark against dark.

"Rest," a soothing voice told him. "You're safe here."

Kellen was too tired to disbelieve. He lay back, letting the hands and voice do as they wished.

"Drink."

There was a cup at his lips, and Kellen was terribly thirsty. It was cool, and only when he had drained the cup did he realize that it wasn't water, but something foul-tasting and bitter. He choked and tried to push it away, but it was too late, and he was far too weak to fight. The darkness was back, carrying Kellen away with it.

Chapter Ten

Hunters of the Dark

Kellen dreamed, and his dreams were anything but pleasant.

There was no sun nor moon, but somehow he could see everything clearly.

He looked around, and saw without surprise that he was back in the canyon, but the lush woods in the distance had been replaced by the lifeless, shattered corpses of trees, and sere grasses tufted the ground beneath them. This time, he was alone.

When he looked up, the sky was a swirl of ugly colors, the red of drying blood, and bruise-purple, and the sickly green of an infected wound. It glowed; the strange dim light of the foxfire found in rotten stumps. The breeze carried the scent of carrion.

The Hounds were coming; he saw them plunging among the blasted remains of the trees, hard, shining claws tearing up great clots of dead turf as they ran. Their eyes glowed, the furnace-red of embers. He could see them swarming toward him, not dozens this time, but hundreds, and as they came closer, they began to change. They sprouted long curling yellow horns, their tails became long and barbed, and their smooth granite skins bubbled and erupted until they were covered with scales. And at the last, leathery wings burst from their shoulders and unfurled in an obscene parody of butterflies emerging from a cocoon.

With a shock, he recognized what they had become. They were Demons, just as Lycaelon had promised. He'd summoned them with the Wild Magic, and they'd come.

They reached for him with their clawed hands, dove at him from above on their leathery wings. They were all around him now, circling around him, laughing mockingly. His sanctuary was gone.

"Wildmage—you summoned us with your magic—Wildmage—"

He swung at them with his club, but it changed in his hand into another Demon, writhing around and sinking its fangs into his arm.

He flung the club away and ran.

⌒

HE was back in the City, at Perulan's house in the Artists' Quarter. Kellen's heart leaped with hope as he ran up the steps and hammered on the door. There was still time. He could warn Perulan not to leave, not to go down to the docks—

Perulan opened the door. He was wearing his favorite red

tunic, smiling as he saw it was Kellen. But as Kellen watched in horror, the cloth became tight and shiny, spread quickly all over the writer's body and turned to scales, as Perulan became taller, fanged and clawed and winged.

"I was waiting for you, Wildmage. Come in . . ."

The Demon lunged, laughing. Kellen turned and ran.

HE was running through the forest. It was night. Thorns and brambles ripped and tore at him, and behind him he could hear the howling of the pack as they followed. Just ahead was the canyon, if he could only reach it. But he had to have a weapon to defend himself with.

He stopped, frantically searching, but saw nothing he could use. At last, far ahead, he spotted a branch that he could tear free. But when he reached it and pulled it away from the tree, he saw that it was old and rotting, crumbling away to splinters in his hand. Useless.

And then the first of the Hounds was upon him, leaping onto his back, tearing at his clothes with paws that turned to taloned fingers as it giggled in his ear.

"Wildmage—Wildmage—Wildmage—"

HE woke up.

He was in his own bed in his own room back in House Tavadon. *It was all a dream!*

Relief so intense he nearly swooned filled him. All a dream! The discovery, the trial, the Banishment, and everything that followed, only a dream! A warning, and he'd been lucky to receive it. Now he could—

But when he flung back the covers, he saw that the sky outside was the color of blood and darkness. Green fire laced across the sky, and by its light he could see the Hunt, racing across the garden toward his window.

He ran for the door, but the door was gone. His father had

taken the door away, because his father meant him to die here, die with the Demons he'd summoned.

He picked up a club . . .

—

HE was standing over a Demon. It was dead, and its blood was all over him. He wiped it away, but the harder he scrubbed at it, the more it spread, and everywhere it spread his skin turned black—black and scaled. Demonskin.

He was a Demon, too.

Kellen ran.

—

THE Hounds pursued him, and Kellen ran. They turned into Demons, laughing at him, mocking at him, until, most horrible of all, somehow Kellen was one of them, running with the Hunt, chasing himself, howling with glee as he ran through eternal night on leathery clawed paws, hunting himself down. He would always run, always hunt. He would never be free . . .

Tainted. Unclean. Because of the Wild Magic, just as Lycaelon had said.

Lycaelon had been right. He'd been right about the Banishing, and he'd been right about this. Why would the High Council send so many Hounds, send not one Hunt, but many, if Lycaelon had not been telling the truth about the Demons . . . ?

At last Kellen spiraled down into a deeper sleep, one without dreams.

—

WHAT seemed a very long time later, Kellen woke up.

It was day. He stared incuriously at the ceiling for a long time, aware of being awake but without feeling the slightest need to do anything about it. He realized that he'd felt this way before—once, as a child, he'd caught the Spotted Sickness and run a very high fever for almost a week. When the fever had finally run its course he'd felt just like this, as if all his energy had been burned away by his body's fires. He wasn't sure where he was, and had no clear idea of how he'd come here, nor did it really matter to him. To think, to remember, to feel, all would take more energy than he had.

It was a pleasant sort of lassitude, a comforting exhaustion, where the body said to the mind, *you* will *rest because you have no choice, you will* not *think, nor worry, because you will not have the strength.*

He was lying on a bed in a small room with walls completely made out of unpeeled logs chinked with white river clay. He could see the ceiling—thatch over timbers—and parts of two walls. There was a window in one of the walls, its shutters thrown open to admit light and air; he had a view of green tree branches, and heard a chorus of birdsong, and the air smelled verdant and sweet. To see anything more would involve moving, and Kellen wasn't ready to do that yet.

He was not completely certain of how he'd gotten here. The unicorn . . . was Shalkan real, or was he a part of the vivid fever-dreams? Memory thrust itself into his present with the sudden unwelcome pain of a thorn in the foot. Remembering made Kellen shudder weakly—but those dreams—the Hounds, the fight—they *couldn't* have been real, could they? He'd been wounded nearly to death, and nothing hurt now. He was very weak, but he wasn't in any pain.

But I am *here, not in my room—I've never seen anything like* this *room in the City. So I* was *Banished, and I escaped the Hunt, so Shalkan must be real . . .*

Just then, he heard soft footsteps behind him, and a young woman came into his field of vision. She was carrying a small wooden tray. Her arrival jarred Kellen further out of his drifting mood of acceptance, for she looked nothing like any female he had ever seen before in his life, dressed as she was in garments that no City-dweller, even the most desperate day laborer, would have contemplated wearing for even a moment. She was . . . she was *un-Citified*. More proof, assuming Kellen had needed it, that he was actually outside the City.

The stranger was wearing a sleeveless calf-length dress that looked as if it were made of some kind of soft golden leather, and her long dark hair was parted in the middle and pulled back into two braids wrapped and tied with leather as well, worn down as no adult woman of the City would ever consider wearing hers. She had a curious face, which reminded him of a cat; perhaps because it was shaped like an inverted triangle, perhaps because her expression was very certain, and very self-composed. He'd never seen a female who had such an air of self-confidence about her—but then as a member of the Mageborn aristocracy, Kellen hadn't met very many females at all. Her soft violet eyes, which seemed large for her face, were fringed by the longest darkest lashes Kellen had ever seen—and suddenly he was positive, not only that Shalkan was real, but that the vow of chastity and celibacy that he had so recklessly sworn to gain the unicorn's aid was going to be more difficult to keep than he'd ever actually imagined.

His body's response surprised him—surely he was far too weak and sick to be thinking of something like *that* at a time like this?

All this went through his mind in the moment it took for her to turn her gaze on him and smile.

"Oh, good, you're awake. I was starting to worry; it's been more than a sennight," she said. Her voice was low and friendly, and strangely familiar—where could he have heard it before?—and her smile warmed her eyes. "Do you think you can sit up?"

Without waiting for an answer, she set the wooden tray on a table beside the bed and moved toward Kellen. Slipping one arm behind his shoulders, she pulled him into an upright position with easy strength. As the bedcovers—a thin wool blanket covered by several supple, beautifully tanned animal skins with the hair still on—slipped away, Kellen realized he wasn't wearing a single thing beneath them.

Reflexively, he grabbed for the blanket, pulling it up

around his waist, and gazed at his hands and arms in puzzlement.

There were no wounds. No bites, no bruises, not even any of the scratches he'd gotten riding Shalkan through all those thornbushes on their flight from the City before the fight with the stone Hounds. He didn't even see the bruises from the way the stone golems had handled him, dragging him out of the Council chamber.

For a moment reality slid dizzyingly around Kellen. Without the proof of his injuries to anchor him, he wasn't sure what to believe. What was real, and what was just a fever dream?

But Shalkan was *real*. He was sure of it. And the City had sent an Outlaw Hunt to kill him and anyone who dared to help him escape the City lands—the Hounds. He remembered almost everything now. But where were the bites, the wounds—the proof of his flight? He didn't even have *scars*.

"Eat now, then we'll talk," the woman said firmly, seeing his confusion. "You've been asleep for a long time."

But not long enough to heal without scars, Kellen thought with a faint pang of fear.

The strange woman sat down on the edge of the bed and helped him feed himself. He was weaker than he'd expected to be, and clumsy; she had to guide his fingers around the wooden mug and help him hold it to his lips, and he could not manage the bowl and spoon at all for very long. The strength just went out of his arm and hand, and his hand shook so much he had to give up on the notion of doing without help. She just waited while he came to that conclusion by himself, then took up the spoon and continued where he had left off.

Defeated, he lay back and let her feed him, but when he had finished the meat broth and the mug of herb tea with honey, he felt much stronger. Strong enough to worry about where Shalkan was, and about what came next, at any rate. He was free of the City, and now he had to figure out what to do next. In fact, he had his entire life to figure out now, and the prospect was daunting.

Free. In all his seventeen years of life, Kellen had never imagined the word could have such a bitter taste. For the rest of his life he was going to have to live with the consequences of a decision made in the flush of youthful bravado and adolescent anger. He was an Outlaw—barring a miracle, he would never see Armethalieh or his father again. And now that he was in this position, he realized that he *missed* the City more than he'd ever imagined he could.

Or—did he really miss the City, or only the comforts and certainty it represented? It was not going to be an easy thing to make his way alone outside the City walls.

For one thing, how was he going to live out here? Unless something extraordinary happened, and this young woman decided to allow him to live with her, he was completely without resources now. He didn't even have *clothing* at this point! No food, no clothing, no place to live, and no idea how he was to get any of those things. He knew nothing about farming, hunting—

Maybe Shalkan could help him. If Shalkan was all right— if the unicorn wasn't in worse shape than *he* had been . . . Kellen had a vague recollection of seeing Shalkan's white fur saturated with blood; it couldn't have been the Hounds', and he couldn't remember if it was his . . .

"Your friend is fine," the woman said, as if she could guess the direction of at least some of his thoughts. "And he was in much better shape to begin with than you were when you arrived. The unicorn says that your name is Kellen, you're a Wildmage, and that you fight remarkably well, but he doesn't know much else. Now, since all I know about you is that you escaped the City and the Outlaw Hunt, and that you arrived on my doorstep in a rather pitiable condition, let's begin at the beginning. Tell me, Outlaw, what's your full name?"

He didn't really want to tell her his life story, but—well— she'd more or less earned some answers by taking him in and caring for him *without* knowing anything about him.

"Kellen . . . Tavadon," he admitted reluctantly.

His rescuer looked startled, as if she almost suspected him

of playing some kind of a trick on her. Her eyes widened, then narrowed, and her jawline tensed.

"Son of Lycaelon Tavadon?" she asked sharply. "The Arch-Mage of Armethalieh?"

"Yes . . ." Kellen admitted warily. It suddenly occurred to him that if the City enforced its rules by such drastic means as the Outlaw Hunt within its borders, it might have enemies outside them.

She knows Father's name. What has he done to her, to her people? Is she going to hate me, because Lycaelon's my father? Or demand some sort of reparation from me? Or throw me back to the Hunt?

"I'm afraid so. Though I'm not exactly in good odor with him, since he's the one who Banished me."

The woman smiled sardonically, looking enormously like Lycaelon all of a sudden.

"A Tavadon—and an Outlaw to boot. Well, I guess Mother's Mountain blood runs true, *little brother*."

Of all the responses Kellen had tried to anticipate, this was not one that had even crossed the threshold of his mind. It was his turn to be startled, and for a moment he wasn't certain he'd heard her correctly.

"Brother?" Kellen said blankly.

"Didn't our loving father tell you?" the woman asked. "That you had an evil sister, and that you'd turned out just like her? I would have thought he wouldn't be able to resist casting *that* in your face, if he was Banishing you . . ."

Suddenly Kellen remembered. His last night in the City—in the cell—his father had said he would come to the same bad end that his sister had. But his sister was *dead,* killed by the Outlaw Hunt years ago!

If Kellen had been confused before, he was at the edge of panic now, as too many new ideas and too much information crowded in on him all at once. It was one thing to say—back behind the safety of the City walls—that he'd welcome new ideas and complete freedom. It was quite another thing, Kellen was discovering, to be handed both things on a platter.

"Uh . . . yes. Sort of. Not exactly," Kellen stammered. "If

you—Are you—" He shook his head just a little, trying to make his thoughts come clearer. "He said I had bad blood, all right; he said that I'd end up just like my sister. I guess you're . . . that sister?" he finished meekly.

"Typical of him," the woman—his sister!—muttered cryptically, staring fixedly at nothing for a moment.

Kellen felt an unsettled mixture of confusion and relief that did much to restore his composure. Confusion, oh my, yes. It wasn't every day that you woke up to discover entirely new family members existed. But relief as well, for this meant one thing for certain; he wasn't completely alone out here. He had a sister—and a beautiful and competent one at that. She *must* be kind; she'd taken in an Outlawed stranger and had tended him. If luck was with him, she'd let him stay with her until he got something sorted out about making his own way out here. She wouldn't throw her own brother out of her house, would she?

And another sort of relief as well, for the moment that she had named herself as his sister, every bit of desire for her had just—vanished. At least this way—since she *was* his sister, even if he didn't really know her—his promise to Shalkan would still be easy to keep.

He studied her more closely, trying to see a resemblance between them. But her hair was dark and straight where his was light and curly, and her eyes were violet to his grey. Still, now that he was looking for it, he could see something of their father in her—more than anyone could see in him, anyway.

He had a sister, right here in front of him. And she was alive. Kellen did his best to get used to both ideas.

"He didn't tell me your name," Kellen offered hopefully.

She sighed and shook her head with disgust. "Typical. He probably drove it right out of his memory. I'm Idalia—just Idalia. I don't claim *his* name. Pleased to meet you, Kellen—again."

She held out her hand, and Kellen shook it solemnly before he took in the full sense of her words. "Again? But we've never met. You were Banished before I was born. You must have been. That's why I don't remember you."

"Wait. I'm going to find you some clothes. I've had plenty of time to prepare them while you were asleep. Then we'll talk. You aren't going to like some of what you hear, so you might as well be patient—and dressed." She got up, then looked back over her shoulder and added, "You'll feel less vulnerable when you're dressed, too, and that will make it easier for you to hear some of it."

Idalia went into the other room and came back with an armful of leather of the same sort and color that she was wearing. She shook it out, revealing it to be a pair of pants—leggings, really—and a long voluminous shirt.

"I wanted to salvage your clothes, but all that was left by the time you got here was a pile of bloody rags, barely enough to make smallclothes with. This should be a good fit, though." She held out her hand to him. "Come on, now, I'll help you stand up."

"But—" Kellen felt himself blushing. He hadn't been dressed by a woman since he was ... well, a whole lot younger than this, anyway.

Idalia dropped the tunic and leggings on the bed and regarded him, hands on hips, an amused smile on her lips. "Oh, come now, brother mine, who do you think cleaned you up, treated your wounds, and put you to bed when you got here? And I bathed you and put you to bed every night until you were six; that ought to count for something."

"But—" Kellen swung his legs over the edge of the bed—still clutching the blanket to him—and stared up at her. "Idalia, I *don't remember you*," he blurted, feeling the fear begin to well up within him once more.

Idalia sighed, and tugged on one of her braids. "I know, Kellen," she said gently. "Father told me he'd do that, just before the Constables came. Look, just think of me as—as a servant, and we'll get this over with."

Kellen flushed. "I still don't remember you. And you don't seem old enough to—to have gone away when you said." Everyone who had cared for him in his childhood had been very, very old; he remembered that much. And his last "Nursie" had departed when he'd been *five*, not *six*.

She shook her head. "But I'm not; I'm only ten years older than you are. I left the City when I was sixteen, a year younger than you are. Banished, just as you were. You were born when I was ten. You were six when I left, old enough to remember me and ask embarrassing questions, since I was almost your sole caretaker until then. So after I was gone, Father tampered with your memories, erasing me from them."

Wildly, Kellen cast his mind back over his childhood. He remembered growing up—alone—in the vast gloom of House Tavadon under the indifferent care of a succession of nursemaids and nannies—none of whom had been Idalia. He remembered falling off his first pony when he was four, and the grand celebration—with fireworks in the garden—when Lycaelon had become Arch-Mage.

He did not remember Idalia. Somehow, Idalia had been taken *out* of all those memories, and a series of strangers put in her place.

"He couldn't do that!" Kellen gasped in shock as he realized just how extensive the changes must have been. *He WOULDN'T do that*, his mind cried inwardly, clinging to that last hope.

"Well, of course he could; it's a simple enough Working," Idalia said with calm reproof. "The Mages use it all the time to take traumatic—or inconvenient—memories away from people. It's all for their own good, of course—and the good of the City." Idalia smiled again, her violet eyes suddenly hard and dark, and once more Kellen could see their father in her. "And if you'd been a good little boy, and agreed to do what they told you, they'd have taken away all the memories that made a rebel out of you and replaced them with memories of conforming. They would have told themselves that it would make you infinitely happier and better off."

"They would?" he asked numbly. "They do?"

The revelation rattled Kellen to his core—but after all he had been through, it didn't really *surprise* him. Only now was he beginning to understand how utterly ruthless the Mages were. If they could kill a man, surely killing his memories would be a minor issue for them.

Idalia toyed with the end of her braid as she watched him closely. "That was one of my problems, you see, all the things that the Mages do to the people for their own good. The other was that we mere females are not allowed to become Mages. We're too emotional, you see." Her lips twisted in an ironic half smile. "As if the Mage Council isn't ruled by every petty emotion there is. Hatred, fear, jealousy . . ."

Kellen barely heard her. He was feeling more than a little sick at the thought of Lycaelon—his own *father*—using magick on him without his knowledge. That was worse than spying on him, lying to him, searching his room to find his Books. He'd been *invaded*, manipulated, changed. And why? Just to eliminate a child's inconvenient questions?

Or to help cover up the fact that Idalia had ever existed at all, to make sure that her influence over him was gone?

Kellen swallowed hard. He'd thought there'd never been an Outlaw Hunt in his lifetime, before his. He'd obviously been wrong. And the question now was, how *many* Hunts had there been? How many of Armethalieh's citizens had been torn to pieces by enchanted stone Hounds—for the good of the City? How many memories had been erased so that no one would even remember the folk who'd been Banished had ever existed?

Kellen shuddered, feeling queasy. Idalia put a gentle hand on his shoulder.

"Those memories that are gone—can they be put back?" he asked urgently, looking up into her face, and hoping he could regain this much, at least. Something more precious than *things*—something lost, something taken from him, something that was *his* by right. Something he wanted back.

Idalia met his gaze, and now there was pity in her eyes. "Oh, Kellen, no," she said softly. "What is cut away by Magecraft is gone forever. It can never be regained. But come on, let's get you dressed," she added briskly, ending the discussion. "You'll feel better, trust me."

Kellen, still stunned by what she had just told him, made

no further complaint as Idalia helped him into the snug buckskin trousers that laced up the sides, and the long, soft leather shirt that fell nearly to his knees. Both were as soft as the finest velvet, and supple as silk, of a warm, golden color, the only ornamentation being the fancy stitching over the seams. They were beautifully, if simply, made.

"You'll need boots, too, of course. I'm working on a pair. They'll be ready soon, but you won't be needing them today. Now lean on me, and let's see if you can walk a few steps," Idalia said. She put an arm around his shoulders and lifted him to his feet with surprising strength.

The floor underfoot was wide pine planks, sanded smooth. Standing made Kellen feel dizzy and light-headed, but with Idalia's firm support he was able to make his way by slow steps into the other room of the cabin.

The outer room was even smaller than the sleeping room, and windowless, but a narrow doorway stood open into the spring sunshine. Most of one wall was taken up with a fireplace made of smooth grey river stones, and a small pine table, a ladderback chair, and a stool filled the rest of the compact space. The room reminded Kellen a bit of what he imagined a ship's cabin must look like, with everything carefully built-in and tucked away to conserve valuable space.

"That fireplace took me all of one summer to build, but it gets cold up here in the winter," Idalia said, nodding at the fireplace as she lowered Kellen into the chair. "When the snows come, you'll be glad of it, believe me."

Kellen was breathing hard, even after walking only a few steps, but he thought he could already feel his strength returning. In a day or two, he was pretty sure he'd be fully recovered. Surrounded by so much newness, he barely even registered Idalia's calm assumption that he'd be here—still here—when the snows came.

From his seat, Kellen could look out the door into the world outside the cabin. The area immediately around the cabin was packed earth, scrubbed clean even of grass. Farther away the ground was covered with scrub and bushes, and then the trees began. The cabin seemed to be set in the center of a woodland clearing, without any other cabins—or for that matter, a road—anywhere in sight. In the center of the cleared area, Kellen saw a ring of large stones with an iron brace built over it. Hanging on the brace was a large copper kettle, its sides blackened with soot. Near to where the trees began there was a large flat tree stump with an axe stuck in it, and some neatly stacked firewood—far more, it seemed to Kellen, than anyone could possibly use.

The whole arrangement seemed neat and orderly and well thought out. Everything he had seen so far impressed him with Idalia's competence, even expertise, in living out here beyond City walls. She would be a good mentor to have.

He'd known her . . . before. He'd been six when she disappeared. He remembered being six. But he didn't remember Idalia.

Don't think about it now, an inner voice warned him. *Now is not the time. Later, when you're stronger. Not now.*

Kellen heeded the inner warning, and carefully turned his mind away from the new wound he'd just been given. Idalia was here now, after all. And there were plenty of things around him to concentrate on.

Without thinking about what Lycaelon had done to him. What *else* Lycaelon had done to him—and all these years, he'd never suspected . . .

As he gazed out at the trees, he saw a flash of white moving through them. Shalkan stepped out of the trees into the clearing, head held high as if scenting the air. He saw Kellen and tossed his head, locking eyes with him to be sure Kellen saw him as well, then trotted back into the trees, tufted tail held high.

"I saw Shalkan!" Kellen exclaimed, nearly losing his balance on the chair. *And he's all right.* A knot of tension Kellen hadn't known he was holding within himself eased. Idalia had said Shalkan was all right, but hearing it wasn't the same thing as seeing it.

"Your unicorn friend? Is that his name? I guess he's sticking around to keep an eye on you, then," Idalia said, unsurprised. She'd gone over to the hearth and filled two wooden mugs, adding a generous dollop of honey to each and stirring briskly. She returned to the table, setting one of the mugs in front of Kellen and sitting down on the stool. "Friendly enough, but won't have much to do with me." She flashed him a smile. "And if you think about it, you'll realize that there's an obvious reason for that."

Kellen stared at her uncomprehendingly. Idalia shook her head, dismissing the subject.

"Now. Suppose you tell me what you're doing here," she said. "The long version, this time. You might as well start at the beginning, even though the beginning is obvious."

"I was Banished," Kellen said, picking up his mug. He was very thirsty, despite what he'd already had to drink, and the sweet tea tasted good.

He looked up and found Idalia gazing at him, obviously waiting for more. The story had seemed complete to him in that sentence, but Idalia apparently felt it wasn't, so haltingly, Kellen began to tell her the rest. He hesitated about telling her *why* he'd been Banished, but Shalkan would not have brought him to this particular place if anything bad could happen to him here, and he had already begun to suspect that nothing he could tell Idalia could possibly surprise her. So he took a deep breath and told her everything—about finding the three Books of the Wild Magic; his first hesitant experiments with them; being brought before the Council when the Books were discovered in his room; casting a Calling Spell to gain Shalkan's help in exchange for a year of continence; their fight against the Hounds.

"I don't remember much after that. And I'm not sure it could have all happened the way I remember, because all the bites and everything are gone," Kellen finished, confused again.

"Oh, they were there, right enough," Idalia said. "Bites—gouges—lacerations—bruises—scratches—broken bones—you looked like you'd been through—well, an Outlaw Hunt. Lucky you were near to my cabin here, when you crossed the border; I'm the only one out here who could have put you back together again." She tilted her head a little and looked thoughtful. "The unicorn probably had something to do with that; it's no secret where I live, and he must have known that after that last border increase, you two would *have* to face the Outlaw Hunt, and afterward you'd need help, and I was the logical person to offer that help."

"I don't understand," Kellen replied, shaking his head. "I mean, I understand that we'd need to find someone and quickly, but I don't understand why it particularly had to be you—"

She raised an eyebrow. "I'm well known as a Wildmage and a Healer out here; it would make the best sense for Shalkan to head straight for me—especially once you were actually injured."

Kellen stared. Idalia . . . a Wildmage? A *female* Wildmage? But *women* couldn't do magick!

Or could they?

Was that just another of the Mages' lies?

What if it was?

Idalia didn't seem to notice his shocked expression, any more than she'd shown any particular surprise or amazement at hearing about *his* involvement with the Wild Magic, although he supposed she'd had plenty of time to get used to that idea already, since he'd come in riding Shalkan, something only a Wildmage would be likely to be doing. He regarded his newfound sister with increased respect.

His sister was a Mage . . . a Wildmage!

"How did you think all your injuries disappeared so fast? I healed you—yes, with genuine, women-can't-possibly-do-it magic," Idalia said. "Wild Magic."

Kellen gaped blankly at her, still trying to get used to the idea of meeting a Wildmage. *Another* Wildmage.

"Of course," Idalia went on, "it was *only* Wild Magic, so I suppose that doesn't count for the Council's purposes . . ." she added mockingly.

"And now I suppose you have a right to hear my side of the story," Idalia continued, "but to tell it properly I'll have to go back a good deal further than you did."

She brooded for a moment, and Kellen took the opportunity to drink as much of his tea as he could before his hand began to shake.

"I suppose it begins with our mother, Alance. Father didn't need to tamper with your memories to make you forget her. She left when you were still a baby, and from what little I remember of those days, he never let her see much of you at all. I suppose after he saw how I turned out, he was afraid her Mountain blood would contaminate you." She sighed. "Sometimes I wonder what the two of them ever saw in each other, but I suppose everyone wonders that about their parents. Still."

She shook her head. "I would *like* to believe that at least at some point they loved one another, but for all I know, it was a political alliance for him."

"But you were old enough to know her—" Kellen ventured cautiously. "He always said my mother was dead . . ."

Idalia grimaced, dismissing Kellen's half-voiced question. "Here's what I do know for sure. Alance was the daughter of a Trader from the Mountains. The Mountain Traders used to come right down into the City, but after Alance left the City again they stopped and started trading only through Nerendale village. I'm not sure why, or if her leaving had anything to do with that. I'm also not really sure why Father didn't try to make me forget her, either—maybe he thought it wasn't worth bothering with, me being a mere female. And then again, perhaps he was right about the 'bad blood' in both of us coming to us through her: if Mother really was a Wildmage, perhaps she was able to cast a spell to make him simply forget about it. Anyway, no matter how it came about, I remember her, and what she told me about how they met.

"Before Father was Arch-Mage, Alance came into the City with a trading caravan of the Mountain-folk. He was already on the Council then, though not yet Arch-Mage, overseeing the licensing of new goods for the markets. She said she fell in love with him, and when her caravan left, she stayed. I was born, and then, ten years later, you were born."

Kellen was putting together the chronology in his mind.

"Was she happy? I mean, I can't see F—*Lycaelon* with a wife."

Idalia gave him a measuring look. "I suppose they must have been happy at first, but once you were born, he changed toward her—I was only a child, but I do know he became very strange around that time. He separated us from her, did everything he could to keep me away from her, and put both of us in the care of a nurse I didn't much like. The nurse was very strict, always lecturing me about how I needed to be a proper lady if I was going to grow up to marry well."

Idalia laughed, but there was little humor in the sound. "Now, up until that point, I had always assumed I would become a Mage like Father. When the nurse came, I was swiftly disabused of that notion. And when I demanded to know why not, I was informed that it was the destiny of a Mageborn girl to marry a Mage—since only the finest Mageborn son would do for Lycaelon's daughter—and produce lots of sons to grow up and become Mages. You can imagine how much I enjoyed hearing that!"

Kellen winced. "I'm sorry," he said awkwardly.

She shrugged. "It doesn't matter now. Anyway, Mother came to me in secret one night when you were about a year old—there was a tremendous party for your Naming Day, and of course I wasn't let to attend. I'd thrown a furious tantrum over it and been sent to bed without supper, locked in my room so I couldn't sneak out and cause trouble. I cried myself sick, of course, and then in came Mother, dressed in the strangest clothes I'd ever seen, with a pack on her back just like a street merchant.

"She told me she was going away—"

"She ran away?" Kellen gasped.

Idalia nodded. "Not dead, no matter what you were told. She ran away. She told me she was going away, and that I would never, ever see her again. She told me that she loved me, and you, and it was not because of anything that either of us had done, but that she must go, because she had come to realize that Lycaelon loved his magick and his reputation more than anything else in the world, including her. She said

I must be brave and careful, and that no matter what happened, I must never, *ever* speak of her again to anyone, even to you, because that was the only way you and I could be safe."

Perhaps because Kellen *hadn't* known his mother, he found it easy to sympathize with her plight. Perhaps because he knew now just how vindictive Lycaelon could be, he understood. But he saw the masked pain in Idalia's eyes, and heard the hurt in her voice. It had been different for her . . .

"I begged her to take me with her, but she said that Father would never let me go, because I was his daughter, and that this was the only way. Then she kissed me and left. I tried to follow her, but she'd locked the door again. There was nothing I could do but cry myself back to sleep."

"I'm sorry," Kellen said again, wishing he could make some of that pain go away.

But Idalia shrugged, and a kind of veil dropped over her expression. "In the morning, as soon as I could get away from the nurse, I sneaked into Mother's rooms, but they'd all been tidied away, and every trace of her was gone, as if no one had ever lived in those rooms at all. I waited sennights for someone to even mention that she was gone, but no one ever did. *Ever.*

"I was so frightened by their silence that I did exactly as Mother said, and never said a single word about her, so perhaps that was why Father didn't think he needed to bother with erasing her from my mind. Or perhaps there was a spell after all. Or perhaps a little of both—you already know how mysteriously the Wild Magic works."

"Oh, yes," Kellen agreed bitterly. "And things are always, 'out of sight, out of mind' for Lycaelon. As long as there's no reason for him to *act*, he's far more concerned with all that business of being important than with anything in his household."

"I'm not surprised," Idalia replied. "Well, after that, I devoted myself to making life hell for a succession of governesses and to protecting and taking care of you; Father devoted his to becoming Arch-Mage; and you grew up into an adorable little boy. And the one thing I wanted most in the entire world was to become a Mage myself.

"Of course it was unthinkable. I'd been told that, loudly and repeatedly. Nevertheless, it was the one thing I wanted most in the entire world."

Kellen eyed her with speculation. "Why is it that I just *know* you wouldn't take 'no' for an answer?"

She smiled thinly, but continued without a comment. "Of course it was as unthinkable when I was in my teens as it had been when I was a child. I'd heard all the arguments— women were too emotional, too frivolous, not smart enough, but they all boiled down to one: there'd never been a female Mage in Armethalieh before, and so of course there could never be one now. So I sneaked into the Records Room of the Council Hall to search through their archives, since unlike the Library at the Mage College, which I knew I'd never be able to get into, the Council Hall isn't surrounded with wards to keep any mere mortal from setting foot in it. All I had to do was make sure I went on a day when the place was full of foreign Traders. That was easy enough; some of them always get lost, and if they were triggering wards all over the place there'd be no peace for the high-and-mighty overlords of the City!

"Besides, it was the records of the Council itself I was after. I figured if I could find a record of a female Mage in the Council Histories, that would be enough precedent for my own training, and if I could find *no* record that any woman had ever been apprenticed and failed, I could always argue that if there had *never* been any female Mage-candidates, how could the Council possibly know that women didn't make good Mages and couldn't control their emotions?

"That was when my Books came to me. I found them there on the shelves, crammed in among a bunch of bound copies of minutes from some ancient meeting."

"Your Books?" Kellen gaped at her. "There? In the Council Records Room? What did you think they were?"

She gave him a sidelong look. "I knew *exactly* what I had of course—I'd read all the way through Father's library by the age of twelve and I knew the *Ars Perfidorum* practically by heart. I knew they were supposedly Anathema, but I didn't care. If the Council and Father were so wrong about females, why should they be right about this? And unlike High Magick, I wouldn't need tutors, or textbooks, or special equipment, or years of practice before I could become a Wildmage. I started practicing Wildmagery before I even finished reading *The Book of Stars*."

"You did?" Kellen felt his estimation of his sister rising again. Brave and fearless Idalia!

Idalia finished her tea, and put the empty cup down on the table. "Yes. Stupid of me, I know. Of course the Council caught me, and pretty quickly, too. I was lucky not to be executed out of hand, but the Council does love its pretense of fairness and mercy. Just as you did, I found myself tried and Banished, standing outside the City walls, waiting for sunrise and the release of the Hunt. Since I was a female, and not terribly important to them or to Father, I wasn't given the option to recant, either, just a half-chime trial, a couple of bells in the cell, and out the gate like the trash I was."

Kellen winced, imagining the scene very clearly. Idalia didn't see it; she was looking down at her empty cup.

After a moment, she went on. "Unlike you, I'd done a little more digging in the Council archives before I'd found my Books. I knew exactly what was going to be coming after me when the Outlaw Hunt was released, and I had no intention of being anywhere that the Hounds could go. So I did a more specific spell. I asked for the power of flight, so that no matter what happened, the Hounds couldn't possibly reach me.

"Of course, since I'd made such a specific request of the Powers, things didn't work out quite the way I expected them to."

He saw a tiny change in her at that moment, a subtle relaxation. Well, the painful part of the narrative was probably past, now.

"It never does, you know. You'll find that out soon enough if you haven't already. I found myself transformed into a Silver Eagle, and the price of the spell was that I must remain in that form until I could find a mate and raise a brood of chicks before I could transform back again. What made that difficult—other than having to wait for mating season—was having to find a Silver Eagle mate. Silver Eagles live in Elven lands, and even there, they are very, *very* rare. It took me three years to accomplish the task. But—oh!—being able to *fly . . .* "

Idalia stared off into space, her expression dreamy as she remembered. Then her eyes focused on Kellen's face again, and she smiled teasingly, reaching out to pat his hand.

"I rather enjoyed it. Once I got used to it, of course. Eggs are certainly a better way of having children than the way we do it. At any rate, once my price was paid, I was free to change back whenever I wished, so I went to the Elves, made my situation known, and changed back to myself—which is a lot better than ending up stark naked on a cliff in the middle of nowhere, don't you think?"

"Better than I did," Kellen said glumly, staring into the dregs of his now-cold tea. He'd almost gotten himself and Shalkan killed. All Idalia'd had to do was spend three years flying around Elven lands as an eagle, probably having all kinds of interesting adventures.

"I don't think so," Idalia said, putting a comforting hand on his shoulder. "The essence of proficiency at the Wild Magic is economy of price. Your price was rather minimal compared to mine. It's hardly your fault or Shalkan's that the Council lost their minds and sent so many Hounds after you. I've read their records, after all. A regular Outlaw Hunt is thirteen Hounds, one for each member of the Council, and from what you've said, it sounds like they sent five or six times that number after you, and Shalkan said—and he should know—that they were preparing more. You ought to be flattered."

"But I got Shalkan involved, and I almost got him killed!" Kellen burst out.

Idalia held up her hand. "Wait a moment. *Think.* These things don't happen by accident. There are no accidents in the Wild Magic. Now, I don't know anything about Shalkan, and it's impolite to ask, but I suspect that helping you was *his* price, either for something that Wild Magic did for him in the past, or for something that he's asked for in the future."

Once again, Kellen stared at Idalia in surprise. That notion had never even occurred to him.

She smiled. "In any event, you ought to be flattered that the Council cared enough to try to kill you so thoroughly. Father must be furious, losing both his children to the Wild Magic this way. I guess Wildmagery runs in our blood. I really do wonder if Mother practiced?"

Kellen said nothing, and Idalia shrugged, dismissing the question. "I suppose we'll never know."

"I suppose," Kellen said, sounding sulky despite himself. "Not that it matters if Wildmagery runs in my blood or not. I'll never know any more about the Wild Magic than I do now. My Books are back in the City. The Council's probably already burned them."

"Think so?" Idalia said, grinning now, with the look of someone who knows something. "Your pack's under the table here. Look in it."

Kellen ducked his head under the table. There on the floor, next to the bloodstained remains of his old boots, which Idalia was using as a pattern to make new ones, was the scraped and battered day-pack that Kellen had carried out of the City. Amazingly, considering everything, it was still in one piece. He dragged it toward him and pulled it open.

There was a compartment in it that he hadn't noticed before. He pulled it open. Inside were the three Books. *His* three Books.

Kellen pulled them out and stared at them in disbelief. They were his; the same ones he'd bought from the vendor at the Low Market in the City. He knew every crease and dent.

"But—" he said, even though he was getting awfully tired of saying it. They weren't here. They couldn't be. The Council would have been insane to send the Books off with him instead of destroying them—and besides, he'd opened that backpack several times since he'd left the City, and before that, in the cell. He was sure he would have noticed the compartment, and the Books.

Wouldn't he?

Idalia smiled as if she'd just given him a present—and in a way, she had. Kellen was amazed and astonished—and comforted in ways he hadn't expected—to have his Books back. He wasn't finished learning from them yet—he wasn't sure if he ever would be.

"Once the Books find you, they can't be parted from you for long," Idalia said. "That's the way the Wild Magic works. Even if someone tries to burn them, they'll survive and get back to you somehow. Only you can choose to give them up."

Kellen stared down at the three slim handwritten volumes in his hands. He didn't doubt her, though it was an amazing revelation. The Books would find him no matter what happened. The Books would look after him.

That being true, in a way they were almost alive—like the power in the Wild Magic that chose the price the Wildmage would pay for each spell, the Books themselves were part of some intention so large and hidden that Kellen had no idea of what it might be.

The thought made him subtly uneasy, though he wasn't quite sure why, and suddenly he remembered the terrible creatures in his dreams. Demons.

Abruptly, in the same way that he *knew* when he cast a spell of the Wild Magic how to pay the Mageprice for his spell and what it was, Kellen *knew* that Demons existed. Never mind the fact that he'd never encountered any mention of them in his unauthorized reading through Lycaelon's library, nor that Anigrel hadn't mentioned them during any of his tutorials, nor that he'd never encountered any Defense Spells against them, Kellen suddenly *knew* the creatures from his fever-dreams were real, at least in some way.

And try as he might, he could not forget what Lycaelon had told him back there in the cell—that practicing the Wild Magic led inevitably to involvement with Demons, to madness and alliance with the Dark. It had been easy to scoff then—but he'd still been safe behind Armethalieh's walls.

There'd been truth in his nightmares. He knew that much.

Had Lycaelon Tavadon lied—or hadn't he?

I don't know, Kellen thought miserably.

He looked at Idalia.

If anything in Lycaelon's words had been true, she was the last person in the world he could turn to for help.

She said Shalkan won't come near her. Is that *why—the* real *reason?*

"You're awfully quiet all of a sudden," Idalia said.

"I guess I'm just tired," Kellen answered awkwardly.

"Well, let's get you back to bed, then. I should have your boots finished by tomorrow, and then we can try something really strenuous, like a walk outside," Idalia said cheerfully.

⟶

HE hadn't actually felt tired—that had only been an excuse to be alone with his thoughts—but the walk back to the bed really did take the last of his strength. Kellen was half-asleep before Idalia helped him out of the leather clothing. He was only barely aware that she had pulled the covers up over his shoulders, and was completely asleep only moments afterward.

He half woke later, hearing her moving around in the room, and tried to speak, but found he couldn't make his mouth form coherent words.

"Go back to sleep," she told him as he stirred sleepily. "I'll make up a bedroll here on the floor."

Well, if that was what she wanted to do . . . it was her home, after all. Kellen gave no further thought to it, and let sleep take him.

Chapter Eleven

Reborn to Magic

When he woke again it was morning, and wonderful food smells filled the air. For a moment Kellen was disoriented, unable to remember how he'd gotten here and why the Morning Bells hadn't woken him, then everything settled into place as memories came flooding back. Banishment, the Hunt, awakening, discovering he had a sister. This was Idalia's cabin, outside of City lands. And he would never hear the bells of the City of a Thousand Bells again.

Reflexively, his hand went to the Talisman around his throat.

It was gone, of course, stripped from him the night of his Banishing, and its absence made Kellen oddly uneasy.

It's gone. That means you're free now, he told himself sternly. But without it he felt more naked than he did without his clothes, despite the fact that now that he knew what it *was,* he hated the very thought of it.

He put the thought from his mind, swinging his legs over the edge of the bed. Idalia had left his new clothes where he could find them, and he was able to don the unfamiliar garments without too much difficulty. He was much stronger than yesterday, though still a little light-headed, but he was able to walk to the other room unsupported.

"Good morning, sleepyhead," Idalia greeted him cheerfully from where she knelt at the hearth. "I thought you were going to sleep the day away!"

Kellen looked around, puzzled. From the position of the sun, it wasn't *that* much later than he usually woke!

She laughed, seeing his baffled expression. "Country ways, little brother! Up with the sun; no Magelight here, and you can't do chores by candlelight. But don't worry; I don't plan to put you to work right away. Come on, sit down. I baked this morning—in your honor, I might add—and I want to see how these boots fit."

When Idalia had mentioned boots, Kellen had been expecting something like the horsemen's boots he'd seen in the City—knee-high gleaming high-heeled things of brightly polished hard-finished leather—but what she brought him was something more like leggings with feet. They were identical to the ones she was wearing, and Kellen realized he should have expected that, but he still hadn't fully come to terms with what living outside of the City truly meant.

No shops. No merchants. No one to buy things from—it was either make it yourself, or do without. Unless you could find someone who would trade with you for what you wanted. Would anyone traffic with an Outlaw?—Two Outlaws?

The boots were flat-soled, with several thicknesses of leather pierced and sewn to heavy deerskin uppers. A long wide tongue of leather came almost to his knee, and the long outsides of the boot wrapped over that. Flat buttons, made of disks of polished antler, were sewn up the sides of the outer flap; at first Kellen had thought they were for decoration, but Idalia showed him how to take a long narrow piece of heavy buckskin and wrap it around the boot, using the horn buttons to keep it from slipping. At the top, she tied it and tucked the trailing ends under neatly.

"Now you do the other one," she said, getting to her feet.

As his sister busied herself by the fire, Kellen struggled with the other boot. He couldn't seem to keep the sides in place as he wrapped the garter around it; though the leather was thick, it was soft enough not to stand by itself. It was evident, however, that Idalia intended to let him work it out for himself, and after several frustrating tries, Kellen finally managed to secure his second boot.

As he straightened up again, Idalia set breakfast on the table in front of him—hot stew and tea. There was a flat loaf and stone crocks of butter and honey already on the table.

"Go ahead—I ate hours ago." Idalia sat down opposite him, carrying her own mug.

It was good food, and Kellen was hungry, but it wasn't what he was used to seeing at breakfast, and somehow that just seemed to underscore what a big change there'd been in his life. He wasn't ill-mannered enough to complain, but Idalia seemed to have no trouble sensing his thoughts.

"It's a big change from life in Armethalieh, isn't it, Kellen?" she asked—kindly, but shrewdly.

He nodded, spooning up stew to save himself from having to articulate a reply. He was alive, and that was a great gift—so great, that it hardly seemed polite to grumble about the terms.

The food was good—if unfamiliar—and the more he ate, the more he realized just how long it was since he'd had a decent meal. He reached for the bread, breaking the loaf open and loading a piece with butter and honey. The honey was thick and dark, unlike the pale golden stuff he was familiar with.

"Wild-gathered," Idalia explained. "I'll show you how, when the proper season for it comes. The butter comes from goats, not cows—I trade for that. It's not a bad life, Kellen. Just different from what you're used to."

"And you live out here all alone?" Kellen asked, swallowing a large mouthful of bread and honey.

"Hardly," Idalia said. "But you'll have plenty of time to meet the neighbors, so to speak. First we need to knock some of that City polish off you. And there's a lot more you need to know about the Wild Magic before the next time you have to cast a spell."

Well, he had no doubt of that. In fact, the more he saw of Wild Magic, the less he felt he knew about it.

"Finished?" she asked. He nodded. "Good. Come on outside. There's a few things I want to show you right now, while you're still fresh and alert."

Kellen got to his feet, his hands still sticky with honey, and followed Idalia out of the cabin. At the door she picked up a large wicker basket, its contents hidden beneath a length of mottled woolen fabric, and pointed to a wooden bucket where he could wash his hands.

"No indoor plumbing here." She sighed. "Of all of the City luxuries, all the things I actually learned to get along without quite nicely, I do miss that, and a lot more in winter, let me tell you. Well. The necessary pit is over there—see that cairn of white stones? That's so you can find it in the dark, if you need to. I'll be over there, by the chopping stump." Her eyes twinkled. "That will give you a *little* privacy, anyway."

Kellen blushed, then followed her pointing finger and took care of what needed to be taken care of, though the accommodations were hardly what he was accustomed to. And he couldn't even begin to imagine what it would be like in the dead of winter . . .

When Kellen arrived at the stump, Idalia was kneeling beside it, the wicker basket at her side. She motioned for him to sit.

"First lesson: keystones. You know what a keystone is?"

Kellen sat, feeling the warmth of the stump even through two layers of leather. "No," he said. Despite the fact that everything around him was different, this bore an odd family resemblance to his lessons with Undermage Anigrel. He'd hated them. He'd never imagined that he'd miss them. But he did; not that he'd want to go back to them . . . but it was something he was *used* to, and it didn't seem right, the middle of the morning, not facing Anigrel.

Idalia smiled. "The funny thing is, you wore a keystone, or a kind of one, all your life, until the day you were Banished, and so did I. At its simplest, a keystone is a device for harvesting and storing power. The Talismans the citizens of Armethalieh wear are designed to harvest and store the tiny amount of power the average non-Mage possesses—when you take your Talisman to the Temple of the Eternal Light each New Moon and trade it in for a new one, the Mages harvest the stored power and use it for their magick."

"Anigrel told me that," Kellen muttered. *I didn't like it then, and I still don't.* "They're a damned cheat!"

"Yes," she agreed heartily. "They are. But like all the things that the City Mages use to harm people, at root they're just a tool, and tools can be used for good or ill."

He thought about that statement; he decided she was probably right. Even taking someone's memories could be used for good, if the memory was of something so terrible that it would drive them mad. But you would have to be *so* careful about that, because pretty soon, if you didn't hold yourself to the strictest of standards, you'd be meddling with people's minds in other ways . . . "for their own good" . . . which was what the Mages were using as a rationale for everything they were doing *now*.

"Since you know what the Talismans really are, you're halfway there," Idalia said cheerfully. "Our keystones are a little different, though. For one thing, *we* don't steal the power from the unknowing like a swarm of leeches."

She reached into the basket and took something out. She took Kellen's hand and drew it toward her, palm up, uncurling the fingers so she could place the object in his hand.

"*This* is a keystone," Idalia said.

Kellen looked down at it. It looked nothing like the elaborate golden Talisman he'd used to wear around his neck; in fact, it didn't look magical at all. It was a small white quartz river stone, perfectly ordinary. He held it up to the sun, looking for runes and carvings, and found nothing. Only the surface was frosted; through gaps in that, he could see down into the clear inside of the stone. He looked at Idalia inquiringly.

"A rock?" he asked dubiously.

"We can use almost anything, but crystals and gemstones are easiest to work with," she told him. "Keystones—even if the Mage Council does use a version of them—are not in themselves a bad thing. We can use them, too. High Magick and Wild Magic both require payment, even if they don't call it 'payment' in High Magick. The power to change things has to come from *somewhere*. In High Magick, it comes from the citizens of the City as well as from the Mages themselves—which wouldn't be so bad, if the citizens were told about it and given some choice in the matter." She shook her head.

"You probably already know that part of managing the costs of a spell of the Wild Magic can be done by banking personal energy against a future request. The way to do that is by storing your personal energy in a keystone—or several keystones, as each one will only hold so much energy—and then emptying them at need. Of course, using a keystone costs more in banked energy than if you cast a spell in the regular way—probably because stored energy isn't 'coming from the heart,' but sometimes, especially for small things, it's just more practical to use a keystone in order to avoid Magedebt." She smiled. "After all, you don't want to have to go out rescuing a nest of fledgling birds, as it were, every time you want to use a little Finding Spell! So I'm going to show you how to make a keystone."

"Now?" Kellen said, recoiling. After what it had taken to get here, he wasn't sure he ever wanted to have anything to do with magic—High, Wild, or any other kind—ever again.

"Relax," Idalia said, looking amused at his skittishness. "It won't hurt. And it isn't a spell, so there's no question of paying a price for the work. Just relax. This won't hurt. If there was ever *anything* harmless in magic, this is it—why, once you've made the stone, *I* won't be able to use the power in it. You, and only you, will be able to access it."

Unlike the Talismans . . .

"What you need to do is feel your way into the stone. Pour yourself into it, the way water pours into a cup, and when you pull back, just leave a little of yourself behind." She gave his hand an encouraging pat. "I'll show you now."

Kneeling before him, she clasped her strong callused hands over his, folding his reluctant fingers around the stone. "Relax," Idalia repeated firmly. "This stone has been used before. It knows the way."

For a long moment nothing happened. Kellen felt awkward and a little silly; all he was aware of was his surroundings—the sunshine, the fresh air, the birdcalls, and the unfamiliar trees. Despite his previous experiences with the Wild Magic, a part of him insisted that this wasn't magic. Magic was incense and incantations done in the hours of darkness, elaborate memorized rituals and hours of painstaking preparation. It couldn't be this simple, this natural.

Then the stone seemed to grow warm in his hands, as if the blood that flowed through his veins were flowing through the stone as well. He felt a faint distant tugging—and then, as if some instinctive part of him had gotten the idea—he *pushed* . . .

—And then Idalia's hands were on his shoulders, steadying him as he slid sideways, suddenly dizzy and weak. He leaned against her, blinking dazedly, feeling as if he'd just run for miles.

"Too much too soon, little brother!" Idalia said, laughing and ruffling his hair. "You don't do anything by halves, do you?" She plucked the keystone from his fingers and dropped it back into the basket.

"I guess not," Kellen said weakly. He took a deep breath and sat up again, pushing the dizziness away with an effort of will. "So that's how you charge a keystone?" he asked, trying hard to sound as if it were the most natural thing in the world.

"Usually it's not so dramatic," Idalia answered dryly. "Usually, the Wildmage doesn't try fully charging a stone when he's still recovering from a mauling. But yes, that's how it's done. They won't replace the personal price the Wildmage has to pay for the larger spells, of course. But they're a help."

"Idalia." Kellen hesitated, then plunged on. He had so many questions, and even if he wasn't completely sure he could trust her answers, there was no one else he could ask. "Why *is* that? Why does the price . . . change? Why is it so, well, *peculiar*? I did two different Finding Spells, and both times, the price was . . . well, it was nothing like anything I ever studied in the High Magick. And I didn't exactly get what I asked for, either."

"I think it's all a matter of balances," Idalia answered slowly, as if she had to think hard before she spoke. "I'm not ᴐure. I've worked most of this out from *The Book of Stars,* which—as you've probably discovered—is the most difficult to understand of the three Books. I believe that what our own power does is enable us to make our requests of—some Great Power. I can't explain it any better than that."

"The Eternal Light?" Kellen asked stumblingly. The Eternal Light was the only Great Power he'd ever heard of.

"Nothing that bloodless and impersonal," Idalia said dismissively. "The High Mages like to make everything abstract and completely removed from the real world, but I don't think the Powers that made us are anything like their Eternal Light. The Elves have their own explanations and names for it all, and they're nothing like the Eternal Light. Better, I think." She brooded for a moment. "Let's just call them 'the Gods,' and leave it at that. And I think the Gods need people here in the world to make minor adjustments now and again to keep things running properly; the Elves say that They don't meddle in the affairs of mortals lightly, and that when they choose to, They need mortal hands to do those things—but that They will neither command nor compel, only make an exchange. That's why we end up doing what we do to pay for our spells.

"As for why we get what we need rather than what we specifically ask for . . . I'd say it's a little more like a gift than a business transaction, even though we do have to pay for it. They're looking out for us. Helping us—I don't know—become *better.* Or at least giving us the tools to become better, if we want to be."

She paused for a long time, looking thoughtful. "I also think—though, mind, I don't know for sure—that when we use keystone energy to pay for spells, that energy is used by the Gods to some other purpose of Theirs elsewhere. So They need what humans send Them, but it isn't being directly returned to our world in any way we can see. Not like when you cast 'from the heart,' and pay in this world with a task the Gods set."

Like promising a year of chastity to a unicorn, Kellen thought. Try as he might, he couldn't imagine how *that* was going to be of any use to anyone, including him.

"It makes my head hurt." And he'd thought the High Magick was mind-numbingly esoteric!

Idalia smiled. "Tell you the truth, it makes mine hurt too, sometimes. I haven't met very many Wildmages who really understand it. But that's enough theory and practice for one day. I'll tell you something you never heard in Armethalieh: magic can be fun. That's another reason to store power in keystones; so you can use it to have a little fun."

"Huh," Kellen said disbelievingly. It hadn't been fun so far. Exciting, yes, but looking back, there had not been a lot of what he'd call fun.

"Seriously. I'll prove it," Idalia assured him.

She got to her feet in one smooth motion and reached down into the basket once more. She lifted out the folds of fabric— as she swirled them through the air, Kellen could see it was actually an ankle-length hooded cloak of thin grey wool— and draped it around herself.

And vanished.

"Hey!"

Kellen jumped to his feet in alarm, staggering just a little in the hasty movement. Idalia was *gone*.

"Like it?"

She reappeared behind him, the cloak draped over one arm. Kellen stared at her, knowing he was gaping at her like a country fool in a wondertale but unable to keep from doing it. This was *magic*—magic of the sort that only existed in books and scrolls and Festival-day plays!

"It's a *tarnkappa*—a cloak of invisibility. I made it a while back when I was still thrilled by being able to create things with the Wild Magic whenever I wanted to, with no one around to care whether I did or not. When I'm wearing it, no one can see me—or hear me, or smell me. Oh, it has its practical uses. I use it to take game in the dead of winter, when quarry is scarce and easily spooked. It's about the only magical contrivance I have at the moment," Idalia said, her eyes dancing with glee at his reaction.

"Why?" Kellen asked bluntly. "I mean, if you *can* make

more things like that, why don't you? *Make* indoor plumbing, if you miss it?"

Idalia shrugged. "The thrill wears off, once you get used to the idea that you can work Wild Magic openly, whenever you like," she said simply. "I have everything I need now, and luxuries—well, they don't seem as much of a priority. But that's enough about magic for one day," she said briskly, folding the *tarnkappa* back into the basket. "Wait here, and I'll bring you something to do." She grinned now. "If you're going to eat my food, brother mine, you're going to have to help me put it on the table."

She walked off toward the cabin, carrying the basket.

Kellen watched her go, frowning faintly. After a few moments he sat back down on the stump again, thinking hard. Idalia, he was coming to realize, was very good at changing the subject when it started to get into matters she didn't want to discuss.

And Kellen—as he was also starting to realize—was very good at thinking about forbidden subjects.

Take the Elves, for example. They'd gotten off that subject mighty quickly when Idalia had been telling him her history! But something about everything she'd told him about how she'd ended up here just didn't make sense. Why was Idalia living out here in the middle of nowhere—in a cabin that didn't even have indoor plumbing—when she could be living with the Elves in their Elven city? Everybody knew that the Elven cities were places of fabulous luxury and decadence, where Elven enchantresses practiced their forbidden wiles on any human men unfortunate enough to fall into their perfumed clutches. And, Kellen supposed fair-mindedly, Elven men did the same for human women, if they could catch them.

So why wasn't Idalia still living there? It obviously wasn't because the Elves had a problem with Wildmages. She'd gone to them for help when she turned back into human form, so they were evidently familiar with the Wild Magic and its effects. She must have lived with them at least for a little while afterward. Why hadn't she stayed with them?

Kellen knew a little about Elves from his studies in the City—though, just as with unicorns, when he came to think about it straight on, he didn't know much. And most of that was from wondertales.

Fiction. Probably not a reliable source.

Not that *anything* he'd learned in Armethalieh—he was coming to suspect—was very reliable.

So what had he learned from his lessons?

He thought carefully. Not much there, either.

What he did know that might be considered potentially reliable came not from his schoolbooks and histories, but from his religious instruction in the Temple when he was much younger. Elves were one of the Nonhuman Races strictly banned from City lands. Occasional Elven trade goods did still arrive in Armethalieh, by way of the Mountain Traders, though their price was beyond the reach of all but the wealthiest of the Mageborn. Elves lived for a very long time, maybe forever, in forests far to the west. They didn't have any particular magical abilities—not like human Mages—but they were enchantingly beautiful, and if a human ever saw one, the Elf would use that supernatural beauty to lure him to his doom, because, like all the Nonhuman Races, they were essentially inferior and corrupt, poor copies of humanity allowed to exist by the Eternal Light for instructional purposes.

Only they didn't seem to have lured Idalia much of anywhere, now that Kellen came to think of it. And if the doctrines of the Eternal Light were as false as the rest of the teachings of the Mages, then Kellen thought he'd better consider the rest of what he'd been taught pretty carefully before trusting—or acting on—any of it.

"Here you are."

Kellen looked up as Idalia returned with a sack and a small iron pot. "Emya roots. They need to be peeled for stew. When you're done peeling them, take them down to the spring and wash them, then fill the pot with water and bring it up to the cabin. I've got some other chores to do, but this should keep you busy and out of trouble. There's bread and apples inside if you get hungry, and—try not to injure yourself too badly at this chore while I'm gone, brother mine. And remember, a little work is going to help you recover faster."

With that she walked off, leaving Kellen staring down at a knife—his own penknife, as a matter of fact—an iron pot, and a burlap sack half full of lumpy brown roots.

They were going to eat *these?*

He picked one up and inspected it dubiously.

"Good eating, those."

Shalkan appeared, seemingly out of nowhere, reached over Kellen's shoulder, and plucked the root delicately out of Kellen's hand.

"Mmm . . . crunchy," the unicorn observed, mouth full.

"Hey! I'm supposed to be peeling those for dinner," Kellen objected.

"Then I suggest you get started," Shalkan said imperturbably, mouth still full.

Kellen looked around. Idalia was nowhere to be seen. He sighed and reached for another root, watching Shalkan out of the corner of his eye lest the unicorn steal this one, too.

Shalkan looked perfectly healthy. Idalia hadn't said anything about healing him; either she hadn't needed to, or she hadn't felt it was worth commenting on.

"I'm glad you're okay," Kellen said, feeling awkward. "You . . . *are* okay, aren't you?"

The unicorn, mouth still full, let Kellen's question pass without comment.

I guess that's a "yes," Kellen decided, and bent his head to the task at hand.

He quickly realized what Idalia had meant by her parting comment. The brown exterior of the root was slippery and tough, hard to cut into. It was going to be quite easy to cut himself while peeling these things if he wasn't careful. The interior was waxy and white, smelling faintly of apples and onions. Kellen supposed that cooking would improve it.

"So," Shalkan asked when he'd finished chewing. "Is freedom everything you hoped it would be?"

"It's different," Kellen said, hoping he didn't sound too

grudging about things. Shalkan's continued presence in his life was another thing he wondered about. It was all very well to assume that the unicorn was here to make sure that Kellen kept his half of the magical bargain he'd made, but surely Shalkan had other ways of knowing that, even from a distance? Was there another reason that Shalkan was sticking so close by—and was there even the faintest possible hope that Shalkan might tell him what that was if Kellen asked him directly?

Probably not.

"And now that you have it, you don't like it?" the unicorn asked archly.

"I said—*ow!*"

In his moment of irritated distraction, the knife had slipped, scoring a thin slice across the end of one of Kellen's fingers. Kellen stuck the wounded digit into his mouth and sucked on it mutinously. "I said," he mumbled around the finger, "that it's different."

The pain subsided. He removed the finger from his mouth and inspected the cut. It wasn't very deep, and the bleeding had already stopped. Kellen took a deep breath, knowing already from the unicorn's tone that Shalkan wouldn't stop prodding at him until he was properly answered. "I don't know yet whether I like it—being free and out of the City— or not. I don't know much about it yet. But I know one thing; it's better to be here than dead. And I know another; it's better to be myself, with all of my memories—or most of them, anyway—and my mind intact, than to be Lycaelon's obedient puppet with half my mind gone. Now, since I don't have a lot of choice about being here and 'free,' I guess I'd better try my best to like it, hadn't I?"

"A good answer," Shalkan said, nodding. "And lesson number one about surviving in the Wild Lands, Kellen: always pay attention to everything around you and especially to the task at hand."

Then Shalkan added, soberly, "Even—or perhaps especially—when people try to distract you from your purpose."

WITHIN a few days, the rhythm of the days with his sister had settled into a pattern. They rose at an earlier hour than he would ever have considered possible in the City, but Kellen rapidly came to appreciate the sheer beauty of the dawn here in Idalia's forest. There were no bells, but every day began with a chorus of birdsong long before the sun was visible, with mysterious threads of fog weaving among the quiet trees. The light gradually increased, and there was a sense of anticipation in the air as the new day began. Then, suddenly, the glory of sunrise—and Idalia took care that they both paused for a moment to appreciate and evaluate it, for the sunrise often gave a clue to the weather for the coming day.

Then he joined her in putting together breakfast, watching and learning the art of cookery, which at the moment was as esoteric for him as that of magick would be for the common Armethaliehan. Then—then the day's work began, a series of alternating chores and lessons in various aspects of the Wild Magic. And even if he didn't *consciously* remember her from his childhood, there was some sort of visceral memory remaining that made Kellen feel more comfortable with Idalia than he had ever felt with anyone else.

That was a bit unnerving at first, but it did make life with someone who was otherwise a total stranger a lot easier. Though life in the Wildwood was hard, based on unremitting physical labor dawn to dusk, Idalia didn't ask any more of him in the way of physical labor than he could do, though she certainly didn't ask any *less,* either.

On the other hand, when he watched her swinging an axe, chopping the wood for the fire that cooked their food and warmed them at night, Kellen felt rather guilty that a lot of the time *he* was lying about doing nothing while a woman did the work, and was just as glad, all things considered, when she did give him things to do.

And every day, as she showed him some other small and practical use of Wild Magic, he began to realize that she'd been telling him the simple truth upon his arrival: here in the

Wildwood, she *was* particularly noted for Healing Spells. Given how she had healed him (and presumably Shalkan), Kellen didn't find himself actually surprised to learn that, and slowly, almost without his noticing, his amazement that a *female* could do magic faded completely away.

Of course women could do magic. Didn't he see his sister doing magic every day?

⟶

"WILD Magic is especially good for healing—almost anything is a Healing Spell when you come right down to it," Idalia told him a sennight after his arrival, as she used Wild Magic to heal the ankle he'd strained while fishing in a rocky-strewn brook, explaining to him that she was also going to strengthen it so that he wouldn't repeat the injury.

Though Kellen had thought he was in pretty good physical condition from his rambles about the City, he wasn't used to clambering about on the uneven ground out here in the wilderness, much less in the treacherous streambed of the shallow stream that ran behind the cabin, and had turned his foot on a hidden stone. As usual in these lessons, he sat on the chopping stump, and she on the ground, looking up at him. He wondered if that was a deliberate choice on her part, to make the lessons as little like the ones with Anigrel as possible, though of course she could have no idea what those had been like. Anigrel had always looked *down* at him from a position of authority. Idalia managed to have the authority without needing to make an issue of it.

"Something like this is trivial, and I can use a keystone to supply all the power I need, but for more substantial injuries, sometimes there is a substantial price to pay. Now, that's often paid solely by the Wildmage."

She held her hands around his ankle, and Kellen could feel a soothing warmth radiating from them that was far more than just the heat of her hands.

"That hardly seems fair," he objected. "The Mage isn't getting anything out of it!"

"Ah, not necessarily," she corrected. "The Mage—or Wild-mage—often gets paid in goods or services; that's part of the whole system of barter out here. Now, as it happens, besides that payment, or instead of it, the Wildmage can share out the price the Wild Magic asks for the healing with her patient, if the injury is severe enough," she explained. "Providing the patient is conscious, able to think clearly, and willing, of course. For that matter, the 'cost' can actually be shared among several 'people,' such as the patient's friends or relations."

He blinked at that. "Really?"

"Well, think—it's not that different from using Talisman-power to do something that really *does* benefit everyone in the City," she pointed out logically as she let go of his ankle and flicked a curious insect away with one hand. "There—try standing on that foot now."

He did, and was delighted to discover it didn't hurt and really *did* feel stronger.

I wonder what the cost was of healing me after the Hunt, though, he thought, when he suddenly remembered how badly he'd been hurt. *He* hadn't been conscious to consent to accept part of the cost—nor had he had a crowd of "friends and relations" to share it with, either. What had the cost been to Idalia?

"And you know, of course, that the High Mages of Ar-methalieh do a fair amount of healing; at least, the common ones do. The difference between what the Wildmage does and what the High Mage does *now* is that the Wildmage is bound to tell the patient and anyone else potentially involved in a spell that she would like help in sharing the cost, and then ask formal permission to do so," she continued. "Whereas the High Mage just uses Talisman-energy he's already taken and stored, without asking permission."

Something about the way she phrased that caught his attention. "What do you mean, *now*?" he asked.

She looked up at him thoughtfully. "I'm not altogether certain that the High Mages have always just taken power

without the knowledge or permission of the people of Armethalieh," she admitted. "Maybe in the past, when the population was lower, they used to ask—" She shrugged. "But to get
back to what *we* do, precisely because of the emotional connection, when the price is shared among a number of those
who are connected with the patient, the price that the Wildmage pays is minimal."

"What's 'minimal'?" Kellen asked suspiciously, sitting
back down again.

"It depends on the extent of the injury, and how quickly it
needs to be healed." Idalia watched him from under her long
lashes. "If it doesn't need to be mended *quickly,* just mended
without scarring or other permanent changes, then even the
cost to the Mage is minimal, and it's all keystone work—
which is one of the reasons *you* slept for a sennight, brother
mine. If, however, it needs to be healed right that moment,
then the cost is a lot higher, and a circle of supporters is a
necessary thing. The more supporters, the lighter the cost, and
it amounts to pain-sharing, usually, some personal energy
lost, and a lot of weakness, because *their* strength is given to
the patient just as their life-energy is—"

"Ahem," Shalkan said from his usual observation point
across the clearing. "I believe that you are going to have an
opportunity to demonstrate that very point in a moment."

Idalia looked at him sharply, but before she could ask any
questions, the underbrush at the edge of the clearing rustled
and parted.

And Kellen had to stop himself from staring and gaping
like a farmer on his first visit to the City markets.

He'd never even seen *one* unicorn before he'd summoned
Shalkan. Now here was a whole *herd* of them! They slipped
into the clearing, moving with the same uncanny silence that
he'd come to expect from Shalkan; there were a dozen of
them, at least, all dazzlingly white, all incredibly beautiful—

Except for the one in the midst of them, supported by a
larger unicorn on either flank, and hobbling on three legs.
The fourth leg dripped dark blood, and dangled uselessly.

"Kellen!" Idalia snapped. "Go help that colt—I can't touch him—"

Kellen started, and hurried forward to lend his shoulder to the injured colt, who was quite young indeed, surely not even a yearling. The unicorn colt was clearly spent; his eyes were glazed with pain and exhaustion, and the glory of his coat and budding horn dimmed.

Idalia ran back to the cabin to collect a basket of herbs and other things. Kellen helped the poor trembling thing to kneel, then lie down; the left hind leg was broken, horribly so; two jagged ends of the bone had come through the flesh and the whole thing just hung limply in a way that suggested the pain must be nearly unbearable.

"He stepped into a rabbit hole while galloping, Wildmage Idalia," one of the adults said gravely as Idalia knelt at the colt's side. "Can you—?"

"Of course, and much more easily since my brother is here." She nodded at Kellen. "Little brother, I can't touch this young fellow without consequences; I can do the healing, but you'll have to do the manipulation to put the bones back into place."

"Manipulation?" Kellen gulped. The mere sight of the mangled leg was making him feel sick, and he cringed inside each time it whimpered in pain. He'd been hoping he could sneak away; surely she didn't mean him to—

She did. "You'll have to straighten the leg and align the bone and hold it in place while I work," she said, and it was clear from her tone of voice that she expected him to agree.

The colt made a pitiful mewing sound that wrung his heart, and he found himself saying "Of course," even though inside he was thinking, *Oh, no!*

"And you?" she asked, looking at the adult unicorns.

"The usual, of course," said the spokesman, and the others all nodded. "He'll lose the leg, else, if not his life. What else are families for?"

Kellen watched closely as Idalia created a pocket-sized fire and quickly brewed something over it, then, at her direction, he held the colt's head up and helped it drink the warm con-

tents of the bowl. After that, Idalia used a touch of the Wild
Magic and a keystone to make it sleep, and Kellen breathed
easier as its keening whimpers died away to soft snores.

But his work had barely begun.

Now Idalia produced splints and bandages from her work-
bag—since, as she explained for Kellen's benefit—the healing would go much more quickly and easily if the bones were
close to where they were supposed to be, and Kellen, working
at her direction, set the leg.

What he had to do nearly made him faint for a moment,
feeling the unicorn's blood on his hands, pulling the leg this
way and that until all the broken pieces of bone slipped back
beneath the skin, feeling—and *hearing* the shattered pieces
slip and grate over each other. He thought it would never be
done, and he really did come awfully close to losing his control over his stomach more than once. If the colt had been
conscious and writhing in agony, he would never have been
able to bear it, he knew, but through it all the young unicorn
slept peacefully.

At last Idalia was satisfied, and talked Kellen through the
process of splinting the leg to hold it steady. When he was
finished, Kellen sat back on his heels, sweating heavily, feeling as exhausted and light-headed as he had after the initial
flight from the City with Shalkan.

"Kellen, you've done enough; I *won't* ask you to share in
the price of this healing," Idalia said then, as he sat there,
nauseous and sweating, his hands and arms covered in blood,
wanting to leave and unable to move. "But if Shalkan—"

She glanced over at Shalkan, who shook his head. "Not
possible," the unicorn said, with genuine regret.

She didn't question that, though Kellen was a bit annoyed;
why shouldn't Shalkan help, after all? Wasn't this a colt of
the same species? Instead, after Kellen had rested for a few
moments, she had him collect one hair from the tails of each
of the adults and the colt, added a hair of her own, and dab-
bled the entire bundle in the blood that had pooled beneath
the colt's leg. Kellen took the opportunity to back away, but
not very far. He simply didn't have the strength.

Then she pricked the ball of her thumb with her knife, and squeezed out a drop of her own blood, holding the now-bloody bundle of hairs under her hand so that the drop of blood fell on it and mingled with the unicorns'.

As Kellen watched, curiosity overcoming nausea, Idalia closed her eyes, then held up her hands, palms out, at shoulder height, and for a moment, he wondered just what it was that she was up to. This was nothing like anything the two of them had done together.

Then Kellen suddenly *felt* power flare up all around them. And just as he did, a fainter wall of power sprang up, encircling them.

A wall? Not quite—as he stared at it, startled that he could see it at all, he realized that it wasn't so much a *wall* as half a sphere, inverted over them like the bowl of the sky. It shimmered like heat haze in the sunlight, like the barrier that protected the harbor of Armethalieh.

Now Idalia dropped the bundle of hairs on the fire, and instead of the stench of burning hair that Kellen had expected, a scent not unlike that of incense arose from the coals.

Idalia closed her eyes again, held her hands palm-up in her lap and her lips barely moved as she whispered some spell Kellen couldn't hear.

And at that moment, Kellen sensed something that was entirely outside of his experience, with High Magick *or* Wild Magic—

It was the sense that Something was with them, inside the half sphere with them, and it was speaking to them. But not to all of them, only to Idalia and the adult unicorns. He, Shalkan, and the colt were left out of the conversation—if conversation it was—entirely.

Then the Presence was gone, winking out as if it never had been there at all. Idalia spread her hands over the colt's leg, and they began to glow with a verdant green fire, so rich and powerful that it made Kellen long to gather up two handfuls for himself and eat it like a double handful of sweets. There was a heady aroma in the air, of new-mown hay, of the breeze after a rain, of every flower in the world in bloom at the same time. And there was *energy* free-flowing all around them—a wonderful energy that filled Kellen with a sense of incredible well-being.

Right before his eyes, through the gaps in the splint, he could see the raw flesh of the colt's leg knit together; he heard a faint grating sound, and sensed that the bones were knitting in a way he would never have thought possible. So *this* was what Idalia had done for him . . . who was, at that point, a mere stranger!

In a shorter time than he would have thought possible, it was over. Idalia made a gesture, and the half sphere surrounding them vanished, and with it, the energy that had swirled inside that sphere. She smothered the little fire, and there was nothing to show that she'd ever done anything, except for the blood on the colt's leg.

She poked Kellen. "Well, go on. He won't be needing that now."

"What . . . ? Oh."

Kellen scuttled forward, still on his knees, and quickly removed the splint he'd so painstakingly applied such a short time before. The colt's fur was still matted with dried blood— there was something so *wrong* about seeing blood on a unicorn!—but now the flesh beneath was whole and unblemished, as if the injury had never occurred at all. He backed away again.

The adults nudged the youngster awake, and the colt got unsteadily to its feet.

"Wildmage, our thanks—" the spokesman said with such fervent sincerity that it brought a lump into Kellen's throat.

"It was my privilege, bright ones," she replied gravely. And a moment later, they were all gone, vanishing just as Shalkan was wont to vanish, passing into the forest without being seen.

"Well," Idalia said, sounding tired, but very satisfied. "*That* was a major healing. What did you think?"

He asked the first question—blurted it, really—that came into his mind. "Why couldn't you touch them?"

And Shalkan brayed with laughter.

In fact, the unicorn was *so* convulsed that he literally fell to his knees and gasped for breath. "Why—why—why—" Shalkan panted, and every time he glanced over at Kellen's increasingly indignant face, he went off again.

Idalia had her face hidden in both hands, and her shoulders shook, but she was not, as Kellen momentarily feared, weeping. When he touched her shoulder, she raised a face full of mirth to his.

"Kellen!" she managed, around her own choked laughter. "*Think!* Why can't I get near Shalkan? What happened when I was an eagle?"

For a moment he just stared at her, unable to see what being an eagle had anything to do with not touching unicorns. Then it hit him. She'd had to find a mate—raise a clutch—

"But—you were an eagle!" he spluttered. "That couldn't count—you were a *bird!*"

"Oh, believe me, it counted," she choked. "It surely counted!"

Of course she couldn't get near Shalkan, or the other unicorns. She wasn't a virgin. Idiot that he was, she'd *told* him that was the reason—well, almost told him—that first time he'd been awake, and he'd been too dense to take the hint.

And all this time, he'd been afraid it was because the Wild Magic had somehow tainted her . . .

He felt his face grow hot with embarrassment, as much over that unfair assumption as for his stupidity.

"Mind—" she said, between stifled snorts of laughter, "virginity is as much a state of mind as it is of the body. Someone who is physically still virginal but is thoroughly nasty-minded could no more touch a unicorn than I—and someone who was still utterly innocent mentally *could,* no matter what had happened to their body. It's a matter of knowledge, too, I suppose—" She took one look at his face—which was probably an accurate reflection of the shock he was feeling—and convulsed into peals of giggles again.

Kellen wasn't sure whether to be furious, embarrassed, or just to go into the cabin and stay there for the rest of his life.

How could he possibly have been so thick-witted? *How?*

"Ah—" he said, trying desperately to change the subject—*his* turn to want to do that now, because he really did not *want* to find out anything more about his sister's sexual adventures—"if it's not violating some promise or something—what was the price of the healing this time?"

Idalia—eyes streaming with mirth—took a deep breath, obviously deciding to take pity on him. Shalkan was still snickering and shaking his head in wonderment, though the unicorn had managed to regain his feet again.

"Ah. The price. My part is to clear a fouled pond of the dead deer that has fallen into it; the unicorns can't purify it until the carcass is gone, and they won't be staying in this area for very much longer," she said, quickly getting herself under control. "Most unicorn families like to travel, you see; they were lucky they were close-by—relatively speaking—when the colt was injured. I can't tell you what the price was for the colt's friends and relatives, but it was trivial compared to the healing." She looked fairly satisfied, actually; surprisingly so for someone who had just agreed to a task probably easily as nasty as cleaning that cistern had been . . .

"I'd like to help. If I'm allowed that is," he added hastily.

Idalia looked a little surprised but quite pleased. "Why, Kellen, that's very kind of you! I accept, but I want to go find the pond first and see what kind of tools we'll need. Meanwhile, there's something else you can do, right now—"

She got up off the ground and went back to the cabin with her basket of herbs and whatnot, scooping up the bloody bandages and splints as well. Kellen had already learned that here in the wilderness you didn't throw things away lightly. Anything that could possibly be reclaimed and reused would be, as it was almost always easier to reuse than to make new.

She returned with a couple of empty baskets and a leather bucket and handed them to him. "If you'd be so kind, go off with Shalkan and see what you can find in the woods. It's summer—there might be berries, and if you can find enough we'll have pancakes and berries for dinner. I always find that

I'm as hungry as a wolf after a healing, and especially hungry for sweet things."

"Of course," he said, wondering if she was trying to get him out of the way for some reason . . .

But no, probably not.

"Anything else you'd like me to look for?" he added.

She looked wistful "Oh—mushrooms—if you're lucky enough to find mushrooms . . . I haven't had a good mess of stuffed mushrooms in so long . . ."

It was his turn to laugh, and he did. "I'll look. And I'll see what else I can find to eat, too."

"You won't need to worry about picking anything poisonous, not with me with you," Shalkan said, a little smugly, coming a few steps closer. "And I daresay I'm as good as one of those truffle-hunting dogs at sniffing out nice bits to eat."

"Truffles?" Idalia asked, the longing so naked in her voice that *both* of them laughed. "Now, I *won't* hold you to that, and I won't get my mouth set for anything in particular. Whatever you bring back will be more than we have already. And the walk will do you good, strengthen that ankle some more, and give you more woodscraft practice."

"Then, we'll be off," Kellen said instantly. Having just embarrassed himself so thoroughly in front of Idalia—and found out things he'd just as soon not know, come to that—he'd just as soon be somewhere else for the next little while. "We'll be back when we've got something to show you."

And without waiting for her answer, he strode off into the woods, making Shalkan trot to catch up.

Chapter Twelve

Apples and Apparitions

This was the first time Kellen had been very far from the cabin since his recovery, and even with Shalkan by his side, he felt rather alone. It was a different kind of aloneness than the kind he had faced in the City, where he'd been surrounded by people every waking moment, and his constant quest had been for *privacy*. But there, at least, irritating as it had been, he'd been protected—by the City Watch, by the fact of being the Arch-Mage's son. He couldn't have gotten into trouble—not real, point-of-death trouble—in Armethalieh, not really. The Watch was always keeping an eye on things, and if he'd really gotten in badly over his head, all he would have needed to do was reveal who he was, and everybody within sight would have been crawling all over themselves to do whatever he wanted and see him safely home. Oh, he might have gotten his pocket picked—that had happened to him a number of times in his early days—but that was just about the worst thing that had ever happened.

But here it was different. Except for Idalia . . . and Shalkan, of course . . . there didn't seem to be another person for miles. It seemed very odd never to see any other people, not to hear the sound of voices all around him, the sound of horses, and carts, and the City bells.

And the problem was that he really *was* alone, both physically and mentally, more alone than he'd ever been in his life, grappling with a problem no one could solve for him. Not Shalkan, and not Idalia.

Kellen was pretty sure by now that he could trust Idalia, trust her intelligence and her judgment, even if she *didn't* always tell him everything. After all, why should she? He was ten years younger than she was, and she had a lot of experiences behind her that maybe she wouldn't want to talk about to someone like him. He liked her a lot—more each day. He was in awe of her—not only her magic and her woodscraft abilities, but her plain common sense.

The trouble he had was that even though all those tales of Demonkind had seemed like nonsense back in the City, they weren't anything to be laughed at anymore. There'd been those dreams, for one thing. And for another, Idalia *herself* had said something in passing, but with a wary look over her shoulder, about Demons.

Now, if Idalia spoke of Demonkind without any irony—and given those awful dreams—Lycaelon must have had something behind his warnings, after all.

Idalia had been working with the Wild Magic for a long time—at least ten years more than he had, so if it was going to turn her to the Dark, it had certainly had plenty of opportunity to do that already, and if it had, surely he'd have seen *some* sign of it by now. And Shalkan *did* like her. It was just that Idalia wasn't, well . . .

After the healing this afternoon, Kellen could hardly believe how stupid he'd been. Shalkan didn't avoid Idalia because she was a Wildmage gone bad (and it should have occurred to him that Shalkan wouldn't have brought them both straight here if there *had* been something wrong with her) it was just that Idalia wasn't, well, a virgin. (Kellen winced. How in the name of the Light had he managed to miss that? But she'd been a *bird*. Being a bird didn't count . . .)

Resolutely, he turned his thoughts away from the subject. He had his vow to consider. He shouldn't even be *thinking* about things like that! Anyway, Idalia just wasn't. And that mattered a lot to unicorns, apparently—look at the way she'd been unable to touch the colt, even though it would have made things a whole lot simpler in the healing today if she hadn't needed Kellen's help. And what if he hadn't been there? What would she have done then?

Really, he should have put two and two together the moment the whole herd appeared, looking for help.

Sometimes I am so dense . . .

But no matter how hard he tried, he still couldn't get his father's parting words out of his head, and the fact that Idalia wasn't any kind of Demonspawn or Darkmage didn't solve Kellen's problem, not really. Lycaelon's words and his own fever-spawned nightmares still haunted him and plagued him with doubts to which there didn't seem to be any easy solution.

Because out here, outside the City walls, nothing was simple or straightforward anymore. Every answer turned out to be a gateway to more questions, more ambiguities. And instead of being given rules to follow, he was presented with choices. Idalia had said that the Gods used the Wild Magic to give Wildmages the tools to help them become better—if they wanted to become better. But that meant that down deep inside, it was still up to each of them to choose how to use those tools. That meant Lycaelon could still be right—that the Wild Magic might open the path to Demonkind by giving Wildmages the power to choose to be good or evil, and the freedom to make the wrong choice.

And Kellen wasn't really sure he knew himself well enough to be sure he was safe—that in becoming a Wildmage, he wouldn't end up exactly the way his father had said he would. Surely nobody started out using the Wild Magic *intending* to get involved with Demons? So how could you know you were going to get into trouble before it was too late to turn back? He already knew he'd made some really stupid decisions in his life. What if choosing to become a Wildmage was another one?

What if—not now, but in ten years, or even fifty years, if he managed to live that long—he did something really really horrible just because he didn't have the sense to stop using the Books *now*? How could he know? How could anybody know? Was *that* why the High Council forbade the study of the Wild Magic? Were they actually (for once in their twisted little lives) *right*? What if the Wild Magic really *was* dangerous—not for everyone, but just for a few people—and you couldn't know who those people were going to be until it was too late? If that was true, wasn't it best to just forbid *everyone* to use it, just in case?

But what if that wasn't true? Why should the Council be right about this when they were wrong about everything else?

How would he know before it was too late?

Maybe it was already too late.

Kellen sighed glumly, which earned him a sidelong glance from Shalkan, although the unicorn didn't comment. Once they'd left Idalia's cabin behind, there was no sign of civilization at all, and he was startled to find how much he missed the familiar walls and roads and buildings he'd grown up with all his life. Even in the large parks in the City that were designed so that all you saw were trees and flowers—no buildings at all, not even the City towers—everything was carefully planted and manicured and *designed.* You never forgot that someone had planned it. Out here, everything was just growing with no plan or pattern to it. Trees fell down, and nobody came to tidy them away. Flowers grew wherever they wanted to. No rules, no order, and no sign that any human had ever done anything here. It was all . . .

"Messy, isn't it?" Shalkan asked. "No, I can't read your thoughts," he added, regarding Kellen's guilty and startled expression. "Or, let's say, I can't read them in the normal course of things. But you wear your thoughts on your face, City-child."

"As bad as that?" Kellen said despondently.

"You'll learn," Shalkan said kindly. "And there's no reason for you to expect to like something you've never seen before, just because you think you ought to like it. Give yourself time."

"But what if I *don't* like it?" Kellen burst out. "What if I *never* like it? What if I always hate it? What if I should have stayed in the City after all?" He looked around at the forest, at the untidy ramble of trees and vines and flowers. Everything was in full leaf, the season racing forward toward high summer. Maybe it was pretty, maybe it was even beautiful, but *his* eyes longed for *patterns.*

"Do you think that's likely? There's beauty and wonder here beyond the stunted dreams of City-folk. And things you never knew existed. You only think that you know all that's to be found out here. Look."

Shalkan was pointing with his horn. Kellen looked sharply in the direction that he pointed.

At first all he saw was a patch of blue sky framed by the branches of two large oaks, but then, as he stared, it seemed to shimmer and glisten, becoming half-solid, shining like glass or water, with the merest hint of rainbow. For a moment he thought he glimpsed a spectral shape, winged and vaguely human, but then it vanished again, and there was only air.

"That—What—" Kellen gasped inelegantly. "I *saw* something . . . didn't I?"

"A sylph," Shalkan confirmed. "A creature of the winds. They ride the currents of the air, and with their help, you can influence the weather. She's not the only creature out here that you've never seen before—and that wouldn't ever go near the City walls. But come along—I know where there are some nice juicy apples."

"It's too early for apples," Kellen protested automatically.

"Come and see," the unicorn said with a wise and amused glance. "You just saw a sylph, are you going to disbelieve in my apples?"

Well, when Shalkan put it *that* way . . .

To Kellen's surprise, Shalkan led him to a wild apple orchard, where the trees were indeed heavy with ripe red fruit. Kellen started forward, hefting his basket, but Shalkan immediately stepped across his path, blocking his way to the trees.

"You might want to ask the owners if they're willing to part with some first," Shalkan said gently.

Kellen looked around, wondering if he'd missed seeing a hut or cabin concealed in the undergrowth.

"Look harder. Look at the trees. Remember the sylph," Shalkan said, giving Kellen a warning nudge with his shoulder.

Kellen did as he was bid, and suddenly he could see

them—women, sitting in the trees, looking down at him with
amusement. Their skin was pale green, like new leaves, their
long hair the emerald of the leaves of high summer. They
were crowned with apple blossoms, and every single one of
them was quite naked. They appeared to be perfectly comfortable in that state, and for a moment, Kellen had the disoriented feeling it was *he* that was the one who was foolish
for being clothed.

"Oh . . . no," Kellen whispered, appalled.

"Apple-dryads," Shalkan said matter-of-factly. "Tree-
spirits, tree-guardians. Not all trees have them, of course, or
we'd be up to our hocks in dryads; no, only a few select trees
are inhabited by dryads, though they do a certain amount of
tending of *all* the trees in their domain. This is their grove.
And their apples, of course."

The dryads came down from their trees; not so much
climbing as gliding, and began pacing deliberately toward
him. Their long hair swirled around them with a life of its
own, now concealing their bodies, now revealing them, a
breast here, a thigh there. Kellen would have turned to run,
but now Shalkan backed around him, blocking his retreat.
They clustered around Kellen, plucking at his clothes as if in
perplexity, and giggling at his horrified embarrassment.

"I—I—I didn't know," Kellen stammered, blushing hotly.
To his horror, he was surrounded by naked grove-maidens
and not quite sure where to look. "I'm sorry." The head of
the tallest of them barely came up to his shoulder, and their
pale green skin had the hard glossy sheen of a polished, un-
ripened apple. Unlike the sylph, which he hadn't been quite
certain he was seeing, the apple-dryads seemed as solid and
real as Idalia.

"Ladies, this is Kellen," Shalkan said, and Kellen would
have been willing to swear the unicorn was smiling. "He's
new here; he's Wildmage Idalia's brother—and he's under a
vow of chastity, so have pity on him."

The apple-dryads drew back a little, regarding Kellen and
Shalkan gravely out of dark eyes the color of apple-tree bark.
Kellen had recovered his composure enough to realize that

they weren't quite naked—or rather that they were, but that they weren't quite human; their slender nakedness, while giving the strong impression of femininity, was the featureless androgyny of a sculpture, or a doll. Vaguely, he supposed that only made sense. After all, they only *looked* human. He cleared his throat, awkwardly.

"I'm sorry I was going to steal your apples," he said. "I mean, I wasn't going to *steal* them. I was just going to take some, and I didn't realize that they were yours. I mean, Shalkan brought me here, and I figured he wanted some, and I knew my sister would like them . . ."

One of the dryads—she seemed to be the leader, though Kellen couldn't quite say how he got that impression—spoke. Her voice was like rustling leaves, and contained no human words, though Kellen felt that his apology was accepted.

A gift for you, human child, and for your sister, on whom be honor. This time he heard the words clearly inside his head, as though she were making an effort to be sure he understood her.

Suddenly the dryads whirled and went sprinting away, each to her own tree. There was a wild rustling of leaves and a great deal of giggling that sounded more like bubbling water than girlish laughter, and a few moments later several of them returned, carrying apples, which they reached out and placed into his basket amid much jostling and amusement. Before he could even begin to stammer out his thanks, the dryads had dashed away again, leaving him staring down at their gift—not as many apples as he might have gathered for himself, but all of them gleaming and juicy and without flaw.

He looked around, but now, no matter how hard he stared, once more the orchard was only an orchard, with no dryads to be seen. He looked at Shalkan, doing his best to make sense of what had just happened. Without the apples in his basket, it would have been easy to dismiss the last few minutes as an especially vivid waking dream, an aftermath of his injuries.

"What can I do in return?" he asked. Gifts required gifts

in return—that was the first lesson both of magic and good manners.

"Bring them water in a dry year," Shalkan answered approvingly, as though Kellen were an especially apt pupil. "Not this year—the rains have been good. But always respect the forest."

"I will," Kellen answered humbly. Humility seemed in order; and so did a lot more consideration than he *had* been giving to his surroundings! Things weren't what they seemed here—and he'd certainly never look at an apple the same way again!

⌐

AFTER that, the two of them moved onward, deeper into the forest. Now that he was getting used to *looking*, Kellen realized that the forest was not the empty unoccupied place it had first seemed to be. In fact, the creatures that were only hinted at in his High Magick lessons seemed to be everywhere, and Kellen was sure that he and Shalkan were constantly being watched. Gathering cress by the bank of a stream at Shalkan's direction, Kellen looked down into the water and found more than his reflection looking back. Something that could only be an undine stared into Kellen's eyes for a long moment before flitting away.

Undines and sylphs . . . that's two of the four Elemental Powers that I remember from my lessons in the High Magick. The other two are salamanders—fire—and gnomes—earth. He wondered where dryads fitted into the scheme of things. *I'm not sure I'd want to meet a salamander in a forest, but I wonder what gnomes look like? I would have paid more attention to my lessons if Anigrel had ever said the Powers were real live creatures . . . but the High Magick always taught that they were abstract concepts, symbols of the elemental forces of Creation that Mages work with, not . . . real. It's like Idalia said. The Mages take everything and squeeze the life out of it, turn it into entries in a ledger. No wonder the High Magick is so bloodless and boring!*

But it still works. Kellen remembered the Hound-golems and shuddered.

While gathering mushrooms—holding each one up for Shalkan's approval before adding it to his basket—Kellen came across a door in the base of an oak tree. It was only six inches high, but aside from that, it looked just like any other door that Kellen had ever seen. He straightened up and turned to Shalkan.

"How did they get here? What are they all doing here?" he demanded, making a sweeping gesture that took in the door, the dryads, the sylph, and everything else he'd seen in the forest.

"Your folk don't own the world," Shalkan replied reprovingly. "They just claim they do, sometimes." He shook his head. "Creatures of Magery are far more vulnerable to Magery's effects than humanfolk are. They're here because they were driven outside the bounds of City lands by spells, some of them. Your—ah, pardon me, not *your*—*the* High Mages don't care for creatures that they can't control, and they don't care for things that might remind their citizens that they don't own and rule the world of nature *or* the world of spirits, and that they share the world with creatures that don't abide by their rules. Most of the Otherfolk here in the Wildwood were chased out by Hounds. None care to remain where they aren't welcome."

Kellen looked back at the minuscule door, wondering which of the half-mythical creatures from his neglected studies lay behind it. Something tiny that built doors just like human doors, at any rate. Maybe someday he'd get to meet it.

Reluctantly, he turned and followed Shalkan.

He'd thought that by escaping the Outlaw Hunt and leaving City lands he'd be outside the influence of the City, but it didn't look like that was the case. If the City had pushed these creatures out of their homes by claiming so much land, then *that* was an influence, too, one that could be felt far beyond the bounds of the City. What if the City kept claiming *more* land? Where would they all go?

It wasn't *fair*.

IT was midday when they reached Shalkan's goal; an immense clearing in the center of the forest, filled with a vast welter of thornbushes that bore a suspicious similarity, to Kellen's eyes, to those Shalkan had charged through so many times during their escape. He regarded it dubiously.

"What's that?"

"Blackberries," the unicorn answered happily. "Oh, come now, City-child. Where do you think black-cap jam comes from? It doesn't grow on trees in little pots. It comes from bushes like these—well, not quite like these. This particular patch is special. It bears fruit out of season, and the most delicious fruit in the whole Wildwoods, I'll wager. Come along. There's plenty for everyone."

"There aren't going to be any more dryads, are there?" Kellen asked suspiciously, still holding back.

"No," Shalkan answered. "Only brambles—but that's why you're wearing all that leather. And a few scratches are a small price to pay for blackberry jam. And blackberry pie. And blackberry griddle cakes. And—"

"Okay, okay—I get the idea," Kellen said, laughing. He was starting to suspect Shalkan of having a sweet tooth, and even Kellen could smell the sugary scent of the fruit from where he was standing. Unlike some of the things he'd gathered today—including what Shalkan said were truffles, which Kellen couldn't imagine *anyone* wanting to eat!—it actually smelled familiar—like the baskets of the blackberries sold in the City markets. But instead of reminding him of home and all that he'd lost, the scent of wild blackberries made the forest seem like home—or like a place that could come to *be* home, anyway.

He set down the large shallow gathering basket and unslung the berrying bucket from over his shoulder, advancing warily toward the berry bush.

"Bears and birds have gotten most of what's on the outside," Shalkan said helpfully, "but there are still plenty of berries inside the thicket."

Resigning himself to a few scratches, Kellen got down on

his knees and began pushing his way inside. He quickly realized that this wasn't just one bush, but a cluster of bushes
grown together—and Shalkan was right; though the outsides
were picked almost clean, here inside the bushes were still
heavy with fruit. It wasn't as difficult to get inside as he'd
feared, either; the way the bushes grew together made a sort
of tunnel for him to push his way into.

He quickly stripped a handful of berries from their twigs
and popped them into his mouth. They were warm with the
sun, and the flavor was intense, piercingly sweet. Greedily,
he wolfed down another handful, before reluctantly realizing
he ought to share his bounty.

The next several minutes were occupied with Kellen feeding himself and Shalkan, as he stripped the fruit from all the
bushes within reach. The unicorn took the fruit directly from
his hands, and Shalkan's lips were soft against his palm. Soon
berry juice had stained Shalkan's muzzle a startling red-
purple, and Kellen's fingers—and probably his mouth, he
imagined—were much the same color.

"I suppose I ought to pick some to bring back, too," Kellen
said when both of them had eaten their fill.

"I suppose you ought," Shalkan said with mock sternness,
swishing his tufted tail back and forth. "I don't think you're
really the container Idalia meant those berries to come home
in. It shouldn't take you more than an hour or so—that's half
a bell to you, though you're really going to have to stop
thinking in City measures. I'll be back before then, and we'll
still have plenty of light to get back to the cabin by. You'd
better tuck that gathering basket in with you, though—you
wouldn't want squirrels to get those apples."

From the look on Shalkan's face, Kellen doubted that
squirrels were what the unicorn was thinking of, but Kellen
was in no mood to ignore good advice, no matter how cryptic.
He crawled out from under the brambles and dragged the
heavy gathering basket back in with him deep under the
bush—it would have to be a *very* determined squirrel who
went after its contents now—and concentrated on filling his
leather bucket.

He heard the unicorn trot off, but intent on his task, Kellen didn't pay much attention. Shalkan wouldn't leave him here alone if this was a particularly dangerous place, and so far nothing he'd met in the Wildwood had seemed likely to offer him harm. He'd seen deer and rabbits, and supposed that where there were deer and rabbits there must be things that ate them—foxes and wolves and bears and even mountain tigers—but so far he hadn't seen so much as a paw-track, and he knew from things Idalia had said that the great predators tended to be shy and unwilling to exert themselves, not attacking unless they were wounded and starving, or the odds ran very much in their favor.

The bucket filled slowly, even though Kellen now conscientiously tried to keep from eating the berries instead of collecting them, and he slowly worked his way toward the center of the patch, lying almost full-length in order to reach the lowest twigs, where the unharvested berries were thickest.

He was totally engrossed in his task, focused entirely on the world a few inches from the end of his nose, when suddenly several terrifying things happened at once.

Kellen felt something seize him by the back of his pants and drag him out of the thicket—straight through the brambles. He dropped the bucket, flailing for purchase as he was swung through the air and dropped rudely to the ground beside the thicket.

A voice—a booming, baritone voice—rang out above his head. "Oh, ho, you grubby little thief! What do you mean by sneaking in here to steal Cormo's berries?"

Kellen stared up at his attacker, and for one blurred befuddled moment he thought he was seeing a man on horseback. Then he realized what he was really seeing.

A Centaur.

The Centaur towered over Kellen. Though from his hooves to the crown of his head he was not very much taller than Kellen, his horse limbs were stocky and heavily boned, and his human torso was muscled like a blacksmith's. Like the apple-dryads, once you took a good look, he didn't look quite human—the proportions were a little off, somehow, though Kellen didn't think this was quite the time for a detailed inspection—and his face was flat and wide with a heavy brow ridge and flat cheekbones. His eyes were black, narrowed now with anger and suspicion.

He wore a sleeveless tunic of goatskin, with the hair left on so that the brown goat hide blended with his chestnut flanks, wild hair, and heavy beard. He stamped one massive hoof menacingly, and Kellen scrambled backward, out of reach of immediate peril.

"I'm very sorry," Kellen gasped. "I didn't realize—" He stopped himself just in time. Cormo had said these berry bushes belonged to him, but Shalkan would never have brought Kellen here to pick berries if these bushes belonged to anyone. After all, he'd been careful to warn Kellen about the apple-dryads. Was this a bluff? He got to his feet, watching Cormo warily. "Perhaps we can work something out? I'd be happy to—"

"Perhaps you will give me what you stole, and I will let you escape without the beating you so richly deserve!" Cormo snarled, taking a menacing step closer. Those hooves looked as large as dinner plates, and very heavy. "Everybody knows these bushes belong to me! Everybody!"

"But that's the thing," Kellen said, thinking quickly. "I'm new here. My name's Kellen. I'm staying with my sister Idalia down at her cabin—maybe you know it? I don't know a lot about the forest, and I certainly wouldn't want to trespass in anybody's farms or gardens. Or berry patches."

"Idalia." Cormo suddenly looked worried, but tried to hide it. "She's your sister, you say? Well—"

Just then Shalkan arrived, vaulting a fallen log at the edge of the clearing with the grace of a leaping deer. His sides worked as if he'd been running hard, but when he walked up to Kellen he sounded almost bored.

"Is there a problem here?" Shalkan drawled, sounding for all the world in that moment like one of the Senior Apprentice Undermages back at the Mage College—a particularly dandified fellow who cultivated a pose of great world weariness and took great delight in making trouble for the Students.

He tilted his head to the side, and his horn flashed in the sun. "I see you've met my friend Kellen, Cormo. Idalia will be interested to know he's encountered you."

Cormo took one look at the unicorn and backed up, shaking his head as if bees were swarming about it. "There's plenty here for everyone, I always say," Cormo muttered, turning and stomping away. "Don't know why everyone has to make such a fuss." He crashed off through the underbrush, still muttering to himself. Kellen couldn't make out all the words, but thought he caught something about "damned unicorns."

He turned to Shalkan, light-headed with relief. "Glory, am I glad to see you!"

"It looked like you were handling things well enough on your own," the unicorn observed. "What happened?"

Kellen explained. "—and when I mentioned Idalia, he suddenly got very cautious. I think he would have let me keep the berries, even if you hadn't shown up."

Shalkan snorted derisively. "There's no 'let' about it—Cormo doesn't own this berry patch, and he knows it! He's a notorious bully—and a lazy one at that, to want you to do his picking for him. He comes from the village a few miles from here—the one that Idalia trades with. It's a human-Centaur village, actually. Most of them are good quiet farmers, just like folk anywhere, but a few of them are like Cormo. Once he found out you were Idalia's brother, of course, he didn't dare offend you. Well, to be honest, he didn't dare do anything that would offend your sister."

"Why not?" Kellen asked curiously.

Shalkan chuckled. "Centaurs can't learn magic. It's not a case of an old wives' tale or a Council proscription or tribal custom—they really can't. Some think it might be because they're closer to beasts than humans are—not in reasoning power, or intelligence, and certainly not because they don't have a soul, but in their *natures*—and obviously the beasts can't do magic at all. Mind you, they're so strong, they don't need magic most of the time! But if they need serious healing from something that might well injure them permanently or even kill them, they need to come to a Wildmage like Idalia—and there's no other Wildmage anywhere closer than the High Hills that *I* know of. Except maybe you."

Kellen laughed. "All I'm good for is finding lost cats, and getting myself kicked out of Armethalieh."

"We'll see," Shalkan said. "You're young yet. And now there's been quite enough excitement for one day. We've got plenty of foodstuffs, and I think it's about time to be getting back."

It took less time to gather up the spilled berries than it had to pick them, and now Kellen was very glad the other basket had been hidden in the brambles, as he suspected Cormo would certainly have been happy to steal it.

So even though there's magic here, that doesn't mean everyone is good and perfect. Still . . . unicorns and sylphs and undines and dryads .and Centaurs . . . what next? Dragons?

〜

KELLEN and Idalia spent the next day—starting out well before dawn—clearing out the fouled pond, a nasty task that reminded him more than a little of clearing Perulan's cistern. Kellen could smell the pond long before they reached it—it smelled like food gone bad. Worse than food gone bad, actually.

"I can see we're going to find someplace else to have our picnic," Idalia said, wrinkling her nose at the stench. "But once we clear the muck out, the pond will bring itself back fairly quickly."

"What do we need to do?" Kellen asked, looking at it with disgust. The bloated, rotting carcass of the deer floated, half-submerged, in the center of the pond, surrounded by green scum and the half-eaten decaying bodies of dead fish. More dead fish were washed up against the edges of the pond, and the reeds and grass were brown and withered. They'd both come wearing heavy packs containing the tools they'd need—seines and buckets and rope and shovels—but Kellen wasn't sure anything short of a miracle could revive this place.

"First, let's get our tools in order. Then, you get to move the deer. Drag it a good way from here. Trust me, someone or something will want it, even if we don't! If nothing else, the vultures will. I'll leave the fish closer by—they'll stink, but most of the folk and the furred and feathered around here won't mind that, actually. And they'll be gone back to the earth in a day or two—or into somebody's belly."

Kellen grimaced, looking at the floating corpse. He hated the thought of actually touching it, but as it turned out, he didn't have to. One of the things Idalia had brought in her pack was a coil of light rope. After a few tosses, she managed to get it around one of the hind legs, and then handed the coil to him.

Then she took a keystone out of her pocket, and held it between her palms for a moment.

A thread of light—scarcely brighter than the sunlight, and just barely visible—wound rapidly around the carcass, until it had spun into a sort of cocoon.

"There. Now it won't fall apart while it's being dragged away," Idalia said. "Remember what I said about keystones? This is the sort of thing they're good for; making something to take the place of something we *could* do with a physical object like, say, a net. Except that we don't *want* to touch that thing, and the spell is very temporary, so it won't need much power."

He nodded; that made perfect sense.

Idalia motioned to him to start pulling. "You're stronger than I am. Drag it off someplace—away from water. Just keep the rope taut, and shake it free when you're done."

To Kellen's relief, Idalia's plan worked. He was afraid that the carcass was going to be too heavy to move, but once it was out of the water, he was able to keep going in what was more or less a straight line. He dragged the gruesome corpse several hundred yards into the forest, wondering where an appropriate location to deposit it would be. Mindful of Shalkan's lessons, he didn't want to be a bad neighbor and leave garbage in front of somebody's house. But it was very hard to tell just what was a house and what wasn't, here in the Wildwood.

Finally he came to a place that looked reasonably deserted to him. "Is this okay?" he asked aloud, feeling just a little foolish. "Does anyone mind me leaving this here?"

There was no response. He took that as assent—or else there wasn't anything living here but ordinary wildlife. He dragged the body to within a few feet of him and then shook the rope vigorously. As Idalia had promised, the loop widened again, and after a few tries, he was able to flip the rope free and coil it up again.

When he returned to the spring, Idalia had unpacked and laid out the rest of their gear, and was busy pinning her long braids up on top of her head. Except for a tight band of linen around her breasts and a hip wrap, she was naked. He gulped, and tried not to stare. She seemed oblivious to his embarrassment.

"Well come on," she said, "get your clothes off. You don't want to get your leathers all mucky. Cleaning them of this stuff would be almost impossible—and they'd smell like dead fish forever!"

He was just glad he *had* something on under the leathers!

The pond was *dead,* unfortunately. He wasn't sure how long the deer had been in it; long enough to kill everything that couldn't escape, anyway. Once they'd used the green willow sieves to seine the dead fish and most of the scum and dead water plants out of the water, it was time to switch to shovels to dig up the dead plants surrounding the pond—muddy work, but easy. Fortunately, the pond hadn't been a very large one to begin with.

"Now what?" Kellen asked, when that was done. By now the day was well advanced, and he was glad enough to be wearing as little as he was.

"Now," said Idalia gaily, "we bail!" Picking up one of the

buckets, she waded carefully out into the middle of the pond.

Kellen watched as she scooped up a bucket of murky brownish water and flung it toward the trees, then shook his head and followed suit. If there was anything more useless than trying to bail out a spring-fed pond, he couldn't imagine what it was, but if that was what Idalia wanted, then that was what he was going to do. Cautiously, he followed her into the water.

At least it was cool, after what they had been doing, and kind of fun, as the two of them competed to see who could throw the contents of his bucket highest and farthest onto the dry earth beyond. And after a few minutes, Kellen could see that the level of the water in the pond was actually starting to drop.

"When it fills again from the spring beneath, the water will be fresh," he said, finally realizing what Idalia was doing.

"That's right. And when it's fresh enough, we'll restock it. Now keep moving, lazybones!"

Idalia wasn't satisfied until the soft silt was showing in places at the bottom of the pond, then she finally called a halt, wiping her sweaty forehead with the back of her hand.

"Okay, that's enough for now. Let's go for a swim and have lunch while it fills. There's nothing more we can do here till then."

"Swim? Where?" Kellen was intrigued.

"Come on. I'll show you. You bring the food. I'll bring our clothes. I'm not getting dressed until I'm clean again."

As both of them were mud- and silt-covered over most of their bodies, and hot and sweaty as well, Kellen could only agree with that plan. He followed Idalia, and received another surprise.

She led him through the woods, and soon he heard the sound of rushing water. They came to a place where a small waterfall spilled down into a deep rocky catch-basin, which in turn overflowed to make the stream where he had seen the undine the day before. The whole basin was in full sunlight. Idalia sighed happily.

"It's a good place to swim—and it's warm!" She dropped

their clothes in a careless bundle and ran forward, arcing into a graceful dive that made almost no splash as she entered the water.

Kellen eased the pack off his back and set it beside the clothes. Though Armethalieh was a coastal city, no one swam in the ocean, but Kellen had learned to swim in the huge public swimming baths that were kept full of spell-purified seawater, and he'd enjoyed it. This was an entirely different matter, however. He'd gotten used to drinking wild water— but swimming in it?

You were just wading in much worse—and you couldn't even see the bottom there! he told himself sternly. Here the water was crystal pure all the way to the bottom, where sunlight played over a bed of tumbled white river stones. Kellen suspected he'd discovered the source of Idalia's keystones. He shrugged, and jumped in, far less gracefully than his sister had.

She'd said it was warm. It wasn't. It was cold—Kellen sank all the way to the bottom, where the water was cold as winter rain—and the force of his inelegant plunge forced cold river water up his nose, adding insult to indignity. He flailed to the surface, coughing and sputtering.

"I forgot to ask if you could swim!" Idalia called from the other side of the basin, laughing at the expression on his face.

Kellen shook his head, snorted, and struck out experimentally for the far side of the basin. The fresh water wasn't as buoyant as the salt water he was used to, but his swimming skills served him just as well, and he had to admit, the water wasn't *that* cold.

"It's nice," he said when he reached her. "And I *can* swim."

"Good," Idalia said. "Then you won't mind if I do—this!"

She ducked under the water, swift as an otter, and an instant later, Kellen felt a tug on his ankle as she yanked him sharply beneath the surface.

A spirited game of tag ensued, one that didn't end until both of them were breathless and clean. Finally, panting happily, Idalia flung herself out on the bank to dry.

Kellen joined her, prudently unrolling one of the blankets they'd brought and spreading it to sit on, but there was no need of a towel in the warm summer sunlight. He sat cross-legged on the coarse wool, savoring the peaceful moment.

"Nice, isn't it?" Idalia said without moving. Her eyes were closed, and her skin, tanned a deep bronze, undoubtedly by many days like these, made her as much a part of her surroundings as the trees of the forest.

"You weren't happy in the City," Kellen said without thinking.

"Not for a moment," Idalia answered, without hesitation. "I hated it. Everybody always telling me what to do, and say—and think. I suppose it's different if you happen to be born male. But not much different, I imagine, if you're a thinking person at all."

Kellen wondered. Maybe he just wasn't a thinking sort of person. He'd been happy enough for most of his life—he'd still be happy there, if he'd been lucky enough not to have been born into a Mage family, he imagined.

He frowned. Or would he? The restrictions might be subtler and less obvious for the non-Mage families, but they were still there. There were rules and restrictions for *everyone,* when it came right down to it. And the basic *idea* of the City was wrong—lying to people for some fraudulent notion of "their own good." Taking away their ability to choose for themselves, so deviously that they didn't even know it was being done.

"The Mage Council is evil," Kellen said.

Idalia sat up and opened her eyes.

"Well, *there's* a merry thought! Where did you come up with that one on a day like this?"

But Kellen was not going to be distracted now that he had things figured out in his own mind. "The Council is evil. The way they run the City is evil. They don't let the people choose for themselves. They just herd them, like—like sheep!"

"And you think they ought to be free—like we are?" The question sounded casual, but was it?

"Well . . . yes," Kellen said stubbornly.

"Do you think that's what they want?" Idalia asked.

I don't care what they want—I want what's best for them!
Kellen was about to say, when it occurred to him that the
Mage Council probably would use the very same argument
in its own defense. He grimaced.

"I don't know what they want. But I do know that they
haven't got any idea of what the Council does, or how, and
if they did know, a lot of them probably wouldn't like it very
much. I think they ought to be able to choose. I think they
ought to be able to buy anything they like in the markets, or
read any books they like. And I think that if they want to
leave the City, they ought to be able to."

"All you want is to change the whole world, eh, younger
brother?" Idalia smiled, and reached out to tug at his damp
curls. "Mind you, I'm not saying that you're wrong. I'm just
reminding you that things need to be thought through before
you do them. And if you're going to change something that
has been going on for as long as the way they do things in
Armethalieh has, you'd better have something ready to put
in its place that is something everyone can agree is an im-
provement. Remember what it says in *The Book of Stars*: 'If
you would change a thing, first understand why it exists.' "

She rolled onto her knees and pulled the pack over to her,
lifting the flap and beginning to remove their lunch. "Come
on, let's eat. I'm starved."

AFTER they'd eaten, they were both dry enough to dress,
though neither of them bothered with their shirts. They went
back to check on the progress of the pond, which Idalia
judged to be refilling nicely. The last of the muck had settled
on the bottom, and the water was a little murky, but not so
much that Kellen didn't think it would clear.

Some of the fish they'd tossed out on the ground were
already gone, and a lot of the stink had blown away. Idalia

sniffed the air experimentally, and then suggested a walk through the woods.

"I want to introduce you to some of the neighbors, and see where I can find some water plants to transplant to the pond," she told him.

"I've never planted a pond," he offered. "What are we looking for?"

"Sedges, reeds, catkins, marginal plants—and water lilies. If we put in just a few clumps, the marginals will spread by themselves, but the lilies all died, and since the pond's in direct sunlight, the fish will need something for shade, and to give them protection from predators. We'll have to get some help to find and plant lily bulbs. In the meantime, maybe we can find some floating plants to shade the fish. The frogs and turtles can find their own way back," she added darkly. "I'm not catching frogs, even with selkie help. You can spend days chasing frogs," she said, in a voice that seemed to come out of hard-won experience.

"Selkies?" Kellen asked, fascinated. That was a new name—he wondered just what kind of creature belonged to it.

"Selkies," Idalia confirmed. "Selkies and undines live in the stream—and otters, too, of course, though they're not Otherfolk. In the woods you'll find dryads of various species, not just the apple-dryads you found the other day."

She gave him a sidelong glance, and he felt his cheeks growing warm.

"That's what Shalkan said," he replied, hoping she hadn't noticed his blushes.

"Well, they're by no means the only thing that lives in the forest. Pixies, fairies, brownies, and fauns—they're very shy, so I'm hoping they'll come out when they see I'm with you. It can take a long time to meet everything that lives here— some folk only come out at night, some sleep through the summer. Some you wouldn't *want* to meet, like *duergar* and goblins and trolls, though I don't think any of them have stayed around here. They were pushed out of the settled lands by the Great War, and even after all this time, I don't think they'd be foolish enough to come back."

"What was the Great War?" Kellen asked, at the same time Idalia said:

"Oh—look!"

Kellen looked where she was pointing. A butterfly—no, a hummingbird. But it glowed, with a light softer than a firefly, though still bright enough to be visible even at midday, as it hovered among a bank of wildflowers.

"A pixie," Idalia said in a quiet voice. "Some people think they're fairies, but they're not."

As Kellen watched, the first tiny glowing figure was joined by three more. He blinked. Was that a—a humanlike body attached to those rainbow wings? They hovered among the flowers for a moment, then darted off. Idalia sighed happily. "I'm glad they're still here. There was a bad storm earlier this year, before you came, and I was afraid their nest had been destroyed. They make a kind of honey that I use in some of my medicines—it puts the patient right to sleep. I wouldn't want to use it in my breakfast tea, though."

"Can you talk to them?" Kellen asked, fascinated.

"With patience and practice," Idalia said, moving on.

As they walked, she pointed out other landmarks, including another tiny door like the one he'd seen before. It was, Idalia explained, the door to a brownie's house. She didn't know much about them, as they were terribly reclusive, but they seemed to live very much as humans did, in homes that were miniature copies of human dwellings—except for being built into the bases of oak trees. According to Idalia, a long time ago they had lived *with* humans, doing household tasks in exchange for food, but both of them found that hard to imagine.

He wanted to ask Idalia about Demons, since she seemed to be in such an expansive mood. In Armethalieh, they'd always been a nursery tale to scare little kids into behaving. But then Lycaelon had spoken of the Demons as if they'd once walked the streets of Armethalieh and might be back at any moment. And then there were the dreams. The Demons in Kellen's dreams were not very much like the Demons that were whispered about to frighten children into good behavior. The creatures in his nightmares were to those bogeymen as a sparrow was to an eagle. Since having those fever-dreams, Kellen was disinclined to scoff at the notion of Demons.

If Lycaelon had been lying in a last-ditch attempt to scare Kellen into submission, Idalia would tell him the truth, he knew. But somehow it had never seemed to be the right time to bring the subject up. But Kellen was starting to think there was never going to be a perfect time, and today seemed better than most.

He'd just opened his mouth to say something when he heard the sound of heavy hooved feet coming toward them. He stopped, but Idalia didn't seem at all concerned. She continued walking forward.

A female Centaur appeared on the path before them, a set of panniers slung across her back.

Like Cormo, she had a broad, heavy-boned, swarthy face and black eyes, but there all resemblance ended. Her chestnut hair was neat and combed, braided and held in place with a set of elaborately carved wooden combs. She wore a pleated linen shirt with bright woolen embroidery along the low-cut bodice and sleeves, and her tail was braided with bright ribbons.

There was a necklace of the sort called "beggar-beads" in Armethalieh about her neck—a long necklace of multicolored glass and stone beads, no two alike, looped several times around her throat and dropped into the cleft between her heavy breasts. Under the panniers, she had a colorful hand-woven wool blanket with heavy fringes flung over her haunches.

"Merana!" Idalia said cheerfully. "How good to see you! Did you see? The pixies are back!"

The Centauress smiled. "Indeed I did, Idalia—I'm going to their tree now to trade for dream-honey . . ."

Her gaze traveled past Idalia to Kellen and she regarded him with frank—and open—admiration. It might be difficult to judge Centaur ages, but Kellen got the feeling that she wasn't very much older than he was.

"So . . . this is Kellen. We've heard rumors about him, Idalia, as I'm sure you figured. Tell me, when are you coming to Merryvale again—and bringing your handsome brother?" Merana smiled and licked her lips.

Kellen blushed hotly. Centaur or no, she made him think things he knew very well he ought *not* to be thinking, not with the promises he'd made to Shalkan! And the more he tried to untangle his thoughts and make them travel in chaste and continent directions, the more lurid they became, until all he could do was stare at his feet and hope he was struck by lightning. Soon.

To his relief, Idalia laughed and walked up to Merana, linking arms with her and strolling with her ahead of Kellen—he could hear the two of them talking as they headed up the trail, and only hoped they weren't talking about *him*. It was bad enough that Shalkan had told the dryads about his vow—if he was going to have to tell every female he met about it for the next four seasons, well, he didn't think he could bear it.

I'll go back to the cabin. I'll lock myself in the bedroom, hide under the bed, and Idalia can feed me through the window for the next thirteen moonturns, that's all. Or I'll find a deserted mountaintop where nobody goes and live there, he told himself desperately.

A few minutes later, Idalia was back.

"She's an awful tease, isn't she?" Idalia said, winking. "She's got all the boys in the village chasing after her—frankly, I don't see how she has the time to flirt with all of them, but she does. She's the apprentice to the village Healer—plenty of work there, between bringing babies—human and livestock both—and setting bones. But I saw she was embarrassing you, so I figured I'd give her a little gossip, then get rid of her. All I had to do was remind her that Master Eliron would be wondering what took her so long to send her on her way."

"Thanks," Kellen mumbled, still flustered. "I guess this

vow isn't going to be as simple to keep as I'd thought."

"That's sort of the nature of them," Idalia agreed gravely. "Come on. We'd better go looking for those plants."

Catkins were easy enough to find, and Idalia assured him they only needed one or two clumps, since the plants would spread quickly to take over their new home. While she gathered the fat roots with their swordlike leaves and their trailing root stems, Kellen dug out a few clumps of grass and reeds, digging deep to make sure he got most of their roots. And they were lucky; in a little pond they found enough water-cabbage that it covered the entire surface; Idalia quickly pulled in plenty of the leaf clumps with their trailing bundles of hairy roots, heaping them carefully in her basket. Armed with their bounty, they returned again to the pond.

"Just about full enough to stock," Idalia decided, floating the water-cabbage out into the center of the pond. They'd quickly begin to "calve," sending babies out on shoots that would break off when the baby got big enough, and naturalize in their new home.

Kellen was left with the muddier task of planting the reed bundles, and once he was done, felt his labors had earned him a question or two.

"Idalia," he began hesitantly, "I've been meaning to ask you. You talk about the Great War, something I've never heard of, and the Otherfolk that were driven out of the settled lands by it. Those creatures . . . does that include . . . Demons?"

"Hush!" Idalia said fiercely, rounding on him. "Never mention them here!"

"I—But—" Her sudden vehemence took him by surprise. "You don't mean you *believe* in them, do you?" he said. Suddenly, once again, such a belief seemed so childish, so unreasonable. Demons were things for nursery shadows and wondertales, not the bright light of the forest.

"Of course I do," Idalia said in a low voice, taking a step toward him. "They're real. Kellen—"

"They are!" an aged voice whispered fearfully. "Oh! Terrible real, they are!"

Crouched among the bushes at the edge of the trees was one of the Otherfolk. From Idalia's references, and his own studies, Kellen guessed it to be a faun. It was a creature about the size of a two-year-old child, humanlike to the waist, but with a goat's haunches. Its pointed ears were long and hairy, and goat horns grew from its brow, curling back over its skull. A small neat beard edged its jaw, adding to the goatish appearance. Unlike the Centaurs, whom Kellen could imagine to be very civilized despite their hooves and tails, the faun wore no clothes, and seemed far closer to the wild creatures of the forest than it did to the forest's more civilized and humanlike inhabitants.

Though he had no real experience with the races of the Otherfolk, even Kellen could see that the faun was very, very old. Its curling horns were as dark as winter leaves, and its hair and pelt were streaked with grey. Its face was as withered and dark as an old apple, and long ago it had been terribly injured—one eye was gone, leaving a web of white scars behind, and the faun's shaggy haunches were dappled with white scars, relics of terrible wounds.

And it was so frightened that it trembled all over, so frightened that Kellen could hardly believe that it was still standing there, speaking to them. The horror in its single, wide eye sent a chill down Kellen's spine, and out of what depths of its soul the faun found the courage to remain and warn them, Kellen could not imagine.

"Never speak of Them," the faun begged, quivering in terror. "Never speak of Them—never! Or They will come here, where it is safe, and pleasant, and turn it into—I dare not say!" Having frightened itself thoroughly, the old faun turned and ran, vanishing into the undergrowth as if it burrowed its way into it.

Idalia sighed, watching him go. "You see? Poor old thing. He came over the mountains years ago—long before I settled here. Something terrible must have happened to him there, but Piter never talks about it. I wish I could heal him—but he would have to ask, and he never has. I think he's afraid of hurting me—if I healed him, I'd find out how he was hurt,

you see, and I would be as terrified as he is—or so he believes." She sighed again. "Poor creature, to be so afraid.
Every year I wonder if this winter will be his last."

She turned away and began assembling their packs, but
Kellen kept staring in the direction Piter had fled. The faun's
terror had been so real that Kellen felt his own heart beat
faster in response, and for the first time in a long time the
memories of his fever-dreams were sharp and urgent.

"Can we—talk about this?" he asked his sister timidly.

"Definitely. But later." She cast a look over her shoulder,
as if to make sure they weren't still being overheard. "Later,
when it's—safer."

And it did not escape Kellen's attention that she said
"safer," not "safe."

Demons *were* real. Lycaelon Tavadon hadn't lied.

And if that much was true, maybe the rest of what he'd
said was true in some way as well.

Chapter Thirteen

The World Without Sun

Upon arising each day, Queen Savilla first took a cup of
spiced *xocalatl* to warm her, then allowed her slaves to
dress her in a diaphanous chamber-robe, cut low in the back
to allow freedom for her wings, and low in the front to expose
her . . . abundant charms.

The Endarkened did not *sleep,* precisely—not as the Bright
World races understood the term—nor did they age and die,
save by misfortune and violence. He Who Is had granted
them the boon of endurance, but like all such boons, it must
be paid for, and so, at regular intervals, adult Endarkened
retreated for a period of deep contemplation that might—

were a human to witness it—be likened more closely to death than to sleep.

Their young had no need of this sort of rest, of course, and even the oldest Endarkened could set the need for rest aside, for a time, without ill effects. But to forgo it altogether was to court first madness, then the loss of power.

It was best not to be foolish.

Without the lights in the sky of the Bright World to mark the passage of days, time passed in its own strange way in the World Without Sun, its course marked by the magic that was the very heartbeat of the Endarkened, and by the rhythms of the bones of the Deep Earth that was their place.

When the Queen went to her rest, so did her Court. In the World Without Sun, Queen Savilla was the Sun and the Moon, the dark radiance from which the world took its light.

Each rising, as her slaves dressed her hair, and buffed and gilded the talons on her hands and feet, Savilla heard gossip and petitions . . . first from Court favorites, then from the Ministers of her Realm.

All information was important to Savilla, and she despised no source of it.

The softbodied Brightworlders that could not adapt to life in the World Without Sun—and the absence of those Bright World lights—sickened and died. Fear and pain kept them healthy for a time, of course, but even the hardiest of Brightworlders were brief-lived and fragile.

It was always necessary to acquire more.

And that was a matter constantly in Queen Savilla's thoughts from her first waking moment, since for her plans to proceed against the Brightworlders required the constant expenditure of magic.

Not the great and terrible magics of days gone by, that had caused the Brightworlders to cringe and tremble and fear the power of the Endarkened . . . and to organize against them. No, Savilla's plans involved subtle webs of treachery, no less effective for that they went quite unnoticed by the soft stupid Brightworlders. Like the slow dripping of water that could wear away stone . . . or build mighty pillars beneath the earth, her magics worked unseen and unnoticed by their victims.

But magic required energy. Energy came from blood and pain. Blood and pain came from the torture of slaves . . . and where did the slaves come from?

Raids upon villages in the Wild Lands and the High Hills were simple enough to plan, but must be conducted with care, lest the Endarkened bring themselves to the attention of the Wildmages who lived there.

Isolated wanderers, whether travelers, traders, or outlaws, could always find themselves lured away from safety, whether by one of the Endarkened in disguise, or by one of their human agents. That was simple enough, and always entertaining, but the numbers of slaves gained were far too few for the purposes of Endarkened magic.

Slaves could certainly be bought outright, for not every land abhorred the concept of slavery—but again, the constant disappearance of slaves into the north might eventually attract unwelcome attention.

And there was something so spiritless, so unsporting, about simply *buying* one's prey!

She would have to consider the matter.

Carefully.

"—SO you see, my Queen, while it is not *precisely* a crisis, it is, perhaps, awkward," Cerbael said charmingly.

Cerbael was Queen Savilla's Master of Revels, his business the orchestration of the public ceremonies and entertainments of the Endarkened Court. He was entertaining and inventive, and had never, in all his long centuries of service, first to her father, and then to her, sought any higher position. He was, as he had once told Savilla with as much honesty as any of their kind could summon, already king of the only realm he cared about, and no one could give him anything he wanted more than what she had already given him.

She would destroy him if he ever failed to amuse her, of course. And he would turn on her if she withdrew her favor and support. But until that time, they trusted one another . . . in their fashion.

"M'mn." Savilla stroked the head of the goblin at her feet and did not reply directly. Its bulging silver eyes were closed to slits in the dim light of the chamber, and its blue-grey skin glistened with gold-infused oil. Erlaon had given the creature to her as a present, and Savilla had decided to be amused at the obvious and clumsy attempt to court her patronage.

One of her human servants approached the goblin too closely, and the little creature, startled, hissed and spat. Green venom spattered the slave's grub-pale skin, and the Brightworlder fell to the floor, writhing in agony. Moments later, its pale body stilled.

"There," Savilla said in pleased tones. "That should solve a few of your problems, Cerbael." She put her hand on the goblin's collar to keep it from moving toward the corpse. Goblins were greedy creatures, always hungry, and Ixit was perfectly capable of eating the entire Brightworlder all by itself.

Cerbael laughed appreciatively at his Queen's jest. "I do not think Filendek would be content with this for long—and it's hardly worth his greatest efforts, don't you think, Majesty?"

"True," Savilla admitted with a fond smile. "We shall have to find him something worthy of his skill. Well?" she demanded of her other slaves, who cowered back, staring in horror at their fellow. "Will you clean this up? Or will you join it?"

Her dressing-slaves scuttled to obey.

After Queen Savilla had heard all Petitions of the Dressing Chamber—and acted upon those which it pleased her to act upon—she allowed her surviving slaves to dress her more formally, and went, as was her custom, for a walk in her gardens.

Of course nothing grew here. Savilla would have been quite offended if it had. Elsewhere in the World Without Sun there were vast farms of strange pale fungus in their infinite varieties, tended by slaves and hosts of the Lesser Endarkened. There were soft writhing worms and lakes of glowing blind fish and tunneling insects for whom the kiss of the sun was fatal, all of which the Endarkened considered delicacies.

But Savilla's garden was different.

Here colored crystals had been coaxed from the ground by magic, in much the same way that flowers sprang from fields of rot and decay in the World Above. And within each crystal, Savilla had trapped some moment of agony of one of her special victims, so that she could cherish it always.

She strolled along the twisting paths, brushing her fingers along the stones and wakening the stored memories into life with a touch of her magic.

—Here, the moment when one of her pet Darkmages had torn the horn from a living unicorn. No Endarkened could touch the creature without dying, and so the beast had thought itself safe enough, but it was not safe from Savilla's Darkmage. How it had begged, pleaded, *reasoned* with the man, telling him what his own eventual fate would be! But all in vain . . .

—Here, the Darkmage's own death, when Savilla had grown tired of him. How she had enjoyed taunting him, reminding him of how he had killed the unicorn, reminding him that everything it had told him had been true, that he could have saved himself had he only *listened* to it instead of killing it . . .

It was so perfect, placing these two stones next to each other, so that they could stand in rebuke to one another for all Eternity, though the minds and souls and deaths that had gone to make them were long expended, gone to fuel her magic.

Which reminded Savilla, once more, of her problem.

She seated herself on a bench cunningly wrought of human bones—some of the younger members of the Court made quite a hobby out of crafting things of what the Endarkened's victims left behind, and some of their pieces were quite artful—and devoted herself to considering the problem.

Problems, really. A ruler had so many problems to deal with, and not one of them could be neglected. Even the tiniest, the most seemingly inconsequential problem, could be the tear in the wing that made it useless in flight.

There must be a way to solve so many minor problems at once. Even Filendek's problems must not be slighted— Cerbael had been quite right to bring them to her attention, for the chief cook was an artist, and his complaints would be seen as setting a certain *tone* for the entire Court.

Filendek was quite beside himself at the emptiness of the larders, and the lack of delicacies to set upon Savilla's table. No faun, no selkie, no naiad, and the stocks of human and Centaur—in the cold-larders and in the fattening pens—were (so he said) dangerously low. As for unicorn, it had been a long time since *that* flesh had graced one of the Royal banquets, and no one at the Endarkened Court had tasted Elven flesh since the last War.

It was sad, really, to see the simple elegancies of life dwindle away even as you watched. But let her plans go as she would have them, and all would be well again, the Court returned to the height of its glory. Their larders would be full, and they would have no need to conceal themselves from the notice of Wildmages, lest their plans be discovered before the proper time.

But until that moment came there was much to do.

She thought back over her morning's reports. Their campaign against the Elves was going well, so now it was time to cause Armethalieh to do something foolish. Her agents there assured her that the Arch-Mage had been ever more unreasonable since his son had turned Wildmage and been Banished . . . perhaps there was something in that she could use to solve her own small difficulties, for as the Arch-Mage went, so went the City.

Savilla smiled, and set the thought aside to ripen.

⌐

"WHAT do you suppose, my love, I would do if you betrayed me?" Savilla said to her son.

She smiled lazily as she felt Prince Zyperis's body tense against hers, then relax with an effort.

"I would never betray you, my mother, my Queen, my love," Zyperis protested. He kissed her shoulder.

She chuckled throatily. "Of course. But only suppose."

The two of them were quite alone in Queen Savilla's private retiring chambers, sprawled upon a circular couch of saffron-dyed silk. The spicy scent of the fabric, heated by their recent exertions, filled the chamber, and the Prince's wings were spread over both of them like a perfumed cloak.

"You would destroy me," Zyperis said. His tone was uncertain, as if he were not quite certain this was the answer she wanted. Good. Uncertainty was the beginning of submission . . . and of wisdom.

"But what if you were beyond my reach?" Savilla said playfully, reaching up to stroke his back with her gilded talons. "What if you had escaped me? What then?"

"Then, dearest Mother, you would track me down, no matter where I had fled, and crush me utterly, no matter what you had to do." From the faint note of relief in Zyperis's voice, he had decided this must be a game. "Nor would you stop until you had done so. And for that reason, I would never flee . . . nor betray you."

No, my son, you would not flee. Nor would you betray me unless you were certain you could win all in one throw of the counters, and render me powerless, Savilla thought with a faint spark of pride. Her son had greatness within him, and for that very reason, she must watch him carefully.

"The Arch-Mage Lycaelon Tavadon's son has betrayed him . . . and fled," Savilla said.

"And does the human Mage pursue?" Zyperis asked with lazy interest.

He moved away from Savilla and off the edge of the bed. Getting to his feet, he walked over to a small jeweled table where a wine service stood waiting. He poured two jeweled golden cups full and brought them back to the bed, handing one to her and waiting until she drank.

"The human Mage does *not* pursue," Savilla corrected him

gently. "The human Mage acted in accordance with the finest instincts of fatherhood—he condemned his son to death—but the Outlaw Hunt could not pursue the Mageborn boy beyond the boundaries of the City lands."

Savilla did not know whether or not Lycaelon Tavadon knew what had happened to his Outlaw Hunt and his errant son, but her sources of information were far finer than Armethalieh's, and she did. The young Wildmage had lured a unicorn, and between them they had destroyed all the stone Hounds that the City had sent to kill him and escaped into the Wild Lands beyond the City borders.

What would Lycaelon Tavadon do if he knew?

He would want to pursue the boy, of course.

But the High Magick, by the terms of its initial creation, simply would not work outside the borders of the lands claimed by the City.

If Lycaelon Tavadon wanted to be able to chase down his Outlaw son with High Magick, he was going to have to get the High Council of Armethalieh to extend the borders of the lands the City claimed.

And doing that would drive hundreds—no, thousands—of fresh victims right into the Endarkened nets, solving all their problems at once.

Savilla sipped at her wine.

"As a mother myself, I feel for Lycaelon Tavadon. I know he would want to know where his son is, and what he is doing. Of course he has spies in the High Hills, but I'm afraid they're not quite as efficient as they could be.

"Do you love me?" she asked suddenly.

"As I love power and pain," Prince Zyperis said huskily, his voice thick with renewed desire.

"Good," Queen Savilla said. "Now. Here's what I want you to do . . ."

GAREN Miq was a tinker and a peddler—a mender of small odds and ends, and seller of this and that—whose route took him all the way to the border, through every small farming villages there was. His favorite stops, of course, were the lowland villages that made a fruitful apron around the Golden City, and he always tried to make sure that his last stop before winter set in was Nerendale, where the trading post was, for Garen didn't like to travel during winter, and always picked a likely village to spend the months of cold and wet somewhere dry and warm. Nerendale was said to be as close as you could get to living in the Golden City herself—didn't it have an actual Mage living there full-time, after all?

But if Garen played his cards right, he wouldn't have to just wonder about what it was like to live in Armethalieh. He'd live out the rest of his days there—as a real, Talisman-wearing citizen, with hot water in his house, fires that never went out, a roof that didn't leak, and all the other wonders of the City of a Thousand Bells, his, free for the asking.

If he only served the Arch-Mage loyally and well.

Garen Miq was a seller of oddments, but he was also a spy. For many years he had served the Arch-Mage Lycaelon Tavadon in that capacity, wandering through the hills and villages and reporting any information that he thought the Arch-Mage should know—of heresy, of Otherfolk within the City lands, of unrest or dissatisfaction with the wise and just rule of the Mages.

He never saw the Arch-Mage personally, of course. Oh, no. That wouldn't be right. Garen Miq had never even been within the walls of the Golden City. Not yet. The man who had come to him many years before—a member of the Arch-Mage's personal staff, of course, wearing the grey robes of a High Mage and carrying the staff of authority—had told him that citizenship would be his reward after long years of faithful service, and given him the means by which he could make his reports—a small ball of golden glass, barely the size of a ripe apricot.

"Only speak into this ball, and it will be as if I—or the Arch-Mage himself—hear your words, Garen Miq. So speak wisely and carefully," the Mage had said.

It was Garen Miq's greatest treasure, proof that he was more than he seemed, and he guarded it carefully.

TONIGHT he was drinking in an inn in a village called Delfier's Rest, at the westernmost edge of the forest. It was a wild, uncouth place, as so many near the border were; people were careless with the Law here, and Garen had seen Other Races here in the past.

Even the name of the inn skated perilously close to heresy, as he'd already reported. The Inn of the Invisible Unicorn? What sort of a name was that for a proper inn?

Still, the mead was good, and the beer was excellent. And the kitchen did a very nice rabbit pie. If it only didn't *snow* so much here in the wintertide, Garen would even be perfectly willing to winter here if he had to, though Nerendale, being closer to Armethalieh, was naturally better.

It was already late summer, and in a sennight—a fortnight at the most—he would have to turn eastward again, lest winter catch him far from Nerendale's comforts. There had been little reason these past few moonturns to speak into his golden orb—in the spring, several farmers had reported seeing a pack of stone dogs running through their fields, and Garen had duly reported that, since it was unusual. But he had no doubt it was Magework, for were not the streets of the Golden City itself filled with statues that walked and talked like living men? Undoubtedly the dogs had been sent on Mage-business.

He was considering one last tankard of ale before retiring to his rooms for the night when a stranger sat down at the table across from him.

"Am I intruding?" the stranger asked. "I hope not. I've been on the road all day, and I confess I'd hoped for a little company at the end of my journey. And you look like an interesting fellow."

His raised eyebrows and conspiratorial smile indicated the rest of the folk in the common room of the Invisible Unicorn, and Garen Miq had to agree—with a small flush of pride—

that no, none of them were what you'd consider "interesting fellows" at all. Farmers and laborers from nearby villages mostly. Not one of them was like him—practically a citizen of Armethalieh.

"Please," he said. "Make yourself comfortable. I'd be glad of the company myself."

The stranger summoned the tavernmaid over and ordered two more tankards of ale—"and brandy—good brandy—if you have it." Garen saw him pass a coin into her hand, and heard her gasp. He recognized it—his eyes were sharp—as City minting, one of the legendary Golden Suns of Armethalieh herself!

Garen wondered what the girl would do with it. The stranger could probably buy every keg in the Invisible Unicorn—and the wench herself—for the wealth that single coin represented . . .

"You've come from the east, then?" he asked, congratulating himself on the casualness of his tone.

The stranger smiled—he really had the most charming smile—and the golden handsomeness that spoke of noble breeding. "Ah, best not to say too much about some things," he said. "Not everyone would take it in the proper spirit. But no harm in exchanging names, now, is there? I'm Henamor Lear. And you . . . ?"

"Garen Miq."

The tavernmaid returned with a wooden tray. On it were their tankards, plus a squat stone bottle and two smaller cups—silver!—as well. She set the items on the table and bobbed a hopeful curtsy at Henamor as she withdrew.

Garen raised his tankard and drank—was it his imagination, or was the ale of a far better quality than his last tankard had been?

Henamor had taken out a small silver knife—of a finer quality than anything that had ever graced Garen's stock—and cut away the wax seal surrounding the cork on the stone bottle. With great care, he withdrew the cork, and poured one of the small silver cups full, sniffing at it delicately and then smiling.

"Ah. An unexpected surprise, and pleasure. I'm sure you'll find this an unanticipated change from what you're forced to deal with here in the rural outlands." He poured the second cup full as well, and passed it toward Garen.

Generally Garen did not care for brandy. He found it harsh and biting, and its only virtue was that it got a man drunk far more quickly than wine. *This* brandy, however, was nothing at all like any he had ever experienced—mellow and fiery, with no bitterness to it at all.

"More what you're used to, eh?" Henamor said with a congenial chuckle.

"I . . . yes," Garen said. Suddenly he very much didn't want his new friend to lump him in with the boors and country bumpkins that surrounded them. He *wanted* to seem to be the sort of fellow who drank this kind of brandy as a matter of course.

"Well, we must all make sacrifices . . . *for the good of the City.*"

Garen nearly choked on his drink. Was Henamor hinting that he was actually in a situation similar to Garen's—an agent of the Golden City?

He'd better not say anything. The penalties if he made a mistake would be too dreadful to contemplate.

But oh, only imagine if it were true! Obviously, this man was a full citizen, and had mistaken Garen for the same. How wonderful to think that his years of study and sacrifice had borne fruit, just as he had always hoped . . .

⌁

IN his guise of Henamor Lear (he had not been able to resist using the name, and the real Lear was long past complaining), secret agent of Armethalieh, Prince Zyperis stifled his laughter with an effort. How very easy it was to fool these brutish, half-bestial humans! It didn't even require any more magic than was necessary to disguise himself as one of them. Why, the gullible fool—who was, in fact, one of Lycaelon's own handpicked Undermages, his true memories hidden behind a spell-screen until his field assignment should be complete, or unless true danger threatened him personally—*wanted* to believe "Henamor." He *wanted* to think he was special, and superior to these simple farmers, when in fact Zyperis could tell no particular difference between them.

Other than that Garen had power, of course. And if the situation had been otherwise, he would have taken very great delight in charming Garen Miq entirely into his clutches and then ripping the spell-screen from his mind, allowing him to know just who—and what—had beguiled him. So many of the High Mages were so *conservative* . . .

But today he acted at the word of Queen Savilla, and his dearest mama had other plans entirely for Garen Miq.

Fortunately for Garen Miq.

So Prince Zyperis went on pretending to be Henamor Lear, implying that Lear was a High Mage of the Golden City, traveling in disguise, and that Garen—foolish softskin!—was Henamor's equal in all things. He plied Garen with excellent and only slightly spellbound brandy, and he talked.

Oh, yes, he talked.

"No doubt, dear Garen, you saw the Outlaw Hunt go by this spring—or heard of it at least? It is a terrible thing when a citizen is Banished—worse by far when it is the Arch-Mage's own son!"

He leaned forward, placing his hand over Garen's confidentially. By now the man was more than a little drunk, but not so drunk that he did not hear every word—and would not report them all to his masters.

"The Arch-Mage's son was Banished?" Garen breathed, sobering a little at such a shockingly intimate piece of gossip.

"Oh, yes," Zyperis/Henamor said confidingly, lowering his voice. "They're keeping it very quiet, of course—and quieter still that the boy escaped the Hunt. He's living just the other side of the border, with his sister. Near a Centaur village— Merryvale, I think they call it. Someone here would know where it is . . . for the right price. I suppose he thinks he's safe enough."

It was amazing just how much Brightworlders could resemble goblins when they really tried—without, of course, having any of the little creatures' more endearing characteristics. Garen Miq looked very much as if he were about to swell up and explode, and his eyes were as round and bulging as fishes' eggs.

"Are you sure?" Garen said in a strangled whisper.

"Dear fellow, I saw him myself," Zyperis drawled. "No mistaking Kellen Tavadon—or his sister. Go see for yourself, if you doubt me. It's only a couple of days from here, I expect."

"I will," Garen said boldly.

But Zyperis knew he wouldn't. That would involve *crossing* the border, leaving the boundaries of Armethaliehan lands. Garen wouldn't know why he was so reluctant to do that, though Zyperis did. If Garen Miq crossed the border, the spell-shields on his mind would crumble away once he was beyond the boundaries of the High Mages' power. He'd remember who and what he was.

Can't have that, now, can we? Who knows what might happen? A nice, plump little Mage like you, reeking of power, wandering around all alone out here . . . some Demon Prince might swoop down and carry you off and do hideous things to you . . .

But it was not to be, Zyperis reminded himself with regret. Garen must deliver his message to his masters and return to them safely. He could not even disappear after his message had been delivered. There must be no possibility that Armethalieh might be distracted from the course upon which Queen Savilla wished to set her.

Perhaps another time.

At length the bottle was finished, and Zyperis, with the excuse of the need to make an early start, got to his feet. By now Garen was anxious to be free of him as well; Zyperis knew that he had some article of magick about him and would be making an immediate report.

And Zyperis intended to console himself for having had to forgo the pleasure of devouring the Mage-man . . .

ALL that had still been available when he'd arrived at the
Invisible Unicorn had been either a private room or a pallet
on the floor of the common room, and for the safety of his
wares, Garen Miq had chosen the private room. Now he was
very glad he had, even though a private room was ruinously
expensive. In his little room at the top of the inn, Garen
bolted the door, lit a lantern from his stores, and drew forth
his speaking orb.

Prudence warred with excitement. Perhaps he should wait
until morning, when his head was clearer, to report his news.
But no. He knew that he must tell this news at once. Tomorrow he would make inquiries about the *precise* location
of the village of Merryvale and report that too, if he could.

He withdrew the leather pouch from around his neck and
pulled out the orb. Unwrapping it from its silk coverings, he
warmed it in his hands. As always, it glowed brighter than
could be accounted for by the available light. He took a deep
breath.

"This is Garen Miq." He never knew if whoever heard his
words could just *tell* it was him, so he always began with his
name. It was unnerving, speaking this way. He'd never quite
gotten used to it. Like speaking to the Eternal Flame, only
more so, since the orb never said anything back.

"I am in the village of Delfier's Rest, near the border. Tonight, in the Inn of the Invisible Unicorn, a traveler named
Henamor Lear came to me and told me that the Arch-Mage's
son, Kellen Tavadon, is alive, and living with his sister over
the border, near a village called Merryvale . . ."

He told the orb everything he could think of, hoping he
had not been lured into error somehow, tricked into reporting
untruths . . . but if he *had* been, that, too, was information that
the Arch-Mage would need, since he would now know when
and where and how it had happened. And Garen had reported
it very promptly. Surely that would count for something.

But deep in his heart, Garen was certain there was no error.
There *had* been Hounds coursing the uplands this spring—

the farmers had reported it. Had the Arch-Mage's own son been fleeing them?

But how could he have escaped? Not only were the Mages of Armethalieh wise and good, they were all-powerful.

He finished speaking, and replaced the orb in its silk wrappings, and then in its leather purse, and hung the purse once more around his neck.

He would not think about it any further. These were things beyond the ken of a simple tinker and peddler. He would sleep now, cushioned by his new friend's very good brandy. In the morning he would ask his questions, and then he would take the road in the direction of his next destination. He had many leagues to go before winter came, but his heart was light, for Garen Miq knew that this night he had struck a mighty blow for the good of the City.

THE tavern-wench had been watching him all night. And why not? He'd bought the most expensive swill this wretched hovel boasted, he dressed in silks and jewels, and he'd paid in gold and never asked for change. And it had amused Zyperis to wear the form of one of the human Mageborn, a form that the softskins reckoned alluring.

"Is there aught else I can do for you, noblesir?" she asked, catching up with him as he headed toward the door that led toward the innyard.

"It seems too early for bed," he said, letting his voice linger on the last syllable, "but I grow weary of sitting and the moon is bright. I thought I'd go for a walk in the forest. Perhaps you would care to accompany me?"

She glanced over her shoulder, but it was late by now and few patrons remained in the common room. She tossed her head and favored him with what she must think was a seductive smile. "I'd like that, noblesir."

It would be a long time before she was missed, and longer still before anyone remembered she'd left with the stranger who'd been drinking with Garen Miq all night, and who had never come back to the inn. By then, Garen Miq would be long upon his road eastward.

Her body would never be discovered.

By the time Prince Zyperis was finished with her, there wouldn't be enough left of it to recognize as a human woman, and the forest scavengers would take care of what was left.

IN the World Without Sun, Queen Savilla watched the threads of her weaving slowly draw together.

And smiled.

Chapter Fourteen

Storms and Bright Water

On the whole, Idalia was rather pleased with her little brother. He could so easily have been sullen and intractable, spoiled and softened by City luxuries. Granted, he was no Wildlander yet, but he was willing to learn, and ready to contribute what he could to the household. Oh, sometimes he sulked, and sometimes he brooded, and often enough he whined, but that was in the nature of the adolescent male, and Idalia had expected a certain amount of temperament out of him. The wonder was, there was less of it than she would have anticipated.

Summer had come and gone, and in the past dozen sennights, Kellen had settled fully into the life of a forester of the Wildlands. With Idalia's help and guidance, he'd begun work on an addition to Idalia's cabin, for with winter coming on, they'd need more space—even if it was only enough space for a second bed.

But even though the first frosts were still sennights away, the days were already perceptibly shorter, and work kept both the young Wildmages occupied from dawn till several hours after dusk. There was always wood to chop—logs to fell for the walls of the addition and firewood to stockpile for the coming winter as well—food to hunt and to forage for, clothes and tools to make and mend, and in addition to all of that, not a day seemed to pass that did not bring someone to Idalia for healing or advice.

And every time Kellen was sure that the world held no more surprises, something always came to jar him out of his complacency.

Take the weather, for example.

Of course the seasons changed in the City. There was even rain—though always at night—and sometimes fog. Snow fell sometimes in the winter—though never on the streets and walkways, of course.

But the sort of violent weather that Idalia described so casually was something that Kellen had never imagined experiencing, and the first time that rain had fallen during the day, he'd been so indignant over losing a day's work that Idalia had laughed quite hard.

Last night a storm—the first great storm of the autumn—had thundered through the Wildwood, waking both of them from their sleep. After the first thunderclap, Idalia had turned over and gone back to sleep, but Kellen had been unable to. He'd sat up for a long time afterward, listening to the fury of the storm battering at the walls of the cabin, startling in shock at each crash of thunder and flare of lightning, unable to believe that Idalia was just sleeping through it all as if it were nothing. It seemed impossible to him that the little cabin could withstand such battering without being swept away; he imagined Demons riding each thunderbolt, seeking him out.

But not even the roof leaked.

At last he was reluctantly forced to admit that if Idalia was sleeping so soundly, this must be normal—though down deep inside, Kellen wondered indignantly how anything this noisy and chaotic could possibly be normal. He made himself lie down again, and sent himself to sleep imagining what would happen in the City if such a storm ever came to play among the bell towers of Armethalieh . . .

The High Council would have a *fit*.

In the morning, Kellen discovered that even though the storm had been what Idalia called "normal," the high winds it had brought with it had still caused a certain amount of destruction. The two of them had spent most of the forenoon repairing the storm's damage: rebuilding the woodpile and the cairn beside the necessary pit, and locating those objects that had been blown away by the wind. It had taken a Finding Spell to locate the cauldron, which had gotten itself lodged between the branches of a tree . . .

⌐

IDALIA watched Kellen moving about the cabin's grounds with an amusement she tried very hard to conceal. She still remembered her own shock at encountering untamed weather for the first time—something not permitted to occur in Armethalieh—and Kellen still seemed rather surprised by it, to judge from the silence with which he finished his part in repairing the storm damage and resumed his work on the addition to the cabin.

Fortunately the lashings on the tarp had held fast, or they'd be looking all the way to the High Hills for it, if Idalia was any judge of winds. The storm had been strong enough to take down half the woodpile, after all. She picked up a broom and turned toward the house. There was soot and ashes all over the main room, courtesy of the winds that had gotten past the dampers and blown down the chimney, and it wouldn't sweep itself out the door.

"Idalia! Idalia!"

A troupe of fauns—the little creatures almost never traveled anywhere alone—came rushing into the clearing, tumbling over themselves with the frantic urgency of their mission. They looked around wildly, spotted her, and bounded over to where she stood by the chopping stump, arranging themselves in a semicircle in front of her.

"Idalia!"

They looked up at her with panic in their eyes, in a state she rarely saw in the normally carefree fauns.

"Idalia!" they chorused, and began to babble.

She quelled them with a glance, then looked around and spotted several she recognized. "Jakar—Redmouse—Malky—what do you need today?"

All of them started talking at once.

"The Lady—"

"The Lady in the Woods—"

"The Oaklady—"

"She's hurt—"

"The treelady's hurt—"

"Lightning struck her—"

"Struck her tree—"

"The Oaklady's tree—"

"And she's hurt—"

"Come, Idalia—"

"Will you come—"

"She needs help—"

"She needs healing—"

"You're a Wildmage Healer—"

"And she's hurt—"

Idalia was used to interpreting the fauns' chatter, and she had no difficulty in extracting from their babbling the information that, somewhere in the woods, an oak-dryad's tree had been struck by lightning and she had sent the fauns for help.

By now, attracted by their clamor, Kellen had come from his own work to see what was going on. Today he was involved in the delicate task of splitting the logs that would become the cabin floor and then planing their surfaces until they were as smooth as possible. Once the log planks had been fitted into place, there would be more smoothing to be done. Though last night the violent thunderstorm that had lashed the Wildwood with wind and rain had made it seem as if the end of the world had come, the day had dawned clear, and that heavy tarp had kept the wood dry enough for Kellen to work.

The sennights of hard physical work had put a great deal of muscle on his long lanky frame, just as the constant exposure to sun and wind had darkened and weathered his skin even as it added streaks of gold to his curly brown hair. Idalia doubted that any of his City friends would recognize Kellen these days, dressed as he was in nothing but a pair of deerhide trousers and his heavy leather moccasins, and with his long dark gold hair tied back in a length of buckskin.

"What's going on?" he asked curiously.

Did he need to know how serious this was? *Probably not.* "An oak-dryad's been hurt, and you can't move a dryad too far from her tree, or she'll die. I'm going to go see what she needs," Idalia answered briefly. "There's no need for you to go. You stay here and keep on working. I'll send one of the fauns back for you if I need you."

Kellen grinned, his teeth white against the new darkness of his skin. "And here I thought I was going to get a rest."

"A change is as good as a rest, so if you want a rest, brother dear, you can finish chopping the kindling. Or charge some of those keystones. Both need doing," Idalia answered tartly.

"I think I'll stay with the logs." Kellen waved, and headed back to the sawhorses. Idalia went into the cabin for her healing-kit, and then hurried after the impatient fauns.

⌐

IDALIA followed the fauns through the trees, her workbag slung over her shoulder. She had to admit, if only to herself, that it was a relief to be more or less alone for a change. Kellen never seemed to tire of asking questions—though she did have to admit, he'd made a lot of progress since he'd gotten here. And it was true that if she'd had someone like herself to question when she'd begun learning the Wild Magic, she'd have asked just as many questions. If only he was as open to it as she had been . . .

If she were to make a guess, she'd have said it *frightened* him, though that hardly seemed possible . . . *He* might not think so, but in her opinion he was as brave as a young lion.

She sighed inwardly, shifting her heavy pack as she ducked to avoid a low-growing branch. She knew, just by seeing his progress over the past few moonturns, that she'd been a better Wildmage at his age than he was, and she knew, without vanity, that she would always be a hundred times the Wildmage Kellen would ever be.

Something in him always holds back—it's as if he's afraid of it, but Kellen has as much courage where it counts as anyone I've ever met.

I must say, I'm baffled. There was no reason for anyone to be *afraid* of Wild Magic, no matter what the High Mages said. *He holds back; he won't commit himself, but to be a Wildmage, you must have the magic in your bones and blood, understand it so deeply you don't have to think about it any more than you have to think about breathing. You have to* become *the magic, until nothing happens around you that you're not aware of, as if the world around you is merely an extension of your own body. As* The Book of Stars *says, "You will come to live within my pages, and my pages are written on your heart."*

But not on Kellen's, apparently.

Was it only fear? Or was there something else going on? Whatever it was, she suspected poor Kellen would never come to the magic through the same route she had taken. It would seem, all things considered, that her little brother's destiny was to become something quite different from your ordinary sort of Wildmage.

I do wish I knew what it was.

Her musings were interrupted by their arrival at the oak-dryad's grove.

The oak was the Queen of the Wood, and the oak-dryads were the greatest of the tree-spirits, but the great trees were particularly vulnerable to lightning, and last night's storm had not been kind to the grove. Idalia could see that the ground here was littered with many branches torn loose by the storm winds—Nature's rough mercy, pruning the weaker branches now before they were layered with a heavy coat of winter's ice and snow—but that was only minor storm damage, part of the cycle of Life, not why she'd been called. On the largest of the oaks, one of the great branches was sheared half away from the trunk, half-charred by the lightning strike that had done it, exposing the heartwood to insect damage and frost-kill.

Its dryad sat slumped on the ground before the tree, her skin as pale as the heartwood and her ash-brown hair tangled and tumbled. She was surrounded by her sisters, their healthy golden skin and hair a sharp contrast to hers. The brownie families who made their homes in the dryads' oaks stood in clumps in the clearing, wringing their hands and murmuring mournfully, and Idalia could see more fauns watching from the bushes at the edges of the clearing.

This is bad, Idalia thought to herself with a sinking heart. The dryad was in shock from the damage to her tree, and the tree itself might very well die slowly over the winter if the damage to its trunk wasn't seen to immediately.

"Here she is—here she is—here she is—" The fauns who had brought Idalia rushed ahead of her into the clearing to join the dryads, some of them climbing into the lap of the wounded one to offer their own rough comfort. As if their arrival had been a signal, the other fauns came crowding into the clearing. Idalia followed more slowly, taking in the damage to tree and spirit, assessing it, making a plan . . .

One of the healthy dryads came to meet her.

Can you heal her? the oak-maiden asked silently.

"Yes," Idalia said aloud. "Who will share the price?"

The dryad looked surprised for a moment. *All,* she answered. *All will share,* she answered, with a gesture that encompassed the inhabitants of the clearing—brownies, dryads, fauns.

"Do you all agree to this?" Idalia asked, raising her voice a little so that all could hear. "Will you all share in the price of this healing?"

There was a clamor as every voice—even the dryads' silent

ones—was raised in agreement, and Idalia winced as the shrill voices of the brownies pierced her skull. But the Wild Magic could not take what was not asked for and freely given. She walked forward through the crowd of Otherfolk, and knelt before the suffering dryad.

"Shoo," she said gently to the faun sitting in the dryad's lap, and the small creature reluctantly squirmed out of the way.

Idalia reached out and stroked the dryad's cheek, then took the dryad's hands in her own. They were ice-cold, with no trace of the vibrant green life Idalia associated with dryadkind.

Kellen always thought of the Wild Magic as hard, as something you had to invoke and pursue with spells and proper forms, but for Idalia it was as simple as stepping aside from her workaday self, entering the greater Soul of the world around her, and letting it well up within. The Wild Magic was a thing of harmony and balance; the presence of evil or injury called it into action as much as any will of the Wildmage. She felt its presence; felt it seek out its price from all who shared in the healing, understood her own part in that payment, and felt health and strength and wellness flow through her from someplace *Beyond* into the dryad.

It was as simple—and as mysterious—as that. Idalia was the portal through which Something reached to set the world right with her help and consent, and in a timeless moment it was done. Strength and healing flowed into her and out again in a glorious and intoxicating verdant river. It poured into the grey void at the dryad's heart, and gradually filled it. She saw the dryad's skin flush gold with health once more, and rocked back on her heels as the Grove-Queen rose to her feet.

The fauns cheered and turned cartwheels, and the brownies threw their caps in the air.

*Ah, my poor tree. . . . * the Queen said sadly, running her hand along the bark.

Idalia stood up, staggering a little with weakness. But only a little, and only for a moment, for her work was not yet over, and the Wild Magic would not permit her strength to lapse while that work remained unfinished. She caught her balance, and walked over to inspect the split in the trunk.

"As to that, my part in this is to repair your tree, my lady. Once I've taken that branch off, and sealed over the heart-wood with tar and river clay, your tree should stand fast for many seasons more," Idalia said, smiling.

Tar would seal the wound, forming a sort of bandage, keeping insects and fungus out. Clay would protect the vulnerable heartwood and give the tree time to build new defenses, and cutting away the split branch would prevent further damage.

"I'll come back tomorrow and take care of it; I need tools that I don't have with me."

It was a while more before Idalia was let to leave, for the brownies pressed scores of thimble-sized tankards of mead upon her, and several thumbnail-sized loaves of acorn-meal bread, and the fauns brought her handfuls of berries, only slightly crushed. All in all, it was late afternoon before she returned to the cabin.

⌁

NOW she was tired; the Magic had no more need of her, and she felt as drained as if she had run for leagues.

Kellen was waiting to greet her, looking impatient.

"Where have you been?" he demanded. "It's been the whole afternoon—"

"I was working," Idalia answered tartly—a bit more sharply than she'd intended.

Kellen looked immediately crestfallen, and Idalia felt guilty about being so short with him. "I healed the dryad—her tree was struck by lightning in that big storm that came through last night. I shared out most of the price of the healing, but I'll have to go back tomorrow and see what I can do about fixing her tree, so I'm going to need to use the tools for the day. I suppose," she added with a smile, "you're going to get your holiday after all."

"But I'll help," Kellen said quickly. "I'd like to help. If that's all right, I mean."

"Surely," Idalia said after a moment's pause. "I can always use an extra pair of hands."

Kellen's eagerness to help shouldn't surprise her, she realized after a moment. He was a *good* lad, after all. No matter what Lycaelon had tried to turn him into. Yet somehow, every time he demonstrated his basic generosity of spirit, it surprised her. Maybe she'd lived alone for too long at that.

⌒

THE two of them spent the following day at the dryad's grove cutting away the dead wood from the oak-Queen's tree and sealing over the exposed wood. Though an axe and saws were not the sort of implements that would normally be welcome in a dryadic grove, this time they were tolerated (though the dryads could not look at them without shivering), and Idalia and Kellen bent to the work.

It was quickly obvious what part of the price that the brownies and fauns were paying. The brownies brought tar—they used it in waterproofing, milking rising sap from pines in the spring in the same way that they milked maples, boiling it down into tar. The fauns came back with handfuls of river clay when she'd done sealing the breech with the tar.

It was hot work—autumn might be on the way, but the late-summer days were still warm—but when Idalia looked at the finished job, her arm draped companionably over Kellen's shoulders, she was filled with a deep satisfaction. What could be better than helping and healing, setting right what had gone wrong in the world?

She knew that Kellen felt much the same way that she did—that he could sense, at least a little, when something was out of balance and needed to be fixed. But there was still something deep inside himself that he didn't trust to always make the right choices.

And until—unless—that last barrier came down, until Kellen really trusted his own instincts, there would always be a barrier between Kellen and his magic.

⟜

IT had been a good day. Kellen had actually enjoyed the work; he had found of late that he really got a great deal of pleasure out of physical labor, especially as his muscles had strengthened to the job.

Maybe I should have been a stone-breaker or a bricklayer after all, he thought, wondering what Lycaelon would say if he'd seen his son sweating like a common mortal. It had been fascinating to see the reclusive little brownies up close as well, and the oak-dryads were more dignified and less inclined to tease than their sisters of the apple orchard.

"I think I'll fill up the big cauldron and heat some water," Idalia said as they walked back to the cabin that afternoon. "I think we could both use a hot bath—or at least a good scrub."

Kellen grinned, and reached out to flick a scrap of drying river clay off her cheek. "Sounds good to me. But I'll carry the water and get the fire started if you'll make some of those dried berry scones to go with the rest of the leftover stew."

"Deal," Idalia answered promptly. Kellen had learned to do a number of new things well since he'd come to live with her, but cooking wasn't one of them. "Just let me wash this clay off my hands first, or you'll be eating it along with the scones." She turned toward the cabin.

But the sound of hoofbeats back down the trail alerted Kellen that their plans were about to be changed.

"Wait. Someone's coming." Kellen slid his heavy pack from his shoulders and turned back the way they'd come.

Idalia frowned—evidently *she* hadn't heard anything—but as she was about to question Kellen further, there was an enormous crashing noise from the underbrush, and a big chestnut-colored Centaur burst into the clearing.

"Idalia!" he roared. "You've got to heal me! *Now!*"

Kellen and Idalia both stared in astonishment, for this was

possibly the most unlikely creature to come seeking Idalia's help of any in the Wild Lands. It was Cormo, the Centaur bully who had attacked Kellen at the berry patch when he had first arrived in the Wildwood, but it was difficult to recognize him now. Cormo's face and chest were badly swollen with a mass of beestings, and the Centaur was covered in half-dried black mud besides. It looked as if he'd tried to doctor himself—and failed—before coming to Idalia for help.

"Heal me—now!" the Centaur repeated in a menacing growl, taking a limping step toward her.

"That's no way to ask for help," Kellen replied angrily, and leaned down to reach for the pruning hook beside him on the ground, but Idalia put a restraining hand on his arm and took a step forward.

"Hello, Cormo," she said coolly. "What is it that you want?"

"Are you deaf, woman?" the Centaur bellowed, this time so loudly that it made Kellen wince, though Idalia gave no indication that she'd even noticed. "I'm *hurt*! You have to heal me with your Wildmagery!"

"Do I?" Idalia actually managed to sound amused; Kellen was impressed. "And do you expect me to do it for free?"

"You have to," Cormo growled, taking another step toward her. "If you're afraid of the cost, make the brat share it—I don't care! But I know your kind—you heal anyone who comes to you for help—and you don't want word to get around that you refused to help me, now, do you?" He took another step toward her, and now Cormo was standing so close to Idalia that he could reach out and shake her like a rag doll if he chose to.

Idalia simply smiled, refusing to give in to the veiled threat or even take a step backward. Kellen was amazed. And impressed. He'd have gone for a weapon by now; he wouldn't trust that bully any further than he could throw him!

"I have some herbal salves, and I'll gladly doctor you with them free of charge, Cormo. But if you want me to use my Wildmagery to heal you, you must agree to accept half the price, and I will take the other half."

Cormo shook his head and changed tactics. He tried to smile conciliatingly, difficult as it was with his face so swollen it resembled a ripe gourd. He pawed the ground, and his voice took on a pleading, whining tone.

"Aw, come on, Idalia, be a friend! It's just a *little* healing, and it really hurts—a lot! You can't honestly expect me to pay half the price on top of all this pain, can you? I could go blind if you don't heal me right now!" By now the whining was annoying enough that it put Kellen's teeth on edge. "You wouldn't want that to happen to your old buddy Cormo, would you?" he wheedled.

"Half the price, or no magic," Idalia said implacably.

"Damn you!" Cormo snarled, lifting one heavy hoof. "Something bad could happen to that precious brother of yours when he's out in the woods alone, you know!"

"Not if you go blind," Idalia said with a small cold smile. "You know, I've heard that if enough bee venom reaches the brain, a person can go deaf *and* blind . . . that is, if they don't just die outright. You really should let me go get my salves, if you don't want to take half the price and let me use my magic." She took a step toward him, and amazingly, the Centaur backed up a pace.

Of course, he's a coward, Kellen realized. *Most bullies are.*

"I wouldn't count on anything happening to me in the woods, either, Cormo," Kellen added, trying to put menace in his own voice. "I never go anywhere without my axe these days."

Cormo whimpered pathetically, backing up even farther. "Aw, I didn't mean anything! I'm out of my head with pain, can't you see that? I need healing!" He looked hopefully at Kellen.

Kellen just shook his head. Even if he knew how to heal someone using Wild Magic—and he didn't—he had no intention of interfering between Idalia and Cormo.

"All right—all *right*!" The last of the Centaur's bluster collapsed. "But I'll tell everyone at the village how cold and cruel you were to a dying Centaur, Idalia, and see how many people come to you for aid then!"

"Go ahead," Idalia said amiably. "I can use the rest. So you agree to take half the cost of the healing?"

"Yes," Cormo muttered, defeated.

"All right, then. Lie down. I can't do anything for you up there. Kellen, go get me a bucket of water and a rag. I'd like to get this mud off him and see what I'm working with."

Kellen didn't like the thought of turning his back on the Centaur, though he doubted Cormo had any fight left in him, but he reluctantly did as he was asked. By the time he returned, Cormo was lying awkwardly on his side, and Idalia was kneeling beside him.

Gently—ignoring Cormo's whimpers, grumblings, and moans that she was killing him—Idalia gently wiped away the caked mud from the Centaur's chest and face as Kellen watched. It looked to Kellen as if the Centaur had been up to his old thievish tricks again, and this time he'd had the poor judgment to try robbing a bee-tree when the bees were all at home. Cormo's face and chest were a mass of red welts, and one hand was so swollen it looked like a water-filled glove. Mud was supposed to be a sovereign remedy for a beesting, but all the mud in the riverbed wouldn't have been enough to draw the poison from Cormo's stings when there were this many of them.

But as Idalia gently washed the mud from the angry red welts on the Centaur's body, Kellen could see the redness and the swelling fade away as well. When she was finished, not a trace of the injuries remained.

And she didn't cast a circle. Kellen saw the familiar glow of the sphere of protection about them, but he knew now that it was only meant to keep out evil things, and anything of good will could pass it; it was, in that way, quite unlike the sort of circle the High Mages cast, which nothing and no one could pass. When she was finished, not a trace of the injuries remained, and the sphere of light faded and was gone.

And she didn't uncast the circle, either, or say any words, or anything. She just . . . did it, Kellen marveled silently. He'd watched Idalia do healings before, but now it was as if for the first time he actually realized what he was seeing: that

Idalia could do magic—at least healing magic—without any visible preparation whatever. It was as if she were *always* inside a magic circle, always in the presence of whatever Gods oversaw the Working of the Wild Magic.

It didn't frighten him—by now he knew his sister too well for that—but it did give him a lot to think about. If this was what becoming a true Wildmage was, it was something Kellen didn't think he was ever going to be: someone who cast spells as easily as they breathed. He knew in that moment that he would never have Idalia's power—he might as well wish to be Arch-Mage of Armethalieh! For him, the magic came slowly, and with great effort, once he'd gotten past the simplest of spells and cantrips. But by the same token, he knew the Wild Magic was still drawing him to itself for some purpose of its own.

I just wish I knew what it was. If I'm not supposed to become like Idalia, then . . . what?

"There," she said with a sigh, dropping the rag into the bucket and getting to her feet. "All done."

"That?" Cormo said suspiciously, rolling onto his stomach and pulling his feet under him. "That's it? Doesn't seem like so very much. Certainly not worth all the fuss you made about having to pay for it, Idalia."

Idalia laughed, stepping back to give Cormo room to get to his feet. "Oh, but a bargain's a bargain, Cormo, and we'll each keep our side of it. Your part of the price for this healing is to help Mistress Haneida haul her cart to and from the market for a year and a day. Mine is to inform the elders of Merryvale of that price—*personally*—to see that they enforce the conditions."

Cormo lunged to his feet and shook himself all over, switching his tail vigorously. "Oh, no, Idalia, don't trouble yourself—I'll be happy to take care of that for you!" he said quickly. "It would save you the trip—and it would be such a small thing to do to repay you for all your kindness, that—"

"Oh, no, *friend* Cormo," Idalia interrupted, smiling wolfishly. "I'm quite willing to pay my part of the price. My part

is to inform the elders of your village *personally,* and believe
me, I'm more than happy to pay it."

"In fact," Kellen added virtuously, "I'll help you, Idalia.
I've never seen the Centaur village. I'd like to."

"You'll love it," Idalia said, turning to him with a smile.
"We can get a good hot meal and a proper bath there. I'll
get some things I'd been saving to trade and then we can be
on our way."

THEY reached the gates of Merryvale about an hour before
sunset, but for almost an hour before that they'd been walking
through the groves and fields that belonged to it.

Harvest was still a few sennights away, and the orchards
and fields were filled with ripening crops and the villagers
who were tending to them. Young children, both Centaur and
human, stood out among the trees and in the fields armed
with tall straw-brooms to scare away birds. They waved excitedly when they saw Idalia, and Idalia waved back. Some
of them, released from their duties by their elders, ran on
ahead to inform the village of the approach of the visitors.

Kellen stared at the neat orderly fields in wonder as they
passed. Each field was edged in low stone fences topped with
split rails. It seemed like a lot of extra work to him, but Idalia
told him that the stones came out of the plowed field itself—a
new crop each spring—and were stacked along the boundaries to save the farmers the work of carrying them farther
away. The rail fences helped to keep the sheep and cattle out
of the crops as well.

As they came closer to the village, he saw other buildings,
which Idalia also identified in answer to his incessant questions—sheepfolds and cow-byres, dairies, communal barns
for hay and grain, a shearing-barn. Most were, like Idalia's
cottage, made of logs or rough-hewn planks, and thatched
with straw. Old roofs were a silvery grey, new ones the color
of pale gold. Gold patches marked the spots where roofs had
been mended, and he actually saw a thatching crew at work

on one of the dairies, packing in the straw bundles and cutting them with their curved thatching knives.

"And on the other side of the town, up along the river a way, is the cider-house and the mill, and the blacksmith's! So many questions, little brother! Don't tell me you've always nourished a secret desire to become a farmer!" she finally said, caught between irritation and amusement.

"It's not that," Kellen protested sheepishly. "It's just that . . . I've never seen anyplace like this."

Though Kellen knew of the lowland farming villages that had supplied Armethalieh with food, he'd never seen anything other than the illustrations in books of wondertales, so Merryvale was as strange and alien a world to him as the Wildwood itself had been. No one possessed thatched roofs in the City, and there were very few wooden buildings. Armethalieh was a city of stone. "And humans and Centaurs live here? Together?"

Another thing he'd been told—it was one of the central teachings of the Temple of the Light—was that humans and the creatures he'd learned to call Otherfolk (instead of Lesser Races) could not possibly live together in peace because of the utter incompatibility of their natures.

"Yes, yes, and yes," Idalia said. "And we'll be there soon—look, there's the gate, just ahead. And dozens of people, all of whom will be delighted to answer *all* your questions."

She pointed up the road, and Kellen could see the palisades of the village ahead. Idalia had told him that the Centaurs were famed for their wood-carving skills, and the walls of Merryvale were certainly proof of that, for certainly only master craftsmen would waste their skills decorating the walls of a village.

The walls and gates of Merryvale gleamed as smooth and polished as fine cabinetry. At this distance, they looked as if they had been carved from the trunk of one great tree, weathered by time and the passage of the seasons to a soft mossy grey-green. The entire surface had been made smooth and even, the logs planed smooth and fitted together in just the way Kellen was planning to fit the logs for the addition to the cabin floor, and then a design had been carved into the resulting smooth surface. As they got closer, Kellen could see that it was a depiction of a harvest festival, with flower-garlanded Centaurs and humans carrying baskets of fruit, bushels of wheat, barrels of drink, and the carcasses of deer, pheasants, and rabbits to a communal feast.

"Oh," Kellen said softly, enchanted. "That's—amazing." He wasn't just talking about the artistic quality of the carving. There it was, depicted for all to see—Centaurs and humans living together, happily and at peace. And while he'd realized that everything the Temple taught was carefully designed to serve the ends of the Council and the City, and so probably wasn't actually true, it was one thing to know that in theory, and another to see the proof right in front of you. Idalia grinned and poked him in the ribs with an elbow.

"Thought that would shut you up."

The gates—wide enough for two large carts to pass through them side by side—stood open, and Kellen could see no guards or soldiers anywhere.

"Isn't anybody going to stop us?" he asked when they reached them.

"Why?" Idalia said blankly. Then her gaze filled with understanding and compassion. "Kellen, this may be a city—well, as close to one as the Wildwood gets—but it is not like *the* City. Nobody's going to ask for your name and family here, demand your address, or make you show your citizen-token. They don't even have a City Guard. People come and go as they please—except you, Cormo," she added abruptly, reaching out to put a hand on the Centaur's arm. "I think it would be better if you stuck around until we saw Haneida and the Council, don't you?"

"I . . . of course, Idalia. Happy to," Cormo said with ill-concealed gracelessness. The three of them walked together through the open gates.

There they paused for a moment. They were standing in what Kellen guessed must be—from his limited reading of the pastoral romances that had been popular in Armethalieh—

the market square. On three sides of the square were rows of neat one- and two-story whitewashed thatched-roof cottages, and here in the center of the square was a well, with a windlass and bucket, surrounded by a curved stone trough with a rim wide enough to sit on. All around them, people were going about their everyday tasks—or so Kellen supposed, as it was all new and unfamiliar to him. Everything he could see was built wide enough and high enough to accommodate Centaurs as well as humans, and Kellen wondered what he'd see if he looked inside some of the cottages. Stalls? Or beds?

"Idalia!" a familiar voice squealed, off to the right. There was a thud of hooves on the packed earth of the square as they turned toward the source of the voice, and Merana pranced to a stop in front of Idalia. "Oh, you've come to visit! And you've brought *Kellen!"*

The young Centauress curveted like a restive filly as she turned to gaze flirtatiously at Kellen, but now he was prepared for her and her ways, and was able to keep his composure a little better than he had at their first meeting. He just smiled, and made sure that he kept Idalia between him and the apprentice Healer.

By now a crowd had started to gather around the visitors, humans and Centaurs greeting Idalia by name and darting curious—and none-too-friendly—looks at Cormo. Evidently Cormo was not nearly as well thought of as he had boasted. Somehow, Kellen wasn't at all surprised.

"Idalia." An old man in a long worn blue robe, its knees stained as if he'd been kneeling in his garden all day, made his way through the crowd. His hair was silvery white and very long, done in a braid that trailed down his back. A small neat beard adorned his weathered face, and there were lines formed by laughter and smiling around his eyes. He was leaning on a long staff, its wood polished with years of use, and he gently moved Merana out of the way with a hand on her withers as if he was well used to her ebullient nature.

"We are both delighted to see you, child—and in such company." He raised his eyebrows, looking over Idalia's shoulder at Cormo. The Centaur male looked very much as if he wished to slink away, but didn't quite dare.

"Master Eliron—just the person I was hoping to see," Idalia said. "You are still on the Council, aren't you?"

So *this* was Merana's Master? Kellen had made the assumption—obviously a mistaken one—that the old Healer must be another Centaur.

"Nothing short of death will make them accept my resignation, so they tell me," the old healer said with a gentle smile. "But surely you cannot have need of my services in either of my capacities, not with a Wildmage of your own to call upon?" he added, nodding toward Kellen.

"Nothing like that," Idalia assured him. "But I healed Cormo today, and I have a price to pay as my part of the healing. Tell me, is Haneida here, by any chance?"

Eliron looked surprised by the question. "Why, yes. She came to see me this afternoon, and I persuaded her to accept my hospitality for the evening. As I hope you and your brother will as well. It's too long a walk back to that cabin of yours to make tonight."

"We were hoping someone would tender us an invitation to stay," Idalia confessed cheerfully. "And you set a fine table, Master Eliron. Could someone fetch her, if it wouldn't be too much trouble"—she held out a minatory hand to Cormo, who looked as if he was going to bolt—"not you, Cormo!—then I can pay my price and spend the rest of the evening in amusing myself. Kellen is eager to see your village."

"As we are to show it to him," Master Eliron assured her gracefully.

"I'll go," Merana offered quickly.

She half reared and pivoted neatly in place on her hind legs, then moved nimbly off through the crowd, which was already buzzing with expectancy at the prospect of great revelations in store. Several others at the edges of the crowd also faded off to spread the word that something terribly interesting was about to happen, and as word spread, the crowd grew, until Kellen was sure that everyone in all of Merryvale was crowded into the market square. As he looked around, he could see people crowded at the open windows of the cottages that had upper stories as well, leaning out of the windows and looking down into the square. If Cormo had wanted to keep the terms of his price a secret, there was no way he was going to be able to do it now.

Which was probably *exactly* as Idalia had planned, the clever thing.

A few minutes later Merana returned, walking slowly and carefully. Seated on her back was an old woman whom Kellen guessed must be Haneida. She sat very straight and held her walking staff across her lap. The crowd parted to let them through, and when they reached Eliron and Idalia, Merana knelt gracefully to let Haneida dismount. The old lady looked around the square, her blue eyes bright and sharp.

Kellen thought she looked amused. He also had the distinct impression that she was not going to be much surprised when she heard Cormo's price.

"Well. All this fuss can't be for one old lady, now can it? Or is it that young Cormo has been up to more mischief than usual?"

"He'll be up to less in the future," Idalia said, stepping forward. "This afternoon I healed him with the Wild Magic, and Cormo accepted half the price. His price was this: that for a year and a day, he is to help you haul your cart to and from the market, Haneida."

There was a moment of silence, and then the market square exploded with laughter. Cormo growled low in his throat, flushing dark with embarrassment. He stamped his hooves fretfully, hating to be the butt of the joke, but did nothing else. Kellen guessed there was nothing he *could* do aside from stand there and take it. For all that Idalia said that Merryvale didn't have guards the way Armethalieh did, he guessed the village must have some way to keep the peace, and a lot of the folks in the crowd, human and Centaur both, looked big and strong enough to make even Cormo think twice about any bullyragging he might want to get up to.

Haneida laughed until she doubled over, clutching at her staff for support. "Oh, my!" she gasped, wiping tears of mirth from her eyes. "Cormo doing honest work for once! It was worth living this long to see that!" She hobbled stiffly over to the Centaur and stared up at him. "Who knows, young man? Perhaps you will grow to like it. And you'll find it a sight easier to be given a honey-loaf warm from the oven than to skulk around my window trying to steal them from the cooling racks!"

Cormo stared down at her, his face blank with surprise. "You'll *pay* me?" he said in shock.

Haneida reached up with her staff and rapped him smartly on the shoulder. "Pay? Who said anything about paying you, my young scallywag? You've *been* paid, in the coin of healing. But when a friend does me a kindness, I do a friend a kindness in return. Besides, it's hungry work, making that long trip from my cottage down to the market and back, and I don't intend to see you go hungry for it. Now. I'll see you in three days, at sunrise, at my front door. Don't be late. And be clean!"

"Yes, ma'am," Cormo said, as meekly as Kellen had ever heard him speak. Haneida turned away and regarded the crowd. "I suppose none of you have homes and dinners of your own to go to?" she said tartly. Waving away all offers of assistance, she began to make her way slowly back the way she had come.

The crowd, sensing that the show was over, began to slowly break up and disperse. Cormo, too—at a nod from Idalia—took the opportunity to make his escape, though as he edged his way through the crowd and out through the Merryvale gates, he kept darting bemused looks over his shoulder at the retreating figure of Haneida, until her slight stooped figure was lost in the crowd.

"He's not altogether bad," Master Eliron said quietly, for Idalia's and Kellen's ears alone, "but like so many, he will try whatever he can get away with."

Idalia shrugged; now that she had discharged *her* price, Cormo was no longer her problem. "I'd hate to try to get away with something while Haneida was watching *me*, Master Eliron. And with the whole village knowing that he is

under an obligation, it should be no great difficulty to see
that he stays honest . . . for a year and a day at least. After
that, who knows? Maybe he'll figure out that working for his
keep is actually easier than the course of theft and bullying
he's been following."

"Only the greatest of Mages can see the future," Master
Eliron agreed solemnly, "and the future is not always so very
cooperative as even they might wish. But come. I have spent
a long day in my stillroom and herbarium, and will be glad
of a chance to stretch my legs—and you have said your
brother wishes to see something of our village."

"We've come to do some trading as well, before winter
sets in," Idalia said. "But that can wait for tomorrow. Most
of all—and I think, first of all—I've promised Kellen a
proper hot bath."

Master Eliron laughed. "And so you shall have one, both
of you. Merana, take our guests' packs to the house, and tell
the cook we will be two more for dinner. Come, Kellen. I
can show you at least a bit of Merryvale on the way to your
bath."

HALF an hour later Kellen was soaking up to his neck in
the first hot bath he'd had since . . . well, he really couldn't
really remember when, since he wasn't sure he could really
count hasty dips in the laundry tub back in Armethalieh, and
it felt wonderful. He didn't even care that it was a communal
bath, and that he was sharing it with Master Eliron and several of the other men of Merryvale, while Idalia basked in
similar accommodations on the woman's side of the bathhouse.

He was up to his neck in a large steaming copper-sheathed
wooden tub, and he didn't care if he never left it. The hot
water was easing aches and pains he hadn't even realized
were there until they were gone.

This was the last—and hottest, and largest—of the three
tubs in the Merryvale bathhouse, the one you got into when

you were clean. The first, a small, tepid, and rather murky tub, was just for rinsing off the worst of the muck and clay: that one you stood up in and scrubbed with a soft brush while pouring water over yourself from a dipper while an attendant topped up a second—fresh—tub with hot water. Kellen had to admit that after a morning spent packing clay and tar into the side of an oak tree, followed by a long cross-country hike, it had been a necessary step.

The second tub was warmer, and big enough to sit down in. That was where you scrubbed yourself clean with soap. While the soap wasn't the dainty colored and perfumed hard-milled stuff he'd been used to in the City, it was also a far cry from the tallowy blocks of harsh yellow stuff he'd gotten used to using at Idalia's. While it still smelled rather more like tallow than flowers, at least it didn't turn his skin red and raw.

Once Kellen was thoroughly clean, the attendant—since it was Kellen's first time at the bathhouse, he'd been assigned a personal guide—conducted him through to the main room of the men's side, where he climbed a short ladder into the enormous wooden vat they called the "soaking pool." The water was kept constantly hot by a bed of coals beneath it—with new coals brought as the old embers died—and constantly full with new infusions of water. At this time of day there weren't too many people here, but Master Eliron told him that sometimes there were so many people waiting that the attendants had to come and turn people out after half an hour.

"Especially in winter, when it seems as if the bathhouse is the only place in Merryvale that is really warm, especially to these old bones," the Healer said with a sigh. "But you won't have experienced one of our upland winters yet, will you?"

"No, sir," Kellen said contentedly, steam rising about his face. "I only just came here a few moonturns ago. But I like the Wild Lands very much. Especially your village. I've never seen anyplace like it before."

Idalia had promised there'd be time for a proper exploration of Merryvale tomorrow before they left, but on his way here, Kellen had already seen enough to fill his head with wonders.

Compared to Armethalieh, Merryvale was tiny and primitive, but spending most of a season living in a rustic cabin in the wilderness with Idalia had changed Kellen's standards for comparison. He was now able to see that on its own terms, the little village was quite sophisticated—and a very happy place, as far as he could tell.

While Armethalieh traded constantly and uneasily with the lands across the sea and the lands Beyond the Forest, Merryvale supplied nearly all its own needs, from cloth woven from the wool of its own sheep and the linen threads spun from its own flax, to honey from its own bees, fruit from its own orchards, and grain from its own fields. The villagers kept cattle and pigs and domestic fowl of all sorts as well, and for the very few things that they didn't produce for themselves, they had a fairly simple method of obtaining them.

From what Idalia had already told him, and the conversation of his companions in the soaking pool, Kellen was able to figure out that Merryvale traded with other villages farther west of Merryvale at the yearly Midsummer Fair, a fortnight-long gathering that attracted people from hundreds of miles around, including the Mountain Traders.

Kellen would certainly have liked to have seen *that*, but it didn't take much thought to figure out why Idalia had delayed his first visit to Merryvale until the time of the Fair was safely past. The Mountain Traders still traded with the farming villages that served Armethalieh, and if Lycaelon Tavadon didn't much care what had become of his daughter, the same could not be said of his interest in his son.

It might be comforting to believe that Lycaelon assumed that the Outlaw Hunt had taken care of Kellen for good and all, but Kellen doubted it. Lycaelon could easily have scryed the Hunt, or viewed it through the eyes of one of the Hounds, and the High Mage probably knew very well that Kellen had been left wounded, but alive. If he'd been furious enough to send so many Hounds in the first place, he would still be

looking for a way to end the embarrassing problem of his
wayward son once and for all.

If Kellen had been seen at the Fair, if word somehow got
back to the City that Kellen had recovered and was living in
the Wildwood, well . . .

He didn't know exactly what would happen, but he was
pretty sure he wouldn't care for it. And neither would anyone
else who could even have been considered to have helped
him.

But those were unpleasant thoughts, and this was a most
pleasant place. Idalia's foresight had protected his where-
abouts for now, and Kellen had the shrewd notion that any
attempt by Lycaelon to use High Magick to locate his son
would meet with failure . . .

After all, High Magick had been no match for the power
of a unicorn's horn.

At last—after what seemed far too short a time to Kellen—
it was time to get dressed again. His clothes had been cleaned
for him while he bathed—not a usual service of the bathhouse, but as the attendant had cheerfully explained, he and
Idalia were honored guests. He toweled himself dry in front
of one of the large iron stoves that kept the soaking room
warm against the evening chill, and then dressed in smallclothes that had been washed and dried, and leathers that had
been brushed completely clean.

It was a level of service that he had accepted unquestion-
ingly, growing up in House Tavadon, but now it made Kellen
oddly uncomfortable. He had been waiting on himself for so
long that it now seemed as if he was receiving something he
was not entitled to, though Master Eliron's clothing had gotten the same treatment.

Master Eliron tied the laces at the throat of his blue robe
shut, and seemed to divine Kellen's unease and the cause of
it.

"Don't worry," the Healer said, patting Kellen on the
shoulder. "These services are available to anyone who wishes
to pay for them, and your sister has already paid their cost."

"Um . . . okay. Good," Kellen said awkwardly. He wasn't

sure which made him feel worse: worrying about it, or being reassured about it.

He didn't have long to fret over the matter though. Idalia appeared in the doorway, her dark brown hair shining-clean and braided back into a single tail with a length of glossy red ribbon. She regarded the two of them, fists planted on hips and an expression of mock-fierceness on her face.

"Well, come along, lazybones! The two of you may want to spend the entire evening stewing like prunes, but I'm hungry! And Merana won't thank you for making her wait to catch up on the gossip!"

By the time they reached the street, Kellen realized that he was hungry as well. Hungry? That was too mild a word; he was ravenous. The sun had gone down behind the hills, but the long summer twilight still lingered, and many of the cottages had set out lanterns before their doors, the candles gleaming softly through the translucent oiled-parchment walls of the copper lanterns. It was easy to find their way, even though many of the streets were far narrower and more twisty than any of the streets of Armethalieh. The village might be built for both humans and Centaurs to live in, but obviously not to wander through in crowds.

Master Eliron's house was on one of the wider streets—which made a great deal of sense, since the Master Healer must receive a great number of visitors of both races. It was a fine two-story cottage, and the shutters of the lower windows were thrown open, releasing a number of savory smells into the evening air.

Kellen's stomach rumbled loudly and Idalia snorted with rude laughter.

"Now, now," Master Eliron said peaceably. "It's a nice change to welcome a pair of healthy appetites to the table—and if memory serves, you've never been shy of your food, eh, Idalia? Or are you still barely eating enough to keep a bird alive?"

She laughed, as at an old joke, and Kellen realized that she must have told Master Eliron about having been turned into a Silver Eagle. The realization gave him a peculiar feeling, but he shrugged it off. Why shouldn't she tell him? There was no stigma to practicing Wildmagery outside the City lands, from what he'd seen. Idalia practiced it openly, and everyone accepted it as a normal part of life. Nobody was yelling for the Priests of the Light to shield them, or for the High Mages to come and protect them—not that the High Mages would, since the humans were living with Otherfolk. And not that Armethalieh's protection was anything that you'd *want* . . .

It was all very confusing.

There's so much to learn! How am I ever going to even live long enough to learn it all?

KELLEN tried very hard to stop himself thinking about Armethalieh, but somehow he couldn't seem to. It had been easy while he was living out in the woods with only Idalia for human company, since everything was utterly different from life in the City, but Merryvale was just enough like Armethalieh that it reminded him of the place that had once been home, while at the same time being so very different that it stood in the most extreme contrast. Here, Master Eliron's servants and apprentices sat at the same table as the Master and his guests—or, in the case of the Centaurs, *stood*—and were treated as members of an extended family. To accommodate the Centaurs' greater height, the table was higher—Kellen could have stood comfortably at it himself—and the chairs for the two-legged guests were more like high stools with backs. Kellen caught himself thinking that was unreasonable—couldn't the Centaurs kneel, or something?—but then realized it would be more unfair to expect the Centaurs to accommodate the humans, when it was easier for the humans to accommodate the Centaurs. It was City thinking, the idea that humans were the pinnacle of Creation, that made him think otherwise. And that sort of reasoning wasn't fair.

Kellen sighed and concentrated on his food, wishing he didn't think so much about problems that didn't seem to have

any solution. The food was certainly a welcome distraction—
hot oven-baked yeast-breads (the thing he'd missed most, living out in the woods), roast chicken with stuffing, a wide
selection of tasty vegetables, and beef. Digging into his meal,
Kellen realized he'd gotten very tired of venison, rabbit, pi-
geon, and fish.

At first, looking down at the unfamiliar tools beside his
place setting, Kellen hadn't been quite sure what to do, but
he quickly realized the courtly table manners drummed into
him in House Tavadon had no place here, and emulated the
style of those he saw around him.

He was saved from any embarrassment by the fact that
Idalia was eating as heartily as he was, with a pragmatic
attention to her food that would have given their father heart
failure. But so was everyone else, even the old Healer, and
Master Eliron's cook was insisting that everything on the table must be eaten before she would bring out the pies and
Haneida's honey-cakes.

"And don't you a-go sneaking into the kitchen to steal any,
Merana, or I've got a stout stirring spoon with your name on
it, my girl!" the woman said firmly. Merana only laughed and
switched her braided tail, reaching for another roll and the
pot of honey.

⌐

"OH," Idalia sighed at last, chasing a drop of gravy about
her plate with a bit of hot bread, "this is lovely. I only wish
I could cook like this—but I'm afraid I lack three things: the
talent, the time, and the tools!"

"You know, my dear, that's hardly an insurmountable obstacle," Master Eliron said gently. "Were you to come here
to live . . ."

Idalia shook her head in refusal. "We've had this conversation before, my dear. You know I can't. The forest needs
me. How could those I serve out there find me here?"

"I expect they would find you just as they always have,
Idalia," Master Eliron answered. "But perhaps you would

consider coming to us just for a few moonturns during deep winter? The Wildwood sleeps then, and here in Merryvale, with your wants seen to, you could devote all your time to Kellen's training. You would not have to fear being a burden on us, not with the Powers at your command, and it would be good to have a Wildmage living among us." He sighed. "We worry about you out there, with nothing between you and the deep cold but a few walls and a single fire. Do consider it."

"Very well, Master Eliron," Idalia said, with a warm and kindly tone in her voice. "I will consider it."

But Kellen already knew his sister well enough to know that the answer was going to be "no."

Why?

The aged Healer was right: those who needed Idalia's help could find her anywhere. And from what she'd told him about how the Wild Magic worked, she could find work to do anywhere. But she wasn't living with the Elves, and now Kellen knew that she'd had several offers to live in reasonably civilized comfort in Merryvale, and she wasn't living here, either.

Why not?

A not-terribly-pleasant idea occurred to him, and he forced it away.

⌐

BUT later, after much more food, and a long pleasant companionable evening spent in music and good talk around Master Eliron's hearth, when Kellen was tucked up under the eaves on a guest-pallet, the idea returned.

Why did Idalia insist on living out in the Wildwood all by herself?

Was it that she really *was* Tainted after all, and that she feared that Master Eliron would discover it?

He knew it was impossible, but the more Kellen tried to push the idea to the bottom of his mind, the more he seemed to be pushing sleep with it as well, until—bone-weary as he was—Kellen lay wide-awake. He stared up into the darkness, unable to do anything but think.

Lycaelon had said that Wildmagery sent its users down the dark and twisted path to congress with Demons, that the High Magick taught in Armethalieh was the only safe magic for mankind to use.

Of course, everything else Lycaelon and the High Council had taught—and the Priests of the Light—hadn't been true, or so Kellen was discovering, during his Outlaw adventures.

But what if this one thing *was*?

It would be a lot easier if Demons didn't exist. Then Kellen could just dismiss his father's warnings as a last attempt to manipulate him. But Idalia said they did, and while Idalia might refrain from telling him things until she thought he was ready to hear them, she'd never outright tell him anything that wasn't true.

So Demons existed. But did that mean that Idalia had seen them? Possibly even dealt with them?

Or . . . *no!*

It wasn't possible, Kellen told himself firmly. Idalia was a good person. He knew that all the way down to his very bones. She healed people. Healing magic couldn't possibly be wrong. How could something good open you to corruption? That made less sense than anything he'd ever learned in the City . . . and his sister was a much more interesting person than anyone in the City, for that matter. More honest, too. She thought about things, she answered his questions (even if the answer was "I don't know, why don't we see if we can find out"), and she didn't always assume that *an* answer was the only answer, or even the best answer.

As far as Kellen could tell from the time he'd spent living with her, Idalia seemed to spend most of her time helping people, with and without magic.

How could that be bad?

How could *Idalia* be bad?

But . . .

Could she be bad without *knowing* she was bad? Was that even possible?

I just don't know, Kellen realized miserably. *Nothing makes sense. I just know that Idalia's always telling me to trust my instincts. And my instincts tell me there's some kind of connection between the Wild Magic and the Demons. And I don't know what it is. And that scares me.*

And I think Idalia might know what it is.

And I think I'm afraid to ask her.

But if she doesn't live out in the forest alone because she knows that she's Tainted and fears to be found out . . . then why?

Chapter Fifteen

Darkness and Lies

The room was smaller than many in the Heart of Darkness, a room for very private pleasures. The curving walls were covered with closely fitted tiles of amethyst of a flawless purple so dark it was nearly black and overhung with slave-woven tapestries depicting the feasts and pleasures of the Endarkened Court. The floor was thickly covered with silk carpets whose pile was so deep that taloned feet sunk into them as if they were fur. In the cool pale spell-light cast by the enchanted globes in which captured forest pixies slowly died for the pleasure of the Endarkened, the patterns on the floor glowed like a captive garden.

Hanging from a heavily jeweled golden chain attached to a large bronze ring in the center of the ceiling was a large silver and enamel cage, crafted to look like serpents twining over graveyard bones. It was a pity, Prince Zyperis reflected, regarding the three fauns cowering inside, that its inhabitants lacked the discernment to properly appreciate the beauty of their confinement. Still, that would not be a problem for them for very much longer, and the next occupant might have higher sensibilities.

Carrying a large shallow bowl carved and polished from one piece of black obsidian, the Prince advanced to the center of the room and placed it carefully on an iron and ivory table draped in heavy red silk. A sharp knife was already there, waiting.

He paused to savor the moment, and the terror of the fauns, before proceeding.

The war-to-come was going forward nicely. Just as he and Mother intended, the Mage City continued to draw inward even as it expanded its territory, isolating itself not only from the Otherfolk, but also from all outside human contact, wallowing in its own spiritual decay. Lovely.

"Let us see how their plans proceed, eh, my little friends?" Prince Zyperis murmured.

The fauns began to scream.

He picked up the knife and opened the door of the silver cage. Reaching in, he dragged out the first of the struggling, screaming fauns. It was no match for his strength; it writhed in his grip to no avail. It might just as well have been thrashing against the grip of a dragon. With quick efficiency, he lifted it over the obsidian bowl and slit its throat, holding it upside down until the last of its blood had drained into the bowl. The screaming turned to a gurgling, and he feasted on the final dregs of its despair as it felt its life ebbing out of it; horror of the other two as they watched it dying, their own screams now stifled in their throats by sheer terror.

Then he turned to the cage again, and the shrieking began anew as they flung themselves against the bars in a vain attempt to elude him and prolong their wretched lives for another precious moment or two.

The other two talking vermin followed in short order—not from any sense of mercy on Zyperis's part, but because today, the death of the fauns was merely a means to an end. Tossing the last of the tiny bloodless corpses aside, the Endarkened Prince leaned over the bowl of hot fresh blood, peering into its depths.

"Show me what I desire," he commanded huskily. The surface of the liquid shimmered, growing misty and then clearing.

Zyperis gazed down at a village square, where a Lawspeaker in Armethaliehan livery stood on a mounting block, reading out a decree to an assembled crowd of farmers. The words the man spoke came to him faintly, and Zyperis smiled. According to the Prince's spies, in recent months the Golden City had expanded its borders once again, seeking to drive out both Otherfolk and Wildmagery. Such decrees were initially popular, since the Otherfolk had to leave their property behind, enriching the humans who remained, but the City's favor was a double-edged sword, and this village was now feeling the bite of the other side of the City's poisoned blade.

Their Wildmage Healer had left as well, of course. The village had petitioned Armethalieh to send them a new Healer, and today they were receiving their reply.

No Healer would be sent to their village. Any who needed help might come freely to the City to receive it—providing, of course, that they were tax-paying humans willing to wear the City token, and who fit City standards of suitability for help.

The villagers' anger came to him only distantly, but it was a heady vintage nevertheless. Prince Zyperis chuckled, and waved his hand across the surface of the bowl, breaking the link. Now that another village had tasted the bitter along with the sweet, they were ready to receive one of his agents—a trader from the High Hills, perhaps, primed with horror stories of the tyranny of the High Mages, to urge the villagers to desert their homes and fields and migrate elsewhere—outside the City-claimed lands—further isolating and impoverishing the City. All the vast acreage of fertile fields in the World Above did the City precious little good if there was no one there to farm it. And after generations of keeping its own citizens pent behind the City walls, there was not one citizen willing or able to take up that task, even if the City was willing to release any of its own precious citizenry to the labor.

The City of a Thousand Bells was the largest single concentration of humans in the land, the stronghold of High Magick, so its destruction was the keystone of the Endarkened's strategy. Since the War, the Mages had completely lost touch with the adaptability and flexibility that was once humanity's greatest strength, utterly rejecting the Wild Magic and imprisoning themselves within a web of inflexible rules and regulations. That had opened them to Endarkened influence, though of course, they had known it not. A subtle influence, that, a careful nourishing of superiority—first of human over not, then of City over foreigner, then at last of Mage over mere citizen. And then, a more subtle influence, one that suggested, oh, so delicately, that since Wild Magic could not be controlled by the High Mages, it must be dangerous . . . or evil. Now the Mages were utterly certain that there was no situation that could not be dealt with according to their lifeless and unthinking rules. In setting themselves up as the sole authorities within the City, they had cast their rules in stone, and used them to build a wall between themselves and the other races of the land.

And since—thanks to careful coaching by Endarkened agents—the High Mages had determined that all the other creatures in the land were destined to be ruled (if human) or enslaved (if not) by the City, if not exterminated outright, those races' reaction to them now ranged from mere annoyance to utter fury . . .

"Oh, yes," Prince Zyperis said softly, rubbing his long taloned hands together and spreading his wings wide in contentment. "Everything is going forward precisely as it should."

KELLEN had finally dropped into an uneasy sleep— plagued by dreams of Demonic Hounds near morning—and even the chance to see more of Merryvale had not been enough to rouse him out of the black mood he'd awakened with. He hated inflicting it on everyone around him, but unlike back in the City—which he still thought of as "home" in unguarded moments—there really wasn't anyplace he could go off to be by himself until it passed, at least, not until he and Idalia went back to her cabin.

There, if need be, he could make an excuse to go off alone hunting for foodstuffs or wind-felled timber for building or the fireplace. He'd wondered when he first arrived why Idalia wouldn't cut a tree that wasn't already dead—until he'd met the dryads. Now he was glad of it; searching for more wood made a good excuse to get away when he needed to. But that wasn't possible today. All he could do was try to keep to himself as much as possible, and hope that nobody noticed.

He would have preferred to just curl up on his sleeping pallet and hide until it was time to leave, but Idalia had shopping to do this morning, and since yesterday Kellen had been so eager to see the rest of the village, there was no way he could get out of going with her without attracting attention he really wanted to avoid.

Armed with a borrowed basket—Idalia had one too—Kellen trailed after his sister as she made her way to Merryvale's Market Street.

It was a very different sort of market from the ones in Armethalieh. Of course it was smaller—much smaller. That went without saying. Half the places Idalia dragged him to were actual *shops,* not proper markets such as he was used to. And everything was jumbled in together in the same place—fruit and honey and meat and bread and cloth, all crowded into the same little part of town. And there wasn't really very much of anything, and what there was, was—he guessed—pretty crude by Armethaliehan standards.

But not one item there had been passed by the Council. Not one item there had received a license to be sold.

He passed by the door of a sweets-seller. The trays of brightly colored sugar caught his eye, and he stopped, thinking of Shalkan. The unicorn had a notorious sweet tooth, and would enjoy the treat.

But how could Kellen pay for it?

He glanced up the street. Idalia was stopped in the doorway of a spice-merchant's, and from the look of things, she was going to be there for some time.

Kellen went into the small shop. It smelled of sugar, vanilla, cinnamon, and other spices he couldn't put a name to. As he entered, he dug in his pouch for some coins—Armethaliehan coins, and probably worthless here, but maybe the metal in them would be worth something. Only the Golden Suns were bespelled, after all; the lesser coins of the City were only ordinary silver and copper. He pulled them out and held them toward the seller, a middle-aged Centaur wearing a white apron who smiled as he saw Kellen approach.

"I don't know if these are worth anything here . . ."

"What were you looking to buy?" the Centaur asked amiably. From his girth, he was his own best customer. "Say, aren't you Kellen—Wildmage Idalia's brother?"

"That's right," Kellen said. "And I've got a friend with a sweet tooth. I think he'd enjoy some of the rock sugar, or maybe some of the sugar sticks."

"And you wanted to pay in coin?" the Centaur asked, sounding baffled. "Idalia usually pays with weather, and all. Still . . ." He inspected the coins on Kellen's outstretched palm critically. "Never seen anything like them, but they look like good silver, right enough. I reckon one of those'll be enough to buy your friend a fine tummy-ache, if you think that's fair."

"More than fair," Kellen agreed. He handed over the coin, and the sweets-seller took out a square of paper and made up a large packet of brightly colored sugar stick and glittering lumps of rock sugar. He tied the packet up with a length of twine and handed it over.

"And this is for you. A treat for luck."

He picked up a small wooden dish and held it out to Kellen. Resting in the middle of it was a round brown doughy object, its surface coated with powdered sugar.

"What is it?" Kellen asked curiously.

"New from Midsummer Fair. The Mountain Traders

brought it. They say it came out of the Southern Deserts, a spice-bean called *xocalatl.* Try it."

"Something new." Kellen hardly needed to hear anything more. He picked up the unprepossessing-looking object and popped it into his mouth.

It began to dissolve immediately, and the rich taste filled his mouth, bitter and sweet and complex. Like *kaffeyah,* but not quite. He wasn't sure he liked it, but he was glad he'd tried it.

" 'Xocalatl,' " Kellen said, trying the unfamiliar word. "Thank you. I'll remember it."

"Come again," the sweets-seller said genially. "And remember me to your sister."

Kellen nodded and moved on, tucking his package carefully into his basket and hurrying to catch up with his sister.

IDALIA completed her trading in Merryvale by midmorning, and she and Kellen began the long walk back to her cabin.

A lot of what she had traded for would be sent later—bags of flour, meal, and salt, too heavy for them to carry—and some things they would be returning for when they were ready. Kellen had been glad to find that they would be trading a quantity of smoked venison and wood-pigeon pickled in brine for an equal weight of salt-beef, preserved eggs, and dried fish (though Idalia warned him he'd be very tired of all of them by spring).

But what they were carrying home with them was heavy enough, since it principally consisted of two large kegs of nails and some coils of thin thatching rope to be used for the construction of the addition to the cabin. He hoped that Idalia knew how to thatch, since *he* didn't, and from what he'd seen, it would be a difficult task to learn.

If Idalia noticed his unusual silence, she did not break it with any comments of her own. The day was bright and clear—good weather for the ripening crops of the Merryvale farmers.

He wished he could feel as cheerful as the weather warranted. He couldn't help thinking about Demons. Idalia still hadn't talked to him about them, and now he was hesitant to bring up the subject again. If she was falling prey to the influence of Demons, that might explain why she didn't want to live in the village, even for the winter. As long as she stayed away, she could keep her associations with Demons secret, but if she moved there and was around them, *especially* the old Healer, she would certainly be found out.

Maybe the reason the old faun wouldn't let her near was that *he* knew she wasn't to be trusted. Idalia might not know what had happened to the aged creature, but so far as Kellen was concerned, it was as plain as a road-post. Demons—or if not Demons, certainly Demonic creatures—had gotten hold of him and his terrible injuries were the result.

If the faun suspected Idalia of being Demon-tainted, he wouldn't let her get near him. But he *might* try and warn Kellen.

Maybe his appearance at the pond had been an attempt to deliver that warning.

Maybe Kellen's dreams of Demon Hounds were another warning.

IDALIA made much of her payment for the supplies that would see the two of them through the winter in the form of spells to keep damaging weather away from the fields for these last crucial sennights. So long as there was not too much tampering, or too often, or over too large an area, a little weather magic did no harm to the greater balance of field and forest. It was when someone got greedy, wanting everything their own way with no thought to the harm that did to others, that balance was endangered. The spells were very specific; preventing rain (or worse, hail) from falling *on those specific fields* but permitting it to fall anywhere else in the area it cared to. This might mean that the forests surrounding Merryvale itself got all the rain that would have fallen on the village *plus* what would have fallen on the fields, but the point was it was all ending up in the same general area and percolating down into the waters underground. The spell was set to dissipate as soon as the harvest was gathered in, thus further limiting its effects.

Though she'd been aware of Kellen's unsettled mood from the moment he'd awakened that morning, Idalia respected his attempt to keep it to himself. From the vantage point of her ten years' seniority, she well remembered the wild emotional storms of adolescence, and coming into the power of a Wild-mage while at the same time being cast out of the only home you'd ever known hardly made coping with growing up any easier. Poor Kellen! He had a triple burden to labor under! That he managed to be cooperative and cheerful most of the time said a great deal for the essential goodness of his nature.

Curse Lycaelon for a brute and a fool! She had loved her brother dearly as a child, and found the young man even more endearing as he bumbled his way toward maturity, but some-times it was hard to believe he was Lycaelon's son. Subtlety simply was not in his nature. Even Idalia had to admit that Kellen was as easy to read as a page of print, and easier to manipulate.

But Lycaelon had never bothered.

The Arch-Mage simply had not been interested in anything outside of his own desires. If he had troubled to take the little time it would have taken to get to know Kellen *personally,* rather than relying on the reports of servants and underlings, if he had considered spending some part of the time he squan-dered in his endless power-games on his son instead of on City politics, Lycaelon could have had exactly the son he'd wanted. Kellen was so starved for affection he would have done anything for his father if Lycaelon had only bothered to love the boy. Kellen would have grown up to become a model son, a credit to his family name, a promising young High Mage.

And the Books would never have come to him.

Or would they?

What if they had?

Sooner or later Kellen would have started to see that what he was *told* and what really went on in the City didn't match. Especially for anyone who wasn't Mageborn.

But if the Books had still come to him, Kellen would certainly never have studied them.

Or would he?

Idalia frowned, wondering.

Kellen was curious. He was intelligent. Sooner or later, he would *still* have started wondering about the lands outside the City, and when his questions went unanswered, or were answered unsatisfactorily, would he have looked elsewhere?

If Kellen had loved his father and that love had been returned—if Lycaelon had been someone else entirely, or if he had died, and Kellen been raised by another, kinder Mage family—might not the same thing have happened, only to a Kellen devoted to his family, to his studies, to the City? Wouldn't that have been an even worse disaster for him than what had actually happened? Only imagine a Kellen who had *wanted* to become a High Mage, who was trying to be the best son he could be, to please his father, or foster father . . . then coming upon the Books, tempted by them, called to experiment with them, to read them, terribly torn between the two paths, agonizing over his divided loyalties . . .

"Even cruelty can be kindness, if we can only see it clearly." So said *The Book of Moon.* If Kellen had been fated to become a Wildmage, perhaps Lycaelon was the best of all possible fathers for him to have had.

But Idalia knew it would be many years before she would ever dare to suggest such a possibility to him.

⌐

AT last they reached the clearing and home. Kellen slid his heavy pack from his shoulders with a grateful sigh and stretched, working the stiffness from cramped muscles. He glanced toward his neatly stacked tools. They were tucked beneath the same weatherproof covering that kept the building logs from warping.

"I'd better get back to work," he said curtly. "I've lost almost two days, and winter isn't going to come any later because I've had other things to do."

Idalia shot him a considering glance, but she didn't answer him directly.

"Master Eliron was right about one thing, you know—I should be spending more time teaching you Wildmagery than I have." She smiled and shrugged. "I hate to admit it, but that's my fault entirely; I've been selfish. Granted, it has been very good for you to do the work you've been doing here, both because it is turning you from a soft City-boy to a strong and resourceful fellow with many new skills. And I want you to finish the addition because I want my bedroom back—but what I want is not what you need and certainly not what you deserve. I should be teaching you both the skills of the hands and of the spirit. I apologize for neglecting the latter."

He looked at her in surprise; never, in all of his life, had any of his teachers (or his father, for that matter) apologized for *anything*. He wasn't entirely certain what to make of this.

Idalia seemed to take his silence for assent, though. "Come on. Help me get this stuff stowed away. We'll get some cider, and I'll show you how to do another one of my party tricks."

Kellen hesitated, still staring off in the direction of the unfinished addition to the cabin. Idalia came and draped an arm around his shoulders.

"Kellen . . . you don't think I expected you to build it all by yourself, did you? I know you could. I know you could do most of it, by now, but that's not the only thing you're here to do. The villagers helped me put up the original cabin, and once their harvest is in, they'll come to help us finish the work you've started here." She gave his shoulders a little squeeze. "For one thing, we'll need the help of the thatcher— I certainly can't thatch the roof, and I rather doubt that was one of your lessons under your tutor! Meanwhile, you have other things to learn that no one else can help you with."

She might have *told* him. She might have let him know. Here he'd been worrying about it, and all along she'd had plans to get him some help. Or had she expected he *would* be able to build it, then discovered that he couldn't, and only *then* arranged for the help? That was probably it.

"Like what?" Kellen asked, not caring just now that he sounded like a sulky child.

"Come and see," Idalia urged with a mysterious smile.

Kellen was really irritated now. Did she enjoy being so maddening? But—he thought back to the young City-men he knew who had sweethearts, and how they tormented and teased their willing captives. Maybe it wasn't just Idalia. Maybe all women were really like that.

First they went into the cabin, where they emptied their packs—leaving the heavy kegs of nails outside. Idalia hung the coils of oiled flaxen thatching line on a hook from one of the rafters where they'd be out of the way until needed, then carefully unpacked the rest of their treasures.

A new whetstone, and a set of small paring knives for cooking (Kellen had managed to break one of the others in his attempts to learn to peel root vegetables, and besides, frequent sharpening wore down the soft steel with time). Hairpins and straight pins and needles for Idalia, the sugar candy for Shalkan, several small paper packets of spices. Real tea for Kellen, who missed the taste, and a thick roll of velum, drawing charcoal, and a sponge. Cleaned carefully, the velum could be reused again and again.

"I didn't know you'd bought that!" Kellen exclaimed, startled out of his blue funk by the discovery of the drawing material.

"Winter is going to be long," Idalia warned once again, tucking everything carefully away into the cabinets and chests scattered around the room. "You need things to occupy yourself when the snow is halfway up the shutters. I do fancy beadwork and embroidery on shirts and ribbons and take it to trade in the village in the spring, but I don't think that method of passing the winter would suit you, little brother. I find that the hours can grow very long without something to keep you busy. It gets very quiet and lonely here once the snows close us in."

Then why don't you go live in the village? Kellen wondered again, biting down hard on the thought for fear she might be able to hear what echoed in his thoughts so loudly.

But Idalia was occupied with retrieving two tankards from the mantel and the cider-jug from the cold-cellar beneath the floor.

"Now. Come and learn," she said, handing one to him once they were full.

There was a tiny spring-fed pond behind the cabin that they used for their drinking and washing water. Kellen knew that Idalia also used it as a scrying pool—the bottom was littered with keystones, and for a while after he'd found out about that, he'd been a little nervous about drinking water charged with magic—but since nothing bad ever happened, and both Idalia and Shalkan drank the water too, he'd gotten over his case of nerves.

Scrying was something he'd heard discussed before, though the Mages never did it around Students. Idalia had only done the spell a couple of times since he'd come to the Wildwood, and each time she'd invited him to watch and learn. At first, Kellen had thought it would be pretty much a waste of time—from what little Anigrel had been willing to tell him about the workings of the High Magick, watching another Mage do magick was about as interesting as watching someone else solve a Maths problem—but he'd been surprised to discover that he could see and hear everything Idalia did when she scryed. He wasn't sure if that was because he was in some sense her apprentice, or because the Wild Magic was simply more generous in its nature than the High Magick he'd previously studied.

But where the High Mages used scrying to keep an eye on the lands beyond the City, there didn't seem to be a good reason for Idalia to use the spell, for all they'd looked at were places they had already been and could easily walk to. When he'd asked why she was showing him the spell, Idalia told him that scrying wasn't the sort of thing a Wildmage tended to use very often, unless he or she wanted to keep an eye on a friend or loved one from afar, or unless he or she had the feeling that the Wild Magic *itself* wanted it done, though it was a skill that every Wildmage learned.

Since at the moment, she didn't have anyone or anything she needed to watch over, it was more something that Idalia did now and then whenever she felt it was a good idea to do it, letting the Wild Magic itself dictate what the scrying showed her. That still struck Kellen as a rather slipshod way to run a magical system. Doing something whenever you felt like it, rather than by a regular schedule of times and observances—where was the discipline, the craft, in that?

But Wild Magic and High Magick were as un-alike as the Wildwood and the formal gardens of Armethalieh. Both had flowers in them . . . and there the resemblance ended. Applying the standards of the one to the other was a good way to get a headache, as far as Kellen could figure out. He wondered if one of the reasons Idalia was so good at Wild Magic—and he was so bad at it—was because he'd gotten High Mage training and she hadn't. Maybe she had fewer preconceptions to unlearn. Maybe women were just better suited to becoming Wildmages in general, because of their generally more flighty and chaotic natures.

Oh, better not even let Idalia catch you thinking of thinking that! You know *it isn't true, not even a little bit! But there has to be some reason she's so much better at this stuff than I am . . .*

Other than the reason he didn't even want to consider. Not even for a moment. Not even in jest. That he was Tainted. Or she was.

Idalia reached the edge of the spring and knelt down, motioning Kellen to kneel beside her. She rolled up her sleeve and fished around in the spring among the keystones, for all the world like a housewife testing the freshness of hen's eggs.

"Ah. Plenty of power for a few more spells here. And I think it's time you actually learned this one, rather than just watching me do it." She rocked back on her heels and took a deep drink of her cider.

Kellen stared at her in horror. Him? Learn to scry? *Now?* He'd never felt less like doing magic in his life!

"You remember what's involved?" Idalia prompted. "The ingredients?"

"I, uh, I—" For a moment Kellen's mind went numbingly blank, then he remembered reading the spell in *The Book of Moon* and from watching Idalia. "Fern leaf. Cider—or wine, if you don't have any cider. Mead will do, if you don't have either of those. Fruit of the earth, though. Four drops into the water, then float the leaf on the surface."

"Good," Idalia said encouragingly. "And . . . ?"

This was *just* like Undermage Anigrel's lessons, Kellen thought resentfully, for just a moment. Recite back what you've memorized, but never get a chance to use it . . .

But she *had* said he was going to use it. " 'You who travel between Earth and Sky, show me what you see.' But, Idalia, how do you know *what* you'll see?"

"You don't, really," Idalia said. "Unless you're doing a specific search—and remember that the more specific you get, the higher the price," Idalia reminded him. "Oh, you can have something in mind, and then, if you're lucky you might get that, but with the Wild Magic, you see what you need to see, not what you want to see. Even if you don't understand what you see—and often you won't—it's more important to see those things than to just get caught up in serving your own desires. Lately I've been trying to keep an eye on the City—endless Council meetings, mostly about how everyone outside of the walls is a covert or overt enemy of the City— trying to find out if they know you escaped the Hunt. I haven't heard anything about you, though."

She'd been watching the Council? Why hadn't she told him? So he wouldn't worry? And why hadn't she had *him* scrying? Because she knew he'd fail? Or because she knew he'd see . . . something else? Something she didn't want him to see?

"But here," she continued. "There's a nice patch of fern growing over there. Let's see what *you* get."

Now he didn't know *what* to think! First she hadn't coached him through the spell, and now she was telling him to cast it!

Feeling apprehensive and confused, Kellen trudged sulkily over to the stand of fern. He just *knew* this wasn't going to work. He'd just end up staring down at an empty pool of white rocks, and Idalia would be . . . kind, and suggest they try again, or say he was just tired and they should do this again another day—or worse, he'd look down and see a Demon staring up at him, and Idalia wouldn't see it.

Or she would, and she'd know he knew she was in league with them and—

No, she wouldn't be doing this if she was in league with Demons, if she didn't know he was going to fail! So she was setting him up to fail, just like Anigrel used to. That was it.

Kellen glared down at the patch of fern, feeling his unsettled bad mood return full force. This was going to be just like all the times he'd tried to be what Lycaelon wanted, and failed, only then he hadn't cared so much. Now he was going to fail *Idalia,* and that made him angry. She ought to know he couldn't do this. Why was she making him prove it? This stuff came to her as effortlessly as breathing, while every spell he cast ended in disaster, and she just couldn't understand how it could be hard for someone. He'd had enough Wildmagery to get him kicked out of Armethalieh, but aside from that? He couldn't talk to the Otherfolk like Idalia could, or really see them half the time, he didn't have her woodscraft skills, he wasn't one-tenth the Wildmage and never would be, he already knew he didn't have what it took to be a farmer or crafter like they were in Merryvale . . .

Wasn't there *ever* going to be something he was the best at? Ever?

No. He was always going to be Kellen the Second-Best, Kellen the Embarrassment. People had put up with him in the City because he was Lycaelon's son, and now they were putting up with him here in the Wildwood because he was Idalia's brother, and nothing, *nothing,* was ever going to change. Look at all Idalia was going through here in the Wildwood—building an addition to the cabin, trading magic for extra food—just because he couldn't pull his weight. And he knew that somehow, somewhere, deep at the bottom of things where he couldn't get to it, there was something *wrong* about the way things were going now, but there wasn't anything he could do about it.

He hated it. He hated having questions he was afraid to ask. But somehow the time was never right.

Kellen came back with the fern-leaf and, jaw set, knelt beside the pool. With angry efficiency, he flicked cider onto the water, dropped the leaf onto the eddying surface, and quickly muttered the proper words, half expecting them to leave colorful trails of Magefire in the air, though of course they didn't. The Wild Magic just didn't work that way.

Then he leaned forward, glaring down at the bottom of the pool as if it were a personal enemy.

Nothing's going to happen. Nothing's going to happen. Noth—

⟳

THE vision came, so quickly that it seemed to sweep the clearing and the pool away.

The sky was greenish-black, lit by flashes of reddish lightning. He soared above it as if he had wings. Though it was dark, somehow Kellen could see clearly, across a barren plain strewn with jagged boulders that looked as if they had been tossed there by a monster child grown tired of playing with them. He could hear the wind, wailing thinly as it forced its way between the stones. The sound made him shudder. He knew dimly that he should have been cold, but he felt nothing at all.

As in dreams, he knew more than he saw. There was something there. Something important. Something evil. The malignity of it seemed to seep upward. The iciness of it seemed to seep upward, out of the vision, filling his bones with poison.

And ringing the plain was a horde—an ARMY—of creatures more horrible than even those that haunted Kellen's most terrible nightmares, all converging on its center. He could hear them baying, the sound the stone Hounds of the Outlaw Hunt would have made if they'd been given voices.

To look closely at them was to risk madness. And somehow, Kellen knew also that he was there, in the middle of them—

Idalia reached out and plunged her fist into the spring, shattering the vision.

"No!" Kellen screamed, flinging himself into his sister's arms as if he were seven, not seventeen. Idalia held him tightly, and he could feel that she was trembling as hard as he was, and knew that she had seen the same thing that he had. The horror of seeing his greatest secret fears brought into the light, given form and weight and reality, ripped the words from his throat: "Idalia, I don't want to be a monster! Please, please—take my Books! Please!"

"Kellen, listen to me." There was a note of fierceness in his sister's voice that Kellen had rarely heard. "You are *not* a monster. And you are not going to *become* a monster."

He shook his head, holding her tighter. "The vision. You saw it too."

"Yes." Idalia drew a deep breath. "And I saw that you were there. But on the same side as those . . . things? I will never believe that. Never!"

He had to speak. He had to warn her.

"But Father said—"

To Kellen's astonishment, Idalia smacked him on the back of the head—hard enough to sting. She pushed him away, so that she could look into his eyes.

" 'Father said'—'Father said'—" Idalia mocked angrily. "*Father,* in case you haven't figured it out for yourself by now, is a narrow-minded, utterly selfish brute without an ounce of human compassion who would say anything to anyone to get his own way. He told you the Wild Magic would turn you into a Demon, I suppose. Well, I'm telling you now that it is utterly impossible. *Kellen.* Look at me. I'll tell you the truth."

Kellen looked up at her, his eyes filled with hope—and fear.

"This has gone on long enough. There's a tiny grain of truth in Father's words, and I'm going to tell you what it is. The Wild Magic teaches you to think for yourself. I've told you that, and you know it's true. Well, people who think for themselves can get into all kinds of trouble—*including* going over to the Demon side, because yes, there *is* a Demon side, and they're always looking for human tools. But to do that, a Wildmage has to *give up* the Wild Magic and everything that has to do with it. Do you understand, Kellen? No Wildmage can serve the Demons—not without ceasing to be a true Wildmage first. His Books will leave him. Yes, because Wildmages think and act for themselves, they can make bad choices and end up becoming evil. But the Wild Magic won't tolerate evil; when they make that choice, the Wild Magic itself *stops serving them and stops answering them.* The Wild Magic will leave, and something else will take its place. That's all the truth Lycaelon has on his side. All of it. But even a tiny thorn can fester," she added, almost to herself.

"But . . ." Kellen said, gesturing toward the pool. It was clear and empty now, a spring-fed pool, nothing more.

"Did you ever consider you might be there because you were *good*?" Idalia said, more gently now. "That you might be fighting the Demons? Or that your vision might be only, oh, a *kind* of truth, like a riddle, to make you think about things more clearly? Or that it might not happen for many, many years?"

"No," said Kellen simply. "But, Idalia, what if I decide to renounce the Wild Magic and become evil?"

"Then I'll knock you over the head, sew you into a sack, and sell you to the Selken Traders," Idalia said promptly. "I'm sure you won't be able to get into any trouble across the Sea." She poked him in the ribs with a finger. "You're beefy enough now, I should even get a good price for you. Deal?"

"Deal," Kellen said with a shaky smile.

He felt as if a fever he hadn't known he'd been running had broken, or as if an actual thorn had been pulled from his flesh. It was strange, but it was far more reassuring to know that there were actually Demons out there who wanted Wildmages to corrupt than just thinking it might all be his own imagination. Idalia spoke of them as if they were just another danger to be faced, and down deep inside, Kellen had no doubts about his own courage—or hers.

"And at least we know you can work the scrying spell," Idalia said, taking another deep steadying breath. "And very thoroughly, too. Now it's my turn."

"But—Now?" Kellen said in dismay. He'd been sure that after something like that, they were going to call it quits for the day.

"No time like the present," she said briskly. "Though if we end up back there again, I'm breaking out that bottle of mead I've been saving for a special emergency," Idalia added, and she didn't sound at all humorous. "And if that *wasn't* some kind of Teaching Vision, then . . . then we'd better figure out what to do about it, hadn't we?"

"But—But, Idalia?" Kellen asked. He knew this *still* wasn't a good time to ask, but he knew he had to. With that terrible vision still in the forefront of his mind, he knew that the time for doubts and secrets was over.

"Yes, Kellen?"

"If—If it's true—What you say—Then, why do you live here? You could live with the Elves—or, or, if you didn't want to do that, you could live in the Centaur village, and not—not out here in the middle of nowhere where you can't even take a bath? I was just . . ." Kellen stumbled to a halt, knowing he'd asked the question all wrong.

Idalia stared at him for a long moment, her face blank with surprise, then hugged him very hard. "Oh, my poor mixed-up baby brother! You've been tying yourself into knots over *that*? I live out here in the woods because I like to; I know you probably find this hard to believe, but when I'm around too many people, I start to feel uncomfortable and crowded. When you live even in a little village like Merryvale, you have to change what you do and how you act; maybe not by much, but it's a restriction. And I'll tell you another truth, if I lived in Merryvale, people would be coming to me to use Wild Magic for stupid little things *all the time*. I would either annoy them by refusing, or see my time and energy frittered away on nonsense. Living out here—well, they have to think very hard before they come to me." She sighed, but smiled. "It's as simple as that. People *do* like different things, you know. I like living alone, with no one to please but myself, and no one nagging me for love spells." She kissed him gently on the forehead. "Now finish your cider."

She handed Kellen his tankard and went over to the stand of ferns to pluck her own leaf. Kellen drank, and regarded the spring warily, but the water remained still and clear, with no trace of the fire and turmoil of his vision.

He felt a mixture of exhaustion and relief, as if somehow he'd passed a test he hadn't known he'd been set. He believed Idalia, and Lycaelon had also been telling a kind of truth. Studying the Wild Magic destroyed a kind of defense against the Demons, because once you started to think for yourself, who knew what you might decide to think about? But Lycaelon knew nothing about what the Wild Magic *was*—rather less than Kellen actually knew about Demons, really. Everything Kellen had read in *The Book of Moon, The Book of Stars,* and *The Book of Sun;* everything he'd done with his own mixed-up spells; everything he'd seen Idalia do; all pointed to it only being able to be used for good. Unlike the mechanistic High Magick, as far as he could tell, the Wild Magic was self-aware, and that awareness was benevolent. He wasn't Tainted, and neither was Idalia.

So as long as you're really *doing Wild Magic, you're okay, I guess.*

Until you stop.

And if there aren't three other *Books out there . . .*

Idalia came back with her own leaf and knelt beside Kellen.

"Wish me luck, little brother," she said, patting him on the knee.

The spell was swiftly cast, and to Kellen's intense relief, the image that formed was a familiar one: the Council chamber in Armethalieh. He heard Idalia release a pent-up breath, and guessed she'd been a little worried as well.

But their relief was short-lived.

THE full Council was in session: thirteen High Mages seated at the curving judicial bench of black marble twice the height of a tall man, with Lycaelon Tavadon at their center on his black throne.

"Volpiril—Meron—Perizel—Lorins—Breulin—" Idalia named them all softly, going around the half circle.

Mage Breulin was speaking.

"We have had great success in our Northern and Southern Expansions, which, as you know, have been a priority over the past several moonturns. I am now pleased to report that our borders are clean and secure from the High Peaks in the north to the Arid Lands in the south, and we have brought several more of the unaligned villages previously outside our borders under Armethaliehan rule, to a concomitant increase in taxes and revenues. Their integration is proceeding smoothly, and we have been sending City Lawspeakers out to ride a regular circuit to make sure that all Enforcement Proclamations are read out on a timely basis. The Captain of the City Militia has requested permission to recruit and form five new units from the local villages in order to be able to support the Lawspeakers."

The motion was quickly passed, after a short discussion about recruitment policy, and the necessity of sending a Mage with the Militia to take care of any unusual problems right on the spot.

Then Lycaelon rose to speak.

"My fellow Mages. Mage Breulin's news is welcome indeed, for how can the City flourish when our enemies are free to gather outside our walls and plot our downfall? Yet I worry that we concern ourselves with the lesser danger and ignore the greater. While we have been occupied with the admittedly necessary purification of our new northern and southern territories, I have sent my agents westward, and discovered that many who do not wish to accept our wise and enlightened rule are massing there. The Western Hills contain a number of flourishing villages, not only of humans, but cesspits where humans and talking beasts congregate together in direct opposition to the wise teachings of the Eternal Light."

Several of the Council Mages frowned; Breulin stroked his beard, and leaned over to mutter something to the Mage at his right.

Lycaelon nodded approvingly when he saw the frowns. "As you know, our Hunt failed, which could only have happened if the most evil of forces had intervened. The Outlaw made his escape into the west, armed not only with the abomination of his dark magic, but with the deepest secrets of our City. Even now he may be leading innocent humans into error, as well as sharing our secrets with the cunning Other Races with which the Western Hills abound, who will seek our City's downfall and the destruction of the Light for no more reason than that they exist."

"Surely not!" one of the others exclaimed, though not as if he objected, but as if he was horrified.

Lycaelon bowed his head in a fine imitation of sorrow, but from their vantage, Kellen saw he was hiding a smirk. "Our way is hard," the Arch-Mage said, mournfully. "Our resources are few. We are one city, alone, without allies, in the face of the teeming bestial hordes of Darkness and Error. But the Light defends us, and our course is clear: In the name of Humanity, for the sake of our lost and imperiled brethren, we must claim *all* of the Western Hills for Armethalieh and the Light—extend our borders once again, no matter the cost to ourselves, and send forth a Scouring Hunt to purge those lands of the creatures that would usurp Man's rightful place in the world!"

There was a moment of silence, then the rest of the Council was on its feet, cheering Lycaelon as the vision slowly faded.

"BLOODY hell!"

Idalia threw her tankard into the spring and began to swear in low passionate tones. Some of the words Kellen had heard on the City docks; some of them he could only guess at the meaning of. She pounded her knee with a closed fist as she vilified every member of the Council, particularly Lycaelon.

Finally she turned from profanity to language that didn't make his ears burn quite so much.

"That pompous precious prancing ass, that demagogue, that warmonger, that *coward*—simpering around like a maiden whose feelings are hurt and getting everyone else to do his dirty work for him, that—that—Oh, if Mother were only there, she'd *spank* him!"

At last she ran out of words and simply sat there, head down, breathing hard, as Kellen watched her anxiously.

Extend the borders of Armethalieh . . . to here? But that's crazy. We're hundreds of miles from the City. Shalkan had to run at top speed for a night and a day to get here, and a unicorn is faster than . . . How can the City possibly control this much territory?

Of course, the Mages could *claim* it . . . all that involved was the casting of a Boundary Spell. The magickal cost would be high, but that was the City's problem.

And once they'd claimed it . . .

He looked up, and saw Shalkan watching him from the edge of the clearing.

"Is there trouble?" the unicorn asked.

"The City's going to expand its boundaries—to here," Kellen said bleakly.

Shalkan snorted and started back, then stamped his fore-hoof angrily.

"There's nothing for it, then," Idalia said angrily, fishing her tankard out of the spring, pouring the water out, and getting to her feet. "We'll have to warn the villages and move farther west. Into the Elven lands, I guess—they won't dare try to intrude there."

"You mean we're just going to run?" Kellen said indig-nantly, getting to his feet as well. "Just because the City de-cides it wants somebody else's land? Why should *we* move? We should stay and fight!"

"Don't be an idiot," Idalia said blightingly. Then she shook her head, and moderated her tone. "I'm sorry, Kellen—I didn't mean that; I'm angry at *them*, not you. You heard our beloved and most merciful father, though, and you should know what that means. They're going to set the borders and then send a Scouring Hunt. They won't even send out a Lawspeaker with a decree this time to give the Otherfolk time to get away. A Scouring Hunt is *just* that. They'll send Hounds, hundreds of them. You and Shalkan fought two packs and barely survived. How can we—and half a dozen villages full of innocent, unarmed villagers without an ounce of magic among them, at least half of them mere children— fight against pack after pack after pack of Hounds?"

"Well, *they* can run, but *we* should fight!" Kellen exclaimed, feeling his face grow hot.

"And what if all my friends here decide to help us—they will, you know," she replied tightly. "And then, because the ones that *can* fight have stayed, their families stay—"

"It isn't fair," Kellen muttered angrily, kicking at the ground. "We shouldn't let them push us around!"

"If we stay and fight—if we don't warn them—they'll die, and is *that* fair?" Idalia demanded.

Kellen hung his head. "No," he whispered. "But it isn't *fair*," he repeated.

"I know," Idalia said gently, "but it's the right thing to do." She sighed, and upended the tankard, shaking out the last of the water. "The right thing to do is almost always the hardest."

"How—how long do we have?" Kellen asked. His voice shook, just a little.

"Shalkan?" she asked.

"A moonturn at least," the unicorn said, tilting his head to the side for a moment of thought. "They'll have to gather the power to set the Bounds, then gather more to awaken the stone Hounds, even with every stonecutter in the City working day and night to craft as many as they'll need. They'll see no need for haste."

"You don't think so?" Idalia looked skeptical.

"How could the Western Hills possibly know what a special treat lies in store for them?" the unicorn said sarcasti-
cally. He tossed his head. "And we'll need every moment of
time between then and now, so we'd better get to it. I'll warn
everyone I can, but there are many I can't approach. You'll
have your work cut out for you. Don't dally."

With a bound, the unicorn was off.

Kellen looked at Idalia and smiled crookedly, though he'd
never felt less like smiling in his life. To be Banished was
bad enough, but now, to be run out of the Wildwood when
it was just starting to feel like home . . .

"Well, I guess I don't have to worry about finishing that
addition after all," he said, trying to put a good face on things.

"And I guess you're going to get to see the Elves," Idalia
said, doing her best to match his bantering tone. "Come on.
We've got work to do."

⌒

BUT as they turned to the work of preparing to warn the
Wildlanders of Armethalieh's intentions, some of his father's
words came back to him, and Kellen found he couldn't recognize himself in the oh-so-dangerous Outlaw Lycaelon had
described.

Him? Know the deepest secrets of the City? When he'd
wandered through his seventeen years there blind and half-
asleep to everything the Mages did? Lycaelon was just putting on airs, trying to make him seem more of a danger than
he was. He wasn't a danger at all. All Kellen wanted was to
be left alone—but telling the Council *that* wouldn't suit Lycaelon's plans. When he couldn't even save himself from the
Hunt without Shalkan's help? Just who did his father think
he was going to fool?

Maybe it didn't matter. Lycaelon was creating a paper ti-
ger, a bogeyman, out of the only material he had at hand,
trying to make Kellen seem to be the heart and ringleader of
some grand conspiracy of evil with designs on the conquest
of Armethalieh, when in reality he wasn't a danger at all, and

never would be. All Kellen had wanted—all he'd *ever* wanted—was to be left alone—

That wouldn't suit Lycaelon's plans, now, would it?

"He's using me as an excuse, isn't he?" Kellen asked.

Idalia sighed. "If it gives you any comfort, yes, at least partly—though I'm sure Lycaelon also hopes that in extending the boundaries, he'll get another chance to hunt you down as well. But I don't think that's the whole of it by any means. I'm sure that even if you were still tucked up safe in Armethalieh, the Arch-Mage would have found *some* bogeyman to wave in the Council's faces. This can't be a spur-of-the-moment thing." She shook her head. "I just wish that I'd known about this sooner. Shalkan's right. It's going to take every moment we've got to get folk warned and out of here."

"At least I *am* here now, and I know the truth," Kellen replied, setting his chin with stubborn determination. "I'd rather know the truth and be here, facing a Scouring Hunt, than be sitting there, safe, believing his lies!"

⟶

IN his small office just off Arch-Mage Lycaelon's far grander one, Chired Anigrel, the Arch-Mage's own confidential secretary, awaited the outcome of the Council session as he worked his way slowly through a large stack of requisition forms, all of which would require the Arch-Mage's personal signature and magickal seal.

He had no doubt of how the session would go. Lycaelon Tavadon was a persuasive orator, with the strength of utter conviction to lend power to his words.

It is always better that way. Sincerity is the best disguise of all.

And all the better for being no disguise. The Arch-Mage had no hidden agenda, no secret double game that lay beneath the surface of his words . . . aside from the rather charming and innocent desire to bend the entire Council wholly to his will or even dispense with it utterly. No, the secret desires and hidden agendas here within the Council House belonged solely to Lycaelon's so-deferential and self-abasing private secretary and whipping-boy, Undermage Anigrel.

Who would have thought that both of Alance's brats would show the Taint? Since Kellen's—The Outlaw's—Banishment, Lycaelon had been harder than ever to deal with. Anigrel could blot out the man's petty life with a lifted finger, but every day he was forced to pretend that he was a mere Journeyman-Undermage, years away from attaining the exalted dignity and power of a High Mage. If not for the brat's defection to the ancient enemy . . .

Anigrel gritted his teeth in annoyance at the lost opportunity that Kellen's departure represented, and kept himself from blotting the parchment beneath his hand with an effort. If he had only managed to get Kellen under his thumb, and then corrupt him utterly, what a prize for his Dark Lady the boy would have been!

"There are no failures, only opportunities," she had told him when he had told his Dark Lady what had happened, making his report as he did once each month at moondark. It was the greatest risk he took, the one moment of unhallowed magic that the Council might conceivably detect. But his talismans, spells, and wards protected him, and in all the years he had played his double-game, he had so far escaped discovery.

"Lycaelon is vulnerable now. Play upon his fears, make him believe that his son could not have escaped him without being cunning as a serpent and powerful as a Demon Prince. He wishes to make Armethalieh strong; foster those ambitions and make them synonymous with his own prosperity. Make the Golden City hated by all the world."

Her mind-voice was like a caress, wakening a hunger that must go eternally unsatisfied, until he could rise high enough in the ranks of the Mages to slake his lesser appetites in the poorest quarters of the City.

Or until the City fell.

"Soon, my impatient love," his Dark Queen purred in his mind. *"Serve me well and you will have all you desire . . ."*

And so, with an idle comment here, an innocent observation there, Anigrel had worked day and night to turn Lycaelon's anger at his son's defection outward to a hatred of the Free Borderers, and to fan a furious envy at Mage Breulin's successful policies of enclosure into a more grandiose plan of his own. That Lycaelon's agents had received the bit of fortunate intelligence about "The Outlaw's" location at the most opportune moment to make an otherwise harmless boy into a nightmare menace was no surprise to Anigrel; he knew perfectly well who had given it to them, and why. The Dark Lady had agents everywhere, and if she could not have Kellen corrupted and in her power, she would use his mere presence on earth to serve her in other ways. Anigrel knew without envy that he was but a small component in a glorious Working, so that one day the Tree of Night would flower and spread its branches against the sky, blotting out the sun once more, this time forever.

And to his well-concealed relief, at last Lycaelon had taken his careful hints to heart. When the news about The Outlaw came, Lycaelon set Anigrel to immediately preparing the preliminary paperwork for a Scouring Hunt of enormous proportions. The Arch-Mage explained nothing, of course, but after laying so much groundwork, Anigrel didn't find it difficult to guess what lay in Lycaelon's mind.

Soon Lycaelon will come and tell you that he has proposed a glorious campaign against the east to extend the boundaries of the City all the way to the High Hills—incidentally running that dreadful and dangerous enemy, The Outlaw, to earth—all in the name of Purity, and that the Council has given it their full support. Be sure to act surprised, Anigrel told himself mockingly.

Chapter Sixteen

Revelry and Ashes

The next fortnight was a desperate race against time. Every village in the Western Hills was busy with harvest and had few people to spare for other tasks, but everyone who could be spared was sent with messages to still other villages and far-flung crofts, warning that Armethalieh was extending its reach into the Western Hills.

Kellen had gone back to Merryvale a few days later to meet with the Council of Elders. He spent two days there, explaining in detail what Armethalieh's rule would mean to them—not only the taxes and tithes, the restrictive laws about what you could buy and sell, but the fact that nonhuman folk weren't welcome in Armethaliehan lands at all, and mixed villages like Merryvale were considered an abomination by the Priests of the Light.

"But . . . why?" Master Eliron and the others kept asking him, and all Kellen could do was shake his head and repeat over and over: "That's just the way it is."

The debate went on endlessly, as if the people of Merryvale simply couldn't comprehend what he told them. They probably couldn't, he reflected. It must seem utter madness to people who had lived as they had for so many decades.

"But surely—if Armethalieh is a city of Law—we, too, will have rights," the Mayor said hopefully. "We will send the City a petition protesting this violation of our sovereignty . . ."

"And I'm sure they will receive it, Master Badelz, and perhaps even read it. And they will tell you that the Law of the City is for the good of all, and that your rights begin and end with doing as you are told by the High Council. They will tell you that the Otherfolk *have* no rights, because they are not human, and the first thing they will demand is that you cast them out of Merryvale. And if you do not do as you are told, they will treat you as an enemy. Please, sir, remember that they have armed men, trained in fighting, to enforce their rule. What do you have? And they have High Mages, who—well, their magic doesn't require the prices that Wild Magic does; they can make it do anything they want to. You've heard about the Outlaw Hunt—Idalia says a Scouring Hunt is a hundred times worse. They're going to set it on all Wildmages, and all Otherfolk. And if you try to resist them they'll set it on you humans." He swallowed hard. "I am . . . I *was* the son of the Arch-Mage, Master Badelz. I know every Mage on the High Council, and they speak with one voice in this. I know what I'm talking about."

Kellen almost wished he hadn't told them that, because of the way they looked at him then, but he knew he had to convince them at any cost. Idalia was right. If the stone Hounds came here and attacked, there would be nothing left of the village.

But he also knew that the Hounds would be looking for him; and for Idalia most of all, once Lycaelon realized she was still alive. Idalia was right. If the two of them could cross the border into Elven lands before the Scouring Hunt was set loose, perhaps the Hounds wouldn't waste too much of their energy on lesser targets.

"Well, if the colt says that, it's good enough for me," a Centaur named Yadrian said firmly. "I'm taking my family and heading east—now—before some greedy Mage decides to hitch me to a plow!"

It turned out that Yadrian spoke for most of the Centaurkin in Merryvale. By the time Kellen left the village, they had already begun dismantling their houses and shops, preparing to head west to places of greater safety. By the time the first Lawspeakers from the City arrived, the only sign that Centaurs had ever been here would be the carvings on the village walls—and the Lawspeakers and Militia would probably insist those be taken down and burned, Kellen thought gloomily. Not that it would matter much. He thought that even the humans who planned to stay and protest Armethalieh's land-grab would be following the Centaurs and the rest of the Otherfolk within a season or two.

⇌

WHILE Kellen was in Merryvale, some of the other free souls who had heard the news came to visit Idalia. Most were afraid, all were angry—some were even angry for Idalia's sake as well as their own.

"How can they do this to you, girl? I've half a mind to ride down into that City of theirs and fetch that high-and-mighty Arch-Mage a clout on the ear he wouldn't soon forget!" Kearn said.

Kearn was a Mountain Trader, making a last pass into the lowlands before the snows made the passes of the High Reaches uncertain. He often stopped to look in on Idalia, and this year she was even gladder to see him than usual, for Kearn traveled with a hardy string of pack mules, and she and Kellen were going to need mobility and speed for themselves and their possessions to make their way west and over the border ahead of the Scouring Hunt.

At least the Centaurs have their own means of transportation, she thought regretfully.

"Ah, Kearn, if I thought it would do any good, I'd send you to him with my blessing. But the High Council Mages are"—she paused, trying to think of a way to make him understand—"they're the worst possible combination of vices. They're greedy, stupid and scared, and utterly convinced that *they* are the only possible people in the world who can, should, and deserve to sit in authority over others, and that's all there is to it." Idalia shrugged.

"Hard weather for the littlefolk, though," Kearn said sympathetically. "They depend on you, you know. From what I hear, the City won't have any care for them."

"Do you think I don't know that?" Idalia said crossly. "If I stay, things will only be worse for them—and I won't be let to help them anyway with my 'evil magic.' " She didn't bother to remind him that *she* would be under a sentence of death for that same magic. "Besides, most of them are leaving now."

"Aye, I thought the Wildwood seemed a bit thin of company as the girls and I rode through," Kearn said, gesturing through the open door of the cabin to where a string of hobbled mules stood placidly behind a large white-stockinged bay. "So the Shining Folk are leaving as well?" he asked, using one of the many names the Mountain Traders had for the shyer Otherfolk.

"Why should they stay where they are not welcomed?" Idalia asked sharply. Shalkan had spread his warnings far and wide, and the dryads, sylphs, undines, gnomes, sprites, brownies, pixies, and fauns had already begun to leave the Wildwood and the surrounding hills. Even the dryads were leaving, difficult though that was for them; they were taking seedlings of their trees, and going. The land would be less fertile and forgiving in their absence—and wouldn't *that* be an unwelcome surprise for the Mages, who must have gotten reports about how lush and productive the western farmland was?

"But I'm glad you're here, Kearn. You're a trader. I want to trade."

Kearn regarded her with wary interest, for he'd traded with Idalia before, and knew she was a sharp bargainer. "I'm not sure I have anything you want with me this trip, Idalia," he began slowly. "Unless you're planning to come home with me, you and the boy. Not that it isn't a great honor, of course . . ."

"You have the mules," Idalia interrupted, cutting off what promised to be a lengthy speech.

"Sell one of my girls?" Kearn looked shocked. "They're like family! Besides, I need them to carry my own things home."

"But you won't be waiting to take on a full load this trip," Idalia pointed out mercilessly. "You'll be heading home today or tomorrow, with only what you have now, because the news I've given you can't wait a few extra sennights to be delivered. If Armethalieh is claiming the Western Hills, how long until it claims the Western Mountains, and everything right up to the Elven borders? For that matter, you'll have a lot of folk heading out of the Hills up into your mountains *now*—right into the teeth of winter, some of them—humans and Centaurs, fauns, and others of the Shining Folk besides. Your folk will need to make ready to receive them."

Kearn grumbled and stared at the ceiling, unable to argue against the truth she set forth so plainly. "Even supposing what you say is true, I'll travel faster if my girls are lightly laden."

"Which is why I wouldn't bring it up unless I had something that would tempt even a hard-hearted old trader like you, Kearn," Idalia said with a ruthless smile.

She walked into the bedroom and came back with a small folded packet of grey material in her hands. "This."

"Is it a shirt, then?" Kearn asked, getting to his feet. He started to shake his head. "Now, Idalia, you know . . ."

"Not a shirt. Better." Idalia shook out the *tarnkappa* and swirled it around herself.

And vanished.

"Do we have a bargain?" she said a moment later, folding the cloak over her hand. "With this you can take game even in deepest winter—you can't be seen, or heard, or smelled. The cloak for my pick of your mules, plus its tack."

Kearn stared, stupefied by what he'd just seen. "Idalia, this . . . you could buy a hundred mules for magic such as this."

"But I only need one. And you have one to sell. And I don't need this. And you want it. I need a mule, if Kellen and I are going to get out of here with more than we can carry on our backs. And you want it, don't pretend you don't." At any other time, she'd have said that teasingly. Not today. "I can't trade with the village; the village needs all its mules for those that are going to try to escape instead of trusting to the tender mercies of the High Council. And besides that, if the *tarnkappa* stays anywhere in the Western Hills the City Mages will only sniff it out and destroy it because it was made with Wildmagery, so there's no point in trading it to someone who's going to try to stay. So . . . do we have a bargain?"

"And it will never fail?" Kearn asked, holding himself back from reaching for it with a great effort.

"If it is not torn or burned. If it is used wisely—not to kill only for the sake of killing, or to kill what you don't intend to eat or use, or to injure instead of kill. If you use it to do murder, Kearn, then I cannot say what will happen to the spell." She gave him a penetrating look. "Remember; it was made with Wild Magic, and if you use it to do something the Wild Magic disapproves of—there's going to be a price. I made it to hunt with."

"I will do none of those things," Kearn promised fervently, abandoning any further attempt to bargain. "I swear by the Wild Magic and the Hunt Law that I will never use this shamefully. Do we have a fair bargain, then?"

"A fair bargain," Idalia agreed, placing the cloak in his hands. "Now let's go look at the mules."

WHEN Kellen returned from Merryvale, the first thing he saw was a friendly dun-colored mule tied out at the edge of the clearing, cropping away meditatively at the bushes.

"Do we have company?" he asked, sticking his head in the door of the cabin. Idalia was sorting through their belongings, picking the things they would take with them in their flight. The rest would be traded away, including the cabin itself.

Though Kellen could ride Shalkan, Idalia would need a horse to ride, and good horses were expensive. Even more expensive now, with so many people fleeing; he feared it would take everything they owned, or near it, to acquire one. But then again, what were they to do with all the things they could not take with them?

Idalia shook out a blanket, and folded it into a tight packet. "No, she's ours. I believe her name is Prettyfoot. A trader friend of mine came by while you were gone, and I was able

to talk him out of one of his pack animals, for a price. He's
on his way back to the High Reaches now with the news
from the City." She added the blanket to a growing pile.
"How did things go in the village?"

Kellen grimaced. He didn't want to tell her what was only
more bad news, but perhaps if she went to the village, they
might believe her.

Or perhaps not. How much more could be said to convince
them?

"I'm not sure if the humans really believed me about how
bad it's going to get, but the Centaurs did," he said, finally.
"They're already packing up to leave. I think the Mayor's
planning to write a letter of protest to the High Council. Fat
lot of good *that's* going to do." Kellen threw himself into a
chair dejectedly.

Idalia sat down on a stool that Kellen had just finished
before—

*Before we found out we weren't going to have a home to
put it in anymore.*

It wasn't fair. *I was just getting used to this place. I might
even have gotten to like it in winter. It was a good stool,
too . . .*

Idalia shook her head. "When are the Centaurs leaving?"
she asked.

"As soon as they can pack—they're even tearing down
their houses to make carts, some of them," Kellen told her.
He'd been amazed to see them hard at work, dismantling
buildings, swiftly turning what had been walls and roofs into
covered carts, which the Centaurs would pull themselves.

"So." Idalia smiled, and he thought she wore an air of grim
satisfaction. "When the City tax collectors arrive, they'll find
a village full of half-dismantled houses. I wish them joy of
that."

"Huh." Oddly enough, that gave Kellen a little satisfaction
himself. "And just wait until they find out that half the farming around here was done by the Centaurs. So much for *those*
taxes." He wondered just how much farming was going to
get done by human farmers, used to having burly Centaurs

helping with the plowing. "I hope Master Badelz says something about that . . ."

"Well, it won't change the plans for annexation, but maybe it will convince the Council that they'd better keep their greedy fingers off the villages until they can sort out just how much revenue they've managed to drive away," Idalia said, though without much hope. "Perhaps that will confuse things long enough for the rest of the humanfolk to make some real plans about what to do now that the City's decided to become so greedy."

"A lot of them think they can make the City see reason," Kellen answered unhappily. "They think if they just send enough petitions, the Council will realize that they've trampled all over the laws of the villages, apologize, and go away."

"And do they also expect that the winter snows will vanish if they create a law to banish them as well?" Idalia asked acidly, then sighed. "Never mind. Who knows? A miracle might happen. And in any event, if the two of us are gone when the Militia arrives and the Scouring Hunt is set loose, maybe the City won't be in such a hurry to enforce its decrees."

TO Idalia's surprise—though not to Kellen's, who had been in on some of the early plans—visitors began arriving at dawn of the day before the two of them were to leave: not only villagers from Merryvale, but others from villages and steadings even farther away. All arrived bearing the makings of a celebration: kegs of beer and wine and mead and cider, wheels of cheese, smoked hams, loaves of honey-glazed bread.

It was quite *literally* dawn. This, Kellen had *not* expected, though he had been awake and working on the preparations for their own departure the moment there was any light in the sky. Idalia had elected to stay abed a little longer than that, but the first of the visitors arrived with a great deal of noise, despite Kellen's attempts to hush them. And there was no keeping the surprise secret at that point.

"I—I—what?" Idalia stammered, staggering out the door of the cabin, still in her sleeping-shift, with her hair tumbled over one sleep-fogged eye, to stare befuddled at the first of the arriving visitors.

"Well, don't stand there gawping, you witless woman! It's a good-bye party—and we've brought good eating, too," Cormo growled, glaring at her with mock ferocity.

The Centaur was nearly unrecognizable, though for an entirely different reason than on his last visit to the clearing. His hair and beard and tail were neatly combed and trimmed. He wore a new smooth-leather vest, bright with embroidery. His coat had been brushed until it gleamed, and his hooves were oiled, trimmed, and polished. And most amazing of all, he was pulling a two-wheeled cart—he could easily have reduced it to kindling with a few well-placed kicks, had he wished—piled high with provisions for the feast. Haneida sat placidly on the seat, a bright shawl wrapped around her.

"You heard what he said. It's a going-away party," Kellen said, coming up behind Idalia and grinning like a fiend.

He was very well pleased with himself over this; planning the party had given his new friends something to look forward to in all of the sadness of the many departures, a bright spot in a very gloomy situation. He was equally pleased with being able to outwit his sister well enough to keep it all secret.

She turned on him, advancing on him and making him back away into the cabin. "You . . . *brat!* You knew this was going to happen!" Idalia sputtered. She was crimson—he thought *not* with rage, but certainly she was as embarrassed as he'd ever seen her. And suddenly there was a wicked look in her eye . . .

"I knew they wanted to have a party to see you off," Kellen said, turning to flee.

But there was nowhere to flee *to*.

"You *told* them when we were leaving!" she growled, and grabbed for his collar.

He tried to dodge out of reach, but it *was* a small cabin. "I might have—*help!*—told someone—*yow!*—that we were leaving tomorrow! But I didn't think they'd start so early! Honest, Idalia! *Help!*"

But it was no good. She'd backed him into the bedroom, tripped him onto the bed, and pummeled him into submission with the pillow.

"Monster! Beast!" she shouted, punctuating each epithet with a whack from a pillow. "Fiend! Serpent! Brother! Letting me walk out into the middle of that in my shift with my hair in rats! Hanging's too good for you. Much too good for you," she added meaningfully, tossing the pillow aside and crooking her fingers into claws.

And then she tickled him until he was helpless and breathless with laughter.

"It is, it really is," Kellen agreed fervently. "Only just don't *tickle* me anymore!"

"Well, get up," Idalia said unfairly, giving him one last swat with the pillow and bouncing off the bed. She scooped up his buckskins (since he'd been stripped to his smallclothes in order to get water wrestled up from the stream for baths) and flung them at him. "Out!"

Kellen dressed in the kitchen, watching the hubbub through the half-opened door. In the few short minutes he'd been gone, the clearing already looked like it belonged to someone else—people were taking down the cookpit and raking the area smooth, taking the logs that were to have gone to become the floor of the addition to Idalia's cabin and making trestle tables of them instead. He could hear the sound of hammers and saws, and smell the scent of fresh sawdust on the air.

Everything in the cabin but what they were taking with them, from the bed to the walls to the planks of the floor, would be going as well once they left, and already the cabin was far barer than it had been when Kellen came. But Idalia had traded to good purpose in the last fortnight, trading large bulky items for small and valuable ones, until after a number of clever trades and a little payment in magic, she had been

able to buy the neat black mare Coalwind, the pride of Badelz's stables, who was tethered contentedly beside Prettyfoot
in a nearby clearing. The fauns adored her and spoiled her
outrageously, bringing her bunches of clover and dryad-
apples. The mare, for all her breeding and promised turn of
speed, seemed to have good manners and a quiet disposition—a good thing, considering the amount of noise Idalia's
farewell party was going to make, if these early preparations
were any indication.

Kellen was just lacing up his boots when Idalia came out
of the bedroom. She glanced out the door, and smiled weakly.
"It looks like it's going to be a very *large* party."

Kellen nodded. "But most of the folk won't be here until
afternoon, Master Badelz and Master Eliron said," he added
helpfully.

For once, Idalia looked to be at a total loss for words.
"Well. I just didn't expect . . . Kellen, these people are losing
their homes, their farms, everything they've grown up with
and worked for because of me . . . and they're throwing me
a party?"

"And because of me, too, don't forget," Kellen pointed out
reasonably. "Lycaelon left you alone for years. He didn't
even let a summer pass before he started hunting me again.
But still . . . a party's a party. It's done them a lot of good to
have something happy to plan. And it's probably the last
good time these folks are going to see for a while. We ought
to let them enjoy it—when Master Badelz suggested it, I
figured it was as much for *them* as for us. Probably more."

"Yes," Idalia said with a sigh, giving in to the inevitable.
"I guess it is. Anyway, I want you to take these out to Coalwind and Prettyfoot and braid them into their manes. I know
a mule doesn't have much mane, but do what you can.
They're just a couple of simple charms that should keep them
from being worried by anything they see or hear. I don't want
them getting spooked and trying to run off."

She handed him two small clear round lumps of yellow
amber, each strung on a short length of red ribbon. Kellen

could feel warmth and serenity radiate from them—a simple spell of comfort and protection.

"Got one for me?" he asked with a smile.

She raised an eyebrow at him. "You're on your own, brother mine. Try the mead."

KELLEN was relieved to find Coalwind and Prettyfoot right where he'd left them. He was glad to see they hadn't been upset enough to try to run off when all the noise started. Then again—since half of the people making the noise were Centaurs, maybe it had sounded like a normal gathering of their own kind to the horse and mule.

He'd paused on his way out to pick up a small bucket of grain—one of the things Idalia had traded for was grain for the animals, since they couldn't afford to let them wander far enough now to keep themselves in natural forage, and once they were on the road they certainly wouldn't be able to go slowly enough to let them feed themselves. Since he was carrying the bucket, both animals looked up alertly when he arrived. Their ears pricked forward when they spotted the grain bucket, and Coalwind whickered flirtatiously.

He set the bucket down and retrieved their halters from a nearby branch, then haltered both animals before removing their hobbles, remembering to hold firmly to their lead-ropes as he did. Kellen wasn't an expert horsemaster, he wasn't even close, but fortunately he'd spent a little time around his father's stables when he'd been younger—before that activity had been added to Lycaelon's "forbidden list"—and Idalia had refreshed his memory on the important points. Always put the halter on *before* taking off the hobbles. Always feed the two animals far apart (Coalwind was a hog and a thief, and would steal Prettyfoot's grain if she could). Don't walk up behind them. Never expect them to be able to see him, even if he thought he was in plain sight; make quiet noise from a distance. Stay out from under their feet unless absolutely necessary. And get used to slobber, because horses don't have table manners.

Though the rules applied more to horses than to mules (and *none* of them applied to unicorns!), it didn't do any harm to treat the two animals equally. Coalwind was trying to pull toward the bucket, but he led her firmly over to a tree and tied her there with close attention to the knots, then led Prettyfoot to another tree several yards away. Only then did he get the grain and pour it out on the ground where the animals could get at it.

While they were eating, Kellen braided the charms into their manes. Coalwind was easy; the only difficulty was getting her to hold still while he did it, for she seemed to have the idea firmly fixed in her head that if she could just investigate every bit of his clothing, she'd find a treat (which was often the case on other occasions). But he got the charm securely braided into her mane at last. And the warm glint of the amber against her dark coat was a very pretty sight.

But Prettyfoot, as Idalia had predicted, was much harder to attach the charm to. The mule's mane was more like Shalkan's—a short stiff brush running the length of her neck— and there was no possible way he could braid *anything* into it.

At last he settled for tying it onto the halter to dangle down her forehead. He'd thought about tying it into her tail, but she'd probably eat it, and even if amber wasn't going to do the insides of a mule any harm, Idalia would be annoyed to lose a nice big piece of amber as a mule-treat. He thought that would hold, at least for tonight.

And tomorrow they'd be gone.

A peculiar sadness filled Kellen at the thought. Not homesickness precisely, because he hadn't really been here long enough for this place to become home. But it might have become home, given a little more time, and he felt an unsettled grief at the lost opportunity.

Kellen pushed the thought aside. There were others whose suffering and loss were far greater—both now, and in the moonturns to come.

Had the High Council lost its tiny collective mind? He knew the regular citizens of Armethalieh didn't question the Mages' decisions—hell, they didn't even *know* about half of them—but surely they'd *notice* that the City had suddenly decided to claim hundreds—no, *thousands*—of miles of new territory for no particular good reason? The Mages would have to tell them. It wasn't something that could be done out-of-sight, like so many of the Mages' dealings. The City might claim there would be an increase in wealth for the City, but there would also be an increase in cost *to* the City—both magickal cost, which maybe the common folk wouldn't notice, but also the cost in people to send to hold those new lands, which was why the people would have to know: those Militia troops he'd seen in Idalia's vision were going to have to come from somewhere, after all.

And troops had to be paid and provisioned—fed and clothed and given horses and armor and weapons—and the money for all of that had to come from somewhere. New taxes, which maybe the common folk wouldn't notice, but also the cost in people—drawn from the Home Farms, of course—sent to hold the new territory; those Militia troops he'd seen spoken of in Idalia's vision.

And if the villages fought back . . . ? More troops would surely be sent.

Then the cost goes up. And they'll notice that, that's for sure, Kellen thought bleakly. Everywhere he'd ever gone in the City—outside of the Mage Quarter, of course—taxes had *always* been a major topic of discussion. But what would the people *do* about it?

He had no idea.

But—probably nothing. So long as nothing changes for each of them personally, they probably won't care. The Council has kept other things secret, why not this?

It wouldn't be that hard, so long as the Mages were able to keep the fact that there was actual fighting going on a secret. If they actually sent non-Mages outside the walls— Kellen supposed it was possible; he wouldn't put anything past the Council at this point—all they had to do was just remove those inconvenient memories from the soldiers once the men returned, and, oh, tell them they'd been to the Out Islands, or something. Even if people from Armethalieh actually *died*, it could be covered up. Tell grieving relatives that their sons died of a snakebite, or sudden fever, or an accidental fall. All those things could happen in the City. Just make sure that relatives of the dead didn't get together and discover how *many* "accidents" there were. The bodies would be given back to the Light, and the Mages would be able to keep their dirty little secrets.

With careful management, no one would ever find out what was really happening, at least, not in Armethalieh.

Not that anyone ever did know what was *really* happening.

"Not in Armethalieh," Kellen said aloud, watching the mule's ears swivel around to catch the words.

When the animals had finished their breakfast, Kellen took them down to the stream for a drink.

⌐

HE was standing beside them, not thinking about anything in particular, when there was a splash at his feet. He looked down.

There was a selkie in the water. Kellen had seen them only rarely; the sleek, dark-furred, big-eyed creatures were shy of humans, preferring deep woods and twilight, although once they got over their shyness, they were as playful as otters and twice as amusing, because of their keen senses of humor. Many of them lived in or near the ocean, where they were usually mistaken for seals by those humans who managed to glimpse them. This one blinked up at him, its large silver eyes a startling paleness in its dark-furred face.

"Kellen isss leaving?" the selkie asked, its long whiskers bristling as it spoke. "Idalia isss leaving?"

"Yes," Kellen said. He was surprised to see it at all. He'd thought all the river-folk, selkies and undines and water-sprites, were already safely gone, warned by Shalkan and the others who carried his message. "And you should leave, too.

The City is coming. The Mages don't like your kind. They're sending a Scouring Hunt." And even if stone mastiffs couldn't swim very well—not at all, in fact—that hardly mattered, since they didn't need to breathe. Land or water, no place was safe.

"I go," the selkie agreed, speaking slowly and carefully. Its short sharp-toothed muzzle wasn't well shaped for forming human speech—the selkies' own language consisted of guttural barks and high-pitched chittering—but selkies loved all things new and strange, and found the effort of speaking to humans in their own language enormously entertaining. "Take fissshhh, too. *Alll* fisshhh. We take." Its round silver eyes crinkled in merriment, inviting Kellen to share the joke.

Kellen blinked, slowly understanding what the selkie was telling him. All the fish? From all the rivers? Gone?

He began to laugh. "You do that, friend. Take the fish. All the fish. And good luck to you."

The selkie reached up out of the water, extending its paw to Kellen, fingers spread wide. Kellen could see the thick webbing between the digits, the long curved gleaming nails that could shear through the toughest scales. He clasped the hand gently, and felt an answering pressure in return.

"Good-bye," Kellen said. "Fare you well."

The selkie released his hand, and slipped beneath the surface of the water, invisible once more.

Shaking his head in amusement, Kellen led Coalwind and Prettyfoot back into the woods to fresh grazing. In a few hours he'd come back and lead them in closer to the cabin, tying them up securely for the night so they couldn't wander. He had no desire to spend several hours come tomorrow's dawn trying to find them!

"No fear of that," Shalkan said, stepping daintily out of the woods, hidden until that moment, though how something the size of a pony and whiter than new velum could hide that easily, Kellen could never figure out. "I'll keep an eye on them."

"Will you?" Kellen regarded the unicorn with relief. "Thanks. That'll be a great help."

Shalkan dipped his horn, acknowledging the thanks. "I was waiting for you to ask."

Kellen shrugged. "I didn't want you to miss the party if you were in the mood for it. It just seems like I'm asking you for so much already."

"You mean, being your noble conveyance to the Elven lands?" The unicorn snorted. "I'd be going there anyway. If it's a choice between that and facing another dozen packs, I'd say it's no choice at all, my friend. And you'll find the Elves . . . interesting. Humans do."

Kellen would have dearly loved to ask Shalkan more about the Elves, but this was no time to get into one of the unicorn's elliptical conversations. Idalia already blamed him for springing the party on her. If he disappeared for most of the day, she'd probably arrange to have him drowned in a keg of cider. So he abandoned the interesting topic in favor of telling Shalkan what the selkie had told him.

"They'd take the fish from the lakes as well, if they could, as the dryads would take the fruit from their trees," Shalkan said. "The City will find no welcome in the Western Hills when it comes, nor do I think the farmers who remain will have an easy life. They will not thank the City for that."

"No," Kellen agreed glumly. He hobbled the mare and the mule once again, and turned them out to graze, retrieving the bucket from where he'd left it.

"Well, see you later. I'll save you some honey-cakes."

"See that you do," Shalkan said with mock severity, switching his tufted tail. "And if anyone's brought any of those maple-syrup candies, and I find out you didn't save me at least two . . ."

"At least!" Kellen promised, and hurried back toward the cabin.

Shalkan, of course, stayed out of sight with the mule and the horse—he wasn't at all comfortable, Kellen had noticed, with so many people about, most of them (probably) not virginal—and Kellen was just a little bit curious about how Shalkan and Idalia were going to handle traveling in close proximity together, though both of them agreed it was necessary. Finally he decided there was no sense worrying about it. He'd be finding out. And soon, too.

◆

KELLEN spent the rest of the day helping with the preparations for the party. His own and Idalia's arrangements for leaving were all but finished, and there was really nothing left for him to do there. Besides, working kept him from thinking. And there was plenty of work to do: helping to put up the poles that would hold the various awnings and canopies, climbing trees to hang lanterns (knowing he—or some-one—would have to climb them again later to light the lanterns), fetching and carrying kegs and bundles, all the while sniffing glorious smells and stealing tastes of delicacies that would be unveiled later.

And hearing people talk about the days ahead, which sometimes meant hearing more than he wanted to.

◆

"I'M not going without you, you damned foolish old besom," Cormo rumbled, in what was—for him—a quiet undertone. It was entirely audible ten feet away, where Kellen was digging a new firepit.

"And I'm not going," Haneida said peaceably. "These old bones are much too old to be bundled up like a goosedown mattress and hie themselves up into the mountains like some-one's luggage. And what would I tell my bees? I'm staying."

Cormo stamped his hoof. "Then I'm staying too, you senile old half-wit."

Haneida tsked. "Such love-talk! Cormo, your mother fell in love with a donkey. You can't stay, and I won't go," Haneida said reasonably.

"I promised," Cormo growled in dangerous tones. "And I'm not leaving you with nobody to take care of you."

Suddenly Kellen realized that there was more at stake here than one stubborn old woman, and an equally stubborn Centaur. Cormo had promised the Wild Magic to haul Haneida's cart to market for a year and a day. Very quietly, Kellen set down his shovel and went looking for Idalia.

He found her inside the cabin, with several of the village women. All the furniture had already been taken outside, even the bed, and the doors had been removed to serve as tables. Their equipment was in the bedroom; they'd sleep on their bedrolls on the floor tonight and get an early start in the morning. The main room was filled with more provisions; stacked hampers and sturdy boxes, making it look less like a cabin and more like a small supply pantry.

"Idalia, can I talk to you? Alone?"

Idalia excused herself and came outside. It took a few minutes before they could find a place that was reasonably private.

"It's Cormo," Kellen said before Idalia could say anything. "I heard him arguing with Haneida. He's saying he won't leave with the last of the other Centaurs when they go. I know Merana's still here, but that's because Master Eliron's going and she's going with him. But Haneida says she won't leave, and Cormo says he won't leave without her." His brow furrowed with worry; it didn't seem *right* that Cormo should do all the improving he had only to be punished for trying to keep his word and his pledge!

"I think he's worried about what will happen if he doesn't pay his part of the Price for the Healing you did for him, and that's why he won't leave, so if you could just *talk* to him . . ."

Kellen's voice trailed off. Idalia was smiling and shaking her head.

"Brother mine, I love you dearly, but sometimes you can be as sweet and dim as a—as a toffee-covered lantern! I've already spoken to Cormo, days ago—the Gods would never punish someone by forcing them to keep to the terms of a bargain when a situation had changed so drastically. Cormo knows nothing will happen to him if he doesn't stay and pay the price he agreed to—and just between you and me, what he's done for Haneida in the last fortnight has been payment in full! No. The reason he doesn't want to leave her is because he's afraid of what will happen to her when she's left all alone; she still refuses to move down into the village, even though half the houses are standing empty now. He isn't wrong to worry, but she's right, too: she's far too frail to survive the journey into the High Hills with winter coming on."

That put a different complexion on things, but it didn't make things any better, at least from where Kellen was standing.

And Haneida wasn't the only one . . . There were so *many* old folks in the village, too old to move. How would the Militia and the Mages treat them?

For that matter, what would happen to Cormo? "Oh, Idalia, what are they going to do? What are they all going to do?" Kellen asked helplessly.

"Their best," Idalia said grimly. "That's all anyone can do. You, me, Cormo, Haneida . . . all any of us can do is our best. Now come. You're the one who told me that a party was the best medicine for future ills. Smile. It's the least we can do for them. And we owe them that."

⌐

BY late afternoon the farewell party had begun in good earnest, when the musicians began tuning up and the much-awaited cold dishes were finally set out on the long tables. The roasted meats would not be ready for several hours yet, but that hardly mattered. The drinking and feasting would go on all night, from what Kellen could tell.

There would be some speeches of well-wishing, but as Master Badelz had told Kellen when he'd arrived an hour before, it was only a fool who attempted to catch the attention of a hungry crowd. People who had been working or traveling all day were looking forward to food and gossip and lively tunes, not speeches, the Mayor of Merryvale said. A few hours of that, and they'd be ready to listen to the likes of him!

Kellen hadn't seen so many people in one place since he'd left Armethalieh. They filled the entire clearing and spread into the woods beyond—not only humans and the few Centaurs who hadn't yet left, but the Otherfolk that anyone could see: Fauns and brownies, pixies and gnomes. Even those folk invisible to those without a touch of the Sight were here: dryads clustered among the trees, sylphs in the air above them, flower-sprites and forest-fae flitting among the leaves.

Now the musicians, having fortified themselves with a quick visit to the kegs, were tuning up and preparing to play.

One of them was a Centaur, one of the few who had remained. He was the oldest Centaur Kellen had ever seen. His hair and beard and tail were quite white, and his chestnut coat had faded with time to a very pale pink. He moved with the slow certainty of age, and a young blacksmith had to lend his shoulder to help the ancient one gain the musicians' stage, for Centaurs, like the horses they partially resembled, were clumsy around steps of any kind. The crowd watched in hushed expectancy; even Idalia, standing beside Kellen in the crowd, seemed excited.

"Oh, I never thought I'd get to hear Verlin play one last time! You're in for a treat, Kellen," she said happily.

Once settled on the stage, Verlin carefully removed a carry-bag from his shoulder, and extracted the strangest item Kellen had seen. It must be a musical instrument, but what kind? It had strings, but it was too small to be a lute, and the wrong shape besides. Besides, he had a bow in his other hand, and the only instrument Kellen knew that used a bow was a psaltery.

Then Verlin tucked the flat paddle-shaped not-a-lute beneath his chin and began to play.

A wail of unfamiliar sound assaulted Kellen's ears. He'd never heard anything like it in his life, and he wasn't sure if he wanted to now; the sound made him think of riding Shalkan through the midnight forest during his escape and drinking a pint tankard of mead both at once. It took his breath away and made him want to yell and run in circles—at the same time, if possible. The drum and pipe sharing the stage with Verlin joined in, and so did the spectators, stamping and clapping to the rhythm of the music. Some stepped back to watch, others came forward to dance.

Idalia grabbed Kellen's hands and dragged him in among the dancers.

"Idalia—*no!* I don't—" Kellen yelled.

"Relax—you learned this one back in the City!" she shouted back.

And it was true, though there the steps were slow and decorous, and certainly did not involve whirling your partner high into the air to be caught by another. But they were the same steps, and once Kellen realized that, he let the music take him, stamping and whirling through the complicated figures with an ease that made his partners shout and whistle appreciatively.

⌐

"WHAT . . . *is* . . . that thing?" Kellen asked his sister, when the music had changed to a slower piece to give the dancers time to catch their breath, and he and Idalia had gone in search of refreshment. Their progress was slow, for everyone wished to say personal good-byes to the two of them, but at last they had a moment to themselves.

"Verlin calls it a fiddle-faddle. They come from the High Reaches. I'm sure the Mountain Traders have offered them to the City, but I don't suppose they've ever been licensed there." Idalia snorted. "Why ask? Of course they haven't. 'Lute and harp were good enough for our grandfathers, certainly they are good enough for us,'" she said, in a fair imitation of Lycaelon at his most patronizing.

"And flute," Kellen said helpfully. "And one or two other things. We got a bowed psaltery five years ago because we already had the plucked and hammered kind. But, oh, Idalia—it makes such wonderful music! And just think of all the other things out here in the world that never made it through the Golden Gates! Here, and beyond the Sea, and, oh, *everywhere!*"

It just made his heart ache to think of it. All the opportunities lost . . . all the things that could have been, and never were. It was enough to make you weep. . . .

⟶

WATCHING Kellen's rapt excited face as he spoke of Verlin's fiddle-faddling, Idalia blessed the old Centaur for staying behind to play here tonight. Since their discovery of the High Council's plans, Kellen had been dangerously closed-in and angry, and anger was a perilous self-indulgence for a Wildmage.

It was not that those who walked the path of the Wild Magic were expected to detach themselves from human emotion, for that road led quickly to the closed-off asceticism of the High Magick, with all its pitfalls. Wildmages lived *in* the world, not cut off from it, and were expected to participate in all its griefs, terrors, and loves.

But anger was a destructive emotion, more so than any other. It destroyed the capacity for clear sight that a Wildmage needed above all things, and the first thing it destroyed was self-judgment. A Wildmage poisoned by anger might never even know it until it was too late, thinking only that he or she was filled with a righteous need to bring justice and balance back into the world.

That the Wildmage's spells would turn against them and fail them, that the price exacted would be too heavy to bear for a spell cast in blind anger, would be cold consolation to Idalia if the caster was Kellen.

But everything was going to be all right. She was sure of it now. Sometimes Idalia forgot how young her little brother was, how sheltered a life he'd led until the last few moon-turns. He was only seventeen; far too young to bear the burden of guilt for the flight of the inhabitants of the Western Hills into unknown peril.

Until tonight she'd been afraid that the guilt would sour him, the anger work in him like a canker, and his thoughts turn into darker paths. It was enough to unsettle a far older and steadier soul . . . but Kellen could not have responded so to Verlin's music if the toxins of blind revenge were working in him.

She was furious with their father and the Council, and had fought a hard and bitter battle against her own rage to keep it from affecting her. *Why* couldn't Lycaelon leave well enough alone? Kellen was gone from the City; as good as dead to him. What in the name of the Gods was *driving* the man on this suicidal course? The City could never possibly hold the territory Lycaelon so rashly claimed. The Wildlanders would fight back eventually; the western farmers weren't Lycaelon's tame cowed lowland villagers, nor yet his utterly pacified Armethaliehans.

Yes, if they resisted, they would lose. If they fought, they would die. And the High Council might get its own way for a time, "ruling" over lands they had emptied of the people who had lived and worked there.

But High Magick wasn't free for the asking. Like the Wild Magic, it, too, had a price and must be paid for. If the High Council had to spend more and more of its power to pacify its new Western Holdings, where would they go to replace it?

And what would happen when, in the fullness of its ambition, the High Council of Armethalieh turned its attention from the Western Hills to the High Hills?

Idalia smiled her hard wolf-smile. The Mountain Traders had nowhere else to go: their lands backed directly on the Elven borders, and the Elves would not give up their lands for the asking. And even if the Mountainfolk *did* have somewhere they could flee to, they wouldn't: the Mountain Traders had hated the City for generations with a cordial and stubborn hate. They hated the Council and its policies nearly as much as they loved their wild mountains—they would not abandon them for the Elven forests even if that was possible. And the Mountain-folk were far from helpless. By now, most of the Wildmages that had been driven out of every other place that Armethalieh had taken for its own were gathering in the High

Reaches. The Mountain Traders would be able to call upon magical defenders of their own.

Armethalieh would regret its greediness. Perhaps not this year. Perhaps not in ten years. But if it pursued its present policies, the City was in for the fight of its life. Perhaps even a war . . . and that meant the Mages would be using their High Magick on the war instead of at home on the City. Magick that had once gone to provide the most comfortable possible life for the citizens of the Golden City, the City of a Thousand Bells, would be squandered—to the Armethaliehans' way of thinking—invisibly and unnoticeably, far from home and hearth. And what would Armethalieh's citizens say when their comforts were abruptly withdrawn, to no purpose they could see?

There would be trouble. Trouble within, trouble without.

Change.

And it's your own fault, Lycaelon Tavadon. You could have left us in peace, left the Western Hills and the High Reaches in peace, lived out your life as Arch-Mage of the High Council and had everything you ever wanted within those eight walls. But you let greed and pride and anger blind you, and now you're going to destroy yourself.

Along with a great many innocent bystanders.

Idalia sighed. Her shoulders drooped tiredly. She could see it so clearly, not with magic, but as a thing of logic and the mind, the way an Elven *xaqiue*-master could see the outcome of the game once the first piece was shifted on the board.

But things might yet come out differently. All the pieces might not yet be on the board. She could only hope that was true, because the one thing she *did* know was that terrible as the picture her imaginings painted was, there was nothing for her to do to avert the future she saw. The only thing she could do was what she *was* doing: remove herself and Kellen beyond the City's reach, into the land of the Elves.

That it was the one place in all the world she'd sworn she'd never return to was irrelevant. It was the only choice on a short list of possible destinations.

And this should teach her not to swear by "never" and "forever."

＝

THE Mayor's speech, when he finally made it, was short—concentrating entirely on what a wonderful person Idalia was and how sorry they all were to see her go, without one word about the City—and followed by several others by other Guildmasters and village leaders in the same vein. Kellen's suspicions had been completely lulled by the time he was seized and lifted up onto the platform.

He stared down at the sea of waiting faces with dawning shock and horror.

"They're waiting to hear a few words from you, boy," the Mayor said, nudging him gently. "You're her brother, after all."

"Uh . . . hi. I'm Kellen," Kellen said. "I guess you know that."

Appreciative laughter and cheers, with calls of "Good start!" and "Go on!" and "Tell us something we don't know!"

What could he say? Kellen stared out at all of them. He had to say something! "I—" He stopped. Silence spread out from the speaker's platform like ripples from a flung stone. Everyone was looking at him expectantly, waiting for him to go on. He stared around wildly, willing Idalia to come rescue him, but his sister was nowhere in sight. He took a deep breath. He'd faced an Outlaw Hunt, and it hadn't been harder than this.

"I haven't been here long," he said at last. "I wish it could have been longer. I haven't been very many places, but this is the best place I've ever been. Thank you—all of you—for being so kind. For being our friends. For welcoming me and—and giving me a place to belong, even if I didn't get to enjoy it for long." Suddenly inspired, he bowed—a full, courtly, City-style bow.

Everyone cheered. Before they could quiet down and ask

him to say anything else, Kellen turned and quickly jumped down off the platform.

It was almost dark by now, and Kellen took advantage of that to make his way to the edges of the party. He thought about it, and then kept going. There was something sort of *unsettling* in the air. He wasn't completely sure of what it was, but for the first time in many sennights, he was reminded again of the vow he'd sworn to Shalkan. Chastity *and* celibacy. He wasn't sure how or why, but he didn't think either promise would be really easy to keep back at the party, between the music and the dancing and the kegs of beer, wine, mead, and hard cider being tapped in such abundance. Like his own speech, the gaiety had a sharp air of desperation under it, the music more than a hint of melancholy; combine that with a little too much to drink and—

And things might get out of hand. Quickly. Maybe he'd just go and keep Coalwind and Prettyfoot company until things quieted down a little bit.

Honey-cakes. I promised Shalkan some honey-cakes. And those little maple candies.

Kellen stopped a few yards up the forest path, fretting. The sweets would all be gone if he didn't go back for them now. He sighed, looking back at the lights in the clearing. It was quiet out here, and he could hear the music drifting enticingly through the trees behind him. It was a little chilly, and back there were fires and warmth. The air smelled of damp earth, and back there were the scents of cooking meat, mulled ale, and woodsmoke. He knew it would be a bad idea to go back there. He'd gotten away once by doing the unexpected. He couldn't expect to be so lucky twice, and of course everybody wanted to wish both him and Idalia well. And with those wishes came tankards of drink from the men, and kisses from the women and girls. One or two of those farewell kisses had left him feeling flushed and uncomfortable already, and those were from the girls he knew the least . . .

But he'd *promised* . . .

As he stood in the darkness of the forest he realized that it *was* dark here under the trees, too dark to find his way, and the moon wasn't going to be high enough to show him the way to where he'd left the horses for several hours.

Great. Now I do have to go back. Honey-cakes and a lantern...

He looked back at the clearing, and for a moment had the unsettling impression that one of the lights was swelling like a frog about to sing. Then he realized that it was moving. Away from the party. Moving toward him.

Kellen slithered behind the nearest big tree and waited.

Merana came walking slowly down the trail, placing each hoof slowly and carefully. She had a basket over one arm, and was holding a lantern high over her head and talking to herself in a loud whisper.

"Idalia said he'd be out here somewhere. Kellen? Are you here? Kellen?" She held the lantern down near the ground and peered at it, looking for footprints that weren't there, then straightened, and peered at the trees on either side of the path.

"Kellen?" she called in a louder voice. "Are you here? Kellen?"

When Kellen didn't immediately answer, Merana took another couple of hesitant steps down the path, then stopped, fidgeting and whispering to herself again. "She must have been wrong. Why would he be wandering around alone when he could be snuggled under a blanket and a cart with a nice warm willing—"

Kellen decided he didn't want to hear any more, and stepped out from behind the tree. Merana squeaked, and for a moment he thought she was going to rear up like a startled horse.

"Kellen?" she said out loud. "What are you doing here? You gave me such a fright!"

"Sorry," Kellen said. He couldn't exactly say what he was doing out here, because he didn't really know himself. "Idalia sent you to look for me?"

"Uh-huh." Merana nodded. "She packed a basket for you, with a warm cloak and everything. Are you *sure* you don't want to stay for the rest of the dancing and all?" she added pleadingly, switching her tail so that the bells braided into it jingled. "I've—we've hardly gotten warmed up."

He shrugged. "Guess not. It's a great party, though."

"The best," Merana said eagerly. "Almost as fine as Harvest Home—though I don't know as anybody's going to be doing much celebrating of that this year," she added, with a hint of that dark mood that seemed to be underlying everything at the festivities. She set down the basket and held out the lantern. Kellen took it.

"Won't you need it?" he asked.

She shook her head. "I can make my way back by the lights, fear you not. Well, I guess this is good-bye, then. A kiss for luck?" she added hopefully.

Kellen took a step back, shaking his head apologetically.

"I was right then," Merana said with satisfaction. "It *is* a Wild Magic thing! Oh, don't worry—I won't tell. I can keep my mouth shut when I ought. And don't you worry about Cormo, either—Haneida and I have him all settled between us."

"Good," Kellen said, and meant it. "You take care of him. He needs—somebody to boss him around and make it stick, I guess. If he gets that, he just might turn out all right."

"He might." Merana's spirit of mischief must have fought clear at that moment, for she added saucily, "Still, it's too bad you aren't coming back to the party. You'll miss the rest of the dancing—and other things besides."

She turned away, and with a last flirt of her tail, trotted back quickly toward the lights and the music.

It's the "other things" I'm worried about, I guess, Kellen thought doubtfully.

He set down the lantern, and investigated the basket. A warm cloak was folded on the top—not necessary just now, but if he was going to be spending most of the night out in the woods, it might be later. And beneath it, a selection of delicacies from the feast, including a generous number of honey-cakes and several patties of maple sugar.

Thank you, Idalia.

Kellen picked up the lantern and the basket and went to find the animals and Shalkan.

*

"I wondered how long it would take you to figure things out," the unicorn said when he arrived.

"You could have told me," Kellen grumbled, setting the basket down and hooking the lantern over the stub of a branch. The horse and the mule dozed placidly nearby.

"You might have said that the girls would be"—he felt himself blushing—"well, *frisky*. Especially Merana."

"Where's the fun in that?" Shalkan asked. "This was an easy one, and I was nearby to warn you if necessary. There may be others that aren't as obvious, and I might not be around for them."

"So I'm supposed to consider this a learning experience?" Kellen asked, spreading the cloak on the ground and beginning to unpack the basket.

"Are those honey-cakes I smell?" Shalkan responded eagerly.

*

IT was very late—or very early—by the time that Kellen, carrying the empty basket and leading the two animals on their halters, returned to the clearing. The chill had turned to cold, but he'd been more than warm enough in the cloak. He was young enough to think a night without sleep to be a grand prelude to a long day's ride, and in fact he'd even dozed for a few hours before Shalkan had nudged him awake. It was still dark, but it would be dawn in an hour or two, and he knew that Idalia wanted to be on the road as soon as there was light to see by. There was a hint of fog in the air, and a suggestion that in a day or two, there might be rain.

The canopies and garlands were all still there—they, like the cabin itself, would be removed over the coming days and taken elsewhere. The clearing was quiet, if not silent, and far from empty; though most of the partyers had gone home or off to nearby villages there were still a few late revelers remaining, sitting and lying in twos and threes and fours, some sleeping, some talking together in quiet contented tones.

Kellen stopped to tie the animals to a tree, then walked into the clearing. Almost at the cabin door, Kellen passed a tangle of sleeping fauns. They smelled strongly of mead, and some kind soul had rolled them into a cloak. As he watched they squirmed over one another, as blissfully indifferent to their surroundings as a basketful of puppies.

He turned and walked into the cabin.

Just as he suspected, Idalia was already up and dressed, but in clothes he'd never seen before. Gone was the woodland ranger dressed in beaded buckskin, horn, and feathers: the boots and tunic, cloak and breeks Idalia wore now would have looked unremarkable anywhere from the High Reaches to the gates of Armethalieh herself: sturdy wool cloth, dyed with indigo and butternut, sturdy leather riding boots with hard soles and stacked heels to hold the stirrups, with a wide felt hat to shade her eyes and face from wind and weather . . . Idalia looked like a stranger.

She glanced over at his entrance, and saw his startlement, and smiled crookedly. "Quite a different look for me, isn't it? There's a set for you, too. It's what they wear in the High Hills; that Mountain Trader I bought Prettyfoot from felt guilty about his good fortune and threw in a few trade gifts, and then I did a little tailoring. We have a lot of territory to ride through, and we won't stand out as much this way. The boots I ordered in Merryvale; when you're running, it's always a good idea to have boots you can trust. Go ahead; I'll start getting the beasties ready."

She picked up an armful of saddlepads and blankets and walked out. Kellen went on into the empty room that had once been the bedroom.

The shutters were closed and pegged now, and the room seemed close and airless, but a fat candle stuck in a wall sconce gave sufficient light for Kellen to see what he was doing. A similar set of traveling clothes were laid out for him: cloak and gloves, too.

After spending so many sennights in supple buckskin, wool and homespun were scratchy and harsh against his skin, and the new clothes itched. Kellen sighed, stamping his feet into the boots. He only hoped it wouldn't be too hard to get used to them after wearing moccasins for so long.

But at last he was dressed, and there was no more point to delaying. He even spared a moment to wish for a mirror to see himself in, though he knew all he'd get would be a shock.

He pushed aside the deerskin curtain and stepped back out into the main room, his new cloak folded over one arm. Idalia thrust a comb into his hand.

"Comb your hair out, and braid it, or tie it back. You won't want to be combing knots and twigs and heaven knows what else out of it at the end of the day," she said, brushing past him to get at Coalwind's saddle and bridle.

Kellen started in on his hair, and discovered to his dismay that there were knots and twigs in it *now*. But he managed to drag the comb all the way through it at least once, and then discovered that in one of the pockets of his new breeks was a long leather tie-band, ornamented with some of Idalia's careful beadwork. So they wouldn't be leaving the Wildwood completely behind! He looped it around his unruly hair, then picked up the heavy wooden packsaddle, and followed Idalia outside.

The day was already appreciably lighter than when he'd gone in, but the world was still the ghostly no-color of false dawn. Out in the forest, wisps of fog drifted among the trees, like spirits. Idalia had led both animals up to the door while he'd been dressing. She'd just finished tightening Coalwind's girths, and Kellen set the packsaddle on the ground and held the mare steady while Idalia soothed her into accepting the bit and bridle. Coalwind was fascinated by Idalia's trader hat, and kept trying to seize it and pull it off Idalia's head; Idalia finally let her have it for an instant, taking it back once the last buckle was tight.

"There you are, my girl. I'm afraid you'll be less frisky by the end of the day." She sighed. "Of course, so will I."

"Me too," Kellen offered. "It's not like either of us have done a lot of riding lately."

"True enough," his sister replied. "Maybe there'll be a village inn up the road; Greenpoint is supposed to be about a day's ride from here. If we're lucky, we'll sleep indoors tonight, but we can't count on doing that very often."

He nodded, but he couldn't help thinking: *And maybe less often the closer it gets to the time that the City is planning on sending in their flunkies.* Travelers wouldn't exactly be welcome at that point, when more and more fugitives would be on the road. And any one of them might be a City spy.

Idalia tethered the mare once more, and turned to help Kellen with the packsaddle. Prettyfoot accepted it with good grace; the mule was an experienced campaigner, and was used to early-morning departures.

Once both animals were tacked up, Idalia and Kellen made several more trips back and forth into the cabin to load the mule with their supplies. Kellen's discarded buckskins joined Idalia's in the pack reserved for last-minute things; they might well need them again sometime. Idalia tied everything in place with a speed and efficiency that led Kellen to believe that she'd done this before.

"It's easy enough, really," she said when she caught him looking. "You'll learn it yourself, with time. Balance the weight evenly from side to side for the beast's sake, also make sure that there's nothing that can dig or press or gall; just as if you were carrying the load yourself—and just as if you were carrying the load yourself, don't ask them to carry beyond their strength. A mule won't do it, and a donkey can carry a pack bigger than it is, but a horse will try for you until it kills itself. Heavier to the front than the back, just as you would want the weight higher than lower in your own pack. Make sure nothing can shift or crumple. Put the things you'll need on the way where you can get at them without unpacking everything. Make the whole easy to load and unload fast. All it takes is common sense and a little experience. You've got the one, and you'll have plenty of opportunity to get the other."

At last the packing was done, and Idalia went back inside

one last time to see if they'd missed anything. She came out with two steaming wooden cups, and a second hat tucked under her arm.

"Hot cider to wake us up—we'll stop in a few hours for a better breakfast—and your hat. Now you can be a proper Mountain Trader."

Kellen took the hat and placed it on his head. It was thick felt, dyed a deep green to match his clothes—the only other time he'd seen such fabric was in the winter boots some of the City laborers wore—and quite the most outlandish item he'd ever seen. It had two long dangling leather cords that could apparently be used to tie the hat upon the head, so that despite its enormous brim—quite as wide as a cartwheel, in Kellen's untutored opinion—it could not be blown off. It was like wearing one of those round sunshades that fine ladies of the City carried on sticks to protect their lily-white complexions from the sun.

It was rather dashing, actually.

Kellen decided he liked it.

Hat in place, Kellen drank the cider—quickly, before it cooled. He set the cup down on the doorstep, realizing with a pang that it was all real. They were leaving here, *now,* and they were never coming back.

"Let's go," Idalia whispered; there was a harsh tone in her voice that startled him, and he turned to peer at her.

He could see by her face that she was trying hard to be calm, not to give in to the same sense of loss that he felt. She swung quickly up into the mare's saddle and started off. Kellen walked behind, leading the mule.

It might have been some last spell of the Wild Magic, or simple kindness on the part of those revelers who remained, but no one called after them to wish them a final good-bye.

⌐

THEY headed along the path away from the clearing and into the Wildwood in silence as the sky continued to lighten and the morning birds started the dawnchorus. Fog still lingered in hollows and low-lying ravines, but it was dissipating. When Kellen looked up through gaps in the trees to the hills, he saw sunlight gilding the tops of them, and the sky was a pleasant blue dotted with white, puffy clouds.

Eventually Shalkan would join up with them, and Kellen hoped it would be soon: his new boots didn't hurt yet, but that didn't mean he wanted to walk any great distance in them.

The cabin was long out-of-sight, and they were past the farthest point Kellen had ever been to on this road, when Idalia reined in.

"I thought he'd be here by now," she said, in tones of faint puzzlement. "I know I'm, well, hardly a unicorn's usual traveling companion, shall we say, but he did say it would be all right."

Kellen looked around, as puzzled as she was, and finally caught a glimpse of white through the trees behind them. He knew that furtive shape; knew it well, but *why* was it lagging so far behind?

"He's following us," Kellen announced in mingled tones of amusement and disgust. He handed Idalia the mule's leadrope and walked back the way they'd come.

Shalkan stepped daintily out onto the trail and regarded Kellen with narrowed eyes. The unicorn's long equine face was not particularly well designed to convey emotion, but Kellen had never had any particular trouble sensing Shalkan's moods, nor did he now.

Shalkan was irritated.

But at what? What had *Kellen* done to deserve that look? Finally the unicorn snorted. "No hat," Shalkan said flatly, staring at Kellen's head in disgust.

Kellen reached up, slowly, and touched the brim. He'd forgotten he was wearing it, actually, but Shalkan seemed to have taken a complete and irrational dislike to it. To a *hat*?

"It keeps the rain off," Kellen said.

Shalkan put his ears back and switched his long tufted tail.

"It isn't raining. And it *is* an abomination," the unicorn said crossly. "Either get rid of it—or walk."

Kellen looked helplessly back at Idalia. She shrugged, and held out her hand for the hat; he could tell she was having a hard time keeping her face composed. Grumbling under his breath, Kellen unknotted the chinstring and walked back to pass the hat to Idalia, who tied it on the back of her saddle, her face carefully expressionless.

What does he think he is, a fashion critic?

Hatless, Kellen went back down the trail to "acquire his mount."

He was still without proper saddle or tack for the unicorn, and so was riding Shalkan bareback, but so long as they didn't have to run for their lives, he ought to be able to manage not to fall off. The unicorn's fur was still as slick and slippery as ever, but he did his best to balance carefully and not give Shalkan any further cause for complaint. After a moment though, he thought he could guess the real source of the unicorn's bad temper. Shalkan was twitching under him as if he were being deviled by sting-flies. The hat had nothing to do with it.

Shalkan might have agreed to travel with Idalia. He might agree there was a very good reason to do so. But the unicorn was a creature of magic, bound by magic's laws. Just because something was necessary didn't mean you had to *like* it.

He began to have a bit more sympathy for his friend. Apparently the hat was only an excuse for an exercise of irritation, and a way to vent some of it.

Poor Shalkan; Kellen wondered what it felt like. Was it like a rash you couldn't scratch? Or a headache? Or that twitchy feeling he got in his legs when he'd been awake too long and couldn't lie down yet? Or all of them?

"You ride on ahead," Kellen called. Idalia looked back, nodded with understanding, and nudged Coalwind with her heels, increasing the distance between them.

Shalkan sighed, stretching his neck out very long and shaking his head. He also stopped twitching. Idalia was still in sight, and if anything attacked either of them, the other could get there quickly enough, but this arrangement was going to make it rather difficult to have a conversation, other than with Shalkan.

"It really is a very stupid hat," the unicorn said, in as much of an apology as Kellen was going to get.

"Idalia thinks that if we look like Mountain Traders, we'll blend in better," Kellen offered meekly. Although how Kellen was going to blend in at all while riding a unicorn was another question altogether.

Shalkan sighed again. "A good plan, as far as it goes. And the sooner we are over the Border—where there is no need to blend in at all—the better for all of us."

Kellen made no comment. The unicorn followed after Idalia at a sedate walk.

"I'll—see if I can get used to her," Shalkan said after a moment. "This isn't safe."

"No, it isn't," Kellen agreed, and left it at that. But he did take one last look over his shoulder as they crested the tallest hill they'd passed so far. Their little cabin wasn't visible, but in the farthest distance, dim and as tiny as a child's toy, he could see the carved walls of Merryvale. *No longer Merry,* he thought with a sigh. He wondered if he'd ever see the place or any of the people in it again.

It was a melancholy thought.

Chapter Seventeen

Into Elven Lands

They kept north and west, and by the end of the first sennight, Kellen and Idalia were able to ride side by side. If she noticed that Shalkan had early on had problems with her presence, or if it continued to bother Shalkan, neither ever commented except for Shalkan's single, oblique remark at the beginning of the journey.

On the rare occasions that they were able to find a roof to sleep beneath in village, croft, or smallholding—for Idalia's Wildmage skills guaranteed them a welcome everywhere in the Western Hills—Shalkan would leave them an hour or so before they reached it, and if any of their hosts found it odd that their visitors should arrive one mounted and one on foot leading a pack mule, none of them said anything about that, either.

By the end of their second sennight of travel, Idalia informed Kellen that they were unlikely to encounter any more dwelling-places, for though they were still far from the borders, they were close enough to them that no one was likely to settle there for fear of encountering Elvenkind.

By this time, they were well into extremely steep hills—or small mountains, it didn't matter which you called them. Heavily wooded, with nothing for a sign of civilization except the road itself, they had to choose their camping places carefully. Idalia did something subtle that warned dangerous wildlife off, but there were other dangers, including human rogues. By now, in the lands they had left behind, the City Lawspeakers were proclaiming the sovereignty of Armethalieh through every hamlet and village, the members of the Militia were moving in, and the Scouring Hunt was coursing in search of Wildmages and Otherfolk.

Kellen wasn't sure exactly how far the High Council had extended the borders, but one thing he did know for sure was: the one thing the Hunt wouldn't find was him and Idalia. Kellen hoped that the discovery would send his father into a fit of apoplexy.

In their third sennight of travel (as far as Kellen could tell; he was actually starting to lose track of how long they'd been on the road, he discovered), he started to wonder if maybe the smallholders had a good reason for not wanting to encounter Elves.

Until now, the two of them had been traveling through lands fairly similar to those around the Wildwood: a landscape of high granite hills and deep river valleys filled with forests of hardwood and evergreen. They'd had no trouble finding good grazing for their animals to supplement the grain they'd brought, or water for drinking and cooking and washing.

Now that began to change.

It had been late summer when they left the Wildwood; now it was—maybe, if you stretched a point—the very beginning of autumn. The trees should just be starting to turn; the leaves yellowing. Later—the change of seasons was apparently similar to what he'd been used to in the City, only much more intense and extreme—would come the riot of autumnal color, then brown, then winter bareness.

But here the leaves were already withered and brown—too soon. The grass was sere, and the horse and mule mouthed it without pleasure. Shalkan made no complaints, but Kellen had no difficulty in telling that the unicorn was deeply troubled.

Worse followed the farther west they went. The smaller streams were muddy and low; the rivers that should have been swollen with late-season rain ran shallowly at the bottom of their beds. Sometimes they were forced to rely upon Shalkan to find water for them, which meant that Kellen walked while the unicorn roved along the periphery of their path, hunting for water.

The closer they came toward the Elven borders, the worse it got. The grass now was parched and dry, hardly worth the effort of chewing for the animals, and the bushes were withered and skeletal.

Shouldn't it be raining? Somewhere? Where's the water?

But Kellen—no farmer—wasn't quite sure that something was actually wrong, or if it was, how badly wrong. All his life he'd heard about the enchanting, green, misty beauty of the dangerous Elven lands, but so much of the old wondertales had been wrong. It was always possible that the stories had gotten it all backward. And Idalia—whose face became more grim by the day—wasn't saying.

But he was sure of one thing. Idalia had not expected to find things in this condition. And neither had Shalkan.

~

IT was midmorning, somewhere in their second fortnight of travel (Kellen was thinking hard, counting back and trying to remember *exactly* how many days they'd been on the road). They'd left open country behind, and were riding through woodland once more. The warmth of the early autumn day contrasted oddly with the sere winter-bleakness of the barren trees. The forest floor beneath the animals' hooves was thickly carpeted with fallen leaves, and the travelers made a faint crackling, shuffling sound as they moved through the leaf-litter. The road they followed was now a bare little track, hardly a road at all; it wasn't what Kellen had pictured to himself when he'd thought of a road through Elven lands.

The forest seemed much too empty, even to Kellen's un-tutored senses. Not only should there be deer and birds, rabbits and squirrels, but Otherfolk as well: sylphs and dryads, fauns, brownies, pixies, gnomes . . . the animals might flee from mounted strangers, but the Otherfolk should be drawn to both Shalkan and Idalia, and even if he couldn't see them, Kellen ought to at least be able to sense their presence with his Wildmage senses. But these woods were silent and empty. It gave him a very creepy feeling. It felt as if they were riding through a graveyard.

"Declare yourselves," a hard voice said abruptly.

Kellen blinked. A man had appeared out of nowhere, step-ping in front of Idalia's horse.

No, not a man. An *Elf*.

He wore clothing the same winter brown as the woods they rode through, his simple tunic and close-fitting leggings em-broidered with a complicated pattern in grey that would make him impossible to see from even a few feet away, for the stitching mimicked the lines and shadows of the forest itself. He was holding a smooth-polished stave as tall as he was, and a bow and a quiver of arrows was slung over his shoul-

der. Over the tunic was a cowl and hood. The hood was
pushed back now, and Kellen could clearly see the Elf's
pointed ears and shell-pale skin.

Where had he come from? He hadn't been anywhere in
sight before.

"Idalia, Wildmage, and her brother, Kellen Tavadon, also
a Wildmage," Idalia answered promptly. "Seeking sanctuary
in Elven lands, swearing no harm to tree, root, and leaf. Llylance, I See you," she added formally.

The Elven guard sighed with relief and suddenly looked
far less austere. He loosened his grip on his quarterstaff, leaning on it now instead of holding it ready to strike. "Idalia!
By the First Leaf, you return in a good hour! We had word
of your coming. An escort waits to accompany you down
into the city."

"We thank you for your kindness and the honor that you
do us," Idalia said. Kellen had never heard her speak so cer-
emoniously before. He hoped this wasn't going to be something they had to do all the time while they were here.

A second Elf appeared at Kellen's side, also seeming to
sprout directly from the forest floor itself. He was dressed
almost identically to Llylance, save that he held his bow
ready to fire.

Kellen felt his eyes go huge. The Elf hadn't made a single
sound. He'd just been . . . *there.*

"Don't be too impressed; they're just very, very good at
hiding," Idalia muttered, so low that Kellen was sure only he
could hear.

"I See you, Canderil," she said politely.

"I See you, Idalia," Canderil answered, with equal politeness. He released the tension on his bowstring and slung the
bow over his shoulder, retrieving his own stave from . . .
somewhere. Even though Kellen, mindful of Idalia's words,
was watching carefully, he couldn't see how it was done. One
moment Canderil's hand was empty. The next, the stave was
there.

Canderil gestured for them to accompany him. Llylance
simply vanished before Kellen's eyes, and once more Kellen

had no inkling as to how he did it, though he watched carefully.

And now, it seemed, they were free to proceed. Canderil walked beside Idalia's horse, having taken the lead-rope of the mule from her, and Shalkan and Kellen followed behind.

At least things didn't seem to be continuing on the same highly formal level as before. Idalia and Canderil spoke easily and companionably about people Kellen didn't know, very much as if they'd last seen each other a sennight ago instead of after an absence on Idalia's part of what must be several years.

Kellen knew very little about Elves. According to what he'd read in the Great Library when he was searching for information about the lands outside Armethalieh, they still visited the City on rare occasions—hard though that was to imagine—but of course no one outside the High Council would have seen them then. And he knew very little about them from his studies with Anigrel, and trusted what Anigrel had told him even less.

The Priests of the Light taught that the Elves were one of the Lesser Races, made by the Light in imitation of Man to serve as a lesson and a rebuke. From his own unsupervised studies in the Great Library, Kellen doubted that: the Elven race was immensely old and civilized, building great cities while humans were still gathering in tribes. Though people thought of Elves as living forever, in fact they were only very, very long-lived: the average Elven lifespan was on the order of a thousand years, and only at the very end of their lives did they show any signs of age at all. Canderil here might well have watched the first stones of the City being laid centuries ago, and wasn't *that* a sobering thought?

Kellen did welcome the chance to be able to get a good look at one of the Elvenkind without being caught staring, since Canderil seemed to be entirely caught up in his conversation with Idalia, paying no particular heed to either Kellen or Shalkan, as though he saw people riding unicorns every day.

Of course, being an Elf, maybe he did.

And despite his firm intention to disbelieve everything he'd read about Elves in the City histories, the more he watched Canderil, the more Kellen understood why the City-folk, and even the Light-Priests, wrote of Elvenkind as they did.

Like his companion Llylance, whom he resembled as closely as a twin, Canderil was tall and slender. His silky black hair was elaborately braided, and despite that, still fell to his hips. His eyes were as black as midnight, his skin as pale as pearl, and it was clear that Elves never needed to shave (this was a matter for envy, as Kellen *did* need to shave, and both sharp razors and shaving mirrors were difficult to come by in the Wildwood). With his high cheekbones and faintly slanted eyes, Canderil possessed an oddly androgynous yet definitely male glamour, as exotic as it was unsettling.

He was beautiful; there was no other appropriate word for it. And worse, thought Kellen, watching him with an increasing mixture of fascination and discomfort, he was *perfect*. Canderil never put a foot wrong, never made a clumsy gesture or an awkward one. Even just walking beside Coalwind, he looked as if he were dancing.

Even his clothes were perfect. At first Kellen had been a little disappointed by the simple grey-and-brown costumes he and Llylance wore. They seemed too similar to what he and Idalia had worn in the Wildwood, albeit made of finer materials, and of cloth, not skins. But the longer he looked, the more Kellen realized that his first assessment had been too hasty.

The dun-colored cloth was the finest weaving he'd ever seen, a wool as soft as Shalkan's coat. It shimmered softly in the light, and against it the grey embroidery glowed, now silver, now dark, in an ever-shifting pattern that Kellen felt he could be content to gaze at for the rest of his life. And no matter how Canderil moved in it, nothing wrinkled, nothing pulled. He wore his garb like an extension of his own skin.

Kellen had been the son of the most powerful man in Armethalieh. He had despised the luxuries that went with that high office, but he was familiar with them. He knew exactly how much time and skill it took to make clothing one-tenth as fine as this—and if these were such clothes as Canderil wore for hunting in the woods, what did *formal* Elven clothing look like?

The Priests of the Light taught that Elves corrupted humankind and caused them to despair, and so honest folk should shun their company, should they be offered it. And Kellen supposed that in a way that was true. If just watching Canderil walk through a forest made him feel grubby and inadequate, what would seeing a whole city of Elves dressed in their finest clothes do? But one of the oldest Histories he'd read had said it better, he thought: *"The Elves have elevated mere living into a form of Art."*

"When you live for a thousand years, you have a lot of time to get things right," Shalkan said quietly.

"Uh . . . yeah," Kellen said. But he was comforted by Shalkan's assurance—and the fact that the unicorn, as perfect in *his* way as any Elf, had been perceptive enough to give that assurance.

"But I have been rude," Canderil said, turning sideways to regard Kellen and Shalkan. "In my eagerness to hear Idalia's news, I have neglected Sentarshadeen's other guests. I hope you will not think me discourteous. Perhaps there are things you would know, and I would hear your news as well."

It would take Kellen a long time to realize that adult Elves simply *didn't* ask direct questions—if an Elf wanted to know something, the polite method was to phrase it as a statement, which the hearer could—just as politely—choose to disregard. Kellen simply assumed he was being asked a question, and after glancing at Idalia to see if it was all right, launched into a slightly tangled and much edited tale of how he and Idalia had come to be traveling into Elven lands. If more than a touch of bitterness crept into his voice when he spoke about what had been done to him by Lycaelon, well, he hoped that Canderil would understand.

As he spoke, the sere landscape was replaced by healthier woodland, and the empty air filled with the proper sounds of wildlife and wind-in-the-branches. They reached the edge of the trees, and Kellen got his first sight of Sentarshadeen.

The Elven city was built into the sides of a wooded granite canyon. At first Kellen didn't see the houses he knew must be there, but slowly his eyes adjusted, and they appeared, as magically as the Elven woods-guards had.

I guess the houses are just very, very good at hiding, too, Kellen told himself.

The dwellings of the Elven city of Sentarshadeen blended into their surroundings as if they'd grown there: low beautiful cottages of silvery wood, each one unique, each one set into its own garden—but too few to make up a city, and when Kellen studied the canyon wall across the valley floor, he suddenly realized that it, too, was filled with dwellings cut into the living rock itself. Every inch of the canyon wall was subtly carved, to form windows and doors and pathways that so beautifully harmonized with their surroundings that they were not immediately apparent to the eye. There must have been hundreds of them.

In fact, if Kellen had not just spent a season in a true wildwood, he would have mistaken the sight before him for untouched Nature, but it wasn't. It was Nature perfected, touched so lightly and gracefully that what had been done wasn't immediately obvious—but, like Canderil himself, everything Kellen saw was quietly perfect.

A wisp of mist trailed along the side of the canyon; faintly he heard the welcome sound of water.

It's like walking into a dream, Kellen thought in awe. All his previous misgivings were forgotten. He might not be able to live up to the Elves' standards, but he could certainly appreciate them.

Canderil led them down the trail to the valley floor, as Kellen gazed about himself in wonder. Somewhere in the distance he could hear the faint sound of wind chimes, and it seemed the perfect enhancement to this place. The rich autumn light slanted down through the trees, sculpting shadows off the canyon walls in ways that Kellen somehow knew had been planned, as though the Elven designers had taken note of how the sun would strike every inch of the rock every hour of the day in every season of the year, and shaped it accordingly. Though he looked hard to find a flaw—something hasty, unfinished, out of place—he never did, in all the time he spent in Sentarshadeen. Even the stones in the dry riverbed they crossed over seemed to each have been deliberately placed to make their surroundings more beautiful.

It almost seemed—though it was an odd word to use to describe a place where people obviously went about their daily lives, for Kellen saw a number of Elves as they passed, if only at a distance—*holy*. Holiness was a concept that Kellen only understood vaguely, and that in connection with the Priests of the Eternal Light. In Kellen's limited experience, holiness seemed to involve long incomprehensible prayers, discomfort, and a great deal of incense. If that was holiness, then it could have nothing to do with Sentarshadeen. But the word still seemed right to him. The Elven city was a far holier place than the cold and forbidding Great Temple of the Light.

They followed a path—though to call it a path was unfair, as it was as wide as a street back in Armethalieh—that led up the cliff and stopped in front of one of the doors. Canderil set his stave into a bracket that seemed to be made for it, and went up the step to open the door. Idalia dismounted.

"We're here," she said.

Kellen slid off Shalkan's back. The unicorn shook himself and took a few steps, sniffing the air.

"I'll be back later. If you need me, just ask anyone. They'll know where I am." He trotted off quickly, leaving Kellen staring after him.

"There's a unicorn herd here," Idalia said, noting Kellen's puzzled and slightly dismayed expression. "He's gone to join them. Don't worry about him; he probably hasn't seen another unicorn aside from that family I healed a while back for moonturns, maybe years, and he'll have a lot of socializing to do. Come on, help me get our things inside. We're home, for now."

Canderil helped them unload Prettyfoot and Coalwind, assisting them to get all of their belongings inside, then retrieved his stave and led the two animals away, leaving

Kellen and Idalia standing among their bundles in the main room of the guesthouse.

"Home, sweet home," Idalia said in an unreadable tone as she looked around the room.

"Idalia," Kellen said hesitantly, "is this place yours? Have you been here before?"

Idalia took a deep breath, rousing herself from whatever she'd been thinking, and smiled. "No. Not here. And until a few minutes ago, this *was* a guesthouse. But it's our home now. From the moment we took occupancy it ceased to be a guesthouse and will be regarded as ours. That's why Canderil left so fast—Elves have very strict customs about who gets to go into private homes and who doesn't. Now that it's our home, no Elf will ever come in here uninvited—except children, of course: Elven children are so rare that they pretty much do as they please and are exempt from all custom and law. And there are all sorts of customs about who can invite who into whose house, and all that, of course, but being human, we won't be expected to know them, much less be bound by them."

"Good thing," Kellen muttered darkly. He'd had his fill of rules of *that* sort back in Armethalieh!

"Why don't you take a look around?" Idalia suggested. "There are two bedrooms; you can pick one, and then we can get our gear sorted out."

Kellen decided to take her advice. He hadn't gotten much chance to inspect the place before, since they'd been getting their things inside as quickly as possible, but now the need to hurry seemed to be over.

The Elven dwelling wasn't large, but like everything else Kellen had seen here so far, it was perfect. The main room—where all of their gear was now—was large enough to be comfortable, but not big enough to seem grand. Its gently curved walls were painted a rich, warm, vibrant cream. Some of the furniture was built-in—long padded benches of carved and polished wood that ran along the walls, following the curve, a tall armoire that opened to reveal bookshelves and a desk—and other pieces stood arranged against the walls awaiting their need: a pair of comfortable-looking chairs, a stool. In one corner, a tall tile stove was set into the wall, ready to provide both warmth and a place to cook. Opening the doors and drawers of its intricate cabinet, Kellen discovered a teapot and cups; bowls and flatware. All but the eating utensils were of the luminous translucent Elvenware that commanded such astronomical prices in Armethalieh. Kellen held a piece up to the light. It glowed, taking fire from the sun, and its color took his breath away. Reluctantly, he set it back in its place and investigated further, turning up some large, flat, black disks, elaborately embossed with an intricate geometric pattern. He had to lift one and examine it closely before he figured out what it was. Charcoal. Even the fuel here was beautiful.

Kellen brushed his hands clean and turned away from the stove to pick up one of the pillows from the sitting benches. Each was covered in a different hand-loomed fabric and pattern, each somehow perfectly right for the room. The longer he looked, the more there was to see. He set the cushion down gently.

"It's a little stunning when you see it all for the first time," Idalia said quietly.

"Yeah," Kellen said weakly. This wasn't getting him any closer to picking out a bedroom, either.

There were three doors leading off the main room. He chose one at random and opened it.

He'd found the bathroom.

The fixtures were similar to what he might have found back in Armethalieh, save for the fact that they were made of colored ceramic instead of wood, metal, or stone, and seemed to be built into the walls and floor. Kellen inspected the washbasin curiously. There was no ewer, and no place to set one, either. Where did the washing-water come from? And why was there a stopper in the bottom of the bowl?

He pulled out the plug, revealing a hole. No answers there. Set into the wall above the basin were two small wheels. Curious, Kellen turned one.

Water began to spill into the basin through holes in the

rim. Kellen yelped and jumped back, startled, then dipped his fingers in the riling water. Fresh enough to drink . . . and the other wheel produced water as hot as if it had just come from a kettle.

Kellen turned them both off, and regarded the washing bowl in awe. Not even Armethalieh's magic could provide a washbowl that filled with hot or cold water on command and emptied itself besides—and the best thing was, he suspected it was all done without an ounce of magic!

Upon inspection, the small hip-bath proved to fill and empty the same way. He could take a bath—a *hot* bath—anytime he wanted to, without having to haul water or trouble any servants.

Or use magic to heat the water.

And best of all, the necessary also sluiced itself clean with water after each use. No more midnight treks to the outhouse. No more close-stools or thundermugs, a feature of even the most exalted houses in Armethalieh. Everything here was clean and civilized.

Kellen frowned, trying to figure out what the fundamental difference was. In Armethalieh, it was easy to be comfortable if you had magic 'and wealth, but your comfort was purchased at the cost of others' discomfort. But in Sentarshadeen, from what he'd seen so far, everyone could live like the High Mages, and nobody had to suffer for it.

He hoped it was true.

He went back into the main room. He didn't know how long he'd spent in the water closet, but Idalia was gazing at him with an amused expression on her face. Kellen blushed. Of course, this was all familiar to her from her previous time among the Elves, but it was still all new to him.

"I'll take that one," Kellen said hastily, pointing at a door at random. He gathered up as much of his gear as he could manage and shuffled awkwardly toward it, just managing to get the tips of his fingers onto the door latch and toe the door open.

The ceiling here was lower, the room done in shades of browns and greens. There was a large window on one wall,

with a deep window seat before it. Facing it, built into the
wall, its contours designed to harmonize with the shape of
the window, was a tall clothes-chest. Between the chest and
the window was a bed, with another bench for sitting at its
foot. Tucked beside the door was a small desk and stool.
There were lanterns in niches around the walls. If he had
studied the ways to design a room for years, he could never
have come up with an arrangement so harmonious, and so—
ah, that word again!—*perfectly* suited to inducing relaxation.

Kellen dropped his burden on the bed. He'd meant to go
right back out for another load, but the view outside his window drew him toward it. He walked over and opened the
glass-paned shutters. From here he could see out into the
canyon, almost as if he were hanging in space. Though the
opposite wall of the canyon must be as filled with dwelling-
places as this one was, somehow they did not draw the eye;
his mind insisted that he was looking out on unspoiled par-
adise. ·

This must be how the Wildwood looked to Idalia, Kellen
thought with a flash of insight. No wonder she'd been happy
there, Kellen realized. It was her *place.*

He didn't think Sentarshadeen was where he belonged—it
was too soon to tell, anyway—but it was so beautiful it could
make you think you belonged here, no matter where your
true place was. And maybe it could help you understand other
people better. *Because I suppose Armethalieh looks this way
to some people, too,* Kellen admitted grudgingly, if only to
himself.

His reverie was interrupted by the sound of voices—*two*
voices—from the room outside.

"I See you, Idalia," a man's voice said.

"I See you, Jermayan," Idalia answered.

Kellen went to the door of the bedroom and looked out.
There was an Elf standing in the doorway of the house.

Like the woods-guards, Jermayan was dressed in earth
tones, but it was clear that his garments were not meant to
blend in to an autumn forest. He wore low boots of russet
velvet over snug moss-green leggings embroidered with twin-

ing vines in russet and gold. His long hair was held back by a tubular weave of dull gold silk ribbons, and he wore a sheer tunic in palest russet oversewn with bands of velvet of a green so dark it was nearly black.

There was a long pause.

"Will you deny me the comfort of your hearth, Idalia?" Jermayan said at last.

Kellen saw Idalia bite back a sharp retort. "If you think you will find comfort in entering this house, Jermayan, then enter it by all means," she said ungraciously.

Jermayan stepped carefully over the threshold. He took a step toward Idalia, holding out his hand.

Idalia stepped back, refusing the gesture. She kept her face as blank as she could, but Kellen could tell she was both surprised and unhappy to see Jermayan. Why? Kellen was confused. Did he and Idalia have enemies here, too?

Jermayan lowered his hand. "You have not changed your mind? When I heard you had come to Sentarshadeen, I hoped . . ."

"I came because I had no choice," Idalia interrupted harshly. "I would have chosen another destination if I'd known you were here. Why couldn't you have stayed in Ondoladeshiron?"

Kellen felt as if he were watching a game of shuttlecock—or a fencing match. He looked from Idalia's face, everything but her eyes completely expressionless, but her eyes holding a tempest of strong feelings—to the Elf's, *his* face holding such longing that it *hurt*.

"Memories of you were there," Jermayan said simply. "Idalia, my—"

"No!" Idalia raised her hand, and there was such pain in her eyes that Kellen winced. "No more, Jermayan. We are not going to talk about this ever again."

No, Kellen realized. Not enemies. And he had all the answers he ever wanted about why Idalia hadn't wanted to stay with the Elves. Jermayan was in love with her. That much was plain. And Kellen was pretty sure Idalia loved him back, and didn't want to. That just made things more confusing.

"I will respect your wishes," Jermayan said softly. "But I had thought—I had hoped—you had changed your mind. Fare you well, Idalia."

Jermayan turned and left. Gracefully.

Kellen hesitated for a moment, then came out.

Idalia rounded on him. "Get a good earful?" she asked dangerously. Her eyes glittered with anger, but behind the anger was a welter of such powerful emotions that Kellen could hardly believe it was the Idalia—calm, restrained Idalia—he had thought he knew standing before him.

"Well, neither one of you was keeping your voices down." He wasn't quite sure how to react to this new creature facing him. "You want to tell me what's going on with this Jermayan? I think I've got a right to know—I am your brother, after all," Kellen reminded her. He only realized how pompous and hateful the words sounded when it was too late to take them back.

But she didn't tender him the set-down that his stupid demand deserved. "I met Jermayan in Ondoladeshiron just after I turned back from being a Silver Eagle. I fell in love with him then. He thinks he loves me. And he's going to have to get over it, because it can't go anywhere, and I told him so at the time," Idalia said, her voice painfully flat.

"But—" Kellen protested, unable to understand why she should be saying anything of the sort. If *she* loved Jermayan, and the Elf loved *her,* then what was stopping them? "But, Idalia—"

"*Think,* Kellen," she interrupted him. "In another fifty or sixty years, I'll *die.* Jermayan will live for another *nine centuries*—and Elves mate for life. Do you think I'm going to condemn him to live what amounts to his entire life alone after I'm dead? What kind of love would that be? It isn't fair, and I won't do it!"

Her eyes filled abruptly with tears, and she turned away and ran into the other bedroom, slamming the door behind her.

Kellen crept up to the door and listened. He thought he

could hear Idalia weeping on the other side. *But Idalia never cries.*

And she never thought she'd have to see Jermayan again, either, another part of Kellen said.

He wasn't sure what to do. What he did know was that there wasn't anything he could do or say to comfort her—or to change her mind, either.

And he was pretty sure she'd rather he wasn't around when she came out, so that they could both pretend that the last few minutes had never happened. So how could he arrange that?

After a moment's reflection it occurred to Kellen that this would be a good time to get out and take a look around the rest of the Elven city. Nobody'd said that wouldn't be a good idea, and he thought he'd like to know a good deal more about Sentarshadeen and the folks who lived here, before he managed to make any *more* stupid mistakes.

And I'd really like to get away from Idalia so she can—

He stopped himself just as he was thinking *"get over it."* She wasn't going to get over it. She wasn't *ever* going to "get over it." But he could take himself off so she could pretend she could. So this would be a good time to get out and see the sights. There were several hours of light left.

And who better to tell him about Sentarshadeen than the people who—so Idalia said—were exempt from all local customs? He wondered how hard it would be to find a kid around here.

Taking a last look around the disorder of the common room, Kellen went out, closing the front door carefully, and very quietly, behind him.

⌒

HE went back down the cliff footpath, to wander the twisting paths along the cliffside among the small houses. This time he saw a number of adult Elves going about their business (all of them ignored him, very politely), but he had no intention of approaching any of them. He was looking for someone quite different.

Idalia said there weren't a lot of Elf-kids. If I were a kid, and I didn't have anybody to play with, where would I go?

He'd been walking for about half an hour, Kellen judged, mostly upstream along the riverbed—there was a trickle along the very bottom of the bed, mostly for decoration, he guessed—when he saw the boy.

The Elf-child was playing by himself down in the muddiest part of the streambed, and just like any other child, mud had gotten all over his skin and his clothes. His black hair was cut short, just brushing his shoulders, and Kellen was amused to see that there seemed to be mud there too. In fact, with a little work, the kid could probably get the *rocks* dirty. He was concentrating intently on something between his feet. Kellen saw something flicker on the surface of the water, passing him where he stood—a tiny boat made of folded colored paper.

He walked over to where the kid was squatting in the water. The boy was wearing a kilt and vest, and sometime this morning they'd been cream-colored, Kellen guessed. Since then, they'd suffered about as much as you'd expect at the hands of an active five-year-old—at least, the Elf-boy *looked* about five. For all Kellen knew, he might be fifty.

"Hello," Kellen said, and waited to see what would happen.

"I see—" The boy looked up and saw Kellen, and his black eyes widened in delight. "I know what you are! You're a human!" the boy said delightedly, jumping to his feet and scattering the rest of his paper boats in his excitement.

"My name's Kellen," Kellen said. "I just got here a couple of hours ago, and I was looking for somebody who could show me around the city."

"I could!" the boy said. "My name's Sandalon, and I know where everything is! I'll show you." He took Kellen's hand and began to lead him back along the river. "You're hot," he commented. "And you're an awfully strange color. Are you feeling all right? Do all humans wear clothes like that all the time? Are you going to wear clothes like that while you're here, or are you going to wear proper clothes? We can start with the kilns, because they're firing today, and that's always educational, Nurse Lairamo says. Are your ears really round? Is it true that humans eat raw meat?"

Eventually Sandalon's questions slowed down enough for Kellen to be able to actually answer them, and ask a few as well—it seemed that Elves knew as little about humans as humans did about them, only they were too polite to say so, if Sandalon's innocent questions were anything to go by— and so Kellen learned about the firing kilns and the orchards, and pretty much everything Sandalon knew about Sentarshadeen: which was quite a bit, since no one hindered him and everyone looked out for him. Kellen found himself the target of sharp glances more than once, but since the boy was obviously enjoying himself in Kellen's company, nothing was said.

Kellen discovered that the cliff walls weren't as solid as they looked, either—there were canyons cut into them, which in turn led back into a whole deeper set of valleys, almost like a labyrinth. Kellen's woodscraft stood him in good stead now: if he'd come here directly from Armethalieh, he'd have been completely lost among all the twists and turns almost at once, but spending a season in Idalia's woods had taught him the skills to be able to find his way back to his starting place fairly easily.

"And this is where *I* live," Sandalon said happily, pointing, after he'd spent most of the afternoon showing Kellen the high points of Sentarshadeen.

Kellen looked out across a meadow covered with short silvery grass. Set in its center was the largest Elven building Kellen had yet seen, a low, deep-eaved house built of silvery wood and pale stone. Age and strength radiated from it, as from an ancient living tree, and Kellen would not have been at all surprised to discover dryads living here.

"Come," Sandalon said, pulling at Kellen's hand. "I'll show you."

Kellen followed him across the grass.

The portico floor was covered with an intricate design of

slatted wood, and by the time Kellen and Sandalon reached
the doors, the soles of Sandalon's sandals and Kellen's boots
were clean and dry. Though he knew this must be a very
grand house by Elven standards, there was no sense of things
being huge just to make people feel insignificant. There were
double doors, wide enough so that several people could enter
at once, but the doors themselves were not the towering
things they would be in Armethalieh. They were simply the
proper size for their function, just as the house seemed to be
the proper size for its function, whatever that might be.

Sandalon pulled one of the doors open—the door latch was
of age-smoothed bronze, in the shape of a twist of vine-
stock—and sketched a quick bow in Kellen's direction.

"Be welcome in this house and find comfort at our hearth,"
Sandalon said. The words came out in a rush, as if the boy
was repeating an only half-understood (as yet) lesson.

"Um . . . thanks. Thank you," Kellen said. Sandalon
seemed to be waiting for Kellen to go first, so Kellen stepped
past him, into the house itself. He thought he heard Sandalon
breathe a sigh of relief and follow him inside.

"Here's where we live—me and Mother. And Father, too,
only he isn't here right now."

The main entry hall extended the entire height of the house,
and there was a skylight in the ceiling to let the daylight down
into the hall. Directly below the skylight was a reflecting pool
and fountain (empty now), its intricate mosaic of colored tiles
depicting fish swimming in a river. At the back of the hall,
two curving staircases mirrored one another, framing a doorway with sliding panels that echoed the entryway. On both
sides, galleries opened onto the main hall, so that people in
the rooms above could look down to see who had entered.
The walls were hung with tapestries that would each have
commanded a mage's ransom in Armethalieh. The colors
glowed jewel-bright, and the weaving was finer than anything
Kellen had ever seen.

Kellen would have liked to stay and gawk, but Sandalon
was already halfway up one of the staircases, and Kellen had
no choice but to follow.

He was starting to get a pretty good idea of what was going on—and who Sandalon was—so it wasn't much of a surprise when—after another quick tour of several rooms—they ended up about where Kellen expected.

"And this is my mother's dayroom," Sandalon said, opening the door.

The first impression Kellen got was that they'd stepped outdoors again. The walls were made of glass—hundreds of tiny panes, all held together in a bronze latticework—and the room seemed to hang in space, surrounded by a lacework made of light and air.

The second was that Sandalon's mother was the most beautiful woman Kellen had ever seen.

Here was the beauty of the Elves as Kellen had read about it: as regal and distant as the Moon, as dangerous as fire. She was seated on a cushion, with a writing desk on her lap, wearing an elaborate gown of green and silver, embroidered with sinuous, twisting designs that seemed to catch and hold the eye, the edges of her trailing sleeves and the hem of her skirt ornamented with heavy silver lace as substantial as jewelry. Her black hair was braided with pearls and a bright green gem Kellen had never seen before, and she wore rings on every finger. She looked up when the door opened, and for a moment Kellen was caught in her gaze. It was like seeing Shalkan for the first time—just as transfixing; like being terrified without fear.

Then she set aside her writing desk and held out her arms to her son, and the moment passed.

"Here is my child—and here is half Sentarshadeen upon his clothes," she added good-naturedly. Sandalon climbed into her arms and hugged her unself-consciously. She paid no heed to the mud on him, and the havoc it was making of her gown.

"I see someone whom I have never seen before," she observed.

Kellen made his lowest and most formal bow. If this wasn't the Queen of the Elves, he'd eat the hat Shalkan hated so much.

"I am Kellen Tavadon, brother to Wildmage Idalia," he said, choosing his words carefully. "I am told that you were all expecting us for some time, so I hope that my presence is not an intrusion."

The lady inclined her head graciously, at one and the same time acknowledging the truth of his words and welcoming him.

"Please forgive me, but as I am a stranger here, I had no idea where this fine young fellow was leading me," he said, with a faint smile at the boy, "and no one has yet told me how to address you."

"My name is Ashaniel, Kellen, and by right of Leaf and Star I am Queen over the Nine Cities. But the Elves have long memories, and do not require constant reminders of our rank and titles." In a human's mouth, the words would have been a false disclaimer, like as not. In hers, it had the ring of truth. "And now, the hour grows late, and I think, perhaps, you have not had the opportunity to truly settle into your home as yet. We would be honored if you would consent to share our evening meal with us."

Kellen had been sure he was on his way to a polite dismissal, so the change of theme caught him by surprise.

He managed not to gape. He managed to bow. "I—Yes. Thank you. I would like that very much, Lady . . . Ashaniel."

"Good."

She sounded pleased. She actually sounded *pleased.* She rose to her feet and set Sandalon on his. "Now my son will wish to go and make himself presentable, and perhaps you will enjoy the opportunity to see something of the House of Leaf and Star before dinner."

Now this *was* a dismissal, for servants—at least Kellen was guessing they were servants, for Queens must have servants—had appeared while Ashaniel had been speaking. Sandalon skipped past Kellen, and took the hand of a woman standing in the open doorway. She was dressed in deep blues and violets, and regarded her charge with a fond smile. Kellen found himself facing an Elven man who regarded him with a visible absence of expression. He was dressed in similar

colors to the woman, but not closely enough for Kellen to be
sure it was house livery, and he was as richly jeweled as a
prince.

"There are things of great interest to be seen in this direction," the man said, gesturing.

Kellen followed.

He listened to a number of indirect remarks about the
length of his journey and the difficulties of the road while
they wandered through the halls before he realized his guide
was suggesting it would be a really good idea if he cleaned
up before dinner. Once he figured that out, he suggested it
himself, and felt an almost tangible sense of relief radiate
from the Elven man. He was quickly ushered to a sitting
room.

There was a large ornate sand-clock on a table in the center
of the room. His guide moved to it quickly, making some
quick adjustments with a series of crystal partitions that slid
through the bowl. Kellen was fascinated to see you could
change the amount of sand that could pass from one half of
the clock into the other half, setting the amount of time that
you measured.

"When the sands run out, I will return," the Elf announced,
bowing slightly. He upended the clock, turned, and left.

Kellen watched the sands run for a moment, then looked
around. As he'd suspected, another door led through to a
bathing room, enough larger than the one in the guesthouse
to contain a table and chair as well. And there he received
another surprise.

There was a suit of clothes waiting for him, neatly laid out
over the chair, and a pair of soft ankle-boots set beneath it.
He held up the tunic curiously. It would be a good—if
loose—fit. And more, it was clearly designed to be a little
loose.

Just as well, Kellen thought. He wasn't sure he was cut
out for the tight-fitting clothes he'd seen the Elven men wearing—it'd be too much like going naked, and he'd never cared
for the tight-fitting fashions of the City, after all. And he was
just as glad to be able to get out of the clothes he'd been

wearing since—well, since he and Idalia had left the Wildwood, actually. If he hurried, he'd have time for a quick bath before his guide came back to conduct him down to dinner.

Dinner.

For the first time that day, his thoughts returned to Idalia. Would she worry when he didn't come home? He wondered if there was some way he could call the Elven servant back, maybe send her a message . . .

But he couldn't think of any, just offhand. And knowing little more about his hosts than that their very long lives were hedged about by rigid etiquette and protocol, he didn't know what would offend them.

Idalia knew the Elves far better than he did. He'd just have to hope she'd guess that wherever he was, he wasn't in any trouble.

He set the plug in the tub, turned the taps, and began to undress as it filled.

A short time later, damp, dressed, and smelling faintly of flowery Elven soap, Kellen stood watching the last of the sands run out. He'd folded his trail-clothes as neatly as possible and left them on the chair. He could come back for them later.

Although, if *these* were the sort of things he was supposed to be wearing around here, he really didn't *want* those old clothes!

KELLEN had been stuck with attending more than a few formal banquets at his father's house, and deep down inside, he'd been expecting and dreading that this would be more of the same: a lot of people he didn't know, a lot of boring conversation about things he didn't care about, and too much really unpleasant food to try to figure out how to eat while he worried about his table manners.

Dinner at the Queen's Palace was nothing like that.

There probably was a grand formal dining room for state occasions here somewhere, but Kellen didn't see it that night.

The four of them (the Elf woman that Kellen supposed was Sandalon's nurse, Lairamo, ate with them) sat together at a comfortable unpretentious table in a room whose enormous, leaded-glass windows were open to the first breath of evening. The walls were inlaid wood, carved to mimic the living forest, and done with such attention to detail that it was hard to tell in the mellow, dusky twilight where the forest he could see outside the windows ended and the carved forest on the walls began. Lanterns hung from the carven tree branches, casting a soft golden light over the table.

The tableware was simple as well, plain silver with sinuous curves—but jewel-encrusted gold would be vulgar, Kellen realized. The plates and cups they ate from were Elvenware, but a form of it that make the examples that he'd seen in the City—and the pieces in his and Idalia's house—look as if they were made out of mud. The pieces on the Queen's table were so light and glowing they looked almost ready to float away, and Kellen was nearly afraid to touch them.

The food was wonderful as well—simple and fresh, with an emphasis on perfectly ripe vegetables and fruits, wonderful breads, savory meat. There were no cleverly disguised, complicated dishes, no culinary oddities. You didn't have to guess at what it was, or how to eat it, either. Kellen found himself starting to relax, as Ashaniel led the conversation into safe easy topics that centered around Sandalon's day and how he'd spent it. The Queen obviously adored her son, and Sandalon was both young enough to think everyone should find Kellen as fascinating as he did and naive enough to be unaware that describing someone in the manner of a new menagerie animal *might* be less than flattering. More than once, Kellen caught Ashaniel suppressing a fond parental smile.

But the smiles quickly faded, and Kellen realized that Ashaniel had a lot more on her mind than being kind to her son's new friend. The Queen was worried about something—badly worried, if even Kellen could pick up on it—and doing her best to hide it.

The last course was raspberries served in frozen cream, accompanied by tiny cups of a dark sweet wine for the adults, and a large mug of berry-cider for Sandalon. The child lingered over his drink, unwilling to finish it, until at last Ashaniel regarded him sternly.

"It is time for you to seek your bed, my young son," she said in a voice that brooked no argument. "I do not think our friend Kellen plans to leave us soon, so you need not fear he will be gone before you wake again. And it is time for you to sleep."

Sandalon looked just as rebellious as any other youngster at being told to go to bed, but he promptly drained his mug and got to his feet. It was obvious that however defiant he might feel, he would *behave* obediently. Everyone stood, and Sandalon bowed—first to his mother, then to Kellen—before allowing himself to be led off by his nurse.

"Will you come and see me tomorrow?" Sandalon asked, stopping at the doorway and looking over his shoulder.

Oh, bless the little fellow—Sandalon sounded positively mournful!

There was a sudden wariness in the air, and Kellen realized both women were looking at him intently, though he didn't know why.

"I will," Kellen promised. "Or you can come and see me. I had a good time today with you!"

Sandalon beamed, and the momentary tension Kellen had sensed disappeared. "I will!" the boy promised. "Thank you!"

"He is very young," the Queen said apologetically, when Lairamo had led her son away. "And—often lonely."

Now what was that *all about?* Kellen wondered. *Surely they weren't afraid that I'd reject the kid?* He'd spent far too many lonely hours as a child himself to do anything of the sort! And how he would have *loved* having an older boy to look up to and have as a mentor!

"I suppose I should be getting home," Kellen said when Ashaniel didn't say anything more.

"Stay a while, if you would. I would talk with you for a few moments," she said.

The bald statement rather startled Kellen—it was the first time today an Elf had ever been that direct. Perhaps because she was the Queen, she felt she could afford to go straight to the heart of the matter.

She gestured to Kellen to follow her, and led him out of the dining salon through another door than the one Sandalon and his nurse had used.

As far as Kellen could tell after all the twists and turns, the room they ended up in was directly beneath the glass room Sandalon had brought him to earlier. Here lamps were lit against the darkness, and a small fire burned in an elegant stove made of the same translucent Elvenware they'd eaten their dinners from. It was built to suggest a phoenix rising from flames, and the flickering of the real flames within gave the tile flames an eerie semblance of life.

The room was small and intimate, a room for private councils. Ashaniel motioned for Kellen to close the door behind them, and sank gracefully down into one of the chairs, gesturing to Kellen to take the other. There was a small table between them, with a tall green and silver decanter and two cups. She poured them both full and handed one to him.

Kellen sipped cautiously, tasting apricots and cinnamon, but no alcohol.

"I beg that you will forgive my rudeness, but I am desperate," Ashaniel said. "You have named yourself Kellen Tavadon. I have heard of another who once bore the name Tavadon, who has lately been a guest in our lands."

Ashaniel waited, looking at him.

Elves don't ask questions. He didn't know where the unexpected intuition came from, but Kellen suddenly realized it was true. He hadn't heard a direct question from anyone here today but Sandalon—and hadn't Idalia said that children were exempt from the Elven code of etiquette?

"You mean my sister Idalia." He *hoped* she meant Idalia. It was all so difficult trying to maneuver around this Elven reticence—

Well, Idalia had said that humans weren't expected to know the rules. He took his courage in both hands and plunged in. "Your Majesty—Ashaniel—I'm sorry. I'll be happy to tell you just about anything I know, but you're just

going to have to ask me. I don't want to be rude, but—" He
gestured helplessly. "I'm not very bright, I'm afraid, and I
just can't manage to make out what you want to know if you
won't ask me directly."

"It was I who did not wish to offend," Ashaniel said, looking uneasy, yet relieved. "I do not wish you to feel unwelcome here, or to hold yourself treated as a criminal or one
without family."

"I won't," Kellen assured her. "But I know . . . I *think* I
know there's some kind of trouble here. There are things you
want to know. And everything will go a lot faster if you just
ask."

" 'Ask.' " Ashaniel set her cup back on the table, regarding
him gravely. She folded her hands in her lap, as if preparing
herself to play a difficult game. Perhaps, for an Elf, it was.
Perhaps, because they lived for such a *very* long time, speaking directly and asking questions was as difficult as mastering
an auctioneer's rapid-fire patter.

"Is your sister Idalia with you?" the Queen asked.

"Yes," Kellen answered. "We both had to flee the Wildwood; we left just ahead of a Scouring Hunt. She's staying
with me at the guest house."

"Is it true that she has come here at last to live?" Ashaniel
seemed to be choosing her words as if this were a riddle game
that required absolute precision.

"Yes. I mean, I think—" But he got no further.

"Holy Stars be thanked!" Ashaniel gasped, bending forward and covering her face with her hands. He could see the
golden leaves in her dark hair tremble with the force of her
suppressed emotion.

Kellen would have been less shocked to see a stone statue
get up and walk—after all, in Armethalieh, he'd seen that
happen many times. Ashaniel had seemed so remote, so untouched. He'd seen at dinner that she was worried, but this
was more than worry. Under that serene exterior had been
nothing less than panic. Maybe there still was—but for some
reason, these people thought that Idalia held an answer to
their problem. The only answer, perhaps.

"We are in desperate trouble, Kellen," Ashaniel said simply, raising her head and composing her features once more. "I do not know what to do. My husband, Andoreniel Caerthalien, has been away for moonturns, searching for a solution to our plight, but this very day I have had a message from him: he has found no answer."

She rose to her feet, and turned away to gaze out through the darkened windows.

"You have seen the state of the land as you rode through it on your way here. The land is starved for water. There has been no rain. The drought has gone on since the spring, and nothing we can do will break it. Our magics are very small: long, long ago, we surrendered all our part in the Great Magics to the Gods of Leaf and Star in exchange for long life and peace, and now, what power we retain is not enough to save the land we hold and love."

It sounded to Kellen as if she were talking about a pact of the Wild Magic—paying a price in exchange for a boon. Did that mean Elves had been human once? Did it mean humans had made a bargain like that with the Gods—or that they'd had a chance to make a bargain and hadn't, and so kept their ability to do magic?

But Ashaniel was still speaking.

"I do mean *save* it, for I fear, Kellen, that the land is dying, and if it dies, there will be no reviving it. We have only just been able to keep the forest and fields near Sentarshadeen and our own herds and flocks alive by carrying water from the five springs to the fields, and to the roots of each tree in the Flower Forest, but if a wildfire should start in the arid lands beyond our home forest, there will be no stopping it before all—the woods, the home forest, our city—is destroyed."

She was right, Kellen knew, nodding in agreement. Back in the Wildwood, he'd seen the damage a flash-fire could cause even in a normal well-watered forest. And no matter how much water the Elves had carried to their home woods, if Sentarshadeen was surrounded by a million acres of burning forest, it just wouldn't make any difference. And winter was coming, and winter meant storms. He thought of the dryad's lightning-struck tree back in the Wildwood, and what would have happened if the Wildwood had been as tinder-dry as the country he and Idalia had ridden through for the last sennight. And even without a lightning storm, high wind could bring disaster, if it carried a spark from a cook-fire or lantern into dry grass.

"I can only hope—when Idalia hears of how it stands with Sentarshadeen—that she can—that she will—help us," Ashaniel finished brokenly.

"I can't promise that she can help," Kellen said carefully. "I can promise that I'll talk to her and tell her what's going on. And that we'll try."

He thought back on Idalia's careful nurturing of the Wildwood, of all the things they'd done there, and not always because it was a part of a price. He couldn't imagine Idalia *not* wanting to help, even if she weren't living here. And she *was* living here—they both were.

And that might make things even worse.

If some of the drought-dry woods were on the other side of the border—the side of the border claimed by Armethalieh . . .

Was the High Council foolish enough—mad enough—to try to burn them out if they knew they were here? Did they know about the drought?

"We'll do everything we can," Kellen said simply. "So tell me as much as you can about the situation, would you? Just when did you know there was something wrong?"

The Queen leaned forward earnestly, and began.

⌒

A servant escorted Kellen to the door of the House of Leaf and Star, and bowed politely as he left. On consideration, Kellen wasn't entirely certain it had been a servant—Queens ought to have servants, but Ashaniel wasn't anything like Kellen had expected a Queen to be, except that he was already sure he was half in love with her. Certainly Sentarshadeen was nothing like Armethalieh at all.

Though the sun was long set by now, the way before him was not dark. Lanterns and torches were placed at frequent intervals along the path to light his way—though Kellen was relieved to see, after his conversation with the Queen, that all of them were completely enclosed, to keep any stray spark from flying out. Then again—these were Elves, who seemed constitutionally incapable of doing anything without thinking about it for a very long time. Maybe they'd always done things this way.

More lanterns stretched off into the distance, dwindling into sparks that seemed to hang suspended in space like a cloud of multicolored fireflies. For one dizzying moment the meadow before him seemed to change places with the heavens above, and Kellen could imagine himself walking through a field of softly glowing stars, shining not with the cold blue-white radiance of the night sky, but in all the pale beautiful colors of spring. Many of the lanterns that he saw had walls of colored glass—blue and pink and green and yellow, and even, here and there, a surprising pale violet. Some were even inset with mirrors, so they sparkled and flashed like fireworks as he passed them, while others were filled with reservoirs of perfumed oil, making the night smell as sweet as a garden at noon. No two of the Elven lanterns were alike, Kellen discovered. Some were topped with whirligigs that flashed and spun from the heat within; others had softly chiming bells attached. Every lantern he saw was different, each one a work of high art, worthy to grace a museum or a palace.

He retraced his steps toward the former guesthouse, taking his time. If Sentarshadeen had been beautiful by day, it was completely enchanting by night. It was difficult to believe that none of this was accomplished by magic, but he saw—and sensed—no hint of magic at all.

It was very strange. Armethalieh was a city filled with magic—yet it was entirely ordinary, even prosaic—and the High Council toiled day and night to keep it that way. Sentarshadeen had very little magic about it, yet it was the most magical city Kellen had ever seen, a place of enchantment and wonder.

Several times as he made his way home Kellen saw Elves tending the lanterns nearest their doors. Apparently it was each householder's responsibility to take care of the lanterns nearest their own homes, and he hoped someone was doing it at his and Idalia's house.

When he reached home at last, he was pleased to see that they had: two large golden lanterns in the shape of summer squash hung outside their door, glowing a deep rich gold. Light spilled through the windows of the common room, and through the clear glass panels inset into the door.

Kellen opened the door and stepped inside.

Idalia was lounging on one of the long padded benches along the wall, surrounded by pillows, reading a book. All of their gear had been neatly tidied away, and the house now looked as though it had been theirs for years. A grey cat had appeared from somewhere and was tucked under one of her arms, purring contentedly. Idalia had pulled the stool over to serve as a low table, and a steaming cup of tea was resting on it, along with half an apple.

She looked up when he entered, raising an eyebrow non-committally, and only then did Kellen remember that when he'd gone out he'd been wearing a different set of clothes entirely.

My clothes! I forgot all about them. . . .

He wondered what the Elves had done with them. Thrown them out, probably.

"I'm sorry I'm late getting back," he said. "But I was invited to dinner . . . at the House of Leaf and Star." He couldn't resist a certain amount of smugness at the news.

"Ah." Idalia gently set the cat aside and sat up—it yawned and stretched, then curled up in the warm spot she'd vacated. "And how did you and Sandalon get along with each other?"

Kellen gaped. He watched as Idalia kept herself from snickering with a visible effort, then pulled her face straight.

"You'll soon find, Kellen, that it's impossible to keep a secret in Sentarshadeen—or anywhere else in the Elven lands, for that matter. The Elves are masters of all the arts—and gossip is also an art form. Not only did three people stop by this afternoon to pass the time and tell me Sandalon had made a new friend, but when Astallance brought your other clothes back from the Palace, she told me you'd been invited to dinner." She smiled then. "I would have expected that, anyway; the Queen is famous for her hospitality and if you hadn't been invited today, you *certainly* would have been tomorrow. The only reason I wasn't, was because I haven't left our house." Now she raised an eyebrow. "I told you that in their way, the Elves are sticklers for etiquette. Until I go into public, I don't officially live here. Or rather, there is a strange female human who is a guest here, who may or may not be Idalia the Wildmage."

"Then you know about the drought already?" Kellen asked, not sure whether to be relieved or disappointed.

Idalia leaned forward, her smile fading.

"Perhaps you'd better come and sit down and tell me *all* about your day," she said. "Don't leave anything out just because you think I might have heard it elsewhere."

Kellen sat down beside her and told her about meeting Sandalon and then Ashaniel. He told her what Ashaniel had told him—that there had been drought since spring, that it had begun when the spring rains failed to arrive, and nothing the Elves could do could end it. He told her how tinder-dry the forest was, and traced for her (as well as he could remember) the territory affected, in all directions, as far as the Elves themselves knew it.

Idalia listened intently, and with growing worry of her own. It was clear that although she had heard some of this from other sources, she had not heard the whole, and that what she had heard had only served to increase her concern.

"And she asked if you'd help. I said you would—I said I'd *ask* at least, and that I'd try—was that all right?" Kellen finished anxiously.

"Of course it was," Idalia said absently, patting his knee. "I'll do what I can, and by that, I mean I will try *everything* to help them. We both will. If Sentarshadeen should fall . . ."

She left the sentence unfinished, gazing off into space, her mind obviously elsewhere. "Go to bed, Kellen. You've had a long day, and tomorrow will be just as long."

It wasn't the dismissal of an adult to a child; it was said in a tone of comradely kindness, a gentle reminder that the excitement of being in this amazing place would carry him only so long until it ran out and left him staring exhaustedly into space.

It was hard to remember with all that had happened since then, but this morning Kellen had been on the road, and had gotten up before dawn to feed and water the animals before the day's ride. Since then he'd spent much of the day walking all over Sentarshadeen with Sandalon, so even though it was only just a little while after sunset, he realized that Idalia was right. He *was* tired, and going to bed actually seemed like a good idea.

A very good idea, in fact. Idalia had been wiser than he, to spend the afternoon and evening here, quietly, resting.

"You're right, as usual," he said, and found himself yawning. "Very right," he added, and took her hand for a moment, giving it a quick squeeze before he got up. She looked surprised, then touched, and squeezed her hand back.

The lamps in his room had also been lit, and his Mountain Trader clothes were folded neatly on the bed, cleaned and brushed, just as Idalia had said. Even his boots had been polished.

A quick inspection of the drawers and cabinets as he put away the clothes revealed that Idalia had stowed away the rest of his gear, and someone had made him a gift of a few more sets of Elven guest-clothes, including a dark blue nightrobe of some weaving that was as soft as fur. Kellen removed his Palace-clothes and slipped it on, marveling once more at the simple perfection the Elves brought to everything they did.

There was a bowl of fruit and a slender carafe of juice on the table beside his bed, and on the small desk beside the door, his copies of the three Books of the Wild Magic were stacked neatly. The bed was turned back, and soft linen sheets gleamed invitingly. He hadn't slept in a bed this fine since he'd left the City.

But even tired as he was, Kellen realized that he wasn't quite ready to sleep. He picked up *The Book of Moon* and the desk-lantern and went over to the window seat, opening the windows to the cool of the night. He came back and quenched the other lanterns, so that the room was in darkness, the only light coming from the lamp beside the book and the gentle radiance of the city's many-colored lanterns spilling in through the window. He set the lamp carefully on the sill and settled down to read.

Simple spells of seeing and finding and knowing: most of the spells of the Wild Magic were contained in *The Book of Moons*, the first of the three Books—it was the art and craft of using and adapting them, the philosophy behind them, that were held in *The Book of Sun* and *The Book of Stars*. You could start to practice the Wild Magic within minutes of picking up the Books, but it would take you a lifetime to understand it. He'd barely begun.

His thoughts drifted away from the Book in his hands as he gazed out through his window into the lighted city below. Standing in the Low Market in Armethalieh, holding this Book in his hands for the first time, could he have ever imagined he would be here? Could he even have imagined this place existed?

Standing outside the Delfier Gate, hearing it barred behind him forever, would he have thought it was worth Banishment to come here and see what he had seen?

Yes. But not worth all the lives of those people the High Council is going to make miserable by annexing their lands just to try to get at me.

That's the problem, really—I don't mind paying the price, but is it fair that another price should be extracted from people who don't even know me?

No. Not if the Wild Magic was involved. The Wild Magic could ask you to pay any price it chose, up to and including your own life, but it would never, *never*, ask you to pay another's life. You could not pay what you did not own, not in the Wild Magic.

But he hadn't *asked* to come here. He hadn't made any bargains with Wild Magic. So was their involvement due to Wild Magic, or was it only coincidence?

Or did Father plan to annex the Wildwood all along?

It was possible. It was more than possible. In retrospect, Kellen now recognized the seeds of greed and avarice in his father, a desperate need to be numbered among the great Arch-Mages. Perhaps, just as Idalia had said, Kellen's defection was only the excuse, not the cause.

He hoped so. All the grief and pain for others that had been and was being unleashed hung heavily on his heart.

And this strange drought, this dangerous weather—he wondered if the reason Idalia had brought them here was part of another price, for she surely hadn't been *willing* to come. He knew the Wild Magic was powerful, but he'd still barely begun to learn about it. Could it truly be powerful enough to bring an end to this terrible drought in time?

And if it was, what would be the price of that? And who would pay it?

Chapter Eighteen

The City Never Sleeps

Lycaelon Tavadon paced irritably behind his throne in the Council Chamber, waiting for the Twelve to arrive. This meeting was not of his calling, and he did not expect it to go well.

The news his agents had brought him over the last sennights had not been good. It had, in fact, been a catalogue of disasters, each more baffling than the last.

The Scouring Hunt had been called up and sent forth—at

great cost to the Mages and their stores of hoarded energy. A handpicked troop of Militia and Lawspeakers had ridden out ahead—though the Hunt would overtake them and finish its cleansing work days before they arrived—to bring news of Armethalieh's will to its newly annexed dominions, stewards to govern them and assessors and tax gatherers to make sure that the crofts and villages were smoothly integrated into the great family of Armethaliehan lands. When they arrived in lands newly humbled by such an awe-inspiring display of Mageborn power, its inhabitants should be deeply grateful to receive the City's protection.

Even though the City itself had visited the terror of the Scouring Hunt upon them . . .

And The Outlaw would be taken, run to ground, with the just vengeance of the City exacted upon him at last.

But that wasn't what had happened.

The first news to reach Lycaelon as the remains of the Scouring Hunt came limping home was the worst: The Outlaw had escaped once again. Somehow the miserable whelp had *known* the Hunt was coming and had fled before it, vanishing beyond the Hunt's power to follow, for by the laws of the magick that had given the Hounds life and power, they could not follow their prey outside Armethalieh's newly expanded borders.

And just as bad, so Lycaelon discovered from the minds of the stone Hounds—for with the proper spells, a Mage of sufficient power could see and hear all that a Hound had seen and heard while Hunting—the boy had help in his wickedness, an ally whose name Lycaelon had forgotten long ago, to his cost.

Idalia. His daughter. His treacherous Banished *Wildmage* daughter.

The Outlaw Hunt sent after her years before had returned, baffled, unable to find her. How that could be, he had not then, and did not now, have any idea. But when there was no word of her for two entire years, he had assumed that she must have died in that grace period between dusk and dawn. Even near the Delfier Gate, after all, the wilderness was dangerous, and there were rogues aplenty and wild animals who could have removed her from the world before the Hunt had been released. She might even have chosen to die by her own hand, rather than face the life of an Outlaw or the terror of the Hunt.

But clearly—so he saw now—she had not run afoul of misfortune. Somehow she had escaped, and not content with escaping justice, had obviously found some way to infect Kellen with her twisted madness from afar, and then claimed him for her own in the moment that the City's protection had been lifted from him.

Someday, girl, I will find you both. And when I do, I swear by the Eternal Light, there will come such a reckoning as will make even your Tainted soul tremble!

The door to the Council chamber opened, and the rest of the Council began to arrive, austere and magisterial in their grey Council robes: Breulin, Meron, Volpiril, Perizel, Lorins, Arance, Ganaret, Nagid, Vilmos, Dagan, Isas, Harith.

A herald announced each one as he entered the room, and an Undermage servant waited beside each one's chair to serve him.

Volpiril, Light blast him back into the Darkness, looked positively gloating at the current turn of events, though he did his best to look austere and dispassionate. Isas and Harith were, as always, Lycaelon's creatures, and would back him no matter what he did, but Breulin and Perizel both had a dangerous streak of independence, and the news from the west had been shockingly bad.

Within the Council there were always undercurrents of alliance and jockeyings for position. And it was, disturbing though the thought might be, entirely possible for the head of the Council and the chief Arch-Mage of Armethalieh to be deposed, set aside, forced to yield his place to another. It had not been done in decades. It had *never* been done to a Tavadon.

Two for him, three against him, and every member of the Council, Isas and Harith included, was both ruthless and ambitious, and each had sources of information nearly as extensive as Lycaelon's own. Each of them had reviewed—as was their right—the experiences of the golems of the Scouring Hunt . . . the ones that had returned, at any rate. Too many of the creatures the Council thought invincible had not returned at all, and that after The Outlaw had somehow managed to utterly destroy all the packs sent against him.

And since this new campaign was all by Lycaelon Tavadon's orders, the Arch-Mage himself was to blame.

"Gentlemen, shall we convene?" Lycaelon said smoothly, masking his unease as he settled into his seat.

This was a special session of the Council, but the business of the City still had to be dealt with first, for the good of the City. Several smaller matters were raised and handled quickly and efficiently, but Lycaelon could feel the current of tension and expectation running beneath it all, like a riptide beneath the still surface of the sea. Everyone in the room knew what the true purpose of this meeting was.

"And now, the last item on our agenda for this afternoon. The Western Campaign," Lycaelon began.

Normally they would have heard the reports of the Mages who rode with the Militia in person, but those men were still in the field, and besides, this was too delicate a situation to discuss in the presence of anyone outside the High Council. The field Mages had reported by scrying-glass to Lord Arance, who had worked the spell that had trapped the sendings in the clear golden sphere of Farspeaking until they should be released with a counterspell.

"Before we hear the reports of our Undermages in the west, perhaps it would be helpful to us all to review what we already know about the situation," Lycaelon said. "The people of the west have a long history of contempt for the civilizing benefits of citizenship in our City."

"We know that those damned upstart western rabble are nothing but a pack of savages," Lord Ganaret said fiercely, leaning forward. "If you ask me, the Hunt should have scoured them *all* off the land!"

"Now, Ganaret," Volpiril said smoothly. "What would there be to tax in that case? Not that there seems to be anything to tax in any case, if what we have heard so far is true. It seems that Arch-Mage Lycaelon's well-known humanitarianism has led him into trying to bring the benefits of civilization to people who simply aren't ready to receive it." High Mage Volpiril sat back in his chair, well pleased with his opening remarks. "Only the savage would destroy his own food, shelter, and belongings and flee into the wilderness rather than accept the rule of the civilized."

"Crops burned in their fields . . . whole villages gone overnight . . . it's Demon-magic, that's what it is," muttered the aged Lord Vilmos. Vilmos, it was well known, saw Demons beneath every bed and in every chamber pot.

"Now, Lord Vilmos, I think you go too far," Lord Isas said hastily, with a quick glance at Lycaelon.

"Obviously The Outlaw found a way to spy upon our councils, as I warned you he would," Lycaelon interrupted, turning the discussion back in a more appropriate direction. "My lords, this squabbling ill becomes us. Surely these are only minor setbacks. The villages will accept our benevolent rule with time. Arance, let us hear the reports from the field."

Lycaelon would have suppressed them if he could, already having a fairly good idea of what the full versions of those reports contained, but his power in the City was not that great. The Arch-Mage led the Council, but he did not rule it. If Lycaelon only had his way, he would dispense entirely with the entire pack of shortsighted nattering fools, fit only to raise power for his use, and shepherd Armethalieh to her destiny as the Golden City should be guided, with wisdom and vision!

His wisdom. His vision. He alone had the foresight to envision what must be done. And he alone had the strength of character to sacrifice anything and anyone, even his sole son and heir, to preserve the safety of the City.

But it was not possible. And he was certain the others' sources of information were nearly as good as his own. There was no purpose in wasting his energy on a fight he would surely lose. Better to let the reports enter the record, and plan how to turn the information to his advantage later.

Arance stood, and set a large black box on the table before him. He opened it to reveal a golden sphere of flawless crystal, which he lifted out and raised gently, his lips moving silently in the complicated counterspell that would release the stored energies contained within it.

The sphere rose into the air and hovered at man-height over the center of the chamber. It began to spin, faster and faster, until it vanished, and in its place stood an Undermage in field robes, his form faintly golden and transparent.

"My lords of the Council, I speak to you from the Western Hills, and bring you news that makes ill hearing. We have come today to a village called Merryvale, but the gates are barred and they will not give us entry. They have refused to allow a steward to be set over them, and have given us a petition to be delivered to the Council, requesting that you allow them to live in peace under their own laws. They have refused to supply us with fodder for our animals or food for our men, nor can we supply ourselves, for the fields and orchards surrounding the village are stripped bare. There is no game in the woods, and no fish in the stream. Our supplies are running low. Several of the men have been badly stung by bees as well. Since we cannot stay here, we are moving on to the next village as quickly as we can." The image faded, to be replaced by another, and the report went on.

In every place the delegation from Armethalieh went, the story was the same—or worse. Some villages were gone entirely, with nothing to show they had been there but hearthstones and the village well. When crops had not been harvested down to the last seed, they had been thoroughly spoiled by wildlife, though the travelers saw not so much as a single bird.

Misfortunes abounded. Equipment went missing, horses strayed or went inexplicably lame, supplies were lost. The only wildlife that ever appeared was never anything that could be hunted and eaten—it was inevitably something that would plague them. Flocks of starlings appeared overhead just at mealtime, and anything that wasn't covered was soon contaminated by droppings. Mice got into the supplies, foxes stole them, and more than once a weary and unsuspecting Mage or officer climbed into his bedroll only to discover that a wildcat had been there first . . . and had left evidence of its displeasure behind.

Everywhere the Armethaliehans went, the news of their coming had somehow gone before them, and no one wanted to see them. If the Mages had not used their magic to force the few villages they encountered to feed them, the Armethaliehan delegation would have starved, but every time they did use the High Magick, the accidents that befell their party increased.

"I see no recourse save to return to the City, Lord Arch-Mage. We await your orders."

The figure of the last Undermage vanished upon the conclusion of the last report. The spinning crystal sphere reappeared, and slowed until once more it hovered, motionless, in the air. Lord Arance summoned it back to its box, enclosed it once more, then sat down.

"It seems the west is not as willing to accept the benefits of civilization as is the north and south," Breulin commented dryly. "My lords, we are dangerously overextended—and for what? A wasteland. Where is the fertile granary you promised us, Arch-Mage Lycaelon? Where is The Outlaw? Where are the hordes of inferior beast-folk who supposedly lived alongside of the human villagers, corrupting them with their insidious presence? We have poured out magic like water on the desert sand—first to expand the boundaries, then to create the Scouring Hunt—and it has brought us nothing."

There was a general mutter of agreement, and Lycaelon realized with a faint sense of despair that he had lost. The Undermages' reports were damning. The Council would never agree to the further investment of resources needed to secure the Western Hills for Armethalieh. He could scarcely blame them, for at this point, it had been all loss and no gain.

One by one the members of the Council—all of whom had cheered him so ardently when he had proposed his plan originally—rose to speak. Each of them supported Breulin's position—even Isas and Harith expressed timid misgivings at the united opposition shown by the westerners, and the cost of overcoming it. The City's resources and magickal reserves were dangerously low, and it would be the work of long moonturns to rebuild their reserves again without disturbing the populace.

Last of all, Volpiril rose, smiling benignly.

"Knowledge is never wasted," Volpiril—treacherous, subtle Volpiril!—began slowly. "I believe the Arch-Mage has served the City well. It is good for us to know who our enemies are, and how much they hate us. How else can we know the depth of our own need for protection? And the Scouring Hunt has surely swept the borders clear of rabble for a season at least. Let us rejoice in that." He smiled benignly on the assembled Council, Lycaelon most of all. The Arch-Mage gritted his teeth in silence, but not without effort. The impudent Darkspawn! How *dare* he speak in such patronizing tones!

"But let us also heed this warning against rashness and the dangers of trying to protect too much at once. As the Arch-Mage said in his stirring speech—which I'm certain we all took to heart—the Golden City is the City of Man, a flickering candle in the darkness of bestiality and error that surrounds it. We dare not let this precious Light go out, even though we naturally grieve to see fellow humans suffering and in peril.

"And so, it is my recommendation, which I place most humbly before this assembled Council, that we take instruction from our momentary weakness, and return our borders to their ancient, hallowed, and historic limits, abandoning our new territories. Now and always, Armethalieh the Golden must stand alone, perfect and pure! To the walls—and not one ell beyond!"

Volpiril sat down again amid murmurs of approval. There was a moment of expectant silence.

It was some small consolation, Lycaelon thought sourly, to see Breulin looking as irritated as he felt himself at Volpiril's pretty speechmaking. It was true that the City's food supply would not suffer—the farmers had no other market for their crops, after all. They would continue to bring them—but now, they would want to be paid for them.

And if ever there had been a moment in the history of the City when the actions of the Council had virtually handed anyone who had even *thought* of rebellion the signal to do so without fear of reprisal, this was it. Why should *anyone* outside the City bother to pay his just tithes and taxes now?

"It will undoubtedly come as a great surprise to the villages of the Delfier Valley to discover they are no longer to be taxed or claimed by the City, but undoubtedly the visionary Lord Volpiril has some way to replace those lost revenues as well!" Lycaelon muttered, just loud enough for his fellow Mages to hear.

He waited, but no one rose to speak in opposition to Volpiril's plan. And he would not demean himself. If they could not see the disaster they were brewing for themselves, *he* would do nothing more to save them from it. Let them reap the consequences of their folly. Let them see what ignorant, foolish children they really were. Let the dark days come, let all see them for what they were, and when things were darkest, let all turn to him, Arch-Mage Lycaelon Tavadon, let them *beg* him to save them from the consequences of their thoughtless arrogance and pride—!

"I call the vote," Lycaelon said. He extended his hand, palm down. Disapproval.

It went as he thought it would go from the moment Volpiril rose to speak. With ten in favor and two abstentions, his dissenting vote was overruled.

The Council would abandon its new territories, pulling back its boundaries to the City walls themselves.

But this was not the end, Lycaelon vowed silently. He would accept neither this defeat nor the City's loss. Someday—someday *soon*—in the name of the City, the Council would reclaim all the lands Lycaelon had been forced to forfeit in its name today.

And more.

Much more.

⌒

ANIGREL had received advance warning of the disastrous failure of the Scouring Hunt—more than Lycaelon had, for his information had come a fortnight ago, when he had filled his iron bowl with dove's blood and herbs to make his regular moonturn's report.

He had learned then with a mixture of dread and glee of the Hunt's utter failure, and the defeat of the proud Armethaliehan army that rode in its wake. Glee—because the City had drained every reserve and overextended itself severely to mount the attack, leaving itself exhausted and vulnerable, easy prey. Dread—because failure on such a vast scale required scapegoats, and Anigrel knew perfectly well that his own position in Lycaelon Tavadon's household was less secure than it had been before The Outlaw's Banishment.

After all, private secretaries could be had for the asking, and he certainly wasn't needed as a tutor anymore.

Today's emergency Council session could only mean that the Council was meeting to review the reports from the field, admit what each of them had known a sennight ago, and fix the blame.

"There are no failures, only opportunities." He only hoped it was possible to grasp the opportunity in this.

"Anigrel!"

Arch-Mage Lycaelon strode into his private office, his aura crackling with barely leashed rage. Anigrel rose from behind his desk and appeared in the connecting doorway.

"Lord Arch-Mage." He schooled his face to a meek expression of bland deference. "The meeting did not go well?"

For a moment Anigrel thought Lycaelon would explode—literally burst into a thousand pieces, like a Founding Day firework. But somehow the Arch-Mage kept his composure in the face of Anigrel's goading. Such seemingly innocent remarks were one of Anigrel's few pleasures, and a necessary part of his masquerade, Anigrel told himself, because they were just the sort of thing someone with no inside knowledge of events *would* say.

"The meeting did not go well, Light blast Volpiril into cold Darkness and the rest of the Council with him for their foolishness," Lycaelon snarled. "Volpiril says, in his 'wisdom,' that if the Western Campaign has been such a failure, the only thing we can do is abandon *all* our lands, including the Home Farms!"

It was just as well that Lycaelon was so angry he paid no attention to Anigrel at all, for the momentary surge of shock and elation must surely have set its mark, however briefly, on Anigrel's features.

"You should have seen Breulin's face when the Council agreed to that; he will think twice about supporting that viper next time."

Lycaelon sounded savage in his satisfaction at that—well, Breulin owned several of the Home Farms, and now he would have to go without the protection of the City if anything untoward happened out there. More to the point, if his servants and laborers elected to defect and keep everything the farms produced for themselves, there was nothing Mage Breulin would be able to do to enforce his will.

Now Lycaelon shook his head, the energy that his anger had generated running out of him like water from a cracked jar. "But it is done. Our borders are our walls, as it was in the beginning. The proclamations will go out as soon as they can be enscribed."

"This is . . . strange news, Lord Arch-Mage," Anigrel said slowly. And important enough to report immediately, without waiting for the usual time.

"Strange indeed. But I will not let their blindness defeat me." Lycaelon's voice hardened. "You have taught me the value of perseverance, eh, my young friend? And now, Anigrel, I am tired. Bring me tea."

Anigrel hurried to do as he was bid, his mind turning on what this meant to his own mission.

"There are no failures, only opportunities!"

And this would be a great opportunity indeed . . . for the Dark Lady.

FROM the habit of years, Idalia woke a little before dawn. She could feel the life of Sentarshadeen all around her, like a melody played just below the threshold of hearing, but mingled with it, terribly, was a *wrongness,* a discord—faint still, but holding within it the potential to grow stronger with time.

The drought had disturbed her ever since she'd seen the first signs of it as they rode toward Sentarshadeen. Drought and flood were both aspects of the balance of Nature, for Nature was not gentle with her creatures, and sometimes the ways she achieved her balance were necessarily harsh. But a natural drought was a thing that was long years in the making, a thing of scant rains, not *no* rain. The High Hills were a country of long dry summers, wet springs, and soaking autumn rains, and a dry summer could extend somewhat into either side of spring or autumn without overmuch harm. But there had been no rain this spring at all, and now none this autumn, and that was not natural.

And more troubling than that, rivers that should have run fast and deep into Elven lands, full with melted snow from the High Peaks, were dry as well.

Perhaps ending the drought would be a simple matter, requiring nothing more than a simple—though powerful—spell. The whole of Sentarshadeen would eagerly share the price, Idalia knew. She only hoped it would be that easy.

Best to find out for sure, then, instead of worrying about it.

She rose and dressed, some imp of perversity causing her to reject the sturdy silks and woolens her hosts had provided in favor of her own buckskins. Let her be seen for what she was: human, and mortal, and Wildmage. Later she would wear the silks as a matter of courtesy, of thanking her hosts tacitly for providing them, but first impressions were important, especially here, and she meant them to think of her as she intended to *be.*

And Jermayan . . .

No. She would not think about Jermayan, ever again. And

if the man had a scrap of good manners left to him, he'd arrange matters so their paths never crossed. It was for the best. The man was an Elven Knight. He was used to making hard choices. He'd just have to live with hers.

An unbidden thought intruded. *I only hope that* I *can . . .*

She shook it off, moved quietly across the main room, to look in on Kellen. He was sound asleep, tangled up in the blankets as though he'd lost a fight with them. She felt a fond smile cross her lips. Kellen slept like a hibernating bear; there was very little chance she'd wake him, no matter how much noise she made.

She quickly brewed her morning tea. She had no appetite herself, but she set out a plate of breakfast pastries for Kellen to find when he awoke. There'd been many visitors last night while Kellen had been out exploring, and at the moment, the larder was full enough to withstand even the onslaughts of a growing teenager's appetite.

Kellen . . . Idalia remembered her first experience in Elven lands and sighed. Last night, when Kellen had come back from the Palace, his eyes had been so full of stars it was the Gods' own mercy he'd made it home at all, and walked *through* the door instead of into it! The Elves were so beautiful, so kind, their protracted lives so seemingly perfect . . . it was easy to fall into the trap of thinking they were always right as well.

And they *certainly think so, after all. It's easier to shift an overburdened mule than to get one of the Elvenborn to change his mind!* "Stubborn as an Elf" . . . now *there* was a new maxim for the City fathers to din into younglings' heads! And it took you forever to notice, because, when one of the Elvenkind disagreed with you, all they ever did was smile and change the subject, and it could take a person forever to figure out that there'd been an argument . . . and you'd lost.

She would never lose her admiration for them, her respect for their wisdom and knowledge, and her affection for them— but Jermayan had served her one good turn. She was no longer blind to their faults, either as individuals or as a race.

But all this cloud-gathering wasn't getting her anywhere, and the sun was almost up. Idalia finished her tea, washed out the cup, and left the tea-things out where Kellen would find them. Then she picked up her walking-staff, filled her pockets with charged keystones, and left their lodging.

She took a quicker route than Kellen had followed the night before, up past the House of Leaf and Star and into the orchard beyond. Even at this early hour, Elves were already hard at work carrying water to the fragile trees. She greeted several of them by name, but did not stop to do more than exchange the briefest of greetings. The sooner she had her answers, the sooner her real work could begin. And with their usual sensitivity to her, they understood that she had an urgent task, and did not delay her beyond the simplest of courtesies.

A few more minutes' walk brought her to her goal: one of the ever-flowing springs that supplied the water for all of Sentarshadeen, located in the meadow beyond the Queen's Orchard. Without rain, these were the *only* sources of water for the city. There were five of them, as she remembered: Alcemil, Caldulin, Elassar, Helanarya, Songmairie. This should be Songmairie. Helanarya and Elassar were under Sentarshadeen itself, their waters sent by wind-driven pumps to course through the miles of pipes whose results had so delighted Kellen last night.

A wide path of smooth stone led up to Songmairie—laid down, Idalia guessed, when it had become necessary to bring water carts to the spring several times a day—and the verge of the spring itself was edged with a decorative pattern of stones and tiles. Grass—lush here, so close to the water source—grew up between them.

She looked out over the meadow, but there were no unicorns to be seen at this hour, though she knew that quite a large herd lived in Sentarshadeen, since Elves and unicorns often lived together. Centuries ago, during the Endarkened War, Elven Knights had ridden unicorns into battle against the Endarkened hordes and their allies. All memory of that war had carefully been edited out of texts in the City, and it was so long ago that Idalia doubted that any of the Elvenkind now alive remembered it personally. But the memories of the Elves were very long, and their recorded memories of Demonkind longer still, and it was never safe to forget the Shadow.

She knelt and drank from the spring. The water was icy and pure. But not enough—even if Sentarshadeen held ten times its population, and all of them labored day and night—to water enough acreage to save them from disaster. All it would take would be one good grass-fire, one lightning strike . . .

One out-of-control salamander, a high wind, or just another year of no rain. And no reason for it. It was raining in Merryvale, and that's east of here, toward the sea. Why shouldn't it rain here?

Still kneeling, she emptied her pockets of keystones. She dipped each in the spring—water called to water—and then arranged them around her in a rough circle.

She cupped her hands again, filling them with the spring, and scattered the water around her, moistening the keystones a second time. Earth-magic and the spells of Finding and Calling required the caster's blood and the fruits of the earth as tokens of intent, but weather magic was the magic of air and water, and did not use those symbols as a bridge between the power of the Wildmage and that of the Gods.

She touched her wet hands lightly to her lips, blowing over them gently, and let the power well up in her, concentrating on her need and her desire.

Rain.

Kneeling in the earth, feeling its thirst, Idalia smelled water, tasted water, willed water to *be*. It was time for rain— the harvest was in, the land was ready to rest, to sleep. Time for rain, to bring the autumn leaves down from the trees and ready the earth for winter and snow. She could feel it—in the air, just over the peaks, in the distance—and called it to her with the intensity of a woman calling for her lover. *Come to me, Beloved, and give me rest.*

Nothing.

After a long fruitless struggle, Idalia opened her eyes with a sigh. Not so much as a shift in the wind. The keystones were drained, and the sky was still an empty arid blue.

More than any other, weather magic required patience and care. A storm couldn't be whistled up for the asking—not out of a cloudless sky, at least, and certainly not without paying a greater price than Idalia cared to. To change the weather was more a matter of a series of gentle nudges over time, more like herding sheep than lighting a fire.

But if her spell was going to have any effect at all, she should have felt *something*. And she'd felt nothing at all. It wouldn't matter how much power she used, or how many folk she shared the price among, she knew: the result would be the same.

The wind would not shift. The rains would not come.

Idalia's shoulders slumped.

This is no natural drought.

She'd suspected as much, after hearing Kellen's story the night before—Ashaniel would not have been so disturbed by a natural change in the weather. The Elves had seen so many droughts in the course of a lifetime that a natural drought would simply be met with a sigh, a hope that the Gods of Leaf and Star would set things in balance soon, and some careful conservation until the drought was over. They were sensitive to the health of their land as humans (other than Wildmages) were not; they would have known if this drought was like the others that had come and gone in the past.

They had—as she had—felt the subtle *wrongness*. They had known that no natural dry spell would give rise to that feeling of imbalance.

And that meant that someone was causing this.

High Mages? It wasn't impossible. Would Lycaelon attack the Elves indirectly this way, perhaps to drive them farther away from the City and the lands it claimed? It would be a clever way to do it, since he could, if challenged, easily deny any such thing, even to the Elves. High Magick, stolen as it was from all of the citizens of Armethalieh, and learned according to strict formulas, did not *have* a signature in the way that Wild Magic did, identifying who the Mage was that set it in motion.

But much as she'd like to place all the evils of the world at Lycaelon's doorstep, until the City had claimed and pacified both the Western Hills and the High Reaches, they had little motive for starting a war with the Elven lands—and war it would be, the moment the Elves discovered who was behind the drought. And Lycaelon could not have set a spell of this magnitude alone. He would have needed the backing of the rest of the Council.

No. Idalia abandoned the idea reluctantly. Though the City might yet be discovered to be behind this, the Elves had other enemies. Enemies older than the City, and more powerful . . .

Wearily, Idalia gathered up her empty keystones and got to her feet. Figuring out who was responsible for this would take a lot more work than she'd already put in. She'd have to rest first, and then make her plans—and weave her spells— very, very carefully.

If her suspicions were true, she could not afford even the slightest of mistakes in her hunting.

KELLEN slept deeply and well on his first night in Sentarshadeen, his dreams untroubled. When he awoke at last, it was to the gentle tickle of whiskers on his face, as the grey cat that seemed to have adopted them investigated him curiously.

A glance out the window told him he had slept far later than he could remember sleeping in—well, it would have to go back to before he began formal schooling. In the Wildwood, the day and its tasks started with the dawn, and back in the City, Kellen had always been in a hurry to be out of the house by Second Morning Bells at the latest in order to avoid Lycaelon.

But here there was nothing pressing that *had* to be done, and no one to avoid.

He lay there for a few minutes, examining the feeling and not certain how to label it, while he gave the grey cat the thorough head scratch she demanded. He was sure there were things to be doing here in Sentarshadeen, but at the moment he didn't have to do any of them. It felt peculiar.

The cat seemed to find some fault with his attentions, for she suddenly gave a violent sneeze directly into his face and bounded off through the window Kellen had left open the night before. "Now, there's gratitude!" Kellen said, half annoyed, half amused. "You ought to belong to Lycaelon."

Yawning, Kellen got up and went in search of Idalia and breakfast.

He found breakfast—a plate of cold pastries, and tea-things laid out for him on the table beside the hearth-stove—but no Idalia. Her room was empty, the bed neatly made. Obviously she had gone out several hours before, leaving him to sleep.

He filled the kettle and put it on to heat, and while he was waiting for it to boil, he washed and dressed, being careful to use as little water as possible and marveling once again at the comfort and efficiency of the Elven plumbing. No shivering outdoors as he had in the Wildwood or waiting around for servants to bring water as he had back in the City. Everything was just *there*, exactly when and where you wanted it.

Clean and dressed—after a little hesitation, he'd chosen one of the new Elven outfits that had been left for him—he ate, savoring the unfamiliar Elven spices, while deciding what to do with his day. The view from the balcony was just as amazing this morning as it had been last night; now he noticed something else, the *sound* of Sentarshadeen.

In Armethalieh, he'd grown up listening to the harmonizing of the bells that marked the rhythms of the City's days and seasons; in the Wildwood, he'd become accustomed to the way that random birdcalls, water sounds, and the song of the winds in the leaves created a background "song," of sorts.

Here in Sentarshadeen, the magic of the bells of Armethalieh had somehow been grafted onto the sounds of the

Wildwood. The song of the forest, added to the wind chimes, the wind bells, and wind harps in the gardens, created a music unlike anything he had ever heard. Beautiful, peaceful—he wondered what it would be like if there wasn't a drought. Surely there would be the voices of a thousand fountains, waterfalls, and the great voice of the river as well, adding yet another note to the consort.

Then, as he finished his breakfast, a breeze brought him the *scent* of Sentarshadeen—or at least, the scent in drought time—and it was as subtle as the song. As in the Wildwood, Kellen could smell the aroma of warm grass and green leaves, but with a hint of sweet herbs and foreign spices added, a suggestion of something in flower. The scent was refreshing, but again, he wondered what it would be like if there wasn't a drought, and lusher flowers were in bloom, roses and phlox, and the water lilies of the ponds.

The scent, the sound, the sight, called to him, and Kellen felt a restlessness come over him. He didn't want to just sit around waiting for Idalia to come back, not with a whole exotic Elven city to explore. He supposed Sandalon must have had lessons this morning or else he would already be here; well, Sandalon would certainly be able to find Kellen anywhere he went, if what Idalia had told him about the Elves' penchant for gossip was true. And meanwhile, he'd take this chance to get a better look around. If everybody knew he'd had dinner at the Palace last night, they might be a little more forthcoming today.

⌐

KELLEN wandered along the canyon floor, peering in at the half-hidden houses as he passed and hoping he wasn't being too rude as he did so. From all that he'd seen yesterday, Kellen had gotten used to the idea that all the Elves were fabulously wealthy by human standards, but what he saw today confused him. Some of the houses he passed, while obviously lived-in, were nearly empty, and so tiny they consisted of only one room.

Were these Elves poor? Or had they just chosen to live without possessions? Nothing he saw anywhere, even in the smallest houses, looked shabby or of poor quality, and everything he saw had the serene beauty of Nature—nothing cluttered, nothing out of place, everything where it was meant to be. *Harmonious.* Kellen wasn't quite sure where the word came from, but it certainly fit. The Elven city was the visual counterpart to a piece of music: everything exactly where it ought to be, every portion necessary, nothing wasted, nothing too much.

Some of the houses had tiny gardens planted around them, and as Kellen passed one house, he came upon an Elven man watering his garden with a bucket and dipper. Kellen slowed down, then stopped to watch.

The man was very old, Kellen realized. His long braided hair had lightened with age until it was the blue of storm clouds, and his body had the wiry slenderness of age. He was wearing a simple loose tunic and trousers, and his feet were bare. He looked up as Kellen approached, and regarded him with bright-eyed interest.

"I see you, Kellen Tavadon, friend of Sandalon."

"I see you, gracious sir," Kellen responded, trying to copy the little half-bow he'd seen last night at the House of Leaf and Star. He started to ask a question, and stopped himself just in time. Asking questions was the height of rudeness here, he was starting to realize. But maybe he could get his answers without asking questions.

"I'm walking through the city because it's the most beautiful city I've ever seen. I have never seen an Elven city, for I have spent most of my life in the city of Armethalieh. I confess that I'm curious about both your city and your people," Kellen said, after a long moment's thought. *Approach the subject obliquely, that's the key,* he thought to himself encouragingly. He was rewarded by a faint smile from the elderly Elf.

"Huh," the old man said, as if speaking to his plants. "And they say humans have no manners. Come and sit a moment in my garden, Kellen Tavadon, and listen to an old man talk to his plants, if it would please you."

"It would please me and honor me very much, goodsir," Kellen replied, cheered that his first attempt at Elven manners had succeeded so well.

The old man came over to the edge of the path, ushering Kellen into his garden. There was a low wooden bench placed along the wall of the house where it would catch the morning sun, a bench made of wood carved in the sinuous lines of a curving vine and as soft and silken beneath his hand as an Elven cloak. Kellen seated himself carefully as the old man returned to his watering.

"Here is eyebright, which will soothe the weariness brought on by late nights over books, and goldcap, which makes a soothing tea, and purple hand—you will remark the shape—which is an excellent poultice for bruises. And you are a Wildmage."

The last was stated as matter-of-factly as the names of the herbs, so it took Kellen a few moments to figure out that it might be a question.

"I . . . yes. No. I don't know, not really," he managed, feeling, somehow, that nothing less than the absolute truth was needed here. "I have the three Books, and I read and study them, and I—I do my best. I haven't been studying as long as my sister, though."

"Yet quite long enough to be filled with questions about where the Wild Magic *comes* from, for that is the nature of humans, to always be filled with questions." The elderly Elf appeared to be addressing his herbs, not Kellen. "It is in the nature of the world that if something is absent from one place, it merely goes to another, and as there are no questions among the Elves, it follows that humans must ask twice as many questions to make up for it," the old one said, smiling down at a set of rosemary bushes, then looking up at Kellen, still smiling. "Perhaps."

"I think you might be right," Kellen answered, smiling back.

"Then it may be that you would be good enough to satisfy

an old man's curiosity, Kellen Tavadon, and tell him where the world comes from," the old one said, moving slowly along the rows of plants with his dipper, pouring out a small measure of water onto the roots of each.

"The world doesn't come from anywhere," Kellen said, confused. "The world just *is*."

The ancient Elf nodded, satisfied. "And so it is with the Wild Magic, young Kellen. The Wild Magic just *is*. Root and leaf, world and magic, you will never have seen a leaf without a root, or a root without a leaf, in the proper order of things. As I tend my garden, so do the Wildmages tend the world, by their bargains and prices keeping the world as much in balance as I with my hoe and dipper. Anyone in Sentarshadeen will tell you the same, for we are a long-lived people, who have not yet forgotten the Beginning of Days."

"Then—" Kellen stumbled to a halt, unable to think of any way to phrase what he wanted to know so it wouldn't come out as a question. "I would like to hear more about the Wild Magic, and the history of the Elves," he finally said.

"Come another time," the old man said agreeably, setting the dipper back in the now-empty bucket, "and I will tell you of the Beginning of Time, long before our race had met your own, and of the Great Queen Vielissiar Farcarinon, who riddled with dragons and learned the secret of making the bargain that gained the great boons of peace and long life for our race. If you lose your way, ask any you meet the path to Morusil's house, and they will be happy to bring you to me."

"Thank you," Kellen said, getting to his feet. He was starting to get used to the Elves' ways of putting an end to a conversation by now, though he wasn't sure he was ever going to get used to their indirect way of asking-without-asking, and answering questions you hadn't asked. He bowed to Morusil, and stepped out onto the path again, continuing on his way.

The path led onward, toward the river, by a different route than he had followed yesterday. He saw no one else in the gardens as he passed them, but perhaps the folk who lived here were indoors—or perhaps they were elsewhere, workng. He supposed that even Elves must work . . .

His conversation with Morusil, short and inconclusive though it had been, had certainly given him a lot to think about, even if he hadn't answered any of the questions Kellen had really wanted to ask. The Elves were a lot like the Wild Magic itself in that way, Kellen thought. But as far as he could tell, it seemed as if the Elves thought that the Wild Magic was actually the magic of the entire world, and that when he and Idalia—and the other Wildmages, who must be around somewhere, even though Kellen had never yet met one—were making their bargains and paying their prices, they were actually bargaining with and paying to the same force that was responsible for, well . . . *everything*, from twigs to unicorns.

Leaf and root, Morusil had said. World and magic, two sides of the same coin, indivisible. All part of the same thing, with the Wild Magic, the magic of balance and healing, to bind them both together.

And somehow, the Mages of Armethalieh had just managed to . . . forget . . . that, if they'd ever known it.

Why? How? When?

Kellen frowned. There was something on the tip of his mind, something he'd heard once, and almost remembered . . .

But the thought was gone before he could chase it to its source. He shrugged. He could ask Idalia about it tonight. Or he could ask some of the other Elves, assuming he could figure out how to do that without asking any questions. Hadn't Morusil said that anyone in Sentarshadeen would tell him about the Wild Magic? He thought he'd see if the old man had been right: he could stand to learn a lot more about it—and as soon as he could—if he was going to use it to help the Elves.

But right now there didn't seem to be anyone tracking him down with demands that he *do* something. Not even the Queen.

Maybe Elves, with their centuries of life ahead of them, rarely saw any reason to hurry.

If that was the case, he supposed he could afford the time for a leisurely amble along the byways of Sentarshadeen, retracing the paths he'd taken yesterday with Sandalon and learning new ones.

Besides, Idalia was probably looking into the situation already; *he* surely didn't know enough to determine what was causing this drought! He wouldn't even begin to know where to start, and as for actually doing anything about it—

I think I'd better leave that up to Idalia. If there was a place for him in the solution, she certainly wouldn't be slow in telling him about it! After all, she hadn't hesitated for a moment in getting him involved in everything he didn't actively and strongly object to.

And I did tell her that I had promised my help already. Given that, Idalia would probably send someone to fetch him the moment she had anything constructive he could do. *I might as well enjoy my holiday while I've got it,* Kellen decided, walking on.

Slowly the form of the Elven city began to take shape in his mind. It was a thing of gentle curves and meanders; where a human city would have broad straight avenues, imposing vistas, and large dignified public buildings, the Elven city seemed designed to present small quiet opportunities for reflection, and often Kellen saw no houses at all, though he was sure he must be in the middle of many of them.

But even in the middle of so much quiet beauty he saw evidence of the specter that hovered over Sentarshadeen. Fountains that should have been sparkling in the sun stood dry and empty; reflecting pools that once held water had been carefully filled with patterns of colored sand instead; tiny bridges arched over dry stones instead of over trickling streams. Though these substitutions would hardly have been noticeable in a human garden, in an Elven one, the tiny imperfections among all that was perfect sounded a jarring note. Tumbled stone and tiled basins were meant for water. As they were, they did not fit. They were not—quite—harmonious enough. The more he saw of such substitutions, the more determined he was to restore Sentarshadeen to what it had been before.

He'd grown so used to the absence of water that when he heard the sound of running water coming from a house up ahead of him, it took him several minutes to believe his ears. Feeling faintly alarmed and very curious, Kellen hurried toward the sound.

There was a house set back away from the road. The path leading up to it was made of rough-surfaced tiles, each a different shape and color, with strong raised designs upon their surfaces. The house was tiled as well, its entire surface, even the roof, covered with an intricate mosaic of handmade tile, until it resembled some giant fantastic creature from one of Kellen's bestiaries—a manticore or a basilisk, perhaps, or even a sleeping dragon.

In addition to the trickling and splashing, Kellen could hear a peculiar creaking and groaning sound coming through the open windows. Intrigued and a little concerned, he came closer and looked inside.

It was a potter's studio, Kellen realized with relief. The peculiar sounds came from the spinning potter's wheel. An Elven man was bent over it, his back to Kellen, busy with the clay, while his bare feet worked the pedals that kept the wheel spinning. He was bare to the waist, his hair bound up in a turban of dark blue cloth. His hands and arms were covered with ghost-white clay.

Two walls of the studio were lined with shelves, on which stood pieces of pottery in every stage of completion, from those that looked as if they'd just come off the wheel, to others, gleaming in jewel colors, that looked as if they were ready for Queen Ashaniel's table. On the third wall, Kellen could see a row of deep sinks, into one of which water trickled and splashed. It was that sound that had drawn Kellen here.

"Drought or none, it is water and fire that shapes the clay," the potter said without looking up.

How did he know I was here? Kellen wondered. But the potter hadn't said anything that indicated he didn't want Kellen to remain, so Kellen continued to watch, enthralled.

The potter dipped his hand into a water bucket at his side, and returned it to the clay again.

He was making a bowl, Kellen realized. He watched in fascination as the clay thinned and flared out under the potter's hands, very much as if it had a will of its own, until it went from a muffin-shaped doughy lump to a wide flaring shape.

The potter lifted his hands from his work at last and let the wheel slow.

"It will crack as it dries." He addressed the pot, not Kellen, and there was a faint tone of regret—or, perhaps, disappointment—in his voice. "The clay is too soft to hold such a shape unsupported. But when it does, I will return it to the slip and try again, and perhaps one day one of them will not." He rose to his feet and turned.

"I see you, Kellen Tavadon. Be welcome in the house of Iletel."

"I see you, Iletel," Kellen answered formally. "It is a pleasure and a privilege to see a skilled artist at work."

Iletel smiled, opened the door for him, and then went to wash off the clay in the sink, take down his hair, and don a loose linen wrap-tunic in pale shades of peach and pink, while Kellen gazed around the studio.

Everything was arranged with an eye to the order and perfection he had come to expect here, even in so messy an environment as a potter's workplace.

"These pieces are wonderful. I have never seen such beautiful things as I have seen in Sentarshadeen," Kellen said honestly.

"It is a great pity we no longer trade with the City as we did when I was younger," Iletel said, "for it was a great pleasure to sell beautiful things to humans, as it is always a joy to instruct the young. I am sad that our two races no longer speak together as we once did."

"So am I," Kellen said feelingly. "That's one of the reasons I'm here—because I know that the Elves know many things I wish to know." He sighed. "I am very glad that the Elves *do* find joy in the instruction of the young, for I would rather that my presence was not considered a burden."

Iletel's smile broadened. "Your presence, Kellen Tavadon, would not be a burden to anyone who is wise. The wise know well that wisdom must be shared, or it grows stale, and that even the wisest can learn new things from the young."

Well, that was encouraging! "I spoke to Morusil this morning," Kellen ventured, "and he told me that everyone here knows something about the Wild Magic. I'm hoping to find out why they no longer remember it in the City."

Or, Kellen amended conscientiously, if only to himself, why they didn't remember it properly—or lied about it if they did.

Iletel smiled. "So direct! I had forgotten that consequence of your brief lives," he said in an amused tone that warned Kellen he had come a little too close to overstepping Elven etiquette. "But come, Morusil's student. Perhaps it would please you to view my latest works, and afterward join me for refreshment. It is nearing my hour to take tea."

Kellen blushed, and assented, wondering if he'd ever really get the hang of the indirectness of Elven manners. Iletel conducted him around the small studio, showing off the various examples of his work—and to Kellen's surprise, finding fault with most of them.

Several pieces that Kellen thought were perfect Iletel announced were only waiting to be broken up so that their clay could be reused "—for there is truly no purpose in keeping those things which are less than perfect—do you see this flaw here? Terrible. And here, where the glaze ran and puddled. A child's error; the temperature in the kiln was uneven that day. But they will be reborn again, without flaw."

As Kellen had suspected, Iletel had made the tiles Kellen had seen outside as well, though when Kellen praised them Iletel dismissed them as journeyman work, too unimportant to speak of. All his work now was in the translucent white shell-clay with which he had been working when Kellen entered. It was harder than earthenware, and translucent when fired. Larger pieces, Iletel told Kellen, were often cast instead of wheel-worked, because the clay's thin shapes were unstable while wet. But Iletel still experimented with larger shell-clay pieces on the wheel, for that, he explained, was how one learned.

He spoke of glazes and firing times with an artist's love and passion, and showed Kellen a few pieces a friend who worked in cast shell-clay had given him: a tiny perfect unicorn, its tufted tail coiled over its back, with shell-pink horn and hooves; a selkie leaning on a rock, a wriggling trout caught in one splayed hand. Every detail was flawless, so real Kellen could almost imagine they breathed.

Long before Kellen tired of seeing the wonders of Iletel's art, the Elven potter led Kellen through the studio into an inner room whose windows looked out on a wooded hillside of birch and pine. The birch trees had already gone yellow with autumn, though of course, being in Sentarshadeen itself they were well watered by the Elves, but the pines, Kellen was relieved to see, were also still a healthy green. Pines were fragile trees, fast-growing and (comparatively) short-lived. They had shallow roots, and were often the first to suffer the effects of drought, Idalia had once said.

"Their roots are strong, by the mercy of the Forest," Iletel said, seeing the direction of Kellen's gaze, "and by the grace of Leaf and Star, our valley has been spared the worst of the fell weather. But should there be another year of drought, even they will begin to suffer."

Iletel indicated that Kellen should seat himself on one of the long benches that seemed to be a standard feature of Elven homes. As Kellen did, Iletel knelt and busied himself at the tile stove, heating water and preparing tea. Kellen cast about for a safe conversational subject.

"I haven't been studying Wild Magic for very long," he said, as self-deprecating as Iletel, "and my sister Idalia is a much better Wildmage than I am, but both of us are going to do all that we can to help make the rains come."

"That makes good hearing," Iletel said, his back to Kellen. "Each day, all who can be spared from other tasks go to carry water to the trees of the rim and to the farther fields. Even I shall go in a few hours to do what I can, though it is so little in the face of the forest's need."

So that's where everyone is! Kellen tried to imagine the amount of work it was to carry water—presumably by hand—to try to keep the forest alive, and couldn't. *And the wondertales all make it seem as if all the Elves do all day is play music and games, and sing and dance . . .*

A few moments later Iletel rose, bringing Kellen a cup of steaming tea that smelled strongly of roses and herbs, and seated himself with his own cup in a chair facing him.

"But, if I understand your need, you come to us to learn something more of the history of humankind." Iletel frowned, just the tiniest bit. "Now I fear from what you do not say that the Wild Magic is another thing the City has forgotten—or has cast aside. This gives me reasons for why the City of Armethalieh no longer trades with us. Perhaps they fear Wild Magic, as they evidently fear us, as the harbingers of chaos and confusion."

Kellen shifted uneasily in his seat. Iletel's indirect assessment was uncomfortably close to the mark.

"But once again it is their brief lives, Wildmage, that lead them into misunderstanding and error," Iletel continued gently, his free hand moving in a graceful gesture of apology. "So far from being the magic of chaos and confusion, the Wild Magic is ultimately the magic of order, as Morusil will have told you already. But it is an order that encompasses the whole world, you see, and so it cannot be a form of order that the ordinary human being can easily grasp," Iletel said, his dark eyes regarding Kellen compassionately.

Kellen nodded, although *he* only half grasped what the Elf was talking about.

"You must understand, Wildmage, that the ordinary human, or even these High Mages who have lately appeared in Armethalieh, is essentially a selfish creature. It is a consequence of having such brief lives, I fear; and not to be wondered at. Humans barely reach maturity before they begin to die: it is not surprising that all they are interested in is the form of 'order' that best suits and benefits each of them alone—or perhaps, if they are the wisest of their kind, an order that benefits their fellows for the duration of their own brief lifetimes. But their lives are so *very* short that even such magnanimity is barely better than the most insular selfishness."

Kellen nibbled on his lower lip, wondering if he should be feeling slightly insulted. Of course, Iletel didn't *mean* to be insulting, but—that attitude seemed, in its way, a bit condescending . . .

Iletel continued on, earnestly. "Yet you must understand, as we Elves do, that one could not expect it to be otherwise, Wildmage. One cannot expect a creature to glimpse the Eternal when its whole brief span of years is spent in being born and dying almost before it has a chance to live." Iletel looked very somber.

I don't know . . . Idalia seems to have figured it out all right. And Master Eliron. And whoever wrote the Books in the first place, and all the Wildmages who've learned from them.

Iletel sighed. "It breaks my heart to imagine it. There is no time to dream, to plan, no time for Art . . . all of their lives are spent in one blind hurrying rush into death, without one moment to think or reflect on any of the things that give Life meaning or beauty."

He shook his head, regarding Kellen with grave pity. "I think you are very brave, Kellen Tavadon, to reach beyond your brief span of years through your magic—but then, as a Wildmage yourself, you are far from ordinary. The ordinary human, man or Mage, lives every moment in terror of the death that is rushing toward him in less than a century of years—such a creature could not possibly be expected to see things with the same perspective that we Elves can. And so, in the human City, they have turned away from the vast and eternal beauty of the Wild Magic to a simpler, more immediate, more *selfish* magic better suited to the briefness of their lives. You wonder why they have rejected the Wild Magic in favor of this self-indulgent magic of their own creation, but the explanation is obvious to any of the Elven-born: no short-lived creature could be expected to love something that confronts it with its terrible impermanence."

Iletel was clearly quite sympathetic to the terrible fate of humans. It showed in his tone, and in the grave way he regarded Kellen. "And so the Mages of the Golden City hate the Wild Magic and its wielders for showing them what is no more than the truth of the world. But you must not blame them for it, as we do not. It is simply their flawed human nature. They are no more to blame for their fears than the wasp for its sting."

Kellen sipped his tea, his mind too full of new ideas to be able to frame a coherent question in the fashion Elven good manners dictated. He was dazzled by the notion of the High Magick being something that had "lately" appeared in Armethalieh—lately by *whose* standards? Iletel's? Did that mean they used to practice the Wild Magic in Armethalieh . . . and stopped? Lycaelon said the High Mages had once studied the Wild Magic, before banning it as being too dangerous . . . was that what he'd *really* meant? That they'd used to *practice* it? That there used to be *Wildmages* in Armethalieh? Kellen felt as if he were swimming—and not very well—in a sea of new ideas.

"But not all humans are like the ones in the City," Kellen protested weakly. "Idalia and I both came from there."

"And both of you left, neither in your own time and season," Iletel pointed out reasonably. "There is as much variation among humankind as among the flowers of the field, perhaps, yet when the gatherer brings them into her garden, she will choose those whose traits please her and grow only those, casting out those who hark back to their wild cousins. So it is with humans, who cultivate themselves like flowers. Do not yearn to be what you are not, Kellen, rather rejoice that you are more than they."

It all made very pretty hearing, since who *wouldn't* want to hear that they were special and gifted, far better than the people they'd grown up with, especially if those same people were the ones that had thrown you out of Armethalieh and then tried to kill you, not once but twice? And it all seemed so reasonable, especially while Iletel was talking.

BUT later, after a little more polite conversation and a promise to come again bringing Sandalon, Kellen wasn't quite as sure. He wandered onward through Sentarshadeen, trying to sort out all the things he'd just learned in his mind. It was a very comforting explanation. A very soothing explanation. But Kellen had been offered a very great number of comforting, soothing explanations for things in his life, and had rejected them all.

Iletel seemed so satisfied with his explanation of how things were . . . just as satisfied as the Light-Priests and the Mages had been with *their* explanations, back in the City.

Wasn't Iletel's thinking that most humans couldn't handle the Wild Magic because they just weren't good enough the same thing as the Mages thinking that all *women* couldn't handle the High Magick because *they* weren't good enough?

Or was it?

The more he learned, the less he knew, Kellen realized. He wasn't sure of anything anymore—except one thing.

Once, the Wild Magic had been practiced in Armethalieh. Then they'd stopped, and invented the High Magick, and declared that nobody could be allowed to practice the Wild Magic anymore. If he put Iletel's explanation and Lycaelon's explanation together, that much seemed to shake out of it as unvarnished truth. But all that knowing that much for sure did was leave him with more questions.

He walked out past the House of Leaf and Star (the Elves might call it that, but Kellen still thought of it as a palace) turning over the conversations with the two Elves in his mind.

Both Iletel and Morusil had been very kind, and filled with Elven politeness, and Kellen certainly had a wider perspective on things than he had before, but he wasn't entirely certain it was a better or more accurate one. Iletel might say that humans had abandoned the Wild Magic because they were essentially self-centered, but that didn't quite make sense if the only Wildmages left in the world were human. Maybe that wasn't true either, but the Elves weren't Wildmages (at least not anymore), the Centaurs couldn't do magic at all, and Kellen hadn't met any representatives of any more of the Other Races yet, so he wasn't sure whether any of them might be Mages or not, or even if any of them still existed. The unicorns were certainly magical creatures, but if the unicorns could get the Elves out of the fix they were in, well, there was a whole herd of them living in Sentarshadeen as from what Idalia said, and there still wasn't any rain, so Kellen guessed they couldn't help. Maybe unicorns could just do specific unicorn-magic things, the way an apple tree could make apples, which was fine if you wanted apples (or unicorn-magic), but he guessed bringing rain didn't fall into that category.

Kellen frowned, looking down at the path. There wasn't even a stray stone to kick to relieve his feelings. How had everything gotten all tangled up and *separated* this way?

Something must have happened to make things the way they were now, with the Mages of Armethalieh practicing the High Magick—and having invented it in the first place because they didn't think the Wild Magic was good enough, or something. But if the Wild Magic was a force for good—and Kellen no longer had any reason to doubt that—why couldn't the two magics exist side by side in the same place? He didn't *think* the High Magick was a bad thing, necessarily—or it wouldn't be if the Mages didn't insist it had to be the *only* kind of magic that was allowed to exist. And if the High Mages were willing to pay their own price in their own power for their spells, instead of always making someone else pay for the spells they did. There *was* that. Kellen frowned.

So why *had* the High Mages thrown the Wildmages out of Armethalieh, really? Why *couldn't* the two kinds of magic exist side by side?

Sighing heavily—he didn't have an answer for that, and he suspected he wouldn't get one from the Elves, either— Kellen passed the Palace and found himself in an orchard.

Apple trees, he thought, though the fruit was long off the trees. He looked for dryads, but didn't see any, and felt oddly disappointed.

He was more than rewarded for that lack, though, when he got past the orchard to the meadow beyond. Scattered across the grassland was an entire herd of unicorns, more than he could easily count.

He hadn't known they came in colors.

The one closest to him was a stallion. The stallion's coat was as red as a woman's hair, but his ears, mane, horn, socks, and the tuft at the end of his tail were jet-black—yet somehow luminous, like black opal, with a fire somewhere deep within. He'd been grazing, but when Kellen stepped through the trees his head came up. He stared directly at Kellen for a moment—his eyes were the same deep violet as Idalia's— then turned his back and went trotting back to the main herd.

The unicorns were all the different colors Kellen associated with horses, only more so: brighter, more intense, more vivid. There was a grey that looked like polished silver, one with a golden coat the exact shade of meadow-honey in sunlight; a unicorn mare with a coat so black the sunlight struck blue highlights from it. Though he saw several pure white ones, none of them was Shalkan.

They all were more intensely *alive* than any other creature he had met so far. And they all had that luminosity that made Shalkan so heart-stoppingly gorgeous, as if they carried their own little lights around inside of them. It was pure joy just to watch them move, and while he watched, he was able to put everything that was troubling him to the back of his mind for a while.

"Looking for me?" a familiar voice said from behind him.

Kellen jumped (though he knew better; sneaking up behind him was one of Shalkan's favorite games). "Not exactly. Just . . . looking." He turned around, though he was reluctant to abandon the sight of the herd. Though how many people had seen even one unicorn, let alone a herd of them?

"And how are you enjoying your visit to Sentarshadeen?" Shalkan asked, in tones of impersonal politeness.

"I'd like it better if it were raining," Kellen said honestly.

"So would the Elves," Shalkan agreed somberly, shaking his short roached mane. "And aside from that?"

"It's amazing. Everything's so beautiful, so clean. And even if they don't have any magic . . . or not much . . . they've accomplished such great things. It's so much better here than in the City!" Kellen said enthusiastically.

"Of course, it all depends on what you like," Shalkan said agreeably.

"Well, since nobody's trying to kill me here, I'd say that Sentarshadeen is better than Armethalieh," Kellen said, feeling slightly cross. He wasn't sure why it bothered him so much when Shalkan agreed with him, but it always did. "And at least they're willing to talk about the Wild Magic here, instead of just saying it's an abomination."

"Then you're learning a lot," Shalkan said, still in that same maddeningly neutral tone. He began to walk out into the meadow, and Kellen followed, somehow feeling he was in the middle of an argument that he was losing.

"I guess so. But if I'm right about what I'm learning . . . if they used to practice the Wild Magic in Armethalieh, and stopped, then *why* did they stop?"

Shalkan swung his head around and regarded Kellen steadily. "Maybe you should ask the Elves."

Kellen snorted rudely. "Have you ever tried *asking* the Elves anything? By the time you figure out how to be polite about it, they're discussing the weather or something!"

"Weather's important, when you're having the wrong kind." Shalkan stopped at the edge of a spring, and drank.

Kellen admired the decoration around the edge: river stones and fieldstone and tiles, all arranged in a harmonious whole, just the way everything else he'd seen here was.

"And maybe it's something they don't want to talk about," Shalkan continued when he'd finished. "Or maybe they have other things on their minds. Or maybe you just have to figure out how to ask the right questions. It shouldn't be long now, at any rate."

"What . . . ? *Hey!*" Kellen shouted indignantly. But Shalkan seemed to feel there wasn't any point in continuing the cryptic conversation. He trotted away, head high, moving faster as he went until when he reached the herd he was covering ground in the bounding deerlike leaps that were the unicorn's fastest gait. The rest of the herd seemed to take inspiration from Shalkan, for in an instant, every single unicorn, from the flame-red stallion to a pair of leggy hornless foals, was bounding along after Shalkan, as smooth and flowing as a flight of birds. In moments the herd had vanished among the trees.

Kellen stared after them, feeling disgruntled. Every time he thought he was about to get an answer, he ended up being sent off down another blind alley, it seemed to him.

"Kellen! *Kellen!*"

He turned back in the direction he'd come just in time to grab Sandalon out of the air and spin him around as the boy leaped toward him.

"Where did you come from?" Kellen asked, too late to keep himself from asking the question.

But Sandalon didn't seem to notice—or mind. "I came with the water cart—see? They're coming to Songmairie where the unicorns drink to fill it so they can water the trees and the flowers. I get to help," the boy finished importantly. "*Everyone* gets to help. Lairamo says that if we don't give them drinks, the trees and flowers will wither and die."

He pointed behind him, and Kellen saw the water cart coming slowly toward them along the stone path. It looked like an enormous wine-vat on wheels, much wider than it was high, drawn by four patient horses, nearly as ordinary as any Kellen might see on the streets of Armethalieh, though beautifully groomed and matched. Walking along with it were six Elves, all carrying buckets. Two walked at the horses' heads, while the others followed behind.

"Then I'll help too," Kellen said, "if your friends don't mind."

"They won't mind," Sandalon said positively.

And in fact, the Elves seemed to welcome Kellen's help, for filling the water wagon from the spring was backbreaking work, and all had to be done by hand. The drovers backed the wagon into position—it would be much harder to turn and move once the barrel was full—and then unhitched the horses, turning them free to graze while the work was done.

Then all that remained was the simple but far from easy work of dipping each bucket into the spring, carrying it to the cart, lifting it to whoever sat on the edge of the barrel top to pour its contents within (all took turns at that, even Kellen), taking the empty bucket back, and doing it again.

Over and over and over.

Sandalon carried a bucket as well, though his was a much smaller one than the others, suitable for a child's strength. Every once in a while, instead of pouring their water into the barrel, one of the Elves would take a bucketful a little distance from the spring and pour it onto the grass instead of into the vat. Kellen supposed that made sense: the meadow wasn't getting any more water than any other place in Sentarshadeen, and there was no way to water all of it.

As they worked, the Elves talked quietly among themselves. Kellen caught scraps of the conversation: the pulley system that hauled water up the south wall had broken, and it would be several days before it could be fixed. Another spring in the outer forest had gone dry, so water would have to be brought from within Sentarshadeen instead. The forest creatures had suffered badly over the long dry summer, and had been driven to raid the Elves' crops in ever-increasing numbers to feed themselves. This was bad enough, but with winter coming on, the predators were following their food supply closer to Sentarshadeen than ever before. Where mice and rabbits and deer had come, wolves and lynx and bear would follow—perhaps even ice-tiger.

Kellen wondered how much the Elves' problems had been added to by the Scouring Hunt, but he didn't want to say anything before talking to Idalia. Beneath its fine clothes and fancy manners, Sentarshadeen was a city under siege, and everyone shared the same fears.

Everyone in the water party was dressed similarly, in the form-fitting leggings, low boots, and close-cut tunics that

Kellen was coming to consider to be Elven working clothes—though there was hardly anything about them, from their color to their exquisite decoration, that was the least workaday—and Kellen had been surprised, on first glance, to find that two of the group were women. Aside from their clothing, it was very difficult for Kellen to tell any of the Elvenkind apart, and impossible to guess their ages, though one of the two women had a sort of aura about her that made Kellen think she must be, well, *mature* by Elven standards. All the time they were working he kept finding her regarding him critically, as though something about him displeased her.

Sandalon had tired of the labor a while before, though he'd kept at it far longer than Kellen had expected before going off to play near the horses, returning every so often to fill his bucket again. Kellen thought the young Prince must be very lonely; he'd seen no other children at all, let alone any near Sandalon's age.

When the Elves stopped to rest and refresh themselves, Sandalon came eagerly back to Kellen's side—and to Kellen's unease, the woman who'd been watching him ever since she'd arrived took the opportunity to draw near as well. She smiled at Sandalon, but studied Kellen in expressionless silence for a long moment before she spoke to him.

"Those colors do not suit you at all, Kellen Tavadon. Come to my shop, and I will make you more suitable clothing."

Kellen blinked. He'd been expecting something else—maybe a veiled insult about how a short-lived round-ear was no fit company for an Elven Prince.

"Those greys, that shade of brown . . . with your coloring; unsuitable. You should wear warm clear colors: blues and ambers to waken the color of your hair and eyes. Perhaps red, though I think that would be too daring—though you have good skin, if you will only take care of it, and not allow the sun to age and damage it. Violet, perhaps, though it would have to be the proper shade of violet. I will see what I have in my stores. Green, if you must have it, though every fool of a human forester will insist that only green may marry with brown, as if folk were trees. *I* would not dress you in green, myself." She shook her head firmly.

Where had all this come from? And *why* all this business about colors and skin *now*? "I'm sorry?" Kellen said. "I don't quite understand . . ."

Sandalon was hungry, and bored by the conversation as well. He went to the back of the water cart, where food was being handed around. Now he came back with two full silver tankards, both much too large for his small hands, carrying them with intent concentration. Kellen saw what he was doing, and intervened in time to prevent disaster. Sandalon smiled up at him, relieved.

"You give one to her," he told Kellen in confidential but clearly audible tones. "She's older."

Kellen handed one of the tankards to the Elven woman, who accepted it gracefully. He looked at Sandalon again, still holding the second tankard. Sandalon was a child, but he was also a royal Prince, and no one who'd grown up in the Golden City could be ignorant of the way rank and privilege worked.

"And you keep the other one, because you're older than me," the boy said helpfully. "I'm only five. You're lots older than that."

Kellen kept the tankard, though it didn't seem quite reasonable to be waited on by an Elven Prince. He glanced back at the Elven woman, and saw her trying very hard to stifle a proud smile.

"And you are wondering who I am," she said. "Why, I am the woman who made what you are wearing now, as I made for your sister and all who pass through our lands as guests. It is a challenge I enjoy, the crafting of garments for those I have never seen, and may never see. But now I have seen you"—her expression turned fierce and stern—"and I will not permit this mismarriage of form and cloth to be seen about Sentarshadeen any longer. Tomorrow morning you will come to the shop of Tengitir, Kellen Tavadon, bringing all your clothing with you, so that I may determine what will best suit you."

Kellen would rather have argued with Shalkan than with

Tengitir, he decided—though, if he were in the middle of a drought and facing annihilation, he thought he'd be able to find better things to worry about than the color of somebody's *clothes*. He nodded meekly, hoping that whatever she was willing to give him to wear tomorrow, it wouldn't be the sort of skintight things the Elves themselves wore. And that the visit wouldn't take too long or be too embarrassing.

But maybe she'd be willing to talk about something other than cloth and colors while she was working. All the Elves seemed to know something about magic and their own history, and maybe Tengitir would know something about Armethalieh's history as well, or know someone who would. At least this time he'd have all night to figure out some questions-that-weren't-questions.

⟳

IT took a few more hours of hard work before the water cart was filled. The team was brought back from its grazing and hitched to the wagon again, and the cart started moving slowly back down the path.

"Do they do this every day?" Kellen asked Sandalon. It was nice having at least one friend in Sentarshadeen that he didn't have to watch every word with.

"Three times a day," Sandalon said proudly. "It goes all kinds of places, but most of the time, people just bring smaller ones like that—"

He pointed, to where another pair of Elves were approaching the spring. They were pulling a light two-wheeled cart, similar to the ones Kellen had seen in Armethalieh, where a running man pulled a single-seat carriage for one of the rich and powerful to ride in.

No one was riding in this cart, however. It contained a large water barrel, like the ones outside the poorer houses in Armethalieh for catching rainfall. But even the rain barrels here (if that's what it was) were as beautiful as the fine furniture in rich men's homes back in human lands.

"But there's running water in the houses," Kellen said, baffled. "Why are they coming here for water?"

"You can't water *everything* from your house!" Sandalon said, in tones that suggested *everyone* knew that.

"I guess not," Kellen admitted meekly.

"Come on," Sandalon announced. "Let's go see the unicorns! I'm not supposed to come out here alone, but you're with me."

Kellen agreed. He couldn't imagine that anything harmful could manage to find its way into the Elves' canyon home, and if it did, either the unicorns would deal with it, or the two of them would have the sense to run from it before it could catch them.

He hoped.

HE ended up carrying Sandalon home to the Palace on his shoulders—which delighted the boy—since otherwise, as Kellen eventually realized, there would always be "just one more thing" for Sandalon to show him, and Kellen could tell by the angle of the light that the day was rapidly coming to an end. He wanted to get home himself and talk to Idalia about the things he'd found out—and guessed—today, and ask her a few questions. Well, more than a few, actually.

Lairamo was waiting at the door, looking as worried as Elves ever let themselves look.

"He hasn't been any trouble, really," Kellen said quickly. "He was showing me around the woods, and I guess I lost track of the time. I hope I haven't kept him out too late."

Lairamo smiled, looking relieved. "No, of course you haven't, Wildmage. If Sandalon is with you, then we know he is safe indeed."

"And if he's looking for me tomorrow, I guess I'm going to be at Tengitir's shop," Kellen added, swinging Sandalon down off his shoulders. "At least in the morning."

"I want to watch!" Sandalon announced. "Kellen is going

to get new clothes, proper clothes, so he doesn't look
like a—"

"That is for your mother to decide," Lairamo said firmly,
whisking Sandalon behind her skirts before the boy could
finish his sentence. "Perhaps it would please you to take a
cup of wine at our hearth, Kellen. I'm certain Prince Sandalon
has marched you over more territory today than all the armies
of Great Queen Vielissiar Farcarinon." ·

He wanted to—he badly wanted to see the Queen again—
but Kellen had the feeling that this was simply a polite offer
that was made without the expectation that it would be accepted. And he hadn't seen Idalia since last night; *she* might
be getting worried, if no one had known where he and Sandalon had been all afternoon.

So he decided on declining, gracefully. "Thank you, but
my sister will be expecting me, and I believe she will have
many things to tell me by now."

Ah. He was getting better at reading the Elves. That *was*
polite relief on the nurse's face.

"I bid you good evening, then," he said. He tried a bow,
and congratulated himself that it was a little less awkward
than yesterday's. Maybe he'd get the hang of this place eventually.

"And we, you," the nurse replied, and with a friendly nod,
turned and chivvied her charge away to his supper and bed.

⟵

ON her way back to her lodging after her visit to Songmairie, Idalia stopped several times for supplies. Odd that it
would have seemed to anyone who was only familiar with
the wondertales about Elves, there was a little market in
Sentarshadeen, full of stalls where Elven farmers and crafts-
folk brought their wares—though admittedly, most Elves preferred to barter than purchase outright. Time, after all, was a
commodity of which they had a significant supply. Even in
the midst of drought, the stalls were occupied, and bargaining
was going on at the usual leisurely Elven pace.

Each handsome stall was different, though all were shaded with awnings, each awning was different as well. Some stalls were created in stark simplicity, some in an amusing froth of ornament; all delighted the eye.

Idalia made her selections with care. Food and wine and a selection of ciders, of course, for any worker must take care of his tools, and one of the most important tools of a worker in magic was their own body. Another stop at a store that sold toys and games of all sorts, where she bought a set of the small polished counters for the game of *gan*.

Idalia had no interest in playing *gan*, today or any other day—the rules were very simple, but the game itself took an Elven lifetime to learn to play well—but there were 144 counters to a *gan* set, small round cabochons of polished agate no bigger than her thumbnail, and she needed them for what she was about to do. The Elven proprietor sold them to her with barely concealed curiosity, though she was ostensibly engrossed in a game of *xaqiue* with a friend. By now everyone in Sentarshadeen knew Idalia was here, and that she'd agreed to use the Wild Magic to aid the Queen. Everything Idalia did would be food for gossip before the sound of her footsteps had died away in the street.

And Jermayan would be sure to hear all of it, for *she* knew that he had not yet left Sentarshadeen, and indeed, had no intention of doing so.

Furious with the sudden direction of her thoughts, Idalia forced the thought of him from her mind once more.

By the time Idalia reached her own doorstep, it was piled with neatly wrapped bundles from the tradesmen whose shops she'd stopped at; she'd carried many of her own purchases, but not all. She set her walking staff outside the door and went inside, then spent a few minutes tidying the things away. Knowing that Sentarshadeen was her destination, she'd taken care to bring a few trade goods that would be of interest in Elven lands, and a Wildmage's credit was always good. If nothing else, charged keystones could serve as currency, for though the Elves had given up their part in the Greater Magics long ago, they still retained a facility with the small magics of hearth and woodland, and charged keystones were better than gold.

Idalia wasn't really sure what the Elves *did* with the keystones, though they seemed to value them—she'd told Kellen once that only the Wildmage who had charged a keystone could tap its power, and as far as she knew, that was true. Maybe the Elves were the exception to the rule; all she knew was that she had always found charged keystones eagerly accepted among the Elvenkind, for whatever reason, and so had not worried too much about not being able to pay her and Kellen's way.

But she had not expected to be riding into a disaster of this magnitude, either, and that changed everything. Certainly while she was doing her best to deal with it, no one would be asking either her or Kellen to pay for anything, at least not in tangible goods.

Before beginning her task, she forced herself to eat and drink and meditate for a while, fortifying herself for the work ahead, then selected a large flat cushion and placed it in the middle of the floor and seated herself upon it, facing west, the bag of *gan* counters in her lap. She spilled them out into a pool in her skirt, taking a moment to admire how the sun spilling through the windows made them glow and sparkle.

Red agates and grey; stones of shining black and golden yellow; creamy white and deep moss-green . . . She ran them through her fingers, hearing them click against each other and feeling their smoothness, slowing her heartbeat and her breathing, readying herself for the task ahead.

Sinking down deep within her own mind as her heartbeat slowed, Idalia imagined herself at the center of a wheel. Spokes radiated out from it: thick spokes for the cardinal points: west, south, east, north. Slenderer spokes between them cross-quartering the wheel: southwest, northwest, northeast, southeast . . . And between them, spokes still finer still, until the room in which she sat was gone, and in her imagination Idalia sat at the center of a silvery wheel, a compass-rose of sixty-four petals, all radiating outward from where she sat.

She began in the west, searching for the source of the wrongness, the binding of wind and weather that she sensed lay behind the unnatural drought. In the spokes of the wheel she felt the sorrow of the Elves, their weariness and despair, but those things were natural, and she ignored them, seeking farther, deeper . . .

There were flickers of shadow, faint hints of wrongness. Each time she sensed one, Idalia took a stone from her pile and set it on the floor in the direction the sensation had come from, and continued searching.

IT was still a little too light for the lighting of lanterns, more late afternoon than evening, but Kellen's stomach was still on the dawn-to-dusk schedule that he and Idalia had kept in the Wildwood, and it was his stomach's opinion that it was time and more than time for dinner, preferably something involving a whole roast ox. He found his way home more quickly than he had the day before, hoping Idalia would be there. It would be a great relief to talk to someone he could ask a direct question of.

He wondered how she'd spent her day, and if she'd have any news about the drought, and what they were going to do about it. Certainly her sources of information—both magical and about Sentarshadeen in general—ought to be better than his. He just hoped that old boyfriend of hers had the sense to keep out of her way, because if not . . .

Well, it didn't really bear thinking about.

But when he opened the door to the house, all was so quiet that for a moment he thought Idalia wasn't there at all. The great room was in shadow, but when he looked closely, the last rays of the afternoon sun spilling through the door showed him Idalia sitting in the middle of the floor, with a large fan of pebbles spread out on the floor beside her right hand. And the whole room smelled—though that wasn't quite the right word—of magic. He wasn't sure how he knew, but he was certain of it.

And at that moment, the world changed for him.

I am *a Wildmage* . . .

It was one thing to be called "Wildmage" by the Elves—and even at that Kellen felt as though he were masquerading as something he wasn't—and it was something quite different to be forced to acknowledge by the evidence of his own senses that it was true. He *was* a Wildmage, able to sense the currents of magic.

"Idalia?" he asked hesitantly.

She'd been sitting with her head slumped upon her chest as if she were asleep. Now she took a deep breath, straightened, and opened her eyes, looking up at him.

"Kellen," she said, and blinked, and then added irrelevantly: "Look at the time."

What has she been doing? It had to be something to do with the drought, of course, but what?

She took a deep breath, stretching and uncoiling from where she sat—carefully, Kellen saw, so as not to disturb the pattern of the stones spread around her. "Let's have some light. And I expect you're hungry." She blinked again, and then said, as if surprised, "So am I . . ."

"What were you doing?" Kellen asked, following her toward the stove. He made a wide detour around the stones on the floor, feeling as if he were avoiding a wasp's nest.

"Looking." She glanced toward the floor and her expression tightened unhappily. "And finding, though finding out *what* I found and what it means is going to take a lot more looking. And how was *your* day?"

As she spoke, Idalia took a long metal wand that contained a braided wick and lit it at the hearth, then used it to light several of the lamps, banishing the darkness.

He wondered how much she would really hear if he spoke to her. "I talked to a lot of people today, actually. I went out to the spring beyond the Palace—the one the unicorns drink from—and helped fill one of the water wagons. I also met the woman who made my clothes while I was helping to water the forest, but—"

"But, what?" Idalia asked, turning, and raising an eyebrow at him.

He sucked at his lower lip, trying to articulate what had bothered him about the encounter. "She doesn't seem to think much of them, so tomorrow I'm going to go to her shop so she can make me new ones—and that just doesn't seem right. I mean, Idalia, doesn't it seem to you that there are better things to worry about at a time like this than whether I'm wearing the right color tunic?"

"Not for Elves," Idalia said—rather grimly, Kellen thought. "Elves are . . . perfectionists," she said, as if she was choosing her words with care. "If you stay here long enough, you'll find that there's no such thing as 'good enough' to the Elvenborn. They have a strong sense of, well, I suppose you'd call it 'fitness.' And until something meets their standards, they don't leave it alone—no matter what else might need doing at the same time."

"But . . . now?" Kellen asked, bewildered. "With the drought, and everything?"

"Elves do not hurry," Idalia said, taking a large pie from the sideboard and sliding it into the oven to warm. "They live a thousand years. They don't have wars, other than the Flower Wars—not recently at least, and not in any way we humans understand the concept. So . . ." She shrugged. "For most of them—not all, but most—there is never a sense of urgency about anything, and they can be so narrowly focused on their own personal obsessions that they weigh things like the drought and clothing design in equal importance. That is the negative side; the positive side, of course, is that they take a very long view of anything, and what may seem like a crisis to one of us is, often rightly, seen by one of them as little more than an inconsequential ripple."

"I guess it's hard to see much wrong with that," Kellen said uncertainly.

"Whereas," Idalia finished, with a wan smile, "something that is an ongoing offense to the eye and an irritation to the senses of all beholders, like an ill-fitting tunic, is a fault that should be corrected immediately."

Kellen snorted, though privately he wondered if some of Idalia's refusal to even *talk* to Jermayan was because of just those things.

He'd seen a great deal more than he had realized in the time he'd spent in the Wildwood and Merryvale. He'd seen flirtations and light-loves, and true-loves and courting couples, and above all, the deep devotion of the happily mated. He knew what love looked like, at least, from the outside, and he knew Idalia loved Jermayan. Caring for him as deeply as she did, and if Elves really *did* mate for life, how *could* she want him to spend centuries alone after her death? Now, if it had been him, he'd try and figure out a solution of some kind, but, well, it was her choice, and not his when it came down to it.

But if Jermayan was as much of a perfectionist as, say, Iletel or Tengitir, and spent as much time on things that didn't seem to matter one way or the other as far as Kellen could tell, he'd drive Idalia crazy in a year, let alone in sixty or seventy. So maybe that was a factor, as well.

Still, in every way he'd yet seen, the Elves were so much *better* than humans that sometimes since he'd come to Sentarshadeen he felt almost ashamed to *be* human.

⌒

IDALIA sat down beside the table, gazing back at the pattern of stones on the great room floor. North. There were tiny flaws in the balance to the west, only a few, and hints of trouble in the south and east—the direction of Armethalieh—but almost all of her stones had been laid out toward the north. That was the direction in which the trouble lay, and that was where she had to go looking next. *Not* in the direction of Armethalieh and the Council.

And that was a great pity. Countering the meddling of High Magick would have been trivial to what she feared—and making trouble for Lycaelon would have been immensely satisfying.

She glanced at Kellen, who was foraging among the drawers and cabinets of the food storage with the same single-minded interest as a bear in a honey-tree. She'd been doing her best to hint to him about the way the Elves' minds worked before he got himself too badly hurt, but she doubted she was getting much of anywhere. Right now, all Kellen could see was the perfection of Elven ways, but like anything else living, the Elves had their faults, too, stubborn inflexibility being chief among them.

Compared to some among the Elves, Lycaelon Tavadon is vacillating and spineless.

But Kellen wasn't worldly-wise enough yet to catch a hint. She supposed he'd just have to figure it out for himself—and he'd be wildly indignant when he did, too; as indignant as he'd been when he discovered the High Mages acted out of self-interest more than disinterested justice . . .

"You look tired," Kellen said bluntly, turning back to her with the makings of a young feast in his hands. "Look, come sit down and I'll feed you."

"I've been working," Idalia said, taking a seat at the table as he laid out sliced vegetables and meat, bread and cheese.

"And you found out the drought's not a freak weather thing?" Kellen asked.

She blinked. For a boy who was normally as thick as two short planks—to borrow a popular Merryvale saying—he did have disconcerting flashes of insight, portents of the man he would someday become.

"Yes," Idalia admitted. There was no reason to keep the truth from Kellen; he'd be involved in the thick of it soon enough. "It isn't a natural thing. Ashaniel suspected as much; I suppose you must have guessed that. That was why she was so worried, even frightened. And rightly—to tie up the natural world like this requires an immense amount of power. I tried to call the rain today, and couldn't manage so much as a shift in the wind. That was proof: something, somewhere, is holding back the rain and doing it deliberately. Unnaturally. Now I have to find out who and where, if I can. I made a start on that today, and eliminated a few possibilities."

"What can I do to help?" Kellen asked. Idalia blessed him

for the bravery of his offer; she knew how wary Kellen still was of the Wild Magic—afraid, in fact.

It was the City still working in him, as much as he'd want to deny it. Armethalieh hated change: everything the High Mages did "for the good of the City" was to keep change from happening there, even the natural normal change that occurred everywhere. And the Wild Magic was all about change: every spell a Wildmage cast changed him or her in some way, small or great. Deep down inside Kellen sensed that. And no matter how much he said he accepted it; no matter how much he said he'd cast off the chains of the City; he was still fighting against it.

It was a battle no one could fight for him. The City's poisons would have to work their way out of his system naturally. Even telling him she knew what he was going through would do as much harm as good, Idalia suspected.

"Nothing, yet," she answered. "It's delicate work, like following a trail through a forest. I'm not sure how long it will take, either. I don't know what I'm going to find, but whatever I find, I do know it won't be pleasant."

She sighed and leaned forward. Kellen moved behind her, putting his hands on her shoulders to rub the tension out. "At least now I know it's nothing to do with the City. It's coming from the north. All the signs point to that."

"What's north of here?" Kellen asked idly. "All the maps in the City don't even go as far as the High Hills. Hah! What am I saying? They don't even go beyond the *walls*."

Idalia sighed, feeling the muscle knots loosen. If she wished for one thing, it was that she and Kellen could have more time together before they were plunged into the trouble she saw coming.

"North of the Elven Lands? Mountains. High desert. And . . . trouble."

She did not yet want to tell him how *much* trouble. Let him enjoy his first few days among the Elves, and revel in their wonderful city.

He'd find out the truth soon enough. They all would.

Chapter Nineteen

The Fruit of the Tree of Night

If only the High Mages knew how pleased with them she was at the moment, it would surely vex them unutterably, Queen Savilla thought delightedly. It was Armethalieh, with its foolish adventure, that had filled the slave pits in the Heart of Darkness to overflowing with refugees fleeing from those lands that the Mages had chosen to claim for their own. Ah, bless them! There had been no need to go a-hunting, with so many refugees simply *flinging* themselves into the traps.

And the cream of the jest was that after flushing such choice game into the waiting nets of the Endarkened, Armethalieh had renounced its new holdings. The witless fools that had attempted to elude the High Mages' tyranny need not have fled at all. The Golden City had hazarded much and gained nothing, while the Endarkened had profited by a rich new supply of slaves and toys; a deep reservoir of pain and suffering from which to draw power in the seasons to come.

Prince Zyperis had brought her the news this very morning, and sweet hearing it made indeed. As Armethalieh withdrew to the shadow of its own walls, weakening itself with its every deluded effort to make itself strong, so Sentarshadeen continued to wither and die, as certain as the Armethaliehans that it was the center and the pinnacle of Creation, and once each could have saved the other, did they only know . . .

But the seeds of discord and distrust had been sown well by Endarkened hands, centuries before. There were no Wild-mages in the Golden City now to come to the aid of the Elves, and Armethalieh would never look to the Otherfolk for her salvation.

Savilla saw to it that her slaves dressed her with exceptional care that day, oiling her wings with glittering unguents to make them shimmer, painting her horns and talons with gold leaf, and choosing her finest jewels for her adornment. The dungeons were filled with candidates for her attentions—since the Ingathering, there were enough vermin and failed slaves to allow every member of the Endarkened Court a pleasant diversion or two—but Savilla had business to attend to today, not pleasure. Her youngest nephew, Goraide, was training several of the more promising candidates they'd captured, preparing them for a future spent serving the Endarkened. It was her duty to attend, to oversee the work and offer the guidance of a more experienced advisor.

Her duty, and her pleasure.

THE slave quarters were above the Palace levels of the Heart of Darkness, placed so that in the event that conflict should reach the Palace itself, the bodies of the slaves would serve as one more barrier to the invaders. Even so, they were deep underground, so far within the twisting labyrinth of the World Without Sun that no Bright World captive could ever find his way unaided to the world he had left behind. This was the first lesson captives were taught: escape was impossible. Submission was the only salvation.

Everything here was designed to reinforce the simple lessons that were the basis of the lives of slaves: submission, pain, despair. The ceilings were low, the passageways narrow and stark, the cells bare and cold. All was dim to Brightworlder eyes. Families had been carefully separated, lest they give comfort and strength to one another. The youngest children had already been taken away to be raised in Endarkened crèches deeper in the Palace. When they were grown, they would be the best and most trustworthy slaves of all, for they would have known no other way of life than that of the World Without Sun, and fed from childhood upon the fruit of the Tree of Night.

But taming the wild-caught adults could be most reward-
ing . . .

She heard a groan of pain from one of the cells, and paused
to glance in. A male Centaur was being shod by an Endarkened farrier. He'd already had his tail docked short and been
gelded; his haunches were spattered with rusty streaks of
blood.

Savilla nodded her approval. Centaurs were useful beasts
of burden, but took care and patience to tame, and the males
were particularly unruly. Once he'd been shod, walking
would be agony, and without the constant attention that only
his new masters could provide, he would be permanently
crippled, his hooves split and festering. Still, the big chestnut
was a magnificent beast, and Savilla had rarely seen this
method of bringing the creatures under Endarkened control
fail. It was a great deal of trouble, but worth it in the end.

Savilla moved on.

SHE found Goraide in one of the main Training Chambers,
with half a dozen of the more promising young human males.
Their skins were still an odd parti-color—brown where they
had been burned by the sun, lighter where they had been
covered by their clothing—but in time it would all fade to
the proper pale shade of slaves who lived their whole lives
in the World Without Sun. Not as pale as that of the Elvenkind, but it had been long—too long—since the Endarkened
had enjoyed the pleasure of entertaining one of the Elves.

Soon, perhaps, that time would come again. If the Elves
could be forced to abandon their cities, they might be as
easily caught as these creatures had been. And then the halls
of the Heart of Darkness would echo with an eternity of rare
feasting and sport, as a thousand past injuries were repaid to
the last full measure . . .

The humans stank of terror—as well they should, for since
their capture, every experience they'd had was carefully
planned by their masters to cause them to despair. They hard-

ly realized it, but even now Goraide was subtly manipulating
their minds, undercutting their will and imagination so that
soon they would be unable to see any other possibility than
blind unthinking obedience to their new masters.

And the best of it was, he was using their own fears, their
own anger, to fuel his spells. When anger was gone, and only
fear and unreasoning despair remained, a slave's training was
complete.

They cowered back as Savilla entered the room.

"Did I say you could move?" Goraide asked gently. "Who
moved first? Tell me, and the rest of you will not be punished."

Savilla watched with interest. The lad had good instincts.
Were the humans ready to betray their own already?

There was a moment of indecision.

"He did—it was him. Cadin moved first," one of the males
said. He was a well-built, dark-haired creature; the slaves
Goraide was seeing to were intended to serve the Royal
Court, and thus were the most comely and vigorous of the
captives.

"No! It was you! Not me! Dairt lies!" Cadin lunged for
Dairt, but stopped when Goraide spread his wings with a
snap. All of them froze where they stood, staring at the young
Endarkened Prince in helpless terror.

"Well," Goraide said, regarding his slaves pleasantly. "You
cannot seem to agree. Perhaps you are not as obedient as I
had hoped. I will give you some time to reconsider. Now,
kneel to your Queen." He folded his wings and turned his
back on them, walking over to where Savilla stood as the six
slaves all dropped to their knees.

"Your Majesty," he greeted her respectfully, bowing his
head. Behind him the slaves were arguing in low vehement
hisses that they thought their masters could not hear. There
would be time enough to awaken them to the folly of that
assumption later.

"Nephew," Savilla said warmly, spreading her wings to
enfold him in a silken caress. "You're bringing them along
very well—turning on one another already? How lovely."

Goraide smiled. "They blame one another for their capture, Aunt Savilla, and I have encouraged them to hate and distrust one another even further. Despite that, they know that if *all* of them do not please me, none of them eat—and I keep their rations short."

"An excellent plan," Savilla agreed. "And I have delightful news for you to share with them." She lowered her voice to a whisper only Goraide could hear. "They have fled from their homes and into our hands for nothing. Armethalieh has just renounced all claim to the Western Hills and withdrawn to the City gates. Had they only stayed where they were, they would be safe in their own beds today."

Goraide's yellow eyes gleamed with pleasure. "All this— for nothing? Oh, they'll be so pleased to hear it!" His tail lashed back and forth with glee. He turned back to the slaves.

"You—come here." He pointed.

Dairt got slowly to his feet and shuffled reluctantly forward. Goraide put an arm around his shoulder and leaned down so that his mouth was near the slave's ear.

"It was you, wasn't it, little soft one, who made the trouble? You're afraid, and that's good. Fear is the beginning of wisdom. But you belong to us now, down here in the dark, and you must always do exactly what pleases us, because your Brightworld Gods have given you to us as a present, did you know that, little Dairt?"

Savilla saw the human's eyes flicker with fear and confusion.

"Do you know how I know that?" Goraide went on, in the same gentle confiding tones. "Because I know how you came here, Dairt. You were running away from the High Mages, because Armethalieh was going to take over the High Hills. And so you ran to us. But Armethalieh changed her mind. She went home to her own walls and left the High Hills alone. You didn't have to come here at all. You could have stayed right where you were, inconvenienced for a time, but safe." As Goraide spoke, Savilla could see him weaving the subtle strands of magic around his words, drawing power from the human's horror and despair to make the man believe him utterly.

"But you did come, Dairt. So it must have been because you wanted to come, to live with us and serve us. And now you will. You will never see the sun again. You will live here, with us, to serve us in any way we choose . . . and it was all your own free choice."

The human was gasping and whimpering by the time Goraide finished speaking, shaking his head in denial but unable to disbelieve. His eyes filled with tears—Savilla had always found that to be one of the odder and more charming things about humans, that they wept for nothing more than a harsh word or two—and he swayed on his feet, his knees buckling. Goraide steadied him, his long talons digging harshly into the human's soft skin.

"Soft one, soft one . . . you have what you came to find. There are pleasures to be found in service." Goraide turned the human's body against his own and kissed him full upon the mouth.

Savilla watched with interest as the human's body shuddered in protest and then stilled, the callused hands clenching and opening as Goraide's hands moved possessively over the soft unscaled body, leaving faint red welts upon the skin.

Yes, her nephew had a fine touch with these matters, one almost as good as Prince Zyperis's.

⟵

HIS visit with the Elven seamstress had been less stressful than Kellen had expected—and shorter, as well, since Tengitir wasn't really interested in any of Kellen's opinions about what clothing he should have. She'd made him stand in the direct sunlight that spilled through the skylight of her workroom as she held various swatches of fabric up to his skin to gauge the effect of the colors, taken a large number of measurements, confiscated most of the Elven clothes Kellen had been requested to bring with him (although she had allowed him to keep one outfit, to his mild surprise: a set of tunic and leggings in an odd steel-grey, almost the color of storm clouds.)

And just as well, Kellen realized on reflection, as Tengitir would have seen no reason that he should not leave the shop wearing nothing but his skin rather than leave in what she considered unsuitable clothing. Once she was done taking his measurements, she told him to be on his way. Kellen, happy to make his escape, quickly dressed in the steel-grey tunic and leggings, and got out of Tengitir's shop as fast as possible.

At least he still had his buckskin clothing, and the Mountain Trader outfit, and he wondered, as he was measured and remeasured, if perhaps he ought to just take to wearing the buckskins again, since Idalia was mostly wearing hers.

Because as hot and scratchy as it is, he thought as the seamstress held up yet another series of swatches to his face, *the only way anyone will get me into that Trader outfit again is at knifepoint . . .*

All in all, his visit to the Elven seamstress could have been a great deal more embarrassing. The only bad part about it was that Kellen hadn't gotten a chance to pose any questions of his own.

Sandalon had been there, of course, offering his own suggestions about the items Kellen should have for his wardrobe for various esoteric Elven events. Kellen supposed he should be just as glad he hadn't really understood most of the suggestions. What was a Flower War? And a Winter Running Dance just sounded exhausting.

Tengitir vetoed all of the young Prince's suggestions, gently telling the child that "I don't believe we are going to be holding any of those this year, Sandalon, what with the drought."

Just as well he wouldn't be getting outfits for either one, Kellen thought.

He spent the rest of the day entertaining Sandalon—and, not incidentally, helping several of the water-carriers in their tasks. Now that he knew more of what to look for, he could see that everyone in Sentarshadeen was completely occupied in keeping the valley that held the Elven city irrigated. And in the time they could spare from that task, work parties toiled in the forest beyond the canyon rim, fighting the losing battle to save the forest beyond.

Kellen promised himself that first thing tomorrow he'd see about formally joining one of those work parties. He might not be able to help Idalia in her work right now—he was only a half-trained Wildmage, after all—but there was no reason for him to be completely idle.

He only hoped that Tengitir had included work clothes in his new wardrobe—and that he'd be able to recognize them if she had. The new clothes she was promising him didn't look very much different to Kellen than the old ones—except in color—though it did seem that they would have more decoration, but then again, he really didn't care. He had more important things to think about.

If there wasn't anything really suitable for working in, his Wildwood buckskins would do just as well. He might not be able to hold his own in any discussion of Elven art, history, or fashion, but he could pump water and carry buckets as well as anyone. And it wasn't as if he could disguise the fact that he was human, so there wasn't really a lot of point in trying.

But in fact, as far as he could tell, his humanity really didn't seem to bother the Elves overmuch—or if it did, the Elves were far more polite about it than a bunch of humans would have been if the situation had been reversed, Kellen thought gloomily.

He didn't expect to see the new clothing anytime soon, but in fact, the first of the replacement items for his everyday wardrobe was waiting at his lodging when he arrived back there again that same evening. All that really mattered to Kellen was that the pieces were *not* (to his great relief) the skintight clothing he saw the Elves wearing, though he guessed they were pretty enough. He *did* wonder how Tengitir had gotten them done so fast, though.

The next morning, Kellen—who, with Idalia's help, had found something suitable among the clothes Tengitir had sent

after all—joined a work party, and was assigned to a work
detail in the Rim Forest to the west.

⇌

AT the canyon rim, a system of wind-driven pumps forced
the water from Sentarshadeen's five springs up above the canyon wall into reservoirs and holding tanks. The tanks had not
been built for this emergency, Kellen discovered, though the
method of filling them had. Normally they were filled naturally by the rains, and kept as an emergency reserve against
fires. From there, the water was pumped by hand into smaller
barrels and taken out into the forest . . . when the pump system worked.

Kellen gathered that it had been built in a hurry, on a much
larger scale than the Elves' usual projects. What he did know
was that it was breaking down more and more frequently as
parts wore out. And if it stopped working altogether, there
would be no way to get enough water from the five springs
of the canyon floor to the rim.

Watering a forest by hand. It's insane. It's impossible.
But they had to try.

Kellen spent most of his time in the days that followed
with the various watering parties, working to save the forest
around Sentarshadeen. It was important, necessary work, and
since he couldn't help Idalia with what she was doing, he
might as well do what he could. His labor was appreciated,
too, and if Elves weren't as fulsome in their verbal thanks as
some humans might be, he found tokens of their appreciation
whenever he got back to the house, in the form of blister
salves, liniments, and bath salts to ease the aches of one who
had hauled more than his share of heavy buckets.

Today—it was now the fourth day after his arrival in Sentarshadeen—he was working with Canderil and Llylance in
Coral Section. By now, every tree in the forest was marked
with a small patch of color on the trunk, so that no one watered a tree twice in any given term. Yesterday Kellen had
gone around his circuit alone, refilling the watering troughs

for the few forest animals that remained in the area. The Elves had tried keeping the forest pools full, but by now the drought had gone on so long that the water simply sank away into the parched ground, so now there were wooden troughs scattered through the forest for the animals to drink from.

It wasn't enough. Nothing was. The wild animals were so parched that they were drinking at the troughs in full daylight, ignoring the presence of Elves and human about them, predator even drinking side by side with prey.

"THIS one," Canderil said, stopping the cart.

Kellen stopped—it was his turn to pull the cart—and sighed in dismay. Even to his untutored eyes, the tree didn't look all that healthy, and by now he supposed the Elves knew every tree in the forest personally. He straightened, easing his shoulders as Llylance knelt and carefully scraped away the sheltering cover of fallen leaves from the roots of the tree, then dipped a bucket of water from the cart and poured it out, conscientiously working his way all around the tree's roots. Kellen could see the Elvenborn's lips moving, and supposed Llylance was saying a prayer for the forest. The earth beneath the leaves was so dry it was almost white; the water pooled on the surface for a moment, then sank away as fast as if it had been poured into sand.

When he was done, Llylance carefully replaced the covering of leaves again, and they went on.

Kellen didn't know how many colors the Elves could distinguish, but he knew that none of the trees was being watered very often. The Flower Forest in the canyon below was being irrigated with a series of trenches and canals, the water to fill them being pumped directly from whichever spring was nearest, but you couldn't do that with thousands of acres of wild forest. They weren't even really keeping the outer forest alive, Kellen knew—if anything, all the best efforts of the Elves could manage was to help it die more slowly.

But just because that was all they could do was no reason

to stop doing it. After all, Idalia might find out how to bring the rains back. Or something else might happen. They had to keep trying.

It usually took several barrels of water to irrigate a section. They'd emptied the first one, and were returning to the Rim for more water when Kellen spotted a familiar figure running toward him.

Sandalon.

Despite his work schedule, Kellen tried to spend as much time as possible with the Elven Prince—the kid was as curious about humans and the outside world as Kellen was about Sentarshadeen and the Elves, and besides, Kellen liked him, and knew the youngster was lonely—but it was barely midmorning, and right now Sandalon should be busy with his lessons.

"You've been running," Kellen said, barely turning the obvious question into a statement at the last minute for Canderil's and Llylance's benefit. *He* might be a scapegrace, rag-mannered round-ear, but there was no reason to give anybody the idea he was a bad influence on the Prince, Kellen thought with an inward grin.

Though who was a bad influence on whom might be a matter of opinion . . .

"They want you—at the House—of Leaf and Star—" Sandalon said, getting his message out between gasps for breath. From the look of things, he'd been running since he left there, and his face was a mixture of apprehension, a little fear, and pride at being entrusted with so important a message.

"Whoa!" Kellen said, reaching out a hand to steady the child. "Start from the beginning."

"They want you there," Sandalon repeated impatiently. "Father's home. And Idalia's there. And Ainalundore, and Tyendimarquen, and *everybody*. There's going to be a big meeting and they want you because there's something important. And I looked all over for you!"

The names meant nothing to Kellen, but they obviously meant something to his companions from the looks the two adult Elves exchanged.

"You had better go," Canderil said. "Ainalundore and Tyendimarquen are two of the Advisors of Leaf and Star."

"Fast," Llylance added. "And as you are," he added as an afterthought, in case Kellen had harbored any notions of going home and changing his clothes.

Kellen winced, just a little. He was hot and sweaty and dusty after a morning spent hauling water for the trees, and even Elven-made work clothes probably weren't suitable for this occasion. But if they said to hurry . . .

Maybe he could wash up when he got there before he saw anybody. He picked up Sandalon, to the boy's great delight, set the child on his shoulders, and strode off.

⌒

BUT when he arrived at the Palace, rather out of breath himself after hurrying most of the way across the city—fortunately Sandalon had gotten tired of riding and wanted to run on ahead—he was met at the front door of the House of Leaf and Star by someone he didn't recognize and hustled quickly along passageways he hadn't seen before into a chamber somewhere in the center of the Palace.

Unlike every other Elven room he'd ever seen, this one had no windows at all, even in the ceiling. It was completely circular, and hanging from the walls were thirteen narrow banners of brightly colored silk, each bearing a single elaborate symbol worked upon it in shining silver. Most of them were completely unfamiliar to Kellen, but one almost seemed to be a version of the Great Seal of Armethalieh. A complex chandelier of mirrored lamps suspended overhead rendered the windowless chamber as bright as day.

In the center of the room was a large round table. If it was made of wood, it was no wood Kellen had ever seen—pale as snow and gleaming like shell. Inlaid in its center, of some shining material so bright it seemed to be lit from within, was a symbol Kellen had seen elsewhere here in the House of Leaf and Star, and on one of the banners here; he supposed it was the symbol of the royal house.

There were nine tall, thronelike chairs with mosaics of colored glass set into their backs arranged in a semicircle around the far side of the table. Eight of them were filled.

Ashaniel was there, and so was Idalia. To Kellen's great surprise, so was Morusil, though Kellen barely recognized him in the elaborate robes and jewels he now wore. Kellen didn't recognize anyone else, though the man sitting next to Ashaniel was undoubtedly Sandalon's father, the Elven king Andoreniel Caerthalien, and two of the other five Elves had to be Ainalundore and Tyendimarquen.

Andoreniel was, well, *kingly*, and Kellen instinctively recoiled from that air of authority before realizing that there was no cruelty or malice in it. Andoreniel might be a powerful ruler, but there all resemblance to the Arch-Mage Lycaelon ended. This was a man who ruled his subjects through love, law, and unwavering justice, not through fear, malice, and subtle treachery.

My father could have been like this man, Kellen thought. But the realization brought only a faint regretful sadness, before that too was swept away by curiosity as to why he had been summoned.

As he stood there, Kellen heard the doors close behind him. One of the gorgeously robed counselors rose from her seat—by now Kellen was getting fairly good at telling male Elves from female, at least most of the time—and came to the door, sliding several bolts into place. As she did, the King raised his hand, drawing a small shape upon the air, and the symbol in the center of the table flared even more brightly for a moment. Kellen felt a sense of *pressure*. Something—something magical—had just happened. He glanced toward Idalia, who smiled reassuringly.

"Now we are all present. The chamber is locked and sealed, proof against all intrusion and spies," Andoreniel said. "We may begin."

"Come and sit down, Kellen," Idalia said in a low voice, indicating the empty chair beside her. Reluctantly, Kellen took his seat. He still wasn't entirely sure why he was here, and he felt incredibly grubby and out of place. They were probably all staring at him, wondering what the gardener was doing here. He and Idalia were the only ones wearing ordinary clothing, and she wasn't sweaty and filthy from work in the forest.

For a moment all of them regarded one another without speaking.

"I have found the source of your problem," Idalia said at last. "I know why nothing the Elves have done has broken the drought."

There was a stir of consternation from the Elves, and Kellen wondered why Idalia didn't just come out and *say* it, if she had the answer. But she almost seemed to be hesitating, as if when she gave that answer, it would change everything, and not for the better.

"Someone has created a kind of magical dam or diversion in the mountains to the north, forcing the natural weather patterns to shift. To the north of here, the high desert is getting soaked with what ought to be Sentarshadeen's rainfall, as the clouds pile against an ethereal barrier created by baneful magic. This does as little good to the desert and its inhabitants as the drought does to the Elvenkind. And while that barrier remains, no drop of rain will reach Sentarshadeen."

Suddenly it seemed as if all of the Elves wanted to talk at once. Andoreniel held up his hand for silence.

"If you know who is causing this, Idalia, you must tell us," he said gently.

"I'd hoped I was wrong, but I'm not," Idalia said, still unwilling to come to the point. "I made very sure of my facts before I came to you, Andoreniel. But there can be no possible doubt. Shadow Mountain wakens again. It is they who have caused your drought."

The name meant nothing to Kellen, but the Elves all recoiled as if Idalia had just emptied a basket of poisonous snakes onto the center of the table.

"Now that I know what's wrong, I can craft a spell to fix it," she said, hurrying on, before any of them could break their shocked silence. "It will be tricky work and demand a very high price—"

"Of course we will pay it, Idalia!" Andoreniel interrupted staunchly. "All the price, if we can, yours and our own. Only show us how."

Idalia smiled wanly. She looked exhausted, Kellen thought, more so than he had ever seen her, and if there was still spellcasting to be done, her work had hardly begun.

"I will," she promised. "If I could not count on the cooperation of all of you, the task would be doomed to failure before it began. But I told you this wouldn't be a simple matter, and it isn't. I can craft the spell here, but it can't be cast here. It will have to be placed in a keystone which will have to be formed by magic. That much I can do, with your help. Then the keystone has to be carried to the place where the Barrier is, and triggered there to release the counterspell— by a second Wildmage." She glanced toward Kellen for a moment. "Naturally, it will be Kellen who goes into the mountains with the keystone."

Me? Kellen did his best not to look as stunned as he felt, and hoped he succeeded.

"But surely you should go instead, Idalia." One of the Elven councilors seated beside Morusil spoke up for the first time. "Kellen is barely more than a child."

"Perhaps in Elven terms, Tyendimarquen," Idalia answered—rather sharply, Kellen thought. "But he is equal to this challenge and I would gladly trust my life to him. And *you* will have to, because I will be needed here. Once Shadow Mountain's spell is broken there will be storms across the land such as perhaps even you have never seen. And when the spell-dam is broken and the rains come, I will have to be here in Sentarshadeen to call the weather back into its normal patterns once more, and shelter the city from flood and wind. Unless you want Sentarshadeen to drown instead of wither away, you'll need me to guide the weather from the moment the Barrier breaks, and I do not know when that will be. Or you can start building boats."

Kellen barely heard the rest of what Idalia was saying.

He'd been stunned at first at the notion that *he'd* been chosen to perform this vital task. He'd gotten used to following Idalia around for so long that it was a shock to think of going off alone to do something so important. What if he failed?

But now that it was starting to sink in, he was excited. And proud. And relieved, in a way, because there finally *was* something he could do, something constructive, something more than carrying buckets.

And something that Elves can't . . .

He couldn't help that thought, but there it was. Elves couldn't do this; Elves couldn't be Wildmages. Of all of the folk here in Sentarshadeen, only he and Idalia could do this. And Idalia was needed here. She'd said so. And that left him.

He could do this—he knew he could. Idalia wouldn't have chosen him if she didn't think he could. At last, here was something he could do *because* he was a Wildmage, something he could do that no one else could!

"True enough," Ashaniel said gravely, inclining her head and regarding Kellen for a moment. She glanced around the table at the other counselors, seeming to reach some sort of silent consensus.

"You cannot mean to send him off alone," Tyendimarquen said in disbelieving tones. "One blow from an Endarkened claw, and our hopes would lie in ruin."

"It is in my mind that perhaps we would be overhasty in sending Kellen off into the mountains entirely alone," Morusil said slowly, speaking for the first time. "But a large escort would only draw the same attention that—as you rightly point out, Tyendimarquen, my esteemed friend and colleague—we very much wish to avoid. So perhaps the escort of a single Elven Knight would be the best compromise between recklessness and caution."

"A foolish compromise, if the barrier itself is guarded by Endarkened warriors," another counselor said.

"I do not believe it is so guarded," Idalia said thoughtfully. "The Endarkened have counted perhaps too much on the fact that you would not discover the source of your trouble. Why waste their resources guarding something they think is perfectly safe? What is more, the Endarkened, for all their evil, are not stupid. I believe they would know better than to draw attention to the source-point of their barrier by heavily guarding it. The faster we—and Kellen—can move against them, the less likely it is that they will figure things out in time to mount such a defense as you fear, Ainalundore."

"Very well," the King said, reaching a decision. "Kellen will go, with a single Knight to accompany him. Tomorrow he rides, and now, let every hand be turned to help him on his journey. It is decided."

The King rose to his feet, and sketched the same symbol in the air as before. There was a change in the air of the room, as though they'd all been in a sealed jar, and somebody had just opened it. One of the Elves—Kellen realized he never had found out all their names—went to unbolt the door again.

It was all over so fast. I thought they'd be talking for hours . . .

Evidently Elves *could* decide things quickly, when a fast decision was what was needed.

It seemed as if he'd barely sat down, and now, suddenly, he was being sent off alone, the deliverance of Sentarshadeen in his keeping. He was going to rescue the Elves by magic—him, Kellen Tavadon.

Unbelievable.

"Come on, Kellen, on your feet. We've got to get you to the armory," Idalia said, pulling him out of his chair.

"Huh?" Kellen said inelegantly, roused from his reverie.

"Armory? Where they fit you with armor? You're going up against Shadow Mountain; you can't do it in a silk tunic, you know. You've got a lot to do before tomorrow morning, and so do I," Idalia said.

"Tomorrow? He didn't really mean that," Kellen said, dropping his voice to a whisper, as the King and Queen were still on the other side of the room, giving orders to their counselors.

"He did. You'll see. The Elves can do things in a hurry when they want to. Come on," Idalia said.

Morusil was moving away from the knot of Elves around

the King and Queen. He stopped in front of Kellen as the three of them reached the doorway.

"It grieves me to know I will not have the opportunity to tell you more of my stories, young Wildmage. But perhaps upon your return we will all have more leisure," Morusil said, and laid a hand on Kellen's arm in a gesture that was at once protective and fatherly, and the comradely reassurance between equals. "I think, perhaps, there is a great deal you should know, in the fullness of time."

"I'd like that very much," Kellen answered.

Idalia stared after Morusil as he left, then back at Kellen. "I didn't know you knew him," she said curiously.

"I met him while I was out walking around the city. He was out watering his garden. I didn't know he was one of the royal counselors."

"He ought to be. He's the Queen's uncle. Now come on."

⌐

IDALIA was right about Elves being able to do things in a hurry when they wanted. Less than an hour later Kellen was standing in the armory, having his first-ever suit of armor fitted to his body.

The process was a lot more complicated than the morning he'd spent at Tengitir's getting new clothes.

All Kellen knew about armor was that it was heavy, expensive, took several moonturns to make, and was designed to keep you from getting killed by somebody who had a sword, mace, spear, or bow. And that even if the Elves did have a spare suit of it lying around, it wasn't going to fit *him*.

It turned out that the only thing he was right about was the last. There wasn't a spare set of armor in his size lying around the armory, but it looked like he was going to have a full suit of Elven armor by tomorrow morning anyway. And—as he soon discovered—Elven armor was almost as light as a suit of clothes.

They began by taking wax molds of his arms and legs, bending thick sheets of warmed and oiled beeswax over his

bare arms and legs and pressing it into place, then carrying
the pieces away into the mysterious inner regions of the forge.
Kellen was allowed to get dressed again, but not to wander
very far; the Master Armorer told him he would be needed
for fittings again almost at once.

As it turned out, Kellen had too much to occupy him in
the interim to be able to wander anywhere at all, even if he'd
wanted to. Elven armor was designed to be worn over a narrow quilted undertunic and leggings, and Tengitir was sent
for to supply that. The measuring began all over again, for
apparently the measurements she had taken for suits of clothing were not the right ones for the undertunic.

And there were a few items Kellen would be needing that
did not have to be made.

An Elf named Ṭandarion entered, carrying a tray on which
lay four swords. Kellen was obscurely relieved to see that
none of them was jeweled. Jeweled swords were all very well
for wondertales and Festival plays, but this was real life.

"Fortunately we had been forging for the Flower Wars next
spring, so there are several here to choose from. Even the
King's command could not forge a sword overnight," the
Master Armorer said. "Choose whichever pleases you best,
Kellen. All are fine weapons, suitable to your needs."

"But how do I—I mean, I've never handled a sword before. I would welcome your advice," Kellen said awkwardly.

The Master Armorer smiled indulgently. "Try them all. I
believe you will know the proper one when you heft it."

Doubtfully, Kellen did as he was told. He lifted each of
the swords in turn, flourishing them in the way he'd seen
swordsmen do in plays back in Armethalieh. He had no idea
of what to do with one, really, but he supposed it came with
the armor, more or less. All of them were light, moving
through the air like an extension of his arm. He was sure
each of them was sharp. How could he possibly choose?

But he kept coming back to one in particular. It just felt
better in his hand than the others. It wasn't that it was
prettier—all of them were beautiful, in the simple perfect way
of Elven things. It wasn't much different in size or shape

than the others, and Kellen had no way of judging what was
a good size and shape for a sword blade anyway.

It just *felt* right.

"The body sees what the mind cannot." The Book of Stars
says that. Okay. "I'll take this one."

"An excellent choice, Kellen. I'll send it to the cordwainers
to have a scabbard made immediately."

*"Immediately." Now there's a word I never thought I'd
hear around here.*

Just then Shalkan walked in.

"Shalkan?" Kellen said, surprised. He wondered if everyone in the forge was, well, fit company for a unicorn, so to
speak. But Shalkan seemed comfortable enough.

The unicorn tilted his head, regarding Kellen. "Did you
think you were going alone? Or that you were going to be
the only one wearing armor?" Shalkan said. "The great Elven
Knights used to ride unicorns into battle. You may not be an
Elven Knight, but I suppose I'll have to get used to that."

Kellen watched with interest while Shalkan discussed his
needs with the Elves. Kellen realized with relief that this time,
when he rode out with Shalkan, he'd be doing it with a proper
saddle; the Master Armorer took Shalkan's measurements,
and in a few moments, several sets of saddles and barding
had been brought for Shalkan to choose from. That, in itself,
would have been a pretty amusing idea, if Shalkan hadn't
been so deadly serious about it—the *mount* choosing the saddle and harness, instead of the rider!

Kellen had seen horses in armor at parades in Armethalieh
on high Festival occasions. Shalkan's armor was quite a different matter. For one thing, the unicorn was built nothing
like a horse. For another, the unicorn was a thinking, reasoning, independent creature, not a beast meant to be controlled
by a rider. Kellen gradually came to realize that it made good
sense for Shalkan to choose his own protection; he was the
only one who could say what was, and what was not, comfortable for him.

Shalkan chose armor that covered his chest and shoulders,
leaving his legs and haunches free. The lower part of his long

sinuous neck was encased in a long collar of interlocking rings that moved and flexed as fluidly as Shalkan himself, lined in sheep's wool to prevent chafing. The armorer urged him to add a *shanfron* to his armor, a close-fitting piece that went over his head and cheeks and latched beneath his throat and muzzle, and in fact Shalkan tried several. But in the end Shalkan rejected them all, saying they were too confining.

Privately Kellen thought that was too bad, as the *shanfron* had looked very dashing.

"We will finish these pieces and have them ready for you by tomorrow, Shalkan," Tandarion said.

Shalkan bowed his head. "Green for the lacings and ornaments, I think," he said gravely. "To match my eyes, of course."

Kellen wasn't sure whether the unicorn was serious or making a joke, but the Elves seemed to think it was a perfectly reasonable request.

Once they'd removed the armor, he wandered over to Kellen.

"Nice sword."

"Not that I know the first thing about using one," Kellen said under his breath.

"Just think of it as a large, pointy, sharp-edged club," Shalkan said helpfully. "You're good with a club. If you can't actually cut at an enemy properly, at least you can bash him with the flat of the blade. And now, if you'll excuse me, I have a few more arrangements to make before tomorrow, and *your* work here has just begun." He pointed with his horn, and Kellen saw the Master Armorer and several apprentices coming out of the forge area with several pieces of what could only be Kellen's new armor.

THERE was a helmet, a sort of collar, pieces to cover his chest and back, and long metal sleeves with segmented elbows, held in place by gauntlets so meticulously jointed that Kellen could touch each finger with his thumb, just as if the gauntlets were leather instead of metal. The closer he looked at the armor, the more small interlocking pieces he could see: it was as unyielding as any of the hard metals (quite harder than bronze, though it didn't seem to be steel), but nearly as flexible as his own skin. The armorers swore a man could dance wearing this armor, but Kellen wasn't looking forward to trying. It might be much, much lighter than anything he'd ever seen of the sort before, but that didn't make it *light*.

The entire surface of the armor was ornamented, or would be when it was complete, with subtle patterns that were almost like the pattern of wood grain.

"It adds strength, you see," one of the armorers told him, seeing his confusion, holding up a finished piece of another suit of armor for Kellen's inspection. That one didn't have a wood-swirl pattern, though; its surface pattern looked more like clouds, or billows of smoke.

"A good beginning, though of course much more work will be needed. You may remove the armor if you wish."

Kellen pulled off the helmet (there would be feathers, he'd discovered to his dismay, in a green to match Shalkan's ornaments) and slipped off the belly-and-back pieces, which were all he'd had on at the moment, the others having already been returned to the forge for more work. It looked like it was a good thing he was going to have an actual Elven Knight with him, because otherwise he wasn't sure how he'd get in and out of all this stuff every morning, even if most of the parts did stay permanently connected to each other once the armor was finished.

But at last, late in the afternoon, the Master Armorer told him he was no longer needed for the work to continue. The armor would be ready for him by the time he was ready to depart.

Rolling up the quilted undertunic and leggings to take with him, Kellen left the armory.

HE went directly back to the house, hoping Idalia would be there. To his great relief he found her lying on one of the long benches in the living room, reading her copy of *The Book of Sun* and eating an apple, the grey cat under her arm.

"Are you all right?" he asked.

"Better than I will be later tonight," Idalia said matter-of-factly, sitting up. "Don't look so worried—with all the Elves of Sentarshadeen providing the energy to create the counter-spell and the keystone, all I'll really have to do is provide energy to channel their power, the skill to craft the spell, and the ability to put it in place. The cost to us all will be no worse than if we'd all worked nonstop for a few sennights, but compressed into an hour or so. We'll all be exhausted once the spell is cast, but it will be worth it. That's why *you* are not going to be participating in what we're going to do tonight. You'll need all your resources for what comes after."

Kellen sat down beside her. The grey cat, dislodged from her previous comfortable position, climbed into his lap, settled down again, and started purring. He stroked her fur absently.

"What *does* come after?" Kellen asked. "Tomorrow, I mean."

"Go where I send you and release the spell there. I'll know more exactly what you're looking for and how you'll find it—and what to do when you get there—once I've done my part tonight."

"That doesn't seem, well, very *exact*," Kellen said dubiously.

Idalia reached out and ruffled his hair comfortingly. "If you wanted exact answers and detailed instructions, brother dear, you should have stuck with the High Magick. That's not what our path is about. Now . . . don't you have some packing to do? Or are you going to be like one of those adventurers in the wondertales, going off on his knightly quest with nothing more than a shining suit of armor and great expectations?" She gave him a gentle shove and lifted the cat from his lap. "Don't worry about food—the Elves are taking care of that, and the mule to carry it. But don't forget your Books, or you'll just have to hunt through everything you've brought to find out where they've gotten themselves to. They won't allow themselves to be left behind, you know."

*

FORTUNATELY Kellen by now had a certain amount of experience with long journeys and the small comforts that made such travel tolerable. Even more fortunately, he and Idalia had been in Sentarshadeen less than a sennight, and his bedroll (and other equipment) were still tucked away in the corners of his room, along with his share of the traveling packs.

Despite all that, it took Kellen a long time to decide what he'd actually need. Too many thoughts kept intruding: of the adventure (or possibly disaster) that lay ahead, of the magic to come tonight, of the thought of actually *wearing* a suit of glorious Elven armor. Would he look silly—or grand?

And, occasionally, darker thoughts. Just what *was* Shadow Mountain? Who were the Endarkened, and did they live there? And why did they hate the Elves? Was he really going to have to fight? He'd never really fought anyone—other than the stone Hounds—before in his life . . .

In the Council chamber this afternoon, Idalia had made it all sound like such a simple matter: go to the source of the spell and use the keystone she would make tonight. And at the time, it'd seemed very simple: an adventure, in fact. He'd triggered keystones before—anytime he used their stored energy to fuel a spell, in fact. That part didn't worry him overmuch.

But he knew it couldn't be *quite* as simple—or as easy—as she'd made it all sound. Just finding out what was causing the drought had exhausted Idalia, and whatever was going to happen tonight would be a further drain on her. But whoever it was at Shadow Mountain who had caused the drought in the first place had meant to destroy Sentarshadeen and everyone in it, so just finding out how to stop them had to have been the easy part, if anything in all this could be called easy.

That meant there must be traps and barriers between Kellen and undoing their spell that he couldn't even begin to imagine right now.

And whoever had set the spell certainly wouldn't want it undone. If they found out about him, they'd certainly try to stop him. Just like the High Council had tried to stop him from leaving the City lands.

For just a moment, in his mind Kellen was back in the pocket canyon facing the Outlaw Hunt. Suddenly he was glad—very glad—that Shalkan and one of the Elves would be going with him. And he was beginning to wish that he'd be going with an entire Elven army, instead . . .

Chapter Twenty

A Circle of Silver Fire

That evening, just after lamp-lighting time, Kellen and Idalia went down to the meadow beyond the Palace, carrying lanterns to guide their way. Tonight, all of Sentar-shadeen was dark. No one remained behind in the Elven houses to tend the lamps, and it would be folly to leave them unattended.

But the meadow itself was bright, for every Elf in the city was there, and the meadow had been ringed with lanterns.

There were no unicorns to be seen anywhere in the meadow, for the work to be done tonight belonged entirely to the Elves. Kellen didn't really understand why—perhaps, just like him, the unicorns would have a different role to play in the days ahead.

He looked around.

The Elves all wore long robes in pale colors, the fabrics seeming to shimmer in the twilight as if they glowed as well. Kellen could hear the faint susurrus of conversation among

the waiting Elves; a quiet sound considering the size of the
crowd.

Idalia stopped him outside the edge of the ring of lanterns.
She was carrying her walking stave, but aside from that, she
hadn't made any particular preparations that Kellen had noticed.

"Remember, Kellen. Once this starts, I don't want you being a part of it. You'll have your price to pay later, and trust
me, you'll pay as much as we do here and now."

"I remember," Kellen said.

Privately, he hardly thought it was fair. Whoever would be
riding with him tomorrow would be in the circle tonight, part
of the spell, contributing their power to its success. Why
couldn't he be here as well?

Still, it was Idalia's choice, and he would accept that.

"And besides," she went on, with a sideways smile at him.
"You *do* have one very important part to play here tonight."

"Thought so," Kellen said in satisfaction, pleased. Then:
"What?"

"When the spell is complete—you'll know when that happens—and the keystone appears, you need to take it and wrap
it up carefully in a protective cloth. The Elves have spent all
day preparing it. Ashaniel will have that; I think I see her
now. Keep the keystone safe, and don't unwrap it again until
you're ready to use it. The cloth should keep Shadow Mountain from being able to sense the keystone, which will serve
as another layer of protection for you. One thing that we *don't*
want is for them to know you're coming, and the keystone's
presence in the world might as well be a blazing torch to alert
them."

That reminded Kellen yet again that he very much wanted
to ask just what Shadow Mountain was, and why it—or
they—wanted to destroy the Elves, but just then Idalia started
moving through the crowd. She handed her lantern to someone at the edge of the gathering, and Kellen quickly followed
suit with his own. Fire was still a danger, especially with so
many people gathered here together.

Everyone stepped back to give Kellen and Idalia room as they approached. Kellen had never been so conscious of being the center of attention, though he told himself it was really Idalia who was the focus of everyone's concern tonight. His part would be played out in the future, out of sight, and suddenly he was glad of it. There was a downside to being the center of attention; if you fouled up, there was no second chance to try again and do it right. He wouldn't fail (of course!) but if he did at least there'd be no one there to see, and maybe he could get that second chance after all.

Because of the way Sentarshadeen was built, even now Kellen wasn't really sure how big the city was, but tonight he knew how many Elves lived here. Hundreds. More than he could count. They filled the entire meadow, all the way back into the trees.

At the center of the crowd a small open space had been preserved. A large five-sided flat tablet of white stone had been set upon the grass, and a small bronze brazier had been placed atop that for Idalia's use. The space was ringed with more torches.

Ashaniel approached them as they reached the edge of the open space, holding a small bundle of dark fabric in her hands. She held it out to Idalia. "Here is the spell-caul for the keystone."

Idalia took it and passed it to Kellen, thanking Ashaniel absently. Kellen could tell his sister's mind was already elsewhere, on the work that was to come.

Curious, Kellen inspected the bundle in his hands. It was a large square of heavy red silk, embroidered in the same color as the fabric. His fingers tingled as he touched it, and it seemed somehow colder and heavier than it ought to be. Magic. Sewn to the outside was a pair of long tasseled cords, so he could tie the bundle shut once he'd wrapped the keystone in it. He folded the fabric up tightly again and tucked it under one arm.

Now all that remained was to create the contents.

He remembered Idalia's lessons about withdrawing himself

from a spell in order to deny his power and energy to a Working. *The Book of Sun* also spoke of starving the will and refusing consent; Kellen had thought those injunctions related only to making bargains until Idalia explained that all aspects of a spell were in some sense a transaction: giving power to the spells of another, accepting a spell cast upon you (for good or ill), sensing the effects of a spell cast by another. If the Wildmage refused to participate in the transaction, depending on his own power, he could minimize or even negate the power of the spell entirely. All these things were aspects of shielding, and Kellen's abilities in that area were going to get a serious workout tonight. Maybe he wasn't such a "nonparticipant" after all; it would take a great effort of will to avoid being drawn into a working this large.

Idalia stepped into the center of the ring of torches, and as she did, silence spread outward in ripples through the waiting Elves, until the only sound was that of the wind through the trees.

As Kellen watched, she knelt on the center stone and prepared her spell, piling a few leaves and a sharp knife beside the brazier filled with tinder.

Then she rose to her feet and began making her Circle, marking it with her staff.

He knew far more now about the physical components of Wild Magic than he had back when he'd first helped Idalia heal the unicorn colt. A Wildmage's Circle was an acknowledgment that the world had boundaries, and that the help he or she summoned came into the world the Wildmage knew and served from elsewhere. It also functioned as a reminder that in calling upon the forces of the Wild Magic, the Wildmage was leaving behind the world he or she knew. In Calling Spells, no forces except those the Wildmage had called could enter the Circle; in Finding Spells, it served as a point of departure on the path that would lead the Wildmage to his goal. On those rare and dangerous occasions when the Wildmage was compelling something to appear before him, the Circle served as a beacon to guide it and an enclosure to imprison it, subject to the Wildmage's will.

But in Kellen's experience, the Circle was always invisible except to magical senses, or at most a line scratched in the earth by a stick or a knife.

This was different.

Where Idalia walked, a white glow sprang up behind her, a glow as intense as Magelight. And when she had finished, there was a ring of bright white light defining the circle she had marked, its silvery radiance as intense as the noonday sun. Kellen closed his eyes and could still see it through his closed lids.

All around him the Elves seemed to sigh. They began to sing in a strange unfamiliar tongue, swaying gently as they did, their voices rising in a high sweet chorus that vibrated through Kellen's body like the carillons of Armethalieh. He felt himself begin to sway as well, felt the song resonate within him, calling to something deep inside him that longed—demanded—to answer it.

He suddenly realized he couldn't be here. Not in the middle of the Elves, not standing so close to Idalia's Circle. Blindly, he turned and pushed his way through the crowd, forcing his way through the unresisting bodies entirely by touch.

The Elves didn't seem to notice, but Kellen was gasping for air by the time he reached the edge of the crowd. He looked around—anywhere but at the Circle—breathing deeply and hugging himself tightly to try to shake off the mesmerizing trance state. It felt as if he were trying to force himself awake from the deepest of sleep; he pinched himself—*hard*—welcoming the sharp immediacy of the pain as something to anchor himself to.

When he was sure he could resist the lure of the rising power, Kellen looked around. He found he was standing on a small rise among the trees, where he could look down on the ceremony behind him. The Elves still sang, but now the sound was something outside him, separate from him, a thing he could shut out with an effort of will. It was unearthly, the kind of song that no human throats could ever form. Not with harmonies built a hundred choruses deep, and so perfectly attuned that even the thought of discord was impossible.

The center of the Circle was only a hazy silvery glow, as bright as if the full moon had come to earth, but Kellen did not need to see Idalia to know what she was doing, for most spells of the Wild Magic followed a similar pattern. She would have kindled a fire in the brazier and used it to burn the appropriate herbs and leaves, along with a few drops of her blood. That was the sacrifice of Power Within that linked the Wildmage to the Power Without, like priming a pump—a metaphor Kellen had neither known nor understood until he had seen pumps in Merryvale.

And somehow the Elves were singing their own power into the spell as well, linking themselves to each other and to Idalia. Kellen could feel that even as he held himself back from it. Unlike the ordinary folk of Armethalieh, who had power, but could neither sense nor use it, though the Elves could not *use* their power, they not only could sense it, they knew it, intimately and well, and could direct it to the skill of one who *could* use it.

The song had begun slowly, a call and response, the melody sweeping around the circle of Elves as the counterpoint followed in its wake. But gradually the counterpoint died away, as more and more voices took up the melody alone, and the melody simplified, until all the voices below sang as one, a single, simple, heart-piercing phrase of unutterable sweetness, repeated over and over in a language Kellen didn't understand.

And step by step that song line shortened as well. Three beats, then two, and Kellen felt the spiraling tension coiling upward, demanding release.

One single note soaring toward the stars, until he thought he would go mad, or the stars themselves would shatter—
—and then—
Silence.
Darkness.
Release.

Kellen staggered backward, as if something he'd been pulling against had abruptly disappeared. He realized that the spell was cast, and that now he needed to get down to Idalia. He forced himself to move.

It was harder, this time, to make his way through the Elves. As Idalia had predicted, they were exhausted by their sacrifice of power to the spell. Some had sat down where they were, others were leaning against the person next to them for support. All of them seemed somehow disoriented, drained. Kellen pushed through them as ruthlessly as he could bring himself to, navigating by the faint steady glow of torchlight ahead of him.

Idalia was kneeling on the white stone, a dark object a little larger than one of the Elven lanterns between her knees. Though it looked nothing like the usual sort of keystone from the quick glimpse he got of it, there was no denying that was what it was. The object *drew* him, in the same way that the Elven song had drawn him, but this time he did not resist the pull of it. He entered the circle, not a particle of his attention on anything *but* the object, none to spare even for Idalia.

Hide me! the thing cried out to him. *Shelter me, cover me, protect me now!*

Kellen quickly dropped the spell-caul over it, swaddling whatever it was up firmly in the red silk—it was surprisingly heavy for its size—taking care to wind it so deeply in the soft folds that nothing could possibly "leak" out to betray its presence. He finished by tying the tasseled cords firmly around it.

When he looked up again, Idalia had collapsed completely, lying unconscious on the ground.

Kellen took a step toward his sister, but he wasn't quick enough. A male Elf had stepped out of the crowd, stooping and lifting Idalia into his arms as though she weighed nothing at all.

It was Jermayan.

The Elf stared challengingly into Kellen's eyes, as if daring him to object to his presence.

Now Kellen was torn between duty and duty. He knew

that Idalia didn't want to have anything more to do with Jermayan, but at the moment Idalia was in no condition to complain. Kellen couldn't carry her *and* the keystone. And no one else seemed to be in any condition to care for her . . .

Before Kellen could think of what to say, Jermayan turned away and began carrying Idalia back in the direction of her and Kellen's house.

Kellen clutched the silk-wrapped bundle tighter and followed.

It looks like they're well matched in one thing. They're both about as stubborn as each other, anyway. He sighed. *Well, if he wants to do this, and it makes him feel useful . . . he's a grown man. I guess he's a grown man. He looks old enough to make up his own mind about making himself miserable, anyway.*

Though true night had fallen while the keystone was being created, Jermayan had no trouble finding his way along the narrow unlighted paths that lay between the unicorn meadow and Kellen and Idalia's house, and Kellen found himself having to hurry to keep up with the Elf. If Jermayan had not been dressed entirely in white, it would have been even more difficult.

"You can slow down, you know," Kellen finally said, a little breathlessly. "There's no rush—I don't think Idalia's going to wake up anytime soon. And thank you for taking her."

Jermayan abruptly slowed, allowing Kellen to catch up with him.

"No, she is exhausted," Jermayan said tenderly, gazing down at Idalia's face, her head cradled protectively against his shoulder. "But I would not wish to place you in the position of having permitted my attentions to your sister, should she learn I have taken this service upon myself."

"What you and Idalia do—or don't do—is between the two of you," Kellen said hastily. "She wouldn't listen to me anyway." *And since I didn't even know I had a sister until Shalkan dumped me at her front door a few moonturns ago, and since she all but told me off for trying to nose in when*

*you first showed up on our doorstep, I'm sure not going to
start telling her how to run her life now.*

Jermayan smiled faintly. "Great wisdom in one so young,"
he commented.

"Besides," Kellen added, after a moment, "what do *I* know,
anyway? Somebody who keeps company with unicorns
doesn't have a right to a lot of opinions about people who—
ah—*can't.*"

He thought he heard a faint chuckle from Jermayan, but
he couldn't be sure.

They continued onward in a more companionable silence
until they reached the door. Kellen opened it, and Jermayan
carried Idalia inside. Kellen was glad they'd left a couple of
the lamps burning; he hadn't anticipated coming back with
so many burdens. He quickly set the wrapped keystone down
on the padded bench.

"Show me to her room, of your grace," Jermayan said, and
Kellen went to open that door in turn.

Kellen turned back the covers and Jermayan laid Idalia
carefully down on the bed, gazing at her for a long moment,
his face unreadable. Kellen could feel the tension of things
unsaid and emotions denied fill the room like water running
into a cup, so intense it made his head hurt.

"Cover her warmly, and watch over her," Jermayan said
abruptly. "See that she sleeps undisturbed."

Jermayan left—not seeming to hurry, in the fashion of
Elves, but gone so quickly it would have been easy to imagine he'd never been there at all. Kellen removed Idalia's
sandals—she might be willing to sleep in her clothes, but not
in her shoes—then covered her and closed the bedroom door,
blowing out the bedside lamps before he left.

He picked up the keystone and went to his own room,
tucking it securely away in his pack, then went to light the
lamps outside the door. Elsewhere in the canyon he could see
other scattered points of light, as the Elves who had wearily
returned to their homes had done the same.

He built up the fire in the stove and rummaged through the
cabinets, setting out a meal for Idalia if she woke up during

the night. He realized he was hungry himself—he'd been too excited to eat earlier—and cut himself a slice of cold venison and dried-cherry pie, washing it down with a tankard of cold berry-cider. Eating dispelled the last of the eldritch feeling he'd gotten from being in the meadow, as if a wind had blown him free of cobwebs. And paradoxically, it left him that much more free to worry.

Now that Idalia's part was done, the keystone made and charged, his part of the task seemed that much closer to beginning. In a few hours, he and Shalkan and one of the Elves would be on their way, riding into the unknown. Kellen was sure he couldn't possibly sleep, but it would do no harm to lie down for a few hours . . .

∽

"WAKE up, sleepyhead!"

"What . . . ?"

Kellen came groggily awake out of muddled dreams, thrashing and struggling. The dreams that had seemed so vivid a moment before dissolved instantly, leaving him blinking in confusion.

He didn't remember falling asleep. But the last time he'd looked out the window of his bedroom, the sky had been black. Now the sky was grey-pale, and Idalia was standing over him, wrapped in a violet house robe the color of her eyes. There were dark circles beneath those eyes that were only a shade or two lighter, but otherwise she seemed quite healthy and alert for someone who had been drained to the point of unconsciousness only a few hours ago.

"Tandarion just came to bring your armor and sword. I've made tea. While you eat, I can tell you what to look for and how to trigger the keystone when you reach the Barrier. Then . . . it's all up to you, Kellen."

Her words brought him fully awake as even a bucket of cold water could not have. Kellen sat up quickly, unable to believe he'd actually fallen asleep. "You know?"

"More than I did last night. And you'll learn more on the way. Now come on."

She picked up a bundle and tossed it at him—the quilted undertunic for his armor, and the supple leather socks that went beneath the armored boots, and left Kellen alone.

He carried the bundle off to the water closet—one thing he was going to miss on the road was the convenience of Elven plumbing—and as he washed and dressed, Kellen felt odd memory-echoes of the last time he'd dressed in unfamiliar clothing for a long journey into the unknown. It was not so long ago—little more than a moonturn—that he and Idalia had left the Wildwood heading into Elven lands. But then they'd been heading out of peril into safety—or so they'd thought then. Now Kellen was leaving even Idalia behind, going from the near-safety of Sentarshadeen into—

—into grave danger indeed.

Suddenly he *knew* that, out of the blue, and a chill of apprehension came over him, shaking him to the core and making him shiver.

This is not a wondertale. It's dangerous. Really dangerous . . .

Suddenly the glorious Elven armor was no longer just something to look good in; it was something to keep him from getting hurt.

Or killed.

He sat down at the table in the common room and accepted a cup of tea, though he didn't think he could eat anything. Idalia produced a comb and began braiding his hair—by now it had grown long enough to make a short club at the back of his neck.

"You'll want to wear it this way," she said. "Otherwise your hair will just get caught on the inside of your helmet. Now. Where to go. You'll be riding north, toward the High Desert. Do you remember that vision you had, the first time you tried scrying?"

"I don't think I'll ever forget it," Kellen said, with an inward shudder.

"I've been thinking about it, and I'm not sure it was meant

to be a representation of an actual event—more the symbolic
representation of the damage the Barrier is capable of causing—but I think the place you're looking for looks something
like that, at least in essence, so you should know it when you
see it. As for how you'll be drawn to it, well, the magic that
has created the Barrier has imposed a unnatural sort of order
on the natural world, and that kind of power leaves footprints
of a sort. What you need to look for as you ride is abnormal
patterns, things that are orderly in a way that Nature isn't
when left alone. The Barrier is the source, and the closer you
get to it, the more abnormalities you'll see."

"Like what?" Kellen asked. Despite his misgivings, the tea
had awakened his appetite, and he reached for one of the
morning pastries Idalia had set out on a plate on the table.

"Swirls of birds overhead that are flying in an odd pattern
and can't seem to break out of it. Animals—especially small
ones, like mice or squirrels—that are running aimlessly in
circles or performing repetitive motions over and over.
Swarms of insects, especially noxious ones, or ones that don't
belong. Anything that seems wildly out of place. Anything
nasty. Anything rotten, dead, or dying that has no business
being there."

"But how will I know?" Kellen asked. "I saw new things
in the Wildwood every day, and we're miles to the west of
that. I could guess wrong."

"That's what you'll have Shalkan for. And whoever's going with you. They'll know what's out of place if you don't:
Shalkan, especially, will be sensitive to the kinds of
wrongness that you're looking for. And trust in the Wild
Magic. When you're not sure, use Finding Spells to show
you the way. But be careful about that. Using the Wild Magic
may alert Shadow Mountain to your presence, so be sure to
move on when you've done that."

It seemed, thought Kellen, that he was to be going off like
a wondertale knight on a quest after all, looking for something he wasn't sure how to find, guided by mysterious signs
and portents. He tried not to show the unease he felt. Idalia
had said to trust in the Wild Magic, and Kellen already knew

how much power it possessed. Once he began, in a way he'd be a part of Idalia's spell as well. He had to trust that.

"Okay," Kellen said, taking a deep breath. He had a thousand questions, but he knew they were mostly for his own reassurance. Idalia had already told him everything he really needed to know. "And when I get there?"

"You'll see another keystone—I'm not sure exactly what it will look like, but I do know that you'll know it beyond a doubt. When you've found it, you'll need to take *your* keystone and place it on top of the Shadow Mountain keystone, then trigger the counterspell. You'll do that by the same method you use to charge a keystone, only in reverse: this time you need to tap your keystone, but instead of pulling the power into yourself, you need to channel it directly into the other keystone."

Kellen thought about it for a moment, reviewing the steps of the spell for triggering a keystone's power in his mind. "Sort of like a healing, except instead of passing spell-energy into a living being, I'll be passing it into a second stone?" he said. Suddenly something occurred to him. "But, Idalia . . . you made the keystone. You charged it. You said that only the Wildmage who charges a keystone can use the energy within it. How can I . . . ?"

Idalia smiled encouragingly, and the expression only made her look more tired.

"This time it won't matter. This isn't an ordinary keystone. It's holding the stored power of everyone in Sentarshadeen, not just mine, and more than that, besides. And the second keystone won't want to receive it, so you'll need to work to maintain the link between them and force the power from your keystone into the other one. But once it happens, it should happen fast." She gave the top of his head a pat. "Now let's get you dressed."

Kellen crammed the last of a third pastry into his mouth and came to stand in the middle of the room. His armor lay in neat gleaming piles on the cushioned bench, as perfect as any of the finished pieces Kellen had seen the day before in the armory. He couldn't imagine how Tandarion and the others had finished it so fast. Even with "small magics," the armory must have been working all night—and that after everyone there had lent power to Idalia's spell.

Kellen felt suddenly very humble. *I'll be worthy of everything you've all sacrificed for this. I will!*

Idalia quickly helped him into his armor, explaining what she was doing as she fitted the pieces over his body.

"Don't worry. You'll be able to put it on by yourself with a little practice. Just remember: chest and backplate first, then leggings, then sleeves, then collar, then boots, then gloves, and you're done. I don't think you'll need to wear the helmet; you should be riding through Elven lands today."

There were indeed feathers on the helmet, but Kellen was relieved to see that it was only a short brushy crest. He held the helmet up for closer inspection. The feathers were pale green, with the glittering iridescence of a hummingbird's down. They didn't seem to be dyed in any way. He set it down again, wondering what bird the feathers had come from.

"Here's your surcoat—no Elven Knight should be without one," Idalia said with a determined cheer that seemed very forced, holding up a length of heavy sea-green fabric. She helped him slip it over his head. It hung down loosely to his knees in front and back. It had the shine of silk, but was much heavier, like a strong linen canvas, and there was a subtle pattern in the weave.

"And here is your sword, gentle Knight."

The sword Kellen had picked out yesterday had indeed had a scabbard made for it as Tandarion had promised. It also had a swordbelt and baldric, a strap going over his shoulder and attaching to the swordbelt.

If the sword itself was plain, the swordbelt, scabbard, and baldric more than made up for it. They were of green leather, stitched in pale green silk the color of his surcoat (and, as Kellen suspected he was going to find, the same color of Shalkan's saddle and decorations) and stitched with silver wire and, to his faint dismay, studded with green moonstones.

he sword and scabbard could be unhooked from the sword elt easily.

Kellen raised his arms so that Idalia could slip the belts to place and buckle the swordbelt. When she was done, the vord hung at Kellen's left hip. He reached down and clasped e hilt experimentally. The armored fingers of his glove osed over the hilt as fluidly as his unencumbered hand ight; it felt as if he were wearing heavy leather gloves, thing more. Kellen sighed in relief and appreciation, reasing the sword and taking an experimental step. The armor oved with him, heavy but not awkward.

Idalia went to get his packs.

There was a tap on the door. Kellen went to open it, finding at even in armored gauntlets, he could still manage the task f clasping the door handle and turning it. Perhaps the Chief rmorer had been right about being able to dance in it as ell.

Shalkan was standing outside, saddled and ready. It seemed congruous to see the unicorn wearing a saddle and armor. he saddle and armor didn't make the unicorn look more like horse—quite the opposite. It just made Shalkan look as if were wearing some sort of unconvincing disguise. Partly, ellen supposed, it was because when you saw a saddle, you xpected to see a bridle and reins as well, but there was ablutely no reason for a unicorn to wear them. A bridle and ins were to control an animal, and Shalkan wasn't an aimal—or if he was, it was only in the sense that Kellen as an animal. Shalkan was a person with hooves.

And Kellen had been right about the color. The seat of halkan's saddle, the stirrup-leathers, the silk cords that knot-d the bands of his armor together, and its sheepskin lining ere all dyed the same shade of green as Kellen's surcoat nd the equivalent parts of his armor.

"I see you're ready to go," Shalkan said, regarding Kellen ith approval. "Very nice. We'll be meeting our escort at ongmairie."

"I'll go with you that far," Idalia said, following Kellen

out the door with his packs slung over her shoulder. "Some
one has to carry the luggage."

⌐

WHEN they reached the canyon floor, Shalkan stopped.

"Time to mount up," he told Kellen. "You *do* know hov
to use stirrups, don't you?"

"Of course I do!" Kellen said in automatic protest, thougl
in truth he hadn't ridden horses very often, and Shalkan wa
nothing like a horse.

But the Elven armor was just as flexible as its designer
had promised, and Shalkan was far stronger than any horse
He set his feet and stood rock-steady as Kellen slipped hi
left toe into the stirrup and swung his right leg determinedl
across Shalkan's back.

Instead of the narrow slippery surface that Kellen had beer
forced to contend with when riding Shalkan bareback, the
saddle gave him a wide comfortable seat, and the stirrup
gave him someplace to put his feet and a way to brace him
self. The broad curl of the saddle in front of him would giv
him something to hang on to, too, if Shalkan broke into on
of his bounding runs.

There was a place at the back of the saddle to hook hi
helmet, so Kellen did.

"Tuck your knees in," the unicorn said sternly, lookin
over his shoulder. "You ride like an arthritic granny."

Meekly, Kellen did as he was told.

Subconsciously, Kellen had expected that everyone in Sen
tarshadeen would turn out to see him off, but it seemed tha
the Elves had too much of a sense of propriety for that. The
early-morning streets were deserted.

He wasn't certain for a moment whether he was disap
pointed or relieved. He finally settled on the latter. It was on
thing to daydream about setting off on a quest amid cheerin;
crowds; it was quite another to have a crowd come to se
you off when you were not altogether sure you were goin;
to be able to do what you were supposed to do . . . and ac

tually, didn't know *what* you were supposed to do, when it all came down to cases.

As they passed the House of Leaf and Star, in the distance he saw Sandalon standing forlornly in an open window, watching them ride out.

"He will miss you," Shalkan said quietly.

"I'll miss him," Kellen said. He raised his hand and waved. He didn't care if it was bad manners. Ashaniel would forgive him.

The boy waved back energetically, and Kellen saw Ashaniel come to stand beside him. He forced himself to turn away and not stare after her like a moonwit. Sandalon would know that he'd said good-bye, and that was enough.

The spring was deserted when they arrived.

Unconsciously, Kellen expected to see the landscape veiled in mist, but the air was far too dry for that. Everything was bright and crystal-clear. Idalia set the packs down and looked around.

"I wonder . . . ?" she began.

An Elven Knight in dark gleaming armor was walking toward them from the direction of the Palace, leading a black horse and a white mule.

Jermayan.

Jermayan was going to be his escort?

This could be more than awkward.

The Elven Knight stopped in front of Idalia, gazing down at her. Idalia met his gaze steadily, and once more Kellen could feel the air was full of intense but unspoken communication.

"Take care of him," Idalia said at last.

Jermayan bowed silently. Idalia turned away and walked off quickly, her back straight. Jermayan picked up Kellen's packs and added them to the mule's burden, lashing them down firmly, then mounted his own horse.

There was a long pause as no one moved.

"Where are we going?" Shalkan finally asked.

"Oh. *Oh.*" Kellen blushed hotly as he realized he was the only one who knew. "North. Toward the High Desert."

Jermayan silently turned his horse and rode off. Kellen and Shalkan followed.

⮐

KELLEN had thought that his own armor was the most elegant thing he'd ever seen, but that was before he got a good look at Jermayan's—and he had plenty of time to study it, because Jermayan didn't say anything as they rode, and given the Elf's look of stony concentration, there didn't seem to be much point in trying to start a conversation.

He's statuesque, all right. Lycaelon's stone golems are more expressive.

The Elven Knight's armor—what Kellen could see of it beneath the deep blue surcoat Jermayan wore—was lacquered in a dark blue glaze the color of the midnight sky, through which silver stars embossed on the armor's surface shone and twinkled. It was more elaborately pieced than Kellen's was, and fitted Jermayan like an elegant suit of clothes, and there was a crescent-shaped shield that matched it—down to the design of silver stars—hanging from his saddle. His horse's armor matched Jermayan's exactly, from *shanfron* to crupper.

The Elven destrier was as much a creature of perfection as Kellen had expected, the exquisite counterpart for Jermayan himself, and leagues beyond the noble beasts Kellen had seen pulling the water carts. With a broad forehead, elegant nose, proudly arched neck, and impeccable carriage, it was every bit as handsome as its rider, and considerably more animated. Once Jermayan had given it their direction, he left its reins slack upon its neck, as if it were intelligent enough to be trusted to find its own way.

It was not, Kellen decided, inspecting it closely, actually black, though it had seemed that way at first. Rather, the destrier was the darkest possible shade of smoke-grey, a color Kellen had never seen before in a horse.

Even the mule that followed placidly behind the destrier at the end of a long lead-rope was attractive, though in an endearing fashion rather than an elegant one. Its ears were rounded, its muzzle small and neat, its eyes limpid, and it resembled nothing so much in Kellen's opinion as a very large baby rabbit. And there was no mistaking it for anything but a creature of Elven breeding, or Kellen would eat his new armor, feathered helm and all.

After long inspection and consideration, Kellen decided that the mule wasn't exactly white (especially next to Shalkan), but actually the palest shade of new cream, from pink nose to silken tail-tuft. He was surprised to see water kegs among the mule's cargo, until he remembered how hard it had been for him and Idalia to find water on their way into Sentarshadeen. Once the water they carried with them was gone, they would have to rely once more on Shalkan to find them water until they reached the edge of the drought area, and to make sure it was pure and fit to drink as well.

⌐

FOR a long time they rode in silence, Jermayan in the lead. Soon enough they had left the Flower Forest of Sentarshadeen and even the outer forest that the Elves were able to tend behind them. Now the effects of the long drought were written plain on the autumnal landscape, so much so that Kellen wondered if even rain could revive it once the keystone he carried had done its work.

The day, as usual, was clear and cloudless, and Kellen felt uncomfortably warm in his armor, though Jermayan seemed perfectly at ease. At least they weren't riding out in high summer: the weather might be unnaturally dry, but the sunlight was the mild sun of autumn.

After a while Kellen began to wonder if they were going to ride all the way to the Barrier—wherever it was—in a polite and chilly silence. From what he'd learned of Elves during his brief stay in Sentarshadeen, it was perfectly possible.

Especially with this Elf. Kellen didn't know very much about Jermayan, and from the way things looked right now, Jermayan didn't intend for him to learn any more.

At least he'd have Shalkan to talk to.

But after a couple of hours, Jermayan reined in, dropping back to ride beside Kellen.

"There is a matter I would raise with you, Wildmage," Jermayan said, breaking the long silence. "And then I would go on to speak of other things."

"Ah . . . surely," Kellen replied. He felt slightly relieved that Jermayan had said something, even though he was fairly sure he wasn't going to enjoy whatever the conversation was going to be about. Whatever it was, it was still better than silence.

"In Sentarshadeen, in times of peace, it is entirely appropriate for civilized people to behave in a civilized and decorous fashion," Jermayan said, in tones that suggested that this was not a matter for debate. "But we are not now in Sentarshadeen, nor is this to be a peaceful journey. We are riding into battle, and it is appropriate for us to behave as warriors do."

"Yes," agreed Kellen politely, because what Jermayan said seemed self-evident. But he got the strong feeling that he didn't understand all of what Jermayan meant to say.

"Excellent," Jermayan said, sounding relieved.

Shalkan made a noise that sounded suspiciously like a snicker.

"I coughed," the unicorn said innocently, when Kellen glared at him.

"Now, as to the second matter. I understand that only you can trigger the counterspell to destroy the Barrier, but is there some reason I do not know of that only you may know how to find it?"

Kellen stared, jaw dropping with shock. *Jermayan had just asked him a direct question.*

Jermayan shook his head with a sigh, seeing Kellen's expression. "Wildmage Kellen, I just explained matters to you, and you agreed. Civilized rules are for civilized times and places. We are at war. You humans are *always* at war. Surely a sennight among the Elves has not civilized you so much?"

Kellen gathered his scattered and perambulatory wits. "No, I . . . it's just a surprise, that's all. I thought you *couldn't* ask questions."

Jermayan regarded him with a haughty expression, one eyebrow raised. "That, Wildmage, is akin to saying one *cannot* be rude. One chooses not to be, of course." Seeing Kellen's stricken expression, Jermayan obviously decided to take pity on him. "Questions are . . . very direct. We of Leaf and Star consider them a form of coercion, not to be used in civilized times and places. But when one rides to war, one must be . . . more efficient."

"Yes. I . . . okay. Yes. That . . . seems reasonable." Kellen didn't know whether to be relieved or not. Well, he certainly shouldn't *show* it. "I . . . Just . . . tell me when I stop being efficient and start being rude, okay?"

"I shall try to bring myself to do so," Jermayan said, with another faint self-possessed smile.

Kellen thought for a moment about what Idalia had told him that morning, gazing northward as he did. "I'm not sure exactly where we're going, really," he admitted. "It's kind of a case of knowing it when I see it. Idalia told me the sort of signs to look for, but I'll need your help and Shalkan's to recognize them."

Quickly he explained the underlying theory about the Barrier, and the unnatural patterns it would produce in the natural world.

"So that's the best idea she could give me of what we're looking for," he finished. "If we don't see anything like that in a day or so—or if we think we're missing the signs or might be going off in the wrong direction—I'll try a Finding Spell to locate our route. Idalia said that was something to avoid if I could, though. She said it would attract attention."

"Then we shall hope that Shadow Mountain has grown proud and careless," Jermayan said grimly. "And now, we should stop as soon as we come to a good place for stopping, for Valdien needs rest if Shalkan does not, and there is something I must begin to show you, for all our sakes."

IN a short while more, they came to an oak tree standing alone in what must have once have been a lush deer meadow. But if the oak had ever had a dryad, she was long gone, and the grass around the tree was nothing more now than greyish stubble that crumbled away into dust beneath the hooves of the animals as they rode over it. The tree itself was bare of leaves, looking sere and winter-blasted out of season.

Jermayan swung gracefully down from Valdien's back, but though he tied the mule carefully to one of the tree branches, he made no effort to tether his destrier in any way. Valdien followed him about the way a dog might, until Jermayan told the destrier to stand. To Kellen's mild surprise, Valdien obeyed, though the destrier continued to watch his master hopefully.

Kellen got himself out of Shalkan's saddle with much less grace, though he managed the feat without tripping and falling.

"Is there anything you need?" he asked the unicorn, seeing that Jermayan was loosening Valdien's saddle-girths.

"Just some water," Shalkan said. "I'll miss Songmairie," he added wistfully.

"Do you know what he's planning?" Kellen asked in a low voice.

"Yes. Don't worry. It won't hurt. Much." Shalkan sounded amused.

Kellen sighed and went to get Shalkan's drink.

Jermayan was already taking both the water barrels down from the mule's back. For a short stop they wouldn't unpack the mule completely, but the water was the heaviest part of her load, and they couldn't leave the load unbalanced.

"The buckets are in the pack on the near side," Jermayan said when Kellen arrived.

Kellen unbuckled the flap and looked inside. It was easy to see which was his; the bucket was green, to match everything else. Well, Idalia *had* said the Elves were perfectionists. He lifted it out. The blue one beneath it obviously belonged to Valdien, but fortunately they wouldn't need to water the horse and the mule until tonight since the weather was relatively cool. Even so, those barrels barely held enough water for a day.

He brought the bucket over to where Jermayan was carefully unscrewing the top of the barrel and dipped it full, then carried it to Shalkan. When the unicorn was done drinking, Kellen carried the bucket back and tipped the last drops down at the base of the tree. It felt odd to remember he'd been doing more or less this same thing at about this time yesterday, with no idea that barely a day later he'd be on the road, riding against Shadow Mountain.

Whatever Shadow Mountain might be. In the flurry of last-minute preparations, he'd never gotten a chance to ask Idalia about that. He frowned. It occurred to him suddenly that Idalia had probably arranged it that way.

Why?

"Now," Jermayan said firmly, summoning Kellen's attention. "You know that we ride into danger. I am expendable. You are not. Without your Wildmage skill to break the spell of the Barrier, all is lost. If I should die, who will defend you?"

Kellen stared at the Elven Knight, hoping he didn't look as disconcerted as he felt. He wasn't sure what he'd been expecting, but whatever it was, it hadn't been this.

"Exactly," Jermayan said, as if Kellen had actually answered. "You will have to defend yourself. Yet at this moment you have no skill with the sword, which is the Knight's weapon. In fact, have you skill with *any* weapon?"

"Not much," Kellen admitted. "I've learned how to use a bow for hunting, and I'm not bad with it."

"There is nothing unknightly about the bow," Jermayan pronounced, to Kellen's relief, "but it will not do when the foe closes in. And so now I will begin to teach you the Way of the Sword, so that you may walk it as far as you can with me before . . . that is perhaps no longer possible. Put on your helm, Kellen, and we will begin."

"But what if I hurt you?" Kellen blurted out, reaching down to touch his sword. He'd held it in his hands yesterday at the armory. He *knew* it was sharp. A dangerous weapon, designed specifically to strike through the armor they both wore. He'd seen swords at Festival-plays in Armethalieh, and the City Guard and the nobles carried them, and of course the Mages used them in the High Magick, but none of that amounted to actual practical personal experience . . .

Jermayan smiled coolly. "It is not possible for you to harm me. I am an Elven Knight. I have been upon the Way since before your grandfather first drew breath. You cannot hurt me. And I promise I will not hurt you. There will be pain, yes. But I will not hurt you. Now get your helm," Jermayan repeated, this time in a tone that brooked no argument.

There didn't seem to be any way around it, and Kellen felt a faint irritation mixed with dread. Had anyone *asked* him if he wanted knight-lessons? Had anyone warned him this was going to happen when they told him to pick a sword back in the armory? No, he was stuck out here in the middle of no-where with a crazy Elven Knight in love with his sister, about to be made a complete fool of just so Jermayan would have something to laugh at. He was a Wildmage, not a knight of any kind! Wildmages weren't knights, anyway—Mages and knights were two different things. He was out here to work magic, not prance around in the heat with a big knife looking like an idiot. Why was Jermayan doing this to him?

Of course he'd fight if there was trouble. He wasn't a coward—he'd fought the Outlaw Hunt, hadn't he?—but it took years to learn to fight with a sword and be any good at it, Kellen knew. Give him a club and he'd do some damage, but a sword . . . ? This was just some complicated Elven plot to make him look stupid, that's what it was.

Jermayan was waiting patiently, with a look on his face that indicated he was prepared to wait right there until the sun set, if necessary.

Kellen set his jaw and went back to Shalkan, and took his helmet from the unicorn's saddle, setting it on his head. As its confining weight settled into place and blocked his peripheral vision, Kellen felt himself starting to panic, and forced himself to take deep calming breaths. He'd *really* impress Jermayan if he tripped over his own feet and fell flat on his face the first time Jermayan swung at him.

He just needs me to prove to him that this isn't going to work, that's all, Kellen told himself calmingly. *Then we can think of something that will.* But he hated the thought that it wasn't going to work, that he was going to fail. It made him so angry . . .

He clutched at the sword hilt, wondering how it could feel so *right* in his hand when he could never learn to use it— knight—Mage—one or the other—not both—when he suddenly remembered something from *The Book of Moon.*

"The Knight-Mage is the active agent of the principle of the Wild Magic, the Wildmage who chooses to become a warrior or who is born with the instinct for the Way of the Sword, who acts in battle without mindful thought and thus brings primary causative forces into manifestation by direct action."

He hadn't been sure what it meant at the time—and he still wasn't—but—

But in the subtle way that Wild Magic worked, he might have remembered that passage now because the Wild Magic wanted him to. So it wasn't one or the other, Knight or Mage. And maybe this *could* work, if he thought of sword fighting as a kind of spell, if he made the conscious *choice* to try the Way of the Sword rather than having it thrust on him. His anger was a warning and a clue: if he was angry, he needed to pay attention and figure out why, because that meant this was important.

Kellen stood beside Shalkan and thought very hard, trying to fight back his anger. He remembered how he'd fought the Hounds. How he'd been angry, more angry than he'd ever been in his life, and then somehow he just hadn't been there. He started to shake, thinking about Jermayan lying dead and broken at his feet, the way the Hounds had lain . . .

No. That wasn't the message his anger was sending him. He needed to not fail in front of Jermayan, not to kill him . . .

Please. Tell me, Kellen thought desperately. He wasn't sure whether it was a prayer, or a spell, or just a hope he could figure out what his own mind was trying to tell him quickly, but whatever it was, it worked. This wasn't about Jermayan.

This was about the sword. About learning to be a warrior. The thought fascinated and repelled him at the same time. It was like when he'd first picked up the three Books of the Wild Magic, only much stronger. It was about using the Wild Magic in a way Idalia had never even hinted at. It might even be wrong. Maybe this was the way that Wildmages went rogue.

No, that couldn't be right. Wild Magic was all about balances. If there was healing, then—did there *have* to be killing?

Maybe. To defend others. He wasn't sure where *that* thought came from, but it felt right. It felt as if it *fit*. Not killing for the sake of it, not for the sake of power, not to impose what you wanted on someone else—but to protect the weak, to defend yourself and others—

Maybe it was like hunting. He hunted and killed; Idalia did, too, for meat and fur and hides, but only for as much as they needed and no more. Balances: death and life, healing and killing. But death and killing—only when you *had* to.

He knew Jermayan was right. They *had* to get to the Barrier. And Kellen needed to be able to pull his own weight if there was any fighting along the way. He couldn't expect Jermayan and Shalkan to protect him.

Maybe the Wild Magic could help him learn the skills he needed. And if it didn't work, he'd be no worse off than he was now.

And if he'd guessed wrong—if he'd misinterpreted everything, if *this* was how Wildmages went bad . . .

Well, then when they got back, Idalia could sew him into a sack and sell him to the Selken-folk, just like she'd promised.

"Kellen?" Jermayan called.

"I'm coming," Kellen said quickly.

He returned to where Jermayan was waiting for him.

Jermayan drew his sword in one fluid motion, holding it

before him in both hands. "Do as I do, Kellen."

Kellen drew his sword, doing his best to copy Jermayan's stance and grip. He concentrated, and felt the world seem to still the way it did whenever he was about to cast a spell or use his Magesight. He thought about the canyon, about the Hounds, and finally let go of his fear.

And suddenly there were two Jermayans facing him. They overlay each other, but one was real, and the other was a colorless phantom. Kellen blinked, knowing he was seeing the phantom-Jermayan in the same way he saw the sylphs and dryads back in the Wildwood.

Then the phantom-Jermayan moved, swinging his sword down, and Kellen—acting entirely instinctively, *acting without mind*—swung his own sword up to block the blow.

Jermayan's sword rang off Kellen's with a jolt of steel. Jermayan had not expected Kellen's sword to be there; he sprang back with a cry of surprise.

For Kellen's part, he had not expected the jarring force of the contact. He staggered backward, the shock jarring him out of the spell-trance, and the flat of Jermayan's blade swept around and caught him with a painful thump along the ribs.

But when Jermayan came for him again, Kellen was ready for him, holding the phantom-image firmly before his gaze, and blocking as it struck. Each time, it moved a fraction of an instant before the real Jermayan did, and each time Kellen's sword was there to meet it.

But no spell-sight could make the sword in his hands weigh any less, or make even light and flexible Elven armor easier to move in. Though they'd been sparring only a few minutes, Kellen was gasping for breath by the time Jermayan stepped back and lowered his sword to rest.

Kellen, grateful that the lesson seemed to be over, fumbled his sword back into its scabbard and pulled off his helmet, dropping it beside him. His hair was soaked with his sweat. He yanked off one of his gauntlets, wiping his face with his bare hand, and staggered over to the tree to lean against it. While they'd been fighting, he'd reacted without thought, just as *The Book of Moon* said, but now that it was over he felt like he'd spent a whole day at the pumping station, or even behind a plow like the ones he'd seen in Merryvale.

Jermayan pulled off his own helmet and tossed it to the ground, then sheathed his sword in turn. He regarded Kellen expressionlessly for a moment, then went over to the mule and searched through the packs for a moment. He came back with a pair of tankards and opened the water barrel again, dipping them both full and handing one to Kellen.

Kellen took his and drained it thirstily. At the moment he found it impossible to imagine getting through an entire battle wearing this stuff. How did people manage?

Jermayan was still staring at him, as though he'd never seen Kellen before. "I know what you are," the Elven Knight finally said.

Kellen froze. For so many years of his life those words, or some variation of them, had made him flinch. They'd always been the prelude to yet another lecture on his many inadequacies. But Jermayan, it seemed, didn't mean them that way. The Elven Knight was smiling at him—a genuine smile at last, one of relief, and something like awe.

"You're a Knight-Mage, aren't you?" The words were spoken in tones of approval, even admiration.

Kellen shook his head wordlessly, unable to speak. He wasn't. He couldn't be. Could he? He didn't even know what a Knight-Mage was! The passage he'd remembered, the business about the Knight-Mages, it was just words in the Book. What he'd done was spur-of-the-moment, something he'd tried out of a desperate desire not to look completely foolish and a need he couldn't explain even to himself.

"You didn't know, did you?" Jermayan asked sympathetically. "I suppose not: Knight-Mages are very rare. Even another Wildmage won't always recognize one for what they are, though undoubtedly you would have figured it out eventually. It is said they only appear in times of direst need. I suppose you simply thought that you just weren't a very good Wildmage."

Kellen nodded, unable to meet Jermayan's gaze. He had thought that, all the time. Idalia'd told him not to worry, but how could he *not* worry about it, seeing what she could do and knowing that the best he could accomplish was so much less?

"Well," Jermayan said, breaking into Kellen's thoughts. "You never will be, not in comparison with a true Wildmage, though you *will* master healing and fire-calling, and other useful skills; they will just never come as easily or naturally to you as to a Wildmage. A Wildmage's and a Knight-Mage's Gifts lie in opposite directions, though both belong fully to the Wild Magic."

That was *exactly* how he'd felt! Kellen clutched the tankard desperately, and some of that desperation must have entered his expression, for Jermayan's face softened further.

"Here," he said, pointing to a fallen limb in what passed for shade under the tree. "Sit—and drink! I will tell you all that I know."

Kellen refilled his tankard and obeyed, hardly able to contain himself. It was nothing short of a miracle, an Elf *offering* to tell him *everything* without having to coax it out, driblet by driblet!

Jermayan settled himself, and took a cautious sip of his water. "A Wildmage," he began, "reaches out to all the world, knowing it intimately, in touch with all of it. A Knight-Mage's gifts turn inward, refining himself, so he cannot be turned away from his path once he has chosen it. A Knight-Mage can withstand forces that would destroy a Wildmage, for his power lies in endurance and the alliance of his knightly skills with his Wildmagery. You will never be what Idalia is . . . but she will never be what you will be, either, Kellen."

"Is it—bad?" Kellen asked, tentatively.

"You mean, can a Knight-Mage be turned to the bad?" Jermayan asked. "That is a foolish question, Kellen. All things can, as you know. But the Knight-Mage, even more so than the Wildmage, must *choose* that path, knowingly, and with forethought, and when he does, the Wild Magic will desert him, and he will retain only his own innermost gifts and training."

So I can't just slide into evil. And it can't just sneak up on me and corrupt me. That was easily the most comforting thought he'd ever had.

He looked down at the sword at his side, remembering the feel of it in his hands. This was his, this skill. The sword was his tool. It felt right in his hands, an extension of himself. And with Jermayan's help . . .

"Never forget this," Jermayan continued gravely. "The Knight-Mage makes the choice of life and death, directly and immediately. Be certain that when you claim a death, your reasons are good ones, the death is necessary, and that, to keep your spirit clean, you *forgive* your foe when you slay him. Anger is not to be shunned. Anger can be useful, and for the Knight-Mage it is a weapon just as is your sword. Good clean anger, full of purpose, will focus you. But as your sword, it can cut *you* if you clutch it to you. Remember that, and when the time when it is useful is over, you must let it go."

Kellen nodded earnestly, vowing to remember. He didn't entirely understand what Jermayan was talking about, but he sensed that he *would* understand it sometime later.

The Elven Knight smiled again, and drained his own tankard. "Now, come. We have some distance to ride. And now that I know what you are capable of, you will not find your lessons so easy."

Kellen grinned at him. Even more than that moment beside the spring, when Idalia had explained the truth about the Demons, he felt a sense of relief so intense it nearly made him weep. A Knight-Mage! There was a *name* for what he was. He wasn't a second-class anything—not a failed High Mage, not a not-good-enough Wildmage. He was a Knight-Mage.

"Just try me, Master."

They returned the water barrels to the back of the mule, and Jermayan retightened Valdien's girths, and they rode on.

◠

"I'M a Knight-Mage," Kellen said to Shalkan, letting Jermayan get a little ahead. For the moment, all his worries about the future, his fears of the battles he still had to face, the Barrier, were all gone. He knew what he was, now, and it was as if a key had been turned in a lock. He knew that the next time he opened his three Books and read them, things in them that had never made any sense to him before would suddenly be as clear as the water of Songmairie.

Learning his new skills wouldn't be easy, he knew that too. But for the first time—the very first time—in his entire life, Kellen felt as if he were finally pointed in the right direction. A Knight-Mage. A *special* kind of Wildmage. It still didn't seem entirely real to him, but the more he thought about it, the more he liked the idea. It would take work—a lot of it, he was guessing—to master a Knight-Mage's special gifts, but what he became would be *his*. Not a second-class Wildmage, doing things that Idalia could do better. A first-class Knight-Mage. *Needed*.

A new thought struck him. "Did you know?"

"I wasn't sure," Shalkan said after a long pause. "I suspected—especially after you managed to destroy two over-large packs of the Outlaw Hunt with nothing more than a big stick—and my not-inconsiderable help, of course. Only a Knight-Mage could have done that. But the choice was still yours to make. You could have refused to be, you know."

Kellen stared down at Shalkan's ears in surprise. The idea hadn't even occurred to him.

It felt so *right*. How could he have refused to be a Knight-Mage?

The same way I could have refused the Wild Magic?

It would have been possible; he could have given in to Lycaelon, burned the Books, gone back to his studies. The Mages would have edited his memories. He might even have been happy.

And if he had?

I wouldn't have been Outlawed, I'd never have come to the Wildwood. Eventually Lycaelon probably would have found a reason to try to claim the Wildwood, but not for a while. So Idalia might not have come to Sentarshadeen until it was too late.

It could have fallen out that way. It could *easily* have fallen out that way. He wouldn't have given in if he'd known they were going to take his memories, of course, but he wouldn't have known about that part, then or ever.

If he'd given in . . .

But he hadn't.

Was *this* why the Books had come to him when they had? So he could be Outlawed and find Idalia? So Lycaelon would expand the borders, chasing both of them to Sentarshadeen, where she would find out about the drought and the Barrier?

And where Kellen could find someone who could tell him what he was?

It made him dizzy for a moment, as if he had gotten a glimpse of a great pattern, of which he was an integral part. It was intoxicating.

And frightening.

Wildmages served the balance of All That Was. It wasn't easy and it wasn't safe. To be fair, nobody had ever told him it would be.

To claim his proper place in that pattern meant danger. But to give it up—would leave a hole in the pattern that would mean—well—maybe disaster, for a lot of people he was coming to know and like. What would happen if one who *could* become a Knight-Mage refused the challenge?

"It is said they only appear in times of direst need." Hadn't Jermayan said that?

"No," Kellen said aloud. "I couldn't have refused."

Shalkan just nodded, and let it go at that.

⌐

THEY stopped at a dry riverbed to make camp late that afternoon. Jermayan looked grim at the sight. Last season, he told Kellen, the broad sandy expanse before them had been a swift, deep-flowing river, one of many that carried the mountain waters down into Sentarshadeen. But with the drought, it had dwindled away to almost nothing. All that was left was a narrow rivulet still trickling along what had once been the deepest part of the riverbed.

Since they were stopping for the night, this time they un-saddled Valdien and Shalkan—fortunately the unicorn was able to tell Kellen what to do—and unloaded the pack mule.

But when Kellen would have removed his armor in turn, Jermayan stopped him.

"It is time for your next lesson," Jermayan said cheerfully. It occurred to Kellen that the Elven Knight had become quite unaccountably better-humored since their first stop . . .

He's enjoying this! Kellen thought, caught halfway be-tween his own anticipation at another lesson and a flash of exasperation at Jermayan's high spirits. *Of course, he isn't the one who's going to get hit.*

But despite the fact that he was tired from the long day's ride, and the fact that he suspected there was a bruise under the armor where Jermayan had managed to land a blow on him that morning, Kellen found his spirits rising to match Jermayan's. There was an indescribable *rightness* that he felt when holding the sword in his hands. And the longer he thought about it, the more sure he was that he had finally found the work he was supposed to be doing.

Was *this* how Idalia felt when she called on the Wild Magic? If so, it was no wonder that she seemed so contented, and so willing to use it whenever she was called upon, even if the cost to her was high. And happy—or at least happy when she wasn't thinking about Jermayan. Kellen only wished there was some way he could tell her that he under-stood at last.

On the dry sand of the riverbed, Jermayan used his scab-bard to scratch out a circle about twelve feet across.

"Here is our dancing floor," the Elven Knight said. "You must try to push me out over the boundary. I will do the same to you. If I succeed, you have lost. If you succeed, I have lost. In battle, it is important never to give ground ex-cept by your own choice, so that an enemy cannot move you into danger. Come now, and we will begin."

Kellen quickly discovered that this was harder work than

simply blocking Jermayan's blows had been. Over and over, Kellen found that he had blocked every blow . . . and still been forced to give ground exactly as Jermayan wished him to.

"How are you doing that?" Kellen demanded as Jermayan stepped back once again and raised his blade in salute, looking down to see his foot once again over the edge of the circle.

"Most warriors step back to block," Jermayan explained, taking pity on Kellen at last. "It is a common instinct, because it helps to absorb the force of a blow. You, knowing this, will use it against your foes. It will help you force your enemy where you wish him to go. Step sideways when you attack, and you can turn him as well, for he will always turn to face you without thinking about it. Now, let us try again, and this time, step forward as you block."

They went on, and Kellen discovered that Jermayan was right. This time Kellen forced himself to push forward instead of stepping back each time Jermayan attacked, and this time Jermayan was unable to force him out of the circle.

But that only meant that the sparring match continued without the breaks that had come each time he'd stepped out of the circle, and Kellen's muscles were not yet hardened to the burdens of sword and armor. If Jermayan was a patient instructor, his kindness did not extend to their physical combat, and if he pulled his blows at the last moment, he showed Kellen no other mercy. As the blows came faster and faster, Kellen's sword seemed to drag at his arms, until at last Kellen saw a blow coming but was unable to get his tired arms up to move his sword quickly enough to block it.

Jermayan pulled back at the last minute, the flat of the sword landing with a gentle click against Kellen's armored thigh.

"A good beginning," he said warmly, stepping back. "Stamina will come with practice, young Knight."

Kellen took a couple of staggering steps backward, his head swimming with exhaustion and his body beneath the Elven armor—how in the name of all that was holy had he ever thought it was light?—soaked with sweat. With shaking muscles, he sheathed his own sword and staggered out of the teaching circle, feeling as if he were barely able to move. He was sure his armor suddenly weighed a thousand pounds.

He twisted his gauntlets to the side and pulled them off, but was barely able to force his cramped fingers to undo the clasps of his helmet. Gritting his teeth, he set the helmet and gauntlets carefully on the ground, pulled off the leather gloves beneath, then moved to unbuckle his swordbelt.

"Not easy, is it?" Shalkan asked, looking on. The unicorn had been an interested spectator at Kellen's first real lesson, but, Kellen had been relieved to find, had not offered any helpful advice—or distractions.

"No," Kellen said, discovering at just that moment that although he could unbuckle the swordbelt, he couldn't reach up to pull it off over his head while wearing the armor. "But I guess nothing worth having ever is," he added, trying to sound as grateful as he knew he would be when he wasn't as hot, sweaty, and just plain *tired* as he was at this particular moment. Until he could get the baldric off, he couldn't get the surcoat off, which meant he couldn't get any of the armor beneath it off.

"Good answer," Shalkan said. "Reach up under the surcoat and pull out the shoulder-pins on the gorget—that's the big neck piece. The sleeves will slip free, then. With the sleeves off, you can reach up to loosen the gorget and lift the whole thing off in one piece."

It was difficult to reach across himself in full armor, but possible. Kellen drew the locking-pins free and slid the armored sleeves down his arms, then unpinned the gorget, and, with a burst of inspiration, bent and wriggled out of the whole mass—armored collar, surcoat, unbuckled baldric, and all, off over his head. He set them down quickly and lifted off the back and breastplate, suddenly impatient to be free of the armor. The quilted padding beneath was soaked through with sweat, and clung to him clammily.

He felt strangely light and unfinished without the weight of the armor, though, as if it had somehow become an extension of him today, and almost regretted removing the last pieces, though certainly not enough to leave them on. He untangled the elements of the armor carefully, folding the surcoat neatly, replacing the locking-pins in their places, and setting everything where he could find it easily in the morning, then went to find a change of clothes.

There was one other important thing he had to do as well.

When they'd ridden out that morning, the keystone had been tucked safely up in one of the mule's packs, but the more he'd thought about the arrangement, the less Kellen had liked it. The keystone was vulnerable. All their enemies really had to do to win was destroy it or get it away from them, and even if he hadn't seen any sign of enemies so far, Kellen couldn't assume that happy state would continue as they rode north.

He dug through his gear until he found the satchel Idalia had given him—filled with herbs and supplies for Wild Magic—and stowed its contents carefully among his other gear. The satchel was just large enough to hold the keystone wrapped in its spell-caul, and he could attach it to his sword belt. He might look a little odd that way, but he'd feel better if he had the keystone with him at all times.

"Good," Jermayan said briefly when he glanced up and saw what Kellen had done.

And after all, he didn't have to say anything more.

By the time Kellen was done making his arrangements, Jermayan had already changed and had started a fire. Kellen changed as well, toweling himself off briskly all over, then rubbing himself with a bag of herbs that Idalia had given him for the purpose in lieu of a bath. The creek here wasn't deep enough to bathe in, and the water was muddy and uninviting besides. At least Shalkan could purify what they'd have to drink later.

As he'd expected upon close inspection, there was a greenish tender patch along his ribs where Jermayan had gotten him. Kellen winced as his fingers explored it. That was going to hurt tomorrow, and if the way the rest of him felt was any indication, it wouldn't be alone. Why did all of his adventures seem to start out with a fresh set of bruises?

He regarded his underpadding unhappily as he spread it out to dry. He hoped there'd be some way to clean it along the way, or after a few more bouts with Jermayan, he was going to smell about as attractive as week-old carrion.

It was starting to get dark now, and Kellen felt the weight of a full day of riding and hard physical work. But he felt much better for being dressed in clean dry clothes with his hair combed out, and whatever Jermayan was cooking smelled good. He picked up the satchel with the keystone— he felt better keeping it where he could see it—and came over to the fire.

"Take off your tunic," Jermayan said, greeting him.

"I want to see how badly you're bruised," he added, when Kellen didn't move, "and without a good application of al-lheal to your muscles, you'll be too stiff to train tomorrow morning, let alone to ride for a full day afterward. Now sit," he said mercilessly. "You can eat *after* you've been tended to."

Kellen pulled off his tunic again and sat, trying not to wince as he folded himself into a sitting position. He was already starting to stiffen a bit.

Jermayan poured, and reached across the fire to press Kellen's fingers around a tall pottery cup. "Tea."

Idalia had always seemed to greet every crisis or stirring event with a cup of tea, and now Kellen knew where she'd picked up the habit. The Elves seemed to feel that every moment, good or bad, called for a cup of tea; Kellen was only surprised that he hadn't been asked to fight with a cup in one hand and a sword in the other, though possibly that would come later. He raised the cup and inhaled, sipping cautiously. The tea tasted strongly of mint, with other musky but not unpleasant flavors beneath, and was heavily sweetened with something that wasn't the honey he was used to.

Jermayan knelt behind Kellen, a large pot of salve in his hand. It was that, Kellen ruefully realized, that he'd smelled heating, and not dinner; it must contain some of the same herbs as the tea did.

Jermayan inspected the bruise on Kellen's ribs critically. "Not as bad as it could be, but you would dislike to ride with it tomorrow." He scooped up a generous dollop of the salve—Kellen watched out of the corner of his eye—and applied it to the discolored area, kneading strongly.

It hurt. Kellen set his teeth and refused to complain as Jermayan worked the allheal into his aching side, working with no more respect for Kellen's flinches than if Kellen had been a bowl of dough. When he stopped, Kellen breathed a sigh of relief—cut short when Jermayan began again on his neck muscles, with as much ruthlessness as before.

"Hey—*ow!*" Kellen exclaimed, despite his best intentions, spilling tea on himself.

"You're tight as a drum," Jermayan said, announcing the fact as if he were discussing the weather. "If you want your body to be able to do what your mind tells it tomorrow, you'll let me work . . . or do you want me to be able to give you a set of bruises to match that one?"

Not really.

Kellen forced himself to try to relax as Jermayan worked the allheal into the aching muscles of his neck and shoulders and arms. Once he got used to it, it actually felt good.

"Now you can dress, and we'll eat," Jermayan said at last.

Kellen straightened up and reached for his tunic, realizing he'd actually almost fallen asleep. The next thing he realized was that he could stretch without stiffness. He felt tired, but that was all. Tired, but *good.* And beneath that, confident. That was something he'd never really felt before, Kellen realized with quiet surprise. He couldn't really remember a time in his life when he hadn't been worried about something—being found out; not living up to expectations that seemed to change daily. But now, when there were *real* things to worry about for the first time in his life, somehow, he wasn't bothered about them. What would come, would come. And he would face it then.

"Allheal is sovereign for ills of the body," Jermayan told

him, holding up the jar where Kellen could see it. "Its herbs can be made into a tea as well, and in that form give strength and rest. It can be used to doctor bruises and small cuts, and to poultice a lame hoof."

"I hope you've brought a lot of it," Kellen said, grinning wryly as he pulled his tunic back on.

"More than I think we'll need," Jermayan said with simple approval.

Kellen shrugged his shoulders experimentally beneath his tunic. They felt fine. "Huh. Jermayan, that stuff *works*!"

Jermayan smiled quietly, and said nothing.

By now it was almost fully dark. Jermayan prepared their dinner, showing Kellen how it was done so that Kellen would be able to take on his fair share of the chores once he'd adjusted to the new routine of lessons and riding. Not that Kellen needed to be shown much, except for the differences between Elven taste and human—different spices and herbs, mostly. He'd taken his share of the cooking at Idalia's insistence that everyone should know how to cook, and that the only way to learn to cook was to do so. Kellen had never been a good cook—and had never mastered baking at all— but he wasn't helpless, especially on the trail.

Since they were heading into unknown lands and could neither expect to find friendly villages nor stop to hunt along the way, Jermayan had brought Elven journey-food. These rations were simple and efficient; compressed blocks of dried meat, fruit, and grain that could be either eaten as they were or cooked to produce a stew.

Kellen was relieved to see that at least for the first night or so, there was fresh bread and cheese to accompany the journey-food, because he meant to fill up on that. He and Idalia had eaten journey-food that she'd gotten from the Mountain Traders on the way to Sentarshadeen, and Kellen remembered it vividly: tough, bland, greasy, and nearly indigestible (as well as nearly indestructible). Even Idalia hadn't been able to make it palatable. Better than starving, of course. Probably.

But when Jermayan passed him a bowl filled with a thick soup, Kellen received a pleasant surprise.

It smelled *good*.

Kellen reached for his spoon and took a cautious taste.

It had spices and flavor, and when he encountered a bit of meat, it was actually chewable. He glanced at Jermayan, hoping he didn't look as startled as he felt.

"It is better if it has longer to cook, of course, but well enough," Jermayan said critically. "Ah, I see from your face that you have experience of human journey-food. Vile stuff. I would not shoe mules with it. Kellen, we Elves have had a very long time to learn to do things properly. If one must travel, there is no need to starve while doing so, and there is surely no need to make every meal an ordeal."

Afterward, all that was needed was to prepare for morning, bank the fire for the night, and to make ready for sleep. Tonight they were still well within the borders of Elven lands, so there was little danger of ambush, and both Valdien and Shalkan slept lightly, so there was no need for either Kellen or Jermayan to stand guard. Later, they might need to find some way to keep watch, but for now, they could rely on the keen senses of their hooved companions.

•

KELLEN slept deeply that night. He dreamed half-consciously; once he realized he was dreaming he struggled against it, for the only dreams Kellen ever remembered having were nightmares of his flight from the Outlaw Hunt, and of Demons.

But these dreams were different. In them he soared in flight over an unfamiliar landscape, looking down upon it as he imagined a bird in flight must view the world.

He realized with a distant sense of discovery that he was looking down at the terrain ahead, and as that knowledge came to him, it seemed he could see it in a way that no human could, as if he were seeing it as something that had been assembled from a thousand different elements, and somehow he could see every part at once. Not seeing the surface, but seeing all the way *through* it, yet seeing all of it, as though he were the architect of its creation.

And as he viewed the scene below him, he had a sense of the land's weakness and strength. It seemed to him that he could feel the baneful orderliness radiating outward from the Barrier he could not yet sense, and feel those things that had fallen prey to its spell as well as those that yet withstood it and remained true to their own natures. In the land below he had a sense of things struggling and dying, and other things resisting . . . so far.

It was as if vast amounts of information were being pressed into his mind, so much that he could not consciously contain it all. The more he tried to grasp what the land was trying to tell him, the more the knowledge slipped away, leaving nothing behind but the impression that it had once been there, until at last, filled with frustration, knowing that he was forgetting important things but unable to stop himself, Kellen awoke.

It was still dark, and the fire was no more than a few dim coals. He could see Shalkan, sleeping curled with his legs tucked beneath him, his head upon his knees, but Valdien and the mule—a pale blur and a dark—were no more than a vague impression of size. That he could see them at all meant that dawn was not far off, though.

Kellen sat up quietly, feeling for the keystone and his sword. They were where they should be. He took a deep breath, calming himself and trying to summon back his dream, but could remember nothing more than the feeling of flight and the memory of being able to see everything about the true nature of the world at once. And that there had been definite signposts of the route they were to take.

He looked around, orienting himself more by the landmarks he'd picked out when they'd made camp yesterday than by the stars, since they were unfamiliar and the moon had long set by now. Even though the dream was fading, enough of it remained to enable him to match the dream-landscape to his real-world surroundings. North and west . . .

he concentrated, dropping into a light trance and trying to bring back the same perception of unnatural order he remembered from the dream. It was hard to put into words—almost a flavor, almost a color—but Kellen knew now that he'd recognize the Taint of the Barrier when he encountered it.

And he had a sense, almost a strong hunch, of the direction to follow. It deviated a little from the course they'd picked yesterday. Today they could see if he was right.

"Is everything well?" Jermayan asked quietly. The Elf Knight had not moved, going from sleep to wakefulness in silence.

"I had a vision." Yesterday it would have seemed silly to Kellen to say something like that. Today the words seemed almost natural. "I think I have a better idea of the way we should go, anyway."

"That makes good hearing."

Jermayan sat up and lit one of the small lanterns they carried with them—Elven cooking fires were designed to produce heat, not light, so they carried lanterns with them as well. By the bright cheery glow of the lantern, Jermayan unwrapped a disk of charcoal and slid it in among the fire's embers to kindle, then got to his feet and stretched.

"We will eat, then prepare the packs. By then, it should be light enough for your morning lesson. Afterward, we can load the mule, saddle Valdien and Shalkan, and ride. Tonight we will still be within the borders of Elven lands, and perhaps tomorrow as well, but the day after, we will be in the Wild Lands beyond, and must be on our guard."

"What's there?" Kellen asked. He lit the other lantern and used it to find the water barrel, setting the lantern down to unscrew the lid.

"It is an inhospitable mountainous land, thinly settled, and that by Men who have never heard of your City, though I believe some Centaurs also live there as well, and may by now have had word from their kindred who fled before the Scouring Hunt. We Elves know little of it; its inhabitants have no love for outsiders of any race, and are fearful and suspicious of anything new or strange." Jermayan shrugged, as if that did not matter, but Kellen was better able to read him now, and he sensed that something about the inhabitants of that wilderness made him uneasy and suspicious.

They should get along just fine with Armethalieh, then, if they ever get together. Why was it that no matter how far away he got from the Golden City, he never really got *away* from it?

Kellen left the lantern beside the water barrel and returned to the fire for the teapot, filling it full at the barrel and bringing it back to hang it over the fire.

"Sounds like we'll have a good time there," he muttered, starting to roll up his bedding.

"Let us pass through alive—assuming our goal lies beyond their lands—and I shall be well content," Jermayan said simply.

Maybe "suspicious" was too mild a term.

⟶

THEY breakfasted on bread and cheese and tea. Valdien and the mule ate grain; Shalkan had bread and journey-rations. By the time all of them had drunk their fill, one barrel was empty and the other nearly so. Jermayan tipped the last of the water from Songmairie into water-bottles, and Kellen rolled the barrels down to the trickle in the creekbed to fill them. Perhaps when they reached the Wild Lands they would be able to do without carrying their own water, but for now it was still a necessity.

He winced inwardly as he poured bucket after bucket of the turbid brown water into the barrels, filling them to the brim. Shalkan was standing behind him the entire time, watching in an eloquent disapproving silence. When the barrels were full, he minced forward, and lowered his horn into each in turn.

As the tip of Shalkan's horn touched the surface of the water, there was a blue shimmer, and the water went from brackish brown to crystal clear, as pure as the unicorn spring itself.

The touch of a unicorn's horn not only destroyed all baneful magic, but could purify water—and any other harmful substance as well. In the City, Kellen had been taught that a cup made from a unicorn's horn would allow its owner to drink even poison safely, a little nugget of information he didn't think he was going to share with his friend anytime soon. In fact, the very thought made him sick now. *Who* could be so vile as to kill a unicorn? Even despoiling one found dead of its horn seemed obscene.

"Thanks," Kellen said.

"I have to drink it, too," Shalkan pointed out inarguably.

By now it was fully light, and time to put his armor on and go to work. It was only as Kellen was settling his helmet into place that he realized he *ought* to be sore today . . . and wasn't. The allheal had done its work. He felt fine.

He hoped he'd be able to say the same thing once the lesson was done.

⤶

BY now the novelty of wearing armor and swinging a sword was past, and he could concentrate fully on the work of learning what Jermayan had to teach him. As a Knight-Mage, a lot of his abilities came from his connection to the Wild Magic, but instincts and innate abilities wouldn't build muscles and hone skills. What Kellen really needed to sharpen his Knight-Mage skills was practice, lots of it, and Jermayan seemed to be prepared to give him an infinite amount. This morning, to Kellen's surprise, they even spent a few moments on extremely simple drills: how to stand, how to hold his sword, how to advance, the basic forms of attack and defense and their names.

"As a Knight-Mage, your body knows these things already, but your mind does not. Therefore, I will tell them to you: once. Try to remember what your body already knows, so that you do not get in your own way," Jermayan said dismissively.

Though the Elven Knight was ruthless in his training, never

letting Kellen get away with anything, and his corrections were *always* swift and painful, Kellen found that he did not resent his new teacher in the slightest. For the first time in his life, Kellen knew that his instructor not only had his own good at heart, with no other agenda in mind (other than keeping him alive), but that he *could* master what he was being taught, if he worked hard. And—also for the first time in his life—it was something that Kellen actually wanted to learn. He applied himself to Jermayan's lessons wholeheartedly, with a passion that would have surprised all of his previous instructors, Idalia included.

At first, these simple things seemed useless, as useless as tracing and retracing the glyphs of High Magick. But then, as Kellen went through the patterns for the third and fourth times, something clicked in his mind.

Because on the third and fourth time—he did them correctly. *Absolutely* correctly. And his body recognized that fact.

What was more, with the recognition came another realization; there was a *good reason* for insisting on perfection in these fighting moves. A perfected movement went as far as it was possible to go in eliminating strain, minimizing the risk of damage, making the most efficient use of strength and energy. Which, of course, was why it *felt* right. This was fighting; obviously he could not completely eliminate injury and damage, and when he actually *fought,* he probably wouldn't be able to do those perfect moves because his enemy wouldn't give him the proper setup. But the more Kellen drilled, the more doing it the right way became habit and muscle-memory.

This wasn't mindless repetition for the sake of humiliating the student; it was mindful repetition to make the movements second-nature, so that he would *never* have to think about them. Because thinking took time, and in a fight, as Kellen very well knew, there never was any time.

Which must be the explanation for that passage of *The Book of Moon.*

And maybe it went a long way toward explaining why he

and Shalkan had been able to fight their way free of the Outlaw Hunt. Because at some point, he hadn't been thinking at all, only letting his body act.

Exactly what *The Book of Moon* said . . .

⸻

"VERY nice," Jermayan said, an hour later, as Kellen stood, winded and panting, in the center of the teaching circle. What mind and heart knew, muscles were being forced to learn—and fast. Kellen was ruefully coming to accept that while the muscles that came from a season of chopping wood and hauling water might be a good foundation for becoming a Knight-Mage, they were only a foundation. Swordplay used those same muscles in an *entirely* different fashion!

"I accept that under most circumstances you will probably not be hit by one swordsman, should only one swordsman attack you. And unfortunately one swordsman is all I have available to teach you with. We will therefore proceed to other matters. Can *you* hit *me*, Knight-Mage?" Jermayan asked.

Kellen wasn't sure himself. The spell-sight showed him where Jermayan was going to strike, but that meant it was only being used reactively. If he attacked, wouldn't that mean Jermayan would have as much opportunity to block his attack as he would have any other attacker's?

"I don't know," Kellen said at last.

"Let us see," Jermayan said. "Come, you have blocked my attacks often enough to see how it is done. Do to me what I have done to you."

Easy enough to say. Kellen took a deep breath and put himself into a trance once more, gazing at Jermayan. Only this time, instead of waiting for Jermayan to hit him, he intended to hit Jermayan. *Hit him,* he told himself.

This time, instead of a blue ghost that moved before Jermayan moved, Kellen saw Jermayan overlaid with a web of red. One spot burned more brightly than the rest. Without thinking, Kellen struck at it.

Jermayan blocked him, of course, but Kellen had already broken off that attack before he completed it, striking at his next red-flaring target. Once Jermayan was in motion, Kellen was always ahead of him, and no matter how many times he was blocked, he kept moving on to the next target.

Until at last Jermayan's blade was not there to block his. Kellen swung toward the undefended target with all his strength.

Wait! NO!

He could not pull the blow, but at the last moment—barely—he managed to shift the sword, so that the flat, not the edge, hit Jermayan's armor. It struck with a solid "clang!" like a hammer hitting a muffled bell, taking Jermayan high on the left thigh.

Kellen staggered back, gasping in horrified reaction when he realized what he had nearly done.

He'd been attacking full-out, because that was the way they'd always sparred. And he hadn't expected to hit Jermayan, because he never *expected* anything when he fought.

But if the strike had gone home edge-first, instead of with the flat . . .

Elven blades were *meant* to cut through Elven armor.

He could have *hurt* Jermayan.

Badly.

Kellen stepped back, the sword falling from his hands to the ground. "I'm sorry," he said miserably. "I didn't think. I could have hurt you."

"So you could have," Jermayan said quietly, and though his voice was calm and steady, his face invisible behind the helmet's guard, Kellen had the sense that the Elven Knight was as shaken as he. "It was my error, Knight-Mage. I will not make it again. And so I think that in future combat, it will be better if we fight with padded blades, lest we do the enemy's work for him."

"Jermayan—" He felt horrible. "I didn't mean—I didn't want—"

Jermayan sheathed his sword and pulled off his helm, then managed a wan smile. "Of course you didn't. Do you think me foolish as a babe unweaned, not to know this? It was *my* fault, to have urged this upon you without forethought myself, and for my folly I shall have a set of bruises to match yours. And—" he added meaningfully, "—think you. You *did* turn your blade in time, though in the heat of combat, and with what, barely a scant two days' true training? You acted with discipline and care. And now, that is sufficient for the morning. We should prepare to ride. There will be another lesson at midday. In which you will learn not to drop your sword when you are surprised."

THIS time they followed the route that Kellen chose, with a midday stop to rest Valdien and the mule and for Kellen to practice again, both his attack and defense. Before they began, Jermayan made sure that both blades were padded, with a layer of tough wadding made from a spare undertunic over each edge and the point, then well wrapped in a thin layer of leather—and for the first time, he carried his shield. Kellen discovered that Elven shields were meant to be worn high on the arm, so that the Knight could still wield his sword two-handed if he chose.

"At home, there would be practice-sheaths to protect the blades—and our armor—but alas, I did not think to bring them," Jermayan said. "It did not occur to me they would be needed."

"Well, I expect you thought I'd barely figure out how to keep from cutting myself on my own sword," Kellen offered.

"True enough," the Elven Knight agreed, to Kellen's chagrin. "But we shall contrive."

There was, of course, no need at all for Jermayan to wrap his own blade as well as Kellen's, but Kellen supposed it had something to do with Elven notions of propriety and fairdealing. As it was, he felt bad about the sacrifice of the undertunic. He just hoped they weren't going to need it later.

Though he tried his hardest, Kellen didn't manage to land another blow on the Elven Knight, but for the first time, a

bout with Jermayan didn't leave him feeling afterward as if
he'd run ten miles uphill in his armor, and Jermayan actually
seemed to approve of his progress. Kellen was feeling pretty
good about things as they went on again.

The feeling didn't last. He'd started feeling unaccountably
nervous as they rode along . . . twitchy, really, as if something
were watching them, but though he kept looking around, he
never managed to spot anything.

They were riding through a forest, one that was suffering
less from the effects of the drought than other places in Elven
lands, as it grew along the banks of a river Jermayan said
was called Angarussa the Undying, which even now ran
strongly, though far lower in its bed than it should have been.

"It runs above caves, doesn't it?" Kellen asked suddenly.

"The Caverns of Halacira are very near here, yes," Jermayan said, puzzled. "The Undying goes down into them and
runs underground for some distance."

"I have to look for something," Kellen said. "Stop." He'd
seen the Angarussa last night in his dream, and something
. . . wasn't *right* here.

Shalkan halted, and Kellen dismounted. He wasn't sure
what he was looking for, but he headed toward the sound of
the river, trying to feel the same sensation he had last night
in his dream. It was frustrating, like trying to listen for music
you weren't even sure was there at all, made worse because
he knew he wasn't going to like what he found, and didn't
actually want to find it.

He walked toward the river, not looking so much as *listening*, until he reached the spot. Or perhaps it wasn't listening, it was *feeling*. The way he felt the Wild Magic.

Here.

He looked down, and discovered he was standing directly
over a patch of low-growing flowers. They looked like tiny
lilies.

"Jermayan?" Kellen called.

The Elven Knight quickly joined him.

"What are those?" Kellen asked, pointing downward.

Jermayan stared at the ground. "They look like starflowers," he said. But he didn't sound at all sure, and his voice was shaken. He stepped quickly backward, off the patch of flowers.

"Are starflowers supposed to be . . . black?" Kellen asked, when Jermayan said nothing more.

"No," Jermayan said with certainty. "Starflowers are—or ought to be—white. Silvery white. And they glow at night. They should be beautiful."

Idalia had said to look for things that were "just plain bad," and the more that Kellen looked at the spreading patch of sooty black flowers, the more he was sure they fit into that category. He didn't know what real starflowers looked like, but these looked wrong. He stepped back carefully out of the flowers.

"What should we do about them? I don't want to just leave them here." He didn't know why, but he knew he couldn't leave those so-called flowers there. They felt—obscene. Or poisonous. Or both.

"Let me," Shalkan said. "If this doesn't work, we can dig them up and bury them."

The unicorn approached the patch of black flowers and knelt so that he could touch them with his horn. As he did, the flowers curled up and withered, the effect spreading swiftly until in a few moments there was nothing but bare earth where the patch of flowers had been.

Shalkan rose to his feet again and shook his head strongly, as though he were shaking something nasty from his horn.

"I suppose this means we're on the right track," he commented blandly to no one in particular.

Chapter Twenty-one

Beyond the Elven Lands

By the end of their third day on the road the travelers had left the borders of the lands claimed by the Elves and were well into the mountains. It was no longer difficult to find water—these lands were not suffering under a magical drought—and the water barrels the mule carried were now empty, to save weight.

But even without drought to afflict it, it was a hard land, one of rocks and hidden springs, near-barren hills covered with sparse grass and scrubby bushes. The small party spent as much time going down as up, often having to detour out of their way in order to find a path that Valdien and the mule could follow. Even a few days and a few miles had made a difference in the weather, and now Kellen was glad of the protection his armor offered in more ways than one, for the days were chilly and the nights decidedly cold.

Kellen's lessons continued—morning, noon, and night—and with every exercise, he became more comfortable with both sword and armor, more confident of his skill, and above all, his endurance, coordination, and strength increased almost with every new lesson. Jermayan was a matchless teacher, patient and firm, and most of all certain of Kellen's excellence.

In addition to the disciplines of combat, Kellen had learned many other things as well—how to care for his sword and armor, how to get into and out of his armor easily, how to cope with the dozens of small chores of life on the road. He realized now how many of those Idalia had handled on their flight from the Wildwood, but now he was learning to take care of them himself.

He was also learning how to care for and even saddle Valdien as well as Shalken—not because Jermayan intended ever to leave that particular task to him, but because, as the Elven Knight constantly reminded him, they could never foresee what disaster might lie ahead. It might come to pass in the future that Jermayan wouldn't be able to take care of Valdien himself, either due to injury, or . . . for some other reason.

Though Valdien blatantly preferred Jermayan's attentions to Kellen's, and made no secret of it, the pack mule was more than willing to become a friend to anyone who fed her and brushed her and cleaned her hooves. Lily, for all the high-flown poetry of her name, was a very tolerant and down-to-earth sort (though Kellen supposed that went with being a mule), patiently enduring Kellen's rather clumsy (at first) attempts at hostlery. But by the time they were out of Elven lands, he could see to her needs as well as Jermayan could, and nearly as fast.

He'd been a little surprised in the beginning to find an Elven Knight so expert at such homely tasks, but as Shalkan reminded him, Jermayan hadn't *always* been an Elven Knight. He'd begun as an apprentice, doing even more lowly tasks. And even in a city as beautiful as Sentarshadeen, garbage had to be hauled away and manure composted for the gardens Kellen had admired so much.

Maybe so, Kellen agreed. But it was still hard to imagine the stately and graceful Elves doing any of those things, even though he'd seen Morusil pulling weeds and Iletel up to his elbows in mud—or potter's clay, anyway.

Though—at least when Jermayan managed to get past his guard and land an especially stinging blow—it was nice to imagine there'd once been a time when *Jermayan* had been getting hit that hard on a regular basis.

TO Kellen's secret relief—if you could call it relief, to see such disquieting things—they saw enough signs of the Barrier's influence along their way to assure them that they were definitely on the right track. One day it had been strange tall structures of mud, as if wasps had built giant nests upon the ground. Jermayan told Kellen that these were termite hills, and that the nest-builders were creatures that rightly belonged to the deserts of the far south.

Another day they had seen a flock of starlings flying far overhead in an intricate unnatural pattern that had gone on for as long as the riders had been able to see them. Starlings normally flew in a pattern that looked, from a distance, like a thick, billowing ribbon going from horizon to horizon, as they left their daytime foraging ground to seek the groves of trees where they would perch overnight in such numbers that they outnumbered the leaves of the trees. This flock still looked like a ribbon, but a ribbon that was looping in on itself until the loops formed a multipetaled flower, and the birds flew the loops over and over and over again. There were birds lying exhausted on the ground under the flock, and more dropped out of the sky even as they passed.

⌒

TODAY they rode through the bottom of a narrow gorge. On either side, sheer granite walls rose straight up; the only way out was straight ahead, through a dense birch forest. The ground underfoot was thick with fallen yellow leaves. None of them was very happy about their route, and it was not one that Kellen would have freely chosen, but there didn't seem to be any other way, not if they were to keep to anything at all like their proper course northward.

Suddenly a flash of blue on the ground off to his right caught his eye. Kellen looked toward it. One of the drifts of leaves at the base of the trees was . . . blue?

"Look there," Kellen said, pointing. "I'm going to go check that. That's not right."

Shalkan stopped, and Kellen dismounted, with far more grace and assurance than he'd exhibited even a few days previously. He walked toward the strange blue leaves, drawing his sword as he did—the gesture was almost second nature by now. Behind him, Jermayan was dismounting as well, telling Valdien to stand.

When he reached the pile at the base of the tree, Kellen prodded it with the tip of his sword.

Not leaves.

Butterflies.

Dead butterflies, blue ones, hundreds of them. They'd flocked here, drawn somehow by the Barrier's power—did butterflies flock, or swarm?—and frozen to death in the harsh northern autumn. He sighed, depressed by the senseless destruction of so much innocent beauty.

"Kellen!"

He whirled at Jermayan's anguished cry, and stared in shock.

Running toward them was a mob of men and Centaurs with swords and clubs.

How . . . ?

Kellen stifled the automatic question. There would be time for questions later—if they survived. He summoned his battle-mind and ran toward the enemy.

He was closest to the group; they reached him—or he reached them—before Shalkan and Jermayan had taken more than a step or two.

Around him, the double-sight overlaid every one of the attackers; he fell into the fighting-trance without effort, and he met the attack of the nearest with no more thought than he had to put into taking a step forward. He had no shield, and his helmet was on Shalkan's saddle; that didn't matter. He automatically adjusted his defense to deal with those handicaps.

Jermayan hadn't had time to get his helm and shield either. And their opponents *did* have helmets, and shields that could turn or even stop a sword, and had the weight of numbers on their side as well. But they were facing an Elven Knight and a Knight-Mage, and their skills and their shields were not enough to protect them. Kellen *knew* that, bone-deep, blood-deep, and gave no more thought to it than that.

Kellen heard the slam of metal upon metal as Jermayan

engaged his foe just behind him, and knew from the shouts and cries of pain just beyond Jermayan that Shalkan and Valdien were attacking as well. *Good,* he thought, then shut out all distraction to focus on his own battle.

He chose his target—a man wearing a shaggy bearskin vest with a chainmail shirt beneath. On his head he wore a close-fitting round helmet with a flat nosepiece, and carried a small round shield on his forearm, but his only heavy armor was a steel collar and shoulder guards. He smiled when he saw Kellen, and in that smile Kellen could almost read his thoughts—*bright surcoat—fancy armor—no helmet—only a boy—easy prey.*

Step and slash, Kellen told himself.

This was different from facing Jermayan in the practice ring. It was almost harder, because his enemy kept backing away, searching for an opening that Kellen wasn't willing to give him, all the while making wild swipes with his sword that had no chance of connecting. After a few seconds, Kellen realized that he needed to lure the man into attacking in order to finish him. He set up an easy patter of parry-right, strike-left, and parry-right, taking his parries farther and farther out away from the proper defensive line, and waited for the man to spot it and think he had found the weakness in his opponent's defenses.

As he'd hoped, the man rushed him, sword held foolishly high. Kellen stepped inside his opponent's swing with ease, felt the man's forearm jar harmlessly against his shoulder, grabbed the sword-arm with his left hand, and brought his own blade down on his foe's undefended shoulder with all his strength.

This time he did not turn his blade when he struck.

The razor edge of Elven steel slipped in between the steel shoulder guard and the steel neck-collar of his enemy's armor, sinking through bearskin vest, chain armor, flesh, and bone, to sever his attacker's arm cleanly at the joint.

The man reeled back, his torso spraying dark blood from severed arteries. He screamed in horror, pain, and shock, falling to his knees in a pool of spreading blood, groping after the limb that was no longer there before he fell over entirely.

Kellen dropped the arm he still held as if it had burned his hand, abruptly shocked out of his battle-trance. The man's screams of pain razored through him and he stood staring stupidly at the blood, and the dying man.

This was no game, no wondertale. It wasn't a practice session. This wasn't like the bloodless destruction of the stone Hounds. This was noisy and messy and *real*. He'd killed a man.

One moment he'd been alive, with a wife perhaps, or a sweetheart, siblings, parents. The next, he was dead.

And Kellen had killed him.

Then Jermayan jumped in front of him, shoving him back just as one of the Centaurs swept a spiked mace down just where Kellen's unprotected head would have been. Jermayan blocked, but the blow had caught him off-balance. The mace slammed into Jermayan's ribs, just where the jointed Elven armor was weakest, and Jermayan fell, crumpling awkwardly to the ground, his coiled black hair spilling free around him in a sudden untidy tangle.

No!

Kellen snapped back into full warrior mode again. Anger spilled around him, but did not touch him. He forgot everything but his training and his purpose. He stepped over Jermayan's body—*always advance*—and forced the Centaur back, away from Jermayan. It reared, striking at Kellen with metal-shod forehooves, and Kellen showed no mercy, crippling it swiftly and then moving in for the kill.

This time he did not stop, did not hesitate for a single instant. When the Centaur was dead he turned, looking for other attackers.

The other Centaur was already down, its belly open in a spill of glistening entrails. Four left, all human. They spread out, trying to keep an eye on Kellen and Shalkan at the same time.

He thought he heard a groan from Jermayan, and rage filled him again; before it could interfere with the battle-trance, he seized it, fed it *into* the trance, and felt it nourish his muscles with new strength, give a sharper focus to his vision.

Kellen circled around, giving them the choice of facing either him or Shalkan, knowing they'd see him as the greater threat—or the easier prey. The possible attacks all converged into one as he moved, the ghost-images coalescing into a single *path* for each man. They'd try to attack him all together, hoping he'd get rattled and careless.

But he wouldn't.

He backed up—Jermayan had also taught him that, to retreat as gracefully and as easily as to advance—leading them away from the bodies and the blood, onto surer footing. Away from Jermayan.

They tried to rush him all at once, but to attack in a group took training, and they only got in each other's way, while the ghost-images told *him* the best way to move to ensure that they tangled with each other. In the space of a breath, he struck while they were still trying to sort themselves out, one after another.

You *could* dance in Elven armor—a dance of death. Kellen moved now as if he wore nothing more than his Wildwood buckskins.

Cut high. Sidekick. Parry on the spin and cut low, parry high. Two were killed outright at the end of that pattern. *High, low, high, rush, hilt to the chin, thrust.* That one he wounded and Shalkan rushed in from the side and finished him. Kellen left his sword in the body and sidekicked the last attacker into Shalkan's path, and Shalkan killed that man by himself, standing over the body with a look of grim satisfaction, horn and hooves dyed scarlet with blood.

It was over. The entire battle had taken less time than the warm-up to a practice session.

Kellen fell out of his trance, and blinked, staring around himself. He wasn't winded, not even close, but he took the moment to breathe deeply, watching the bodies for any sign of movement, for another thing that Jermayan had warned him of was that an enemy might merely pretend death in order to take the supposed victor unawares—or attack in two groups, holding back half his strength.

But as he watched, Shalkan moved among the bodies, testing for signs of life, then raised his head, looking in every direction, testing the air. When he was done, the unicorn shook his head silently. There were no survivors, and no further threat.

Kellen reclaimed his sword. It was bloody from hilt to point, blood dripping from the quillons and the end, as wet as if he'd dipped it into a vat of the stuff. His surcoat was sodden with blood. He shook his head to clear it, feeling as though he were half-asleep, dazed, but knew he did not have the luxury of sinking to his knees and resting as his body suddenly urged him to do. There were urgent matters to attend to and no time for either panic or self-reproach.

Jermayan.

Still carrying his sword—there was no way he could sheathe it in its present condition—he hurried quickly back to his fallen friend and knelt beside him.

To Kellen's enormous relief, the Elven Knight still lived, though he was unconscious from his wound. Blood was seeping steadily through the armor, soaking the edges of the gash in the dark blue surcoat. His breathing was shallow, and his face was far paler than usual, nearly as white as shell-clay.

For one moment, Kellen felt a blinding flare of panic—what should he do? What *could* he do?

But as soon as it had come, it was gone. He knew what to do. He had to heal Jermayan with his magic. Fortunately, Idalia had taught him enough of the Healing spells to manage that. It was a simple spell, but costly—and with Jermayan unconscious, he couldn't ask him to share the cost. Kellen would have to pay the entire price.

Unless . . . ?

He glanced up at Shalkan hopefully, but the unicorn shook his head.

"I can't," the unicorn said, shaking his head unhappily. "I'm sorry, Kellen."

So it was all up to him alone. And when it was over, Kellen would be laboring under some sort of new responsibility or *geas*, as the Wild Magic exacted its payment—and it was barely possible that this price might be something that ran counter to his current mission. On the other hand, if Idalia ever found out that Kellen had let Jermayan take the blow meant for him, and then let him die afterward when he could have saved him, he knew she'd kill him. Twice.

He quickly stripped off Jermayan's surcoat, trying to be as gentle as possible. The armor followed, though it was like trying to peel a crawfish out of its shell. At least he could *see* the pieces of the armor and their fastenings, which was more than he could do when he was taking off his own. Then he lifted the padded undertunic to get a look at the wound. He bit down hard on a pang of nausea as he discovered he had to pull the undertunic *out* of Jermayan's side: the Centaur's mace had been spiked; there were deep punctures in the flesh, and Kellen suspected broken ribs besides. A serious wound, but not as bad as the gash in the surcoat had suggested. One of the spikes must have caught in the fabric and torn it.

I can't cast a circle on bloodstained ground. . . . He looked around for a clean place to cast his circle, then, as gently as possible, eased Jermayan onto his own cloak and dragged him there. The Elven Knight groaned in pain, but did not rouse to consciousness.

Since he was *not* as good a Wildmage as Idalia, there were things Kellen would need to cast the Healing Spell, and thanks to Idalia, he had them with him. Kellen covered Jermayan with his bloodstained surcoat for warmth, then went to Lily and rummaged through her packs, looking for knives, bandages, waterskins, and the leaves and herbs he would need.

The mule was skittish and upset, disturbed by all the blood and trying to pull away. But she was tied securely to Valdien's saddle, and Valdien—trained to war—stood steadily. Kellen was grateful; he didn't have the time to soothe her fears or try to catch her if she bolted. Jermayan needed help *now,* before he bled to death.

He took the jar of allheal as well. Jermayan had said it was really only useful for minor abrasions, but there was a lot of bruising involved in the wound. He wasn't sure how far he'd be able to heal Jermayan, and he wanted all the help he could get.

In a way, though, he was glad that he had something to concentrate on besides what he'd just done. If he thought about all those dead bodies—

So he wouldn't think about them.

"Can you find us somewhere to camp?" Kellen asked Shalkan as he gathered what he was going to need. "Someplace not too near here—with water?"

He still didn't know who'd attacked them, or why—whether they were just common hill-bandits, or something more sinister—and he still didn't have the luxury of waiting around to find out. And even though they'd killed all of them, that didn't mean they didn't have friends who might come looking for them, and even tomorrow would be too soon for that.

"I'll take care of it," the unicorn promised, trotting off.

His arms filled with supplies, Kellen hurried back to Jermayan. He took off his own armored gauntlets and drew a circle around them both with his dagger. Then he built his fire of bits of dried twigs and charcoal from his packs on a patch of earth scraped bare of leaves. When the charcoal had kindled, he sat cross-legged on the ground beside the Elf, and closed his eyes to assume the spell-trance that was so like, and yet unlike, the battle-trance.

Taking his knife he cut a few strands of Jermayan's hair, then added a bit of his own. He curled the strands into a tight lock, then touched them to the blood from Jermayan's wound, remembering what Idalia had done to heal the unicorn colt.

Cautiously, he ran his thumb along the knife blade, wincing as the flesh parted easily. Quickly, he added his own blood to the spell, and dropped the small bundle into the fire, along with the dried leaves of willow, ash, and yew for good measure, burned them along with three drops of his own blood.

Still in that dispassionate state, he closed his eyes again and gathered his own power in a knot around his heart, slowly pushing it outward until it met the physical barrier of the scribed circle with a faint sensation of *resistance*.

Grant me the strength to heal my friend, he promised the Powers, *and I will pay the price for the healing.*

It was done. Now all that was left was to await their answer and hear their price.

He opened his eyes, held in the calm, still center of the trance, to see the faintly glowing dome of his protections above them. He knew he'd done all that he could do with his Wildmagery, and that the rest was up to the Gods, so Kellen began cleaning and bandaging Jermayan's wound as well as he could, wiping the still-oozing blood away with a dampened cloth, applying allheal to the bruised flesh, making a thick linen pad to place over the ugly wound in Jermayan's side.

Kellen wasn't sure how extensive the healing would be—or if he would be granted one at all, after having killed so many men—but the one thing he was certain of was that the Wild Magic didn't look favorably on those who tried to use it as a replacement for everyday common sense.

Suddenly, as he worked, he had an abrupt sense of heatless force pressing down on him, as if giant hands, impossibly heavy, were thrusting down on his shoulders. He felt Power flow through his hands into Jermayan's flesh, and all around him the golden summer sunlight went brilliantly green, as if he'd suddenly been plunged into the heart of an emerald.

He felt the Power flood into him, strong and sweet, intoxicating, and he lost himself in it, forgetting everything, simply *being*, and knowing that beneath his hands, the wounds were closing, blood ceasing to leak from the damaged veins, flesh knitting.

And from somewhere within him there came a voice:

You will know what you must do when the time comes.

Then, all at once, as suddenly as it had come, the sense of Presence was gone. Kellen fell out of the spell-trance, so suddenly that he felt giddy and chilled, and was a little surprised not to feel himself *thudding* down onto the ground beside his mentor.

Huh. He opened his eyes and shook his head a little. The dome of protection was gone—but then, it had done its work and there was no more need of it.

Cautiously, Kellen lifted the cloth covering Jermayan's wound. The ugly oozing gash was gone. Only faint bruises remained, and a few dull silvery marks, as if the injury were sennights, even moonturns, in the past.

Well, I know it worked, anyway.

"That was—peculiar," Kellen muttered aloud, breathing a shaky sigh of relief. He certainly didn't recall Idalia mentioning anything of the sort happening to *her* during a healing. He felt almost as if he'd been forgiven, though he wasn't quite sure for what.

And he was suddenly bone-weary, having paid an immediate price of his own strength for the healing and the protective circle.

Even Jermayan's color was better, the Elven Knight having gone from a swoon into a natural sleep. He was breathing easier as well.

So the healing was more than just cosmetic, it had worked as well as Kellen could ever have asked if he'd dared—even though Kellen had no notion of what his greater price might be for the spell he had worked here today. *So I'll know what to do when the time comes, will I? That's useful, I don't think.*

Kellen sat back on his heels, able to stop and take a deep breath himself for the first time since the fight had begun. He crushed out the little fire he'd built, reaching for his gloves and gauntlets and putting them on again before getting stiffly to his feet. As soon as Shalkan got back, he'd wake Jermayan and they'd move. He forced himself to try to think and plan, though at the moment his head felt as if it were stuffed full of feathers.

How had those bandits—or whatever they were—managed to appear out of nowhere without any of them—even Shalkan—noticing them? Had they had magic? Had they been sent by the enemy? If someone had sent them, more might be on the way.

And if they'd only been bandits and nothing worse, then

at the very least, a valley full of dead men wasn't going to be a pleasant place to camp, and where there were some bandits, there would probably be others, even in Kellen's admittedly limited experience.

And on top of everything else, Idalia had warned him to move on quickly from anyplace where he used his magic, as it was likely to draw unwelcome attention. So whether the bandits had been sent by the enemy or not, he probably had the enemy's attention now—or at least, would have it soon, if he was still here.

Steeling himself against the sight, Kellen went back among the corpses to reclaim the rest of Jermayan's armor and sword. The blood hadn't bothered him while he was fighting—not after Jermayan had been hit—but it was different now. Now the sight of the bodies made him sick, and knowing that *he* was responsible for killing a good half of them, well . . .

For the first time, he was able to count the enemy numbers. Six men and two Centaurs, all looking pretty much like what Kellen imagined hill-bandits would look like; dirty, unshaven, and under their armor, their ill-fitting clothing was clearly stolen from their victims. He took the best of the round shields that the bandits had been carrying for himself—after today, he thought it might be a pretty good idea for Jermayan to teach him to fight with one.

Once he'd done that, he led Valdien and the mule over to where Jermayan was. That took even more coaxing; Valdien was excited by the scent of blood and kept dancing away when Kellen reached for his bridle, and Lily was plain and fancy spooked. But Kellen managed that task as well—it helped that he was far too tired to lose his temper with either of them.

He hoped Shalkan would get back soon; if he didn't, he'd have to find some way to go on without him and meet him on the way. It was already midafternoon, and as soon as the sun got much farther over the canyon wall, it would be dark down here, and Kellen didn't want to chance trying to lead either Valdien or Lily down an unfamiliar trail in the dark.

By the time Kellen was able to lead the animals back to where Jermayan lay—making a wide circuit around the actual battlefield—the Elven Knight was awake and trying to sit up.

"I wouldn't move if I were you," Kellen said. "I'm not sure how badly you're still hurt."

Jermayan grunted and lay back, apparently agreeing with Kellen's assessment.

"The bandits?" he asked tersely.

"If that's what they were," Kellen said doubtfully. "Dead. All of them."

"Good," Jermayan said with satisfaction. He pressed his fingers against his side, wincing as he probed the site of his injury, and then sat up. His face was pale, but determined.

He looked around, taking in the circle drawn in the dirt, the remains of the fire. "It seems I owe you my life," he said.

"I owe you mine," Kellen said, feeling his inadequacy engulf him like a wave. "I'm . . . sorry, Jermayan. I just . . . froze."

And that was when everything fell apart for him.

Kellen dropped to his knees, retching, his stomach heaving, tears streaming down his face as he sobbed between bouts of vomiting. He felt, more than saw, Jermayan getting slowly and carefully to his feet; felt Jermayan kneel beside him, and felt the Elf's hands steadying him as his stomach emptied. He wept for himself, for a loss of something he could not name, for the blood on his hands and his soul. He wept that he had been so weak that Jermayan had been forced to put himself in danger. He wept that he had simply not been *good* enough.

And he wept with rage, at the men who had forced him to kill.

"All the practice in the world cannot prepare you to see a man die," Jermayan said simply when Kellen was able at last to listen. "But you did not let your feelings overmaster you— or we would not be here now."

"But—" Kellen groaned. He'd *failed*. He'd gotten Jermayan hurt, nearly killed! "I—"

"Hush. And listen to one who is briefly your master," Jermayan said gently. "You have crossed a great abyss today. You have chosen death. With your two hands, you have delivered it. Are you sorry?"

"Yes. No. Both." There was nothing left in his stomach, but Kellen remained bent over, gut aching, throat raw, tears still burning down his cheeks.

"Good. It is a wretched thing to take a life, but it was what needed to be done today. These outlaws *could* have turned aside from us; they could have broken off combat at any time, and we would not have pursued them. They did neither. We cannot know if they *deserved* the death they won, but if we had not slain them, they would have slain us, and our task requires that we live. Do you hate them? Do you anger, still?"

That Kellen was sure of. *"Yes!"* He'd killed today. He would never forget that, never forgive it. Never!

"Do not; we cannot know what drove them. Perhaps their minds were not even their own. Let it go. Forgive them."

"How?" Kellen cried in anguish.

"Now they are not your foes. Think of them as men and Centaurs once more."

It was the hardest thing he had ever done, until he remembered that moment of paralysis, when he had looked at the face of the first dying man, and had thought, *He has a wife, friends, parents—*

Then at last he could, and did. The tears came again, and in weeping for them, Kellen forgave them.

"Now forgive yourself," Jermayan said. "You could do no other than what you did."

And Jermayan put a steadying arm around Kellen's shoulders, and waited until he could.

FINALLY, Kellen was done with forgiveness and forgiving; he was empty and exhausted, but he finally felt—clean. As he had not felt since the fight began.

He got to his feet with an effort, then helped Jermayan to stand. They stood for a moment with hands clasped, looking into each other's eyes. Finally, Jermayan nodded, as if satisfied by what he saw in Kellen, and let his hands go.

When Jermayan stood, Valdien hurried to his master's side, nudging at him worriedly. Jermayan put an arm over the destrier's neck, gripping his mount's saddle for support.

"You'll need to clean the swords," he said matter-of-factly. "Scrub the blades down with earth. Pack my armor on the mule . . . I think I will have to ride without it."

For Jermayan to make such a concession meant that the Elven Knight must be far weaker than he wanted to admit, Kellen realized. He said nothing, merely doing as he was told. Most of the blood came off the blades with a few handfuls of earth, and he was able to sheathe them. A thorough cleaning with oil, rag, and whetstone would have to wait, but this would do for now.

By the time he'd repacked the healing supplies on the mule, added Jermayan's armor, helped Jermayan back into his padded tunic and surcoat (the tunic was torn, and both items were bloody, but they could not spare the time to unpack anything else), and gotten a cloak for Jermayan to wear over the padded undertunic, Shalkan had returned, to Kellen's great relief.

The unicorn had managed to wash off all traces of blood while he'd been gone, his fur restored once more to its pristine glistening whiteness. Kellen was grateful for that—there'd been something especially disturbing about the sight of Shalkan covered in blood.

The unicorn took in the situation in a glance and nodded in approval.

"I've found a place that should do. All ready?" Shalkan asked.

Kellen looked to Jermayan. The Elf nodded.

"Good. Let's go," Shalkan said with a wary look around. "We've been here too long already."

Kellen helped Jermayan into Valdien's saddle—another concession that proved how weak the Elven Knight really was, no matter how hard he tried to hide it. Jermayan rode heavily, as if remaining upright took most of his strength.

Kellen hoped they didn't run into anything else between here and the campsite Shalkan had found for them. Jermayan was in no condition to fight at all, and Kellen wasn't feeling much better, truth be told. He swung himself into Shalkan's saddle and landed, despite his best intentions, with an ungraceful thud. The unicorn didn't comment.

—

SHALKAN led them through the trees toward the eastern wall of the canyon. Soon Kellen heard the sound of trickling water, and saw that they were paralleling the path of a tiny stream. After a short while, the sound of the little brook was joined by the louder sound of falling water, and through a gap in the trees ahead, Kellen could see what must be their destination for the night: a wide crack in the canyon wall where a tiny waterfall spilled down from above to fill a cup-like catch-basin before spilling away into the narrow stream.

By the time they reached it, Jermayan was swaying dangerously in his saddle. Kellen had saved his life, but he didn't have Idalia's practice in healing; whatever had happened had been done by the Powers without any help or guidance from him.

He had the feeling that this healing had been a great deal like forcing a lot of water into a pond by flooding it, rather than allowing it to trickle in. The pond got water in it, but a lot was lost in the process.

And there had been no one to share the price of the healing with him, either, which probably made more of a difference. The Elven Knight was still dangerously weak, and Kellen couldn't think of any way to fix that except rest and food.

As for Kellen, between the fight and the healing and the aftermath—well, he was exhausted, and really not interested in anything but rest himself.

And what about attackers on their trail?

The thought made his stomach hurt all over again. *We're not up to another attack,* he thought desperately.

But the campsite Shalkan had found them was easily defensible—there was only one direction from which anyone could approach, and the entryway was not that much wider than the canyon from which Kellen and Shalkan had fought off the Outlaw Hunt. The moment he saw it, he sighed with relief. He and Shalkan could protect it alone if they had to.

Best of all, there was plenty of water. He was thirsty, and knew Jermayan must be as well, having lost so much blood.

As the light faded from the sky, Kellen was wholly occupied with the chores of setting up the camp, since for the first time he had to do it all by himself. First he got Jermayan off Valdien's back and settled more or less comfortably against one wall of the narrow canyon while Valdien and the mule quenched their thirsts. He filled one of the tankards from the spring and handed it to Jermayan, then he got Shalkan out of his armor and unsaddled Valdien. He found a twisted bit of tree growing out of the rock wall at the back of the canyon, and tied the mule's halter-rope to it securely. He was sure that Valdien wouldn't stray—the big Elven destrier behaved more like a large dog than he did like any horse Kellen had ever seen—but Lily had had a hard day, and Kellen didn't want to wake up to find the mule gone. Once she was securely tied, he removed his own armor at last and began unloading her.

After that, all that was left to do was to light the lanterns, build a fire, and feed the animals while the tea was brewing— allheal, he thought, since both of them could use it. Once the animals were fed, Kellen unwrapped a couple of trail-bars for Shalkan and began cutting up another couple to make soup.

By the time that task was done, the tea was ready. Kellen added a large disk of crystallized honey to each cup—they could both use the sugar—and poured the two cups full. Maybe Idalia and the Elves were right about the restorative powers of tea after all, Kellen thought. Certainly nothing had ever seemed so welcome as the thought of a hot cup of sweet tea just now.

He carried the other cup over to Jermayan.

"Drink this. You'll feel better."

"My thanks." Jermayan took the cup from Kellen's hand.

His fingers were icy where they brushed Kellen's own, and his hand trembled.

"You should come over by the fire where it's warmer," Kellen said. "You've lost a lot of blood, and you'll be cold."

"Soon," Jermayan promised. He drank, eyes closing.

"We ought to have died back there," he said after a moment.

"I nearly got us killed," Kellen said bitterly.

"No." Jermayan reached out his hand with an effort and placed it on Kellen's arm. "It was I who nearly got us killed, riding bareheaded and unshielded as if I went to bring in the spring-tide, though knowing that I rode through unfriendly lands with an unblooded Knight-batchelor who had not yet won shield or spurs. Against six Men and two Centaurs . . . it is only because you are what you are that we are here now, Kellen Tavadon. And beyond that: you have put yourself under obligation to the Powers to ransom my life from Death's cold halls. That is a gift of which I am unworthy."

Kellen wasn't really sure what to say to that. "Well, it's not like I could just go back and tell Idalia I'd misplaced you," he said awkwardly. "She wouldn't like that."

"There is much of your sister in you," Jermayan said mournfully. "Her grace, her nobility of spirit. From the moment I first saw her in Ondoladeshiron I knew it was she for whom my heart had waited through all the long decades of my life. Love among the Children of Leaf and Star is no light thing. It is for ever and always. I would not have troubled her with the burden of my heart, did I not know that hers inclined to me as well. Yet she denies what we both know to be the truth." He lowered his head and sighed deeply.

I don't want to hear this, Kellen thought uncomfortably. And yet—

I want them to be happy, and I know damned good and well that neither of them is ever going to be happy without the other.

"I understand that she does not wish to leave me alone and forsaken when the brief span of her mortal years is run, but cannot one so wise understand that I am already alone who has once gazed into violet eyes the color of evening mists? I shall be forever alone without her, my Idalia—would she deny me even the memories of the brief summer's afternoon of our love to warm me through the long cold winter I must spend without her?"

Urk. This was getting more uncomfortable by the moment.

"Every moment we spend apart is filled with thoughts of her," Jermayan continued, with a curiously restrained passion. "It is she who completes me, Kellen—would she be so unfeeling as to refuse me the transfiguration for which her own soul must cry as well? Without love, all the treasures of the world are ashes, and the Children of Leaf and Star know that true love comes only once into every life. How is it that she cannot see that, who can see so much else so clearly? We are meant to be together. It matters not how brief the time, only that it is filled with joy."

"I think the soup is ready," Kellen said hurriedly, scuttling backward toward the fire.

He didn't know if Jermayan had ever said anything like that to Idalia—if he had, it would be just one more good reason for her to not want to have anything more to do with him, by Kellen's reckoning—but he was completely sure he didn't want Jermayan saying anything more of it to *him*. It was bad enough having to read things like that in wondertales—and Kellen *didn't;* he skipped over those parts—but it was a thousand times worse having to hear someone saying them about your *sister.*

Grace—nobility of spirit—soul must cry—filled with joy—I didn't think anybody really talked like that! Kellen thought in disgust. *He must be running a fever from that healing I did.*

He glanced up and saw Shalkan watching him. From the expression on the unicorn's face, Shalkan thought *something* was pretty funny, and Kellen didn't want to inquire too closely about what it might be, Kellen thought in acute discomfort. He'd have been disgusted if it had been another human who was blathering on like that, but, well—Elves just seemed to talk like that naturally.

Like that kind of thing can be spouted off casually.

As he filled the bowls, Kellen cast about in his mind for a subject that would distract Jermayan from the topic of Idalia.

When he had Jermayan comfortably seated in front of the small fire, Kellen deftly took control of the conversation before Jermayan could start talking again.

"Those people we fought today—who do you think they were?" he asked.

Jermayan frowned. "I'm not certain. Perhaps simple brigands, for all that they managed to take us so completely by surprise. This far from human and Elven lands there are all manner of unchancy things prowling. It is a hard land, one that cannot be farmed or husbanded. Though there are a few who are sturdy enough to eke out a precarious living as shepherds, even they are surly, unfriendly, and half-beast themselves. Those who fell upon us today might be no more than the lawless wolfsheads whose meat is hapless travelers—but the fact that they were able to hide so nearly in plain sight and approach us so closely argues that they may have had magical help to do so."

"So they might have been related to these people who set the Barrier? Shadow Mountain?" Kellen said.

Jermayan reluctantly nodded.

Aha! "So who—what—is Shadow Mountain, and why are they—it—doing this?" Kellen demanded urgently.

There it was, the question he'd been wanting to ask ever since the name had been mentioned back in Sentarshadeen and the Elves had practically turned themselves inside-out. What *was* Shadow Mountain? If the enemy was going to be hunting them directly—and now that Kellen had used the Wild Magic outright, he'd been thinking more about that possibility—it was time to stop avoiding the question and find out exactly who and what he might be facing.

Though—now that he came to think about it—everyone, including Jermayan, had been doing a very good job of distracting him from that very question from the moment of the Council meeting back in Sentarshadeen.

There was a long pause. Kellen could tell that Jermayan

really wished Kellen hadn't asked the question, and for a moment Kellen almost withdrew it. But he wanted to know. More than that, he thought he *needed* to know. If he was going to be fighting Shadow Mountain—if they were going to be sending enemies after him and Jermayan—he needed to know what he was up against.

"Shadow Mountain is what the Children of Leaf and Star call the stronghold of our oldest enemy—indeed, the oldest enemy of every race in this world, if only the rest of you knew it. Shadow Mountain is the home of the Endarkened," Jermayan answered at last, very reluctantly.

Kellen looked puzzled. The Endarkened. The name meant nothing to him.

"Demons," Jermayan elaborated. "The Endarkened are what you humans call Demons."

"Demons?"

All Kellen's old fears—fears he'd thought long-settled and put to rest—returned in a sudden rush. Idalia had said the Demons were real. The old faun back in the Wildwood had been terrified of them. But even though he'd been hearing about them since he'd left the City—and even before— Demons still seemed so unlikely, a concept Kellen recoiled from believing in even while it terrified him. They belonged to nightmares, not to conversations like this.

Jermayan seemed to sense his hesitation, and misunderstood its source.

" 'Demon' is the name that Men gave to them in the War, and it is a truly fitting one—or so we Elves decided, once we understood the human concept of Demons. The Endarkened are evil, without exception. They are at least as long-lived as Elves, if not truly immortal."

"They are?" Kellen asked in a whisper. The creatures of his nightmares had certainly seemed unstoppable . . .

"What—what do they look like?" He didn't want to know. Except that he did. He had to know if his nightmares reflected the truth, or only his own twisted imagination.

"Unless they are disguising themselves by magic," Jermayan replied, "they are easy to recognize: they have the horns of goats, the slitted eyes of snakes, scarlet or ebony skin, barbed tails, talons, and often wings or cloven hooves as well."

Kellen shuddered, suppressing a chill of horror. Jermayan's description exactly matched the images in his nightmares. *But how had he known?*

But despite his reluctance to begin, Jermayan was by no means finished with the subject of Shadow Mountain and Demons.

"And unlike other races, *all* the Endarkened are powerful Mages, able to wield a kind of magic that is neither the High Magick of the City, nor the Wild Magic you have learned, Kellen, but magic of a third kind, wholly abominable, and wholly inimical to Life. The least of the Endarkened is an inherent Mage far more powerful than most human Mages, and the most powerful of the Endarkened Mages can cast spells of incalculable power and devastation. Their power comes from the pain and fear of their victims and from the anguish and despair of their victims' deaths. The price of Endarkened magic is paid in the blood and suffering of others, as we learned to our cost in the War.

"So if they are not truly Demons as you humans use the term, you will find, should you learn more of them, that they are close enough," Jermayan said with a bitter sigh.

Kellen knew that Jermayan's unwontedly expansive mood would probably not last long, and that he should learn all he could while the Elven Knight was willing to answer his questions. Suddenly he remembered something Idalia had said to him a long time ago: ". . . *duergar and goblins and trolls . . . pushed out of the settled lands by the Great War, and even after all this time, I don't think they'd be foolish enough to come back . . .*"

"You mentioned a war. There *was* a war, wasn't there? Between the humans . . . and the Demons?" And Armethalieh had made sure that no mention of it had survived in the City Histories. Lycaelon had said as much—something about the Black Days, when Demons had prowled the City itself.

He'd blamed that on the Wild Magic—and though Kellen

now knew that the Wild Magic *couldn't* have been at fault—not in the way that Lycaelon had tried to get him to believe, anyway—his instincts still told him that there was some sort of connection between the Wild Magic and the Demons.

Jermayan smiled just a little, like a teacher pleased with his pupil's quickness, even though the subject itself was a terrible one.

"The Endarkened have tried twice before to conquer all the living things of the earth—once, when only we Elves were there to stop them, and the second time when Elves and Men joined in the Great Alliance with several other races to drive them back to their caves beneath the earth once more. The Great Alliance left scars in the fabric of the world that are healing still: Men only entered the conflict because there were other humans, their enemies, who had been seduced by the promises of the Demons and had allied themselves with the powers of Darkness. There were dragons in the world then, who fought on both sides of the conflict—dragons betrayed by the humans who had bonded with them into slavery at the hands of the Demons, and dragons who faithfully served the Great Alliance. The unicorns played a vital part in that war, because the Demons, being creatures of Dark Magic, cannot survive the touch of their living horns."

Dragons! This was the first time Kellen had ever heard that dragons existed outside of a wondertale! The thought distracted him for a moment—

—but not for long, because Jermayan was still talking.

"The Great War took a terrible toll from all the Creatures of Light. Some races were lost forever, some changed beyond recognition. Some withdrew forever from the sight of Elves and Men. Ancient partnerships that had been forged in the morning of the world were sundered forever . . . It would make you weep, Kellen, did I tell you the story of those days in full, of all that was true and good and fair that passed out of the world then, never to be seen again. Yet in the end we rejoiced, though the land itself was in ruins and the work of rebuilding would be a thing of centuries, for we had broken the power of Shadow Mountain for all time . . . or so we thought then."

Jermayan shivered, and Kellen wondered, had *he* been there? Had *he* seen the Great War? Surely not; he was far too young—

"But you won—" he ventured. "Surely you could have gotten rid of them forever!"

Jermayan shook his head. "What victory we won came at a great price, one that your race is paying down to this day. When the Great War was over, the few human Mages who were left—and there were not many, for the War had taken a terrible toll of any who had the least magical Gift—banded together to found the City of Armethalieh, where they thought they could be safe. They outlawed the Wild Magic, swearing death to any who should practice its arts and driving the few surviving Wildmages who would not renounce their practice far from human lands. There began the creation of the High Magick, and the history of Armethalieh the Golden, City of a Thousand Bells—a city for humans alone, ruled only by the High Magick that the surviving Mages created to take the place of the Wild Magic they had spurned."

"But . . . why?" Kellen whispered, horrified.

"The new High Mages thought that it had been the practice of the Wild Magic that had led to the seduction of their human enemies by the Demons," Jermayan said mournfully, as if he could not believe that the Mages had been so blind. "And so they outlawed the Wild Magic, lest new Wildmages should become the prey of Demons as well. But it was not the Wild Magic that caused those Mages to fall."

There it was, the thing Kellen had been dreading. That Wild Magic was dangerous, that Wildmages could be drawn to the Dark—both he knew to be true, though Idalia said it was not true that a Wildmage could serve the Demons with Wildmagery. But she had not told him *why* Wildmages could be drawn to the Demons . . .

"But—if it was the Wildmages who were corrupted—" he ventured.

"Oh, no, Kellen," Jermayan said, and not in the tone people

used when they were trying to reassure him (which of course had the opposite effect) but as if this was such accepted truth that Jermayan could no more have doubted it than he could doubt that the earth would uphold him. "It was not the Wild Magic that caused those Mages to fall, rather their attempts to escape or subvert the price of Wild Magic that led them down the dark paths. They were Wildmages who did not wish to pay the cost of their power, and so in the end, they paid a far higher price."

He looked narrowly at Kellen. "Do you understand me? They wished power without a cost, at least to *them*. And so, they lost the Wild Magic, and found—that only the Demons would promise what they wanted. And they *believed* that promise, only to find that there was a price, after all. It cost them their souls, all that made them truly happy, and in the end—their lives."

Kellen blinked. *Power without cost to them—but isn't that what the High Mages have now?*

But was it? The High Magick still cost somebody something, and *sometimes* the High Mages used their own power . . .

He thought.

"When we realized what they believed in Armethalieh, we sent them envoys and tried to reason with them, for we knew that the Wild Magic was the only defense against Shadow Mountain, and we could not learn its arts, having given up our part in the Greater Magics long ago. But the humans were afraid. They would not heed us. Fear can make people— anyone—think very strange things. Even Elves," Jermayan finished softly. "And now it may be too late."

"Sleep now," Shalkan said firmly, stepping into the lantern light. "Both of you. I'll keep watch. I've had a much easier day than either of you. Sleep."

It was hard to argue with such good advice. Exhausted by the events of the day—the battle and all that went with it, the spell he had cast, Kellen knew he couldn't possibly stay awake much longer, and Jermayan needed to sleep to finish the work of the Healing Spell. Getting to his feet, Kellen quickly washed their cups and bowls and snuffed the lanterns as Jermayan wrapped himself in his bedroll. A few moments later Kellen did the same.

As he looked up at the stars, he thought about what Jermayan had said. He had his answer at last, at least most of it. He thought about his own moment of weakness just this afternoon, how he'd hated the thought of incurring another Mageprice. But he'd accepted it anyway, because that was the cost of the Wild Magic. You paid for what you got, because in paying your Mageprice you were actually helping to tend the garden of the world, as Morusil said.

Only . . . somewhere in the distant past . . . there'd been Wildmages who hadn't wanted to pay, who'd wanted to do spells without incurring Magedebt, to use their power selfishly, for themselves alone. And they'd turned to the Demons to escape paying their price, to keep from *repaying*.

And so, out of that, had come the High Magick. But while the High Mages paid the price of their spells, they didn't pay it themselves . . .

It was precious little comfort to know that as a Knight-Mage, he had a little more immunity to Demonic entanglement than the average Wildmage. *"The Knight-Mage, even more so than the Wildmage, must choose that path, knowingly, and with forethought . . ."* It was like knowing you were a little more fire-resistant when you were planning to walk into a firing-kiln. Not a lot of real practical use.

And somehow, tangled up in everything else he'd learned about the history of the Wild Magic and the High Magick tonight—and bigger than all of that, really—was the War Jermayan had spoken of, the one the City'd ended up blaming on the Wildmages. Kellen stared at the sky through half-closed eyes, trying to imagine that long-ago war. Dragons . . . what must it have been like, to look up and see the sky filled with dragons in flight?

A few moments later he was asleep.

⟺

THE morning sun woke him, and Kellen realized he had slept far later than usual. He sat up quickly, relieved to note that the exhaustion of the day before had passed.

Jermayan was already up and moving about. The Elven Knight seemed to be almost back to his old self again, though he moved with a bit more care than usual. His surcoat and padded undertunic—and Kellen's surcoat as well—were spread out on the grass, damp from a recent washing.

"They should be dry enough to wear by the time we're ready to leave," Jermayan said, noting the direction of Kellen's gaze. "And fortunately, Elven armor doesn't rust. Tea?"

"Why did you let me sleep so late?" Kellen grumbled, feeling cross and guilty in equal measure, as he rolled out of his blankets. Despite the advanced hour, the air was still chilly, and he pulled one of the blankets around himself, groping for his cloak.

Jermayan tossed it to him, and Kellen pulled it on gratefully, then accepted the cup of tea—a different kind this morning.

"You needed the rest," Jermayan answered inarguably. "So did I. And there were tasks that needed doing. We have been careless and lucky. No longer." He gestured, and Kellen saw that a bow and a large quiver of arrows stood beside Jermayan's armor now, unpacked from their place in the mule's load. "Today we ride fully armored and weaponed, and woe betide the enemy who tries to take us unawares."

Kellen saw that the round shield he'd taken from one of the bandits was piled with his own armor. He barely recognized it, for it had been scrubbed and polished until it gleamed.

"I would say that you have indeed earned your shield, Kellen Tavadon, and I only regret that it is not a more fitting one. Later I will teach you how to make the best use of it. For now it must suffice that you wear it."

So there wasn't going to be a lesson this morning, either. Just as well, Kellen supposed, if they were starting this late, but he did regret it a little. He was wondering what it would

be like to face Jermayan in the teaching circle again after
having fought for real, and having killed. Would it make a
difference? Could he still do it?

But the answers to those questions would have to wait.

Soon enough they were back on their road again, this time
wearing cloaks to conceal their armor—not that any cloak
Kellen wore could conceal what Shalkan was, or Valdien's
armor, for that matter. But anything they could do to conceal
their own armor might help them to avoid further attacks. Or
it might draw bandits to them, who thought them easy prey.
It was a gamble either way.

When they left the canyon and Kellen took his bearings,
returning to their northward path, they found themselves
heading up a narrow cleft in the rock, a track with sheer walls
on either side. After the previous day's ambush, none of them
liked it, but to seek another route would take them days out
of their way, time they could not afford to lose. They had to
act now as if Shadow Mountain knew they were coming, and
in that case, speed was their best ally.

The path was barely wide enough for them to ride single
file. Kellen and Shalkan led. This time Kellen wore his helmet, with the unfamiliar weight of the round shield strapped
to his left arm. The helmet protected his head and face, but
left him feeling closed in, unable to see the world very well
with his side vision cut off. Fortunately Shalkan's senses
were better than his own to begin with. He'd just have to
trust Shalkan to spot any potential ambush.

As in fact the unicorn did, before the sun was very much
higher.

"BACK!" Shalkan shouted suddenly, rearing up and turning
in place.

Kellen took in the situation behind him at a glance. Valdien
couldn't turn on the narrow path, and the destrier couldn't
back up if the mule didn't move. Kellen leaped down from
Shalkan's back and squeezed past Jermayan, grabbing Lily

by her bridle and putting his shoulder into her chest. Speaking soothingly but urgently, he pushed, and to his great relief she backed up readily enough. Valdien followed swiftly, backing neatly, with Shalkan jammed in beside him.

Just as the Elven destrier was starting to move, a stone the size of a young pig hit the center of the trail right where Valdien had been standing a moment before. It landed with enough force to crack it in half, and a second later it was followed by another, only slightly smaller.

The travelers stared up at the walls of the gorge, knowing that if further attack should come, they were powerless to avoid it.

But no more stones fell. After a long moment Shalkan walked forward, looking down at the stones with dissatisfaction.

"I believe that they are gone," Shalkan pronounced. "Having failed to topple us, they had no wish to encounter arrows, I suspect."

"They didn't originate from above," Jermayan said unemotionally, gazing down at the boulders. "Those are river stones—see how smooth? Not boulders from farther up the cliff. And soft enough—that's why the one broke when it landed. They were carried here from some distance away to be flung down at us."

"By who—and why?" Kellen asked.

"These and other eternally unanswerable questions . . ." Shalkan commented with a sigh, shaking his head with a rattle of his armored collar as if flies bedeviled him.

His friend was right, Kellen realized with dismay. They had no way of knowing who was trying to kill them—or why. There were too many possible answers. And what was more, there might be no more sinister reason to this attack except an attempt to kill them and steal what they owned. After staring at the stone for a few moments more, Kellen mounted up, and they reluctantly continued on.

Eventually their path led them out of the gorge into a region of windswept hills covered with sparse grass. What few trees grew here were low, twisted by the constantly blowing wind. In the distance, Kellen could see taller hills dark with trees, and beyond them, true mountains at last, bare rock, their peaks white with snow. Perhaps Shadow Mountain was among them. *I just hope we don't have to go all the way there to find the Barrier,* Kellen thought worriedly. Such a journey would take months—and Sentarshadeen needed rain soon, for the sake of the spring crops.

As he rode, he'd been continuing to think about all that Jermayan had told him the night before—about the War, and the reason Armethalieh had outlawed the Wild Magic, and the Demons. It made a certain amount of horrible sense, and it certainly didn't make him feel any better about his own emerging Wildmage—or Knight-Mage—powers. True, Jermayan had said that the Wildmages who *did* fall to the Demons did so because they wanted to get out of paying the price for their powers and spells . . . but that was a temptation every Wildmage faced every time he cast a spell. Hadn't Kellen himself worried about it when he'd done his Healing Spell for Jermayan? What if the Wild Magic had asked a price that had interfered with him going to trigger Idalia's spell at the Endarkened keystone (and it still could, he knew, because the voice he'd heard hadn't been very specific about what his payment would be) what then? If he refused to pay the price of his magic, was he on his way to being Demon-bait, even though he only refused because it would get in the way of him fighting the Demons and saving Sentarshadeen?

It was all very confusing. And the confusion didn't stop here. Even if he paid his Mageprice this time, it was a choice he was going to face every time he cast a spell for the rest of his life.

It was worse, in a way, than when his fears had just been based on a formless misconception that the Wild Magic might be evil in itself. Now he knew it wasn't. Now that Jermayan had told him about the Great War he knew exactly how a Wildmage got himself into trouble using the Wild Magic, and that was worse, because it wasn't something that you could make up your mind once and for all not to do. It was a decision you had to keep making, over and over.

What if you got tired? What if you got careless? What if you made a mistake?

How could anybody keep making the right choice, over and over and over again, when the choices kept getting harder and harder?

How could *he*?

"We should look for a place to stop and eat," Jermayan said, breaking into Kellen's thoughts. "Perhaps that grove up ahead."

To call it a grove was a serious overstatement, but at least the few scrubby trees would provide some shelter from the wind.

But when they neared it, a Centaur came charging toward them from among the trees, shouting angrily.

He had a thick grey beard, and was wearing a long rough coat of goatskins that draped over his dark bay flanks, the goat hair blending with his own shaggy uncurried coat. He carried an iron-shod crook as well. They couldn't make out his words, but the intent was plain.

"Fool of a shepherd!" Jermayan said angrily, reining in. "Does he think we're after his flock—wherever they are? Look here, fellow—"

Seeing them pause, the Centaur-shepherd stopped as well. He thrust two fingers into his mouth and whistled sharply.

"I don't think he likes your tone," Shalkan commented dryly.

Instantly half a dozen shaggy grey forms appeared out of the grass, loping toward the party purposefully. For an instant, Kellen thought they were wolves, then realized they were instead the largest dogs he'd ever seen—dogs that could easily kill wolves, should they happen to meet any.

"Come on," he said, urging Shalkan into a run. Jermayan followed—with some reluctance, Kellen thought.

Behind him Kellen heard the sound of the Centaur's laughter.

He'd thought that would be the end of it. That *should* have been the end of it: they'd intruded, they'd been driven off, the shepherd should have whistled his dogs back and that should have been that.

But it wasn't.

Shalkan turned and began to circle back, just in time for Kellen to see Jermayan slipping the mule's lead-rein free to give Valdien room to maneuver. She was running flat-out, but even her top speed wasn't as fast as Valdien's, and neither of them could match Shalkan's turn of speed. To Kellen's horror, he saw that the Centaur-shepherd's grey hounds were harrying her, snapping at Lily's flanks. One of them had already drawn blood.

"Hold on," Shalkan said.

He charged directly at the running hounds, head lowered. His horn slid into the nearest hound's shoulder, skewering the beast neatly. He tossed his head, flinging the beast away. It landed with a thud and a yelp, getting painfully to its feet and limping quickly away.

Jermayan and Valdien were sweeping through the rest of the hounds, Jermayan beating them away from the mule with the flat of his sword, Valdien encouraging them to flee with hooves and teeth. Though the hounds had obviously been trained to take down prey, equally obviously they weren't prepared to face this much resistance, and a few more well-placed blows from Jermayan's blade encouraged them to flee back to their master. The one that Shalkan had wounded limped along behind, bloody-flanked.

The moment the hounds broke off their attack, Kellen and Shalkan took off after the mule. Though terrified, Lily was already starting to slow her panicked headlong flight—mules, even Elven mules, were built for endurance, not speed—and Kellen and Shalkan were able to catch up with her easily. Actually catching her was another matter, and Kellen finally had to dismount and have Shalkan drive her toward him until he could grab hold of the trailing lead-rope. They were just lucky she hadn't gotten tangled in it and broken her leg.

She pulled a little against the rope, shaking. "Here now, girl. It's all right. It's all right, girl. You've had a rough day, haven't you, poor girl?" Kellen spoke soothingly, coiling the rope up in his gauntleted hand as he approached her, until she finally allowed him to lay a hand on her neck and stroke it comfortingly. She was trembling and covered in sweat, but she seemed to be all right. The bites on her haunches didn't go very deep—the hounds had been trying for the bite that hamstrings its prey and leaves it helpless, but fortunately hadn't been able to manage it. An application of allheal should see her right, but he wasn't sure that they dared stop for it now.

Jermayan rode up on Valdien, sheathing his sword.

"I should have shot the beast when I had the chance," Jermayan snarled, and Kellen somehow knew Jermayan didn't mean any of the hounds.

"He was only protecting his flock," Kellen answered, not sure the words were true even as he spoke them. He handed the mule's lead-rope up to Jermayan, who made it fast to Valdien's saddle once more.

"Was he? He had a very odd way of doing it, to be sure," the Elven Knight answered angrily. "Come to that, wolf-hounds such as those are more likely to savage a flock than to guard it; they are hunters, plain and simple. I wonder whether there was a flock at all, or whether he was set to watch for us, and lull us off our guard."

"By running out of cover and shouting at us?" Kellen asked doubtfully. Still, it was possible. The shepherd had been quick enough to set the dogs on them—and Jermayan was right—they looked nothing like the kind of flock guards Kellen had seen in Merryvale.

"Come on," Shalkan said pragmatically. "The sooner we go on, the sooner we can stop."

THEY moved on at the pace that the mule set, which was even slower than before; she was having trouble with the trail, and it was clear that her wounds were hurting her. The hill-tops were bare and rocky, and between them were narrow ravines filled with all manner of brambles. The trouble was, you had to go down one hill to get to the top of the next. At the bottom of one such gully they found a stream where they could pause to rest and eat and tend to the mule's injuries, but they didn't linger for very long. Where there had been one attack, there could be another, and all of them knew that whether their attackers were hill-bandits or agents of Shadow Mountain, if the attack succeeded, they would be just as dead.

They rode on, into a cold wind out of the north that howled among the peaks like a damned soul and ate away the faintest trace of warmth.

IT would be dark soon, and they'd reached an unspoken agreement that the next little valley, if it was at all suitable, would be where they would spend the night. Camping on one of the hilltops in the constant wind would be impossible—or miserable at the very least. At least down in the ravine they'd be out of the wind, and warmer.

But they'd barely dismounted when Valdien began behaving skittishly, fretting and shaking his head nervously.

"Trouble," Shalkan said briefly, his nostrils flaring. "I smell something—odd—"

Kellen drew his sword with a metallic grating sound. He cast his eyes to the left, the right. Down here out of the wind it was quiet, and hard to see much in the heavy undergrowth, but Kellen saw no sign of any trouble. He glanced at Jermayan. The Elven Knight had his bow ready, an arrow nocked, but from his puzzled expression, he saw as little reason for alarm as Kellen.

Even the mule had sensed something wrong now. She was grunting and pulling at her lead-rope, ears laid-back.

"Anything?" Jermayan asked tersely.

Kellen shook his head, and concentrated, trying to invoke the battle-trance. Even to Othersight, the ravine seemed deserted, nothing but shadows moving within the branches as the wind above in the tops of the hills stirred the withered leaves down below.

"I could try a spell . . ." he began, feeling as if he should be whispering.

Suddenly there was a crashing through the underbrush and a pale rush of movement. Before Kellen could react, Jermayan had drawn his bow and fired several arrows in an action too fast for Kellen to see.

There was an unearthly scream, and a crashing as something fell to earth and began to thrash wildly. Shalkan whirled, and charged, head down, his horn glinting wickedly. He plunged it into the creature, once; the beast convulsed, and was still.

By the time Kellen joined him, it was over, and the unicorn was shaking his head, flicking his horn clean.

"What *is* that?" Kellen asked, looking down at the body, still outstretched and twisted sideways in its final convulsion.

It was twice the size of the dogs that had attacked them earlier today. Kellen had seen lynxes in the public zoo in Armethalieh, but those were small animals, little bigger than a large house cat.

This was like a lynx grown to giant size. It had long dappled silvery fur, and jutting from its upper jaw, two enormous fangs as long as his hand.

"An ice-tiger," Jermayan said, kneeling beside the body to retrieve his arrows. "Odd that it should be here. They are creatures of the high hills and mountains, rarely venturing this far south."

"Especially this early in the year," Shalkan said, returning from cleaning his horn in the earth. "And *very* odd for it to be attacking us at all. Look at it, Jermayan. A healthy young male, no broken fangs, no injuries . . . it should be attacking its natural prey, not an oddly assorted group of travelers like us. They don't *like* to be anywhere within leagues of humans or Elves or Centaurs either; they're terribly shy."

"Another thing that isn't where it's supposed to be," Kellen said grimly. "But is it just an accident . . . or is this another trap?"

"Were any of them traps?" Shalkan asked simply. "Or were they all just the sort of misfortunes that would have happened to any traveler that passed this way?"

"Either way, we'd better move on," Jermayan said tiredly, getting to his feet. "Where there was one, there may be more."

THEY made an unsatisfactory camp in one of the hilltop groves, keeping a sharp eye out for more rogue shepherds— or anything else. At this point, Kellen didn't trust anything, not a starling, not even a mouse. Before the light failed entirely, there was time for a few minutes of sparring practice with Jermayan, and Kellen was relieved to find that it was still as easy for him as it had been before the battle.

That night Jermayan began drilling him in the rudiments of shield-fighting—how to draw an attacker's blows to your shield, how to fight using your sword one-handed for greater reach. But there was not time for much of that before it was too dark to see, and neither wished to risk a misstep or a foul blow in the dark.

In the morning, they struck camp and moved on quickly, none of them willing to linger in such inhospitable territory. By early afternoon they were crossing terrain that was dangerous enough in its own right, without the help of brigands, bandits, or questionable shepherds.

They weren't trekking now so much as mountain-climbing, their progress slowed to the slowest walking pace by the need to test every foothold before proceeding along slanting, tilting, nearly invisible trails. Shalkan led—the unicorn was as surefooted as a goat—with Kellen clutching the saddle tightly and trying not to look down.

To Kellen's surprise, for all his size, Valdien was nearly as nimble as Shalkan, the Elven destrier able to follow any path Shalkan chose. The mule scrambled along behind, patient and uncomplaining—or perhaps, now that it had escaped the fangs of wolfhound and ice-tiger, desperate to remain with its "herd" and the protection of the two Knights.

"Once these hills were lush with forests," Jermayan said when they stopped to rest. "Sweet-smelling cedars as far as the eye could see, and flowering *alyon*, and fragrant *vilya*. In my grandsire's time, we built ships from the trees that grew here in the Forest of Tilinaparanwira to sail the oceans of the world. Our home was here in these forests, and in the mountains beyond as well. In those days, we thought ourselves masters of all." Jermayan sighed, as if the ancient memory pained him.

Kellen looked around. It was hard to imagine anything at all growing here, let alone trees tall enough to provide the masts for an ocean-going ship.

He glanced at Jermayan. The Elven Knight was smiling ruefully, seeing the expression of skepticism on Kellen's face.

"But my grandsire lived a very long time ago, as the Children of Men reckon time—just as the Great War itself was so long ago that you have schooled yourselves to forget it. We ride now across the lands where many of the battles of that war were fought—and because of that, for tens of your generations, no blade of grass grew from this tainted earth, no bird flew through these accursed skies. Have you never wondered why the holdings of the Children of Men are so few in this land, yet your cities are armed and walled for war? Though you have purged the very hint of it from your histories, there is a reason for those walls, a reason why Men are so few when they breed so rapidly." He closed his eyes for a moment, as if weary. "But now Life returns. I wonder— is it that which has roused Life's old enemy from its slumber?"

There was no answer he could make to that, and Kellen didn't even try. They rode on, with Kellen trying to imagine what this place might have looked like when it was as lush as the Flower Forest around Sentarshadeen must have been before the drought. Jermayan had said the Great Alliance had paid a terrible price for their victory; looking around at a landscape so scoured that grass barely grew here now, Kellen as only now beginning to imagine what it must have been ke.

"Look there," Jermayan said a few moments later, pointing f to the left.

Kellen looked. Halfway down the slope—probably a cou- e of miles away; distances could be deceiving here—he saw a odd row of tall narrow boulders standing in a line on what oked like a gentle sloping plain. Kellen knew from his ex- erience today that that sort of terrain was particularly treach- ous. Either it was gravel over rock, and just as slippery as led glass as a result, or it was a thin layer of topsoil over ranite, which meant that the footing would hold just long ough to give you a false sense of security before giving ay and sending you tumbling to the bottom of the slope.

He took a closer look at the boulders, since they seemed be what Jermayan was pointing at. They didn't look like e rest of the stone around here, which was mostly pale grey ranite. The boulders were black, and looked as if they were ade of something else. He couldn't tell what, though, and ad no particular desire to investigate more closely, having ent most of the morning getting up an incline that looked retty similar to that one.

"That is Ulanya, where the last of the Dark-corrupted drag- ns fell with his Mage. It is said the dragon's bones endure this day. As you see."

"Huh," Kellen said, shaking his head as they rode on. If ose boulders were dragon-bones, Kellen revised his desire see a living dragon. Judging from the size of them—if ey really were dragon-bones, and not just funny-looking)cks—a full-sized dragon must be larger than the Council Iouse where the High Mages met. No wonder both sides in e war had wanted to get their hands on them!

And on the Wildmages who controlled them.

Once again unwelcome worries intruded into Kellen's nind. Why hadn't Idalia told him about the Great War, and e dragons, and why the City had outlawed the Wild Magic nd invented the High Magick to take its place? Why hadn't he explained to him what he was going to be facing? She'd

told him everything else—except the most important thing,
that he was riding off to face an ancient enemy that had a l
of experience in corrupting Wildmages and turning them
its own purposes.

Had she thought ignorance would protect him? Had sh
thought Jermayan wouldn't tell him the truth? Maybe h
wouldn't have, if Kellen hadn't turned out to be a Knigh
Mage. Maybe she'd kept it from him for his own protection
Maybe the fact that Kellen now knew the truth was going
make things go wrong somehow.

Or maybe she counted on Jermayan to tell me the truth
counted on me being brave enough to face it. She had p
plenty of challenges in his path before, and reckoned on h
being able to meet them.

But she could so easily be wrong. She didn't know him
Not really. She didn't know how often he failed or messe
things up.

He couldn't afford to worry about things like this—it wa
too late to change things, and he couldn't unlearn what h
knew—but somehow he couldn't stop himself from con
stantly poking at the problem, as if it were a sore tooth. Th
whole thing was just too big and too complicated, mad
worse by the fact that the more he learned about the Demons
the more formidable an enemy they seemed to be. No matte
how much confidence Jermayan seemed to have in Kellen'
emerging powers as a Knight-Mage and Wildmage, *Kelle*
didn't have the same confidence, not down where it counted
He knew how many mistakes he'd already made in seventee
short years of life, and now, with so many lives resting o
him making all the right choices, he didn't feel any smarte
than he had when his choices didn't matter to anybody bu
him. He'd already almost gotten Jermayan killed once.

All it took was one wrong move.

Just one.

THOUGH Jermayan had been reluctant to talk abou
Shadow Mountain and the Great War initially, as they rod

that day through lands he could have never seen—for Kellen now knew that Jermayan, old as he was from Kellen's standpoint, had been born centuries after the War was over—the Elven Knight spoke of those ancient events as if he had indeed been present at that last great battle between the forces of Life and those of Darkness.

So vivid were his descriptions as he pointed out the landmarks of the conflict that had shaped Kellen's world that it almost began to seem to Kellen as well that he could see the armies marshaled upon the battlefield: humans, Elves, and Centaurs in their gleaming armor, the swift and terrible unicorn cavalry, their bright horns flashing in the sunlight. Overhead, dragons wheeled and soared in the sky, their scales glittering radiantly—red and green, gold and blue and black—and the air seethed with elemental forces, as sylphs and salamanders awaited the bidding of their comrades and allies.

And arrayed against them, the terrible forces of the Endarkened and their slaves: the Darkmages, the *duergar* and goblins and trolls, protected from the sunlight fatal to their kind by the magic of the Endarkened—a protection that might be withdrawn at any moment, should the Endarkened need their power for other things.

"Across that valley—there—in the distance—is a place once called The Field of Sorrows. I do not know if it has a name now. There, the army of Countess Karissa of Avoret was utterly destroyed." Jermayan's eyes were shadowed with sorrow, as if the tragedy had taken place a decade ago, instead of millennia. "Ten thousand warriors, the flower of human pride and knighthood, were gathered there to do battle, and not one of them escaped alive. It was the first great human loss of the War . . . you had underestimated the barbarity of the enemy you faced until then, I think, and thought they would fight by the civilized code of human men. But they gave no quarter, slaughtering the wounded, those who had surrendered, the servants and children who rode with the army . . . all. Not even the supply oxen were left alive, and when our army arrived, too late to aid you, the battlefield was lake of blood too vast to sink into the earth."

Kellen blinked, trying to picture it and failing utterly. It was just too horrible to get his mind wrapped around. And *this* was the enemy they would have to confront!

"When the Count came and saw the place where his daughter had died, he swore that he would not rest until the power of the Endarkened was broken forever and the treachery that had slain his daughter was avenged; that if he must defy Death himself to allow this to come to pass, he would find a way. He was a great Wildmage; how his story ends, the histories do not say, but it was through his tireless efforts that the human kingdoms fought at our side staunchly through all the dark days of the War, though the Endarkened tried constantly to make a separate treaty of peace with you. They would willingly have promised you anything to withdraw from battle, knowing that they would turn on you later once they had achieved victory over us."

How many humans failed to listen to the Count, Kellen wondered. How many thought that a separate peace could be achieved, and been betrayed? There must have been some, or the rest would never have known that Demonic promises were lies.

"But here is a happier tale, if any story from those days can be said to be a happy one," Jermayan went on, pointing into the far distance. "See there, that mountain pass?"

Kellen strained his vision—he suspected Elven eyesight was better than human—and in the distance he could just barely make out a notch between two mountains that might be the pass Jermayan spoke of.

"That is Vel-al-Amion, where The Seven held back the entire army of the Endarkened for three days, until Cirandeiron Istemion and King Damek could arrive. Their names have been lost to history, and so they would have wished it to be, remembered only as The Seven, comrades in life and death, who did what could not be done, and so saved us all."

"How could you forget them if they were Elves?" Kellen asked, since if he'd learned one thing in his time in Sentarshadeen, it was that Elves had very long memories, and kept

xcruciatingly accurate records of their families and geneal-
gies.

"The Seven were not Elves, not all of them," Jermayan
orrected him crisply. "They were of all the races that fought
gainst the Endarkened. And they were not warriors at all,
ut scouts, sent out to patrol in advance of the army to learn
he disposition of enemy forces and to report back."

*Not warriors? Then how could they ever have held against
host of Demons?*

"But this time, knowing what they knew, seeing what they
ad seen, they dared not. They knew the Endarkened host
nust come through Vel-al-Amion, and so they retreated to
hat pass, sending messages to their commanders, messages
hat they could only hope would reach them, knowing they
vould never know if word had gotten through in time. And
vhen all the hosts of Darkness and foul magic descended
ipon Vel-al-Amion, the Demon army found its way barred
>y seven scouts who would not yield the pass."

Kellen found himself profoundly stirred by this tale. Only
couts! Yet they had done what needed to be done, against
ar longer odds than those he and Jermayan faced, against the
Endarkened in all their strength, not the weakened creatures
iiding in Shadow Mountain. If *they* could do it . . .

"No one knows what happened there, though there are
nany ballads of their bravery. I believe that when the En-
larkened saw The Seven could not be easily brushed aside,
hey tried to tempt The Seven to join their own forces, for
hat is ever the way of Demons."

Suddenly Kellen could picture it in his mind, the vast host
>ehind the leaders, the Endarkened leaders offering—what?
t would have had to be more than just their lives. It would
iave to be everything all of them had ever wanted: love,
>ower, riches, fame, *everything* . . .

"But that, too, will have failed," Jermayan said, his voice
illed with awe, "and then, surely, the wrath of the Endar-
:ened commander must have been overweening. Yet The
ieven held Vel-al-Amion, and the Endarkened army could
iot advance through it while their way was barred."

"But how?" Kellen asked wonderingly. "If they were jus scouts, how could they have held?"

"There is much we will never know," Jermayan admitted simply. "It was a miracle, and The Seven gave their lives i payment to the Gods that had answered their prayers for tha miracle. What is certain is that reinforcements arrived in time to catch the Endarkened army while it was bottled up in the pass. 'Then blew the silver horns of the army of Cirandeiro Istemion, then roared the mighty drums of King Damek; bra zen and argent marched the human and Elven armies across the bridge of their hallowed dead to engage the foe . . .' or so the bards would have it. The Allied armies hurt the enemy badly enough to force them to retreat, and the War went on The bodies of The Seven were never recovered. Yet if they had not held the pass long enough for the Allies to get there . . ." Jermayan shrugged eloquently, and said nothing more.

But Kellen thought about that story long and hard as they rode, and he wondered—if it had been him, would *he* have had the courage to stand?

⌒

THEY made an early camp, unwilling to push the tired an imals any farther over such difficult terrain. There was no possibility of finding any place that was sheltered, but at least they'd found someplace flat, a stony hilltop with a spectacular view of the barren sweep of parched hills and the mountains beyond. If they could not be comfortable, Kellen consoled himself, at least no one could possibly sneak up on them.

Not for the first time today, Kellen wondered if they'd overshot the mark or taken a wrong turn. He soothed his apprehension with the promise that he'd do a Finding Spell in the morning before they set off. That would quickly set them on the right path again. True, Idalia had warned him against that sort of thing except in a dire emergency, but—

—but by now their presence here in the Lost Lands couldn't be a secret anymore.

He'd done pretty major Healing Magic on Jermayan, and ven though he'd done it within the protection of his circle, ome of the power had to have leaked out. And he *knew*, eep down inside, that at least one of the attacks on them ad come from the hands, if not of the Endarkened them-elves, at least from their creatures. And since they'd be mov-ig immediately, it wouldn't draw the enemy to their osition.

But the moment he made the decision, doubt set in. What rice would the Finding Spell exact? What if paying it ran ounter to his current mission? What if it was something he ouldn't—or didn't want to—do?

What if it was the first in the series of mistakes that would et him on the path to becoming a Darkmage? What if it onflicted with the price he had yet to pay for Jermayan's ealing? Every time he thought of doing magic, things just ot more complicated! No wonder the ancient Mages had ome up with High Magick, which—

Which has its own prices, and is paid for with stolen en-rgy.

So that wasn't an answer, either.

He performed his part of the chores of setting up camp in haze compounded of equal parts of exhaustion and preoc-upation. Jermayan helped him dig out and collect several nelon-sized stones to build a fire-ring, both to protect their ire and to conserve its heat.

"No practice tonight, I think. We're both tired. And I think ou'll know what to do when the time comes."

The Elven-Knight's words were an unintentional echo of he message Kellen had received from the Wild Magic during he last spell he'd cast, the message he still didn't understand. Remembering that unfulfilled obligation only worried him nore. What would the true cost of Jermayan's healing end p being? Would it turn out in the end to have been better or Sentarshadeen if Kellen had let Jermayan die? But how ould he ever have faced them—Idalia—Shalkan—himself— f he had?

"Ah—all right, if you think that's best," Kellen muttered.

"I think I'm going to take a look around. Stretch my legs while there's still light."

"Be careful," Jermayan warned, but Kellen could tell from his tone that the Elven Knight wasn't really worried. Nothing could approach them unseen up here.

Kellen changed out of his armor into the spare set of clothes and boots he'd brought. Wrapping his cloak tightly around him and belting on his sword—an act that seemed like second nature to him by now—he walked off.

He didn't plan to go far—not even out of sight of the camp—but he'd been telling the truth about wanting to stretch his legs. Spending a day on horseback—or on unicorn-back—was still a kind of sitting, and not the restful kind, either. His legs ached with something that was not quite a cramp, and felt restless, as if they would twitch nervously if he didn't given them the exercise they craved. Strange, how you could be so *tired* and yet parts of you still needed more activity to settle down. . . .

The hilltop was covered with the same sort of dry scanty grass that they'd seen elsewhere; both Valdien and the mule were grazing meditatively. In places the granite beneath showed through, and if that weren't enough, there were occasional horse-sized (and larger) boulders strewn about, as if someone had been using the hilltop for a target a long time ago.

Considering what Jermayan had told him about what sort of thing had gone on around here, maybe someone had. This would be a natural place to make a stand.

He was keeping one eye on the camp, intending to walk a wide circle around it, when he saw the stele.

At first he thought it was just another boulder, albeit a tall and narrow one. Perhaps snow and rain had sheered part of it away, giving it that tall and narrow shape.

But no. When he got closer, he realized that it had been carved into that shape deliberately, and centuries of wind and weather had softened its shape until it looked like one of the natural boulders.

He came closer. There was writing on it—at least, he

thought it must be writing, though the even rows of symbols were wholly unfamiliar.

There was one thing about the stele that was all-too understandable, however, though seeing it came as a complete and utter shock. Carved near the bottom was the glowering, horned, and fanged countenance of a Demon.

"Jermayan!"

Kellen's shout brought the Elven Knight at a run, sword drawn, with Shalkan close behind. Kellen pointed; he was very proud when his hand didn't shake.

Too much.

"Ah." The confusion and alarm eased from Jermayan's face. He peered at the inscription on the stone. "It is a marker, commemorating a great battle fought here, of an Allied triumph over the Demons."

Kellen stared around. Suddenly the empty hilltop seemed somehow populated, as if the armies that had once engaged here had not left.

Maybe they haven't. If any place should be haunted, it ought to be a place like this one.

"Of course, in those days this place had a different aspect," Jermayan reminded him, as if guessing the direction of Kellen's thoughts. "But come. We will eat, and consider what route we may take on the morrow."

Jermayan turned and walked away. Kellen gazed after him. Jermayan seemed awfully *calm* about standing in the middle of an ancient battlefield, a place where Demons had actually set foot. He glanced at Shalkan, but for once the unicorn's expression was unreadable.

Grand. Making camp among the ghosts. I hope at least some of them are friendly.

"I guess we'd better go back," Kellen muttered. He cast a last look at the stele, and followed Jermayan.

Though there was not to be a sparring match that evening, that didn't save Kellen from a long lecture on the theory of combat, which was, in its way, just as helpful as actual physical practice. There was more to battle than hitting the enemy with a sword, he was coming to discover, just as there was more to magic than casting the most powerful spell you could manage. Just as knowing what spell would produce the best result with the least expenditure of personal power was important for a Wildmage, so, for a Knight (or a Knight-Mage), was being able to make your foe do what you wanted—flee or die—with the least risk to yourself and your allies.

"Glory and honor are important," Jermayan said sternly, "but they are not the most important things in the life of a knight. He must always keep his ultimate goal in his mind, and be prepared to sacrifice all other things to that goal. Perhaps even his honor, should such a choice be forced upon him."

Kellen nodded, but he knew his own choices weren't so simple. A Wildmage's personal honor involved always paying the price of his magic, no matter what that price might be. And to refuse to pay that price, as he had learned from Jermayan, would lead a Wildmage down the path of corruption, and into the service of the Demons of Shadow Mountain.

Kellen had the horrible suspicion that what that meant was that eventually a Wildmage would inevitably be called upon to betray one loyalty for another, and he didn't like that thought very much at all. Betray a friend who trusted you for the greater good? Betray a trust to keep a greater one? Betray a secret to save another? But try as he might, he couldn't see any way around it . . . if the need to do so ever came up.

Maybe it wouldn't.

He hoped it wouldn't.

How could he do that and ever feel *clean* again?

But the unpaid price of Jermayan's healing hung over his head, like a sharp sword suspended by the thinnest of threads, and all Kellen could do was worry about a potential disaster he could see no way to avert.

How did Idalia live with this sort of thing hanging over her all the time? How did other Wildmages?

How would he? Or would trying to resolve all the conflicts someday drive him mad?

Eventually their small fire burned low, and it was time for

sleep. Despite the whirl of worries and fears chasing each other around and around inside his head, when Kellen laid himself down, weariness had its own way with him.

Will-he, nill-he, he slept.

Chapter Twenty-two

Visions of the Past

He was awakened by the ring of swords against armor. Kellen threw himself out of his bedroll, staring around himself wildly. Beside the fire, Valdien and Jermayan still slept, undisturbed. Even Shalkan dozed unconcernedly.

"Kellen! They're breaking through!"

Someone was shouting his name. But even as Kellen looked in the direction of the call, he realized it was not him they were summoning. Or at least not the Kellen of here-and-now.

He saw with the strange doubling of Othersight, but instead of single objects, or a simple overlay of lines and symbols, as it usually was, this time it was as if he saw into a whole other world. All around him an army was gathered, beautiful and terrifying, and as in a dream, somehow the moment he saw a thing, he understood everything about it, as if he were seeing it and reading about it in a book at the same time. Part of him knew he hadn't moved at all, that he still lay asleep in his blankets, and did not stand upon the hillside, gazing into the sun.

There was a booming sound in the sky, as loud as a sudden crack of thunder, and when Kellen looked up, he saw that one of the dragons had launched itself into the sky.

Dragons?

He'd wanted to see a dragon. Now he had that wish.

It bore as much resemblance to the lizards of the forest as

Shalkan did to a horse, and as little. Long sinuous neck, tail twice the length of its body, ending in a broad flat barb to help it to steer in the currents of the upper air.

As he watched, its spread wings caught and held the light, glowing like colored glass, for somehow Kellen was aware that even though it was still night where his body truly was, what he was seeing was taking place in the day. The plates of its underbelly—all he could see at this angle, as it caught an updraft and began circling higher—glowed like burnished metal.

And on its back rode the other-Kellen, the one to whom the summons had gone.

All around him the tide of battle surged. Though a part of his mind knew that this was dream or vision, nothing that could touch him now, it was so real that it was easy to forget and be swept up in the urgency that surrounded him, the screams and cries of embattled men and creatures.

All thought of Reality faded away as he looked around himself for familiar forms—for humans, Elves, unicorns—and saw none. To his left, a phalanx of towering figures in faceless red armor, twice as tall as a man, waded slowly into battle, swinging thick black clubs slowly before them and chanting rhythmically in deep rumbling voices. On his right, he heard a rumble of hooves, and turned to see a horde of bizarre cavalry rush forward, overtaking the giants. The animals were ponylike, but squatter and stockier, with cloven hooves, yellow eyes, and hairless skin and tails. They snapped and squealed at one another as they ran, like pigs or rats.

Their riders matched their mounts in a chilling way; just as stomach-churning, as bestial, and as terrifying. They were the size of children, but their bodies were thick and apelike with muscle, and their skins were the dark purple-grey of an old bruise. Protruding yellow teeth, like a forest boar's, deformed their mouths, giving their faces a brutish aspect, and their fingers ended in long hooked claws like a badger's. They were dressed in rough animal skins, with what looked like animal bones braided into their coarse black hair, and they howled maniacally as they rode. Each carried an iron hammer and a long hooked knife thrust through his belt, the weapons dark with old blood.

Were *these* the Allies of whom Jermayan had spoken so proudly? Kellen wondered in horror. He looked behind them, to where their General stood before his bright silken tent, its banners flowing proudly against the sky.

Saw the glorious ornamented armor—

Saw the wings—

And realized, with a disappointment too deep for despair, that the Kellen who fought here today, the Kellen who rode his dragon high above the battle, the dragonrider who shared his name . . .

Fought at the side of the Endarkened.

But he lost. Jermayan said they lost! Kellen told himself desperately.

Across the field, another dragon, then another, launched into the sky.

Fervently, Kellen urged himself to wake up. He didn't want to see any more. But all he seemed to be able to do was move himself from the hilltop—for so it had been, a thousand years ago—down onto the plain of battle itself.

It was horrible.

Here humans and Elves—and other creatures for whom he had no name—fought and bled and died. It was his own battle with the hill-bandits, magnified a thousand, a million times. He couldn't imagine how anyone could plan something like this—or direct it—or be willing to go through it twice. He stood it for only a moment before he began to run. He didn't care what this was—dream, nightmare, vision—he couldn't stand it. If he couldn't wake up, he had to get away.

Above him, the two dragons wheeled and screamed, attacking the third that the other-Kellen rode. Their wings cast flashes of blinding light down onto the battlefield, as though someone overhead were holding a giant reflecting mirror over an anthill.

Suddenly, there was a great ripple of magic across the field, and the light became brighter. With the sudden intuition of dreams, Kellen realized that up until now both armies had been fighting in a sort of spell-cast gloom that the Allied Wildmages had been able to break. He stopped and looked back.

The Endarkened forces were burning.

Not all of them, but enough. The horrible dwarves on their misshapen ponies had burst into flame and were running in circles, screaming, to be easily slain by the nearest Elf or human. The giants had stopped where they stood, toppling to the ground like disenchanted stone golems. Elsewhere on the field, other smoky pillars of flame indicated that there were other creatures of the Endarkened's forces that could not bear the touch of true sunlight either—and whose end was far more spectacular. As Kellen stared, sickened and fascinated, the Allied army began to surge forward, across the battlefield toward the enemy position, regrouping and slaughtering as it went.

It was a great victory.

It was sickening.

It was too much.

"No! Make it stop! No! No—"

"Kellen!"

⌐

HE awoke—for real, this time—to find Jermayan shaking him, a hand over his mouth to muffle his shouts, and Shalkan standing over him anxiously.

"Are you all right?" Jermayan said when he was sure Kellen was really awake.

"I . . . sure. It was just a bad dream," Kellen said, sitting up. But the details of the dream didn't fade, the way dreams did with waking. If anything, they seemed to become clearer, sharper, as if they were an old memory that had just been waiting to be summoned to life.

Had that been him—some ancient version of him? Or had the coincidence of names been no more than that—a coincidence? Lycaelon had always taken pains to remind him that he'd been named for a revered ancestor, that generations of Kellen Tavadons had upheld the honor and traditions of House Tavadon in Armethalieh. He wondered how proud his father would be of the name if he knew . . .

"It must have been some dream," Shalkan commented sourly.

Kellen looked around. It was still full dark, sometime after moonset but long before dawn. Jermayan had lit the lantern, and was making up the fire to brew tea, the Elven panacea for all ills.

"It was," Kellen said in a low voice. He hesitated, not wanting to make things more real by speaking about them. But hadn't keeping secrets caused enough trouble already?

Enough of secrets. If there is something wrong with me, I want Jermayan to know about it, before—

Before it was too late? But what if it already was too late?

But perhaps it wasn't. All he could do was to tell the dream, and let events play out as they would. "I dreamed about the battle . . . the one Jermayan said was fought here. I don't know if it was real, or just my imagination, but . . ." He stopped, reliving the horror of the moment when he realized that the other-Kellen was fighting for the enemy, had actually embraced the fate that Kellen himself feared so greatly.

"Probably a little of both," Shalkan said. "You'd have to be blind *and* deaf not to feel a little of what happened here, but we didn't have a lot of choice about where to stop, really. So what did you see?"

"Monsters," Kellen said bitterly. "Monsters, and dragons . . . they always talk about war like it's such a grand adventure, but if real battles are anything like what I saw, why would anybody ever do that twice?"

"Because the alternative to fighting is worse," the unicorn said somberly. "Or people think it is. And in this case, we know it was. But that isn't what's bothering you, is it?"

"No." Kellen glanced past Shalkan's shoulder. Jermayan was staying politely on the other side of the campfire, keeping busy with the tea-things and pretending not to hear, but Kellen already knew that he wasn't out of earshot. Never mind. At the moment, he valued even the illusion of privacy for what he had to say.

"There was someone there. A Wildmage, I guess—an evil one. With my name. I didn't see him clearly. He had a dragon. And he was fighting for the Endarkened." The words came quick and harsh, and having said them, Kellen felt better and worse, as if he'd managed to gag up a meal of bad meat.

"That's bad," Shalkan agreed, lowering his head to rub his cheek against Kellen's in a quick caress. "But it could be nothing more than your own fears talking, you know."

"I know," Kellen said, trying to convince himself.

"No one knows the names of all the Mages who were corrupted," Jermayan said, coming to kneel beside Kellen and place a cup of tea in his hand. "When we return, I can go to the Hall of Memory and discover what I can, if you wish. But no matter what I find: that man is not you. That you share a name, even a lineage, means nothing. A man is not his bloodline; a man is what he *is*."

"I know," Kellen said miserably. He lifted the cup to his lips and drank, savoring the heat and the unfamiliar spicy flavor. They might be forced to exist on Elven trail-rations, but Jermayan had still packed a dozen different kinds of tea, suitable for every occasion. And the "small magics" of the Elves ensured you could get a hot cup of tea on short notice, even in the middle of the night in the middle of nowhere.

"It just . . . I know it probably didn't even happen, and if it did, it's just some kind of coincidence. But I feel . . . betrayed. It's stupid, but there just isn't any other way to describe it," Kellen said.

"Yes," Jermayan said softly. "And so were the great dragons of the earth betrayed in those days, who bound their immortality to a span of mortal years in a bond of love and more than love such as even we Elves can only dimly guess at, and found that love profaned in unimaginable ways when their Wildmage mates were corrupted by the blandishments of the Endarkened. It was in many ways the worst of all of the betrayals of the War, for the dragons could do nothing but what their mates willed, and so they found themselves fighting friends, battling their own kindred, and could not stop themselves, though their great hearts were breaking. Perhaps it is that sorrow you sense here, Kellen."

"This just gets better, doesn't it?" Kellen said bitterly. It wasn't bad enough that Darkmages were creatures of cruelty and evil—no, they had to ruin the lives of creatures who had even given up *immortality* for them. He took a deep breath and sighed. "Look. It won't be dawn for hours yet, and I don't think I'm going to be able to sleep, but why don't you at least try to? No sense in everybody sitting up just because I'm seeing ghosts."

"Fair words, Wildmage," Jermayan said gravely.

Kellen had thought Jermayan might argue with him, but apparently Jermayan did him the courtesy of assuming he knew what he was talking about. Without further discussion, the Elven Knight took the empty cup back from Kellen and banked the fire again before returning to his bedroll.

Kellen pulled his blankets up around his shoulders more firmly. It was cold out here.

"You can use me for a backrest," Shalkan invited, kneeling down behind him. "Warmer that way."

"Thanks," Kellen said, leaning back cautiously into the unicorn's muscular softness. Soon the small camp was utterly still once more, save for the blowing of the wind and the faint rustling of the grass. The stars were very bright overhead.

He'd wondered if Jermayan might have put sleeping herbs into his tea, but apparently the Elven Knight trusted him to make his own decisions and take their consequences, for Kellen remained wide awake. The memory of the dreamlandscape overlaid the real one he now saw—a thousand years ago the land here had been more even. Forested, as Jermayan had said. Now the terrain was all blasted away to almost bare rock, the gentle slopes he remembered from the dream entirely gone.

And it really didn't matter *whose* magic had done it, Allied or Endarkened, because the end result was the same. What used to be the Forest of Tilinaparanwira was a wasteland, and even another thousand years wouldn't be enough time to make it the way it had been before the Great War. All the survivors of that war could try to do was hold on to what they had left, because even as hard as they'd fought, they hadn't fought hard enough to defeat their enemy once and for all. Shadow Mountain had survived, and the Endarkened were ready to go to war again.

And if there was another war, no matter who won it, would there be anything left at all this time?

If? In the cold hour before dawn, Kellen had the depressing certainty that it wasn't an *if*. It was a *when*. And that *when* wasn't far off.

Chapter Twenty-three

Allies and Enemies

He dozed off finally just as the sky was beginning to lighten, to be awakened as Shalkan moved out from under him.

"Rise and shine," the unicorn said, looking down at him. "It's the start of a beautiful new day."

"I'll rise," muttered Kellen, rolling over on his stomach and hugging the blankets to him, "but I refuse to shine."

And in fact the day was hardly beautiful. Though the night had been clear and icy cold, clouds had rolled in toward morning, and the day had dawned—if you could call it that—cold, grey, damp, and overcast. Kellen gave thanks for the thousandth time that Elven armor didn't rust, but there was no power on earth that could make it warm and inviting on a day like this. Even a mug of hot tea and a bowl of soup did little to cut the biting chill.

He'd been going to do a Finding Spell to seek their path this morning, but after his experiences of the night before, Kellen hesitated to work any magic, still feeling off-balance and out of sorts. If they didn't find any clear sign that they were on the right road by the time they stopped for their midday rest, he'd do one then, but he hoped he wouldn't have to. The thought of the mounting cycle of debt and obligation that was a necessary part of a Wildmage's life still bothered him. In the normal course of things, he wouldn't mind—or not much—but right now, when any Mageprice might take him away from the vitally necessary task of placing the keystone at the Barrier, Kellen grudged any spell he needed to work, for fear its obligation would lead him astray.

You'll know what to do when the time comes. . . . All very well when you were not surrounded by enemies, with Demons sniffing for you, when you were in, say, Merryvale or the Wildwood and the most dangerous creature in the forest was Cormo. And it was easy enough to try and tell himself that since the Wild Magic "wanted" the Barrier broken, it *wouldn't* put an obligation on him that interfered with that.

Easy to tell himself that, but hard to convince himself. It was a matter of faith, he supposed, and he just didn't have a lot of faith in anything or anyone, when it came right down to it.

Not even in himself.

And the consequences of refusing to pay for his magic were not to be considered. . . .

⌐

IT was a relief, coming down off the hillside, to strike a real road at last. It wasn't what Kellen would have considered a road at the start of their journey, but after so long traveling through the Lost Lands, even this narrow beaten track—obviously going from Somewhere to Somewhere, and frequently used by someone—was a welcome change, providing sure footing for horse and mule. The only thing that marred Kellen's relief was that he still hadn't seen any more clear

signs of Endarkened Taint in their surroundings—although
that wasn't altogether surprising, since there wasn't much
around them to see besides rocks and a little sparse grass. It
was hard for either grass or rocks to go awry in any noticeable way. How warped would grass have to get before he'd
notice the Taint?

I suppose it would have to be purple, or something.

There hadn't even been birds in the sky.

Up ahead the trail forked. One branch led down, into a
broad valley, while the other curved off and away around the
side of a rocky hillside. Either could have been the right road.

But there was a third path, almost invisible, a narrow goat
track leading up over the crest of the hill at right angles to
their present course.

You will know what to do when the time comes.

Certainty descended over Kellen like an invisible cloak.
This was the moment the Wild Magic had prepared him for.
Now was the time to pay his Price.

"Which way?" Jermayan said, reining Valdien to a stop.

"This way," Kellen said, pointing toward the hill.

"Don't be ridiculous," Jermayan scoffed. "It goes almost
straight up—and probably back the way we came, besides.
The animals will never make it, and—Kellen! Come back
here!"

But Kellen wasn't listening. *There. There! Something—
someone—needs me. Is in trouble!* He couldn't have turned
aside from the path now if he'd wanted to. And he didn't
want to. "Come on," he said to Shalkan. "We've got to
hurry."

He didn't know where the sudden sense of urgency came
from, but the unicorn accepted it without question. Shalkan
bounded up the goat track and lunged along it, as surefooted
as the goats it was meant for. Kellen clung to the saddle,
ignoring Jermayan's frustrated shouting somewhere behind
him.

They reached the top of the hill, and Shalkan broke into a
bounding run. Kellen didn't know where they were going,

but the demand of his obligation drew him onward, and he followed it without hesitation.

In the valley ahead, there was actually some healthy-looking vegetation, trees, a stream—not lush, by any standards, but far more livable than the country they'd been passing through. Shalkan bounded over the stream, and headed up the hillside, following that goat track around the curve of the hill, and a small stone hut appeared up ahead, just under the crest of the hill, on the lee side—a shepherd's croft, undoubtedly, the sort of crude construction of stone, mud, and thatch that the natives of the Lost Lands might build.

It was the first he'd seen—after their encounter with the Centaur-shepherd, he and Jermayan had steered well clear of any possible locals—but it didn't take any great act of imagination to figure out what the hut represented, and what sort of inhabitant it had, especially with the small herd of agitated goats milling and bleating in the stone pen beside the door. The only question was, why had the magic drawn him here?

Who was it that was in trouble?

Shalkan slowed from his bounding gallop to a fast trot as they drew closer, caution overtaking urgency.

Then, shattering the silence, ringing out across the valley, came screams. A woman's screams, coming from inside the hut.

Kellen didn't have to think twice. He kicked free of the stirrups and vaulted from Shalkan's back, running toward the door of the hut.

The hut was small and dark, but enough light came in through the tiny windows to allow Kellen to see that someone large had someone else—the woman who had screamed, almost certainly—trapped in a corner of the hut, savagely beating her with a short club. That was enough for him. He crammed himself inside—there wasn't a lot of room, and three people seriously crowded the tiny hut—and grabbed the man's arm before he could land another blow.

If the shepherd was surprised to have his beating interrupted by a knight in full armor, he wasn't surprised enough to keep from attacking Kellen. He swung his club savagely at Kellen's head, and only Kellen's helmet saved him from a nasty concussion. The club was thick wood, wrapped in bands of black lead. It was a deadly weapon, meant for killing, and the blow rattled Kellen's teeth and left his ears ringing.

There wasn't enough room here for Kellen to draw or use his sword, but he had his fists, and his armored gauntlets, and plenty of muscles from Jermayan's sword-training and his time in the Wildwood. And he'd taken—and given—enough beatings growing up back in the City to know what to do in a fight.

But this wasn't the place to try.

He wrestled the man around, then rammed his shoulder into the bully's gut and shoved, carrying them both outside. They tumbled over together, but the man was swift, strong, and agile, and scrambled to his feet as quickly as Kellen did.

Now Kellen had room to pull his sword—

No.

Blade against club, however deadly the club—*no.*

He waded in with his armored fists. He took a good pounding—and he added several new dents to his armor, with corresponding bruises beneath—but at last Kellen was able to finish the fight with a solid blow to the gut, followed by a cracking—and heartfelt—punch to the shepherd's jaw.

The man toppled over like a felled tree, measuring his full length on the ground. He was unconscious, and would stay that way for some time, Kellen hoped uncharitably. But he was alive. Which he would *not* have been if Kellen had pulled his sword.

Kellen turned back to the hut, to the shepherd's victim. He had to bend down a little to get in through the door, and in the dimness, all he could see was a huddled female shape in the corner. She was completely muffled in a long dark cloak of homespun with a deep hood. Kellen lifted her gently, hoping she didn't have any broken bones. At least she was alive as well. A few moments later, and she wouldn't have been.

He carried her out of the hut, seeing without any particular surprise that Jermayan had finally elected to follow him. The Elven Knight dismounted and came hurrying forward just as Kellen lay the woman gently on the ground and looked up toward him, about to explain what he'd found when he reached the shepherd's hut.

But to his shock, Jermayan's face contorted with horror and anger, and the Elven Knight drew his sword and lunged forward, intent upon attacking the woman Kellen had just rescued.

"No!" Ignoring his aches and bruises, Kellen jumped into Jermayan's path, grappling with him. A quick glance over his shoulder showed him that the woman was awake and moving, crawling weakly away. There was something not quite right about her face, but Kellen didn't have time to figure out what. Jermayan was far stronger than he was, and determined to free himself from Kellen in order to reach her.

He held tight to the wrist of Jermayan's sword-hand, and held him like a wrestler trying to force his opponent out of the ring.

"Don't you see what she is?" Jermayan shouted in his ear. "She's a Demon! I've got to kill her!"

No. If he was sure of anything at the moment, Kellen was sure of that. The Wild Magic had brought him here. The Wild Magic was Anathema to *anything* Demonic, if Jermayan and Idalia were to be believed. So whatever this *looked* like, the woman couldn't be a Demon.

He had to believe that. . . .

"Think!" he urged Jermayan, holding the struggling Elf's sword-arm in a vise-grip. "If she's a Demon, why was she letting that lout in there beat her to death?"

"To trap us, you fool!" Jermayan shouted in exasperation.

Kellen finally managed to get the leverage he'd been seeking, twisting Jermayan's sword-hand so that he had to let go of the blade or—even in armor—end up with a broken wrist, and with a well-placed shove, sent Jermayan sprawling. When Jermayan hit the ground, he lost his grip on his sword, and it went slithering away over the wiry grass.

But Jermayan didn't give up. He struggled to his feet once

more, obviously deciding that Kellen had to be dealt with before the Demon.

Kellen risked another wary backward glance. The woman was sitting with her back to the hut now, watching both of them with an expression of terror on her face. Her skin was the rosy-red of ripe cherries; her short curly hair a darker shade of the same red, and her ears were as pointed as an Elf's. Pale gold horns sprouted from just above her slanting eyebrows and curved back over her head. Her eyes were the same yellow-gold as a cat's, with the same narrow slitted pupils.

He looked back barely in time to block Jermayan's attack. He knew Jermayan didn't actually want to kill him, and unfortunately there were few things you could do to a man in a full suit of Elven plate armor short of that. But suppose Jermayan managed to knock him unconscious, or tie him up somehow? What would happen to the woman then?

Then Jermayan slammed into him, knocking him to the ground. As the two men rolled noisily over and over, Jermayan's fingers scrabbled for the straps of Kellen's helmet. Kellen gritted his teeth. If Jermayan could manage to get his helmet off, it would be fairly easy for the Elven Knight to knock him senseless.

"*Stop it.* This has gone on long enough." Shalkan's voice wasn't loud, but it carried, and there was a power in that command that shocked both of them into quiet. For a moment Kellen and Jermayan stopped fighting to stare at the unicorn.

Shalkan paced over to where the woman huddled against the side of the hut and lowered his horn until it touched the side of her face.

Nothing happened.

"But the touch of a unicorn's horn will slay a Demon!" Jermayan gasped in shock. He got to his knees, releasing Kellen.

Shalkan knelt down and placed his head in the woman's lap. She flung her arms around his neck and buried her face in his fur. Great wracking sobs shook her.

Kellen glanced back at Jermayan—if there was one thing

all Jermayan's lessons had taught him, it was never to take your attention off your enemy until that enemy was unconscious or dead. Preferably dead, though of course he had absolutely no desire to kill Jermayan.

But Jermayan no longer seemed interested in fighting. He was staring at Shalkan and the woman with an expression as close to utter shock and dismay as Kellen had ever seen on his face, as if everything Jermayan had believed in had been brutally overturned, all in a single moment.

"Still so sure of yourself?" Kellen muttered crossly, rolling to his knees and getting to his feet.

"Apparently," Shalkan said caustically, keeping an eye on them both, "things are not what they seem. And we need to be gone from here before that brute that was trying to kill this child wakes up. Gentlemen, shall we?"

"Go on," Kellen said to Jermayan, still not really willing to trust him too near the woman he'd just rescued. While Jermayan seemed to have had a change of heart—or at least a profound shock—Kellen didn't really trust what he didn't understand. He never would have thought that Jermayan would attack him, after all, and a moment ago, he had. "We'll be right behind you."

As Jermayan silently went in search of his dropped sword, Kellen shook himself like a dog, that being the quickest way to set his armor and surcoat straight.

He sounded, he thought ruefully, like an entire blacksmith's shop falling downstairs.

Not that the noise he and Jermayan had made fighting had been any quieter.

Carefully, he approached Shalkan and the strange woman. He was thankful he'd had the foresight to leave the keystone on the unicorn's saddle this morning—if it hadn't gotten broken in the brawl in the hut, it certainly wouldn't have survived Jermayan's attack afterward.

"Uh . . . hello?" he said tentatively.

The woman raised her head from Shalkan's neck with a gasp, and cringed back. She was much younger than Kellen had originally thought—a girl, not a woman, someone close to his own age. And terrified.

"Don't worry," he said hastily. "I'm not going to hurt you. Nobody is. Not even Jermayan. Not now that Shalkan's proved that you aren't—what you look like."

Very tactful, Kellen.

"He's my unicorn," Kellen added, rather awkwardly.

"It would be more accurate to say," Shalkan drawled, "that you're my boy. But let it pass."

"Anyway," Kellen said, hurrying on, "we've got to get out of here before the bas—I mean, the fellow who was hurting you—wakes up and causes more trouble. Do you think maybe you could ride Shalkan if I helped you mount?" He crossed his fingers mentally as he said it, hoping that would be okay with Shalkan as well. But the unicorn had let her *touch* him . . .

She blinked up at him, doubtfully, as if she didn't quite believe what she was hearing. "I . . . yes," she said in a trembling voice.

Shalkan stood up and backed away so that she could stand, and she reluctantly held a hand out to Kellen. He took it without hesitation, drawing her to her feet.

She was limping badly, unable to put much weight upon her right foot at all, and after a few steps Kellen simply picked her up and set her on Shalkan's back. Shalkan made no objection.

"Free with my favors, aren't you?" Shalkan said in a voice so low that only Kellen could hear.

"Come on," Kellen said, pointing off to where Jermayan and the mule had gone.

NOW that the Obligation had left him, Kellen felt the mild disorientation he'd come to expect after the Wild Magic was satisfied, but that didn't stop him from thinking clearly as he walked along beside Shalkan. Yes, the strange girl looked the way he'd been told Demons looked—red skin, slitted pupils, claws, horns, and all. And Jermayan had certainly thought she was one.

But he'd also said that all Demons were evil, and could not bear the touch of a living unicorn's horn . . . and she'd certainly proven that she could.

And the Wild Magic had sent Kellen to rescue her as the price for Jermayan's healing. And Kellen knew he wasn't Tainted—confused, maybe, but not Tainted. Whatever might happen in the future, whatever his ancestors might have done, he'd so far paid every price the Wild Magic had asked of him willingly. And Shalkan . . . Shalkan was *perfect*.

In a way, it was a kind of problem in Maths . . . you couldn't end up with evil if there hadn't been evil in the equation to start with.

And he *knew* with a conviction too deep and certain to put into words, that she wasn't evil. But what was she, then? Could you look like a Demon, but not be one?

The answers to that would have to wait until they reached a safe stopping place.

The three of them caught up with Jermayan at the point where the goat track plunged over the edge of the hill. Jermayan untied the mule's lead-rope from Valdien's saddle and tossed it to Kellen without a word, then headed Valdien down the trail. He didn't look back, either at Kellen or at Shalkan and his new rider.

Apparently the truce that Shalkan had forced upon the Elven Knight was something Jermayan was finding very hard to bear.

"I'll wait till he's down, then follow him down with Lily. You wait till I've gotten down with her, so falling gravel doesn't spook her, okay?"

"I will," the girl said softly. She'd pulled the hood of her cloak up again as she rode, and her face was in shadow once more, as if she was ashamed to be seen.

Maybe she was. Or maybe it was just good sense. It stood to reason that just about anyone you encountered was going to try and kill you if you looked like a Demon, after all! Unless, of course, *they* were Demons.

Which, if you *weren't* a Demon, but only looked like one, might be even more dangerous . . .

Kellen glanced around. From the hilltop he had a good view of the surrounding countryside, and he could see that the right-hand fork of the trail looped around the hill and seemed to run parallel to it. They might as well take the left-hand fork if they wanted to get anywhere, and no Finding Spell needed. That was a relief.

The bruises he'd gotten from the fight at the cottage were starting to ache, and his skin was probably the color of Jermayan's pretty blue armor in places by now, between the shepherd's club and Jermayan's fists. If there'd been any additional price to be paid for his magic, Kellen was pretty sure he'd paid it—in full.

Valdien reached the bottom of the twisting track. To Kellen's relief, Jermayan didn't just ride on, but waited for the others to join him. Kellen started down, leading the reluctant mule. His metal boots slipped and skidded on the dusty trail, and the mule set her feet and grunted her displeasure, but they reached the bottom without mishap.

He'd hoped—now that the two of them had a little privacy—that they might talk things out, but Jermayan continued to ignore him utterly. Kellen set his jaw. Fine. Let him.

"I'm here," Shalkan said.

Kellen turned and regarded the unicorn, suddenly realizing they had another problem. He wasn't looking forward to spending the rest of the day on foot, and it would slow their speed enormously. On the other hand, he *knew* the girl couldn't walk, and there was absolutely no point in asking Jermayan to take her up behind him on Valdien. He could Heal her, but he wasn't sure he wanted to risk another spell—both because of adding another layer of obligation, and because of the possibility, which seemed much more real now, that the enemy might be watching.

"I can carry both of you. She doesn't weigh much," Shalkan said. "And I'm a great deal stronger than you think. She gets down, you mount, then she gets up again behind you. Simple."

Simple it might be, but it took a few minutes to accomplish, and when it was done, Shalkan's back felt rather . . . crowded. But as soon as they were both settled, Shalkan trotted off, leading the party down the left-hand trail and leaving Jermayan to bring the mule, quite as if *he* was in charge now, and not the Elven Knight.

Perhaps he was.

⟶

IT was only after they'd started off that Kellen realized he'd just assumed without asking that the girl was going to come along with them. It had been obvious he couldn't leave her where she was. Even though he and Jermayan were riding into danger, she'd been in danger when he'd found her.

"Um . . . I know this is a little late to ask, but . . . is there somewhere safe we could take you? Do you have any family?" Kellen asked.

"Safe? Me?" The girl laughed bitterly. "I have no family, or none that would not hate me on sight. You've seen my face, gentle Knight. Is there anyone in all the world who wouldn't slay me the moment they saw it?"

"Well," Kellen said after a moment's thought, "I didn't."

There was a moment of surprised silence from behind him.

"No," she agreed. "You didn't. And your companion does not love you for that, I think. But . . . tell me . . . if you don't mind, that is . . . what are two knights—one of them an Elven Knight—doing here in the mountains? Elves don't usually come here."

Kellen hesitated—not because he thought the girl was Tainted—he was certain she wasn't—but because he wasn't sure he ought to tell *anyone* what they were doing here. But Shalkan settled the matter in his usual pragmatic fashion.

"I don't suppose I need to tell you what Demons are, do I?" the unicorn said.

Kellen felt the girl shudder, even through his armor.

"I thought not," Shalkan said. "And as you probably also know, Demons hate Elves more than they hate any of the other races of the Bright World, and so they've set a nasty spell to destroy the Elven lands, by making sure no rain falls there. Ever."

"Ever?" the girl said. "They—would make a desert of it? *All* of the Elven lands?"

"At least," Shalkan replied.

"Goddess bless—" she said, sounding shaken.

Kellen flicked a glance sideways at Jermayan, who was riding at Shalkan's flank. The Elven Knight's face was set in what was threatening to become a perpetual glower, but there was little Jermayan could do to stop Shalkan from saying whatever he wanted. Even among the Elves, Kellen was coming to realize, unicorns were a law unto themselves.

"So Kellen here, who's a Wildmage, like his sister Idalia, is taking the spell she made to the Barrier that Shadow Mountain has set up to keep the rain from falling. Once Kellen sets Idalia's spell against theirs, the Barrier will fall and the rains will come to Elven lands again. The only trouble is, nobody's quite sure where Shadow Mountain hid their spell. So that's what we're out here looking for. And hoping we find it before they find us, milady."

"But—if you're looking for Demon magic—I think I know where you want to go!" the girl exclaimed in surprise.

"I told you it was a trap," growled Jermayan, breaking his long silence.

Kellen clutched at the front of the saddle as Shalkan whirled, fleet as a cat, to block Valdien's path. Behind him, he felt the girl clutch at his belt.

"One—more—word—" the unicorn said through gritted teeth, "and I promise you, Child of Leaf and Star, that your sweet soprano voice will be the admiration of everyone you meet for the rest of your very long life."

Kellen stared at the unicorn's horn. It had taken on an odd pink flush he'd never seen before. He looked up at Jermayan. The Elf was staring at the horn as well, face pale and eyes wide.

There was a moment's tense silence, as the wind whistled

among the rocks all around them, and at last Jermayan looked away, bowing his head in submission.

Still nobody said anything, and Shalkan didn't move.

"You can tell where we want to go? How?" Kellen said at last, to break the silence. He hated seeing Jermayan being put in such a humiliating position, even if it was almost entirely of Jermayan's making, and probably the politest thing to do, under the circumstances, was to pretend he hadn't noticed anything.

"You know—you can see—I have Demon blood," the girl said painfully.

Kellen waited for another outburst from Jermayan, but the Elven Knight had been thoroughly cowed by Shalkan. Shalkan stayed where he was, and Jermayan didn't even seem willing to move Valdien around the unicorn and continue on their way. It was clear he did not intend to move until Shalkan gave him permission.

"I will tell you the whole story soon, I promise, but I have been hiding from the Demons all my life, and the only way I was able to do it was because I can feel the presence of Demons as a kind of sickness that gets stronger the closer they come. As you can well believe, I've worked hard to hone this gift so that it will give me a sense of the direction from which the danger comes as well. I—if they ever find me"— her voice was shaking—"they will do worse to me than any human or Elf ever could."

Kellen heard the terror there, and he wanted to offer comfort, but couldn't imagine how. Surely Jermayan heard it too! How could he hear it and not be moved?

Because maybe he isn't thinking?

"For the past few days—and now, in the direction we're riding—I have been feeling that same unease," she continued. "Or—would *sickness* be the right word? That something is wrong, Tainted—no, *not* Tainted, merely, but polluted. Not a Demon, but something that tells me that Demonic magic is near, and growing stronger. If we ride toward that, surely you'll find what you're seeking?" she finished in a rush.

It was up to him, Kellen realized in dismay. Jermayan was

too caught up in his own anger and fear to think clearly, and Shalkan couldn't—or wouldn't—make these kind of decisions. Like it or not, Kellen was the leader.

He'd always known that, but somehow it had never been quite so important before. For the first time, Kellen realized how much was riding on the decisions he had to make, and that only he could make them. It was up to him not only to decide to trust this chance-met stranger, but to trust her instincts and judgment as well. To guess, and guess rightly (he hoped), that she was not only a good person, but had the wisdom to use her gifts in the best way they could be used in this situation.

That was what made this a hard choice. It wasn't as simple as deciding whether or not she was good. She *was* good— both he and Shalkan knew that much, even if Jermayan was still unconvinced. What Kellen had to decide now was whether she was smart, and clever, and levelheaded enough to lead them close to trouble but not into it.

The Wild Magic led me to her. But had that been for her sake only, or for all of them? *Was* she a key to this, or only incidental?

"What's your name?" Kellen asked almost irrelevantly, still sitting on Shalkan's back in the middle of the trail as if they had all the time in the world to figure things out.

"Vestakia," she said, sounding surprised.

"Vestakia," he said. He was playing for time, he knew, hoping the Powers behind the Wild Magic would send him certainty, knowing all the while that the decision was going to be his alone, without any outside help. "Have you lived up here all your life?"

"All eighteen years of it," she said. She sounded puzzled now, probably wondering why they hadn't started down the trail again. "I've been alone since my aunt died, and that was four years ago."

"Can you . . . can you tell how far away the Demon-magic is, as well as what direction?" he asked, thinking hard.

"I can tell how far away one of *Them* is, right enough," she answered promptly. "But what you're looking for . . . I

on't know. All I know is that it must be bad, if I can feel
t at all. As bad as the Demons themselves."

His last hope was gone. If she was able to tell them how
ar away from the Barrier she was at any given time, that
vould make following her gift less of a danger. But since
he couldn't, Vestakia might, even with the best of intentions,
ead them right into it without warning.

*But the Wild Magic sent you to her for a reason. She has
he power to take you to the Barrier. Use it.*

"Show us the way," Kellen said, making his decision.

As if his words had been a signal, Shalkan turned back
long the trail.

—

OR the rest of the day they followed Vestakia's halting
lirections as she led them deeper into the Lost Lands. Even
he sparse wiry mountain grass was gone from the rocky hill-
ides now, and the only vegetation was a thick, dry, mosslike
rrowth, or tough lichens. Vestakia said that no one, even
utlaws, came this far into the mountains, and those that did
ever came back.

Kellen could tell that though Jermayan said nothing (his
ilent frustration and anger were nearly palpable), he ached
o accuse her of leading them in circles, but Kellen didn't
hink she was. She'd said that the presence of Demons—or
Demon-magic—made her ill, and she seemed to grow weaker
nd more uncomfortable as the day wore on and the sun sank
vestward. Soon they'd have to find a place to stop, even
hough there didn't seem to be any good ones.

The thought of stopping—of sleeping—anywhere in these
nountains made Kellen profoundly uncomfortable, but what
hoice did they have? He had no idea how close they were
o the Barrier, and Vestakia didn't seem to be sure either.

What he did know was that he'd been right to trust her to
how them the way. There'd been no further signs to indicate
heir path—not very surprising, as there was nothing living
o be warped out of its natural pattern. Kellen knew he could

never have found this route without spells, and he was mor
and more unwilling to cast another spell for any reason.

"Vestakia?" he said when she hadn't spoken for a while.

There was no answer, and suddenly he realized that all he
weight was leaning against his back, and that she was startin
to slide sideways.

Shalkan stopped as Kellen wriggled free of the saddle, jus
in time to catch the girl as she slumped to the ground. H
lowered her gently and turned back the hood of her cloak
She was gasping for air, and her eyes were half-closed.

"Vestakia? Vestakia, can you hear me?"

"I . . . oh, it hurts so much!" She rolled to her knees an
retched weakly.

Kellen hated to badger her, but he had no choice. "Ves
takia, is it near? Which way?"

"There." Still on her hands and knees, she pointed up be
tween two boulders, at a nearly sheer half-dome of rock
"Near. It must be."

"We can do it," Shalkan said, looking the way she ha
pointed. "But not in the dark. And the animals can't do it a
all. We'd have to leave them here."

"Stay here tonight?" Kellen said incredulously, gazin;
down at Vestakia. "She can't!"

"There are some medicines in your packs that will hel;
her. So I suggest you get them," the unicorn said impassively

Kellen got to his feet and gazed up at Jermayan, who wa;
still sitting astride Valdien, gazing down at Vestakia's misery
as if it had nothing to do with him.

"Well? Are you going to just sit there? Do what you cam
here to do and be of some use," Kellen snapped harshly, in
a voice he hardly recognized as his. "Or I'll tell Idalia yo
failed in your task to help me. And how. And why. And sh
can make up her own mind whether or not you were worthy
of her."

Jermayan flinched back as if Kellen had slapped him, an
turned wordlessly away to dismount and unpack the mule.

A heavy weight of oppression seemed to press down or
Kellen's spirit. It wasn't just the deadness of this place, the

loomy sky, the unforgiving stone, though all of those con-
ributed to the feeling. Something bad lived here. Something
nimical to the human spirit. Vestakia was right, or if not
ight, very close.

He had to fight himself to keep from crouching down, from
ooking over his shoulder, from peering at every shadow in
earch of an enemy. Vestakia was already miserable enough;
e didn't want to terrify her.

Kellen turned back to Vestakia, helping her to sit. "You'll
eel better soon, I promise," he said, hoping it was true.
Shalkan says we have medicines with us, and you'll have
hem soon."

Vestakia smiled wanly at him, blinking back tears. "Please
lon't let them get me, Kellen. I'd rather die than that. Prom-
se me."

Apparently his attempt to put on a cheerful face wasn't
listracting her. Well, if this place seemed oppressive to him,
low bad must it be for her?

"I won't let the Demons have you," Kellen promised, re-
lizing with a sinking feeling just what it was he was prom-
sing. *And Jermayan would probably be happy to kill you
vhether there was a Demon around or not.*

He looked up at the sky, trying to decide how much light
hey had left. By the position of the sun, it was a few hours
efore sunset, but darkness came quickly here in the moun-
ains. Even if Shalkan's remedies worked, and Vestakia was
vell enough to go on today, there was no guarantee that dark-
less wouldn't find them halfway along the path, trapped
omewhere in the mountains far too near the Barrier.

But Kellen knew he'd been right, too. The thought of
amping for the night here on the enemy's doorstep was not
nly unthinkable, he suspected it would be impossible. He
hought of the dreams he'd had back on the haunted battle-
ield and shuddered. He wasn't willing to risk more of the
ame—or worse. There might not be any sign of opposition
vet, but the longer they stayed here, the more likely discovery
ecame. No, they'd go on as soon as possible.

Shalkan had wandered off, and was talking to Jermayan.

Kellen would have given a lot to know what *that* conversation consisted of, but the unicorn's voice was pitched too low for him to hear. Jermayan was unloading the mule, and unpacking the brazier. Shalkan collected one of the bags in his teeth and sauntered back, depositing it at Kellen's feet.

"There's a cup, a black bottle, and a wineskin in there. Put an ounce of the contents of the black bottle into the cup, then fill it up with the wineskin. Then have Vestakia drink it. Jermayan's brewing tea." Shalkan's voice was neutral, conveying nothing of what he might be thinking.

Kellen ought to have expected that. Well, if whatever was in the bottle had allheal in it, the stuff might do Vestakia some good. "Listen, just tell me if Jermayan ever *neglects* to brew tea when we stop, will you?" he asked Shalkan, trying for a little humor to at least cheer up Vestakia. "If that happens, I'll know there's either something seriously wrong with him, or it's an imposter."

Shalkan sniggered. Unfortunately, Vestakia didn't seem to notice, or didn't realize he was trying to lighten her mood.

Kellen followed the directions meticulously. The contents of the black bottle smelled strongly of herbs, like fresh-cut hay, and the liquid was the bright green of spring leaves, as thick as berry-syrup. The cup was a small one, obviously not meant for ordinary use. It was made of Elven silver, a silver as bright and soft as pure gold. Kellen handled it carefully.

The wineskin contained nothing more exotic than white brandy. It was clear as water, and turned pale green as it mixed with the herbal draught.

"Here," Kellen said, holding out the cup to Vestakia.

"Oh. I don't want—"

"Please. Shalkan says it will help."

"Drink it quickly," the unicorn advised. "*Really* quickly."

Uncertainly, she took the silver cup, and gulped its contents down as fast as she could. A stricken expression crossed her face, and she exploded into a paroxysm of coughing as soon as she'd swallowed.

"It doesn't taste very good," Shalkan finished mildly. "Un-

ess you happen to be a horse or some other grass-eater. Now
you, Kellen."

"What does it do?" Kellen asked, suspicious now that he'd
seen its effect on Vestakia.

"Among other things, it closes down the magical senses,
though not for very long. You'll need the breathing space.
You may not think you can sense the Barrier from here, but
you can. Drink it."

Vestakia stopped coughing and sputtering. "That was horrible!" she said. "But . . . I feel better now. Thank you." She
took a deep breath that turned into a sigh of relief.

Kellen looked at the cup and the bottle and winced. But
Shalkan had never given him bad advice yet, and if his
mounting despair was due to sensing the Barrier—well, he
needed the help. Much worse, and he'd start weeping over
trifles. Or he'd sit down in the middle of the path and refuse
to go on. Quickly, he mixed his own dose, and drank.

The brandy seared his mouth and throat with choking fire,
and did nothing to mask the incredible gagging bitterness of
the herbal liquor. Even braced for it, Kellen choked and sputtered nearly as much as Vestakia had, swallowing over and
over to try to get the taste out of his mouth. But once the
burning and bitterness subsided, he *did* feel better. Some of
the despair lifted. Now, he was merely depressed.

And who wouldn't be, around here?

Kellen investigated the bag further, discovering it was the
first-aid kit. He pulled out the jar of allheal salve and a roll
of bandages.

"You were limping earlier. Which ankle is it? If I use some
of this on it and strap it up tightly, you should be able to
walk." *I hope,* he added to himself. "I wish I could Heal you,
but I . . . don't dare," he finished, feeling ashamed.

"You couldn't do it right now, anyway," Shalkan said helpfully. "Not after drinking *that*."

"It's because it would call *Them*, isn't it?" Vestakia said,
shuddering. "Never mind. I'd rather bleed to death horribly
than do anything to summon one of Them, and this close . . ."
She shivered again, wrapping her cloak tightly around herself.

"Even without magic, I should take a look at it," Kellen said. "Some allheal will do a lot to make the bruising heal faster." *Assuming that matters, and we aren't all dead before morning.*

Vestakia seemed to see the sense of that.

"This one," she said, thrusting out her right foot. "I twisted it when I fell. He'd never have caught me otherwise," she added proudly.

Kellen removed his gauntlets and eased the boot off. Vestakia was wearing much the same thing the farmers working the fields in Merryvale had been—long tunic, wide calf-length trousers, and heavy boots of rough leather lined in sheepskin. It was the boot that had kept the sprain from being any worse: her ankle was a little swollen, and warm to the touch, but it didn't seem too painful when Kellen prodded it experimentally, asking her how it felt. With the color of her skin, he wasn't sure whether he'd be able to tell if it was bruised or not, otherwise.

"I'm afraid this will hurt a little," he said, as he began to work the salve into her skin. "But it will feel better afterward."

Vestakia winced as Kellen's fingers found a particularly sensitive spot. Kellen cast about for something to distract her.

"You said you'd tell us how you came to be here?" he asked. "This would be a good time." He glanced over his shoulder. Jermayan was taking an *awfully* long time getting the tea to boil.

"I suppose I owe you the tale," Vestakia said, hanging her head. "I warn you, Wildmage, it isn't a pretty one."

"Well," Kellen said lightly, "it's bound to be interesting."

She managed a wan smile. "My father, as you know already, was a Demon. My mother told us that he called himself the Prince of Shadow Mountain, and though all Demons lie, I have no reason to think that this one time he wasn't telling the truth."

Interesting. He wondered why she was so sure, but decided to let Vestakia tell the story in her own way. He could always ask questions later. Beside him, Shalkan was listening with rapt attention.

"My mother was a Wildmage, who lived with her sister in a little village far to the east of here. My father seduced her in human form and got her with child, intending to leave her on some pretext and come back after I was born and claim me for his own. It is a common practice among Demonkind and well known among the Mountain-folk—perhaps you have heard the songs we sing about it?"

Kellen hadn't. Vestakia shrugged.

"It doesn't matter, because this time his plan failed. One night my mother wore a Talisman of the Good Goddess made from braided unicorn hair to their bed. He did not recognize it for what it was, and he touched it. It burned him, and he vanished."

Kellen blinked at that; he'd known that the living unicorns were inimical to Demons, but unicorn *hair*? He filed the information away for future reference. It could be very useful.

"She knew him for what he was then, of course, but by then it was too late." Vestakia sighed. "She was with child, of course, and—and that doomed her to lose the life she had always known, and it would be *only* that, only if she was very fortunate indeed."

"Why?" he asked, because Vestakia had stopped talking.

"If the villagers found out that she had been Tainted by a Demon's embrace, even accidentally, they would put her to death," Vestakia told him flatly. "If they found out she was pregnant by a Demon, they would put her to death even more swiftly—and there was no point in trying to abort in secret what she carried: Demon-children cannot be gotten rid of except by killing the mother. So she faced death twice over for her error—but my mother was a powerful Wildmage, and she was very clever as well, and she was not going to lie down and wait for death."

If she was anything like you, and I expect she must have been, I can certainly believe that, Kellen thought.

"She took stock of her options and resources, and made plans. No one but she knew that she had taken a lover at all, much less that her lover had been a Demon: she would be disgraced in the eyes of the village elders when she was found to be carrying a bastard, but not murdered—not until the child was born and showed unquestionable signs of Demonic Taint. And—she didn't intend to give birth to a child that would grow up to destroy and corrupt all that it touched."

"Well, I can see where that would be a problem," Kellen replied, keeping his eyes on her ankle, and his tone light, but not *too* light. He didn't want her to think he was making fun of her, or not taking her story as seriously as it deserved to be. "I assume she must have had an idea of what to do about it."

"She did," Vestakia said solemnly. "She called upon the Wild Magic to help her."

He blinked. "Oh. My." It was a completely *logical* solution, given that the woman in question was a Wildmage, but how many would have had the courage to take it, knowing that the price asked was likely to be very high, and there was no one to bear it but herself? *Idalia would,* Kellen thought with a flash of pride. But how many others?

"And so according to the ancient ways, because she had asked only for *help,* and not what kind of help, my mother was offered a choice, and a price."

He looked up, then, into those solemn, yellow eyes, and thought that he could guess the choice. But he didn't interrupt Vestakia. Jermayan was eavesdropping, although he pretended otherwise, and he needed to hear this from Vestakia's lips.

"Her choice was that the child to be could be completely hers in spirit, and its father's in body; or its father's in spirit, yet hers in body. So I could look like him, yet be human inside, or look like her, yet be his in every way that mattered—a Demon. No matter which choice she made, she would sacrifice twenty years of her allotted span of years."

He winced. A hard price; a harder choice. "I think," Kellen said aloud, "that she must have been very brave."

Vestakia nodded, accepting his comment as no more than simple fact. "It was—so my aunt always told me later—a hard choice to make, for some claimed that Demons were not by nature evil, and if one could only get an imp young enough, and raise it up in love and law, perhaps its nature could be turned away from Darkness. And if Mama had only taken the choice of having me look human, she could have stayed where she was, among her friends and family, and hoped for the best. Perhaps—so she might have told herself—I could have been turned from my evil ways. And even more temptingly, even if I *was* evil by nature, there was a good chance that I wouldn't begin to work my wickedness until I was grown, and due to the nature of her price, she knew she would be dead by then."

Shalkan made a little, thoughtful sound. "Less risk for her; potentially a disaster for everyone else. Not so much a choice as a temptation?"

"Maybe," Vestakia acknowledged. "Maybe not. Maybe it *is* true that Demons are not evil in nature; maybe she would have been doing all of the world a great service by proving it. If it were only her own fate that was at stake, I believe she might have tried it. But it was not. If the child proved to be evil in blood and bone, if my nature had been unredeemable, she would be risking not only her sister's life and those of everyone in the village—not only with what I might do to them, but in what would certainly happen when my father came for me. And not only theirs, but perhaps the lives of everyone in the surrounding countryside as well, for once Demons are drawn to a hunting ground and find it undefended, they do not stop until they have destroyed everything within reach. Mama saw that one path was easy—for her—and one was hard, but that only one was right. She was very brave," Vestakia finished proudly. "She told the Good Goddess that she would bear a Demon-appearing but human-spirited child, and sealed her bargain."

"Good for her." Shalkan touched Vestakia's cheek lightly with his horn, and she glowed a little at his praise. Out of the corner of his eyes, Kellen caught Jermayan watching, his frown deepening at this further proof that Vestakia was not what *he* thought her to be.

She picked up the thread of her story again. "But I would not be born for many moonturns yet, and she had many plans still to make if we were both to survive, for Mama did not intend for either of us to die—nor for either of us to fall into my father's hands again. She went to her elder sister Patanene, who was unmarried and loved her dearly, and confided all to her, and my aunt was just as brave and strong as Mama. Aunt Patanene got herself put in charge of a flock of goats to be sent out deeper into the mountains for summer pasturage, and Mama went with her. They stole half the flock, and took it away with them deep into the Lost Lands, where they knew they would never be found, walking for moonturns. I was born in a hut the two of them built with their own hands and shared with their little flock."

Two women and a baby all alone in these mountains? And I thought living in the Wildwood was hard! Kellen thought to himself.

"I suppose it was a hard life for them," Vestakia said, in an unconscious echo of his thoughts. "As for me, I never knew any other. Mama's Wildmagery kept us well and safe and fed, and I was always happy, even though the very first thing I learned was that I must never let anyone see me. All was well for ten years, then Mama died, paying her price, and Aunt 'Nene and I were left alone to fend for ourselves. We didn't do quite as well, I think . . . Mama's magic had kept us safe when the Demons hunted me, and when she died, at first we were never sure when they were near. But then, when I . . ." Vestakia hesitated, and looked away, embarrassed. "When I . . . began to become a woman . . . I realized that I could *sense* them when they drew near, because I became ill. Aunt 'Nene and I had reason to bless that gift, many times!

"But it was a hard life, very hard. And when Aunt 'Nene fell ill, four years after Mama died, I wasn't skilled enough to nurse her back to health, and though I called upon the Good Goddess, without Wild Magic, I could do nothing for her but to keep her comfortable and ease her spirit. And she died. So then I was alone."

By now Kellen had finished working the allheal into Vestakia's ankle, and he began winding the linen bandage firmly about her foot—not too tight, or it would cut off the circulation. He only hoped what little he could do would be enough.

How brave she had been! Compared with what she had faced growing up alone and isolated, his own problems as Lycaelon's despised and socially embarrassing son seemed like nothing. He'd spent a lot of time feeling sorry for himself, but he could tell, just by looking at her, that Vestakia had never wasted a single moment on self-pity.

"What did you do then?" he asked. "After your aunt died, and you were all alone?"

"What could I do?" Vestakia asked, with some spirit. "If I sat about and bewailed my lot, the goats would starve, I would starve, and what use would there have been of Mama's sacrifice, of all of Aunt 'Nene's care? I buried her next to Mama, I tended my flock, I went on with my life. I knew how to hunt, I had milk and cheese and butter from my goats, eggs from the wild birds, and sometimes meat. Though you may not think it, there are wild foods growing in these hills, not abundant, but Mama and Aunt 'Nene taught me how to find them. Sometimes I could trade for bread and flour with the other crofters—I wore gloves, and bandages over my face, and let them think I had some horrible skin disease. I managed well enough. I knew the Demons were hunting for me—Mama had warned me that my father would always know that I was still alive, even if he could not tell exactly where I was because of the boon the Good Goddess had granted her, and that he would never give up searching for me. So I hid whenever I felt the Demons nearby, but I dared not leave the hills, or go anywhere there were more people, because I would be killed at once or, and that would be nearly as bad, lead the Demons among people. Mama made sure I learned those lessons well, so that I would never be tempted to show my face to anyone. She warned me that anyone who saw it and pretended not to care *must* be a Demon in human guise; of course, she never lived to know that no Demon

would ever be able to trick me that way . . ." Vestakia sighed
and bowed her head. "When I saw you . . . when you saved
me . . . I was so afraid! I thought my power had failed me
somehow. If Shalkan hadn't been there . . ."

She reached out to the unicorn, and Shalkan stepped forward so that Vestakia could stroke his cheek.

"Usually, of course, the maiden rescues the unicorn," Shalkan commented, and Kellen was pleased to see Vestakia
smile gravely.

"As for what I was doing there in the first place: that was
my home, up until today. A month ago, someone started
stealing my goats. I couldn't let that go on, so I set a trap to
catch the thief, intending to give him a good drubbing and
get my goats back—any of them that he hadn't already eaten,
at least.

"But there was Demon-magic in the air, and I wasn't paying enough attention. I twisted my ankle, and he cornered
me. If you hadn't come along when you had, I'd be dead
now. And so he has *all* my goats, and my hut as well! And
I wish him much joy of them, whoever he is."

Kellen finished wrapping the bandage at the top of her knee
and tied it off to hold it fast. He held up her boot, and Vestakia slipped her foot into it.

Both of them looked up as a shadow fell across them.
Jermayan was standing over them, holding cups of tea. The
Elven Knight's face was a stony mask of disapproval. Kellen
realized that with Elven rigid-mindedness, Jermayan still
didn't believe any part of Vestakia's story—though he'd certainly heard all of it—despite all the proof Shalkan had given
him.

Idiot. He's as blind sometimes as Lycaelon. If Idalia ever
got wind of his behavior—

—*if we make it home again*—

—she would be sure to give him a well-deserved piece of
her mind.

If he amends his behavior, I'll consider not telling her.

Kellen rocked back on his heels, wincing at his own sore-
ness, and reached for the cups. Reluctantly, Jermayan placed

them in his hands. Kellen passed one of them to Vestakia.

Kellen sipped the tea in silence. Considering everything, Kellen didn't think he was going to tell Jermayan that he'd been led to save Vestakia by the Wild Magic, or *why* the Wild Magic had exacted that particular price from him, as satisfying as letting the haughty Elven Knight know that Vestakia's rescue was the price of his own healing would be. It would only irritate Jermayan further, and Kellen didn't need Jermayan any more irritated and upset right now. He needed Jermayan alert and cooperative.

"There's soup," the Elf said reluctantly.

So that's what took him so long. Kellen forgave Jermayan slightly.

"We'll need to eat," Kellen told Vestakia. He got to his feet and handed his cup to Jermayan. He knew Jermayan would want tea as well, and they'd only brought two cups. And he was sure just by looking that Jermayan wouldn't want to drink out of a cup that had been used by Vestakia.

"After we eat, we're going ahead, as far as Vestakia can lead us. From the way she was feeling before Shalkan dosed her, the Barrier must be close by, and the animals can't get up the rock, so we'll have to leave Valdien, the mule, and everything we don't absolutely need here, and hope it's here when we get back." *If we get back,* Kellen added silently.

For a moment Kellen was certain Jermayan was going to refuse, to demand that Kellen find some other path, or decide to strike out on his own. But the Elven Knight merely bowed, the same stiff formal bow Kellen had seen so often back in Sentarshadeen. "As you command, Wildmage," he answered tonelessly, turning away back to the campfire.

"Well, *that* went well," Kellen said, under his breath.

"He hates what I represent," Vestakia said sadly, getting to her feet. She tested her foot gingerly, then put more of her weight on it, her expression relaxing into relief. "Well, I hate it, too. Does he think I've ever been able to look into a bowl of water without hating the Demon that looks back at me?" she added bitterly.

"Hate the Demon, but don't hate yourself," Shalkan said

quietly, "for you are not of their kind. Your mother's Wild
Magic saw to that, her courage, *your* courage. Vestakia, you
have been braver than you think. If one who is wholly human
can be turned to the Darkness willingly, think how much
easier it would have been for you! You would have been
accepted without question; all you would have had to do was
take the easy path, embrace evil, and join your father. You
did not. You are as human as your mother was, brave and
true. And just as *good*."

"No one will ever believe that!" Vestakia cried wildly,
tears starting to form in her yellow cat's-eyes. "Mama said
so!"

"I do," Kellen said firmly, willing her to believe him.
"Shalkan does. And Jermayan will believe in you, too—if I
have to beat his Elf-stubborn head down between his shoulders until his eyes are level with his collarbone to make him
realize it, I will. But we don't have time for that, now. We
have to get up over those rocks before the light fails. Now
come and have some soup. You'll need all your strength for
the climb."

He was talking in part to keep from thinking. It was quiet.
It was too quiet. Surely the Endarkened knew that they were
near! Surely he would not be able to just clamber up to the
top of the rocks, put the keystone in place, and walk away!

But Vestakia had said that the Taint was here, the dark
magic, but not the Demons themselves. And certainly there
was no sign of life here except for the moss and grey-green
lichen. Maybe—maybe by taking up with Vestakia, they had
been able to reach this place before the Endarkened were
prepared?

He wanted to believe it, and knew he dared not. He dared
be nothing less than prepared for the worst.

Except, of course, that "the worst" would be impossible
for anyone short of an army to stop.

Chapter Twenty-four

A Pause Before the Storm

He led Vestakia over to the campfire. Valdien stood nuzzling his master as Jermayan stood eating thick trail-soup from a bowl. Neither the mule nor the stallion wore any trace of tack now. At the moment, the mule did not look inclined to stray, and even if she did, she probably wouldn't go far. If none of them returned, the beasts would have to fend for themselves as best they could.

Maybe they'll make it back to Sentarshadeen. If nothing else, I suppose they'll find their way to where there are some people. The people can't all be like that bastard that tried to kill Vestakia ...

Of course, by his way of reckoning, he was killing a Demon, so maybe I shouldn't call him a bastard.

Except that he was stealing her goats before he thought she was a Demon, so I guess he is.

These and other inconsequential thoughts chased around and around in his mind, and he let them. Better that than think about where they were going and what he might meet.

Kellen ladled more soup into the remaining bowl for Vestakia, and then ate his portion directly from the pot and unwrapped several trail-bars for Shalkan.

Afterward, in silence, he took his heavy green cloak from his pack and pulled it about himself, then took the bag with the keystone from Shalkan's saddle and hung it from his belt.

"I don't think I'll want the armor where we're going," the unicorn said, so Kellen unbuckled the saddle and armor from Shalkan's back as Jermayan retrieved his own dark blue cloak from the pile of packs on the ground, and his bow and heavy quiver full of arrows as well. At least no gleam of their armor would betray them to any watchers.

"How long until your medicine wears off?" Vestakia asked Shalkan in a quavering voice.

"Not long now," the unicorn said gently. "You'd better make as much distance as you can while it still has some effect."

Kellen picked up his gauntlets and locked them into place as Jermayan scuffed out the small fire. And then there were no preparations left to make.

He turned away and followed Vestakia and Shalkan over the crest of the hill, across the shallow ravine, and on toward the rock face. Behind him, he saw Jermayan turn back to Valdien, and stand with his arms around the storm-grey destrier's neck for a long moment. Only then did Kellen truly realize that Jermayan was being forced to abandon someone who loved him and depended on him, and whom Jermayan loved in return—and worse, someone who probably could not survive without him. If they did not come back . . .

Kellen gritted his teeth, forcing the thought from his mind: the image of Valdien, starving, alone, desperately and hopelessly seeking his dead master in this wilderness. They had to go on. There was no choice. More lives than Valdien's were at stake. Many more.

He glanced behind him, in the direction of the sun. A few hours more of light at most, and then they would be in darkness. At least they *had* sun, though it had to fight with the clouds. The way this place felt, it should properly be shrouded in shadows, under a grim, grey, lowering sky, with clouds too thick to actually see the sun.

There was a faint, peculiar, bitter smell to the wind. He couldn't put a name to it. He wondered if the others noticed, and glanced at Shalkan. The unicorn's expressive nostrils were held pinched shut.

I guess he's noticed.

His hand went to the pouch at his belt, where Idalia's keystone waited, cocooned in layers of magical Elven silk, and examined the steep rock slope.

Shalkan crouched on his haunches and then sprang strongly upward. The unicorn's unshod hooves scrabbled for a hold against the rock for a few moments, then Shalkan found his footing and began to climb.

"You're next," Kellen said to Vestakia.

She gave him an effortful smile and followed Shalkan up the steep incline. Kellen waited until he was sure she wouldn't slip back, then got ready to start after her. He glanced back at Jermayan, standing stiff and forbidding behind him. He wished there was something he could say to close the gap that had opened up between them, something that could repair their easy fellowship, but he couldn't think of anything. Jermayan was as stubborn as all the Elves, and wasn't going to change his mind about Vestakia, or be pleased with Kellen for taking her part.

But if Jermayan hated Vestakia, it was because he hated all Demons, and Kellen had no doubt that destroying the Barrier was his highest priority. Jermayan would do what he had come to do.

"It will be over soon—one way or another," he said to Jermayan.

"One way or another," the Elven Knight echoed grimly. "And I hope your human heart has not betrayed you, Wildmage."

Kellen supposed that this was as good as he was going to get in the way of a reconciliation. He turned away and began to climb.

The half-dome was steep, and it was also absolutely bare rock. There was a sort of furrow in it that gave purchase to his hands and feet, and Kellen used it to pull himself up to where the incline was less steep and he could actually move forward in a sort of crablike crouch over the pale stone. Without Vestakia, he and Jermayan would never have found this route to the Barrier, not in weeks of searching.

As he caught up to Vestakia, he could see her shuddering. She would shake for a moment, clinging desperately to some invisible cracks in the rock, then the spell would pass and she would creep forward a pace or two before the shivering started again.

"It *is* wearing off," she said glumly. She pointed, ahead and to the left. "Whatever it is, it's that way."

Kellen looked where she was pointing. They still had to climb a good distance to reach the top of the dome of rock they were on, and he could see nothing beyond that, but what he saw around and behind him suggested more of the same kind of terrain—mountains and high hills, the only vegetation a little moss and lichen at most, the rock scoured clean by the battles of that long-ago war. Once they got to the top here, they might have some serious climbing ahead, and none of them had brought so much as a coil of rope. And worse of all, there was no more than an hour or two of good light left at best.

But they were close to their goal—close enough that they had to press on immediately, because they were already within the pall of Shadow Mountain's influence, and Kellen was coming to suspect that spending very much time here wasn't very healthy for living things. He followed Vestakia and Shalkan. He was relieved to see that the unicorn was staying close to her, but Vestakia seemed to be completely recovered from her earlier beating, and was moving without difficulty.

And they were close to their goal—

Now *he* sensed it; the despair and the bitter ache at his bones had a source, close enough that they had to press on immediately.

When they reached the top of the rock dome, it proved to be no more than the foothill of a true mountain, and Vestakia was miserable for other reasons. She'd thrown back the hood of her cloak, and her ruby skin was beaded with sick-sweat. She was breathing hard, almost panting, holding her stomach as if she were in pain. Kellen wondered if she could go on.

"Still want to take the lead?" he asked. "Or do you need to rest a little?"

"I'm fine," she said irritably, in answer to his query. "It's far worse than this when there's a Demon around."

"There's a path up the mountain," Jermayan said, as if speaking pained him. "Look, there, where that shadow starts, see? It's narrow, and you can barely see it, but it's there." He looked right at Kellen, obviously waiting for a decision.

Kellen looked in the direction that he had indicated, and made out the beginning of a goat track in the shadows around the curve of the cliff. It didn't look very wide, and it climbed rather steeply. If it got any narrower, they'd be edging their way to the top with their backs plastered against the stone wall.

"Then that's the way we go," Kellen said reluctantly. Vesakia nodded, very slightly, confirming his guess that that was the direction of the strongest Demon-taint. It looked like a long climb. Once they reached the top, it would be too dark to return safely. Kellen touched the pouch with the keystone, more to reassure himself than anything else. In his half-formed imaginings of the moment when he reached the Barrier, he'd always supposed it would be full daylight, that he'd be rested and ready for the final fight, not arriving after a long day of brawls, petty squabbles, and climbing up the side of a mountain. His bruises ached, he was tired, and he hated being at odds with Jermayan. Depression weighed him down as if he were carrying a full pack. Despair whispered that he was about to fail. The bitter air burned his throat and made him horribly thirsty. It seemed that Reality always managed to play tricks with your dreams and imagination, turning your fantasies inside out when it made them come true.

Jermayan drew his sword with a hiss of steel. As Kellen turned toward him, the Elven Knight met his eyes and inclined his head ever-so-slightly. Despite his misgivings, Jermayan would follow where he led.

Kellen turned back toward the mountain, and pointed. "Let's go. The sun won't wait for us."

Shalkan led the way, his white fur glowing almost as brightly as it had the first time Kellen had seen him. So short a time, measured in sennights, but it held a lifetime of experiences. Now Kellen was gambling—with all their lives—

that he'd learned the right lessons from them, and was making the right choices now.

Vestakia followed immediately after Shalkan. If the trace of Demon-taint shifted, she would be the one who would know first and be able to alert them to retrace their steps. She would also be the first to know if there were any actual Demons in the vicinity.

That's one certainty, anyway. She might betray us inadvertently, but she won't do it deliberately. If I can't trust a unicorn's judgment, I might as well just throw myself off this rock and be done with it.

Kellen followed her. Jermayan came last, his sword drawn and ready in his gauntleted hand.

When they reached the trail, they saw it was both steep and narrow, a double-handspan cut into the side of the mountain, with a sheer drop on one side and the sheer cliff on the other. There was no way to hurry. Of the four of them, only Shalkan found it even halfway easy going, and that only because he had four feet, not two, to apply to the trail. The wind blew harder the higher they climbed, and seemed to turn colder with every step, until Kellen could feel the ache of cold right through the padding beneath his armor. The sunlight weakened, not that it had ever had much strength in the first place, but it seemed now as if what light there was came to them past a dark veil over the sun's face.

Kellen concentrated every fiber of his being on just managing to take the next step—finding the place he would put his foot, moving it there, testing it with half his weight, trusting it with his full weight, moving on to the next step. He drove every other thought to the back of his mind.

At last they gained the top. It was a relief to step onto secure footing at last, and no longer have to fear that the slightest misstep would plunge one or all of them hundreds of feet down the side of the mountain. Kellen eased his way past the others and looked around.

All during his long journey to reach his goal, Kellen's greatest fear had been that he wouldn't know the place he was looking for when he reached it, but now he realized that

ad been foolish. There was no mistaking it. He'd seen this
lace before. He'd been here in dreams and visions. This was
ne place of all his nightmares. This was the place he had
een that time he'd tried to scry in the forest pool, the hilltop
overed with warring Demons.

The top of the mountain was broad and flat, as if some
mpossible power long ago had sliced its peak off with a
nife. The flatness was scattered with the same huge tumbled
oulders that Kellen had seen at the ancient battlefield where
e and Jermayan had once camped, and now Kellen imagined
n assassin lurking behind every one, ready to ambush them.
he wind whimpered and moaned around the stones, stirring
p dust, the source of the bitter smell. Nothing grew here,
ot even lichen. Sand and stone, grey and black, a landscape
f sterility.

In the center of the wasteland was an enormous conical
airn built of dull grey-black stone, larger than the Great Li-
rary of Armethalieh and as tall as a four-story building, with
 set of stairs spiraling around it to the top. Its base was
inged with more of the boulders that were scattered about
ne mountaintop, as if someone were trying to fence it in. At
s apex stood a glittering black obelisk, the top half of it just
isible from this angle.

But in all of this deadness, the obelisk was alive.

All of the obelisk that Kellen could see from where he
tood was covered with tendrils of greenish energy like min-
ature lightning bolts. They spat and hissed along the surface,
icking out at the wind. They ran over the sides of it like
ome terrible fountain, constantly spewing from the crown
nd running down the sides in an endless cascade like some
ideous toxic wellspring of all that was bad and unholy in
ne world.

This, without a doubt, was the source of the disruption to
ne natural order of the world, the Barrier that he had come
 destroy.

Kellen glanced up toward the sky. Though the day had
een overcast when they started and the clouds had not lifted,
ne sky directly above the point of the obelisk was clear, a

huge unnatural ring of cloudless sky that was now the white of mountain twilight.

This was the place he'd seen in his dreams, or as close to it as Kellen ever wanted to come while he was awake. And there was a *wrongness* about it that wasn't subtle at all.

"Here," Vestakia groaned. "This place."

Kellen turned back to see Vestakia sink to her knees, her face contorted with nausea.

Shalkan managed a few steps toward her and nuzzled her sympathetically, but Kellen could see that the unicorn wasn't in much better shape. The place reeked of Evil.

Now, that particular phrase had occurred in many a wondertale that Kellen had read, and it happened to be a conceit he thought both trite and overwrought. He hadn't really understood until this moment that there was usually some truth behind even the most overused of metaphors. The place *stank*. Not in a physical way, but it was just *wrong*.

It wasn't really something he was perceiving through his normal physical senses, Kellen realized. Each time he tried to focus one of his senses upon the pervasive sense of utter *wrongness,* he realized he wasn't really sensing what he thought he was, but it didn't help. When he concentrated, he could tell there was no particular odor to the place, but the moment he did that, the wind took on a discordant, jangling keening note that was a subtle torment. When he concentrated on the fact that he wasn't really hearing anything out of the ordinary, the horrible smells returned, and when he could shut out both the scent and sound of the place, his eyes insisted that everything around him was tilting and wavering, moving and yet standing still in a way that made him ill to see it. At least he could *pick* which sense he wanted to have abused, more or less.

But obviously neither Shalkan nor Vestakia were able to do even that much. It was simplest to say that the place reeked of evil, and to be honest, Kellen couldn't imagine how the unicorn could bear it. Now that he could *feel* the wrongness of the structure just as Vestakia did, the presence of the obelisk was agony to him and to Shalkan as well as to her

He didn't think either of the others would be able to get much closer to the Shadow keystone.

Fortunately Jermayan . . .

Then he took a good look at Jermayan.

The Elven Knight was leaning on his sword for support, using it as if it were a cane. His hand was pressed to his side where he'd taken the blow from the Centaur's mace, as if it were still fresh and unhealed. His face was pale and set—with pain now, instead of hatred. But Kellen had healed him . . .

Then Kellen realized what must be happening. The Demon-magic was very powerful here, powerful enough to undo Kellen's magic, or at least to suppress its effects. At this moment, Jermayan's wound was suddenly as fresh as if Kellen had never worked his Wildmagery and it had only had a few days to heal on its own. At least it *was* partly healed: it meant that Jermayan wouldn't bleed to death on the spot.

"I'm sorry," he said aloud. *I'm sorry I got the three of you into this. I should have come alone. I'm sorry . . .*

"Do what you came to do," Jermayan said, his voice harsh with pain.

Kellen looked back at the sky. In an hour—no more—it would be dark.

He took off his armored gauntlets and the gloves beneath and set them down on the ground. The chill wind—real or illusion, it hardly mattered—bit into his flesh, numbing his fingers. He flexed his hands, willing warmth and suppleness into his fingers, then reached into the pouch that held Idalia's keystone. He drew it out and unwrapped it.

This was the first time he'd actually had a chance to take a good look at Idalia's keystone.

It didn't look like a standard keystone at all. All of them were round or oval, and small enough to fit into the palm of the hand. Even Armethalieh's golden Talismans were flat rune-scribed disks, nothing like this. The last time he'd seen it—by torchlight, at the unicorn meadow in Sentarshadeen—he'd thought it was black. Now it looked as if it were made of the same opaque white crystal Idalia had always used for her keystones.

It was the size of a small melon. On the outside, it was shaped just like a section of natural mineral crystal, a square six-sided tube that tapered to a six-sided cone at the end. But inside, the keystone had a different shape. Inside, there was a four-sided cup that tapered to a point inside. It would obviously fit right over the top of the black obelisk he'd already seen. The Wild Magic had known what exactly he'd be facing, even if Idalia hadn't.

As he held it in his bare hands for the first time, it began to glow softly.

At that moment, knowledge filled him—the same utter certainty that he felt when he worked a spell of the Wild Magic and gained his knowledge of the Mageprice. Idalia was right he *did* know what to do! He felt as if Idalia was standing behind him now, her hand on his shoulder, lending him her strength as she murmured her final instructions into his ear. He knew precisely what he had to do to use this keystone.

The only problem was that it would require a little preparation.

He set it back gently into the spell-caul for the moment, and set the silk on the ground, and slowly began to remove his armor.

"What are you doing?" Jermayan demanded, his voice tight with pain.

"I can't wear my armor for this," Kellen said. No armor, no weapons, nothing of metal. Anything metallic would attract that power crawling all over the obelisk. He wasn't sure what would happen then, only that it wouldn't be good.

Not that marching up there without armor and weapons was good, either, but he didn't have much of a choice.

He was far from being as calm as he felt, or as certain. Releasing Idalia's spell was no longer something he was going to do sometime in the future, it was now, in the next few minutes, after which nobody, least of all him, would ever again be able to say that he wasn't a full-fledged Wildmage.

If he could do it.

Doubts flooded his mind as he peeled off pieces of armor and laid them aside. After all, who was *he* to be attempting this thing? Even without an army, or even a guard of Demons watching the obelisk in the open, he was certain there were things lying in wait around here. Or at the least, there must be some species of alarm that he would set off when he entered the enclosure. Then what?

A lot of bad things, almost certainly.

What am I doing here, anyway? What possessed anyone to think I was up to this job, when all I ever do is muck things up? Kellen thought despairingly.

When he'd found the three Books of the Wild Magic in the Low Market, he'd had a home and a family and a bright future available for the asking. He'd thrown away all three for stubbornness and willful pride. He was probably never going to see Armethalieh again, and the longer he was away from it, the more he realized how much he missed the City.

No, not the City. He missed what the City *could* have been—a place of justice, and honor, and law. He missed the fact that he'd used to believe that it was. He missed the sound of the City bells on a winter morning, and spice-bread and hot black tea, the small good things that you couldn't get anywhere else. Suddenly he missed them very much.

Sentarshadeen was gorgeous, but—it was full of Elves, who weren't the most *comfortable* of neighbors. Merryvale— well, there probably wasn't much left of Merryvale now, even though Idalia hadn't been able to get any news of it. He longed for the company of simple, uncomplicated humans (and Centaurs) with a kind of craving.

And in a way, he longed for his old life, as well, and the days when his only responsibilities were to be the good son and student his father wanted.

And most of all, at that moment, Kellen realized that the more he learned about the Wild Magic, the more he realized that it really was truly a dangerous thing. Beneficial, yes, necessary, yes, but not a *tame* magic, one with the consequences all laid out in advance, where you could see them before you acted. The Wild Magic demanded belief, a faith that the world's needs were more important than your own comfort and safety, and far more important than your own peace of mind.

And that—well, that implied that it could be dangerous to *him* one day. Someday—and maybe that day was now—it might very well ask a Mageprice of him that would kill him, cripple him, or change him beyond recognition, and the Wild Magic wouldn't care, because it couldn't care, any more than a general could care about whether or not one of the individual soldiers in his army got hurt in war. The general knew that the war itself was worth fighting, that was all. The Wild Magic would bargain whatever it needed to, for the greater good of all—and some would fall in seeing that greater good accomplished. Wonderful if you were one of the survivors, but pretty hard on the ones who weren't.

Piece by piece, Kellen removed his Elven armor and set it aside, as carefully as if he were certain he would be coming back for it. And as he did, a second set of thoughts occurred to him, no more comforting than the first. In neutralizing this spell—if he had the strength, the luck, the will—he would be placing himself—not Sentarshadeen, not Idalia, but *him*, Kellen Tavadon—in direct opposition to the Prince of Shadow Mountain. The Demons, the Endarkened, the creatures that haunted his innermost fears, the monsters that frightened even Jermayan and Queen Ashaniel, that terrified Vestakia, would be hunting *him*.

He'd stood up to the Arch-Mage of Armethalieh—his own father—and the consequences of that had been grim enough to make him wary of the penalties of rash defiance. The full cost of that act was one Kellen was only barely coming to realize, one that he was going to face for the rest of his life. What would be the price of making a personal enemy of the Prince of the Demon Legions of Hell and his allies?

Kellen stood shivering in his underpadding and leather socks. He picked up the keystone again. The crystal was warm in his hands, the only warmth in all the world. It seemed to pulse with sleeping life.

He hesitated, glancing up at the fog of green lightning around the obelisk.

He was afraid. He had to acknowledge that. In fact, he was terrified. Not because he didn't know what would happen, but because he was fairly sure he did. No matter what was to come, it was going to be bad. The only question was, how bad?

For a moment Kellen felt nothing but panic and despair that held him frozen in place where he stood. He *felt* the hatred here, in a way that was hard to articulate. The things that had created this place, the emotion they had for everything that was *not them* was so malevolent that the word *hatred* didn't begin to describe it. Even if he succeeded here—and there was no guarantee of that—nothing would be over. All the four of them would have done was end the drought in the Elven lands and alert Shadow Mountain to the fact that the Elves knew the Endarkened were moving against them and preparing to strike at the World Above once more. Shadow Mountain would still be as powerful. The Elves would still be as weak. Armethalieh would still be as blind and arrogant, thinking of nothing but itself.

Nothing much would change for anyone, except for Kellen. *He* would have made powerful enemies, enemies that would not stop until they had taken their revenge for what he'd done here today. Was even Sentarshadeen strong enough to protect him? *Would* they, if they could?

Would he want them to? Could he live with being the reason why Shadow Mountain brought their agents, their armies, against the Elves of Sentarshadeen?

He looked down at the keystone. He held his future in his hands. He could drop it and run. It would break. If not here, then he could do it once he got to the other side of the cairn, where the others wouldn't see. He could throw it off the side of the cairn. Then he wouldn't have to make this choice. He wouldn't have all the Demons of Shadow Mountain after him personally. He could sneak down the far side, get back to Armethalieh somehow. Lycaelon would forgive him—especially if he renounced the Wild Magic and told him every-

thing he knew about the trouble among the Elves and in th
border lands.

Oh, he could see it so clearly: he could become his father'
favored son again; there'd be some tale put about of hi
having been sent out as a special agent, and he'd be safe
safe, *safe* . . .

But then he looked at Vestakia. She'd struggled to her feet
clutching at Shalkan's shoulder for support. Vestakia ha
lived every day of her life on the run from the Prince o
Shadow Mountain—not hypothetically but really—she'
been fathered by a Demon but had never given up the figh
to be human. He looked at Jermayan, who hated Demons wit
every fiber of his Elven soul, but stood beside a woman wh
looked like one, who had been fathered by one, and did s
now because he trusted Kellen.

Both of them—and Shalkan—were counting on him t
keep his part of the bargain he'd begun when he first bega
to read *The Book of Moon*. He couldn't back out now. Thi
was his price. He wouldn't refuse to pay it.

Maybe I'll die here, Kellen thought in a kind of grim hope
Compared to being the target of the entire race of Demons
death didn't seem terribly bad. Death—or failure—if he die
trying, surely Jermayan would take up the stone (if it wa
still intact) and see the task to its end. Surely, now that he
knew what to do with it, it didn't require a Wildmage to
actually put it in place!

He clutched the keystone tighter, imagining it cracking ir
his hands—accidentally!—knowing that even amid the guil
and horror he would feel nothing so much as relief at the
choice and responsibility that would be taken from him in
that moment. *I'm only a boy! I'm only seventeen!* a voice
deep within his mind shouted despairingly. *I've never done
anything special in my life! I'm not ready for this!*

Part of him yearned desperately to believe that, but even
if it were true, it couldn't be allowed to make a difference
now. Ready or not, able or not, he had to do what he had
come here for, because so very much depended on him.

He turned away from the others and began to walk slowly

across the broken wasteland toward the cairn. Taking the first step was the hardest thing he'd ever done, and it was only after he'd begun to walk that Kellen realized he hadn't even said good-bye. But he knew that if he stopped, or turned back, or spoke, he would never have the strength to start walking again, and so he gritted his teeth and kept walking. If he got back, he'd be able to explain. If they all died here, it wouldn't matter.

He had not gotten more than twenty paces away before the first attack struck him.

Only it wasn't the first attack, was it? They'd been under attack from the moment they set foot on the mountaintop, Kellen realized. Why else would he even have *considered* betraying his friends and going back to Armethalieh?

It was terrifying to realize he couldn't even trust his own thoughts!

I won't give in, he told himself stubbornly. *I WILL take the keystone to the top of the cairn. I WILL do what Idalia trusted me to do. I WILL . . .*

The next attack was subtle as well, though now Kellen was suspicious of everything. It began with pain, but not intense pain, only the dull aching of every muscle in his body. As if he were in the throes of a fever, except that he was so cold . . . as if he had been beaten from head to toe. But the pain increased the nearer he drew to the cairn. His real injuries hurt far more than they should have. Each step was an agony, as if his muscles were filled with lead. Each impact of his foot against the ground jarred his bruises into sullen life, until his whole body ached like a rotten tooth, and he trembled with pain as much as cold.

Though he knew his friends were only a few yards away, that if he turned and looked back he could still see them, Kellen felt utterly alone, as if when he had taken that first step he had somehow passed into a place where they could not follow.

And despite the fact that he was the one who had moved, he felt as if it was they who had abandoned him. He was out here alone, likely to die, and they didn't care.

Jermayan doesn't care about me. He never did. He onl cares about the Elves, about ending the drought. He onl pretended to like me to get me here.

If Idalia was such a great Wildmage, why hadn't she com back to the City for him? Why had she left him to suffer lonely and despised in his father's house? She knew bette than anyone else what it was like, but she had left him there And then, Idalia had left him again, to do this thing that he wasn't ready for, and she didn't care.

Why had Alance left both of them with Lycaelon, knowing what kind of man he was? What kind of mother would aban don her children to a man like that? His mother had though only of herself and the trap that she was escaping. She didn' care either, about either of her children.

Why had no one in all the City cared what Lycaelon di to either of his children? The Law was supposed to be Ar methalieh's greatest treasure, but the Mages set themselves above the Law. No one would interfere in a Mage's persona life, and so—corrupt, petty, vindictive as they were—the Ma ges of Armethalieh were a Law above the Law, and their families suffered for it. And the Mages gave everyone the safe little world that they wanted, no one cared what that cost

No one cared.

He knew his thoughts were petty, unworthy, coming from a part of him that wanted to live at any price, that would do anything, say anything, to get him to give up and turn back. He knew the thoughts came from the cairn, from Shadow Mountain, from the Demons. Kellen ignored the voice, letting it say what it would, letting the words pass over him un heeded. He didn't even care if that inward voice reflected who he truly was. It wasn't who he wanted to be. It wasn't who he *would* be.

He had a choice. He was free.

Kellen walked on.

He kept his eyes fixed on the ground, both to shut out the terrifying sight of the obelisk, and to keep from stepping on a stone. The only thing covering his feet were the thick leather socks he had worn beneath his armored boots. Kellen's feet were quickly growing numb with cold, but if he stepped on a stone and cut himself, or twisted his ankle, he might not be able to walk. And he had to be able to walk, at least as far as the top of the cairn.

Even if he was alone and abandoned. Even if he had no true friends, no family worthy of the name. Even if despair weighed him down so heavily that it felt as if he should be staggering beneath the weight of it. Despair drove him even to tears; he felt them leaking out of the corners of his eyes, but he was too sunk in despondency to care.

At last—he had no idea how long it took—Kellen reached the ring of stones at the foot of the cairn. They were not directly at the base, he saw now, nor did they completely enclose it. There was a gap about six feet wide between two tall stones, and through the gap he could see that the cairn did not rest on the same level ground as the rest of the mountaintop, but at the bottom of a deep pit which began a few feet inside the ring of stones. The sides of the pit were absolutely vertical except where a long sloping path led down between the stones and into the pit.

The cairn was much taller than he'd realized; from where the four of them had stood, they had only been able to see the top two-thirds. He would have to go down in order to go up. Down into a place that had almost certainly been designed as a trap.

Kellen hesitated just outside the tall stones, almost unable to force himself to walk between them. The closer he got to the obelisk, the more he could sense the Darkness radiating from it. The air seemed thick and dirty, heavy now with that bitter scent and taste, making him reluctant to breathe, as if he were accepting the obelisk's foulness into his lungs when he did. With a conscious effort, Kellen compelled himself to breathe deeply. There was no point in half-measures when he was actually going to have to *touch* the thing.

He felt a little better once he did, as if the icy air had cleared his head, and a few good breaths had actually swept some of that despair away from him. He was shivering in earnest now, and his body ached with cold. He wished he

had his sword, or even a dagger, but the instructions that ha
come with the keystone had been quite specific. He coul
bring nothing with him but the keystone. The stone and him
self.

He continued forward, stumbling a little through the stone
down the path to the cairn itself.

In the temporary relief from the wind, it was almost warm
He could still hear it moaning, but at least the cold wasn
cutting through to his bones. Going down was a little easie
than going up, which made it a little easier to resist the spir
itual attack on him, the attempt to make him give up befor
he started.

And in a way, that was heartening. If despair was the De
mons' primary weapon—perhaps the odds weren't as grea
as he feared.

Soon he was facing the cairn itself, and the long windin
grey stone staircase that led to the top.

Here was where the Demons had battled in his vision—
hordes of them beneath a black-red sky filled with gree
lightning. Had his vision been of the past, or of the near
future? Would they come now?

He could feel them, though they were not visible. Thei
presence was everywhere. And one step on the stairs woul
be the trigger that released them.

He almost turned back then to warn the others, though h
wasn't sure even now what he'd say. Why hadn't he tol
them earlier, when there was time?

You're stalling, he realized, and smiled grimly to himself
Stalling didn't make this any easier, and not going up thos
stairs didn't guarantee that the monsters from his dreams and
visions wouldn't come. No matter what he did, they woul
come.

He took a step forward and placed his foot on the first o
the steps.

Suddenly the wind's force increased, changing from a
steady monotonous whine to a howling gale in an instant
But even that was not enough to mask the shrieks, the howls

the tumult of the creatures as they were released from whatever arcane concealment they'd been held in.

He looked back. He could see nothing but the wall of the pit, but he didn't need to see to know what was happening now, this instant.

This was the place of the monsters of his vision, and the monsters were on their way. Imprisoned in the rocks, perhaps, or held in pits, or even materializing out of the thin air, taking the path between the rocks to the cairn, to tear him limb from limb and end the threat of the keystone forever.

He had never had a chance, of course, and he stood there in a state of fatalistic resignation, waiting for them to come.

But fast as they must be, Jermayan and the others were faster. Ill and wounded as they were, it was Jermayan, Shalkan, and Vestakia—not the monsters—who appeared between the rocks that guarded the entrance to the path. They took a stand just between the tall rocks Kellen had passed through. The stones formed a natural gateway to the cairn, and one that could be defended.

As the Seven defended that pass?

He saw Vestakia snatch Jermayan's bow and quiver from his shoulder, and nock an arrow on the string, and fire.

Kellen hesitated, on the verge of turning back to help them. But he had no weapons, no armor, only the keystone in his hands.

It could be that this was what the Demons wanted him to do—turning back to help his friends would certainly doom them, for unless he placed the keystone on top of the obelisk and triggered the spell, all was truly lost.

He trembled in place, almost physically torn in two.

—Longing to run to join them as a Knight-Mage should.

—Knowing his duty as a Wildmage and a Knight-Mage lay in finishing the task he'd begun.

A Wildmage's honor lies in betrayal. Finally I understand.

With a bitter cry, he turned away from the sight of his friends, blinking hard against sudden tears.

They were going to die. Jermayan was wounded, Shalkan and Vestakia were poisoned by the emanations of this hellish place. The three of them could barely stand. How could they fight?

Go on. Don't make them die for nothing.

He took a second step, then a third, up the grey stairs. And then, he began to run.

⊂⊃

"HOW long?" Vestakia asked in a small voice, watching Kellen walk away from them.

"As long as it takes to climb the tower and set the keystone into position," Jermayan answered shortly. He took a step forward, leaning heavily on his sword as he peered after Kellen. His wound—or the hell-spawned magic of this place—must be affecting his vision. The boy seemed somehow *insubstantial,* as though he moved through mist. But no. The rocks around him were as sharp as ever to Jermayan's sight. It was only Kellen who had taken on the aspect of unreality.

He darted a suspicious glance at Vestakia, but the sight of her obvious misery was enough to make even Jermayan think twice about accusing her.

"Where he goes now, even you cannot follow, Elven Knight," Shalkan said. The unicorn sounded utterly weary, and pressed close against Vestakia, as if seeking comfort there.

"Will he die?" Jermayan asked, putting his greatest fear into words.

"We will all die if he cannot do this," Shalkan said flatly. "We three. Sentarshadeen. The Wildwood. Even Armethalieh and beyond. If they cannot be held here, the trickle of gravel that heralds the avalanche will have begun."

When Jermayan looked again, Kellen had nearly reached the rocks surrounding the cairn, moving toward the natural gateway in the stone ring. Yet he could not have gone so far at the slow pace he'd been making in the short time since Jermayan had last looked. Jermayan shuddered. This was a horrible place. Nothing was as it seemed, but all of it was evil, polluted, and vile. The pain of his wounds was a wholesome thing compared to the crawling sense of *uncleanness* that seemed to fill the very air, and Jermayan was neither Wildmage, nor Demon-bred, nor creature of magic. How much worse must it be for the others?

There was nothing to do but wait.

Slowly it grew darker.

"Ah, Good Goddess save us!" Vestakia cried in a high terrified voice, jerking away from Shalkan. "Something is coming!"

Jermayan whirled, swinging his sword up and taking a defensive stance, though the movement made him feel as if someone had plunged a red-hot poker into his side. For a moment he saw nothing, then his keen Elven eyes detected a flicker of shadow at the edges of several of the boulders.

Without thought, he grabbed Vestakia's hand and ran.

The stone ring—they're after Kellen—

Behind him, he heard howling.

Chapter Twenty-five

Battle at the Cairn

The three of them reached the stone gateway and turned to face their pursuers. Jermayan leaned against one of the pillars for support, and as he did, he felt Vestakia reaching under his cloak, pulling his bow and quiver free.

"I know how to use these," she said grimly, slinging the heavy war-quiver over her shoulder. It held six dozen arrows, but she shouldered its weight without difficulty. She strung the bow and nocked an arrow with one swift expert motion.

"This is the only way to the cairn," Shalkan reported, drawing himself up and preparing to fight. His horn had begun to glow: the bright silvery blue of moonlight.

"We have to hold them here for as long as we can," Jermayan said grimly. The pain of his wound was forgotten; an Elven Knight was trained to ignore such things. But it would sap his strength, his speed . . .

He didn't say what they all knew: they were going to die here. The Demon-girl was welcome to his dagger as well as his bow, but they faced overwhelming numbers. All they could do was buy Kellen time.

Running toward them across the broken ground of the stony waste was an army of goblins, their bulging silver eyes squinting against what was to them the painful brightness of twilight and the unicorn's horn. They gibbered and cackled and howled as they ran, opening frog-wide mouths to expose endless rows of shark-bright teeth. Their glistening hairless skins were all the colors of bruises: purple and black and green. Some swung themselves along on their elongated forearms, like the apes they somewhat resembled, others shambled upright, the better to carry weapons. Most preferred to rely on their natural weapons—teeth and claws, speed and strength.

The Endarkened, Jermayan knew, kept them as pets. In the Great War, they had used them as shock troops. They could move through earth as if it were air, and that, of course, was how they had lain hidden until some trap-spell alerted and released them. Goblins would eat anything, and not wait until it was dead to begin. A goblin horde could devour an ox down to the bone in minutes.

Vestakia fired, choosing her targets with both speed and care. Each time she fired, she hit her mark, and the goblins nearby the victim stopped to devour their fallen comrade.

And that was an unexpected help. Fights broke out over the division of the spoils, as members of the horde turned on each other and fought. Vestakia was careful to space her targets, to spread the chaos as far as possible, and to conserve her arrows.

But some got through.

"Back!" Jermayan shouted as the goblin sprang at him. A quick slice of his sword cut it nearly in two, and left it twitching out its life at his feet. He killed four more almost immediately. They were easy to kill, and as long as they didn't get close enough to spit poison in his eyes, or onto his exposed skin, he was safe enough. Their deadliness lay in their sheer numbers, and the fact that they were too single-minded to retreat even when they were being slaughtered. They'd just keep coming.

And sooner or later they *would* wear him down, and poison him. They were strong enough to rip his armor off to get at what was underneath while he lay paralyzed. And then it would be over.

Vestakia ducked out from behind him again and again and began shooting, and Jermayan took advantage of that to throw the dead goblins as far toward the horde as possible.

"They spit poison!" Jermayan shouted at her, afraid suddenly that she might be taken unawares.

"I'm immune!" she shouted back. "I found that out a long time ago! And Shalkan can purge you of poison!"

Jermayan spared a moment for a pang of relief. Another help, and one he had not expected; the unicorn might not be able to *heal* him, but the touch of his horn would neutralize any poison, even from a goblin bite.

So all they had to worry about was being torn to pieces and eaten alive. That was comforting. Jermayan glanced toward the unicorn. Shalkan had a goblin skewered on the end of his horn. With a snap, the unicorn sent the body flying back into the horde.

But the goblins kept coming.

Somehow the creatures decided that Vestakia was the most vulnerable. They feared Shalkan, and Jermayan was well protected by his armor, but they kept taking desperate risks to get at Vestakia, and finally Jermayan realized why.

It's not that she's the most vulnerable. They want her. They must have orders to take her alive!

His suspicion was confirmed when several goblins managed to get past Shalkan and knock Vestakia down. Rather than bursting through the gate after Kellen—or beginning to devour Vestakia on the spot—they grabbed her legs and began dragging her back toward the horde.

Vestakia screamed, a wail of nightmare terror. The goblin horde swarmed forward. But it didn't attack. It was waiting, waiting until it had claimed Vestakia.

Shalkan was too far away. If he came to her aid, the goblins would have the opening they sought without having to wait. They'd pour through the gate and be after Kellen in an instant.

Jermayan sprang forward and grabbed her by the hair. He hauled back with all his strength, jerking Vestakia toward him, pulling her and both the goblins into the air. He got his hands, sword and all, under her armpits and whirled, though the pain of his wound made him cry out in a high-pitched wail of his own.

He cracked her legs like a whip as he lifted her, retreating between the stones, but the two goblins refused to let go. She kicked and struggled frantically, screaming at the top of her lungs, but the goblins dug their claws into her legs and hissed.

With another howl of agony Jermayan caught her up around the waist with his unencumbered arm. Still holding her in the air, Jermayan swung his sword, thrusting more goblins back as they rushed forward to help their horde mates. He wouldn't be able to hold her up much longer— already it was torture—and the moment the goblins got their feet on the ground, the battle for Vestakia would be lost.

Then Shalkan appeared. Almost delicately, the unicorn slipped his horn through the body of one of the goblins. The wound smoked. The goblin convulsed, and Vestakia whimpered as its claws dug deeper for a moment before it dropped off, dead. Jermayan marveled to see that even then, its horde brother still clung to Vestakia, as if having reached the long-sought prize, it could not bear to relinquish it. What price, what price had been set upon her by her Demon father?

All true, Jermayan realized in that instant. *All she said— true.*

The goblin glared at Jermayan, and spat. The poison struck

his surcoat harmlessly and bubbled away, steaming. The vile liquid stank.

Shalkan killed that one, too. Jermayan kicked the bodies away, stumbling backward into the gap again.

The fight over their fallen comrades kept the goblins occupied for a moment, giving the defenders a respite. Jermayan could only thank the Powers that it had been goblins that had been sent against them. Anything else would not have been distracted from battle by food. For the moment, the horde was only a snarling, slavering feeding frenzy, ignoring their real foes.

"Can you stand?" Shalkan asked.

Vestakia nodded.

"Can you fight?" Jermayan asked.

She nodded again, blinking back tears.

"I thought—I thought—" Vestakia gasped.

"Not—while—I'm—here—" Jermayan snarled, his voice shaking with pure rage. How *dare* those unclean things think they could steal one of his battle comrades from beneath his arm, a woman who had stood beside him in this place of death and hell, and that he, Jermayan of the House of Leaf and Star, would stand by and do *nothing*?

He thrust her dropped bow into her hands and turned away, letting his fury flow into his sword, banishing weakness. The horde surged forward again, and Jermayan's sword filled the air with sprays of goblin ichor.

⌒

THE moment of respite passed, and the horde came again, and they fought. Another moment of peace, while the dead were eaten, and then another wave. It was now too dark to make out the individual forms of the dark-skinned goblins, even by the light of Shalkan's horn, but as far as they could see, the plain was filled with hungry watching silver eyes that glowed brighter as the darkness deepened. The howling of the goblins was loud enough to drown out even the ever-present moaning of the wind.

The space before the stone gateway was clear of the dead. Under cover of their attacks, the goblin horde tidily dragged away its dead to devour them. But there were always more goblins, and the monsters were always hungry, and every moment the battle continued, true night drew closer, and true night was the time of the goblins' greatest power. How long since Kellen had begun his ascent? Had something gone wrong?

How much longer could they hold the gateway?

"Jermayan!" Vestakia shouted over the yammering howls of the goblins. *"I'm running out of arrows!"*

⟜

UP and around the circumference of the cairn he went, and as he did, the wind slowly increased again as he drew level with the surface of the plain. His legs ached so badly he thought that he would surely never be able to rise if he fell; his side burned, and Kellen hardly seemed to get any air at all from the panting gasps he pulled into his lungs. The wind itself was his enemy, tearing at him, blurring his vision, trying to rip him off the stairs or freeze him in place. It seemed to Kellen now as if the source of the wind was the obelisk itself, as if it blew *out* of the obelisk from someplace not of this world. The wind was colder even than before, and with each step Kellen took the force of it increased, until it was blowing so hard that he had to lean into it and press himself hard against the side of the cairn to keep from being blown off.

As if from a great distance, he could hear inhuman yelping and the sounds of battle. If he looked, he would be able to see it as well, down over the plain, but he refused to look. He could not afford to be distracted from his battle with the obelisk; it took all his concentration to keep his footing on the stairs against the ceaseless hammering of the increasingly frigid wind. Kellen's teeth chattered uncontrollably; tears that now owed nothing to grief streamed from his eyes and froze along his cheeks and lashes. He gripped Idalia's keystone hard against his stomach and prayed that it would hold together as fervently as he had once hoped it might crack.

And then, as a further torment, grit began to pelt him, mixed with the wind, as if the force of the storm were starting to dissolve the cairn itself. Fine sand at first, that left him blinking and half-blind, but soon heavier sand that left his skin feeling raw, then good-sized pieces of gravel and small rocks that hammered his skin, leaving bruises and even drawing blood. He could taste grit between his teeth, on his tongue, feel it in his nose, in his lungs, choking him. He pulled his undertunic up over his head. It was hard to breathe through the heavy quilted material, but as he heard the wind-driven sand hiss over its surface, Kellen was glad he'd done it. Better to be half-stifled than arriving at the top of the cairn blind. Slowly his tears washed his eyes clean.

He was even gladder to have done it when the sandstorm became heavier, quickly escalating from fine grit to stinging particles that left his exposed skin feeling raw, and good-sized pieces of gravel and small rocks that pelted his skin stingingly, and even drew blood. At this rate, he'd be dodging boulders soon.

And he needed to protect the keystone as well as his eyes and lungs. Kellen quickly tucked the keystone under his shirt, and turned toward the wall so it was protected by his body. It was as icy against his skin as it had once been warm against his hands. He ducked his head beneath his tunic, turning his face against the wall, and crept, crabwise and even more slowly, up the stairs. The sand made them slippery, and he knew that Something was hoping he'd fall and break the fragile keystone.

As he'd feared, small stones were soon joined by larger stones, as the fury of the gale—or the intelligence behind it—tore off pieces of the mountain and flung them at Kellen. He groaned as fist-sized chunks of rock struck him—on the shoulders, the ribs, the leg, hammering against the bruises the shepherd's club had made. Only that morning? It seemed an eternity ago. At least the howling of the wind and the booming of the rocks against the stone shut out all sound of the battle below. If it was still going on. If all his friends weren't dead already. If Vestakia hadn't been taken, kidnapped into a slavery and torture she feared more than death. *Please, let that at least not have happened.*

I won't look back, Kellen promised himself. *Whatever happens, I won't look back.*

He couldn't believe he was doing this. And it was so unfair for the enemy he faced to be throwing *rocks* at him in addition to hurricanes, monsters, and all the rest. It seemed so petty, somehow, so much like the action of something that saw him as a mere nuisance, an insect—or as if he faced, not a dignified enemy that fought with solemn strategy, but a petty spoiled child that had lost its temper.

Or else that he meant so *little,* that he was so unimportant, so meager a threat, that the enemy deemed it sufficient to batter him with a few rocks, figuring he would turn tail and run.

That, as much as all the pain, the uncertainty, the grief and despair, nearly broke Kellen's spirit.

Only his anger at the insult saved him.

Anger is a weapon, as much as your sword.

"I'll—show—*you!*" he snarled through clenched teeth. And went on. Slowly, agonizingly slowly, blind, aching, terrified, but now, above all else, angry, he went on.

The worst part was when there was no more wall beside him. Kellen realized that must mean he was near the top of the cairn. Groping blindly, his head still muffled in his tunic, he slid his hand along the wall in front of his face, upward until he touched emptiness. The wind pushed at his fingertips with the force of a wave of water. If he tried to simply walk up to where the obelisk was, the wind would pluck him off and hurl him to the ground.

Very well. Then he would crawl.

Kellen got down on his hands and knees and crawled up the rest of the stairs, brushing the sand away carefully from each step before him. It caked on his abraded hands, and every time he wiped them clean on his tunic, one after the other, always keeping one hand wrapped tight around the keystone beneath his tunic, fresh blood welled up from a thousand tiny scratches. And the wind still blew, cold enough to leach all sensation from his flesh.

He reached a flat place, and crawled out onto it, pushing against the wind.

Suddenly the wind stopped.

"Well, you make a fine sight," a voice said from somewhere above him, sounding amused.

The voice was elusively familiar.

Kellen dragged his tunic down around his neck and stared, blinking, into the watery green light.

He was facing . . . himself?

Another Kellen stood on the other side of the obelisk, grinning down at him nastily. The point of the obelisk came just to his heart level. This Kellen was sleek and manicured—no one would ever call his smooth brown curls unruly!—and dressed in the height of Armethaliehan finery, from his shining half-boots of tooled and gilded leather to his fur-lined half-cape and the pair of jeweled and embroidered silk gloves tucked negligently through his gleaming gilded belt. The cape and gloves were in House Tavadon colors, of course. No one would ever forget which Mageborn City House this young man belonged to, not for an instant.

Slowly, Kellen got to his feet, though his cramped and aching muscles protested. Instantly, Other-Kellen clapped his bare hands over the point of the obelisk, blocking Kellen's access to it.

"Think about what you're doing," Other-Kellen urged him. "*Really* think about it. Now, before it's too late. You've had a chance to taste freedom, and you've found it's a bitter wine. Only power can make it sweet, but you already know the responsibilities that power brings. Even the powerful aren't really free—everyone serves someone, or something. The only real freedom we have is of choosing our master, and most people don't get even that. But *you* can choose."

"I don't serve anyone!" Kellen said angrily.

"Oh? And you a Wildmage," Other-Kellen said mockingly. "I should think you would have learned better the moment you opened the Books."

Kellen snapped his mouth shut abruptly. If this was a fight, he'd just lost the first battle. He *did* serve the Wild Magic, and so far he'd done exactly what it told him to do, no matter what that was. How free did that make him?

"You've made some bad choices in the past," Other-Kellen continued smoothly. "Even you're willing to admit that. Wouldn't you like the chance to just undo them? To go back and start over, knowing what you know now? To make it right? You can have that. Erase the bad choices but keep the wisdom you've gained. Few people get that opportunity."

Other-Kellen smiled, and for the first time, Kellen could see his father's face mirrored in this stranger's that was his own. The sight shocked and distracted him, even in this moment and in this place. Assurance . . . competence . . . or just corruption?

No. Temptation—there it was. Even if he'd never put it into just those words, wasn't it exactly what he himself had thought so many times of doing?

"You left Armethalieh because you rebelled against Arch-Mage Lycaelon's plans for you, but you know better now, don't you? The life of a High Mage has its compensations— and the High Mages were right to want to build safeguards against the prices and bargains the Wild Magic required," his doppelganger said, his voice as silken and sweet as honey, reasonable and logical. Kellen himself had never sounded like that. "What's so wrong with trying to improve something? They still practice magic, and they still give their citizens a good life—and if life in the Golden City is too restrictive, well, when you're Arch-Mage, Kellen, you'll be able to make all the changes you've dreamed of, and make the City an even better place to live, one where the citizens have choices."

That shocked Kellen so much that he almost dropped the keystone. Of all of the things he had imagined and fantasized about, that was *never* one that had occurred to him!

"And you *can* be Arch-Mage," the double said, persuasively. "You *have* the gift and the talent; your father isn't wrong about that! If everyone must serve, then choose your service. Serve the City. Go back now, beg your father's for-giveness—it won't be that hard; he needs you to shore up his own failing prestige. He'll be grateful when you turn up again, full of repentance! Give up the Wild Magic. That won't be hard, either, will it? Step back into the life you *should* have had, and work for the good of Armethalieh. You'll have everything you wanted. All you have to know is where to look for it. And you know that now, don't you? You've learned. You've gained wisdom. Wouldn't it be a shame not to be able to apply it, to be able to give others the benefit of your experience? To help them? You'll be able to keep your memories, of course—what good is experience if you don't remember it? And you won't be wholly without resources. Or allies. Just think of all you can do for the City when you return . . ."

Kellen stared in horrified fascination at his doppelganger. Was this really him? The person he could have been—or could still be? If Lycaelon had been able to create the perfect heir by magick—If, a year and more ago, someone had asked Kellen what he wanted to be, and he hadn't thought clearly enough—

To help them. Even against the Demons? If he did this, could he even turn the City to help the Elves, and forge a new Alliance as in the old days?

But Jermayan would know what had happened—

Shalkan *surely* would—

"Your companions are already dead. You have no one to consider but yourself. No one will know what happened here but you. Isn't it time you did what *you* want, for a change? Here is your future, Kellen. You have but to reach out and seize it. Power—glory—mastery—fame—everything you can imagine, even love. It can all be yours. And you will receive nothing but praise for your actions."

Now Kellen looked away, down toward the plain below, but he could see nothing at all of the battle that might still be raging there. Everything below the top of the cairn was covered with a thick layer of yellow-green fog. It was as if the rest of the world had vanished. Quickly he looked back at his doppelganger, suspecting a trick, but Other-Kellen had not moved. His doppelganger smiled at Kellen sympathetically, as if guessing the direction of Kellen's thoughts.

"But if you go through with this foolish adventure that you have undertaken at the behest of others, your future will be set. If you think you have troubles now, you can't even begin to imagine what your life is going to be like afterward— assuming you don't die right here. Think of the Demons. They know your name, Kellen. The Queen and Prince of the Endarkened know who you are." The double's voice caressed the names. "They know all about you, and they'll find you wherever you go. You won't have an easy death, or a quick one. They *love* Wildmages. They love to *play* with them and their power. Torment—oh, for them, it is the highest form of Art, and they have had millennia to perfect it. You won't die, but you will long for death with all of your being. For years, Kellen, for *years* . . ."

Other-Kellen shuddered in mock-sympathy, his eyes never leaving Kellen's face. Kellen trembled, remembering his nightmares, knowing they must have fallen far short of the truth.

"Oh, you might survive triggering the keystone. You might even manage to get back to Sentarshadeen alive, I'll grant you that. And I'm sure your friends the Elves will do their best for you. But it hasn't really been much of a best so far, has it? They couldn't even manage to save themselves without a Wildmage or two to help. And when it comes right down to it, they're going to take care of themselves and their families first once the trouble starts, aren't they? So it's just going to be you and Idalia, all alone with no one to help you, and how long do you think the two of you will survive? After all, you two are only humans, and blood is, as the saying goes, thicker than water. If anyone is protected, it will be other Elves, not a couple of barbaric, mayfly humans who can't even manage a conversation without being rude and uncouth."

The doppelganger snickered, and Kellen flushed, remem-

bering his stumbling attempts to converse with anyone in
Sentarshadeen other than the child Sandalon.

"I wouldn't say we're friends, exactly, but I would say I'm
the closest thing to a friend you've got. Right here. Right
now. *Think* about it, Kellen. This is your last chance. After
this, you have no choices left. *Think*. Use what you've
learned. They've all tried to keep the truth from you—even
Idalia—so you wouldn't know what the stakes are. Think
how hard you've had to work to find out what little you have.
Why is that? So you wouldn't know enough to make a fair
choice," Other-Kellen said.

Fair, Kellen thought bitterly. *Nothing about this is fair.*
Nothing had ever been fair and out in the open, from the
moment he'd found the three Books in the Low Market, and
hearing all his secret fears and unworthy hopes in the mouth
of this manicured popinjay was the least fair thing of all.

He remembered Jermayan telling him about The Seven—
how when they'd faced down the Endarkened army at the
pass of Vel-al-Amion and first beaten them back, the Endarkened had tried to seduce them to the Dark.

As one of the Endarkened was trying to seduce him now.
This, then, was their last line of defense, and the most compelling of all.

"Well . . ." Kellen said, walking closer and lifting the keystone in his hands as if he were about to hand it over. "I
guess I really ought to be smart and do what you say."

The Other-Kellen smiled triumphantly and relaxed, certain
of its victory.

"But I'm not going to!" Kellen shouted.

He brought the keystone down—hard—on the doppelganger's hands. It howled and recoiled as if it had been
burned, jerking its hands back from the point of the obelisk.

And in that moment, it . . . changed.

The Other-Kellen was gone. In its place stood a Demon.

It—*she!*—towered over Kellen, her wings spread wide. He
caught a confused glimpse of blood-red skin, of horns and
claws, but she was barely there for an instant, for in the moment that the Demon had released her hold on the obelisk,

Kellen slammed the keystone down over the tip of the stone.

The instant Idalia's keystone touched the obelisk, the Demon howled in fury and vanished, her cheated rage a whiplash across his senses. For a moment he was blind and deaf in a paroxysm of pain. He cringed, but kept his hands on the stone.

They had not counted on his experience with being lied to. And perhaps that was the greatest weapon Lycaelon Tavadon had given to him.

I know a lie when I hear it, you bastards.

Kellen trembled all over, realizing in that moment how close the Demon had come to winning. But it hadn't.

Now it was up to him. Despite everything he had already gone through, the hardest part was still to come. He took a deep breath and reached down into the keystone with his Wildmage senses, touching the power waiting within. The power leaped toward him eagerly, but Kellen knew that *he* was not to be its destination. Gently he turned it toward the obelisk.

He felt the obelisk's resistance, and pushed harder, adding the last of his strength and all of his will to the keystone's power, forcing the link into being. It was like healing an unwilling subject, if such a thing were conceivable.

One by one, the obelisk's defenses gave way. Kellen felt the triggering force begin to rush through him and into the obelisk. He kept his palms pressed against the keystone's sides; without him to maintain the link, the spell would be broken before the Barrier was breached. And all of it—the journey, the others' sacrifice—would all have been for nothing.

Then, breakthrough. And his body spasmed, convulsed, his mouth going open in a silent scream. It was nearly impossible to keep his feet; he wouldn't have been able to if his muscles hadn't all locked at once, freezing him in place; head flung back, back arched. He felt as if he were being struck by lightning, a bolt of energy that somehow went on and on and on, searing its way through him.

His hands were burning. He stood the pain as long as he

could in silence, but then he had to scream. Holding the keystone was like clutching red-hot metal fresh from the forge, and there was no respite, no mercy. He could smell the pork-like scent of his cooking flesh, could feel blood running down his wrists as blisters swelled up and burst, and then, in a thunderclap of agony, the fire was everywhere, coursing through his veins with every beat of his heart.

Kellen howled unashamedly, great wracking sobs of hopeless agony. And he held on. Perhaps it was stubbornness, but he had always been stubborn. And he would not give the Demons this victory.

I'm going to die.

Suddenly he realized that was the price of the spell, the rest of the cost. It must be. A Wildmage's life. Idalia must have known when she created the spell that the price of casting it would be the life of the one who triggered it. His life. Kellen felt a flash of pride in his sister at keeping the painful secret so well.

But he would have to consent. No Wildmage could give up that which belonged to another—not without turning to the Dark.

She had known the price of the magic, but she could only have hoped he would pay it.

If that's the price, he shouted silently to the Powers, *then I will pay it! I wish I didn't have to, but I swear I pay it willingly and without reservation!*

But more than ever, having surrendered his life, he yearned to keep it. To see the sun again, to feel the gentle summer wind, to walk through the forest or drink a cup of morning tea. But all those things had their price, and so did keeping them. And some prices were too high to pay. The price of his life would be the destruction of all those things, soon or late. The price of keeping his life would be victory for the Endarkened.

No. *Never.*

My life for the destruction of the Barrier. A fair bargain. Done. Done!

Then the pain was too great for thought.

As if it were made of flesh, not stone, the obelisk began to warm. Beneath his hands, seen even through his closed eyelids, it glowed an unhealthy green. The ground started to tremble beneath Kellen's feet, and a low rumbling sound filled the air, growing louder, becoming a roar, then a wail.

Abruptly the obelisk began to swell, its stark lines distorting as if the malign power it contained was backing up inside it, filling it beyond its capacity. Its swelling carried him upward; he collapsed against its surface, clinging to the keystone, and still it swelled. Now the stone was a baneful pus-yellow color, nearly spherical. Kellen lay upon its surface, unable to preserve the thought of anything beyond the need to maintain the link.

The whole cairn shook like a tree in a windstorm.

The wail rose to a scream. The toxic light flared lightning-bright.

And for Kellen, there was sudden darkness and a release from all pain.

Chapter Twenty-six

Storm Wind and Silver Feather

Waiting was the hardest thing.

No matter how many times Idalia told herself that Kellen had the more difficult and dangerous task, her own part—waiting for the Barrier to fall—ate at her self-control.

There was nothing she could do until the Barrier *did* fall, and the fact that she spent her days in comfort and safety while the two men she loved most in all the world—Kellen and Jermayan—rode off into danger did nothing to soothe either her nerves or her temper. And if Shadow Mountain should capture them, Idalia knew very well that the Endarkened would account both an Elf and a Wildmage—not to mention a unicorn—very great prizes. Jermayan and Shalkan would certainly die horribly. As for Kellen . . . death by torture would be the kindest of the things the Endarkened would do to a Wildmage who fell into their hands.

She thought about Jermayan often as the days passed. It was safe enough now, she thought bitterly. He was probably going to die making sure Kellen reached the Barrier alive. Why had she been so stubborn, so proud, so arrogant?

Stubborn as an Elf . . . When you came right down to it, everyone, Elf and human, had the same life span. They lived until they died, that was all—and with Shadow Mountain moving against the Bright World again, the lives of Elven Knights would be measured in years, not centuries.

A few days, a few hours, of happiness would have been something—a gift to him, a gift to herself, something they could have shared, a moment of sweet fulfillment with which to defy the monstrous Darkness that Jermayan was even now laying down his life to destroy.

Her thoughts were bleak, anguished, and the passing of the days only increased her despair.

Even if they succeeded, she would probably never see either of them again. The energy released when the spell was triggered would be . . . well, *she* did not know enough even to guess at the effects. Add to that the power of the unbound weather patterns, unleashed from their unnatural binding . . . lightning, hurricane, gale-force winds, and there, high in the mountains, in winter, snow. Heavy snow.

How could two men and a unicorn, probably wounded, battered, definitely alone, ever hope to survive even a single night in a blizzard?

Even success would not guarantee their safety, or their lives.

And so Idalia took care to keep entirely to herself in the days that followed Kellen's departure, lest her unhappiness contaminate the hope that was growing in Sentarshadeen with each passing day.

IT was over a sennight since they'd been gone. Idalia had been restless all day, wandering far beyond the city, into the Flower Forest beyond the House of Leaf and Star. There were no flowers now. She could feel the sorrow of the trees and plants, their slow withering starvation and death, and her helplessness in the face of their need was like a fresh grief. The narrow canals the Elves had dug to bring water to the forest held only dampness, for the five springs were not inexhaustible, nor were there enough Elves in Sentarshadeen to man the pumps to fill the canals every day.

Who shall live and who shall die? They have had to make so many choices already, and if my spell does not succeed, if Kellen and Jermayan do not succeed, they will have to make more . . .

Sick at heart, Idalia turned away from the slowly dying forest and crossed the unicorn meadow again. It was nearly lantern-lighting time, the bright, ever-cloudless sky dimming as the sun set. She should go home, and rest. Tomorrow morning she would come back here, to the spring called Songmairie and do as she did every morning. She would cast her Seeking Spell to see if the Barrier was down. Perhaps tomorrow she would scry as well, but she had been afraid to do that for fear of what her spell would show her. Like the Elves, Idalia wanted to hope until all hope of hope was gone.

Suddenly there came a pulse of magic so strong it staggered her; a lightless flash perceptible only to her Wildmage senses, but it blinded and deafened her to all else for one incredulous moment.

Kellen has triggered the keystone!

Wild hope and sudden fierce joy filled her. *He's gotten through!*

She stood, staring northward, fists clenched, willing him to hold out, to keep the link true until the spell was complete. She hadn't known she'd be able to sense it, but the keystone was part of her, formed of her magic and linked to her, and so she'd felt that first fierce uprush of energy as the keystone began to give up its spell. But now . . . nothing.

Nothing but hope, and her faith in all she knew Kellen to be.

Idalia turned and began to run.

She was back in less than half an hour with her tools and a full bag of charged keystones. Heart hammering, hands shaking, she dipped each in the spring and began to lay them out in a circle around her. There was a bag of crystallized honey-disks in her tool-bag as well, used for sweetening tea, and as she worked she pulled one out and popped it into her mouth. She'd need the energy, now and for the rest of the night. If the spell had worked.

Please, you Gods who shape the world. Let it be so!

She paused for a moment, waiting. But the spell would run fast once it was triggered. If it had worked, she would be able to sense the results now. Or the failure.

Once more—as she had done so many days ago—she dipped water from the Elven spring and scattered it around herself, touched water to her lips, raised her dripping hands to the sky, and called to the rain.

Hesitation. Confusion. And then . . .

Haste. Urgency. Frenzy. Need. Long-penned forces boiling across a barrier that had suddenly been cast down, roaring through the parched and empty halls of air with the force of a landslide, carrying a tidal wave's worth of water with them, shedding it indiscriminately and violently on the desert-dry land below . . .

Kellen had won! The spell was cast. The Barrier was down. And all the pent-up rain that belonged to Sentarshadeen and the Elven lands was coming this way.

Fast.

She needed to slow it. Holding the clouds back would mean heavy snows for the mountains—that couldn't be helped. She must hold cloud-packs over lakes and rivers as much as possible, and let them gently into the Elven lands to provide the gentle soaking rain the forests needed, or else the rain would do as much damage as the drought had done. Keep storm systems from forming to minimize as much as possible the devastating winds and lightning storms that could still set tinder-dry woods ablaze even through the rain . . .

She had time to think carefully. Even the fastest-moving storm system would normally take several days to reach here from the mountains. This storm was coming as if sucked through a vacuum—the abnormally dry air saw to that—but she had time—barely, but enough—to be sure she made the right decisions.

This was not the sort of weather-working Idalia usually did, giving a gentle nudge to normal weather patterns. These weather patterns were abnormal to begin with, and she was trying to set them back into their normal ones. If she simply dissipated the force of the storm when it reached here, and broke up as much of it as she could as far away as she could reach, the pattern of the weather should quickly return back to normal, and Sentarshadeen wouldn't be drowned by flooding in the process.

She took out another honey-disk and crunched it between her teeth with nervous need. There weren't enough keystones in the entire world to provide energy for the work she had in mind. And it wasn't much more than a sennight since she'd called upon the Elves to lend power to the forging of the keystone she'd sent off with Kellen. She couldn't call upon them to share in a spell-price twice in so short a time. Many of them were still recuperating from the last Working. She knew they would help her willingly—and if they did, this time there would be deaths. She would not have that on her conscience.

It's all up to me, then.

She ate another honey-disk, thinking about what she needed and what she would pay. She would not set a price—it was always safest, and if she refused the bargain, she would be free to try again. But she must think carefully about what was needed before she began.

What was the most important thing? *The Book of Stars* said that all true magic came from the heart, and after she had thought about that for a long time, she had realized that one of the things it meant was that in every request a Wild-mage made, there was one thing that was most important, the central element from which the rest of the request came. Focus on that, and see what else you could leave out. That was the most elegant way of working magic. Simplicity.

The weather patterns needed to be returned to normal. That was the most important thing. But in this case, it wasn't the only thing, because the Elven lands had to be protected from the damage that the weather would do while it was settling back into its normal patterns. She couldn't ask for either one without asking for the other, not and be certain of getting both.

So what was the best way to ask for both?

To ask for the strength to do it yourself. She knew she had the skill. All she lacked was the power. The Wild Magic would grant her that—if she was willing to pay the price it asked.

It would be a high price. She knew that already, even before the spell. The more specific you were, the higher the price.

Would it be worth it? Mageprices could be bitterly hard.

She looked around. How could she even ask? The flooding would drown everything in the canyon. It would destroy the city. And the forests and grasslands for hundreds of miles around were still tinder-dry. When lightning struck them, they'd burn. It wouldn't matter how hard it was raining. They'd burn.

She'd promised to protect the people of Sentarshadeen from that. She'd sent Kellen to the Barrier to end the drought, knowing how dangerous it was, knowing that the journey would probably take his life, knowing that if he lived to reach the Barrier, the spell would almost certainly *ask* for his life— and that Kellen, being Kellen, would give it freely, even joyfully. What was one more sacrifice? With power came responsibility.

With great power, greater responsibility.

She opened her work-bag and took out a tiny brazier and a bag of herbs. She set the small cake of charcoal into the brazier's pan and called it alight with a snap of her fingers, then burned her herbs. As she did, she formed her intention clearly in her mind, and asked her boon of the Gods.

To give me the strength to help the rains come gently and safely, and to return the weather to its rightful pattern, repairing the damage done to it by the Barrier. She did not specify the price she was willing to pay.

When she heard the Mageprice that was her magic's cost, Idalia took a deep breath and lowered her head for a moment, closing her eyes tightly. For a moment she was tempted to refuse. Surely there was another way, a different spell she might cast!

But now the choice was hers. After a moment, she raised her head.

"I accept," she said in a hoarse whisper.

She felt the heavy sense of *listening* depart—the sensation Idalia always associated with the making of the bargains associated with Wildmagery—and then there was only the sense of competence and ability, the deep ever-filling well of Wildmage power, hers for use.

She got to work, putting the thought of the bargain aside.

She reached out with her heightened senses, touching the storm.

It was as if she were in Silver Eagle form once more, riding through the air on great, long-feathered wings. But now she was larger than any Silver Eagle ever hatched, her body so vast that she could sweep thunderheads aside with one beat of her great wings. She flew into the heart of the storm itself, shepherding the clouds where she wished them to go, spreading them across the landscape, slowing their eastward rush.

Again and again she dove into the heart of the storm, feathered shepherd to her dark woolly sheep, but instead of bunching them, she kept them well separated, and instead of hurrying them, she slowed them—though, also like sheep, they resisted her efforts, trying always to return to their own ways despite her best efforts.

Idalia lost all track of time. There was only the glory of flight, and the necessity of the task. The storm wind buffeted her, flinging her thousands of feet toward the sky in one instant and tumbling her toward the ground in the next moment as if she'd suddenly lost her wings. Each time she recovered and doggedly returned to her work, though her phantom muscles began to ache with exhaustion. It must be done. There was no one else to do it.

And she had made her bargain.

THE first fat drops of rain on her face woke her from her trance. It was day, but heavily overcast.

Idalia opened her eyes slowly, blinking against the light. She was cold, and ravenously hungry. The first drops of rain were joined by more until it was raining steadily, and in moments Idalia was soaked to the skin. Rain! She'd never felt anything so wonderful.

ALIVE . . . ? she thought in confusion. *But—*

Ashaniel was standing over her, in the middle of a half circle of Elven courtiers. All of them were gazing down at her with expressions of identical worry.

Idalia stared up at the sky. Day. But it had been night when she began.

"I must—" her voice came out in a hoarse croak. She coughed, and licked rain from her upper lip, and tried again. "I must have been here all night."

"Idalia," Ashaniel said, very gently, "you have been sitting here for *three days.*"

HE smelled wet earth. The scent puzzled Kellen, drawing him slowly toward consciousness. How could earth be wet? It had been dry for as long as he could remember.

Wondering drew him back into his body, and he became

aware of the sensation of cool hands bathing his face with a damp cloth. His raw skin stung, but the motion of the soft cloth felt good, and he smelled the faint spicy scent of allheal tea. He opened his eyes.

"He's awake!" Vestakia cried. "Jermayan! He's awake!"

Kellen tried to sit up. The effort produced the sensation that someone had lashed his back with a bundle of hot wires. He could not feel his hands at all, and in a distant foggy part of his mind, he knew that was a good thing. He groaned faintly, and relaxed again, only then realizing that his head was in Vestakia's lap. He blinked. It was a great effort.

He and Vestakia were in a cave. Not very far in—he could see the entrance from where he was. Outside, he could see that it was raining, a hard, steady, soaking rain.

Rain!

Jermayan appeared in the doorway, ducking his head to clear the entrance. The Elven Knight was stripped to the waist, his hair tied back with a length of rag. He smiled in relief when he saw Kellen, and quickly came to kneel at his side.

"How are you feeling?" he asked.

"I'm alive," Kellen said, sounding baffled, even to himself. "But . . . I thought . . ." *The Other-Kellen said you were dead. But that was a lie, just like all the rest of it, just a lie to get me to give in.*

And I thought I was supposed to die. Wasn't that the price of the spell?

Or was just being willing *to die enough?*

I don't understand . . .

"You thought we were dead," Jermayan said. "And I must say, without this young lady and her skill with a bow, we might very well have been." Jermayan paused to exchange a look of warm comradeship with Vestakia that left Kellen gaping in shock. Things had certainly changed while he'd been unconscious!

"But once you destroyed the cairn, the goblin army fled, and your healing regained its power. Once we found you, we got out of there as fast as we could. Fortunately Shalkan was able to light our way back to Valdien and Lily, and praise the powers of Leaf and Star they'd stayed where they were left," Jermayan said. Kellen could hear the relief in his friend's voice.

"We bandaged you up as well as we could," Vestakia added. "Your poor hands! And I thought of bringing you here—this is one of the places where I hide from the Demons. And at least it's dry."

"And there's plenty of fresh meat—if you like goat," Jermayan added, smiling as if at a private joke. Vestakia giggled.

"Do you think you can sit up?" Jermayan asked.

"No," Vestakia said firmly. "I'll lift him up." Gently she cradled Kellen in her arms and raised him into a half-sitting position. Abused muscles shrieked in protest, but he managed to keep from crying out.

Jermayan produced the inevitable cup of tea and held it to his lips. Kellen drained it thirstily, and then another, and then a large bowl of broth. He felt better after that—not well enough to try moving on his own for anything short of a Demon attack, but better.

"My hands," he said, once Vestakia had returned him to a supine position once more. "You said they were burned. I can't even feel them. Can I . . . do you think . . . will I be able to hold a sword again?"

"You are a Knight-Mage and a Wildmage," Jermayan answered with a smile. "The healers in Sentarshadeen are very good—and Idalia is there. I believe you will. But now, let us savor our victory. It hasn't stopped raining once in the last three days," Jermayan said, sounding satisfied. "And if it rains so out of season here in the Lost Lands, then the drought must be truly broken in the Elven lands as well. And as for Demons, my girl, your days of hiding from them in caves and under rocks are over. You're coming back to Sentarshadeen with us, and any Demon who comes after you will have to answer to me. As will anyone else," he added meaningfully.

"To all of us, I think," Shalkan said, stepping into the cave.

The unicorn was covered in mud, but looking very pleased with himself.

Kellen sighed with relief, feeling himself relax completely. The Barrier was down, his friends were friends with each other, and he was alive. He couldn't stop grinning, even though it made his sand-abraded face hurt a great deal.

"We did it!" he said. It was finally starting to seem real to him.

"Yes, we did," Shalkan said approvingly. "And once you're well enough to travel, we can bring the good news to Sentarshadeen . . . although I suspect they already know, somehow," the unicorn mused, switching his sopping tail back and forth.

"It will be a wet trip back," Jermayan said cheerfully. "And I'm sure there will be floods and mudslides and—well, it doesn't matter. We did it, all of us. The Barrier is down, the drought is ended. We've broken the power of Shadow Mountain."

Vestakia dipped the cloth in the bowl beside her and began to bathe Kellen's face again with the allheal tincture.

"Thank you," she whispered, bending over him. She kissed him, light as a butterfly wing, upon the forehead, then replaced her lips with the soothing cloth.

And suddenly, Kellen was anything but soothed. Suddenly he felt a peculiar *unsettled* feeling in the pit of his stomach, and was utterly conscious of Vestakia's presence, her nearness, in a way he hadn't been even a moment before.

Now that he realized he *was* going to live after all, there was the matter of the future to deal with. And he was starting to get the feeling that his vow of celibacy and chastity was really going to be a lot harder to keep than he'd thought.

A *whole* lot harder.

QUEEN Savilla was angry.

In the Heart of Darkness, her anger was more dangerous

than sunlight, more deadly than the touch of a unicorn's horn. All who lived in the World Without Sun feared her fury.

Save one.

PRINCE Zyperis entered the private pleasure chamber of his Queen. The mosaic floor of gold and polished skull-ivory was red and wet, for Queen Savilla had been about her Art for many hours now, slaking her disappointment upon the bodies of those captives who could not be broken or subverted. There were a dozen creatures in various elaborate and ingenious forms of restraint scattered about the chamber, so that Savilla could move from one to the next as her fancy struck her. Most were still capable of screaming, the Prince noted with a connoisseur's eye, though naturally none dared. To make the slightest sound would be to draw Savilla's attention to them once more. There was only a faint pleasing background music of gasps and whimpers, stifled sobs, and the steady beat of the barbed lash that the Queen was using on the current object of her attention, a once-unruly Centaur.

The creature was far beyond standing under its own power, but all six limbs were held fast by a seemingly delicate cage that could be adjusted almost infinitely to provide the Queen full access to any part of its body she wished to torment, without protecting it from her attentions in the slightest.

Prince Zyperis noted, with interest, that Queen Savilla was so thoroughly engaged in her amusement that she hadn't noticed his arrival. That must be rectified. The Barrier was down, the rain had returned to the Elven lands, the Endarkened's plans had been utterly ruined, and even the blood and pain of several of the captives in his own dungeons had not been enough to take the edge off his anger and despair. He needed more. He needed danger.

"One weak and uncertain Knight-Mage, dearest Mama, yet you could not convince him to cast aside his pretty pebble and join his fortunes to ours? How droll."

QUEEN Savilla turned away from her victim. Only one creature in all her kingdom would dare to speak to her like that. With a snarl of rage on her lips, she turned to face her arrogant son. For a moment her eyes burned white-yellow with the force of her passion. Then, with a change of expression so sudden it came as a shock, she licked blood from her claws, and smiled.

"Ah, Prince Zyperis. And your own plans on that day went so well, of course? When may I greet my dear granddaughter Vestakia, and welcome her to our Court?"

PRINCE Zyperis growled. His great wings trembled as he fought his temper. Tweaking the Queen's tail was one thing. A true battle for dominance was something he did not want.

Yet.

"They will pay," he whispered in a low, shaking voice. "The Elves—the accursed Wildmages—my love, we were *so close* . . . !"

He could not help himself. To have the one thing he longed for with a longing that was torment snatched out of his claws in the moment of victory! He felt tears of rage burning his eyes.

"And now we must begin again," Savilla said firmly. With a gesture, she banished her servants from the chamber, then went to him and drew his head down against her bosom, stroking his hair and his wings as he wept tears of outrage and fury against her blood-red skin. "But come, let us think of more soothing things for a time."

She recalled her servants, and together they dispatched Savilla's victims one by one.

IT was good to do things together, Queen Savilla reflected. It gave you insight into those who might one day become your enemies, against the day when you might need to destroy them. Meanwhile, the cheated rage that burned in Zyperis's soul was balm to her own. Let others grieve as she sorrowed, for the victory that had been taken from them by the arrogance and pride of a young Knight-Mage. She had spoken no more than the truth when she had told Kellen Tavadon that he had doomed himself. She would make sure of it. Everything and everyone the Knight-Mage loved would die, and he would die with them. Slowly. But only *after* he had watched her extract the last drop of pain from the ones he cherished.

At last the two of them reclined together, taking refreshment as they watched human servants clean away the disorder. In some ways, this was the sweetest pleasure of all, for Savilla took care that the servants chosen for this task were the newest ones, those it was still possible to shock, and their reactions—oh, but they tried so hard to hide them, knowing their masters were watching!—thrilled across her senses like harp-song.

"What now?" Prince Zyperis asked, in a tone that marked him as sated, but unsatisfied.

"Now the Elves know to fear us once more," Queen Savilla said, popping a sweetmeat into his mouth. Her expression was distant, her voice brooding, her anger banked but far from quenched. "And that is . . . unfortunate. If the Elves have renewed their ancient Alliance with the Wildmages, who knows how many they may call to their banner? But fear not, my darling, my love. I do not hazard all on one stroke of the lash. There is still the Golden City, and my agents there may yet prove to be the most useful of all . . ."

―

IT had been a moonturn since the rains came—not that the moon was visible through the clouds—and it hadn't stopped raining once in all that time. Sentarshadeen had turned from a city of gold to a city of silver with the long-delayed autumn rains, becoming a city of streams and fountains once more, losing its desert aspect as its growing things awakened into life, even in autumn. The snows would be heavy this year, even this far south, but by spring, all would be well.

It had taken Idalia several days of rest in the House of Leaf and Star to recover from her cloud-herding exertions, and the knowledge of her Mageprice still weighed heavily on her, even though she had come to realize it would not be asked of her immediately.

But when?

Would she have any warning at all?

Dared she make any plans for the future?

There is no future, Idalia told herself with a sigh. *Or—not one any of us can plan for.* Yes, Sentarshadeen was safe— from drought and floods. But now Shadow Mountain knew that its ancient enemy was aware of it once more, and another attack would inevitably come. Over the winter Andoreniel and Ashaniel would have to send envoys to the other Elven cities, to their allies, and to the other Wildmages, to tell them that Shadow Mountain was moving against the Bright World once more. And someone would have to at least *try* to warn Armethalieh.

Oh, Jermayan—I wish you were here, so I could tell you what a fool I have been! She had spent so long thinking of the centuries he would live beyond her own—but an Elven Knight was not likely to live very long at all, once the Elves went to war with the Endarkened once more. Their two lives, now, were *exactly* the same length.

If only he were here, so she could repair the damage her pride had caused them both.

But as one sennight, then two, passed without sign of him, or Kellen, or Shalkan, her hope for their survival dimmed. She began to accept that they were dead, lost in the aftermath of the fall of the Barrier. If not for the fact that a Wildmage's scrying was a notoriously uncertain method, more likely to show you what you ought to see than what you wanted to see, she would have tried that, and used it to search for them.

Another day or two without word, and she would try it anyway, and see whatever sights the Wild Magic brought her. Whatever revelations it sent could be no more painful than not knowing.

⌒

THE morning she had made up her mind to scry, Idalia awoke, as always these days, to the drumming of the steadily falling rain and the distant music of Elven rain-chimes. No day since the coming of the rains had passed without some sort of celebration—though the Elves knew as well as Idalia did that war was inevitable, they were pragmatic enough to know that one must rejoice when and where one could. She had declined a dozen invitations in the past fortnight to rain-picnics and rain-dances and rain-concerts of all sorts, lest her bleak mood contaminate the happiness of the celebrants.

She swung her legs over the side of the bed, shivering in the damp morning chill—everything always seemed to be damp, now—and hurried into the common room of her little house to build up the fire, pulling a heavy shawl around her shoulders.

The grey cat hurried ahead of her, springing up to huddle against the warm stove and complain, plaintively, about the weather. Idalia smiled.

"It will be warm soon, Greymalkin. And you would have liked it less if the rains had *not* come, I promise you."

The cat sneezed, disagreeing emphatically.

The stove began to radiate heat, warming the room. Idalia filled the kettle and set it on the fire, then wandered over to the window and looked out.

The river at the bottom of the canyon was full once more. If she opened the window, she would be able to hear its strong purling music, and soon fish would return to its waters. Across the canyon, she could see the forest. The moonturn of rain had stripped the last of the autumn leaves from the trees, but even bare-limbed, the forest looked healthier than it had before, and the evergreens had begun to regain their dark healthy green. The canyon wall itself was silvery with water, gleaming in the diffuse morning light like polished glass. Tiny rills and freshets of water jumped along its face as they trickled down, spraying out into the air in tiny outbursts engineered by the canyon wall's long-ago designers. It all looked entirely natural, yet Idalia knew that everything she saw was the work of subtle Elven artifice.

The kettle was hot now, and Idalia made tea.

She dressed in her fringed leathers. A thick cloak of oiled wool and her Mountain Trader hat would keep off the worst of the rain, and Idalia hated being encumbered.

She filled a bottle with the rest of the tea, and wrapped a couple of breakfast pastries to eat later, tucking them into her shoulder bag. She added a pouch of charged keystones, a tiny flask of wine, and a leaf of dried fern, enough for the spell. If she held her cloak out over Songmairie, she should be able to still the water enough to use it for her scrying. In an emergency, a Wildmage *could* scry in a simple bowl of water, but the most power—and the best results—came from using natural pools, and today Idalia wanted all the help she could get.

Greymalkin accompanied her as far as the door, scolding her in a plaintive voice for her abandonment before retreating to the warmth of the stove. Once outside, Idalia took a deep breath. The air smelled strong and alive, and she could hear the purl and plash of fountains, the ting of rain-chimes, and the deep peal of rain-drums. The city made its own music.

Idalia made her way slowly through Sentarshadeen, briefly greeting the Elves she passed. The small gardens that were a feature of many Elven homes had suffered least from the drought, but even these were brighter and more alive thanks to the natural rain. She did not take the fastest or most direct route to the spring, but paused frequently to admire fountains and pools, shut down and emptied during the drought, and now brought to life once more. It was as if the city had been reborn in water.

At last her slow progress brought her to the unicorn

meadow. Here the rain had worked the greatest change of all, banishing the silver from the grass and turning the whole meadow a rich deep dark green the color of emeralds. The unicorn herd was scattered across it, grazing greedily, their coats glossy with rain. The scent of the fresh grass was almost overpowering, as if its greenness were a palpable thing.

The path of smooth stone leading up to Songmairie was gone, though the decoration around the lip of the spring itself remained. In the distance, Idalia could see an Elven work party moving among the trees of the Flower Forest, gently filling in the irrigation canals. Soon the trees would come into leaf again; the fragrant *alyon* and the flowering *vilya* would bloom, even in the depths of the coming winter. Even now, if she concentrated, Idalia could smell the scent of the forest, wood and rising sap and new growth mixed with the cinnamon scent of the wet unicorns.

This was peace, all the more precious because it was about to be swept away by war. Idalia stood there, watching the herd, feeling the moment heal the bruised places in her soul.

Suddenly the herd's quiet was shattered. They scattered in all directions as a young Elven scout, mounted on a red unicorn stallion, plunged through them, heading for Idalia. Both scout and rider were soaked to the skin. The unicorn stopped a good distance away from Idalia, prancing skittishly, nostrils flaring.

No virgins here, Idalia thought, amused in spite of herself.

It lowered its head and shook itself like a dog, spraying water everywhere and nearly unseating its rider before raising its head and regarding her with bright turquoise eyes.

"Wildmage!" the young stallion said excitedly. "People coming from the north! One of them's Shalkan!"

Shalkan? One of them? Great Powers, does that mean— "Is—It would be interesting to know if you might have seen anything else," Idalia said, pleased to find her voice was steady and that she could still summon the proper forms of Elven good manners.

"Shalkan. His rider. And Jermayan with Valdien as well,

Wildmage," the young scout said, her voice high with excitement. "Queen Ashaniel bid us come and tell you at once."

"I will go now and thank the Queen for her courtesy," Idalia said gravely. She bowed to the unicorn and his rider. The stallion, taking this as permission to leave her uncomfortable presence, immediately dashed off, forcing his rider to emit an undignified yelp and clutch at his neck for support. Idalia turned her back quickly and pretended not to see, hiding a smile.

Kellen was alive! Kellen was coming home!

And Jermayan . . .

She would see him again! And this time she would not be a fool. Whatever time they could have together—hours, *minutes*—she would take as the great gift it was and make every moment count.

Shrugging her bag higher onto her shoulder beneath her cloak, Idalia squelched off through the wet grass toward the House of Leaf and Star.

Oh, Jermayan, come soon!

UNDERMAGE Anigrel made his residence in one of the buildings on the grounds of the Mage College that had been established for those few Mages who, for one reason or another, could not or did not choose to live in the opulent demiplaces of the Mage Quarter.

Some were not of Mage-birth, and thus did not have family homes in the Quarter. Some lacked the wherewithal or the inclination to maintain such an expensive establishment. Some had been asked by their families to situate themselves elsewhere, either temporarily or permanently. Thus, the buildings of the Mage Courts were the residence of the young, the less-than-prosperous, the eccentric . . . by the narrow standards of Armethaliehan society, of course. All were Mages, from Journeyman to High Mage, and it went without saying, vastly superior to any of those who had not the talent and the Gift.

The moon was dark again tonight. Anigrel hurried home from his duties, intent upon his evening's task.

His chambers consisted of two small rooms on the top floor of the building, a study and a sleeping chamber. The bathing room was down the hall, and Anigrel took his meals elsewhere. No servant ever came to trouble the quiet of these rooms, though there was little to find, should anyone think of doing so: only the books and apparatus that any working Mage might own, and a small curious iron bowl, easily overlooked. Lycaelon's private secretary spent little time here.

He entered the room—the door panel dissolved at his touch and re-formed behind him—and crossed to a chair. There he sat, and waited.

Slowly the sounds of activity in the building around him—they would be inaudible save for the intercession of the spells he had laid down years before and renewed each moonturn—died away. When all was silent, Anigrel got to his feet and went to a small casket. It was not kept locked. Locks implied valuables, and long ago Anigrel had learned that the best way to keep something hidden and safe was in plain sight. Misdirection was the greatest protector.

On the table in the center of the room, he set out the small iron bowl and a sharp steel knife. It was his penknife; it would not do to allow an object such as a knife to gain too much sense of purpose. That in itself could betray him. Thus, the knife he used for his darkest magic was also the knife he used for the humblest of his everyday tasks.

His preparations made, Anigrel crossed to the window and opened it. He picked up his wand from the top of the bookcase and drew a careful sigil in the air; an ordinary sigil of the High Magick. It glowed brightly in half-a-dozen colors, then slowly faded.

A moment later two plump sleepy pigeons fluttered down onto the windowsill. With lightning swiftness, Anigrel reached out and grabbed them. Closing the window with a gesture, he carried the pigeons over to the table and beheaded them over the bowl, one after the other, with the sharp steel knife. His gestures were quick and neat. He had been doing this for a very long time.

Anigrel had first seen the Dark Lady as a child of eight, in a mirror in his father's study. He had been her devoted servant from that moment. With her aid he had come quickly into his inheritance, for siphoning another's life force without their knowledge was the first of the things she had taught him. No one had thought Torbet Anigrel's early death was in the least unusual, and from that moment, young Anigrel's sense of power and purpose grew.

Once the bowl was full, he set the birds aside. Another spell would dispose of them once his work here was done.

He bent over the fresh blood, eager for his communion.

A blast of furious rage struck him, its force enough to fill his head with agony. Tears of pain streamed down his cheeks and he clutched at the table, his manicured nails digging into the wood, marring the finish. Disjointed images poured into his mind, frightening, hideous beyond bearing, until he screamed for them to stop, *begged* for them to stop.

Suddenly the connection was gone. Anigrel fell to the floor and huddled there, weeping. She was angry with him. His Dark Lady was angry with all the world.

Because of The Outlaw. Because of *Kellen*.

Somehow Kellen had hurt her, hurt Anigrel's Dark Lady. He could not imagine how such a thing was possible—that Kellen, Lycaelon's Tainted whelp, could summon the power to strike out at such power, such perfection, such beauty . . . but he knew she could not lie, not to *him*.

His purpose was clear. As the worst of the agony receded, Anigrel realized that as always, he had gained much wisdom from the mere touch of her mind. What he had learned would become clearer to him in the days to come, but for now, he knew one thing absolutely.

Kellen Tavadon must die.

It would be difficult to persuade Lycaelon to renew the Hunt for his rebellious son, now that The Outlaw had taken refuge in the Elven lands, but not impossible. Lycaelon

wanted to bring the Council to heel, to regain his lost prestige, to unseat Lord Volpiril from his present position of
smug superiority before Volpiril managed to topple Lycaelon
from power completely.

What if proof came to light that Volpiril had conspired
with The Outlaw? How else could the border lands have gotten word of the Scouring Hunt in time to prepare a defense?

Proof would be difficult to arrange, but not impossible.
Anigrel must move carefully. But for his Dark Lady's sake,
it would be done.

"There are no failures, only opportunities."

And now Kellen Tavadon would have the opportunity to
die.

Chired Anigrel would make sure of it.

About the Authors

MERCEDES LACKEY is the author of the Heralds of Valdemar and Elemental Masters series from DAW books, the Bardic Voices (in collaboration), the SERRAted Edge, and Bedlam Bards series from Baen Books, and the Halfblood Chronicles from Tor Books, along with many other solo and collaborative works. Her hobbies include needlework, jewelry design, beadwork, and dollmaking. She lives in Oklahoma with her husband, co-author and artist Larry Dixon, and far too many parrots for a peaceful household.

JAMES MALLORY is a professional ghostwriter with several books to his credit. Under his own name, he wrote the three-part novelization of the Hallmark *Merlin* miniseries: *The Old Magic, The King's Wizard,* and *The End of Magic.* Born in San Francisco, Mallory attended schools in California and the Midwest before moving to New York to pursue a career in writing. From an early age Mallory has been fascinated both with the Arthurian legends and their historical evolution, an avocation that triggered a lifelong interest in fantasy literature. Mallory's interests include hiking, comparative religion, and cinema.

ABOUT

About the Authors

Look for

To Light a Candle

The Obsidian Trilogy:
Book Two

Now available from Tor Books

In *To Light a Candle*, Kellen learns that while he may already be a Knight-Mage, and a hero, he still has much to learn . . .

Chapter Two

The House of Sword and Shield

*T*he *Book of Stars* said that *"The Knight-Mage is the active agent of the principle of the Wild Magic, the Wildmage who chooses to become a warrior or who is born with the instinct for the Way of the Sword, who acts in battle without mindful thought and thus brings primary causative forces into manifestation by direct action."*

When they had discovered that this was what Kellen was, Jermayan had told him that a Wildmage and a Knight-Mage's gifts lay in opposite directions; that while a Wildmage reached out to all the world, a Knight-Mage's gifts turned inward, so that he could not be turned away from his course once he had chosen it. Because of that, Kellen's abilities in Wildmagery would never be as strong as Idalia's, but Jermayan also said that a Knight-Mage could withstand forces that would destroy a regular Wildmage, for the Knight-Mage's true power lay in endurance and the alliance of his knightly skills with his Wildmagery.

Kellen wasn't surprised to find that *The Book of Stars* seemed to make a lot more sense now that he knew what he really was.

"Only when you cease to try, will you achieve. Only when you cease to seek, will you find. Only when you are emptied, will you be filled."

If that wasn't exactly what finding the Way of the Knight-Mage was like, he'd eat his boots. It gave him a kind of comfort, to know that whatever might come to pass, it was somehow within the sphere of the Wild Magic.

THE House of Shield and Sword was located on the southern edge of the city. It was out beyond the firing kilns, separated from the city proper by a dense plantation of balsam-bough trees. A whole pocket canyon spread out before Kellen and Idalia, its floor rich with tall grass. The forest, he realized, had been planted—and carefully tended—to screen its opening. Horses grazed loose in the meadow, their coats shiny with rain.

About halfway down the canyon floor was the House of Sword and Shield.

Like all Elven architecture, it blended into its surroundings so harmoniously it seemed to have grown there instead of being built. Unlike the House of Leaf and Star, it was all of simple golden stone except for the roof; one story, and with the high-peaked roof making it look even lower and wider.

"Why is it out here in the middle of nowhere?" Kellen asked.

"You'll have to ask Jermayan," Idalia said, amused. "I think he's coming now."

She pointed. A rider was coming toward them. Jermayan and Valdien.

Today the Elven Knight wore no armor at all, merely a simple tunic and leggings in dark green beneath his raincape, with soft boots to match, and Valdien wore only a simple halter. Elf and destrier moved as one being, and Kellen wondered absently if he could learn to ride a horse, and if he could ever manage to equal Jermayan's easy grace.

"The student approaches," Jermayan observed. "I promise, Idalia, that he will be returned to you . . . reasonably unscathed."

"Oh, don't bother on my account," Idalia said cheerfully. "As the *Book of Stars* tells us, 'There is nothing worth knowing that is not bought without effort or pain.' I'll see you later." She turned away, walking back through the pines.

Jermayan dismounted from Valdien and slipped the halter from Valdien's head.

"Come," Jermayan said to Kellen, beginning to walk back toward the House of Sword and Shield. "It is time for your proper training to begin."

Valdien followed Kellen and Jermayan like a hopeful pet, occasionally nudging Jermayan in the back.

Kellen felt a flutter of nervousness at the pit of his stomach. It wasn't that he doubted his own skill—he didn't; he was a Knight-Mage after all. But all of his experience with formal training of any kind had been disastrous, and all of a sudden he was afraid that this was going to turn out the same way.

"Jermayan—" he said, "I asked the Council a question this morning."

That surprised a startled laugh from Jermayan.

"To allay your fears, there will be times within the House when questions will be encouraged, for War Manners are taught here along with all the other arts of War. You will learn all that we can teach you, my word on that, Kellen."

By now they had reached the doors of the House. Jermayan turned to Valdien and dismissed the stallion firmly with a pat on the shoulder. The stallion lingered for a moment, for all the world as if hoping to be invited inside, then turned and trotted off with a reluctant sigh.

Kellen realized that the building was taller than he'd thought, the height of the indoor riding-rings back in Arme-thalieh. The doors added to that impression; they were tall enough to admit two mounted knights riding side-by-side. Jermayan opened one tall narrow panel, and the two of them stepped inside.

"Be welcome in the House of Sword and Shield, home to all who bear the sword for the Nine Cities," Jermayan said formally.

Kellen looked around.

The first thing that caught his attention was the ring of steel on steel. In the center of the room, four armored Knights whirled and danced around one another, swords flashing in a deadly pattern of light and motion. Kellen studied them, his attention caught. Were three attacking the one? Was it two against two? It was impossible for him to tell; they moved so fast. . . .

Then a fifth man, unarmored, wearing dark-green robes, his hair the silver-blue of great age, walked into the midst of them. All four immediately put up their swords. The man began talking, too low for Kellen to hear.

"Belesharon is one of our greatest teachers of the sword," Jermayan said quietly. "His father once trained a Knight-Mage. He looks forward to meeting you."

Kellen blinked, slowly reasoning it out. If Belesharon's father had trained a Knight-Mage, that meant that Belesharon's father had fought in the Great War, since that was the last time there'd *been* any Knight-Mages. He looked away from the armored Knights, unwilling to draw Belesharon's attention to him any earlier than he had to.

Although, if he could actually ask Belesharon questions. . . .

Including the four in armor, there were about twenty Knights in the room. Some of them, to Kellen's vague surprise, seemed to be female, though he supposed there was no reason they shouldn't be. He didn't really know enough about the way Elves did things to know whether they cared about things like that or not. All the Knights were dressed just as Jermayan was—loose tunics, pants, and soft boots, though the colors varied from pale green to deep yellow to red.

Jermayan took Kellen's arm and led him out of the entryway, onto the stone floor of the hall. Belesharon had concluded his instructions to the armored knights, and turned to face Jermayan.

"I See you, Jermayan," he said, bowing.

"I See you, Belesharon," Jermayan said, bowing in return. "I bring you Kellen Knight-Mage, who comes from the lands of Men to learn what you can teach him."

"I See you, Kellen Knight-Mage," Belesharon said. He did not bow, but studied Kellen with cold black eyes.

Kellen bowed deeply. "I See you, Belesharon." He rose

from his bow and studied the Elven swordmaster in return.

He'd thought Morusil was old, and until this moment, Morusil had been the oldest Elf Kellen had ever seen. But next to Belesharon, Morusil was a mere child. Up close, Belesharon's bone-pale skin was spiderwebbed with the fine lines of age; his eyebrows nearly white. Perhaps Elves had run shorter centuries ago, or perhaps age had shrunk him; Belesharon was as small as a child, making Kellen feel lumpish and ungainly as he had not since his days in Armethalich.

But no matter how old he was, there was nothing of infirmity about the ancient swordmaster. His eyes sparkled with alert intelligence, and his movements—as Kellen had seen previously—were lithe and swift.

"Well," Belesharon said after a moment. "Staring gains only so much. Bring practice swords, Ciradhel."

One of the green-tunic'd teachers hurried off.

"I don't understand," Kellen said. Always a safe enough statement when dealing with Elves.

Belesharon snorted. "When one undertakes to teach a student, young Kellen, one begins by judging his quality. We will spar. You will attempt to strike me, holding nothing back. If you fail in this, I will know. And you will no longer be welcome in my House."

"But—" Kellen glanced at Jermayan with indecision bordering on agony, but Jermayan's face was unreadable.

He remembered facing Jermayan at their streambed camp, and nearly killing the Elf by accident simply because neither of them had been prepared for the scope of Kellen's newly-awakened Knight-Mage powers.

Kellen bit his lip, thinking very hard. Killing or injuring the master wouldn't be a very good start. . . .

He bowed.

"Master Belesharon."

"The fool speaks. Come, take your weapon and face me. Choose either."

Ciradhel had returned, carrying two practice swords similar to the ones he'd seen the yellow-garbed students working out with. They were the length and shape of Kellen's own sword, but made entirely of wood.

But even a length of wood could be deadly in the hands of a Knight-Mage.

Kellen bowed again.

"If you like, I am a fool. And you have trained fools and children for a very long time, so you will understand when I say that there is a saying among my people that nothing is foolproof, because fools have too much ingenuity. I do not wish to hurt you."

Now Belesharon bowed, his eyes twinkling with amusement.

"Such courtesy! Such respect for age! Your rascals would do well to heed it, and have more consideration for an old man who is nearly on his deathbed. Young Kellen, your honesty and thoughtfulness do you credit, and I honor the truth of your words. Therefore, our contest will be closely watched, and if I am in danger, my students will intervene. You, however, must look to yourself."

Kellen bowed again and reluctantly took the sword that Ciradhel held out to him. He'd hoped to avoid the match altogether, but this was a good compromise.

He hoped.

Belesharon took up his own practice sword and strode to a practice circle marked out on the stone floor. Kellen recognized the dimensions as being equal to the ones Jermayan had marked out on the ground when his training was just beginning. The rules were simple: stay inside the circle at all costs.

Reluctantly, Kellen took his place in the circle. The four armored knights, swords drawn, stood just outside it. Jermayan was the only one who seemed concerned—but then, Jermayan was the only one who'd seen him fight. Kellen realized with resigned dismay that all other activity in the hall had stopped. Everyone was watching.

Grand. Either I end up looking like an uncouth barbarian, or else I do something like I did to Jermayan. And either way, I'm in trouble.

"Now we shall begin your education," Belesharon said. He raised the wooden practice sword in a fluid salute.

Kellen copied the gesture, at the same time summoning up his spell-sight. At once there were two separate Belesharons: the living man, overlaid with a web of glowing red showing Kellen how he must strike, and a glowing ghost, indicating how Belesharon might move.

That's never happened befo—

WHACK!

Kellen yelped and jumped back, jarred entirely out of battle-mind in time to see Belesharon step back into ready position. There was a stinging welt on his upper thigh.

"Too slow, Knight-Mage," the swordmaster commented mildly. "Perhaps you still think to spare my old bones."

Not any more, old man.

Resolving to ignore the peculiar doubling of his spell-sight, Kellen summoned it once again. No matter what else it showed him, it still showed him where to hit.

This time he struck without warning—the match was already begun, after all—but somehow, instead of a clean hit, he missed entirely. Belesharon swayed out of the way at the last moment.

Kellen paid no attention, moving on to the next target, and the next. But instead of one clear possibility, his spell-sight showed him a dozen, forcing him to think, to choose—

Forcing him out of battle-mind. Forcing him to be only Kellen.

Each time he summoned it anew, only to have it stolen away again. He realized as the match wore on that Belesharon could have hit him a dozen times. He realized everyone in the hall knew it too. The best he'd been able to manage had been to stay in the circle.

He began to feel a dull desperate anger. *I'm better than this! I have to be!*

Because if he couldn't be good enough, people were going to die.

Focus!

He fed his anger into his magic, making it his tool. The

enemy's confidence was also a weapon he could use. Once more he summoned up his spell-sight, then reached beyond, to the Gods that made the patterns, the Gods who sent both Knight-Mage and Wildmage into the world.

And struck.

There was a gasp and a hiss of steel from outside the practice ring. Kellen realized he had closed his eyes. He opened them.

His wooden blade was pressed against Belesharon's ribs.

The swordmaster's blade rested gently against the side of his neck.

The swordmaster withdrew his practice blade.

Kellen stepped back shakily, lowering his own blade. He only hoped he hadn't struck very hard.

"A most instructive bout, young Kellen," Belesharon said, bowing with no evidence of discomfort. "Of course, you would have been dead as well, but I think time and practice will remedy that defect. And now, if you will be so good as to don your armor, we shall see how you fare against multiple attackers."

Belesharon handed his sword to the nearest Master, and turned to go.

Kellen barely remembered in time to bow. He felt as if he'd been running for several leagues. Uphill. Carrying Shalkan.

"This way." Jermayan stepped into the circle and led him out through the gathered crowd. Half of them were staring at him as if he were a Demon Incarnate, and the other half were talking among themselves in excited whispers, too low for him to catch.

"You *hit* Master Belesharon," Jermayan said quietly.

"I didn't mean to," Kellen said. "I mean, I *did*, but—"

Jermayan slid open a panel in the back wall and ushered Kellen into a small room with wooden walls that were shallowly carved in an intricate geometric pattern. Jermayan went over to a part of the wall and pulled it out, revealing it to be a drawer.

"Here is your armor and sword," Jermayan said, lifting out

the familiar pieces and handing them to Kellen.

Kellen began removing his clothes, surprised to find they were sodden with sweat.

"I hope I didn't hurt him," he said, pulling on the leather underpadding for his armor.

Jermayan had opened another drawer and was removing his own armor. He stopped and looked at Kellen quizzically.

"You have no cause for concern. But it was . . . startling."

When both of them were armored, they returned to the main hall. Everyone ignored him so thoroughly that Kellen thought he'd rather have been stared at. The story of the bout was probably going to be all over Sentarshadeen by nightfall—in fact, given the Elves' penchant for gossip, it was probably already making the rounds.

Jermayan led Kellen back to the teaching circle, where Belesharon was waiting with the four armored knights. Belesharon glanced up when he saw them, and his face crumpled into an almost comical frown of disapproval.

"This armor is a disgrace to the House of Sword and Shield," Belesharon said. "I see no enamelwork, no gilding, no jewels. It is the armor of a brigand or a hill-bandit, not a knight."

Jermayan had said that direct speech, even questions, were permitted in the House of Shield and Sword, but this was rude speech even for a human.

"Forgive him, Master Belesharon, but it is the only armor he possesses. It was made in a day, and there was no time to finish it properly," Jermayan said.

"Then let another suit be made, one more suitable," Belesharon said irritably.

Kellen winced inwardly. Jermayan looked great in gleaming sapphire-colored armor that looked like expensive jewelry. But he didn't think he would.

"Suitable perhaps, for an Elven Knight, Master Belesharon," Kellen said. "But I am human; my people are simple, as am I. Please forgive my presumption, but as Elvenware is simple, yet a perfect blend of form and function, it seems to me that for a human, and for me in particular, there should be no more adornments than there are upon a perfect bowl. I am—my people call it a *virgin knight,* one who is untested in battle. If one wears the map of one's experiences upon the metal he is clad in, then mine should be unadorned. And—forgive me again, but I have an emotional attachment to speak of as well. This is the armor I was wearing when I found out I was a Knight-Mage. I should like to keep it just as it is."

"The human child is bold and stubborn," Belesharon observed to no one in particular. "He contradicts me in my own house. Well! Perhaps it is for the best."

Kellen had the oddest feeling he'd just passed another test.

"Now. Dainelel, Kayir, Naeret, Emessade, and Jermayan will attempt to kill you, just as in a real battle. All swords will be in practice-sheaths. I will award injuries. It is not necessary to remain within the circle."

Ciradhel brought Kellen and Jermayan practice-sheaths—the others already had them. Jermayan showed Kellen how to fit the heavy leather sheath over his blade and bind it over the guard so there was no possibility of its coming loose during a practice bout. With these in place, even the lethally-sharp Elven swords were safe to use.

What does he mean, 'award injuries?' Kellen wondered.

Then there was no more time to wonder, as the bout had begun.

His main advantage was that—having just seen him fight Master Belesharon—Dainelel, Kayir, Naeret, and Emessade were cautious about engaging. But the Elves knew how to work together as a team, not getting in each others' way. Quickly they spread out, encircling Kellen, forcing him to defend himself from every side at once.

But unlike Belesharon, the images they presented to his spell-sight were clear and precise. . . .

"Dainelel, Naeret, you are both dead. Retire from the field, if you please." Master Belesharon's voice came to Kellen distantly as he whirled to block an attack from behind, and turned about—too late!—to respond to an attack from Jermayan.

"Kellen, you have taken a disabling cut to the thigh. Drop to your knees, if you please."

"What?" Kellen shook his head, not understanding. The other three had withdrawn, swords at rest, waiting.

"Kayir's blow got through. I judge it was quite strong enough to have severed the tendons of the leg. You cannot stand, but you can still fight. Drop to your knees, if you please," Master Belesharon repeated.

Feeling rather foolish, Kellen did so. Fortunately, the Elven armor was flexible enough to permit the move.

On his knees, unable to maneuver much, Kellen was easy prey, though to his secret delight he was able to "kill" one more of his attackers before receiving a "fatal wound."

If this had been real, I'd be dead now, Kellen thought soberly.

Jermayan helped him to his feet.

"Perhaps you would share what wisdom you have gained this day in the House of Sword and Shield," Belesharon said, when Kellen was standing before him once more.

Despite aches and pains and the fact he was dripping with the sweat of exhaustion, Kellen grinned beneath his helmet. From the way his head hurt, some of his opponents had managed to land more than a few blows, though he hadn't felt them at the time. Kellen's adversaries had used their feet, fists, and shields, as well as every part of their swords against him. Only the protection of his armor had kept Kellen from collecting a spectacular set of bruises this afternoon, but his muscles were certainly convinced he'd given them a splendid workout.

"I have learned that I need to learn a very great deal, Master," Kellen said honestly.

Belesharon smiled. "Good. Jermayan, take this callow youth to pick out a horse. And come early tomorrow, Knight-Mage. You have much to learn."